MW00344491

JERUSALEM FALLS!

A Monk's Tale of the First Crusade

1095 - 1099

By Thomas Esson Ewing

Copyright © 2019 by Thomas Esson Ewing

All rights reserved.

No part of this publication may be reproduced, distributed or transmitted
in any form or by any means, including photocopying, recording or other
electronic or mechanical methods, without the prior written permission of
the publisher, except in the case of brief quotations embodied in reviews
and certain other non-commercial uses permitted by copyright law.

For permission requests please contact Canoe Tree Press.

Published 2019

Cover image: *Taking of Jerusalem by the Crusaders by Emile Signol*
Printed in the United States of America
Print ISBN: 978-1-7338384-7-4

Canoe Tree Press
4697 Main Street
Manchester, VT 05255
www.CanoeTreePress.com

PREFACE

history has always been my first love, ever since I was very young. It was also my first career. I taught Asian Studies at Leeds University, England. My specialty was the northern Chinese frontier, authoring a book, *Between the Hammer and the Anvil? Chinese and Russian Policies in Outer Mongolia, 1911-1921* (Indiana University Press, 1980) and several academic articles published by European and American universities.

Twenty or so years ago I happened to read a popular history of the First Crusade (1095-99). I was absolutely captivated. Those four years seemed to embrace the entire human experience: superstition, intrigue, heroism, savagery, blind faith, avarice, bigotry. It was all there. Thereafter, I began reading, upwards of 120 books and articles, primary and secondary sources directly or indirectly related to the subject. I took voluminous typewritten notes which literally filled a banker's box, tens of thousands. My intention was to write a novel. I started twice and surrendered twice. I found myself lapsing into a sort of default mode—writing an historical account but without the imagination a novel demands. I concluded I was absolutely devoid of talent. That may yet be true; others will judge. I stored the box away, at times considering trashing it to make room on the shelf but just couldn't bring myself to do it.

In 2017 I traveled to China to attend the wedding reception of my son Ross and his bride Tian Hui-jun. It was a long flight, nearly a day there and a day back. I needed something to read. A friend recommended two historical novels by Robert Harris, *Dictator* and *Conspirata*, both about the Roman orator Marcus Cicero. On reaching home I decided to try one last time. What persuaded me was this: Many novelists, in my opinion, use history merely as a backdrop in which to set their stories. As a reader I may have been diverted but invariably was left with only a vague sense of the underlying history. Harris wrote differently, weaving his story *around* and *through* historical events, thus both entertaining *and* enlightening the reader. That was the kind of novel I wanted to write. I needed to try.

Jerusalem Falls! is a story of the First Crusade told through the eyes of a twenty-five year-old Benedictine monk who embarks on this great pilgrimage to Jerusalem in the spring of 1096. Because of my background as an historian I have tried faithfully to recount the major events without compromising historical accuracy, though not infrequently being forced to reconcile the contradictory accounts of the original sources to produce a plausible and coherent narrative. I have also added "historical notes" and maps in the appendix to add context.

This has been truly a labor of love for over twenty years. I wish to thank the following people who have tirelessly read each chapter always providing invaluable critiques: Christopher Ewing, Col. Jerry Lauzon, US Army (ret.), Peter Wall, and, not least, my son Alexander Ewing for producing the historical maps.

But, above all, I want to thank my brother Zan E. Ewing for his continuous encouragement even when this novel was a mere concept and his many insightful suggestions as the manuscript progressed. This book would not have been possible without him.

It is to him I dedicate *Jerusalem Falls!*

PROLOGUE

My name is Oderic of Rheims, son of Rainald also of Rheims, a spice merchant. Despite my father's wish that I become a spice trader, God called me to His service. I became a monk in the Priory of La Charité sur Loire in Francia.

In the Year of Our Blessed Lord, 1095, I heard the call of His Holiness Pope Urban II to rescue Jerusalem from the pagans who for so long had persecuted true Christians and denied them from worshiping at the altar of the Holy Sepulchre. My heart was joyous. I thought of the 24th Psalm:

> *He who has clean hands and a pure heart,*
> *who does not lift up his soul to falsehood,*
> *who does not swear deceitfully.*

And with that, I left my priory to join the Great Pilgrimage, now called a "Crusade". With faithful diligence I made daily notes intending to write a chronicle of our Christian great deeds. In 1099, on the capture of Jerusalem from the Saracens, I returned to my priory and began to compose. But in doing so I could not reconcile our Christian behavior with the "clean hands" and "pure heart" the Bible commands. My faith in God's compassion and His love were unshaken. The fault lay not with Him. It lay with man's greed, lust, and brutality.

I set aside my work and went into seclusion for several years. I have now read chronicles of that crusade. They are blemished by the blind loyalty of the authors to their patrons, by mindless credulity, by excessive piety, or by ignorance for their reliance on hearsay, all glorifying the evil deeds of our own *milites Christi*, "Soldiers of Christ". I decided the historical record must be corrected.

It is now thirty years since leaving Jerusalem. My hand is withered from age and required the services of a young scribe, Brother Samuel, a monk of La Charité, to take my dictation. There will be those who condemn this book for what, in their view, is a slavish devotion to fact rather than to faith. You must judge for yourself. But as the Apostle John said: "*If we say we have no sin, we deceive ourselves, and the truth is not in us.*"

I was an eyewitness to all events related here. This is a true and accurate account.

This ends the Prologue of *Jerusalem Falls!* Book I begins.

BOOK I
MY EARLY LIFE

I was born in the year of our Blessed Lord 1070 on the feast day of St. Michael the Martyr. Five years after my birth my father enrolled me in the cathedral school of Rheims, famous for the rigor and breadth of its learning. I studied for seven years, mastering all subjects of the *trivium* and the *quadrivium*. Classes were taught exclusively in Latin, which I learned both to speak and compose exceedingly well. I studied Greek and by the time I left was able to read and converse passably well. It was then I discovered my rather precocious aptitude for languages, something which would serve me well later. My father, a spice merchant, was particularly eager for me to master calculations, a necessary skill for conducting international trade. My progress in that discipline, however, disappointed him.

Business for my father, I believe, was good. Though expensive, spices were eagerly sought by the wealthy for they served so many uses: preserving food, improving the flavor of dishes, their medicinal properties, and not least according to popular belief their efficacy as aphrodisiacs. He had a small shop in the city, directly below our home, in which he prepared and sold his wares. After school I often helped him, less because I was interested in trade than just the pleasure of being with him. Perhaps I should have better used that time to master mathematical *formulae*.

At the age of twelve my father had business in Mainz. He asked me to accompany him. I gladly agreed, welcoming an opportunity to experience the world. I had no idea how profoundly that journey would change my life. We spent a night in the guesthouse of the Priory of La Charité sur Loire on the road to Mainz. I was overcome by the hospitality and piety of the monks. Equally, their conventions intrigued me: regular religious offices beginning at matins in the early morning to compline at night before the monks retired for bed; their long hours of perfect silence during which they communicated only in a complex system of sign language. I could not quite dismiss that experience from my mind.

At Mainz we stayed for three days with Samuel ben Meier, a Jewish business associate of my father, also a spice merchant. I liked him immediately; he was to become a second father to me. During that time, my father and Master Samuel consulted together on matters of trade.

Uninterested in the subject, no doubt yet another disappointment for my father, I explored the city. The Rhine was especially fascinating, such a contrast to the diminutive river that flowed through Rheims, the Vesle. I would sit on the bank staring at the river traffic and wander among the quays watching dockers load and unload cargo to and from barges.

One evening before our departure my father invited me to take a stroll with him. We walked quietly down the street. He broke the silence.

"Samuel likes you and sees great possibilities in your future, as I do."

"I like him too, father, though I don't understand what exactly he sees in me."

Father waved his hand dismissing my doubts. "Samuel has agreed to accept you as his apprentice . . . of sorts. What I mean by 'of sorts' is that local bishops never enforce apprenticeship contracts between Jews and non-Jews. However, this is an advantage for you will be bound only by a gentleman's agreement between Samuel and me. It can be broken at any time without penalty."

I thought on this for a moment. "How long would I serve under Master Samuel?"

"Perhaps three years," he replied, "but that depends on you and him. After you complete your apprenticeship, you will return to me and we will consider your future. What do you think?"

"I don't understand, father. Have I disappointed you in some way that you would wish me to live so far away?"

Father gently placed his arm around my shoulders and pulled me closer. "No, no, no my son," he whispered. "This is a marvelous opportunity, a chance for you to learn my trade under a different master with different ideas. But also by living with Samuel here in Mainz you will learn Teutonic, more importantly Hebrew as well. There are Jewish merchants in every city from here to Constantinople to Jerusalem and beyond. The traders of Francia cannot speak Arabic; Arabic traders cannot speak our language. Jews can communicate with one another across every boundary and border. And if you can converse with Jews throughout the world, there's no limit to your future in commerce."

I began to shudder with emotion. "I will miss you terribly."

"And I will miss you my son. But we will be together again soon." I never saw him again. He died two years later.

For the next three years I lived with Master Samuel and his wife Rachel. They treated me as their own son, occasionally referring to me as their "favorite gentile", terms they used with great affection. I shared that affection. I learned both Hebrew and the language of Germania. Master Samuel taught me so many things about his craft: how to grind spices to their proper grades; the culinary and medicinal properties of every spice he sold—cinnamon, pepper, tumeric, coriander, cumin, and others; how to present and sell them in his small shop fronting the street underneath his living quarters. He even took me to Venice to secure a contract with another Jewish spice merchant for the supply of herbs and spices more diverse than those he already sold. Three years passed quickly and happily.

But during those years, especially in the last, I became restless, wandering along the banks of the Rhine and into the woods near Mainz after my duties for the day were completed. Something was missing. I came to realize that, while perhaps my heart was full, my soul was empty. God was calling me to His service. It was time to leave. We had a tearful farewell. I promised never to forget them and that I would return. I kept that promise ten years later. Under tragic circumstances.

I journeyed to La Charité sur Loire and there became a monk.

This ends Book I of *Jerusalem Falls!* Book II begins.

BOOK II

MY LIFE AT LA CHARITÉ SUR LOIRE

Prior Damian Summons Me. Preparations for a Journey. Father
Benedict Falls Gravely Ill. The Relic of Saint John Exposed. Father
Benedict's Illness Diagnosed. Departure from La Charité.

Prior Damian Summons Me

It was in the year of 1085, at the age of fifteen years, that I entered the Priory of La Charité sur Loire. Soon thereafter I pledged my vows to a monastic life and became a novice. The next ten years of my novitiate were rewarding, especially the last five during which I served as a scribe in the priory's *scriptorium* under the watchful eye of its precentor, the beloved Father Benedict, a priest no less worthy than Noah of Genesis: "*A righteous man, blameless among the people of his time, and he walked faithfully with God.*" Father had on several occasions encouraged me to become ordained but I felt I was not ready to accept the burden of becoming a full choir monk. I was content with my station. In the summer of 1095, however, under his gentle yet relentless pressure, I consented.

It was October of that year that my life changed once more. From the fourth to sixth hour of every day the priory's *customaries*, our rules of order, permitted monks to read, a welcome respite from near continuous services throughout the day, from matins in the morning before even the sun rose to compline at night. I didn't want to read that day. My mind was focused elsewhere. I was close to completing my translation of *De Symptomatum Causis*, "On the Causes of Symptoms", by the Greek physician and philosopher Galen of Pergamon of Roman antiquity. I possessed both a copy in the original Greek produced by a scribe in a Byzantine monastery and a Latin translation. My training in Greek at the cathedral school of Rheims was sufficient for me to recognize the errors of the latter, too many for the work to be reliable. I obtained permission to be excused from reading and return to my work in the *scriptorium*—as a scribe copying ancient manuscripts I held an honored position in the priory allowing for occasional deviations from the regular order.

Father Benedict was curious how I was progressing with Galen. He stepped behind me, leaned over my shoulder squinting intently at my manuscript. He lingered for several moments. "Exquisite calligraphy," he whispered. "Who will do the illuminations? Garnier, I suppose? His depictions are so faithful to the subject and his inks so wonderfully vibrant."

"This has yet to be decided," I answered. "I think it will be a challenge. Galen explains the imperative of the four humors being in balance for perfect health. I am not sure how one can reproduce blood, yellow bile, black bile, and phlegm in a miniature."

"Hmm. I see your point. But I must say that I never understood the value of copying such a text, even though with reluctance I approved it."

I protested immediately. "We have no medical text in our *armarium*, indeed few books at all. "Yet we have an *infirmarium* in which we treat the sick and wounded. The *infirmarius* would benefit from reading the science of Galen."

"You must understand," Benedict replied quite firmly, "that sickness is the product of sin. It is God's just punishment. Sincere repentance and devout prayer are the only remedies, not false science even if derived from antiquity. If I could make the decision again, it would be different. I would have instructed you to write the life of one of our church's saints, Saint Apollonia perhaps, a martyr to our faith whose teeth were torn out for refusing to renounce her belief in Jesus Christ. Prayer to her is the only certain remedy for toothache and diseases of the gums. Although," Benedict pausing to reflect, "even more beneficial for the afflicted would be a pilgrimage to the Church of Santa Maria in Rome where her sainted head reposes in a reliquary. Our priory's *armarium* is spare of the lives of saints. This would have been a welcome addition. And," he added with emphasis, "it would advance our knowledge of medicine as you appear to wish."

I said nothing, fearful that Benedict might require me to cease my work. "But, my son," he said reassuringly, "you are nearly done and it needs to be completed." I swelled with relief.

"Tell me, Oderic, have you thought about your next project?"

"With your permission, Father," I answered, "I am thinking about writing the life of Saint John the Martyr. He was never formally canonized of course but he is our own local saint nonetheless."

"Yes, yes. His hand is in a reliquary on our church's high altar. But I know little of his story," Benedict answered.

"I too am uncertain of all the details of his life. I know only this: When three hundred years ago the Muslims conquered Alexandria and the territory around it, they forced Christians to convert to Islam on pain of losing a hand. John, may his saintly name be preserved, refused to deny Christ. Thrice they severed his hand, but thrice through the intercession of the Holy Mother of God his hand grew back."

"Oh yes," Benedict exclaimed excitedly, "the story is now coming back to me. Did they not cut off Saint John's head?"

"That is true," I answered. "But how the Muslims were unable to cut off John's hand three times, it being restored, and yet successfully cleave his head is a mystery to me. I believe that God had tested John's endurance and faith until finally He decided to call him to His bosom."

"Certainly so! Certainly so! Our Lord is wise and merciful," Benedict responded eagerly.

"However, as you know," I continued, "Saint John's legacy did not die at Alexandria. Some forty years ago Estienne, Vicomte of Bourges, made a pilgrimage to Jerusalem. On his return, he visited Alexandria and made the acquaintance of a Muslim who showed him Christian tombs in a catacomb under the city. There he saw a sarcophagus on which were incised the words 'John, a martyr to his Faith in Jesus Christ.' With the Muslim's help Estienne raised the lid and found a single hand, the body missing. He brought it home with him. Pilgrims from great distances travel to our priory seeking the healing power of this precious relic for all ailments of arms and hands. We can thank Vicomte Estienne for funding our priory before he died and for donating Saint John's hand. Without both of them we would not be here."

"You are a true son of La Charité," Benedict said. "Of course, I must reflect on this newly conceived undertaking of yours but the *armarius* would doubtless be pleased to add such a book to his collection." Benedict then came to the reason for his visit with me. "Prior Damian has requested your presence at his office. You must go now."

"Do you know why?" I asked with a mix of curiosity and anxiety. Such an invitation from the prior to a junior monk was highly unusual.

"No. He's waiting for you."

* * *

Damian's office adjoined the east transept of the church. The door was open. I timidly stepped in beyond the threshold, stopped and stood silently. I had never visited it before, perhaps no other monk either since it was reserved for consultations between the prior and the priory's senior officers, the *obedentiaries*: the subprior, sacristan, precentor, almoner, cellarer, and others. I was apprehensive. The room was dimly lit, only one window, a small rectangular opening in the stone wall, and a candle. As my eyes adjusted I could discern to my left a single table on which lay various documents, presumably relating to priory business. At the far end, directly opposite me, was a desk behind which sat Damian. He seemed deep in thought studying what appeared to be a letter in his hand. I waited. Damian finally looked up.

"Oh, it's you, Oderic. I hope you have not been standing there long. I didn't hear you. Come in. Come in." Damian rose from his chair and came around the desk to greet me. I bowed and gave the *benedicte*, "May the Lord bestow His blessings on you."

"And on you, my son," he answered. He offered his ring which I kissed.

Damian was an elderly man, rather stooped in frame, with deep lines in his face and a prominently bent nose—caused by an accident, I heard, when as a lay brother at the Abbey of Cluny before becoming a monk he was harvesting in a field and was struck accidentally by the handle of a scythe. But this description is insufficient. He had served as prior for ten years, beneficent and just, although occasionally curt in speech to the foolish—he suffered the lame in body but not those in mind. He was, nevertheless, much loved by all the monks of the priory.

"Come," he said. "Sit with me. I have a task for you . . . well, for us both."

There were three chairs in the office. He pulled two up and positioned them at angles to one another. He motioned for me to sit. "I have just received a letter from Abbot Hugh of Cluny," his finger pointing to a document on his desk. "He has summoned me, as well as all *obedientiary* priors subject to the abbey, to a plenary chapter meeting at Cluny. His Holiness Pope Urban II will attend. He will also consecrate the high altar of its basilica. This is a great honor and Abbot Hugh wishes us all to be present." Damian paused in momentary reflection. "But there must be something more. I have heard that the pope is now, as we speak, traveling through the lands of Francia in the south—Provence, Burgundy, Auvergne, Toulouse, and others—visiting churches and monasteries. Abbot Hugh informs me that His Holiness has sent letters to all the bishops and abbots to attend him in council at Clermont."

"At Clermont? What's in Clermont?" I asked.

"I don't know. Hugh intimates that the pope's message will be important but he does not clarify the purpose." Damian paused again. "I want you to accompany me there and after that to Cluny. I would like you to make all travel arrangements. You must plan a route that will allow us to enjoy the hospitality of Cluniac priories on the road; this will relieve you of the burden of finding accommodations. The journey will likely take a month."

"Who will be traveling with us?" I asked. "I assume the claustral sub-prior, your chaplain, the chamberlain, and some brother monks?"

"No. Just you and me."

I was startled. "Why me? I am merely a scribe without holding any responsible portfolio in our priory. I do not understand what value I can bring to this mission."

"The plenary chapter meeting in the abbey will be attended by all Cluniac priors," Damian explained. "Matters of consequential business will be considered. With age, my mind has become less retentive than it was. I will surely forget at least some of the decisions made there. I need you to take notes of the proceedings. You will require several wax tablets."

I went silent. Damian could see that I was disturbed. "What is it?" he asked.

"Just the two of us? I must plead with you to reconsider. I am of course honored you would ask me to accompany you. It would be a blessing to worship in the Basilica of Cluny, unrivaled I'm told anywhere in Christian lands."

"Then what troubles you?"

"Father Prior, I beg you to forgive my bluntness." Damian waved his hand indicating permission for me to speak further. "These are increasingly perilous times. The old order seems to be collapsing. There is civil strife everywhere. No place is secure. Brigands frequent our highways, robbing and killing. And many of these villains are not mere bandits. They include nobles who poach not only on the poor but on one another, seeking every advantage by ruse or by the sword. I cannot guarantee your safety alone." Damian looked down at the floor in thought. I believed this my opportunity to press the point. "Nobles not only assault other nobles. They even have the temerity to assault men of the cloth. You have heard of Lambert, Bishop of Arras?" Damian nodded. "Then you know he was kidnapped near Provins by a robber lord, Guarnier of Trainel, I believe, and held for ransom. He was released only through the personal intervention of the pope who threatened to excommunicate him. You are a prior, custodian of a prosperous priory, an attractive target for anyone seeking mischief, common brigand or unscrupulous lord. You *must* have an entourage to protect you."

For a moment I thought I had given Damian pause. I hadn't. "These are perilous times indeed," Damian agreed. "And I understand your anxiety. I think, however, the dangers you apprehend for us both are likely exaggerated. The Peace of God declared by the Church will provide our security. Remember too that we are doing the Lord's work. He will protect us." I thought to myself that this so-called "Peace" had not benefited the Bishop of Arras. Further efforts to dissuade Damian from what I sincerely believed to be a dangerously ill-conceived plan would be fruitless. I looked up at the crucifix on the bare wall above Damian's desk and made a quick and silent prayer.

"We must leave in two weeks' time," Damian instructed. "You will make all arrangements: a cart, a horse, perhaps a sumpter mule for excess baggage, food for the two of us as we travel between priories, and a sufficient supply of clothes. You must consult with the chamberlain regarding our daily needs, especially clothing, and with the sacristan whose help will be needed to select formal ecclesiastical vestments for me—after all, we will be in the presence of the pope. I would also like him to find an appropriate gift for Cluny's basilica from our treasury to grace its high altar for the pope's consecration. You may dispense with the normal silent hours. Your task is difficult enough without being restricted to signing."

Damian rose from his chair and briefly placed his hand on my shoulder knowing I was in distress. We exchanged *benedictes*. I left to begin immediate preparations.

Preparations for a Journey

It was mid-morning. The air was crisp with the smell of fall though warmed by a bright sun. As I approached the priory gate, the porter emerged from his small shed. He squinted at me, cupping his hand over his forehead to shield his eyes. I drew nearer.

"Good morning Father." I nodded in response. "Are you leaving the priory?" he asked, the porter's principal responsibility to prevent unauthorized passage into or out of the priory.

"Yes. I have permission from the prior."

"Not many monks leave the priory. Pretty rare. Guess they don't let you out much."

I nodded in agreement. "Nevertheless, I have a charge from the prior and cannot tarry here."

"And what 'charge' is that?" he asked hesitatingly. "Forgive me Father, but the last time I let a monk through he too said he had permission from the prior. Turned out he didn't. Went to a tavern in the village. 'Fraternized', they said. Got caught." I heard that at a chapter meeting such accusations were made. The offending monk explained he was only there to bring the Holy Light of Scripture to wayward women, women who sold their 'wares' out of a tavern. He was defrocked and expelled from the priory. Father, your name, if you please?"

"Oderic. I am a scribe serving in the *scriptorium*. And I assure you I'm on the prior's business."

He began mumbling, repeating my name twice to himself, "Oderic . . . ? Oderic . . . ?" as though trying to recall something. "Hmm. Yes, I've heard of you. A righteous monk, I'm told. I'll let you pass. But you must swear that if anything's amiss, you will vouch for me with the chamberlain. The last time he warned that another dereliction, letting a monk pass through the priory's gates without proper permission, would result in dismissal from service."

"I swear it. You have nothing to worry about."

The porter unlatched the wrought iron gate and waved me through. "Father. Do you know where you're headed? Need directions?"

"I'm going to the stable. I've never been there before."

"Oh, it's a short walk. Take that path to the right."

I thanked him for his kindness, coming soon to the priory's stable housing horses belonging both to the priory as well as to visitors temporarily quartered in the guesthouse. I passed through the paddock holding perhaps five horses grazing on sparse grass oblivious to my presence and walked to the horse barn. A worker inside, I assumed the *connestabulus* in charge of the stable, was just inside the door grooming a horse.

I walked up and gently stroked the horse's flank. "Lovely animal," I said.

The *connestabulus* was bent over, brushing the horse's leg near its hoof. He immediately stood upright, looking at me over the back of the horse. "Excuse me, Father," doffing his hat, "I didn't hear you. We rarely see monks. The horse? It's a palfrey, nice and gentle. Belongs to a nobleman's wife. She and her companion spent the night in the guesthouse and will be leaving shortly. I'm getting the horse ready. Is there aught I can do for you Father?"

"Yes. I'm on the prior's business. I've heard there's a carriage stored here for use by priors. Is that so?"

"Indeed," he answered. "Let me show you. It's right down there," pointing to the far end of the barn. As we walked he gave his name as Piers.

I needed a closer look and gingerly stepped over saddles, bridles, and stirrups thrown haphazardly on the ground, Piers following behind. "I apologize for the mess, Father. I'm a bit shorthanded and haven't gotten around to straightening up the place."

I dismissed the apology. "I'm not here to inspect the barn but to see the carriage."

Even in the dim light and from a distance the carriage seemed incandescent glowing with silver and gold leaf trim that ran along the middle of all four exterior sides, perhaps six inches wide. Above it were intricately painted swirls painted in gold; below, also swirls but differently figured in silver paint. The wooden spokes of the four wheels were luminescent red, the felloes to which the spokes were fixed an equally luminescent yellow. The effect was dazzling.

"It's a beauty alright," Piers said fondly, sensing my admiration.

"How long has the priory had it?" I asked.

"I don't know. At least since I came here, nigh ten years ago. I was told it was a gift from the family of the Vicomte of Bourges."

"May I look inside?" I could see no way of climbing up into the carriage from the front. There were neither footplates nor a perch for a driver, a postillion I assumed who would sit on one of the horses to guide them, and only a small door at the front which was probably intended for ventilation.

"Yes of course. This way." He led me to the back. A short ladder, four rungs, hung on two bright copper hooks just beside the door. He untied the leather strap that secured the lower part of the ladder to the body of the carriage, lifted the ladder off of its hooks, set it on the ground against the door sill. Sweeping away the cobwebs, testifying to its lack of use, Piers climbed up and gently pushed the door open, looking briefly inside. He came down. "We would keep it cleaner but the present prior, and in fact his predecessor, never uses it. Pity."

I then climbed up and stepped inside. There were two benches, easily seating six, of polished mahogany with cushions covered in purple velvet embroidered with gold thread and yellow tassels dangling from the sides. Two windows on either side of the interior wall provided light. Between the windows were immaculately painted scenes from the Old Testament: David with his sling just before hurling a stone at Goliath; Samson between two columns, his arms outstretched against each, ready to take the edifice down; Noah on the prow of his ark, a dove settling down on his hand. It was truly glorious.

"Father, may I ask. Your purpose here is what?"

"Well, I'm taking the prior on an extended journey south, and we need transportation."

"How many are going?" Piers asked.

"Just the two of us, the prior and I. This may be too large for our needs."

"No, no," he quickly protested. "He needs to travel in a manner appropriate to his position. This carriage is magnificent. It represents the wealth and prestige of our priory. It's fit for a bishop!"

At that moment, I realized he was exactly right. Such a sumptuous carriage would excite unwelcome curiosity, not to mention cupidity or worse, that could be met on the road. Something less conspicuous was needed. My response was careful: "The prior is a man without vanity who avoids extravagance. Do you have anything here more modest that would fit his need?"

"Not here," he replied. "I'd suggest you check with one of our deaneries. They use carts for all their farming operations. But I will warn you they will be disappointing." He thought for a moment. "I think the best equipped deanery is just down the road, four miles perhaps," he pointed south. "I would inquire there."

"I'll need a horse. Do you have one available?"

"Yes. Just give me a few moments to fetch and saddle the animal."

As I waited, I continued to admire the carriage. And I thought on Piers's remark: "Fit for a bishop." I became even more convinced that my decision to use a less grand conveyance was correct. I only hoped the prior would agree. The horse came. I headed south in the direction Piers pointed me.

I arrived at the deanery, recognizable by its large stone-built barn next to the road. I dismounted and tethered my horse to a fence. There was a barn a half-bowshot away and next to it a small field where sheep, goats, and cows were grazing, the milk of the latter two used for butter and cheese; a separate corral for oxen used to pull plows; a tannery close by; beehives for the production of honey and candle wax; and several sheds whose purpose I could not discern. The deanery truly reflected Saint Benedict's injunction for monastic life: "Be self-sufficient in all things". The twin doors of the barn were open and I could see two men stacking hay with pitchforks. Hemp bags filled with wheat, oats, peas, beans, and barley, all produce of the deanery, were stacked high against the walls. One of laborers, seeing me, laid down his pitchfork and approached.

"Good day, Father," he greeted me. "We rarely receive visits from monks. I'm Paul, the deacon here. May I help you with your inquiry?"

"Perhaps," I replied. Wishing to avoid an unnecessarily complicated conversation involving the prior, I was more careful with my explanation than I had been with the *connestabulus*. "A fellow monk and I are making a trip, some miles distant, and we require a cart for ourselves and our baggage. Do you have one that might accommodate our needs?"

"Well, I'm not sure I have anything you will find appropriate. Follow me if you would." Paul led me to a large shed behind the barn. It was filled with plows, harnesses, and several tumbrils, two-wheeled carts without rear gates their beds able to be raised and contents easily raked out. They were arranged in two rows, their twin shafts and crossbars resting on the ground pointing inwards. The spacious corridor between was large enough for two men to pull them out of the shed. As he led me down the corridor Paul described the carts. "They're all dedicated to specific purposes. It saves time that way because we don't need to clean each one when its use changes. This one," pointing to the left, "carries fresh vegetables from the fields to the priory," his explanation unnecessary for its use was evident from the dried broccoli flowerets, lettuce leaves, and onion skins scattered over the bed. "And this one," pointing to the right, "is for hauling animal shit, I mean . . . I mean . . . excuse me Father. I intended to say 'manure' which we haul from both the priory's stable and the cow barn to spread on our fields." Again, this cart in particular required no explanation, its service abundantly evident from the odor and dried dung stuck to the side walls. He continued as we walked down, Paul expressing clear pride in his carts: "This one is for hauling hay, this for grain, this for peas, this for lentils," and on it went until, gratefully, we reached the end of the barn. "Well, Father, what do you think? I just don't believe any of them is suitable." But then he paused, having a second thought. He looked up; I followed his eyes. There was a cart hanging by ropes from a rafter, raised and lowered by pulleys. I could not suppose its function or the reason for storing it there other than there seemed limited space on the floor. "You know, this just *might* work. We use it, fortunately not often, for transporting lay brothers who have suffered an accident to the priory's infirmary." Without waiting for a comment from me he walked out of the shed and shouted: "Roland, get over here. I need your help!" The cart was lowered. It was solidly built with a spacious bed, its sides made of rough, weathered planks set horizontally on top of each other secured in place by upright supports. Humble and inconspicuous enough. And fairly clean. I thought it sufficient for our needs.

"This will do", I said.

"When do you need it?"

"In two weeks."

"We can have it ready. Do you require anything else?"

"Perhaps. This cart may not be large enough for the amount of baggage we will be taking. I just left the priory's stable but neglected to ask if they had a sumpter mule. Might you have one?"

Paul chuckled. "No point asking there. They're too grand to stable mules, let alone those used as pack animals. I guess we're less worthy. But yes. We have three. I'll pick one."

"And finally, I'll need a horse to pull the cart," I said.

"Of course. I know just the one. Esther. A mule. She's trained to pull a cart."

I thanked him, remounted my horse and returned to the priory.

* * *

It was late, close to sext. I had not expected to spend so much time at the deanery. The monks would already be gathering in the cloister for their obligatory communal shaving of faces and tonsures superintended by the chamberlain, Father Roderick. I thought this the perfect opportunity to talk with him about travel preparations and the apparel we would need, of which he had charge.

I quickly rode back to the priory, tethered my horse to a rail of the corral, and hastened into the cloister. Fortunately I was just in time and able to slip unnoticed among them. Benches, taken from the refectory, had been arranged in a long row end-to-end. Using hand signs Roderic directed us to separate into two lines on either side of the benches, front and back. Instructions were hardly necessary because such shavings took place on the same day, at the same time, every week. Monks in front of the benches sat down, behind each another monk, at his feet a basin of soapy water in which was placed a razor sharpened earlier that morning in the kitchen ready to begin the shaving at Roderick's signal, all singing in unison a psalm especially dedicated to shaving—there is in the priory a hymn for every occasion and activity. Roderick slowly walked down the row, intently inspecting each face and tonsure for a tuft or even a strand of hair left uncut. An omission resulted in a sharp slap on the shoulder of the offending monk.

The shaving was now completed. The monks returned the bowls to the kitchen and after enduring the cool of the open-air cloister hastened to the *calefactory* where they could warm themselves before the blazing communal fire, one of the few heated rooms in the priory. They would then attend to their regular duties. Roderick and I were alone in the cloister. He had collected the razors in a wicker basket, took them to a cabinet, stored them on the shelves, and then locked it with a key from his chain. He had just placed the chain back around his neck when I decided to speak, with decided apprehension for speaking to a senior officer of a monastery without invitation, even though I had the prior's permission, always invited rebuke, particularly from this one.

The chamberlain was tall, thin as a blade used for filleting perch from the priory's fish pond, and an angular face incised with a perpetual scowl. His speech to monks, especially to novices, was abrupt, caustic, and condescending. We novices had given him a nickname, "ankle-biter". In chapter, however, and only when Prior Damian was present, his manner was decidedly fawning and unguent, always appealing to his own self-interest albeit cloaked in pious humility. I could never understand why he found such favor in Damian's eyes other than the blessed prior saw good in all living things—even if he held a flower in his hands, its petals brown from blight, he would exclaim "Oh what a marvelous life this daisy has led."

"Father Roderick. I must speak with you."

Roderick wheeled around, fully thrusting out his arm with a finger directed at my face, wagging it side to side in an accusatory fashion. "You are speaking during silent hours. Be still! I will report this breach at chapter!"

I was rather stunned by his ferocity, momentarily unable to respond. "Father," I stammered, "I am on the prior's business and under his instructions. I need to consult with you."

Roderick appeared as startled by my answer as I had been by the severity of his reproach for a prior's business was ordinarily transacted by one of his officers, not by a junior monk. But his face was no less tightly drawn than it was before. "What is it? I'm busy."

"Prior Damian is making a trip south to hear a sermon of the Holy Father at Clermont; he intends to travel next to Cluny. He wishes you to assist with his preparations, in particular selecting his daily clothes for this long journey. I think shoes as well. He must wear a monk's tunic for the trip but nothing conspicuous that would attract attention."

Roderick's demeanor softened, albeit only slightly. "Hmm. Prior Damian has not discussed this with me. I know nothing of it. But I shall do as he requests." He paused in reflection, gazing down at the floor. "Let me think, let me think," as he held his hands on both cheeks, spinning slowly around in a circle looking up to the sky, contemplating. "I shall need a wardrobe for myself, of course. The claustral subprior will be coming. Probably the sacristan and maybe the chaplain as well." He hesitated. "Who else?" a question more directed to himself than to me. "The precentor perhaps . . . no. He wouldn't be needed. But no doubt five or so brother monks will accompany us. When do we leave?"

"With apologies, Father Roderick, I am to accompany him alone. There will be only the two of us, none else."

In the time it takes to ignite a spark from flint he flew into a fury, his face reddened, his eyes on fire. "You boy? You? *You* will see the pope?" he snickered. "The shame of it! I cannot stand for this! I will *not* assist!" In that instant Roderick caught himself. I could see it in his eyes. He realized that he was violating *the* imperative of monastic life: absolute and unquestioning obedience to ones prior. His voice immediately mellowed. "When does he leave?"

"In two weeks."

Roderick turned around and walked away. Without looking back "Prior Damian will be ready."

I had few dealings with the chamberlain after that. He died during my pilgrimage to Jerusalem. I did not mourn his passing. I had yet to meet with the sacristan responsible for overseeing donations to the priory, its treasury of sacerdotal vessels, and the prior's vestments. I now dreaded the same unpleasant reaction from him as I received from Roderick. Happily, that proved not to be the case. I explained the purpose of the journey and that I alone would accompany the prior. No objection was raised. He fetched coins from the priory's coffers to meet the expenses of our journey and from the treasury a silver candelabra of beautiful craftsmanship, a gift he thought appropriate for the consecration of Cluny's high altar by the Vicar of Christ. I thanked him effusively, perhaps as much for his kindly treatment as his assistance.

Father Benedict Falls Gravely Ill

Three days later I was at my writing desk in the *scriptorium*. My fellow scribes, Garnier and Roul, were present too, absorbed in their labors. Benedict had come in shortly before and was walking from desk to desk inspecting our work, his hands clasped behind his back as he peered over our shoulders. I was just putting the finishing touches to my translation of Galen, quill in hand with a full horn of ink, when I heard an indistinct murmur, something like "I ache. I ache." Looking up, I saw Benedict stumbling, one hand grabbing the back of a chair to steady himself, the other on his belly. His face was flushed. For moments I just watched, uncertain whether he needed assistance. But then he fell. I leapt up from my stool and rushed over.

"You're ill, Father!" I cried out. "Let me help you."

Garnier and Roul jumped up to help. Together we lifted him into a chair. I was uncertain what to do; my study of Galen had not prepared me for this. "Let's get him to the bench over there in the corner," inclining my head in its direction. "We can lay him down."

With Garnier and Roul on each side of him, their arms around his waist, they lifted him up. He was slight of build so the task seemed easy. That is, until fully standing, his legs buckled and then collapsed under him. They gently set him back down into the chair.

I was nearly hysterical. "We'll need a litter to carry him! Garnier, go fetch one from the *infirmarium*. Quickly!"

In the meantime I went into the kitchen, found a sponge, soaked it thoroughly, and then returned to Benedict patting his face to cool the flush. Garnier returned with the litter. It was placed on the floor and the three of us pulled him off the chair and gently laid him on it. We carried him to the *infirmarium*.

I had never been there. It was a long, rectangular room, its ceiling supported by two arches at either end and two rows of columns running down the center, seven or eight feet apart, forming a wide aisle in the middle like the nave of a church. Under each arch was a fireplace. The ceiling was fifteen feet tall allowing air to circulate freely and several large windows providing natural light. Despite its somewhat grim function a certain cheerfulness radiated throughout. The *infirmarium* was a monastery in miniature, almost completely self-contained. It had its own kitchen in a small adjoining building for preparing special foods appropriate to the sick, usually chicken, perch, grains, nuts, greens, and fruits. The rule against eating meat, rigorously applied to all other monks, was relaxed here. The *misericordia*, the refectory dedicated to infirmary purposes, was in a separate room adjoining the kitchen and was where ambulatory monks took their meals. There was a bloodletting room, a modest cloister for exercise and personal reflection, and a garden dedicated both to vegetables and herbs possessing medicinal properties: rosemary, fennel, sage, pennyroyal, mustard, among others. Ten or so beds were arranged side-by-side, their headboards abutting the wall and end boards nearly touching the columns. Beside each bed was an upright chair and a small table on which would be placed food for those unable to walk to the *misericordia*, a ewer of water with a cup beside it, medicine, and a book—commonly a psalter—used by those well enough to read. Each bed had its own curtain which could be drawn for privacy, forming separate cubicles when necessary. Half of the beds were occupied by elderly monks, not necessarily ill but whose age prevented them from fully participating in daily monastic activities and who required special attention, particularly their dietary needs. Three beds were occupied by monks who suffered from some indeterminate illness, and one by a lay worker whose leg was in a splint, probably broken while laboring in one of the deaneries. Two staff attendants, the *infirmari*, were busy with various household tasks: sweeping the paved floor, wiping down the walls and cabinets, and collecting clothes to be washed in the kitchen's cauldron and then hung to dry in the cloister. Fortunately four beds were available.

The *infirmarius*, master of the *infirmarium*, Guarin, emerged drowsily from behind a curtain, obviously having just awakened from sleep, hobbling on a cane. I had never met him but I knew him by reputation. He was a kindly monk, quite aged. He had been appointed two years earlier, a choice clearly influenced by his mastery of penitential psalms rather than his knowledge of or interest in the medical arts. He, like Benedict, believed that prayer, especially to the Virgin Mary, was the perfect tonic for every ill. Among his duties, the one he particularly enjoyed, was sprinkling holy water daily over patients' beds while reciting prayers. I doubted that he would be my first reader of Galen.

"Where do we lay him?" I asked.

"Over there," he replied. We carefully laid Benedict on the bed and covered him with a felted woolen blanket; I gently lifted his head pushing a pillow underneath.

"What ails Father Benedict? Too much wine at midday dinner?" Guarin asked. I could not tell if he were serious or merely trying to lighten the mood with humor, our anxiety obvious to him.

"No, I think not," I answered. "He collapsed in the *scriptorium*, clutching his belly. I don't know if he merely ate something disagreeable or whether it's more serious."

At that moment another man approached, more alert than Guarin. He walked over to Benedict's bed, bent over, and intently studied him. Guarin introduced him. "This is Geoffrey of Turin. He is a *conversus* and assists me in the infirmary. How long has it been Geoffrey . . . three years now?" Geoffrey nodded without taking his eyes off Benedict. The *conversi* are laymen who in their mature years join a monastery and serve in various capacities. They take the vows of a monk and are thus entitled to wear the scapular but not the complete vows of a choir monk such as I. "He is a 'Doctor of Physik'," Guarin said in a barely concealed mocking tone. "He even attended medical school," pausing, "Salerno, wasn't it Geoffrey?" Again, Geoffrey merely nodded, his concentration unbroken. I was relieved that Benedict was under Geoffrey's care, less because of his pedigree as a graduate of Salerno, renowned for its medical studies including Arabic learning, but because of his undivided attention to Benedict. "He possesses a curious view," Guarin continued, relentlessly, "that herbs and poultices have greater healing powers than prayer to the Holy Mother Mary who has miraculously cured many an affliction, or to Saint Raphael the Archangel, the patron saint of healing." Geoffrey ignored Guarin, continuing to intently study Benedict. Thankfully, Guarin wandered off back behind his curtain, no doubt frustrated that his taunts had not provoked a reaction.

"What ails him?" Geoffrey asked, turning to me.

"I'm not sure. He was clutching his stomach and then collapsed."

"Nausea, perhaps?" Geoffrey asked.

"Yes, maybe. I don't know."

"Let's get him to the *lavatorium*," looking to Garnier and Roul for assistance. "Do you think you can make it with help?" Geoffrey asked Benedict. He nodded. Garnier and Roul, supporting him, took Benedict to a rather small rectangular room with two rows of toilet benches facing one another extending the length of the room. Holes had been cut out every three feet, the excreta falling into a water trough below fed by a stream diverted from the river into the priory's fish pond. No wonder, I thought, the fish were so plump. Between the toilet rows were two stone washbasins. We gently sat Benedict on one of the toilets. In the meantime, Geoffrey had left the *lavatorium*, returning quickly holding a flask in one hand and a chart of some kind in the other.

"Father, you'll need to urinate in this," handing Benedict the flask. "You can finish in the toilet." Benedict complied. Geoffrey held the flask up to the light, squinting at its contents for a few moments, then compared the urine to the colors on his chart. That done, he set the chart down and poured some urine from the flask into a cup sitting on the washbasin swirling it around. He stuck his nose into the cup sniffing and lightly tasting it. His face momentarily squirreled up but then forced it into an impassive mien as though he didn't want to betray his thinking. Tasting urine was such a common diagnostic tool of physicians that I thought Geoffrey would surely have become accustomed to its taste by now, yet he was clearly disturbed. Now I was too.

"What is it Father?" forgetting that a *conversus* is not a choir monk.

Geoffrey looked sharply at me. "First of all, I am *not* a 'father'. I have no children, nor do I want or deserve any," a rejoinder more sarcastic than edifying. "Nor am I a priest. I am a Doctor of Physik! No more! I am satisfied being a *conversus*. You choir monks attend offices all day; you master the psalms, hymns, and litanies. It's enough that I am a physician. Besides, I can't sing. You may call me Geoffrey."

I had unwittingly given offense. "Forgive me, Father, I mean 'Geoffrey', but you seemed troubled by something."

"Return him to his bed," Geoffrey instructed, not responding to me.

Garnier and Roul assisted Benedict back to his bed and then left, returning to the *scriptorium* to resume their work. Geoffrey drew up a chair next to Benedict's bed, his hands palpitating Benedict's stomach, feeling his pulse, placing the back of his hand on Benedict's forehead checking for fever, and raising the blanket to inspect the condition of his skin and limbs, squeezing both arms and legs. After completing his examination, he sat back in the chair, hands folded, staring at Benedict.

"Geoffrey, if you please, I have a question though I don't want to interrupt your work."

"Yes?"

"Do you believe in the power of prayer to cure?" I confess that I was disturbed by Guarin's dismissal of Geoffrey's lack of faith in the efficacy of divine intercession.

"I treat afflictions of the body. You treat those of the spirit. They're different," he answered curtly.

I hesitated to press the question, fearing yet another offense. I continued nonetheless. "You haven't really answered my question."

Geoffrey thought, answering rather carefully. "Of course, anything that strengthens the mind and the will to live is always useful therapy." I was conflicted: God's judgment or Galen's science? I wondered which was more efficacious in Geoffrey's mind. "Enough questions from you," he said gruffly. "I have a patient here requiring my attention. And I have my own questions of him. But he's too weak now to answer them. I'll attend to him tomorrow."

"Do you mind if I'm present?" I asked.

"No, not at all. It might even be comforting for Father Benedict. Do you have a close relationship with him?"

"Yes, quite close."

"Good," he answered. "That may be more helpful than prayer. Be here immediately after chapter." With that, I bid Geoffrey good day. It was now time for quiet reading and study in the cloister with the other monks.

* * *

Chapter the next day was uneventful other than a prayer said for Benedict's recovery. Fearing that I would be late, I hurried to the *infirmarium*. I went to Benedict's bed. He was sitting up, supported by a pillow, murmuring a prayer, barely audible but I could recognize it, the penitential prayer from one of the Psalms:

> *Have mercy on me, Oh God,*
> *according to your unfailing love.*
> *Have compassion and blot out my transgressions.*
> *Wash away all my iniquity and cleanse me from my sin.*

Benedict, looking up at me, interrupted his prayer and smiled weakly. He beckoned me to sit close beside him on the bed. He said nothing, just looking into my eyes. Nor did I, though my own expression showing intense concern and love was speech enough. Geoffrey was making his rounds from patient to patient earnestly inquiring about their conditions. The strict rule against speaking was of necessity relaxed here. He came over to Benedict's bed and settled in the chair beside him. I stood up, stepped to the rear of the bed and remained standing.

"Father Benedict, I have some questions for you. Do you feel well enough to answer them?" Benedict nodded.

"Are you urinating more than usual?" Benedict nodded.

"Do you have dizzy spells?" Again, Benedict nodded.

"What about thirst, more than usual?"

"Yes."

"And hunger, fatigue? Depressed?"

"A little. More than in the past," Benedict answered.

"Father, I have only two more questions. When did the excessive urination and thirst begin?"

"Two weeks ago."

"Hmm. I believe that was when Taurus was ascendant. I can't remember what was the phase of the moon. I'll have to check my zodiac chart for both. Finally, under what sign were you born? I need to know this to understand the physical ailments to which you are predisposed."

"Aries," Benedict replying rather weakly. "Jupiter was then rising. I know this because my father had visited an astrologer about a day after my birth to cast my horoscope. He was pleased about Jupiter because it promised riches and honor for me. I think he was disappointed when I became a monk."

The questions stopped. Geoffrey sat there gazing at Benedict but obviously quietly weighing his responses. "It is too early to provide a diagnosis with confidence," he said. I was surprised. The look on Geoffrey's face when he tasted Benedict's urine and the precision of his questions, all receiving affirmative answers, made me certain that he already knew the source of Benedict's ailment. But Geoffrey was unrevealing.

Geoffrey continued: "Obviously your humors are out of balance. I suspect the culprit is an excess of black bile, a cold and dry humor which can excite melancholy, hence your depression. Bloodletting will release some of that from your body and improve your disposition. We shall begin tomorrow, an auspicious day for the procedure. We raise leeches in our fish pond. I'll catch a few, less painful than a knife across your veins. I will also speak with the keeper of the refectory about your diet. Black bile is cold. Also, when we are young, we are warm and moist but with age we become increasingly cold and dry. Therefore, we will need to counteract with a diet of warm dishes: fried perch, mutton boiled in vegetables, heated wine. Oh, and boiled eggs but no cheese!" Geoffrey stated emphatically. I will also mix an elixir of henbane, mandrake, and mustard as a salve for your belly. This should relieve the nausea." Looking at me, "I'll know more in two or three days. Come back then."

I was about to take my leave when Benedict motioned me to come closer. He had something he wished to whisper in my ear. As I leaned over, I could detect an unusual sweetness in his breath. "I'll miss you." I couldn't interpret Benedict's meaning but it sounded foreboding.

The Relic of Saint John Exposed

I returned to the *scriptorium*. My translation of Galen was complete. I had decided that illumination was superfluous. The manuscript required only binding which I entrusted to Roul. He enjoyed this work more than the tedious labor of copying—sticky, viscous honey flowed faster than writing one sentence with a quill. Roul had already pierced the parchment papers with an awl and was now sewing them together with an iron needle threading the pages together. He would later cover the manuscript, front and back, with wooden boards. I wasn't sure whether the boards would be covered simply in leather or in ornately embroidered fabric. I suspected the former. This was, after all, a manual of science not the life of some revered saint. Nevertheless, I looked forward to the finished product.

I had four days before the prior's and my departure to Clermont. I wanted to begin my biography of Saint John but first needed permission from Benedict, though he was too indisposed to give it. I must see the prior. Besides, something else was on my mind. I went first to Damian's office in the church. It was empty. I was about to leave when I spotted a monk kneeling in an apsidal chapel in deep prayer. There were two on either side of the apse. This one was reserved for the prior, though occasionally an errant monk prayed there when the others were in use. A single candle was lit on the altar, its light flickering dimly. I stepped quietly forward to ascertain the monk's identity. Sensing my presence, he turned his head. It was Damian.

"Hello Oderic. And what brings you here?"

I bowed. "My deep apologies Father Prior. I had no intention of disturbing your prayers. We can talk later."

"No. Now is fine. I finished my prayer. It was to Saint Raphael the Archangel for Father Benedict's quick recovery. How is he faring?"

"I too pray for the best but I fear the worst."

"Well, I hope you're wrong."

I couldn't resist the next question. "Father Damian, with the deepest respect, why were you not praying to our priory's own Saint John the Martyr. His relic is just over there," pointing back over my shoulder to the high altar on which rested a reliquary holding Saint John's hand.

"I suppose I could," he answered. "But Saint John is a local saint, never canonized by the Mother Church. I think that Saint Raphael would be a more powerful, more influential, voice with the Holy Mother of God in Heaven. Let's sit on the bench outside the chapel. We can talk there."

We sat together. "I have completed my translation of Galen. There are yet four days before we leave. I would like to begin another project. However, without Father Benedict's permission I cannot and he's too infirm to give it."

"Does Benedict know of this project?" he asked.

"Yes, he approved it. Well . . . he didn't object."

"That's sufficient for me. Anyway, who am I to dispute the precentor? What project is this Oderic?"

"The life of Saint John"

"Why do you wish to write his life? You're a scribe, a copyist, not a chronicler."

"True," I replied. "But pilgrims come to our church and pray before Saint John's relic. A chronicle of his life would bring more. We are situated on the road to Santiago de Compostela where numerous pilgrims travel to venerate the remains of Saint James. Why should they not stop at our beautiful church to invoke the healing powers of our *own* saint, especially those suffering from afflictions of the fingers, hands, and arms. I have heard that some, after praying, fell into a profound sleep in front of the high altar and on awakening were cured. I'm even told that the arm of one pilgrim, previously severed in combat, was miraculously restored. We might also consider manufacturing and selling pilgrim badges, or perhaps amulets." In my breathless desire for permission I instantly feared that I had overstepped, appealing to Damian's cupidity of which he had little instead of his faith which he possessed in abundance. I pressed no further.

"Yes. Yes. I understand. But how do you know it's authentic? There are stories . . ."

I knew there were questions about the authenticity of relics from the Holy Land, even shared by some bishops. Two churches, one in Rome and another in Amiens, even today claim the head of John the Baptist, one in Constantinople as well. Several hold reliquaries containing the foreskin of Jesus—I wondered whether Jesus grew a new member after each circumcision when he was a boy. There are several shrines possessing the navel of Christ, wooden boards from the manger in which He had been born, the flail with which He had been whipped, the sponge from which He drank on the cross, even the table napkin Jesus used at the Last Supper. But now was not the moment for doubt.

"Forgive me Father. I understand your concern but . . ."

Damian interrupted me. "I realize that every church, every monastery, wishes to acquire as many relics as possible. They enhance their reputations and bring donations enriching the Church. But I am troubled that we may have forfeited faith for avarice. We must beware of relics, including the hand of Saint John, which become the objects of idol worship. Although he believed in the power of relics, Saint Augustine warned against this practice. They must be venerated for their reflection of God's Grace. No more."

I now expected Damian to deny my request until he asked "How confident are you this hand is genuine?"

"I am quite confident, Father. No, I am *absolutely* certain! It was a donation, not a transaction, from Estienne, Vicomte of Bourges, who had indeed traveled to the Holy Land."

"Then I approve. How do you plan to proceed?"

"I have heard that Estienne's daughter, the Dowager Cateline and mother of the present vicomte, though aged, is still quite alert of mind. She may provide information regarding circumstances of the recovery of Saint John's hand by her father. Such information would be helpful to my *Life*. I would like to ride to the family's *palais* in Bourges to visit with her."

As he sat there meditating, I continued. "Prior Damian, I have one more request to make. I have made all transportation arrangements for our journey. I first inspected your carriage at the stable. It is grand. Even magnificent. But you are esteemed for your lack of vanity both here and elsewhere. I fear that you may regard the carriage too magnificent for our trip on the highways." Here, I was pandering to Damian's humility. I also hoped that the words "magnificent" and "highway" would remind him of the dangers of which I had warned him.

"True. I am a humble servant of the Lord. But I detect your real purpose is to avoid attention on the road." I said nothing. "So, what would you have us use?"

"I have arranged for a modest cart from a deanery," I answered with hesitation.

"I surrender. I surrender," he said with a smile.

* * *

On approaching the priory's gate, the porter emerged. "You again? This is the second time in as many days. On the prior's business I suppose?" laughing genially. "Do you know your way?"

"This time I do." He unlatched the gate and I walked quickly to the stable.

On arriving, a horse was already saddled, a groom about to mount it. Piers saw me.

"Hello Father. What can I do for you today? Here to take another look at the carriage?"

"No," I answered. "I need a horse to take me to Bourges. Do you have one?"

"Well, here's one. My groom was about to take it out for an exercise. But a ride to Bourges would more than suffice."

The day was cool, a blustery wind blowing from the north and clouds blocking the sun. I was wearing my winter cape which gave some warmth and protection, though insufficient. I knew it would be an unpleasant ride thirty or so miles. When I arrived in the town, I needed directions to the *palais*. I saw a tavern and decided to make an inquiry there. I tightly covered my head with my cowl, required by our *customaries* when a monk leaves his monastery though I had dispensed with that during the ride enjoying the wind through my hair. But I was now in a town. On entering, the patrons stared at me, a monk in a tavern quite extraordinary, stopping their chatter and swilling their wine. I inquired of the keeper who was helpful, leaving as quickly as I could.

I reached the *palais*, two miles from town, a stone manor house from which the vicomte, with his steward and bailiff, managed his estates and tenant farms. In the distance I could see a village of houses, timber-framed walls of wattle and daub and roofs thatched with straw. There was a church, the singular stone structure in the village and the tallest, easily visible from afar. The *palais* was surrounded by a modest wall, sufficient to deter thieves but no more. I passed through the gatehouse without challenge. Dismounting, I walked up to the entrance, a pointed arch, its double-hinged doors underneath similarly shaped, was impressive for its stout oaken planks set vertically with decorative metal studs spaced every two inches in a horizontal pattern from top to bottom. There was a small square aperture cut into one of the doors covered with a metal lattice grill. I rapped on the door. Moments later a face, peering suspiciously at me appeared from behind the grill.

"Yes?"

"My name is Father Oderic. I am from the Priory La Charité sur Loire. I would like to see the dowager if she's available."

"Does she know you're coming?"

"No, she doesn't, but if you would ask her, please, to do me the honor of speaking with her. I wish to discuss her father."

"Wait here," the doorman answered in a somewhat surly tone.

After what seemed an interminable time, made especially unpleasant by the cold and wind, the doorman reappeared. "The dowager will see you. Follow me."

He led me past the great hall on the first floor up a flight of stairs to the solar. He opened a door and announced me. "Father Oderic of La Charité sur Loire here to see you Madame." I could hear a voice from inside "Enter."

The room was modest in size. At one end was a small fireplace, framed with colorful tiles, producing a blaze warming the entire room. At the other end was an entrance to another chamber, partially concealed by drapery, her bedroom. It appeared that the solar was hers exclusively, the rest of the *palais* occupied by the current vicomte and his family. Rich tapestries hung on the walls each depicting a hunting scene: a boar, spear dangling from its side, writhing in pain, its thick neck extended and twisting, mouth wide open baring four incisors as huntsmen from a safe distance watched impassively; wolfhounds eager for a kill followed by three horsemen, crossbows in hand, taking aim at a stag only feet away from refuge in a copse; a unicorn, its body arched skyward, the hooves of its two forelegs above its head ready to descend with fury on an attacking lion. But, curiously, there was no a biblical scene; nor was there an altar or a crucifix on the wall.

The dowager, a thin linen wimple covering her head, was seated on a stuffed chair, a blanket covering her from waist to foot, and a small table beside her. I bowed briefly. "Thank you, Madame, for seeing me without notice."

She waved off the courtesy. "What can I do for you Father. You've ridden a long way."

"I came with permission from the prior to speak with you about the hand of Saint John the Martyr and your father."

"Ah. The hand of John." I was struck that she didn't refer to him as a "saint". "I'm feeling a bit achy at the moment. I don't know how much time I can give you."

"I'm sorry about that. Have you consulted a physician?"

She scoffed. "A monk? Useless. Their prescription for every ill is the same: prayer and repentance. They offer nothing." I was taken aback by her irreverence but found her honesty disarming. I liked her.

"And the piss-drinkers," she continued, "they're worse. They announce their arrival with bells tinkling from their saddles, all wearing purple hats and red gloves, bowing and scraping like Turkish whores in a Babylonian harem. They drink the piss—they must like that stuff—step outside to stare at the night heavens, cloudy or not, survey the alignment of stars and planets, return and prescribe some vile concoction of herbs promising immediate relief, leave a couple of leeches to suck my blood, collect their three silver *sous*, and then depart. At least the monks don't ask for money."

I wasn't certain how to respond but wanted to redirect the dowager's attention to my purpose. "Your father, Estienne, Vicomte of Bourges, gave us the hand of Saint John the Martyr. I want to chronicle his life and to honor your father for the recovery of the hand."

"Ah," she murmured again. The dowager appeared to fall into a deep reverie, not speaking for the longest time.

"Madame . . . ?"

"I haven't forgotten you, Father. Remind me again. Your purpose here?"

"I wish to write the story of Saint John and also to honor the memory of your father who brought the saint's hand to our priory."

"Oh yes. Of course. I know nothing of John's past." I was struck that again she didn't refer to him as "Saint John". She knew something. I couldn't tell what. "All I know is what I've heard: John was a devout Christian. In Alexandria Muslims seized him. They demanded that he convert to Islam. He refused. They threatened to cut off his hand. Again, he refused. They cut off his hand. But miraculously it grew back. Once more they demanded that he convert. Once more he refused and once more they cut off his hand which was instantly restored. A third demand was made with the same result. The Muslims decided this was witchcraft, that John was the devil. They severed his head. It did not grow back. They left him on the street, I assume to rot."

"What happened next?"

"Some Christians happened upon his body, well . . . both parts, took them into the catacombs of Alexandria where other Christians had their resting places, found an empty stone sarcophagus and laid him there. It was empty, I suppose because once a body has decayed and only bones remain, those bones are stored in an ossuary, freeing up the sarcophagus for another occupant. They chiseled on the sarcophagus an epigraph in John's honor.

"And tell me of your father. How did he come across the hand?"

"My father had taken a pilgrimage to Jerusalem."

Oderic interrupted. "Dowager, I'm curious. Was this to seek redemption for some sin he had committed?"

"I don't know. Perhaps. He did say that he had cut a palm from the River Jordan and planned to show it to the Lord on the day of His judgment to guarantee his own place in heaven. It's over there," pointing to a dried palm frond resting in a vase over the mantel of the fireplace. "That's all I know."

"How did he obtain Saint John's hand?" I asked.

"I understand only this from stories I've heard. A Muslim, a Moor I think, whom my father had befriended told him that the body of a Christian saint named 'John' lay in the catacombs of Alexandria. The Moor led him there. My father saw incised on one of the sarcophagi the words 'John, a martyr to his faith in Jesus Christ'. With his assistance my father lifted the lid, finding it empty but for a single hand. He brought the hand home. It now lies in your church."

Much of this story I already knew. I sensed, however, perhaps from her demeanor and tone of voice, that her telling was too facile, too well-rehearsed, one she had evidently given many times. I suspected there was more.

"What else can you tell me? Forgive me, please, Dowager. I think this is not the entire story."

She became silent. She slipped into another reverie. Long moments passed as I sat there.

"Madame . . . ? Madame . . . ?"

The dowager suddenly aroused herself. "Well, there *is* a second story, never told. I don't know if it's true or not. My father was dying. The night before he passed he called me to his bed."

"And what did he say?" I asked anxiously. She became momentarily lost in thought. Not the same reverie as before, just lost in thought, her eyes unrevealing.

"I don't know what harm will come from telling. Does it matter anyway? My father is dead. I'm an old woman. He told me a second story."

"Which is . . . ?" I asked, my eyes riveted on her.

The dowager rose from her chair and walked to the windows, already shuttered, drawing the curtains almost absent-mindedly, doubtless a routine she followed every evening at this time. She returned to her chair.

"My father was in fact in Alexandria, riding through a city street on his way north. The street was deserted but he could see a Moor being attacked by two thugs. Christian, Jew, or Muslim, it made no difference to him. He had an heroic quality. The Moor was on the ground, the ruffians stomping him with their feet and beating him with their fists as the Moor desperately tried to cover himself. My father had to act immediately. His sword was in its scabbard hanging from the saddle's pommel. There was no time to draw it. He leaped from his horse and raced into the mêlée. As he ran, he pulled his dagger from its wooden sheathe dangling from his belt. He had purchased it in Damascus having heard of the wondrous metal produced by its artisans. It possessed a power—he once showed it to me—the likes of which he had never seen: the pommel made of silver, a globe at the end of the hilt perfectly balancing the weight of the blade, and the *ricasso* just below the quillon finely etched with Arabic writing. It was double-edged to the fineness of a razor. Its function was to pierce and stab . . . I have it . . . somewhere . . . I'm sure I still do." She seemed lost in thought as though she were searching every room of her home in her mind.

She returned to the moment. "But in my father's fury he didn't think of technique; he wanted only to kill. He was in a frenzy like a lion cornered—thrusting, cutting, slicing—killing both attackers. The hand of one of them remained attached to the arm but only by a single sinew of flesh."

She paused momentarily. "He helped the Moor from the ground. This man, though dazed and bleeding, out of gratitude and knowing the Christian eagerness for relics, told him of John's sarcophagus nearby and then led him underground. Together they lifted its lid. So that part of the story—the story about the catacomb—is partially true." The dowager reached down for her tea, rosemary from its delicate aroma, sipping it. "What is *not* true, however, is what my father found in the sarcophagus. Nothing. It was empty. Nor was the name of John incised on the stone. There was no epigraph. Nothing." I was stunned. I had not expected the story to turn so completely sideways on me. All I could ask was what her father did next. "Well, he knew that he couldn't return home 'empty-handed' without a relic of some kind," giggling slightly. "Forgive the dark humor. He returned to the spot of the encounter and cut off the thug's hand, wrapped it in cloth, and stored it in his saddlebag. On the way home he hit on the fabulous story that this was the authentic hand of a saintly man who had died for his faith in Jesus Christ. My father knew this deception would never be discovered, that in the credulity of our age it would be considered holy. Besides, what harm could it do?"

"I would like to know," I asked, "why did he engage in such an elaborate fraud. What benefit?"

"Oh, great benefit in his eyes. He worried about his salvation. His eternal life. Personally, I do not share such worries about my own but he did. He made an arrangement with the present Abbot of Cluny, 'Hugh' I think his name, to obtain absolution for his sins in return for which he agreed to fund a priory with a donation of part of his manorial lands and to donate the hand of John. In return, Hugh promised that every day, in the new priory, the monks would read the Office of the Dead for his soul."

"Yes," I replied. "We do so faithfully. Your father is even buried in our priory's cemetery."

"I know that. My father would be pleased but that was the arrangement. I sometimes wonder what great sin my father believed he had committed. For him, it was not enough to be a Jerusalemite, to have journeyed to the holy city and return with a palm. His penance—and

I believe he felt it was penance—was both to make the pilgrimage *and* to found a priory whose monks would pray daily for his soul. What terrible sin did he commit to require this? I don't know," her thoughts wandering off once more.

She turned her eyes to the curtained window. "Father, it's night and the weather has taken an ill turn. Let me offer you the hospitality of my home. You can return to the priory tomorrow morning. I'll see to it that your horse is stabled and fed." With that, and not waiting for a reply, she rang a small bell on her table. The doorman appeared.

"Goss, please instruct the stableman to take care of Father's horse and show him to our guest bedroom. He will also require an evening meal." After thanking her I wished her a good evening and followed the doorman.

The next morning's weather was a welcome improvement over the previous. The wind had died down and the sun was out, warming me as I walked to the *palais's* stable to fetch my horse. But the ride back to La Charité was a troubled one. I had come to Bourges to discover the story of Saint John. I learned more than I preferred. The relic was yet another fraud. I wished that I had never conceived of this project. My course of action was unclear. I had assured Prior Damian that the relic was authentic. What was I to tell him?

Father Benedict's Illness Diagnosed

On arriving at the priory, I hastened to the *infirmarium* to learn of Benedict's condition and of Geoffrey's diagnosis, though the dowager's disdain for the diagnostic skills of physicians had shaken some my erstwhile confidence in Geoffrey. Benedict was asleep when I came to his bed. Geoffrey strolled over. We exchanged the normal courtesies.

"Have you settled on Father's diagnosis and course of treatment?" I asked.

"No, not yet." This was what I did *not* want to hear.

"You've come earlier than I expected. My investigation into Father Benedict's condition is not yet complete. Soon though. Let's talk in the *misericordia* so as not to disturb Father."

We sat down at a table on benches across from one another. "Did you study the zodiac chart?" I asked.

"No, I didn't and I won't," he replied rather abruptly.

His answer shocked me. I half rose from the bench, glaring down at Geoffrey. "You *didn't!* And you *won't?*" I exclaimed, half shouting. "What kind of 'Doctor of Physik' are you? Tell me! Now!"

"The best. Sit down," he said quietly. "What I will now tell you is the truth but it will be hard for you to hear. I know what afflicts him."

"Is that why your demeanor changed when you tasted Father's urine?"

"Yes. I saw you bending close to Father Benedict's mouth to hear him whisper in your ear. What did you smell?"

"There was an odor from his breath."

"Sweet, like honey?" Geoffrey asked, though from the way he framed the question he already knew the answer.

"Yes, like honey."

"I strongly suspected the cause of Father's true condition when I smelled and tasted his urine. Sweet like honey. My initial impression was confirmed the next day when he said that he was both urinating and thirsting more than usual."

I was startled. "What is it?"

"Diabetes."

"'Diabetes? I've never heard of it."

"Your own Galen was the first to identify this disease and to use the term, though he provided few insights into its symptoms or treatment. It was when I studied at Salerno that I was instructed in the *Canon of Medicine* by the Persian physician Avicenna. His description of the condition is quite thorough."

"But why then," I asked, "did you delay the truth and tell us you needed to study the zodiac?"

"Because patients expect physicians to study the alignment of stars, planets, and constellations in order to arrive at a correct diagnosis. This is a method favored by some . . . no, by almost all physicians. People believe that heavenly bodies dictate their entire lives, from birth to death. Those expert in astrological calculations are given credit, no matter the patient's fate. I practice differently. I rely on physical examination: of the urine, the blood, the pulse, and the body. Even though I quickly understood the true source of his affliction, I needed to invent *some* diagnosis. I hit on black bile. My recommendation for bloodletting by leeches will do no harm. The salve for his belly may well reduce the nausea as hopefully will the diet of hot food. But I required time to contrive some benign diagnosis which would give him hope. His diabetes is quite advanced. And, I must tell you, truthfully, he will not recover. No one ever does."

"Is there nothing you can do?"

"Nothing. You asked about my course of treatment, well I have one. At Salerno we were taught the cardinal rule of patient care: 'Depend on the three physicians: First, Doctor Quiet, next Doctor Merryman, and third Doctor Diet.' I will have to trust in them. The best I can do is to provide comfort."

There was no more to say. I thanked Geoffrey for his honesty and walked out of the *infirmarium*, my legs shaking so badly that I was unsure whether I could make it to the *scriptorium*. But as I staggered through the priory grounds I thought of Jeremiah:

> *Heal me, Oh Lord, and I will be healed.*
> *Save me and I will be saved.*
> *For you are the one I praise.*

God's intervention was my only hope.

Departure from La Charité

The next day Prior Damian and I were to leave La Charité. As promised Paul had delivered both the cart to which our mule Esther was harnessed and a packhorse tied to the back of the cart. Clothes from the chamberlain and other supplies were already loaded in the cart and into twin boxes tied by a rope over the packhorse's flanks; smoked and pickled herring, cured meats, cheeses, oatcakes, salted meats were stuffed in a linen bag; a tent and ground cover in case we were forced to sleep outside; blankets and other miscellaneous. I noticed that the silver candelabra intended for the Basilica of Cluny, wrapped in a red velvet cloth, had been laid on top. It was too tempting a target for highway brigands. I concealed it under the baggage and then threw a tarp over the cart. We were ready to depart.

At the scheduled hour Prior Damian emerged from the cloister's door. I had already taken my seat on the cart's perch. He climbed up. I confess to being a little apprehensive about his reaction to the modesty of the vehicle. Gratefully, he said nothing. In the meantime, all the monks had gathered in two rows just inside the priory gate singing a hymn dedicated to both sending off and welcoming back an abbot or prior. I turned Esther toward the gate. Each monk as we passed in front bowed his head, continuing to sing. Outside the priory I pulled the reins to stop. I wanted to look back for I feared we might never return.

"Esther, walk on," I commanded. We were on our way.

This ends Book II of *Jerusalem Falls!* Book III begins.

BOOK III

JOURNEY TO CLERMONT AND CLUNY

Meeting Paupers on the Road. Pope Urban Proclaims a Crusade. The Abbey of Cluny. An Execrable Priest and a Papal Blessing. Peter the hermit Excites a Village Crowd. Confrontation with Brigands.

Meeting Paupers on the Road

Damian and I departed from La Charité in the latter part of November, Year of Our Lord 1195. I feared that in our open cart we, especially Damian, would suffer from the vicissitudes of weather, the cold and the rain. In my haste to begin our journey I had neglected to inspect the clothing Roderick packed for us. I did not underestimate his punitive nature—would he provide appropriate clothes for warmth and to repel the rain? When we arrived at our first priory's guesthouse, I did search our baggage. He had not. Fortunately, my worries were unnecessary for during the journey both south and then on return the weather was unseasonably warm and dry. I said nothing to the prior but there was rage in my heart. Prior Damian was in *my* charge.

As I guided our mule Esther along the dusty, narrow dirt road, trying to avoid rocks, fallen tree limbs, and potholes, I sang psalms to Damian as is the monks' custom when accompanying an abbot or a prior on a journey. Before long, Damian asked me, albeit gently, to cease. Whether he tired of my voice, preferred to view the countryside undistracted, or sought silence for his own spiritual contemplation, I didn't know. Nor did I ask.

The poverty and destitution of the times were abundantly evident on the road. Harvests had failed yet again due to drought. Bread was available only at dear prices. Some villages seemed partially deserted. I was soon to understand why as we passed numerous small companies of people walking along the road in search of a new home. There were the poor, the aged, the blind, the deformed and the maimed—curiously most heading south, perhaps seeking a warmer clime in which to escape the certain cold coming from the north or to find work unavailable in our region. There were numerous lepers, always in small groups of two or three, bells ringing or wooden clappers clinking to warn of their approach. There were also small bands of children, obviously orphans for they were unaccompanied by parents, who had traveled together for self-protection. As we approached, they would hear the hoof beats of our mule, form into a single file to give us room, remove their head coverings, make slight bows, and then stretch out their hands, palms uplifted, with pitiful calls for alms.

I recall one small incident particularly well. It was the first day of our trip. There was a man limping alone ahead of us. He wore a wide-brimmed straw hat, bare feet, his tunic torn, but most oddly his bare legs below the tunic appeared withered and blackened. I saw many more with similar afflictions on my trip south and again returning north.

"Father, do you see the man in front of us? His legs seem burned. I wonder how?"

"He suffers from 'Holy Fire,'" the prior answered sorrowfully. "Soon, if not already, he will be demented."

"What causes it? God's punishment?"

"Well, I think not in his case. It is the result of eating contaminated barley. Many people have it. A horrible disease. Stop here."

The man limped to us, tightly gripping a crooked staff cut from a bough and shaved of its bark, his hand outstretched. "Just a moment," Damian said as he reached into his purse and handed him a coin.

"Bless you Father. Bless you." He turned and hobbled on.

But then a group, perhaps seven or so in front of us, seeing Damian's act of charity, raced back to us leaving behind a blind man and a cripple who nonetheless hobbled on his crutches as quickly as he could to join his companions. They surrounded our cart, not threateningly though I was unsure, imploring Damian for coins:

"Please Father," one insistently pushing her empty hand forward, "my husband has died and my children shortly after him." Another: "Father, Father, please! I have lost my arm," pointing to his armless sleeve. They were all pressing their way forward pleading their causes. It was a cacophony of begging as though breadcrumbs had been scattered on the ground attracting a swarm of ravenous, shrieking starlings. Damian again reached into his purse handing each a coin. One of the supplicants attempted to grab Damian's purse. I immediately smacked his hand with my fist. Over my shoulder I could see others rushing to our cart from behind.

"We have to leave Father." I didn't wait for approval but shook the reins with one hand and with the other grabbed a light whip to urge Esther forward. We sped away, the packhorse still tied to the cart quickening his gait. I realized that I would have to check Damian's generosity. We would be exhausted of coins before even reaching Clermont if this continued.

"Father . . . we can't . . . "

"I know," Damian said, sensing my thought. "My purse will soon be empty."

Thenceforth, I encouraged Esther with a slight lash of the whip to a swifter pace when I saw paupers on the road. I wanted to relieve Damian of his sense of guilt for not aiding the poor, though I confess the economy of our funds was also on my mind.

Pope Urban Proclaims a Crusade

We were informed at the last priory where we had stayed that the pope was to speak in Clermont's Basilica Notre-Dame du Port at noon the next day. Our departure that morning was delayed somewhat because Damian had matters he wished to discuss with the prior. We entered the principal gate of Clermont, unmanned, and proceeded on a street paved with tightly fitted cobblestone. I needed no directions to the basilica, its spire easily visible. I had expected the streets to be thronged with people eager to hear the pope. But they were eerily empty. We arrived before the basilica. No one was present except one man sweeping the steps underneath its marvelous tympanum, elegantly carved with images of two angels, their wings unfolded, apostles, and Christ.

I called out to the sweeper, "Where is everyone? Where's the pope?"

"Rejoice! Rejoice! He has come. I have even seen him!" he exclaimed, almost deliriously. "Everyone has left to see His Holiness. He was supposed to speak here in the basilica but there was no room. The townspeople have gone to a field outside of town. Over there," pointing to a different gate, east, a short distance away. "You may just make it." I could see men, women, and children hurrying through. We followed them.

Perhaps a mile out of town we came to a large meadow blanketed with wildflowers. It was girded by a hedgerow, people pushing and shoving through a rather narrow gap. I stood up from my perch on the cart to look over the hedge. At one end of the meadow was a wooden platform with three carpenters hastily completing its construction. In front were gathered some three hundred prelates all wearing their birettas, three peaked hats, red for cardinals and purple for bishops; and cappas, capes flowing over their shoulders, the trains reaching almost to the ground, again red for cardinals and purple for bishops. It was a sea of colors rivaled only by the wildflowers. Each prelate held a crozier, a pastoral staff, upright in his hand, quietly conversing with one another. Abbots and priors were present too, less colorful, wearing black cassocks and scapulars over their front and back shoulders, cowls covering their heads. Surrounding the meadow on three sides were townspeople and peasants, some sitting, others standing, laughing merrily as children chased one another, darting in and out between them. It had the spirit of a village fair.

I guided Esther into a side field. It had been left fallow, barren but for clumps of bracken here and there. Horses were either hobbled or tethered to the hedgerow. I assumed they belonged to the prelates. Damian and I alighted from the cart. I left Esther, confident that she would not roam, harnessed as she was to the cart with the packhorse tied behind. We walked to the meadow, carefully stepping over the piles of cow dung not yet dissolved by rain. Damian joined the prelates, several greeting him with broad smiles and signs of welcome, and I the townspeople.

The pope entered through the hedgerow gap. The assembled throng became immediately silent. He was riding a magnificent horse, completely black, its head and tail arched, forelegs rising knee length stepping one after the other in perfect cadence, less a gait than a prance. He was followed by twenty horsemen dressed in the distinctive garb of papal guards, all holding upright spears pennanted with the pope's coat of arms seated in leather holsters beside their stirrups. At the rear, outside the hedgerow, I could see three wagons loaded with supplies all covered with tarps. Two guards leapt off their horses, one racing to the cart returning with a stool which was placed under the stirrups of the pope's horse, both aiding him in the dismount. The moment the pope's feet rested on the ground, the prelates made low bows and the townspeople erupted in loud cheers. In the meantime, the papal guards positioned themselves in a line before the platform facing the crowd standing at attention.

The pope was in resplendent choir dress, from his peaked mitre hat to his red leather shoes. He wore a purple, sleeved cassock reaching down to his ankles, its long train held above the ground by one of his attendants; a shoulder cape fastened with a silver chain over which was draped a pallium, a long sash looped around his neck and over his shoulders hanging down both in front and behind; and a mozzetta, a short cape around his shoulders of red satin trimmed with white fur. One of his attendants handed him his ferula, a papal staff topped with a knob on which was affixed a cross. The pope ascended the stairs of the platform unassisted and then walked slowly to its front edge facing the assembly. A gold pectoral cross set in pearls hanging from his neck by a silver chain swayed rather wildly with each step, so much that the pope clasped it to his chest to still it.

And then an astonishing thing happened. The day had been cloudy with a light drizzle of rain. But when he began to speak there was a momentary break as the sun peeked through, shining its light solely on the platform and on the pope, everywhere around him in shadow. There was an audible gasp from the spectators. It was as though God were directly speaking through him to us.

"*In nomine Patris et Filii et Spiritus Sancti,*" he intoned, making a wide sign of the cross with his hand extended, a blessing to all those present. The prelates in unison responded "Amen". He paused, perhaps to gather his thoughts or for dramatic effect. If the latter, he was successful for a hush fell over the entire meadow. There was not a sound.

"To the faithful heralds of Christ gathered here," looking down at the prelates below him. "To the Frankish nobles, descendants of the pious and victorious Charlemagne assembled in this place," as he slowly scanned the assembly from left to right. "You are the chosen people, beloved by God, and we greet you. We speak this day with utmost sincerity. Grim tidings have reached our ears from brother Christians in the East. Pagan Turks from the heathen lands of Persia have invaded the ancient lands of Anatolia and Palestine and are at this very moment plundering their churches, tearing down their altars and covering them with their filthy excrement. They convert sacred houses into idolatrous places of worship to their false gods. Bishops and abbots, priests and monks are being seized and either killed or sold into slavery. Christian towns have been razed and burned to the ground. There is no devilish deed of which these pagans are not capable. They kill Christian pilgrims who travel to Jerusalem to pray before the altar of Jesus in the Holy Sepulchre suffering beyond measure."

Even from a distance I could see the look of horror over the prelates' faces. There were mutterings among them mixed with subdued voices of outrage. The pope continued but I was unable to hear clearly so I slowly made my way through the crowd, sideling between them and squeezing through. Eventually I was able to get to the front.

". . . and they split open the bellies of the faithful and with their filthy hands pull out their intestines. They squeeze this blood into bowls, force them to their knees, and compel them to drink and declare it the blood of Christ. Those who refuse and those infirm of age and body—their heads are instantly severed and then stuck on sharpened poles for the world to witness. The young and the fair—they sell into slavery or retain for their own abominations, the wickedness of which I cannot describe."

The Pope fell silent, first looking at the ground, then to heaven, and finally to the prelates below. "This must end!" he demanded, stamping his ferula on the platform floor, the echo reverberating throughout the meadow. "*This must end!*" he shouted again, slamming it once again. "God's final judgment is nigh. He will examine the quick and the dead. The wicked will endure eternal damnation in hell. The righteous—paradise. This judgment will take place when our Lord and his Sacred Son sit on their thrones in the Holy Sepulchre of Jerusalem, the 'Navel of the World'. It will not happen until the Sepulchre is cleansed of the putrid odor of heathen Turks. Today I summon all nobles, their horsemen, their men-at-arms, those able to wield a spear, a sword, a bow, or a mace to march to Jerusalem. This is the commandment of Christ: '*If any man will come after me, let him deny himself and take up his cross and follow me.*' We shall be victorious and reclaim the land for which Christ shed his blood! *This is God's will!*"

The prelates at first seemed stunned. There was silence. But then, from the back, I heard one shout "*Deus vult!*" "God wills it!" Then all the other cardinals, bishops, and abbots joined in until there was a crescendo: "*Deus vult!*" Deus vult!" pounding their croziers onto the ground. The pope had been speaking in Latin, a language unknown to the townspeople; nevertheless they sensed the urgency in the pope's voice and his anger. They could also recognize some words: "Turks", "pilgrims", "Jerusalem". Yet they comprehended his message, albeit vaguely. But "*Deus vult*" they completely understood. "*Dieu le veult*" came their response in Frankish. The townspeople began stomping their feet with arms upraised, "*Dieu le veult, Dieu le veult!*" The earth seemed to tremble.

To my right, I saw men and women fall to their knees, some weeping, some shaking with passion as if possessed; others twitching and whispering "*Dieu le veult*". Everyone seemed intoxicated by the pope's words. I looked to my left. They were either kneeling with hands clasped, their faces upwards to heaven, or lying prostrate on the ground pounding their fists shouting "God wills it!" Except one. We were separated by two women, both sitting on the ground, one nursing her child. I averted my gaze. I hadn't noticed him before. A tall man, gaunt, greasy hair, clothed in the ragged tunic one would expect of a peasant who labored in a manorial field. His face was marked by the scars of some disease, his right eyelid drooping halfway down. Even in the open air he bore a stench about him as though he had not washed since he had been dipped in a baptismal font.

An open cesspool would have been more fragrant. We briefly exchanged glances. I detected in the instant our eyes met either keen intelligence or low, sinister cunning, perhaps both. But what impressed me the most was the letter "V" branded on his cheek, "V" for *voleur*, "thief", that and his complete impassivity to Pope Urban's stirring words. He merely stood there. Later I came to know him better. His name was Drogo, formerly a Norman knight, disreputable, a man perfectly loathsome in character as I was to learn in Anatolia.

I turned my attention back to the pope. "I declare to all the bishops and abbots here: Return to your churches, spread the word of our summons. Those who willingly march to Jerusalem shall be known as *milites Christi*, 'Soldiers of Christ'. Only men suitable for battle may go. They shall signify their vow by sewing onto their surcoats a red cross, the *cruce signati*. As Christ said: '*If any man will come after me, let him deny himself, take up the cross and follow me.*' By this cross on your shoulder you shall be known. All your sins will be remitted and you will enjoy the spiritual pleasures of Paradise, even if you perish on land, on sea, or by the hands of pagans before reaching Jerusalem. Those who succeed shall be honored as 'Jerusalemites'. But those who falter, the faint of heart who timidly and under cover of darkness slink away, shall be subject to the sword of anathema. All others need to tend to their families and crops." Again, in unison, the prelates shouted "*Deus vult!*", the townspeople joining them "*Dieu le veult*" without the slightest comprehension of what the pope had said.

"We shall end these petty quarrels in our lands between brothers. Their quarrels must cease! To all nobles, I admonish you thusly: You girt yourselves with the belt of knighthood but are arrogant in your pride. You intimidate the weak. You disturb the Peace of God. No more will a bishop, a monk, priest or nun be seized, at the risk of your excommunication!" I thought immediately of Lambert, Bishop of Arras, as I'm certain the gathered prelates did as well. "No longer will robbers claim dominion over our highways during the day or thieves at night. Henceforth, we shall direct our swords at the barbarians, not at each other. Our energy shall be used to exterminate the heathen vermin!" Once again, the assembly of prelates erupted into "*Deus vult!*" the townspeople following with "'*Dieu le veult!*"

"'God wills it'", Urban continued, "will be your rallying cry. You shall assemble in whatever places you choose on the Feast of the Assumption, August 15, in the Year of Our Incarnate Lord 1096, after harvest. And on that day you shall begin your glorious pilgrimage, crosses in one hand, swords in the other, to recover our Holy Land."

At that point, when the passion he had aroused reached a fever pitch, one of the bishops standing among the prelates handed his crozier to a bishop next to him and in an apparent act of spontaneity raced up the steps to the pope. He knelt down in front of him. The pope extended his hand, the bishop kissing his ring. The bishop said something which I could not hear. Urban placed his hand on the bishop's shoulder and then, gently grasping his arm, raised him up. The two stood side by side facing the crowd.

"This is Adhémar, Bishop of Le Puy. He has just beseeched me for permission to join this pilgrimage. I joyfully consented. I appoint him my legate to the Holy Land and as my *dux* to lead our valiant pilgrim soldiers to Jerusalem. His words shall be as if I spoke them. He will bring us to victory!" The prelates erupted in frenzied enthusiasm as did the townspeople sensing something important had just occurred. More stomping of feet, raising of hands, stamping of croziers. Adhémar smiled, bowed to the pope and then to the audience.

Over the course of my pilgrimage I came to know Adhémar. A saintly man and a warrior-bishop for Christ. He was a fine horseman and had been trained in the use of arms, though during our pilgrimage and even in battle he forebear from using them. It was said that years before Adhémar had taken a pilgrimage to Jerusalem. He was an inspired choice: loyal to Urban's vision of the crusade and the reforms he sought for the church; uniquely able to navigate between the overweening ambitions of crusader princes; and a thoughtful diplomat in dealings between Rome and Constantinople. It was only later, on my return journey to La Charité and while reflecting on that day, I realized that Adhémar's "spontaneity" seemed too well rehearsed. Still, it was dramatic theater.

At that moment, a cardinal, whom Damian later identified to me as Gregory, ascended the platform, fell on his knees facing the crowd and led it in reciting the *Confiteor*. The prelates in unison joined him; the townspeople, untutored in Latin, knelt instead. With that, the entire multitude crossed themselves with an "Amen". The Pope then blessed all who were present, "*Dominus vobiscum*" making a sign of the cross, and bowed his head as though in silent meditation. The sermon was concluded.

A great crusade had been launched.

The Abbey of Cluny

Damian and I returned to our cart and began the journey to Cluny. The trip, six days, was uneventful. As before, we spent the nights in priory guesthouses. I especially enjoyed Damian's and my respites during the day when I would pull the cart off the road and we would sit on a log or grass eating our midday meals. The goat-milk cheeses, produced at our own priory, were especially enjoyable. La Charité had earned a well-deserved reputation for their quality, distinctive aromas, and earthy tastes, some pungent while others more mellow. I would cut wedges for Damian but remove the rinds for myself believing that chewing on tough skin would strengthen my teeth. But most pleasant were my conversations with the prior. We spoke of the pope's sermon at Clermont, of what Damian expected to learn at Cluny, and points of faith disputed by theologians, always abstruse to me. Even today, many years later, I have such fond memories of that time, fresh as though they occurred yesterday.

In late afternoon we arrived at the village of Cluny and passed into the abbey compound through its entrance, two iron gates with a curved stone arch above. Directly to our right was the abbey's guesthouse and stable. My immediate instinct was to head there. But in the distance I could see the basilica, its three octagonal towers at the far end of the structure: a bell tower over each transept and a third tower, similar in design but much larger, between them over the apse. Its enormity and grandeur left me speechless.

"Magnificent," I murmured to myself without intending for Damian to hear me.

"Yes, my son. I came to Cluny many years ago as a novice. I remember the old church. Much more modest. That one was the second; this is the third. Construction began about seven years ago."

"It is so huge. I wonder why?" I asked.

"I think Abbot Hugh wanted a church that would display Cluny's stature. After all the abbey with its hundreds of priories and thousands of monks is the largest monastic system in all Christian regions. As you can see," pointing to the laborers standing on scaffolds still working on both transepts, "it will take years to complete. But when done it will be the largest church in Christendom."

"Well, it must be an enormous expense. I wonder how it's paid for."

"The King of Leon, Alfonso VI, donates one thousand *dinari* a year to its construction. His wife is the niece of Abbot Hugh. Alfonso's father, Ferdinand, was also a generous benefactor to our abbey. Every day at mass the monks of Cluny say a special *collect* for Alfonso, praying for his well-being."

It was a cloudy day, the sun only partially visible. Sunset was approaching and the Office of Vespers would soon be held in the basilica. Even at that moment abbey monks were slowly assembling outside the entrance, ready to file in. I wanted to see the church immediately, just Damian and me.

"Father Prior, may we go inside the church? I would so much like to see it now."

"Of course, but we must hurry." I directed Esther to the front of the basilica and left her there. We walked in. The walls of the narthex, a vestibule between the exterior entrance and the nave, were tiled with marble slabs, rather opaque silver gray with blue swirls, glistening even in the darkened room. Spaced at regular intervals on the tiles were pilasters of polished walnut simulating Roman columns. On the floor stood several wrought iron candleholders, six or so feet tall, each containing pink votive candles, none lit. In the center of the narthex, hanging by a chain from the ceiling, was a lamp with four flickering candles. We walked through the arched door on which were hung two enormous doors elaborately carved with scenes from the New Testament. Entering the nave, the central corridor of the church, I looked up. The ceiling, consisting of vaulted arches supported by columns, their capitals richly sculptured with foliage, was over ninety feet tall. The nave, with double aisles on either side, seemed to stretch limitlessly to the high altar at the far end. I just stared in disbelief. Seeing my reaction, Damian leaned over and whispered in my ear—the grandeur of the basilica's interior demanding silence and reverence—"It's over four hundred feet long."

We walked down the nave to the apse at the far end under which was the high altar, the grandest I had ever seen, tiled in marble with a carved stone trim. Damian whispered again, "The pope himself will consecrate the altar in two or three days when he arrives. A great honor for us." On the three sides of the apse were apsidal chapels gloriously covered with what appeared to be gold leaf, perhaps painted, I couldn't tell, each with its own altar above which were ten-foot crucifixes affixed to the walls. I was so overcome that I knelt down in silent prayer. Damian knelt beside me.

On leaving we returned to the cart and headed back to the guesthouse. We were warmly greeted by its keeper, an elderly monk, who escorted us to our separate cells. There were also lodgings for lay guests, divided for men and women, with a common refectory. As monks, however, we were privileged to take our meals with the community in the general refectory. Our cells were small but adequately furnished: a bed, desk, chair, cabinet for our clothing, and a simple altar of wood with a pad in front on the floor for prayer. I retrieved our baggage from the cart, leaving personal items in

Damian's and my respective cells, and deposited the rest in the care of the keeper of the guesthouse for storing. I then took the cart and packhorse to the stable. After that, Damian and I joined the other monks for vespers. Following mass, we returned to the guesthouse and retired for the night. Visitors staying in the house, even Cluniac monks, were exempted from attending the regular offices. It had been a long day and I looked forward to a restful night, relieved of having to awake in the early morning for matins.

* * *

On the following day Damian was busy with other affairs, both administrative and personal. He had meetings with the abbot and the grand prior to discuss matters relating to La Charité; he also wished to visit with fellow priors, many of whom he had known for years. I was on my own but spent the day fruitfully wandering about the abbey, visiting the bakehouse, kitchen, cellar, almonry, infirmary, and a second church, much more modest than the basilica. I was especially interested in seeing the *scriptorium* and *armarium*. The *scriptorium*, just off the cloister, was similar to our own at La Charité only much larger with more scribes. They were all working silently. I walked from writing desk to writing desk, the scribes paying no attention to me, discreetly looking over their shoulders interested in the subjects of their labors. Each of them was working on the life of one saint or another, some of them producing manuscripts more elegant in their lettering and illumination than Garnier, Roul, or I could achieve. It seemed the works of Galen did not interest them.

However, I was most intrigued to see the *armarium*. It was located in a room adjacent to the *scriptorium*. Damian had told me that it contained more volumes on more diverse subjects than any monastery of his acquaintance. He was right. There must have been five hundred books, perhaps more, covering two walls. Our priory's entire collection could fit on a single shelf. I slowly perused each—the collected works of the Church Fathers: Tertullian, Eusebius, Ambrose, Jerome, Origen; civil and canon law; a history of the Franks and of the Vandal and Lombard churches; a book on the lives of the emperors from Augustus to Theodosius; works by classical historians: Livy, Suetonius, Josephus; books by orators and poets including Virgil, Cicero, Horace, Juvenal, Terence, and Ovid—even Ovid! As I was slowly making my way through, a monk entered the room. Speaking was permitted at that hour.

"I am Gosse, the *armarius*. And you are . . . ?"

"I am Oderic, a monk and scribe of La Charité sur Loire."

"Ah, yes. Father Damian is the prior there, is he not? He and I were novices together, professing our vows at the same time we were. We were blessed with the honor of being ordained by His Holiness Pope Urban, also formerly a novice at Cluny and later grand prior here."

"Indeed?" I replied. "Prior Damian and I came together from La Charité to Clermont and now to Cluny."

"Did you see the pope? Did you hear him speak?" he asked, the pitch of his voice rising in excitement.

"Yes, I did. I thought he was quite eloquent."

"So I've heard. You know, young monk, he will be coming to Cluny two days from now to consecrate our high altar. All of us are eager to greet him." Then he paused, scanning the walls of books, "So, you enjoy our collection, do you? I think I can tell."

"Yes," I answered. Pointing to the shelves, "I have never seen so many books. How did you come by them?"

"Our own scribes produced some, primarily the lives and passions of the saints." That answer did not surprise me. "The others, well, donations from benefactors."

"I am surprised," I said, "but certainly not disappointed at all that you have so many books by Greek and Roman authors, especially the poets."

Gosse sighed briefly. "I myself am surprised that Abbot Hugh allows us to keep them. He's a man of profound piety, very profound, and austere in his personal habits. I'm told that one night, while reading Virgil's *Aeneid*, he fell asleep. In a dream he sensed serpents under his head. He awoke in horror and discovered not serpents but Virgil's volume under his pillow. He cast it on the floor, never to open it again, convinced of the poisonous nature of poetic fiction. But he has said nothing to me. Until then, I shall preserve it here."

"Tell me about Abbot Hugh. I have heard so much but know so little."

"Abbot Hugh, yes," he responded. "A godly man, a saintly man. Pious. He's the sixth abbot of Cluny, installed . . . " pausing to calculate, "yes, some forty-five years ago. At the age of twenty-four. Extraordinary! Wise with a preternatural gift of wisdom. He is humble, even sharing our dormitory at night, no separate room for himself. He is indeed, how shall I say?, a monk's monk and an example to us all."

"Father Gosse, I see you have a reading table here. I have already explored your wonderful abbey to my satisfaction. There are yet two days before the pope's arrival. Prior Damian and I will leave shortly after.

I should like to take advantage of that time to read here. Would that be permissible?"

"Yes, of course," he answered happily. "As a scribe, you surely have the same veneration for books as I."

Gosse departed. I was intrigued by his story of Hugh and the *Aeneid* selecting that to read which I did every day during my stay in Cluny. Except one afternoon. I had thought of Father Benedict. Constantly. Notwithstanding Geoffrey's diagnosis and his dismal prognosis for Benedict's recovery, I knew divine intervention would be needed. Without it, he may die. I had an idea. I walked to the abbey workshop adjoining the sacristy and lay cemetery. The workshop included a smithy in the next room. I entered. The room was hot, a small forge burning with red coals, a worker vigorously pumping air into it with his hand bellows, each time the coals glowing more brightly. Another man, older and more muscular, evidently the iron founder, wore a thick leather apron covering his chest down to the knees intently hammering a horseshoe on an anvil. He had not noticed me enter. Hanging on the walls were tongs, differently shaped hammers each for a specific purpose, chisels, grips, punches and other tools whose utility I could not determine. Particularly attracting my attention were several iron pectoral crosses each with small rings welded on top through which were threaded linked chains. They were all hanging on a single hook. I approached the blacksmith from the front, careful not to startle him. He looked up, inquiringly, laying the hammer down.

"I am Oderic, a monk of the Cluniac priory of La Charité sur Loire. I see you have several pectoral crosses. I am seeking one. Might I . . . "

The blacksmith interrupted, with a suspicious look in his eyes, "And you need one why? Surely you have a smithy at your own priory."

I quickly realized that my task might be more difficult than I initially thought. A different tactic was required—an appeal to authority and shameless flattery. "Well, no we don't. I am with the prior, Damian, and we are here at Abbot Hugh's personal request to witness Pope Urban's consecration of the high altar of your marvelous basilica. I saw it for the first time yesterday. I assume the iron works were yours. Marvelous."

I had not noticed any iron fixtures in the basilica at all but the deception proved fruitful. He broke out in a wide smile. "Yes, most of it is done here: hinges, bolts, door handles, other things too. On a limited scale, mind you, but we're proud of our work. What is it you need?" he asked, his mood now turning more obliging.

"Our precentor is very ill," I answered. "I was hoping to bring back with me a pectoral cross produced by our mother abbey and blessed by the pope as an amulet to ensure his recovery. I see some over there" pointing to the wall.

"You may be in luck. These crosses are intended for our new novices soon to profess their vows. Let's take a look." We walked over to the wall, he taking the crosses off the hook and counting them. "There are eleven here. Eleven, because I was told there would be eleven novices. But yesterday I learned that one will not be joining the abbey. Uncertain why. No matter. That leaves one. You say it's for a Cluniac monk?"

"Yes. I deeply fear for the precentor's recovery. If I may take one and have it blessed by His Holiness, I'm certain his health will be restored. This would be a generous donation from the abbey. Surely the abbot would approve."

"Then take it," he said in a feigned gruff tone. "It will serve a more useful purpose than hanging by itself in my smelly shop."

I smiled, nodded my head in thanks, and stuffed the cross and chain into the pocket of my cassock. I returned to the *armarium* to continue my reading. There was yet a chance for Benedict's life, if only it would receive the pope's blessing.

* * *

I had skipped supper earlier in the day in favor of visiting the smithy but by now I was hungry. It was already close to sunset. I heard the refectory's bell signaling dinner, left the *armarium* and joined the other monks in the cloister where at the far end was the *lavatorium*, a stone trench filled with water running along the wall where we washed our hands. A large wooden cabinet, without doors, stood on either end, its shelves stacked with fresh towels for drying our hands. And then, in procession, one monk closely following another, we proceeded into the refectory.

The refectory was perhaps sixty feet wide and a hundred feet long, far more spacious than ours at La Charité. It was well lighted with thirty-six glazed windows on the northern and southern stone walls. Both walls were richly decorated with colorful murals: scenes from the Old and New Testaments, an immense painting of Christ in Majesty, and a depiction of the Last Judgment under which was a lengthy inscription beginning with "*Ecce dies magnus*", the rest I couldn't read from a distance. There were also portraits of major benefactors to the abbey, one more prominent than the others, I assumed that of Alfonso. Six tables, set end-to-end with benches on either side of the hall, were already laid with napkins, trenchers, and spoons. There was a spacious aisle between the three tables on the right and the left. At the far end was a dais with one table facing us, behind which were four chairs. Only the abbey's choir monks were present, the priors from different regions taking meals in their private rooms.

The monks took their regular places at the table. I chose one that was empty. There was perfect silence for speaking was not permitted at meals, only signing. We remained standing, all facing the center aisle. Abbot Hugh entered. He was greeted at the door by two monks who bowed solemnly to the abbot in the Cluniac manner, holding their backs perfectly straight, bending until their heads reached their waists. One held a ewer with which he gently poured water on the abbot's hands, the abbot rubbing them together as the other monk handed him a towel. Then followed the grand prior, the claustral prior, and Prior Damian in that order, the same washing ritual employed for each. I should have been surprised by Damian's presence but I wasn't. He enjoyed the companionship of monks, no doubt preferring our company to that of supping alone. They proceeded down the center aisle in a file, each monk bowing as they passed. They took their places on the dais, the grand prior to the abbot's right, the claustral prior to his left, and beside him Damian. We sat, bowing our heads in silent prayer.

Immediately below the dais was a lectern. A monk walked up, book in hand, *Lives of the Saints*, and stood behind it. It was December 5, the feast day of Saint Sabas. The lector opened his book to the life of this venerable man. In the meantime, the keeper of the refectory, assisted by three monks, brought trays of food cooked in the adjoining kitchen, first to the head table and then to the rest of the us. No one ate until the *eulogia*, blessing of the food, had been given. As the lector was reading, the kitchen attendants silently ladled stew made of vegetables raised in the abbey's garden, beans, and lentils flavored with animal fat—meat was proscribed for monks, the only exception was for the abbot—onto the individual trenchers, coarse bread produced from barley, and distributed cups of wine and slices of cheese, simple monastic fare. Mustard and vinegar were placed on the tables to flavor the dishes according to the tastes of individual monks. On completing our supper, with our personal knives, we scraped off the crumbs from the table onto napkins to be used by the almoner to feed the poor. The head table, Abbot Hugh leading, stepped down from the dais and in the same order they had entered walked down the aisle as we stood and bowed. We then followed, as silently as we had entered. I returned to the *armarium* to read.

An Execrable Priest and a Papal Blessing

I arose early in the morning in time for mass at prime, looking forward to what I expected to be a thrilling day with the pope present. On the night before, rather late, I heard through my cell window the furious clanging of bells. A short time later there was the sound of hundreds of leather sandals racing across the cobblestone to the abbey's gate. I looked out through my window. Monks had gathered, dressed in white albs readily visible in the moonlight, forming into two lines. Then came the ringing clatter of shod hooves through the gate. There was a line of horsemen, two in front holding lanterns guiding a single rider immediately behind them and further in the rear a retinue of armed horsemen followed by supply wagons, passing between the double lines of monks all singing hymns of welcome. I was certain it was the pope. They proceeded to the abbey's palace. I returned to bed.

On this morning, hearing the basilica's bells ringing for mass, I quickly stuffed the pectoral cross obtained from the smithy into my pocket and grabbed three wax tablets with a stylus for taking notes as Damian had directed. I left the guesthouse with Damian to join the priors and monks on the steps just below the entrance to the basilica. They were already lined up in a processional form, with the priors in front and the monks behind them. Damian excused himself to join his fellow priors. Abbot Hugh officiated over the service, something he did rarely but the pope, sitting in his episcopal chair, was present. On the conclusion of Abbot Hugh's homily, the pope rose and blessed the high altar in front of him.

Following service, we all proceeded to the chapter hall on the east side of the cloister, entering through the parlor and then into the hall itself. The room was thirty-five feet wide and forty-five long, its ceiling supported by two rows of ornately carved columns creating three aisles. At the far end, behind the dais, was an alcove, three feet deep, with a life-sized statue of Christ carved in wood. Along the north, south, and west walls were three stone benches ascending one above the other. The room was spacious enough for the abbey's monks during a regular chapter meeting, but with perhaps two hundred priors in attendance there was seating sufficient only for them and then only with additional benches brought in from the refectory.

Damian had arranged for me to be present and I found a small stool in the corner. After taking our places, we remained standing for some period of time to allow the pope to change from his sacerdotal raiment which he had worn at mass. Finally, the pope, dressed in a simple white cassock and a matching zucchetto, a skullcap made of silk, entered the room followed by Abbot Hugh. We all bowed as they walked to the dais at the end of the room. Hugh sat on his customary high-backed wooden chair, more functional than ornate, its curved arms extending down to his knees. Urban took his seat next to Hugh's, identical in design but much more ornately carved and upholstered in padded red velvet reserved for senior ecclesiastics visiting the abbey. Hugh nodded to the priors indicating they were to take their seats.

The meeting began conventionally enough with a prayer and the lector reading from a chapter of the Rule of Saint Benedict. There followed a discussion of matters of general interest to the gathered priors: harvests, tithes, local seigneurs and bishops attempting to control the elections of priors, and other issues with which I was only dimly conversant. I furiously took notes on my wax tablets. But then it took a decidedly unusual turn. Hugh stood up.

"Today we shall dispense with the regular order in view of the presence of His Holiness. He has blessed our high altar this morning, ensuring its preservation for a thousand years. He wishes to speak." At that all the priors immediately stood and bowed deeply to the pope, who remained seated.

"On behalf of the Holy Mother Church in Rome, we greet all of you. It is such a pleasure for us to return to Cluny. We first professed our monastic vows right here," pausing for a quick mental calculation, "a quarter century ago I think. Father Abbot himself," turning to look at Hugh, both exchanging smiles, "ordained me. Returning here fills us with sweet and the most tender memories. This abbey is indeed the 'Light of the World.'" What Urban did not say was that Hugh had appointed him grand prior, second to Hugh himself. He indeed had an affection for Cluny. "But we have a specific purpose in speaking today, for you as prelates of our Holy Church have a fearful charge, to serve as messengers and advocates of our summons given only days ago at Clermont. A fierce and merciless holy war must be waged to wrest our Holy Sepulchre in Jerusalem from the wicked hands of pagans. From here I leave for Limoges, Tours, Toulouse and other cities to issue the same appeal as I did at Clermont."

"However," he continued, "our mission is broader than that. We must heal the venomous schism that has torn asunder our churches in Rome and Constantinople. For fifty years recriminations have been exchanged between the Roman and Greek churches over theological differences, punctuated by mutual excommunications, excommunications which have only served to poison relations. One of our first acts as pope was to lift the ban on Alexios Komnenos, Emperor of Constantinople. Those differences, some trivial—whether leavened or unleavened bread is to be used in celebrating the Eucharist; others more weighty—whether the Holy Spirit emanates from the Father alone or from the Father and His Son and the question of Rome's supremacy throughout all of Christendom, not just in the West. These are issues of consequence, to be sure."

On saying that, Urban placed his hands on the arms of his chair, half-lifting himself up. "But they cannot and must not prevail over our common belief in Jesus Christ who gave His life for our salvation and in His beloved Father, our Lord. Tolerance, not intolerance, for different usages based on long customs, *must be respected!*", he exclaimed, sitting back down. "Some twenty years ago a Byzantine army was defeated by the Turks at Manzikert. The former emperor himself was taken prisoner. Then Nicea fell to the pagans, after that the sacred city of Antioch, and finally the whole of Anatolia has been unlawfully seized by the heathens. Muslims now occupy Jerusalem itself! Christian pilgrims no longer are able to peacefully journey through Anatolia to Jerusalem for prayer and personal redemption. At our council in Piacenza several months ago ambassadors attended with a personal request from Emperor Alexios for military assistance against the Turks. He fears that without such help the whole of Christendom in the East is endangered. Aiding our brethren, when our common faith is threatened, is not merely our Christian duty. It is essential to restoring amity between our churches."

"At Clermont," he continued, "we called upon all Christian men suitable for bearing arms, whatever their station in life, to march east and there become the instruments of God's will, for in due course, well-nigh, our Lord and His beloved Son shall sit on their thrones in Jerusalem, the 'Navel of the World', in judgment of those passed and those living. The worthy may expect salvation; the rest, the eternal fires of hell. But 'suitable for bearing arms' does not mean country folk who are more accustomed to carrying a harness than a spear. Nor does it include monks, forbidden to draw a sword even to kill a heathen however worthy his death. And no monk may embark on this pilgrimage without the permission of his superior."

"Holy Father, may I briefly interrupt?" Hugh asked. Urban nodded. "I do not encourage," looking directly at the priors, "any of our monks to participate. Their work is too important here. Without their daily prayers this holy campaign may not succeed. Yet . . . yet, if any monk is zealous about joining this pilgrimage, he has my blessing. Thank you Holy Father."

* * *

The pope had finished, but the meeting had not.

"Holy Father, we have two matters on which I may require your guidance. Do I have your indulgence?" Hugh asked.

"Yes, indeed. I would be interested."

"Allow the supplicants to enter," Hugh commanded the porter at the door.

A man with the bearing of a knight walked in followed by three younger men, obviously his sons, side-by-side. He bowed first to Urban and then to Hugh.

"Your Holiness," directing himself to Urban, "my name is Achard of Montmerle." I could see, even from the far end of the room, anger in Hugh's eyes as he glared at the three men behind Achard though he said nothing. "I wish to join my fellow knights on this march to Jerusalem. It is a holy endeavor for which I am willing to give my life." His wish was realized. He died during the siege of Jerusalem. "However, there are great expenses. I have five knights requiring more horses than I currently possess, with new saddles and halters to buy; for my men-at-arms coats of mail, their worn swords and spears replaced. And, all of them must be paid for their service. I request a loan from the abbey."

The pope merely glanced at Hugh indicating that this was Hugh's decision, not his. Both men understood that the costs of embarking on this pilgrimage were significant and nobles often turned to the richly endowed bishoprics and monasteries for loans. "Who are these men behind you?" Hugh demanded. I suspected Hugh already knew.

"These are my sons: Pons, Peter, and Bernard."

"Ah," Hugh's voice dripping with scorn, "I see, Pons, Peter, and Bernard. I have heard of you. The devils of our county. Villains who have attacked our priories and stolen their silver candlesticks to be melted down into coin, no doubt to pay for tavern whores; who have exacted tolls on pilgrims to our abbey merely for traveling on roads, roads to which they have no claim; who have seized even monks and demanded ransom from our abbey's coffers; who have ransacked villages for their meager supplies of grain. *These are your sons?* You are a worthy knight and father indeed!"

At that the three sons fell to the floor prostrate, Achard remaining standing. "*We repent! We repent!*" screamed one, the eldest it seemed, raising his head to look at the pope and then Hugh. "We have been wicked. Very wicked. We have committed those crimes and more. But we were at Clermont and listened to your words, Holy Father," fixing his eyes on Urban. "We saw you cloaked in sunlight while all around you was darkness. We left inspired. On riding home the moon was full and bright enough to guide our horses at night. But gradually the moon darkened as though a shroud were drawn over it. In our astonishment we knew in that moment our Lord was speaking through your lips, that your summons for a Great Pilgrimage was a command from God Himself." He rested his forehead against the floor and then looked up again. In a voice more a whimper than a wail, "Your Holiness, we are committed to changing our errant ways, to behave as Christian knights and to redeem ourselves in your eyes and the eyes of God by marching to Jerusalem. We beg for your mercy!" The pope remained silent, staring, not responding to their plea.

"Your Holiness, may I ask a question?" Hugh asked, shifting himself to face the pope. Urban nodded. Turning to Achard, "Tell me again, how many knights and men-at-arms have you?"

"Five knights and ten men-at-arms, Father Abbot"

"Good fighting men?"

"The best."

"How much do you need?"

"Two thousand *livres* and four mules for our baggage."

"And what guarantee have I that this loan will be repaid?"

"I have three large estates in this district. Their harvests until recently were abundant. I'm certain that they will soon be profitable once more. If I die on this pilgrimage or for whatever reason fail to return, these lands will escheat to the Abbey of Cluny in perpetuity. You may have your own notary draw up a *contractvivum gagum* which will guarantee this pledge."

"And these vile sons of yours will accompany you?" Hugh asked.

"Yes, Father Abbot, they will. And I guarantee to you, on my immortal soul, that their conduct will be unimpeachable."

"Having them out of our lands, leaving us in peace, may alone be worth the price of the loan. Holy Father, your thoughts?" Hugh asked.

"I sense their contrition," he answered.

"Then it shall be done," Hugh said.

Achard's sons rose and with tears in their eyes bowed slowly to the pope and to Hugh. They turned and left the room.

* * *

"There is one more matter, Holy Father." Looking to the porter, "Bring them in."

The porter opened the door. Through it passed a castellan holding a rope tied around the neck of a young man dressed in a peasant's tunic looking bewildered and terrified, the castellan yanking it twice as he walked toward the dais, the man stumbling each time. The prisoner was flanked by two men-at-arms. A look of astonishment immediately crossed the faces of all the priors. Urban and Hugh betrayed no emotion. He was about my age, twenty-five, clear complected, bright blue eyes, quite handsome with an almost angelic countenance. What possible crime could he have committed? At Antioch I learned that his beguiling appearance was a deception, that there was no crime of which he was incapable. The castellan strode up before the dais, bowing with a knee bent first to Urban and then to Hugh.

"I am Aubry, servant to Renaud, Count of Burgundy and of Mâcon, captain of his house guards. I am here at the count's request. This filthy so-called 'priest' is a monk here at Cluny. He committed a crime in Mâcon and my Lord wishes permission to have his hand severed in Mâcon's public square. My Lord believes that it would be salutary for citizens to witness the penalty for thievery and for a different execrable act which I hesitate to describe. Even a priest is not exempt from our laws." In other regions of our land, local lords could have with impunity asserted their own authority in matters such as this. But Cluny and all its daughter priories were unique in their complete autonomy, free of control of secular lords, even bishops, an authority granted and confirmed by successive popes, including Urban. We owed our allegiance solely to the Holy See and no one else. The priors visibly stirred upon hearing that he was a Cluny monk. I could also tell from the intensity of his gaze that Urban was taking a keen interest, perhaps because it involved a cleric. He took control of the interrogation.

"Who is this man?" Urban asked.

"I know only that his name is Peter Bartholomew, Your Holiness. A monk of Cluny."

Looking first to Hugh and then to the gathered priors, "Does anyone know this monk?" Urban asked.

Hugh shook his head and then looked to his *obedientaries*, the senior monks, who were seated side by side to his left, for an answer. The grand prior stood up, first bowing to the dais. "I know him, Your Holiness. He is indeed Peter Bartholomew and until recently a monk of this abbey. Some five days ago he disappeared. I know nothing of his actions since then."

"What crime has he committed?" Urban asked of Aubry.

"The cellarer of my Lord's palace was in town collecting bread for his Lordship's table. He saw this man in peasant's garb with a cowl over his head, almost as though in disguise. But for the fact that his cowl momentarily slipped, revealing his tonsure, the cellarer would not have known that this detestable creature was a monk. He saw him grab a loaf of bread, conceal it in his tunic, and then walk quickly out of the bakehouse. The grain used for the bread was grown on my Lord's land; the mill which ground the flour and the bakehouse that baked the bread are both owned by the Count. Three thefts from his Lordship! The Count demands his right hand!"

"This is a serious charge indeed", the pope said. "Unworthy of a Cluniac monk. Brother Peter, what say you?"

Peter stood here trembling, struggling to speak. "Your Holiness I . . . "

At that, Aubry fiercely yanked the rope downwards, forcing Peter to his knees. "When you speak to the Vicar of Rome you will kneel as a penitent!" Aubry shouted at him and with the heel of his boot struck him in the back to push him further to the floor.

"Your Holiness, all he has said is true. I was without coin. My intention was not to take it for myself but to bring the loaf to a poor Christian woman whom I was told had not eaten in two days. *That* is the extent of my crime. If Christ himself fed loaves and fishes to the poor I could do no less."

"I wonder," Urban musing, looking at Aubry, "is losing one's right hand proportionate to the crime of theft of a loaf of bread, particularly intended for a destitute woman? I believe Father Abbot can deal with this."

Aubry would not allow the matter to rest. "There's more," he said. "The cellarer rushed to our castle and summoned two of my men-at-arms. In their search for Peter, they were directed to the home of a woman, a witch of general reputation, not starving at all. On the contrary, rather plump."

At that Peter cried out "I didn't know she was a witch!"

"Outside the door," Aubrey continued, "they heard the voice of a man both screaming in pain and laughing in joy '*more, more!*' They then burst into the house to see this *priest*," he said sarcastically, "naked, his wrists and ankles tied with thongs to the bed as the witch was flogging him with a whip. He seemed to enjoy it." He looked back to his men for confirmation. They both nodded.

Quickly, Urban's voice became quite severe, now looking at Peter, "Is this true?"

"No! No! This is a lie!. They tried to extort coin from me. I had none! This story is an invention! I swear on the sacred heart of our Holy Mother Mary!"

"*Liar!*" shouted Aubry, yanking the rope up forcing Peter into a standing position. He placed both hands on the uppermost part of Peter's tunic and ripped it apart. He then roughly spun Peter around to reveal his back, welt marks and blood only partially dried.

"Well . . . yes," he stammered. "But I didn't really enjoy it. I wanted to experience the passion of Christ before his crucifixion. By doing this, I hoped . . . I hoped I could feel His agony and become closer to my God."

Urban stood up. Anger streamed across his face. "*You unworthy monk!*" he shouted. "You are an abomination. You did this out of lust, to satisfy some perverse sexual urge. You did *not* do this for Christ. I declare you anathema. No longer may you take Holy Communion. You are henceforth dead to the Holy Mother Church. Begone!" pointing to the chamber door.

Even Aubry appeared startled by Urban's vehemence. "Your Holiness, may we still have his right hand?"

"No," Urban replied. "Excommunication is sufficient. He will burn in hell. That should repay the count for his loaf of bread." Yanking the rope Aubrey pulled Peter out of the room.

Urban looked to his right at Hugh. "Father Abbot, do you have anything further you would require of us? Otherwise, we must continue our mission to other cities."

"No, Your Holiness. I wish you a good journey."

* * *

The meeting was about to conclude with the singing of a psalmody when I decided to speak.

At chapter monks are permitted to voice their opinions, even to disagree with their superiors, albeit always deferentially. I had one moment, only this moment, to save Benedict. Trembling, I stood and with a halting tone of voice "Your Holiness, I . . . I have a petition." All the priors turned their heads to me in astonishment. For a mere monk, uninvited, to address a pope was remarkable; no, unprecedented. I quickly looked at Damian for reassurance. His face was grim. Abbot Hugh's also.

"Yes, my son?" Urban asked in a very kindly manner, giving me a bit of confidence.

Hugh interrupted. "Your Holiness, I did not know of this monk's request but in view of your journey's schedule, you may prefer that his prior and I deal with this matter?"

Urban placed his hand gently on Hugh's arm. "We shall not be separated from our priests. Your name young monk?"

"I am Oderic of the Priory La Charité sur Loire. I wish to tell you that Prior Damian, my superior, has no knowledge of this. If penance is to be done, I alone am responsible Holy Father."

Urban waved the concern away. "No penance will be necessary. Where do you come from Brother Oderic, your birth home?"

"From Rheims. My father was a spice merchant there."

"Ah. Rheims. Warm memories. In our youth, we studied at its cathedral school."

"And I also, Your Holiness," I responded eagerly.

From Urban's expression, I knew we had established a connection. "Brother Oderic, how can we serve you?" he asked in a fatherly tone further fortifying my spirit.

"Your Holiness, Father Benedict, now precentor of our priory, is suffering from a disease. He is likely to die. This is the judgment of his physician. But this surely cannot be God's Judgment for he is as saintly a man as I have ever known. Only Our Lord can save him now. I have with me a cross," retrieving it quickly from my cassock and holding it up, "which I believe if sanctified with your blessing would enable Father to recover from this hateful illness. That is my request."

"Come forward," Urban waved to me.

I approached, stepped up onto the dais, and knelt before him. He extended his hand and I kissed his ring. He signaled for me to stand. "Benedict?" he queried to himself. "Benedict? Yes, we remember him. We spent our novitiates together here at Cluny, did we not?"

"Yes, Holy Father."

"And we were both ordained at the same time by Father Abbot, were we not?"

"Yes, Holy Father."

"A worthy and indeed a saintly man. We would be honored to bless this cross with the sincere hope that it aids in his recovery." He then offered his open hand to receive the cross. With that Urban kissed it, murmured a prayer, made the sign of the cross over it, and handed it back to me. I bowed, backed two steps, turned, and descended down the dais steps. The hall was perfectly still. As I was halfway through the aisle I heard Urban call. "Brother Oderic." I turned to face him. "Brother Oderic, your devotion has touched us." I smiled, bowed, and returned to my seat. As Damian and I walked out of the chapter hall he put his hand on my shoulder and said softly "Well done".

We left two days later. I took advantage of that time to complete my reading of the *Aeneid.*

Peter the hermit Excites a Village Crowd

It was on the third day of our journey that we witnessed a startling event. We were passing through a village, rather large in comparison with others I saw on our trip. I don't recall its name nor is it of consequence. As we entered, we could see a crowd of people, men and women, perhaps a hundred, in the village square, a modest stone church facing it. In the middle of the square was a statue, I believe of some saint, likely one specially venerated in the village, crudely carved and placed on an oversized stone pedestal three feet high. In front of the statute stood a monk, rather short, thin, probably around fifty years of age, wearing a woolen tunic reaching down to his ankles girded with a rope, his feet bare. Unkempt, slovenly in dress, his tunic clearly never having been washed, a face long and lean not unlike that of the donkey he rode tethered beside him. He looked more like a pauper than a priest. Damian was quite curious. "Let's listen. Stop here."

The monk began to speak. "I am Peter. Some call me 'the Hermit'. I have in my hand a letter," waving a piece of rolled parchment, then holding it aloft above his head, "which I received directly from Jesus Christ in Jerusalem when I was on a pilgrimage. I had fallen asleep before an altar in a remote chapel dug out of the hillside of Golgatha where Christ was crucified. He appeared to me in a vision. I walked outside and it descended into my hands from Heaven. I fell to my knees and cried out with joy. The Grace of God enveloped me. It is from Christ Himself *to all of you*," his voice rising, pointing the parchment at the crowd, slowly from left to right, "a command for you to follow me to Jerusalem. There we shall take back our Holy Sepulchre, where Christ was buried, from filthy pagan hands. This is God's will."

The crowd was silent though listening intently. "You have suffered mightily in recent years from drought and famine. You have seen a light in the sky, lasting for twenty days, with a tail shaped like a sword; darkening of the moon; and other events unknown in nature. But they are not unknown to God. They are a message *from* God! You have lived your lives in wickedness and turned your backs on our Lord. *Renounce your unholy lives!*" his voice rising again. "Do you wish to perish in the eternal fires of hell?"

There was a first slight murmurings of "no, no." The murmurings became louder, "No! No!" they cried almost in unison.

"Do you wish to be denied eternal salvation? Damnation is certain! The fires of hell await you! Your sufferings have only begun. A plague of locusts, even worse than that which God visited on the land of the pharaoh in Egypt, will devour your crops. What remains will be eaten by mice and maggots. You will be left to feed on roots in your fields and nuts in your forests! Is this what you want for your children, your wives and husbands? *Tell me!*"

"NO! NO!" they began shouting, some falling to their knees, hands clasped, looking upwards toward heaven.

"Filthy and godless Jews who sacrificed our Lord on their altar of usury foul the air we breathe and bring pestilence and plague to our lands. They will steal your children and roast them for their midday meals. *Is this what you want?*" he shouted.

"NO! NO!" The few who had not fallen to their knees did so now, sobbing and weeping.

"Join me to Jerusalem. God's final judgment is nigh. If we do not restore the Holy Sepulchre into His hands, we shall *all* perish in hell. Let us rid it of the polluted stench of the pagans for the sweet perfume of salvation. Follow me to Jerusalem! There you shall receive God's blessing and his forgiveness. This is God's will!" Peter's arms were outstretched, his entire body shaking.

The crowd was becoming hysterical rising to a crescendo: "GOD WILLS IT! GOD WILLS IT!" they shouted. At that moment I saw Drogo, the verminous wretch at Clermont branded with a "V", standing at the back of the crowd. He began trembling uncontrollably, his eyes wide open almost bulbous, his hands on his cheeks tilting his head from side to side as though possessed. The crowd turned to stare.

"This is a holy man," he cried out, pointing at Peter. "A saintly man of God. He alone can lead us to Jerusalem. Look at me!", Drogo continued, screaming. "*Look at me!*" he screamed again, even louder. "I came here with a clear face, unblemished. But now," removing his hands to reveal his face, "God has touched me with this holy mark, a 'V', the sign of '*Victoire*'. We *shall* be victorious! Christ is with us and will protect us!" With that, he fell to the ground, seemingly unconscious, his arms and legs convulsing in a spasm. Wild, uncontrollable frenzy seized the crowd.

"*Behold this man! Behold him!*" Peter shouted in a final rhetorical flourish. "God has revealed Himself this day. He has promised victory. This is His sign!" Peter did not pause, doubtless fearful of losing the momentum of the almost riotous fervor he had aroused. "Gather all your belongings! Carry them on your back! Pack them in a barrow! Collect your children! Follow me! Follow me to Jerusalem for your *salvation!*"

I had never heard such oratory. His eloquence spellbinding for indeed he had cast a spell over the crowd. People began running to their homes, quickly emerging with what baggage they could assemble in a few moments, and then dashing back to the square where Peter waited, many of the men holding scythes, sickles, and hoes with which to fight the Turks. Drogo had joined them. Peter stepped down from the pedestal, mounted the donkey next to him, nudged it forward with his knees and slowly began to ride out. "Peter is a saint, blessed by God Himself!" some cried. They began crowding around him, tearing at his clothes hoping for a piece to revere, others pulling tufts of hair from the donkey believing the animal holy. Peter slapped the butt of his donkey to escape the crush of people but then, when a short distance away and in safety, he slowed down to wait. The townspeople began following him in a joyful chant: "God wills it! God wills it! To Jerusalem!"

Damian and I sat quietly throughout, watching in amazement as this procession snaked its way through the village onto the road ahead. We waited in silence until it was no longer in sight. The road forked just outside the village. I am certain Damian was as relieved as I that Peter had chosen a route different from our own. We traveled in silence for some distance.

"I don't think this is what the Holy Father intended at Clermont," I said simply.

"No, it's not," Damian answered with a deep sigh, staring at the road ahead. "No, it's not. Just rabble."

Confrontation with Brigands

We traveled several more days. There was scant conversation, even at mid-day meals off the road. I think both of our minds were contemplating the events of the past month and especially what we had just witnessed in the village. As we journeyed I kept wondering why people were so deceived by the words of Peter the Hermit. How many more of this "rabble", as Damian described them, would follow him? What was Drogo's role? A cascade of questions, doubts, and thoughts poured through my mind.

We were about a half-day from La Charité. I was looking forward to our return knowing that I could expect a pittance—an extra serving of fresh perch for dinner, always a small feast when an abbot or prior returns from a long journey. We came to some woods. The sky was clear and the sun very bright but its light intermittent through the trees: one moment I was blinded by darkness, another by the sun's glare. There was never time to adjust my eyes. Ahead, dimly, I could see two men standing in the middle of the road. I had an uneasy feeling. I came to about fifty feet from them. I could now see more clearly. They were men-at-arms, swords hanging from their belts, their shields leaned against a tree, and two horses tethered to tree boughs grazing close by. Their surcoats bore the same coat of arms as the escutcheons on their shields: three gyrfalcons, talons bared, descending on their prey just below, an angry boar.

One of them, taller of the two and evidently in charge, raised his hand indicating that we were to halt. My initial instinct was to shake the reins, lash Esther, and race through but I immediately realized that escape was impossible. I stopped. He walked forward.

"Good monks," he said, "I am Jehan, captain in service to Thomas of Marle, Lord of Coucy. In his name we greet you," his head nodding slighting to us but distinctly without reverence. "We beg your forgiveness, but a slight toll charge must be paid." Without waiting for a response, he began calculating. "Let's see . . . " surveying us, "two passengers, a cart, mule, and a packhorse. Yes. That will be five silver *sous*. And then we shall gladly allow you to pass."

I knew we had only three *sous* left in Damian's purse, the rest depleted from his charity and other expenses on the road. I had hoped to deal with this myself, pleading the poverty of monks but Damian gave me no opportunity.

"How dare you!" he exclaimed with vehemence. I knew then there would be trouble. "We are men of God. And you extort from *us*? This is the King's Road, a public highway. You have no right. Let us pass, right now!"

"Well, I beg pardon, your holy magnificence," he replied sarcastically. "We are posted here to collect tolls and tolls we shall collect. Five *sous*, if you please."

Damian's anger was growing. "And by what authority does this so-called 'Lord of Coucy,'" asking with equal scorn, "have to commandeer this road? We are protected by the pope's Peace of God. You have *no* right to extort money from priests, or anyone else. We won't pay!"

Jehan's eyes narrowed as he glared at Damian. "We are the Peace of God. Without us there is no peace. No, on second thought, six *sous* for you have offended the honor of our Lord. Who are you and what is your business on our Lord's road?"

"I told you before, this is *not* Coucy's road. Not that you have any right to know but I am the prior of La Charité sur Loire. My brother monk," bending his head slightly in my direction, "and I are returning to our priory. Let us pass."

"Oh, a prior. Yes?"

Damian said nothing. "I have heard of La Charité. Another wealthy Cluniac monastery." Looking back at his companion several feet behind him, "What do you think the ransom would be for a prior? A fat purse, no?" The soldier nodded. "We shall escort you to our Lord's castle. He can deal with your insolence. But let me check your cart and packhorse. Perhaps I will find something to reward us for our own time." Jehan walked to the cart. He then grasped the reins which I was holding in my left hand, apparently suspecting that we might try to flee. He was right to be suspicious. I had been silent throughout the exchanges between Damian and the captain. This was the moment I had feared from the beginning. There was no choice but quick action. I clenched my right fist and hit Jehan squarely in the nose. He released the reins and stepped back, his face bleeding. He reached for his sword but was too close to the cart to pull it from his scabbard. He drew his dagger instead and made a step toward me. Blood from his nose was pouring down over his mouth and chin. We were no more than a foot apart. At that moment he started to wipe his face with his free hand but I could tell that his grip on the dagger had loosened. I dropped the reins and with both hands ripped his fingers from the hilt snatching it before it fell. With a wild swing, but one that proved accurate, I slashed his face with the knife. Jehan fell back screaming.

The man-at-arms was watching from a short distance, no doubt confident his commander could deal with a single monk. He quickly thought differently. He pulled out his sword and began running toward the cart. I recovered the reins and shook them furiously, no time to reach for the whip. Esther bolted forward. He was directly in our path. Seeing the mule charging him, he quickly stepped aside but in doing so tripped over vines hugging the ground and began stumbling. I yanked the reins to the left. Esther responded immediately. With a glancing blow of her body she struck the soldier, throwing him down. When we reached their horses I pulled back hard on the reins. Esther slowed and eventually stopped. I grabbed the whip, jumped out of the cart and raced back. I could see Jehan staggering wildly about, his hands clasping his face still screaming

in agony, and the other soldier lying on the ground, it seemed unconscious. I was leaving nothing chance. I untethered the horses and struck
them with quick lashes on their flanks. They raced off.

We resumed our trip, though at a quicker pace than before wishing
to put as much distance as I could between Thomas of Marle's men and
us. Damian was deeply shaken, easy to see out of the corner of my eye.
He spoke not a word to me; I respected his private thoughts. We had no
further trouble that day.

On arriving at the priory, I guided Esther to the cloister door. Damian,
trembling yet, was having difficulty stepping down from the cart; two
monks present outside rushed forward to assist. I took the cart, Esther,
and the packhorse to the stable leaving them in the care of the *connestabulus* requesting that he deliver them to the deanery. Before I left, I nuz-
zled my head against Esther's neck, stroking her forehead, softly thanking
her for her service to Damian and me. In the meantime, I had a more
important errand. I hurried to the *infirmarium* and found Benedict in the
same bed as I had left him but he seemed more frail than before. He was
awake. I pulled up a chair.

"Father, how are you faring?"

"I don't know," he said weakly, his voice barely audible. "You'll have to
ask Brother Geoffrey." I had hoped for more strength in the month I was
absent.

"Father, I have brought you something from Cluny." With that, I reached
into my pocket to bring out the pectoral cross. I gently raised his head
from the pillow and strung the chain around his neck placing the cross
on his chest, straightening it so that it lay correctly. "Father, this cross
was blessed by His Holiness himself who kissed it and said a prayer on
your behalf. It is an amulet and will bring you a speedy recovery," I said
encouragingly.

He smiled, tenderly grasping the cross. "You are a good son, Oderic."

"Father, Prior Damian and I just returned and I have much to do right
now. I must leave you but I will return tomorrow to tell you of the journey.
Such tales I will share with you! Until then, Father."

He nodded. I kissed his forehead and left but with terrible dread in my
heart.

This ends Book III of *Jerusalem Falls!* Book IV begins.

BOOK IV
MASSACRE OF JEWS

Death of Father Benedict. I Become a Pilgrim. My Pilgrimage Begins.
Bishop John Saves Jews in Speyer. A Reunion in Mainz. A Warning
Ignored. A Plea to Archbishop Ruthard. Emicho at the Gates. Massacre
at the Episcopal Palace. A Battle, Rebecca Rescued, and Escape.

Death of Father Benedict

It was the day following my return to La Charité from Cluny, cold and blustery, one moment the wind still, the next howling through the cloister's promenades. We had put on our cloaks to give a little warmth, the sun concealed by thick clouds providing little. Mass at Lauds was over and we were filing through the cloister into the parlor leading to the chapter hall. Waiting for me just inside the parlor was Prior Damian. He beckoned to me. This was the first time we had spoken since the fight with Thomas of Marle's men.

"Oderic," his voice struggling to find the words, his eyes welling up with tears, "*Infirmarius* Guarin just informed me that Benedict is close to death. Someone must maintain a vigil. You have a close relationship with him and your presence I'm sure would be comforting."

I suppose that I should have been shocked by the news but I wasn't. I had sensed in my heart from the previous day's visit that the end was close but I just refused to admit it to myself. "How much time does Father Benedict have? Do you know?"

"Very little. You must go now."

I hurried to the *infirmarium* and drew up a chair close to Benedict's bed. His breath was faint and chest heaving. He was caressing the pectoral cross on his chest. I was close to tears. "Father, how are you doing?" the only thing I could think to say. He didn't respond, just gazing at me, never taking his eyes away. I sat with him through the day and that night, both of us silent. I refused to leave him, periodically dozing off in my chair. Geoffrey brought me some cheese and bread on a platter. As he placed it on my lap I looked up as though asking whether recovery was possible. He simply shook his head. By the next morning Benedict seemed worse.

Geoffrey was standing nearby. I left my chair and walked up to him. "Is it time?"

"Yes."

"Please inform the prior," I said. "We need to move him immediately to the chapter hall." Geoffrey rushed off. A short time later I could hear the hall's bells summoning the community. Two *infirmari* fetched a litter, laid it beside the bed and gently lifted Benedict onto it. They bore him to the hall, I following. When we entered Damian was standing on the dais wearing his full sacramental vestments—a dalmatic over which was a chasuble and an embroidered stole around his neck hanging down over the shoulders to the waist—for hearing confession. The monks were standing also, chanting the *Miserere* invoking God's mercy. The litter was laid on the dais. Damian knelt down before Benedict. The chanting ended. I could see Benedict mouth the words "Bless me Father, for I have sinned," but everything else was whispered, so low that Damian had to press his ear against Benedict's mouth. I could hear Damian say *Te absolvo* as he made the sign of the cross over Benedict. Damian, still kneeling, nodded to the attendants who carried Benedict back to the *infirmarium*. The entire community, led by Damian, followed chanting the *Miserere* once again. We filled the room. I gently pushed my way forward to the front.

In the meantime preparations had been made for Benedict's return. A goatskin shroud strewn with ashes lay beside his bed, two standing candleholders placed at the shroud's foot, both candles lit. He was lifted from the stretcher onto the shroud. Damian knelt beside Benedict to administer the *viaticum*, the last rites. I feared his death was so imminent that he would be unable to complete the sacrament. Damian placed a wafer in his mouth and then tenderly raised Benedict's shoulders and head with one arm and with his free hand held a cup of wine to his lips. A small vial of holy oil, already prepared, was on Benedict's table in preparation for the sacrament of Extreme Unction. I walked to the table, poured the oil into a bowl, and handed it to Damian. Damian dipped his thumb into it and anointed him, on the forehead, chest, shoulders, and hands, Benedict all the time staring intently at Damian. Damian took Benedict's pectoral cross, still around his neck, kissed it and then placed it to Benedict's lips. Damian laid it back down on Benedict's chest. At that moment, Benedict took his last breath. Damian with sweet gentleness placed two fingers over his eyelids closing them. Unable to control myself, I began to sob.

That evening our bells tolled. We all gathered in the church. His body lay in an open wooden coffin before the high altar. Damian asperged his body by sprinkling it with holy water. He had been previously washed and dressed in his habit, over it a cape, night shoes on his feet. His cowl was placed over his face, sewn down to the neck. We sang "Vespers for the Dead". Throughout the night the monks took turns praying followed in the morning by the Requiem Mass. The church's bells rang three times. Six pallbearers, including me, carried his coffin to the priory cemetery, the community walking solemnly behind in procession. A lid was placed over the coffin, nailed down, and then lowered into his grave.

On the following day I went to the *infirmarium* and stood by Benedict's empty bed, just gazing at it. Geoffrey walked up to me, gently placing his hand on my shoulder. "Father Benedict sensed he had only hours to live. He had asked me to take his pectoral cross after he passed to be given to you. He told me that it would not save him but it might you. He didn't explain how. Just before he was to be ritually washed, I took it from his neck and stored it. Somehow, Prior Damian became aware of this and asked me for it. He promised that, someday, you would have it." He briefly squeezed my shoulder, turned, and walked away. That was the last I was ever to see Geoffrey. Over the years I have thought of him many times.

Soon, Father Benedict's intuition would be proven right. His pectoral cross saved my life.

I Become a Pilgrim

For the next three months I was listless during offices, sometimes stumbling over verses of the hymns, more alert when reciting the penitential psalms thinking of blessed Father Benedict believing no one deserved God's Grace more than he. I had returned to the *scriptorium* to begin my new project. During my journey from the *palais* of Vicomte Estienne after my meeting with Dowager Cateline I had struggled deeply whether or not to embark on the life of John. I even doubted that he was in truth a "saint". I had not discussed my visit to Cateline with Damian. He was already suspicious of relics. And I had been so confident. I was in a quandary—Was I to abandon the project altogether? Or was I to follow the traditional, albeit fraudulent, story, the "miracle" of Saint John's hand and its "discovery" by Estienne in "John's" sarcophagus. I had decided on the former course and began copying the "Life of Saint George", the Roman soldier in the emperor's guard executed for his unwavering faith, venerated by Christian warriors. I thought him a worthy subject of my labors.

That is, until Benedict's death. Everything changed. I decided to write the life of Saint John the Martyr with tales that Benedict would have enjoyed reading. Veracity was now secondary. I no longer cared whether he was a saint. I built on the traditional story, embellishing it with invention: How John received a vision from the Virgin Mary near Antioch instructing him to build a church on impossible terrain; he pleaded that he lacked the skills but at that moment the land was transformed. How a church had caught fire, its huge interior crucifix ablaze; John knelt in prayer to the Virgin, heard her sweet voice, and spit on the flames quenching them restoring both the cross and the church. How he happened to meet a pilgrim on the road bleeding profusely from a dagger attack to his neck; John touched the wound healing the pilgrim but now bleeding from his own neck. I even thought, albeit briefly, of John visiting a leper colony outside of Jerusalem, touching each with his hand curing them instantly. But Prior Damian might not appreciate lepers descending on our church with their bells and clappers driving other pilgrims away. My favorite, and one I was certain Benedict would enjoy, was John retrieving the corpse of a young child floating in the River Jordan, laying him on the bank. As he kneeled over the child in prayer a bright light enveloped them both and the boy began reciting the Lord's Prayer. The child's resurrection would especially attract parents with sick children. The more miracles I could attribute to "Saint" John, the more pilgrim traffic would be drawn to La Charité. God would forgive, I hoped, this minor deception in favor of a nobler purpose.

* * *

It was now early spring, April I think, the Year of Our Lord 1096. My chronicle of Saint John had been completed and I gave the manuscript to Damian who earlier expressed an interest in reading it. One day I had an errand that brought me close to the priory's gatehouse. In front of the gate some thirty men and women, including children, had assembled dressed in the characteristic garb of pilgrims but with red crosses sewn on their tunics. The priory's almoner and two assistants were distributing to each a half loaf of bread and a cup of wine. I listened. Their voices were indistinct but I could hear some words: "Peter the Hermit", "Jerusalem", "Holy Land". For reasons I cannot explain even today, I was struck by the same light that had transformed Paul on his road to Damascus. I had a new purpose.

I could not wait, never blessed with the virtue of patience. I rushed to Damian's office. He was in. He looked up and beckoned me to enter. I was breathless, even forgetting the *benedicte*. Before being invited to speak

I blurted out "Father Prior. I want to go to Jerusalem!" He was obviously nonplussed, uncertain how to respond. He too dispensed with formalities.

"Come, sit," pointing to a chair. "Oderic, what is it that disturbs you?"

"Father, I have seen pilgrims at our gatehouse on their way to Jerusalem. I wish to join them. I'm sure God has spoken to me and given me a new mission. I must obey. I would like your permission to leave within the week."

"Oderic, what is this mission about which you feel so strongly?"

"It is to rescue our Holy Sepulchre from the heathens. To restore Jerusalem to true believers. I wish to take up the cross of Jesus and do his holy work. The words of Pope Urban at Clermont inspired me. As did the oratory of Peter the Hermit. I want to join these saintly men, soldiers of Christ, pilgrims of God, imbued with the Holy Spirit who are undertaking this pilgrimage. They are ready to sacrifice their lives for Christ. I can do no less. *Deus vult*."

Damian sat in silence, his eyes fixed on me, then on the floor at his feet, and at me again. I was becoming anxious. I sensed more sadness than surprise. As I reflect back on that conversation, I'm sure Damian was thinking of my youthfulness, my naiveté, my blind faith in the goodness of all Christians. But he chose his words carefully.

"Oderic, you have become a worthy priest. I came to know that especially during our journey to Clermont and Cluny. Though . . . " pausing, "slashing the face of a Christian, even an unworthy one, a brigand, with a dagger was a transgression of your vows." I was startled, never realizing the gravity of my sin in his eyes for he had said nothing before. His mouth then broke into a slight smile. "*Te absolvo*," making a rapid and perfunctory sign of the cross. "You did what had to be done. Recite five penitential psalms and the matter is closed." I was relieved. "But I'm unsure the men in which you place so much faith are as saintly as you believe. They are men. Given to godliness, yes, in some fashion, some of them, in moments, but always clinging to their own interests. They are tempted by avarice and personal advancement as are all men. Beware of them for they will fail you. Beware of them. If they behave as barbarians in their own land, why should they behave any better in the East? There is one other problem," Damian continued. "The pope has decreed that the pilgrimage is not to be undertaken until the Feast of the Assumption, some five months hence. You should wait and obey his injunction."

I suspected that by urging delay his real purpose was to defer my departure as long as possible hoping time would alter my mind. "Father,

I can't," I protested. "Pilgrims are gathering now. They require spiritual guidance. Perhaps I can provide that."

Damian realized that my intention was set. No amount of persuasion would alter it. "I must say, selfishly, that I will miss you. However, I have little choice in this matter. Father Abbot has given blanket permission that all monks who wish to undertake the pilgrimage may do so. You too." With that he reached out with his hand, clasping my arm with a loving touch. Our conversation ended.

My Pilgrimage Begins

It was only three days later that a service was held for me in the church. All the monks had gathered sitting in their choir stalls. Damian stood in front of the high altar. I lay prostrate before him, my arms outstretched. The monks were chanting versicles led by the choir leader, the cantor, with responses, and three collects, my name mentioned in each.

Damian began. "Father Oderic. Do you believe in Jesus Christ Our Savior?"

"I do Father Prior."

"Do you renounce the devil and all his iniquities?"

"I do Father Prior."

"Do you vow upon your immortal soul to march to Jerusalem, to reach the threshold of the saints without fear or falter, and to return to us safely and in joy?"

"I do Father Prior."

"In the name of Jesus Christ and blessed John the Martyr, our patron saint, I bless your journey. May God Himself protect you. Arise Father Oderic." I was surprised that Damian had invoked John, gratified that he had come to believe. I would hold the truth in my heart. No one else need know. There was a higher good.

On the altar were a "script", a leather satchel with shoulder straps for holding food and clothing; a "burdon", pilgrim's staff, perhaps six feet tall, with two iron knobs, one at the top and the other a foot lower, its end a six inch spike; a neatly folded "sclavein", a long woolen tunic reaching down almost to my ankles with a red cross of silk sewn below the shoulder; and finally a wide-brimmed pilgrim's felt hat, its front brim folded and pinned back to the crown. To my surprise I saw two pewter badges fastened on the folded brim, one a scallop shell indicating that the wearer had completed a pilgrimage to Santiago de Compostela and the other depicting the heads of the Three Kings proving a pilgrimage to the shrine in Cologne containing the remains of the three Magi, both famous destinations for pilgrims. Damian sprinkled holy water over each of them in turn accompanied by a blessing, *In nomine Patris et Filii et Spiritus Sancti*, as he handed them to me one by one. There was yet another object on the altar I had not noticed, an iron pectoral cross, Benedict's cross. Damian picked it up and as I slightly bent my head placed it around my neck. I was filled with emotion.

As the monks were proceeding out of the church, Damian motioned for me to follow him. We walked into a chapel, the same in which I had found him months earlier reserved for his use only. "Oderic," he said tenderly, "you must promise me to return safely. You have undertaken a dangerous journey. I shall pray for you every day."

"Father, I thank you. I shall return. But I'm curious. You gave me a hat with badges showing I had completed pilgrimages to Compostela and to Cologne. I've done neither."

Damian nodded. "Yes. True. They had belonged to a former claustral prior. When he died, I kept them not knowing the purpose to which I would put them. I have now found it. These badges will endow you with the authenticity of a devout pilgrim. Perhaps they may help. Perhaps they won't. But they won't hurt. I have two more things for you." With that, he handed me a purse of coins. "You will need this. The trip is not without expenses. But there is something else." He handed me four journals, newly bound in leather, filled with blank pages of parchment. "Keep a daily record of your journey. I want to know everything, recorded every day, until you return. Letters from you would also be welcome."

"I promise, Father Prior. Faithfully. Every day." I bowed and kissed his hand. I kept that promise.

* * *

The next day at dawn I left La Charité. As I passed through the gate the porter simply doffed his hat without questioning my purpose in leaving the priory. He seemed to know. Perhaps the pilgrim's garb. "Good luck!" he shouted after me. I experienced a sense of joy, of liberation, free of the stifling rigors of monastic life. I could be myself, venerate my God, and be part of a community of devout Christians who worshiped easily without restrictive regulations. We could all march to Jerusalem together, retake it from the heathen grip and restore it into God's hands. If at La Charité my "mission" was to prepare for my personal redemption, my purpose now was larger: to ready the East for salvation and the return of Jesus Christ to Jerusalem. It was a feeling not long to last.

Ahead of me, I could see a small group of pilgrims, thirty or so, walking north. Behind me was another group of pilgrims heading in the same direction, all traveling in groups for safety. There seemed to be thousands on the road, as far ahead or behind as I could see. We passed through one town after another. Every time we approached a walled city, one or another of the pilgrims would ask me "Is this Jerusalem? Are we there?" I would shake my head, "No, not yet. More miles." They asked only me, no one else, I think because on my hat were pinned the two badges proving I had traveled more than five miles from my birth village and thus must have seen the world.

With the famines, food was somewhat scarce and market prices dear, made worse by the number of hungry pilgrims on the road. Nevertheless, townspeople, when they saw us, were as generous as they could be with contributions, bringing from their kitchens what they could spare. I also possessed a pouch of coins, though I used them sparingly. Other pilgrims, less fortunate, searched for whatever they could eat gleaned from fields, scavenged from woods, or gathered from kitchen scraps lying on city streets. I hurried to join a group immediately before me. Most had brought all their worldly possessions, either carrying them on their backs, thrown into small carts, husbands pulling them by hand, or into barrows, wives and children walking alongside. Mothers with young children carried their infants in their arms. Many pilgrims walked barefoot, a sign of penance for some sin or a demonstration of deep piety. A few wore iron chains around their waists or sackcloths of coarse animal hair which irritated the skin, their purpose to suffer for Christ.

"Where are we going?" I inquired of one pilgrim.

"I'm not certain," he answered. "We're following that holy goose up there," pointing ahead.

I looked forward. To my astonishment there was indeed a goose waddling in the lead. I needed a closer look. The goose would occasionally stop. The pilgrims stopped, watching anxiously. She would then waddle forward. The pilgrims followed. This occurred repeatedly.

I asked incredulously "Is this goose truly our guide?"

"Yes," was the answer. "She's filled with the Holy Spirit and will lead us to Jerusalem."

"Does she have a name? I'm curious."

"Does the Holy Spirit have a name?" came the sarcastic reply. "But I've heard that some miles ahead another company of pilgrims is being led by a goat who understands the Mysteries of Christ."

The pilgrims followed the goose from a respectful distance. Her behavior was uncanny. She would come to a fork in the road, halt, look right and then left, and then waddle forward. I almost believed she had supernatural powers. At one point the goose wandered off the road and settled on a tuft of grass. She was nesting. All of us gathered around, not moving, just watching. And watching. And watching. Finally, she stood up. She had laid an egg. The pilgrims became frenzied, falling on their knees, their arms uplifted, hands shaking. "This is a holy child of God!" they began exclaiming. The goose of course was startled by the noise but after it subsided wanted to return to her nest. Instead, one of pilgrim picked her up and returned her to the road. With a gentle tap of his shoe on her back feathers he urged the goose forward. Another pilgrim, unnoticed, picked up the egg and placed it in her apron, perhaps to worship it, perhaps to eat it. I hastened forward to join another group, fearful of asking who was leading them. I did decide to avoid the Holy Goat.

Three days passed. In front of us, perhaps five hundred paces away, was a road that merged with our own. Walking on it were some twenty men and women chatting merrily with one another, a small wagon behind them pulled by a donkey. It was unclear who they were. Pilgrims? They were barefoot, yes, indicating they were penitents, but without the customary sartorial indicia: wide-brimmed hats, pilgrim staffs, or satchels over their shoulders. They wore loose fitting woolen shirts and knee-length linen braies, undergarments often worn by peasants in the field. Almost all of them were holding slender wooden rods. They were now in front of us. Leading them was a man, his back to me, holding a large staff on which was affixed a cross. As we drew closer to the town, now just in sight of the townspeople, he raised his staff as though giving a signal to those behind. Suddenly, some of them rushed to the wagon, removed their shirts, and hastily donned sackcloths. When their backs were bared as they changed I could see faint welts, small sacrifices as I soon came to understand for the rewards that awaited them here and in every city they visited. They quickly reformed into rows, three abreast, wordlessly in a very practiced manner. The first row drew bells from their tunics and began furiously ringing them to announce their arrival. The following rows began vigorously beating with rods the backs of the row before it. Each of these blows was greeted with howls of pain and weeping far in excess of the severity of the blows themselves. The final row began singing in unison:

Lord, we repent of our sins.
Deliver us from our evil.
We are your obedient penitents.
We shall joyfully suffer our punishment.
Redeem us, dear Lord,
For your Son's sake.

The leader turned around to inspect his company, ensuring it was properly formed. He bore the brand of "V" on his cheek. It was Drogo again. I hung back, unwilling to be recognized.

"Who are these people?" I asked in a low voice of a pilgrim walking next to me.

"I've heard they're called 'flagellants'", he answered. "They are the truest sons and daughters of God."

Suddenly, the companionship of goose and goat worshipers became appealing to me. I looked back down the road but they were nowhere to be seen, doubtless the waddle of a goose hampering their pace. I could see townspeople gathering along both sides of the street leading into town. They were cheering the flagellants, all crossing themselves. Overwhelmed by curiosity, I hurried forward and walked discreetly behind the flagellants' wagon not wishing to be seen but close enough to watch. Drogo was holding his staff in both hands as though he were Moses prepared to part the Red Sea. He stopped, facing those assembled in front of him. The ringing of bells and beating with rods ceased. All was silent.

"I am Drogo, Messenger of God, the one and true God. I have been blessed with this mark," pointing to the "V" branded on his cheek. "It is a sign of God's Grace on me, *Victoire*," he shouted, "proof that we shall have victory in the name of Christ and reclaim Jerusalem from the heathens. But our Lord came to me in a vision last night. He commanded me to visit your city for He is sorely vexed by your sinfulness and godless ways. You tolerate wickedness and evil. You revile the Lord by word and deed. He wishes to cleanse you as He did Sodom and Gomorrah, to be wiped out from the face of our world, to visit upon you plague and pestilence, to inflict greater suffering than you can imagine!" The townspeople were stunned. Two of them began gasping as though suffocating. "But," he continued as he grasped his staff looking piously heavenward, "our God is a merciful god. You are not beyond redemption. We are the Army of Christ Himself. We have fasted for three days." I thought to myself they looked stout enough. "We require food and lodging. We require coin for our journey to Jerusalem where God has commanded me to lead my congregation. I shall now pray at our Lord's altar in your church," pointing his staff toward the church. "In front of it I shall leave a wagon. It is as holy as the Ark that bore our Lord's Commandments. It requires filling with lentils, beans, cakes, all you can gather. There will also be a box for coin. God will judge you by your devotion. Generous, and he promises bountiful harvests, prosperity in your trades, and freedom from pestilence and plague. Selfishness and adoration of mammon, I admonish you, will result in unspeakable suffering. I shall bend on my knee and report to God that you have fulfilled His Command," he paused sinisterly, "or that you have not."

With that, Drogo walked slowly, doubtless for effect, to the church followed by his company, the ringing of bells resumed along with beatings and wailing. I had seen enough. Charlatans and swindlers. All of them. Was this God's way? I asked myself. Surely not. I left quickly and soon joined another group of pilgrims, uncertain of what new surprises would hold for me with different companions.

Bishop John Saves Jews in Speyer

It was the third day of May. Our road took us through the city of Speyer, into its market square. It was an astonishing sight, quite beyond my powers to describe. In the middle of the square was a gallows with five nooses, the gibbets of two already occupied with men hanging from its transverse beam, their bodies partially eaten by crows. Below it, several feet from the gallows steps, was a large wooden block resting on the stone pavement, half of it carved out for a head to rest. There were shouts from the side streets: "Find the Jews!" I could see men going from house to house—Jewish homes easily identifiable by mezuzahs, small parchment scrolls with Old Testament writings, hanging on door posts—ferreting out their quarry.

With clubs in their hands, they were roughly pulling out every Jew they could find by their arms or hair, the Jews screaming in terror. The hands of each were tied with leather straps, ropes around their waists, and pulled into the city square. One Jew, a somewhat portly man, stumbled and fell face down on the pavement. A burgher, rather slight in frame, was having difficulty dragging him. Another came quickly to his aid, grabbed the rope, both of them pulling the man face down over the rough flagstones, his head bleeding profusely. He and four other Jews were yanked up the steps to the gallows. Other Jews were lined up before the steps waiting their turn. Perhaps the burghers thought this a more sanitary method of execution than butchering them with daggers and clubs. Most horrifying of all was the bodies of nine Jews, lying in a circle, identifiable by the round yellow rotas, or "wheels", sewn on their tunics which Jews were required to wear, lying still on the ground, their tunics punctured from repeated stabbings, the heads of some crushed by the withering blows of clubs. Over them stood five burghers, wealthy merchants distinctive for the fine tailoring of their tunics and mantles over their shoulders. Each held in his hand either a knife dripping with blood or a club similarly stained. All their clothes were splattered with blood.

Two Jews were still alive, kneeling on the pavement. In the middle of this circle was a priest, his head looking up as to heaven and his arms upraised, then looking down and screaming at the kneeling Jews: "You verminous wretches! Christ killers! You shall pay for your sins!" The priest walked up to one, pacing back and forth in front of him, the Jew's head bowed. "Renounce your idolatry! Accept Jesus Christ as your savior! *Do it now!*" he shouted. The Jew was silent. "*Now!*" he screamed. The Jew shook his head. "Then I sentence you to eternal damnation!" stamping his foot. "My vows prevent me from taking a life. But someone else can!" With that, he nodded to one of the burghers holding a club. He was clearly practiced from the blood on his club and with one blow smashed the Jew's skull. Not content with this savagery, he began beating him over and over again even as his body lay still. "Enough!" said the priest. "You've already killed him three times over." "One more won't hurt," the burgher snarled, and smashed his head again, splitting the skull, brains spilling out.

It was now the turn of the remaining Jew. He fared no better. A burgher was standing over him, shouting "Where is your treasure? Your silver. Tell me and you may live!"

The Jew looked up and began pleading, his voice broken by sobs, "Your Excellency, I have no silver. None. I cannot give you what I do not have."

"You lie! You lie! All you Jews lie. *Silver!* Where is it? Tell me!"

"I'm merely a butcher," he answered, his entire body trembling with fear. "I'm not a tradesman. I have no silver."

The burgher's face was wracked with anger. He stepped behind the Jew, grabbed his hair forcing the head backwards and placed his knife against the Jew's throat. "*Your silver! Your silver!*" he shouted.

"I tell you. I have none. Spare my life!" he begged.

The burgher realized he would get nothing from his victim. He looked over at the priest who was watching intently. The priest gave an approving nod. The Jew's throat was instantly slit, blood squirting and gushing.

The burgher released his grip on the hair and thrust him forward onto the pavement in obvious disgust.

At the far end of the square were ten horsemen watching silently, behind them several dozen men-at-arms. They all bore red crosses sewn on their clothes. I recognized one of the riders by the scar on his face. Jehan! I slipped back into the crowd of pilgrims around me not wishing to be recognized. Next to him was evidently his seigneur, Thomas of Marle, recognizable by the coat of arms on his surcoat, three gryfalcons descending on a raging boar, the same I had seen in the woods near La Charité. Immediately to Thomas's left was another horseman, he too bearing on his surcoat a coat of arms, the top half a fleur-de-lis and the bottom a phoenix rising. Most of the shields of the men-at-arms bore the same. I assumed this nobleman was in command. Both Thomas and his companion had been observing the executions impassively, not interfering.

At that moment I heard the ringing sound of iron horseshoes on the pavement, two horsemen leading followed by twenty knights, galloping furiously into the square. One of the two was clearly a bishop, a purple cloak over his shoulders clasped at the neck with a silver broach, the other I assumed to be the city's military governor, the burgrave, armored in mail with sword drawn, his surcoat bearing a coat of arms identical to the horsemen behind him, a depiction of a barbican closely resembling the twin-towered gate through which we had passed. They stopped at the gallows. By this time the two rotting corpses on the gibbets had been cut down. Five Jews were standing on stools, nooses around their necks, the ropes thrown over the crossbeam, a burgher beside each ready to kick it out from under them on a signal from the priest.

"Release the Jews," the burgrave demanded pointing to the men on the gallows. "Now!" he commanded. Without protest, they obeyed instantly. While the burgrave's men positioned themselves in front of the gallows he and the bishop, having seen the small force at the edge of the square, cantered forward, stopping in front of Thomas of Marle and the other rider. I wished to hear the conversation. There was, of course, the danger that Jehan might recognize me but I calculated the chances to be slight. Not wishing to tempt fate I nevertheless pulled my hat over my face as far as I could and carefully stepped closer.

The bishop was the first to speak, directing his attention to what appeared to be the leader of this company. "I am John, Bishop of Speyer. You are?"

"I am Emicho, Count of Leiningen." Then tossing his head toward

Thomas, "This is Lord Thomas of Marle, Count of Coucy."

"I've heard of you both," John responded with a mix of sarcasm and scorn.

"Well," Emicho answered with a grin, "I had no idea we were so famous"

"No. You flatter yourself Count. Not famous," John answered instantly, "infamous, notorious. What is your purpose here?"

"Well . . . " Emicho answered slowly, "we are but humble pilgrims on our way to Jerusalem. We stopped here only to enjoy the spectacle. Though the question did occur to me: Why are we traveling thousands of miles to the East to kill godless heathens when we have so many here? Nonetheless, it was quite entertaining."

"Entertaining?" John answered incredulously. "*Entertaining?* Eleven Jews have been butchered this day. And this is *entertainment* for you?"

"Eleven Jews too few, I think. We would have preferred more. All of them in fact," shifting in his saddle to look at Thomas. Thomas nodded with a sinister grin.

"Your Excellency," Thomas asked, "just how much are the Jews paying you to protect them?"

"Enough," John answered. "But it is of no account. They are not only under my protection but that of our King Henry. Do you plan to interfere?" John asked in a menacing tone of voice, looking at Emicho.

"No. Not at all." Emicho answered with cloying sweetness. "We are just here as witnesses of Christ to see God's wondrous work."

"Then witness!" John exclaimed, yanking the reins of his horse galloping back to the gallows and the burgrave's company. "Arrest all the burghers involved in these killings. Immediately!" he commanded the burgrave's sergeant.

"But how shall I know them, Your Excellency? There are so many."

"You shall know them by the blood on their faces, their hands, and their clothes. Bring them to me!"

The sergeant did as instructed. His men rounded up seven burghers. They stood before the bishop still on his horse, their heads bowed, quivering.

"What about that abominable priest? Bring him here!" John demanded.

The priest was roughly grabbed by the nape of the neck and brought before John. The priest fell to his knees. "Your Excellency. I killed no one. Others did it," looking around to the burghers. "I am a man of God!" he exclaimed. "You cannot kill me!"

John glared at him. "No life is forfeit this day. Sergeant, bind their left arms with the same leather straps used for the Jews. Take them to the block," pointing to the stump below the gallows, "and remove a hand."

The sergeant looked up at John in astonishment. "The priest too, Your Excellency?"

"All of them!" The priest began to wail. "Do it now!" John ordered.

The burgrave's men, all dismounted, untied the Jews, gathered the straps, and then wrapped one around each burgher's' arm pulling them to the block as they screamed and wept. One by one, a hand was placed on the block and one by one a hand was severed.

"Take them to the smithy over there," John ordered, pointing down the street. "No doubt he has hot iron in his forge to cauterize the wounds. I wish them punished. Not dead. After all, I'm not a pagan." John was not completely done. "Gather their hands in a sack, tie it with rope and hang it on a gibbet, the middle one. Let this be a warning to others!" With that, he pulled the reins and galloped off.

I had remained standing where I was, unseen. But I could hear Emicho quietly say to Thomas "Well, this has been amusing. Perhaps more entertainment awaits us in Worms. Let's be off."

With that, the two counts led their men from the square and turned north, towards Worms.

A Reunion in Mainz

I feared for the lives my Jewish friends in Mainz, especially Samuel ben Meier and his family. Emicho's designs on the Jews of Worms were obvious. But I knew his lust for killing would not be satiated there. He would need more. Mainz, further down the Rhine, would be next. I had to warn them.

Mainz was sixty miles away. It was already late, the sun just beginning to set. The pace of my pilgrim companions would be too leisurely and I feared that I would not arrive in time. I could walk alone but the perils were great. I had another idea. I raced to the river and came to Speyer's wharf. A small barge, steered by a single oar, had just docked. The oarsman was unloading his cargo, boxes of merchandise, two men packing them in a wagon. There were several wooden casks sitting on the dock waiting for the barge to transport them down the river. I approached the oarsman.

"I am Oderic, a pilgrim. I need to get to Mainz as quickly as I can. Will you take me? I'm willing to pay."

"Well, I'll be damned," he exclaimed as he looked at me with great curiosity. "A pilgrim in a hurry. But, yes, I can take you to Mainz. Going there myself. Enough room for a scrawny lad like you. Besides, might enjoy the company. Lonely on the river. I won't charge you if you help me load these wine casks onto my barge. Two-man job. I'm Roland, by the way." We loaded the casks.

"Do you have a place to stay tonight, Oderic?"

"No," I answered.

"Tell you what. You can sleep over there," pointing to a folded tarp and blanket in the corner of the barge. "More comfortable than sleeping on the hard ground in the woods. Safer too, I'll wager. I'm staying with a friend in town." I thanked him. "We leave at dawn," Roland said as he was departing.

"Roland," I called after him. "One more question: How long will it take to reach Mainz?"

"Two days I reckon," he answered without turning around. "Tomorrow. Dawn." I laid down on the tarp, a blanket over me, listening to the gentle lapping of waves against the boat like a mother rocking her baby in a cradle. I fell quickly to sleep.

The scenery was spectacular on the Rhine but I was too focused on Samuel and what I feared to be his dismal fate to take pleasure in it. I did enjoy my conversations with Roland and, perhaps recklessly, not knowing his thoughts on Jews, explained my mission and its gravity. I was relieved by his obvious sympathy. We arrived in Mainz at sunset. I heard the cathedral's bells in the distance announcing curfew. The city gates would be closed. Roland allowed me to spend yet one more night on the barge. The next morning I awoke at dawn, either from the glare of the sun in my eyes or the sound of bells announcing prime beginning the day's activities and announcing the city open for commerce. I leapt onto the dock.

"Hey, Oderic," Roland shouted. "You have to help me unload the casks."

"Roland, I can't. My business in Mainz is urgent. I have not a moment to spare. I'm sorry."

He understood. "Well, go on then. Good luck to you Oderic."

I raced into the city through the unguarded gates. The streets were full of people: women doing their morning shopping, forming lines to buy fresh bread, poultry, or beef; servants carrying empty buckets to the communal wells to fetch water for their masters' homes. I had to evade the roaming pigs consuming garbage on the streets and avoid piles of horse and other animal dung lying here and there. The streets were of cobblestone, slanting inward toward a gutter running along the middle for drainage. It was evident there had been little rain in days for the streets were abundant with detritus. The smells were overpowering: dried blood from tanneries, split carcasses and offal from butchers' shops, rotting corpses of cats and dogs lying on the streets, cesspits full of excrement. The air was suffocating. Houses faced one another on both sides of the narrow streets, each floor jutting further and further out until they seemed to meet, blocking out the sky and preventing any breeze from circulating. Oh how I missed the sweet smells of La Charité which refreshed me every morning.

I raced down one street after another: one dominated by drapers, another by tanners, a street for bakers, another for hatters. I was lost. I had expected to find Samuel's home easily even after a years-long absence. Perhaps my memory had become dulled or because the city had grown. I needed directions. The streets were full of peddlers, each hawking their wares all piled in three-wheeled barrows. I approached the nearest, a fish monger. "Fresh eels for sale! Nice perch from the Rhine caught today! Best prices!"

As I walked up to him, he immediately grabbed one of the eels holding it up at both ends to display it for me. "Master pilgrim, look at this fine eel. Only two pennies. How many do you want?"

"None," I answered. "I have business in the Jewish quarter. Can you direct me?"

His face changed instantly, from an unguent smile to a scowl and then to a sneer. "Ah, the Jewish quarter. Don't know why a Christian pilgrim would be doing business with Jews. Filthy lot."

I had not expected such rebuke. "I need to change some money," I stammered in reply, trying to think of a reason for visiting the quarter. I needed his help.

"Well, be wary. They'll cheat you. You give them a silver mark. They'll give you copper penny in return." He then shrugged. "Not my affair. It's that way," pointing north.

I headed in the direction he indicated but with a foreboding deeper than before for the safety of my friends. I soon found myself in the Jewish quarter, obvious from the mezuzah scrolls on the door posts and the yellow rotas on the clothes of pedestrians. The quarter was organized much like the rest of Mainz, each street reserved for specific trades. I found spicery row quickly enough and knew exactly where Samuel's shop was located. His, like others, had two louvered shutters hung horizontally, both closed and locked at night but opened in the morning when business commenced, the top raised and supported by poles, the bottom lowered to serve as a table. Samuel was sitting behind it, wooden bowls of spices in front of him. Behind him was an apprentice, about my age, grinding spices. The aromas were intoxicating. Samuel at that moment was dealing with a customer.

". . . and here," his finger tapping the rim of a spice bowl, "we have dried balm leaves from Gilead in the Holy Land. It's a powerful palliative for women when they are in season and a curative for treating snakebite and ailments of the chest. But here, let me show you this," pointing to another bowl, "cinnamon, from India, far away. Smell it," lifting the bowl under the customer's nostrils. "It will enhance any beef pottage your wife makes. Lovely. And here's one more, cloves, a wonderfully sweet spice especially good with cakes. I've heard in India they use all kinds of delicate spices to flavor their dishes."

The customer pondered. "I'll take the balm, a *livre's* worth," reaching into his purse.

"Good," Samuel said as he weighed the balm on his balance scale. "Crush the leaves with a pestle, mix it with wine, and drink it."

Standing there, I was delighted just watching Samuel. I became deluged with fond memories. I walked to the table. He looked up without recognition and no doubt surprised to see a Christian pilgrim before him. "May I help you young pilgrim?"

"Master Samuel. It's me, Oderic . . . I mean Matthew. It's me!"

Samuel stared intently. His eyes squinting. I could tell he recognized the voice from his past, but from where? I had also changed with age and carried a full beard, not having shaved in weeks. But then, slowly, his face broke out in astonishment followed by joy. "Matthew! Matthew! It's you!" He quickly got up from his table, came around it, kissed me on the forehead and both cheeks, and then embraced me so tightly I thought he would squeeze the life out of me. "You've returned," he said, tenderly, stepping back and placing both hands on my shoulders. "I knew you would keep your promise. Rachel's upstairs. She'll want to see you right away." Turning to his apprentice, "Uri. This is Matthew. I've spoken of him many times." He broke out into a wide smile and nodded, giving me a brief wave. "Come, let's see Rachel. Uri, mind the shop. Matthew and I are going upstairs."

We entered the solar on the second floor. Rachel was sitting at a loom weaving what looked like a coverlet. "Rachel, Matthew has returned. *He's here!*" She embraced me with the same vigor as had Samuel, tears in her eyes. "Matthew, it is indeed you. You've come back," placing her head on my shoulder. On becoming a novice I had abandoned my birth name 'Matthew' in favor of 'Oderic'. I decided to correct names and explain my vocation as a monk later. There was more immediate business.

"Master. We must talk. Now. But I would prefer privately," not wishing to frighten Rachel with news from Speyer. Samuel nodded, sensing my urgency, and wordlessly led me back down to the ground floor, through the shop leading to a patio paved with multicolored hewed stones behind the house. The sky was cloudless and bright blue, the sun warming, a contrast to the dark and cold news I bore. We sat. "I have just come from Speyer." I then related the events there: the murder of eleven Jews by city burghers, how Archbishop John had rescued the remainder of Jews from destruction, that Count Emicho and Thomas of Marle were likely at that moment committing atrocities in Worms, and my fear Mainz would be next. My tone and words were deliberate and my composure steady to give Samuel some confidence in the accuracy of my account.

Samuel sat silently, listening closely without interruption or questions though shifting uneasily in his chair. I finished and looked to him for a response. "I have heard nothing from Worms," he said pensively. "We did receive a missive from the Jews of Francia warning us of dangers presented by these pilgrims. They also reported a massacre of Jews in Rouen some months ago and urged us to fast and pray. But nothing else. Matthew," Samuel continued, looking tenderly at me, "your fears, though heartfelt, may be exaggerated. It's true that a rabble of peasants, many thousands of them, led by someone called 'the Hermit', passed through here a week ago. He bore a letter from the Jewish community in Trier requesting that we provide his people with food. We did so. Otherwise, they did not molest us. He was followed by an army commanded by Godfrey, Duke of Bouillon. We had been told he vowed to kill Jews. Our elders paid him five hundred silver marks to leave us in peace. I've heard that Cologne paid the same. But your information is concerning. Let us speak tomorrow with the parnas of our synagogue, Kalonymos ben Meshullam. You remember him, I'm sure. He will know what to do. In the meantime you look tired. I assume you have no place to stay. Why don't you go upstairs to your old bedroom in the garret and rest. You can stay overnight. Rebecca, her husband David, and their two sons will be joining us for supper later. We will call you down."

"Thank you, Master," I replied. "I had hoped you would offer your hospitality." I lay down but my rest was an uneasy one.

"Matthew!" I heard my name called from below. It sounded like Rebecca's voice. "Matthew, supper is ready. Please join us. Besides, I want to scratch your head," a silly game she and I had played in our youth. It was Rebecca indeed. I came down. She was standing at the bottom of the stairs waiting. We tenderly embraced. "Oh how handsome you've become," she said, stepping back to studiously survey me. "You've grown up."

"The years have favored you, Rebecca," I replied shyly. She blushed slightly. I was twelve when I came to live in Samuel's household and she sixteen. But as I slowly matured into manhood over the next three years I came to think of her less as a sister than, well, something more intimate. I was in love. She had long, black, gossamer-fine tresses, double plaited and deep brown eyes possessing a beauty that had captivated me more with each passing year. But she was a Jewess and I a Christian. Even then I knew a union would be inconceivable. Perhaps that was in part why I became a monk. I cannot tell. The years had indeed favored her, more beautiful than ever. In that instant my affection was rekindled. It would need to be repressed. Until it couldn't.

We all washed our hands in a common bowl and sat down at the table. Rebecca introduced her husband David and two sons Eliah and Jonah, twins, both six years of age. Uri sat with us as well for apprentices are treated as full members of their masters' families as I had been. It was the Sabbath which permitted a more lingering meal. It was a sumptuous repast, the first I had eaten in weeks, delicious challah bread baked that day in a Jewish bakery, a rich stew of vegetables and lamb, and trout which David proudly announced he had himself caught that morning in the Rhine rather than purchased from the fish market. The courses were punctuated with numerous toasts, "for life" followed by the traditional response "and for a happy life." We spent hours talking cheerfully of our lives since I had last seen them. I explained the change of my name. There was special interest in my experiences as a monk. I told them of my work as a scribe, of Benedict, and my journey to Cluny. I decided, instinctively, to omit Clermont and for more judicious reasons I avoided the subject of Speyer.

A Warning Ignored

The next day Samuel and I attended regular service at the synagogue in the late afternoon. I removed my shoes and sat at the back of the hall on a bench feeling a bit conspicuous in my pilgrim's costume. I had forgotten how modest the synagogue was compared with the churches of La Charité and particularly the incomparable basilica at Cluny. It was single-storied containing but one room, a hall with modest vaulted arches and six windows, their shutters opened, on either side of the sanctuary. The floor was paved with smoothed stones, all fitting precisely together, benches lining three of the four walls. In the center was a bimah, a raised platform, on which stood a table from which the Torah would be read during service. The top of the table was flanked on either side with silver menorahs. On the east wall was the Torah Ark, the holiest part of the synagogue, a cabinet in which the Torah scrolls were stored behind an embroidered curtain. The synagogue hadn't changed in years although I recall a dispute over reconstructing the building into a worthier place of worship. However, the idea was dismissed because of fears that a more ostentatious structure would attract unwanted attention from city taxing authorities and excite envy among Mainz's citizens.

At the conclusion of service the congregationalists loitered outside in the courtyard. Samuel and I joined them. Kalonymos was there conversing. We walked up.

"Rabbi, excuse me for interrupting," Samuel said. "do you remember Matthew of ten years ago? My apprentice then. He is now a priest, Father Oderic."

We exchanged the traditional greetings: "Peace be to thee, Rabbi," I said, bowing. "And to thee Father Oderic, a goodly blessing," he responded. "Yes, of course I remember you," he exclaimed, kissing my cheeks and then, looking up and down at my pilgrim's garb. "I gather the pleasures of mixing spices no longer intrigue you," he said smiling.

"No, Rabbi, I found a higher calling."

"Rabbi," Samuel interrupted, "Oderic bears disturbing news from Speyer. I think you should hear what he has to say." We sat on a circular stone bench surrounding a fountain in the courtyard. I reported the same facts I had recited to Samuel, of Speyer, my belief that the community in Worms was already under attack, and my fear that Mainz would be next.

Kalonymos, as had Samuel, listened intently and silently. "I'm distressed to hear of events in Speyer. I think this is a matter to be discussed by the synagogue's council of elders at our regularly scheduled meeting two days hence. Samuel," looking first to him and then to me, "I would like both of you to attend."

Without waiting for Samuel to answer I blurted out: "Rabbi, there is no time to waste! Not a day, not an hour. You must prepare immediately."

"Two days," he said firmly albeit kindly. "Thank you, Father Oderic, for this information. It will be considered." With that, he rose from his seat, gave a brief nod to each of us, and rejoined the other congregationalists in conversation.

As we walked back I said to Samuel "I fear the rabbi is not taking this seriously enough." He said nothing.

A Plea to Archbishop Ruthard

In Samuel's library I saw a copy of the *War of the Jews* by Flavius Josephus, the famous Jewish historian. It was bound in soft leather, the calligraphy wonderfully done and adorned with beautiful miniatures. It was a precious possession of Samuel's but I could see that it had rarely been opened, probably because it was written in Latin and Samuel knew only enough to conduct simple commercial transactions. With Samuel's permission I retired to my room and began reading. I had not gotten far when I heard Samuel calling me urgently to come down.

"Oderic," he said in an agitated voice, "we have just received news from Speyer. The events were exactly as you described. Eleven Jews were slain by burghers; the rest of the community was saved only by the bishop's intervention. Kalonymos has summoned an emergency meeting of the council of elders. They're gathering now. We must hurry!" I wondered why my story had seemed to be mistrusted.

The elders were already seated on benches around the hall's perimeter. Kalonymos was standing silently on the bimah behind the table waiting for us. Samuel and I were the last to arrive. Kalonymos motioned for me to come forward. There was a murmur of surprise and obvious suspicion at seeing a Christian pilgrim standing beside the rabbi in their synagogue.

Kalonymos began. "Under the present circumstances, we will dispense with the normal formalities. This is Father Oderic. Some of you may remember him as 'Matthew', formerly an apprentice of Samuel ben Meier. He is now a Christian priest but a good friend to us all. We have all heard of events in Speyer. Father Oderic was present, saw it all, and raced here to warn us. I would like Father to tell us what he saw." I recounted now for the third time all that had occurred and my fear that Worms was next, after that Mainz. By the time I had finished the suspicion on the elders' faces had visibly changed to one of palpable fear. I returned to sit beside Samuel.

"We must decide what measures should be taken," Kalonymos announced. "I invite opinions." One of the elders stood up. "The news from Speyer is concerning, of course, but we were able to pacify Peter, so-called 'the Hermit', with provisions and he passed through our city without troubling us. Cannot we do the same now?"

Another rose. "We heard that a certain Godfrey of Bouillon was soon to come to Mainz and that he had vowed to kill Jews. Rabbi," bowing briefly to Kalonymos, "you sent a letter to King Henry asking for his protection. He informed us that he had ordered Godfrey to leave us in peace. He did so, induced I'm sure by the five hundred silver marks we paid him."

A third stood to speak. "Rabbi, have you not spoken with Archbishop Ruthard who has guaranteed our safety?" Kalonymos nodded. "If the Bishop of Speyer protected our brothers, so can Ruthard here."

And yet a fourth: "We Jews and gentiles in Mainz have lived together in harmony for many years. We have good relationships with our city's burghers. Our commerce has helped to enrich the city. And of course we pay taxes. The burghers will surely protect us."

The mood of the council was changing quickly, from initial fear to self-delusion and appeasement. I knew better. They had not seen what I had. I could not remain silent. I rose from my bench. "Though not a member of your council, I must speak. You do not know these men, Count Emicho of Leiningen and Count Thomas of Marle. They are thoroughly evil. They cannot be bought or bribed or persuaded. They want nothing less," my voice rising, "*nothing less* than your destruction. They are in Worms, as we speak. I fear the worst. You must prepare for your defense!"

Fate intervened. At that moment a man crashed through the door rushing inside. "Rabbi! My apology for this intrusion but I have ridden all night with urgent news from Worms. May I speak?"

"Yes, come forward."

The rider hurried up to the table, facing the elders, speaking almost breathlessly. "I know not where to begin. A certain count, they call him Emicho, and his blasphemers came into the city, dug up the body of a gentile buried thirty days earlier and then paraded it through the streets claiming this was our work. They also spread a rumor that we had boiled a gentile and poured his remains into the city's well to poison its inhabitants. The townspeople were inflamed. Most of us tried to take refuge in our homes; some fled to the bishop's palace pleading for protection. But marauders went from house to house hunting for us, killing all they could find."

At this point several of the elders stood up staring in horror at the speaker. Angry shouts ensued. "Sit down!" Kalonymos commanded. "Let him continue."

"The errant ones then broke into the bishop's palace killing all who had sought sanctuary. They smashed the doors of our synagogue stealing whatever they could, grabbing Torah scrolls and throwing them out into the street to be trampled. Others not killed were marched into the river where vile signs were waved over them." I understood this to be forced baptism. "I fled, having hid my family in a shed. I think they're safe. But I fear our entire community may be eradicated by now. Mainz will surely be next. The evil ones are only days away." He bowed his head, sobbing uncontrollably, tears streaming down his cheeks.

Panic followed. There were deafening shouts from different elders, each crying out louder than the last, all vying for attention:

"Hide our Torah scrolls!"

"Hide our money!"

"Beg Ruthard for sanctuary!"

"Pay off Emicho and his thieves!"

"We can find refuge in neighboring villages like our brothers in Cologne did. They're safe!"

Kalonymos raised his hand for silence. Gradually the shouts diminished. "All these ideas are worthy of consideration but we must first approach Ruthard for guidance. Father Oderic," looking at me, "would you be willing to accompany me? You could help. You are a Christian priest. You have also lived among us and know our ways. We should leave immediately."

"I will join you Rabbi."

"In the meantime," directing his instructions to the elders, "we must seek God's protection. We shall fast for three days from sunrise to sunset, pray, and give alms to the poor. Surely our Lord will not desert us in this hour of peril."

The elders dispersed to their homes as Kalonymos and I hurried to the archbishop's episcopal palace. The gate was closed but not locked. The gatekeeper, standing just behind it, challenged us for our business. "I am Rabbi Kalonymos. This is Father Oderic. We need to speak with the archbishop urgently."

"Does he know you're coming?"

"No." Kalonymos answered.

"Then you must first make an appointment. Come back later."

I took matters into my own hands. I shoved the gate open so violently that it knocked him back. With a menacing glare, priest or no, I meant business, "We shall pass!"

Kalonymos led the way; he had been to the palace many times before. We entered the audience hall. Standing before us were Ruthard and another man, the burgrave it appeared from his military bearing, sword, and surcoat. Ruthard, hearing someone enter, turned around and looked at us with surprise. "Oh, it's you Kalonymos. Come in, come in. How pleasant. And what brings you here?"

"Your Excellency," Kalonymos began, "we have just received terrible news from Worms. Pilgrim bandits led by a nobleman named Emicho have wiped out our community. I am told reliably that he is on his way here, only days from Mainz. I beg your advice."

"Who is this with you? One of those wicked pilgrims from Worms?" Ruthard asked, with no little sarcasm.

Without waiting for Kalonymos to respond, I decided to take control. "I am Oderic, a pilgrim and monk of the priory La Charité sur Loire. I was not in Worms. I *was* in Speyer and witnessed there the murder of eleven Jews. Rabbi Kalonymos is correct. Count Emicho will soon be here. He is the worst sort of villain. He will bring destruction with him to your city."

"I have heard of events in Speyer," Ruthard replied. "Yes, eleven dead but it could have been worse. I have heard nothing of Worms. Rabbi," looking to Kalonymos, "what is it you wish of me?"   "Your protection and sanctuary for our community in your palace when Emicho arrives."

Ruthard stood there silently, musing. He then turned to the burgrave. "Aldred, what do you propose?"

"Well," he replied, "we have the city's garrison but they will need to be paid. I don't know this Emicho but he surely brings men-at-arms with him. This will require additional protection and expense."

"Yes, certainly," Ruthard agreed. "And I will incur the expense of feeding so many Jews."

Kalonymos decided to intervene quickly before the tally of every cost grew more than the community could bear. "Your Excellency. We are willing to pay. Will two hundred silver marks suffice?"

"Hmm. Yes," looking at Aldred for confirmation. The burgrave nodded in assent. "Yes, I think that will do. Aldred, I propose you send scouts south to watch for Emicho. If they are indeed coming our way, we shall close our city gates and summon the Jews to the palace." Aldred nodded again. Turning once more to Kalonymos, "We shall alert you if they're seen. When your people come, I urge them to bring all their valuables. They'll be safe here."

We took our leave of the archbishop, thanking him. I returned to Samuel's home. In the meantime Kalonymos had sent instructions for the community to gather what weapons they possessed—Jews were not permitted to bear arms—and store them in the synagogue. They were to conceal the Torah scrolls, silver menorahs and hanging lamps. Mezuzahs were to be removed from door posts lest they be identified as Jewish homes, and clothes and valuables to be packed in readiness should they be called to the palace.

Emicho at the Gates

Some days passed. I spent them reading Josephus's history, though in my anxiety it was hard to concentrate. When not reading I wandered about the streets of Mainz looking for any evidence of Emicho's men, a fool's errand I knew but sitting and waiting would not ease my disquiet. On the morning of May 25 I was awakened by muted shouting some distance away. I put on my clothes and rushed downstairs. Samuel was in the solar.

"I just received word from a messenger," Samuel said. "Emicho's troops are outside the city gates. Fortunately, the gates are locked, but for how long?" he said with a shake of the head indicating doubt that they would stay fastened for long. "But worse, Emicho's arrival has stirred riots among the townspeople. They're pillaging some of our shops. Rabbi Kalonymos has summoned the entire community to the synagogue. Oderic, you're safe here. They won't hurt a Christian. But I must go."

"Master, I'll join you. But first I need to check for myself. I'll be there in a bit." I could hear loud and angry voices nearby. I followed the noise. As I hurried down the streets of the Jewish quarter I saw none of Emicho's men but neither did I see men-at-arms from the city's garrison. Rioters owned the streets. I feared the Jews were on their own. Pillagers seemed to be targeting the shops of goldsmiths, silversmiths, bakeries and butcheries—whatever they could pawn or eat—some banging on doors with clubs and fists, others trying to pry open closed shutters with crowbars. I prayed that Samuel's would be spared. Rioters might be less interested in spices.

I had seen enough. I raced to the synagogue. The community had gathered—in the hall, overflowing into the courtyard, and then into the adjoining street. Fear was apparent on every face. I squeezed through to hear.

Kalonymos was standing on the bimah already addressing the congregation as I arrived. ". . . and you must gather your families and possessions including all your valuables. Return here in two hours. I shall escort you to the bishop's palace where we have been guaranteed sanctuary. Those of you who wish to seek shelter in your homes, do so." I thought the latter option a poorer choice though, as events unfolded, it made no difference. "But," he added quickly, "I wish briefly to speak with the elders." I stayed behind at the back of the hall thinking Kalonymos might yet need my help. Kalonymos was silent until all but the elders had left. He moved straight to the point. "I know that the bishop's palace is fortified. It will also be guarded by the burgrave's men-at-arms. But whether it is secure enough to protect against a siege by Emicho is a different question."

I could not help but interrupt. "Forgive me, Rabbi, but during the rioting I saw not a *single* soldier from the garrison. I have little faith in their protection."

The elders began nodding their heads in agreement. Kalonymos continued. "Father Oderic, I share your suspicion. Which is why I asked all of you to tarry here. Perhaps a 'contribution' in gold", a word he used with evident irony, "might persuade this Christian lord to leave us in peace. Your thoughts?" There was quick and unanimous agreement from the elders. "We have consensus. Let us gather all the gold we have and bring it to my home. Today. Perhaps Emicho will see there is more profit in ignoring us than killing us. Father Oderic, may I call upon you tomorrow for yet another service, to accompany me to the camp of Emicho? Your presence may help pacify his animal spirit."

"Yes, Rabbi. Always."

"Good. Then I shall meet you at Samuel's home midday."

Kalonymos arrived with a leather knapsack over his shoulder containing seven pounds of gold. I was dressed fully in my pilgrim's garb—satchel, staff, pilgrim's hat, and even bare feet—I hoped this might, just might, emphasize my role as a penitent pilgrim of Christ in support of Jews. I advised Kalonymos to cut off the rota stitched on his tunic to give less the appearance of a Jew than a prominent merchant of Mainz. Guards at the city's gates allowed us to pass when we explained our mission. We came to Emicho's camp, not far from the city walls, his men sitting in front of fires laughing and singing, all in the language of the Teutons. I saw one tent, rather more sumptuous than the others, in front of which was placed a pole flying a banner with Emicho's coat of arms. The entrance to the tent was flanked by two men-at-arms standing at attention.

As we walked up they crossed their spears to bar our entry. "What is it you want?" one of them asked gruffly.

"We are a delegation from Mainz here to see the Count of Leiningen," I answered, summoning up the most commanding tone I could—now was not the time for timidity.

The guard looked us over suspiciously. "Wait here." He opened the tent's flap and stepped in, closing it after him. I could hear muffled voices from within. Moments later he came back out. "The Count will see you."

We entered. Standing around a table were Emicho, Thomas of Marle, and Captain Jehan. They had been studying a map which appeared to be of the city. Emicho looked up and quickly rolled it. "My Lords," I began, both Kalonymos and I bowing, "I am a pilgrim and a priest from Rheims.

This is Kalonymos ben Meshullam, a merchant and leader of the Jewish community of Mainz. I am here to speak on its behalf." I glanced at Jehan, then quickly averted my eyes. He was staring at me curiously. He knew he had seen me before but where? I had introduced myself as hailing from Rheims and not La Charité for that would surely have exposed me. I was thankful that in the weeks since departing from the priory I had shaved neither my beard nor head.

As Jehan was staring at me, so was Emicho at Kalonymos, making no effort to disguise his contempt. He then turned to me. "I won't ask what a priest is doing with a Jew. You can answer to God for that. What is it you want?"

Kalonymos then spoke, bowing once more to Emicho. "My Lord. In our city, Christians and Jews have lived together harmoniously for generations. We Jews live in our own quarter and cause Christians no complaint. We obey all laws and peacefully conduct our affairs. We wish that to continue."

"Your *affairs!*" Emicho's voice rising, "*Your affairs?* You Jews loan money to good Christians, violating God's law with your usury. You corrupt by stealing their children in the middle of the night, forcing them to convert to your heathen faith. You parade haughtily through the streets offending our Christian feast days. *Your affairs indeed!*"

Kalonymos knew discussions might be difficult. He had not expected such slander. "No! No!" Kalonymos exclaimed in a pleading voice, bowing yet again. "We do none of those things. We worship the same God as you and we Jews, as Christians do, faithfully observe all His laws. Surely, surely we can arrive at some understanding."

"And what sort of 'understanding' do you propose?" Emicho's tone now changing to one of interest.

"I have a letter," Kalonymos responded pulling out a folded parchment from his tunic and handing it to Emicho, "from our council of elders urging all Jewish communities through which you pass to offer contributions to your cause and to honor you." Emicho merely snorted. "Here," Kalonymos pulling the knapsack off his shoulder, "I have seven pounds of gold coin which we offer you as a sincere gift."

He handed it to Emicho. Emicho's interest and that of his companions was now piqued. They opened the bag, eagerly sifting through the coins with their hands. "And what, Kalonymos ben Meshullam, do you demand in return for this 'gift'" Emicho asked. The word "gift" dripped with sarcasm.

"No 'demand'" Kalonymos protested. "No demand, Your Excellency. A gift for your successful march to Jerusalem to fight the Turks, enemies of Christians and Jews alike." Kalonymos paused, "But in return we ask only that you spare our community." The specter of Speyer and Worms was on his mind, obvious to all.

Emicho looked to both Thomas and Jehan, who nodded signifying their consent. "I think this can be arranged. I give you my word as a Soldier of Christ that we shall leave you in peace. You may relax your vigilance. We shall leave in two days."

We turned and departed. But as we walked back to the city I turned over and over in my mind Emicho's words: *"You may relax your vigilance."*

Massacre at the Episcopal Palace

When I returned to Samuel's home, Rebecca and her family were there. They had gone to Ruthard's palace for refuge but the gates were locked. The palace was full, they were told, no more Jews permitted in. Samuel had decided that he and Rachel could not leave them alone. They would share the same fate. We all went to bed early that evening. I was unable to sleep. I kept pondering Emicho's words "You may relax your vigilance," more ominous than reassuring. I arose from my bed and went outside, wandering toward the square near the city gates. I had heard that the burgrave ordered a curfew but I saw nary a single soldier enforcing it. Though rioters were absent, their energy likely spent, there were still people milling about. As I drew closer to the gates, I saw a small group of burghers in heated argument. I approached as closely as I could without becoming conspicuous. While the voices were somewhat indistinct, I heard enough. Some seemed to welcome Emicho's presence and wanted the gates unlocked. Others angrily warned that allowing him into the city would result in the destruction of property, death, and most especially harm to their commerce. The response was chilling, "What of it?" replied one. "Jewish merchants compete with us and steal our business. What have we to lose?"

The burghers ultimately dispersed, all but four who headed toward the city gates. I could see them speaking with the guards who nodded their heads and then opened the gates for them. I returned to Samuel's home and slipped in quietly so as not to disturb anyone's slumber. Samuel was awake, I suppose as unable as I to sleep. He was sitting at a table in the solar dusting off ink from a parchment in front of him and pressing his seal on hot red wax. He bore a serious expression, greeting me solemnly. Without saying a word he rolled up the parchment, tying it with a deep purple ribbon.

"Here is a letter of introduction," handing it to me, "which you may need. Don't ask me why. I don't know. But I feel it. With it you will receive the hospitality of any Jewish home or inn. You have risked your life for us. It is the least I can do. Hold onto it. It may be useful."

"Master," I said, my voice breaking with emotion, "I have done nothing. I don't deserve your gratitude."

"You do, Matthew . . . excuse me, 'Oderic'. I must retire now. Pray for us, Father."

"I shall, Master Samuel, tonight and every night."

I kept that promise. My prayers, however, proved unavailing.

I was awakened at sunrise by loud shouting underneath my window and the sound of axes and clubs smashing doors and shutters. I leapt from my bed, pulled on my breeches, opened the shuttered door and stepped onto the narrow balcony, leaning over the balustrade. I looked down the street as far as I could, my eyes squinting against the glare of the morning sun. I saw soldiers wearing the insignia of Emicho either breaking into houses or running out of their doors arms full of plunder. The burghers must have opened the city gates! Some Jews were being pulled from their homes onto the street by soldiers demanding to know where their valuables were hidden, others were being thrown out of windows. The soldiers were systematically moving down the street toward Samuel's home, house by house.

They were yet half a bowshot away. I still had time. I quickly dressed in my entire pilgrim's regalia and raced down the stairs to the door outside. As I passed by the solar I could see Samuel and his family huddled together, kneeling on the floor in prayer. There was no time to talk. I stepped out onto the porch and stood there, striking the most imposing figure I could, one hand on my pectoral cross and the other firmly on my staff. I knew the practice of plundering soldiers, obscene I always thought: he who first loots a house now claimed it, signifying such with a mark of some kind, any kind, on the door. I quickly removed the scallop pinned on my hat and affixed it to the post where Samuel's mezuzah had hung. Prior Damian had been right—someday it would be useful. I waited. Two of Emicho's men soon arrived. I stood squarely in front of the door.

"Out of the way," one of them snarled, "or it will go poorly for you, pilgrim or no."

"I claim this house for myself," summoning the severest, most commanding tone of which I was capable, pointing to the scallop. For further effect, I flipped the staff upside down, the knob end on the ground, the iron spike upright. I grasped the staff with both hands. They had a choice: treat me as a Christian pilgrim and let me be or treat me as just another plunderer and face a fight. I was ready for either. I stared coldly into their eyes, not moving.

One of them pulled the other's hauberk: "Let's go. There are easier houses to be had."

They moved off to continue their rampage. At that moment I looked down the street to see Thomas of Marle and Jehan, sitting motionless on their horses, staring at me. Wordlessly, they turned and trotted back up the street. I went upstairs to the solar. Everyone was now standing, having heard what happened outside the door, their eyes full of gratitude. "You're safe for now." I said. "But I can't promise how long. Hide yourselves. I must go to the episcopal palace to see what I can do to help. I fear for Rabbi Kalonymos and his flock. I shall return as quickly as I can."

I hurried to the palace. To my shock I saw no garrison soldiers manning the front gate, only a trembling gate keeper. "Where is Bishop Ruthard?" I demanded.

"He left yesterday with all his attendants. The burgrave too."

The Jewish refugees were without protection. I entered the courtyard. Men were standing in small circles, all wearing franged prayer shawls, arms crossed over their chests, bobbing their heads and intoning psalms of penitence learned by heart. Sitting on the floor along the walls were women and children. The men ignored me; the women looking up in terror.

"Where is Rabbi Kalonymos?" I asked one of the women.

Stammering, "He . . . he has gone after the bishop for help."

I knew that Emicho's men would soon be here, the prospect of loot and either converting or killing Jews too tempting. "My friends. My friends!", I shouted out, "you must leave! Now! Soldiers will be here soon! Flee!"

It was too late. At that moment Emicho, Thomas, and Jehan entered the courtyard, one hundred troops behind them. I retreated to a darkened corner of the yard. The Jewish men continued bobbing their heads in prayer, the women holding their children tightly. Emicho stood there, silent, surveying. "*Renounce your godless ways!*" he screamed at them. "Accept Christ or die!" The men continued bobbing their heads, the women clutching their children ever more tightly. They spoke not a word. "Kill them all!" Emicho ordered, drawing his sword. "And I'll start with this one," walking up to a circle, selecting a Jew at random, piercing his neck. The orgy of killing began. Emicho's men fell upon all of them like wild beasts devouring a fresh carcass, the women screaming, the children wailing, the Jewish men bobbing their heads. At that moment some Jews, perhaps twenty, swords in their hands which earlier had been collected at the synagogue, rushed into the courtyard from the inner hall of the palace. They attacked, wildly slashing, thrusting, and cutting with fury but they were tailors, tanners, and bakers, not trained soldiers. Emicho's men made quick work of them. The slaughter of the remaining Jews resumed. Until it was done.

I rushed into the inner court. It was empty but for moaning behind a door. I opened it, stepped inside closing the door behind me. This was Ruthard's audience hall where I had first met him. The sight was horrifying. It was full of dead bodies, from one end to the other—men, women and children, too many to count—lying on the floor soaked in blood, their throats cut. There were perhaps a dozen Jews still alive. Many of them mothers, on the floor, sobbing, murmuring benedictions in comforting tones—the same ones, I knew, that were made when animals were slaughtered in accordance with Jewish law—as they held their crying children cutting their throats with ritual knives, knives unblemished with the slightest nick. Behind each woman was a man—perhaps a husband or father—also with a ritual knife in his hand prepared to slit the throat of the mother when her task was completed. Several did so as I stared in shock. I could not understand what was happening until I remembered the story of the Jewish Sicarri at Masada which only the evening before I had read in Josephus's history. This was the last stand of the Jews against the Romans. There, the Jews, abhorring suicide, preferred to be killed by another Jew than be taken alive by the Romans and forced to accept some pagan cult. Those few who remained alive were ready to be killed by Romans.

Emicho crashed through door, his soldiers close behind. He seemed to look approvingly on the slaughter. Only six Jewish men remained alive. Knives in their hands, they stepped over the dead bodies to attack the crusaders. Knives against swords. It was over in moments. Jehan, a few feet away, saw me standing beside the door. "Oh, the Jew-loving pilgrim again," he sneered. Then he drew closer, too close, and a look of recognition came over his face. "I remember you now. The monk who gave me this!" with a finger tracing the scar on his face from his cheek bone to his chin. With that, I pushed him as hard as I could into the throng of soldiers still rushing through the door. I fled. But as I did so, I could hear Emicho, "Strip them all. Find their gold!"

As I raced through the palace gates, fearful that Jehan would be chasing me, my mind turned to Samuel. I had to get back. I ran as fast as I could but unexpectedly met Uri, Samuel's apprentice. He stopped me.

"Father Oderic. I beg you. You must help me. It's urgent. There's no time to explain now. Follow me!"

Reluctantly, I complied. We ran to the synagogue, stopping at its door. By now I was quite out of breath. Uri tried to open the main door but it was locked. As he was searching for a key that may have been secreted behind a plant or under a rock, he explained his purpose. "There are plans to convert our synagogue into a church. This would be a sin against God! You understand our ways. Help me burn our synagogue down," he pleaded.

"I can't, Uri. I must get to Samuel's house. I fear I have little time."

"I can't find the key," he replied in exasperation. "Then at least help me into the building. I'll do the rest." We were next to a shuttered window, five or so feet above the ground. I took my pilgrim's staff and with its top knob broke through the double shutters. I lifted Uri up through the window and could hear a thud as he fell to the floor inside. In a moment, his face appeared. "Thank you Father. Your service is done. Save Samuel and his family."

A Battle, Rebecca Rescued, and Escape

I ran back to Samuel's home. The shop's shutters were shattered. I looked inside. Clay jars of spices were strewn across the floor, most broken. It seemed less like theft than rage. The door of Samuel's home had also been smashed open. I sprinted up the stairs to the solar. There I witnessed a terrifying sight. Samuel and Rachel were sitting, their heads hanging over the backs of their chairs, throats slit. In front of them was David, his right hand bloodied, on his knees, his shoulders resting on the floor. Decapitated, a ritual knife beside him. I apprehended instantly what had happened: David had killed Samuel and Rachel; some intruder arrived, forced David to his knees, demanded that he convert and when he refused severed his head. That much was clear to me. I looked to the door across the solar. It was hanging askew on a single hinge and partially open. I could hear the weeping of a woman from behind the door, Rebecca, and the sound of men jeering, two voices I thought.

Staff in hand, I carefully pushed the door open fearful of making any noise and peered in. Rebecca was sitting in a chair, wailing, clutching both her sons in each arm tightly to her breast, their throats slit. Her clothes were drenched in blood. Thomas of Marle stood akimbo directly in front of her, Jehan only a few feet behind.

"Well, well," Thomas said in a mocking voice, "what have we here? A fetching Jewish wench. Murderess too by the look of it. I'll wager she's a sorceress. They all are, you know," looking back at Jehan. Redirecting his attention to Rebecca, "Are you willing to accept Jesus Christ as your savior? We *may* spare you if you do," he said with a grin so sinister as to contort his entire face. She said not a word, instead shaking her head vigorously, squeezing her sons ever more tightly to her breast. "Well, I thought not." Thomas then stepped right up to her and snatched the boys in turn from her arms throwing them into the corner of the room as though they were rags. Rebecca screamed, looking in horror at her children in a pile. "If she won't convert now, perhaps we can persuade her, and have a little fun to boot." With that, Thomas grabbed Rebecca's hair, yanking her off the chair onto the floor. Rebecca screamed even louder. He then unbuckled his belt, throwing both his sword and dagger aside, and began pulling his breeches down. He fell down on Rebecca, knees on both sides of her waist as he lifted up the hem of her kirtle.

Rage—absolute rage—was boiling inside me. My fury unquenchable. There was no time to plot or plan. I had to act. Jehan would be first. He was too intent on the drama unfolding to notice me. Like Thomas, he wore a chain mail hauberk reaching down to his knees. I knew the iron spike of my staff could not penetrate it, at best stunning him only momentarily. He wore a simple helmet. I had one chance. One only. And I took it. God favored me. Jehan had not noticed me as I crept forward. With the iron point of my staff I thrust it into the side of his throat plunging it as deeply as I was able. Blood spurted as though a volcano had erupted. As he fell back I yanked the staff from his neck. The only sound he made was a gurgle.

Jehan was dead. It was now Thomas of Marle's turn. He was so occupied with his "amusement" that he hadn't heard the thud of Jehan's body on the floor. Thomas had made little progress for Rebecca resisted furiously, squirming and pulling his hair. "Bitch! Bitch. *Stay still!*" he screamed at her. I could see no vulnerable spot for attack, his mailed hauberk protecting his body and a mailed aventail covering his head, neck, and shoulders. Wild stabbings with the spike of my staff might injure Rebecca. I flipped the staff upright and with the knob at the top began pounding Thomas on his helmet and back. The blows did not have the effect I sought. He rolled off of Rebecca and before I could pound him again stood upright. He reached down for his sword on the floor, drawing it from its scabbard. Were the danger not so great it might have been comical—a knight holding a sword in his hand, his breeches down to his ankles as he stumbled forward to attack me. He swung. I stepped back once more. He stumbled forward again with another swing. I stepped back again. And a third. But with each step he was able to extricate his legs from his breeches. Finally he was free. The fight had been in earnest before. It was now to the death.

I again flipped my staff, the spike in front as I gripped it tightly with both hands. I had now become rather more adept at the use of my unexpected weapon. But I was outmatched. I jabbed the staff at Thomas. He easily parried. I jabbed once more. He deflected again. He seemed to be enjoying the battle, grinning ever more broadly with every parry. "My, my," he laughed as he played with me, "what a little pilgrim warrior you've become," as he slashed my arm with his sword. The wound was superficial and but for the pain didn't impair my ability to wield the staff. Thomas could have struck more deeply but refrained, likely wanting to prolong his enjoyment, taking me piece by piece. "Oderic. Yes Oderic," he said as he playfully slapped my staff with the broad side of his sword, first from right to left and then from left to right. I was having difficulty keeping its point directed at Thomas. "Yes, I know you. Jehan recognized you at the palace when I was killing filthy Jews. You were the one who gave him the beauty mark. Made him look ever so more handsome," he laughed contemptuously.

I suddenly realized that I had been the author of my Jewish family's destruction. Jehan had come for revenge. My fury became white-hot. The contest was unequal, the outcome certain. But Thomas had become overconfident, too playful. He lowered his sword, swinging it slowly back and forth, taunting me. That was my moment. I rushed forward, my staff ramming against Thomas's chest, not penetrating his hauberk but driving him back, a look of astonishment on his face. With his free hand he grabbed the shaft to push it away but I maintained my grip continuing to lunge forward as he stumbled backward. God was with me. Jehan's body lay just behind him. Thomas tripped over it falling on his back. He stretched out both arms to break his fall and in doing so released his sword, clanging to the floor.

Thomas and I were both the same height but I was slight of frame, he larger and more powerful. There was no time to think. With the spike of my staff I stabbed his bare leg. He let out a scream of pain but not so disabled that he couldn't grab the staff holding it tightly in his hand as he reached wildly for his sword. I was unable to withdraw my staff from his grip for another thrust. I flung it aside and leapt onto Thomas's body, grasping his throat with both my hands to squeeze the life out of him. He in turn grabbed my hands with his own to pry them loose. But I was too strong and my rage too intense. He had seen Rebecca's ritual knife when he fell. It was within his reach. He began tapping the floor with his fingers probing for it. This contest would soon be over. I released my grip on his throat, grabbed the pectoral cross hanging around my neck with its long chain, the unlikeliest of weapons, and thrust it into Thomas's eye, pushing down as deeply as I could. He emitted a horrible scream such as I never heard before, like a boar being gelded. He rolled over, and in doing so threw me off. He continued to roll over and over, both hands over his wounded eye, howling. In that brief instant I remembered the tapestry that hung in the Dowager's room: the wounded boar with a spear in its belly.

I jumped up onto my feet and raced over to Rebecca lying on the floor, her eyes focused on her sons. I had to get her to safety. If Emicho's men showed up, both our lives would be forfeit, probably in the most horrible manner. Rebecca was in shock. There was no time to reason with her. I grabbed her hand yanking her up and out through the door into the solar, she saying nothing, still looking back at her children. I was thankful she hadn't seen the bodies of her family. I roughly pulled her down the stairs. I had left my cloak, hat, and satchel at the entrance on entering. I threw the cloak over her shoulders and my hat on her head, an attempt to disguise her as a pilgrim, the best I could do. I picked up my satchel and scallop badge from the doorpost and led her down the street. At the far end, around the corner, was a stable. We headed there but yet had to pass through Emicho's men. I feared a challenge but they were too busy looting and killing to pay us any mind. Fortunately Rebecca was still traumatized—any sound of distress would have brought unwelcome attention.

We came to the stable, a sign above the large doors both in Hebrew and Teutonic. It was empty, perhaps because the stable owner, I assume Jewish, had fled. I had intended to steal two horses. There was only a two-wheeled cart already harnessed to a mule, perhaps in readiness for someone's emergency flight. Ours was the more immediate need. I helped Rebecca up to the perch, climbed up after her, seized the reins and headed quickly for the city gates. Rebecca had been silent throughout our escape, not even a tear. Her weeping would come later.

As we were leaving I turned to look back. The synagogue was in flames. Samuel's family dead. A thousand Jews slaughtered. A community destroyed. I pointed my horse toward Constantinople.

This ends Book IV of *Jerusalem Falls!* Book V begins.

BOOK V
BUTCHERY
ON THE DANUBE

Joining a Caravan. News from the Rhineland. Emicho hunts for Us.
Massacre at Semlin. Retribution at Nish. Our Deception Exposed.

Joining a Caravan

We were five miles from Mainz when, for the first time since fleeing, Rebecca leaned over to me and spoke, her voice barely audible over the sound of our horse's hooves.

"Where are we going?"

"To Constantinople."

"How long will it take?"

"Three months."

She fell silent after that. The sun was falling quickly. We had to find a place to spend the night. I saw what appeared to be a Cluniac priory. However, I wanted to avoid prying questions why a priest would be traveling alone with such a beautiful woman, especially one whose dark hair, eyes, and tawny skin might betray her as Jewish. I knew there had to be a deanery in the vicinity. I calculated that a farmer would be less inquisitive than the keeper of a monastic guesthouse. I saw one in the distance and turned my horse and headed there. On hearing us arrive the deacon emerged from a shed where he'd been working. I introduced myself as a Cluniac monk from La Charité traveling with his sister and explained that we needed shelter for the night and that the priory's guesthouse was full. He asked no questions and allowed us to stay in the barn. I gathered straw for our beds and found horse blankets with which we covered ourselves, my sleep intermittently interrupted by the sound of rats scurrying across the ceiling above.

We left early the next morning. I was concerned about our security and knew that we must join a company of travelers. Ten miles further on, fortunately without incident, we came across a caravan of ten merchant wagons heading south. Although the forest hugged the road they had found a glade close to a creek, pulled off, and circled their wagons for protection. The wagons were rather charming: some simply designed, purely functional with side boards and curved bowtop roofs of linen canvas; others much more elaborate with shingled roofs, carriage lights, shuttered windows, and stove pipes—small homes on wheels. All were brightly painted with pictures of the wares they were selling: furs, tapestries, woolen garments, cooking oil, religious objects, jewelry—bracelets, necklaces, amulets, and talismen. I studied the caravan carefully from the road, unsure whether I wanted to tie my fate to it. My journey from La Charité to Speyer and then to Mainz had taught me the virtue of caution in selecting traveling companions. The merchants were too busy to notice me as they were unharnessing their horses and leading them to a creek for watering. I drew closer.

From one wagon I smelled the sweet odors of incense, spices, perfumes, and herbs. The merchant was just then assisting his wife in stepping down from the wagon's footboard. As he turned around, I saw that he wore a yellow rota on his tunic. A Jew. And a spice trader at that. Perhaps fortune was with us. I climbed down from my cart and approached him, careful not to draw attention from the other merchants. He stared at me with a deeply suspicious frown—a Christian pilgrim bearing the sign of the cross on his tunic. I had to allay his suspicions quickly. I doffed my hat and in Hebrew introduced myself simply as a traveler and Rebecca as my wife. The merchant was obviously surprised, perhaps shocked more accurately, to be addressed in Hebrew by such a stranger. Although still guarded, he relaxed enough to introduce himself as Isaac ben Judah and his wife as Miriam. Isaac peered intently at me, then at Rebecca with some slight sense of recognition which I could not discern.

"How can I serve you, young pilgrim?" he asked.

"We are traveling to Constantinople." I decided to omit the fact that I was trying to rejoin Peter the Hermit. "We would like to travel with you, at least as far south as you are going. I have coin."

"Let's sit and talk first," Isaac suggested, pointing to a fallen log near his wagon but out of sight of the other merchants. We sat, Rebecca and Miriam next to us. Isaac began, getting directly to the point. "I do not know who you are but you may be interested in this. Last evening two mounted soldiers stopped our caravan and inspected each wagon. They were looking for a monk pilgrim and a Jewess claiming they're criminals wanted in Mainz. They headed further south to continue their search but I do not doubt on their return north they will investigate us again. They seemed quite zealous and warned us that anyone harboring these fugitives would be hung." He continued without the merest hint that he knew who we were. "I'm sure you're not the ones they seek, but I thought you'd be interested in knowing." His implication was perfectly clear.

"Do you know who these men were?" I asked.

"No, I can tell you only that on their surcoats they bore an emblem: one-half a fleur-de-lis and the other a phoenix rising."

Emicho! I went silent.

He pursued the subject no further. He didn't have to. His point was made. "It's too late for you to travel further. Camp with us. I think we have enough dinner for four, do we not wife?" Miriam smiled and nodded. "But before that, let's enjoy some splendid wine I purchased in Cologne." With that he fetched a clay jug from his wagon, returning with four pewter cups. And after each toast—"for life," followed by "for a happy life"—I became increasingly talkative. Under Isaac's gentle but persistent questioning, no doubt influenced by the wine, I revealed my entire story. In doing so I mentioned the name of Samuel ben Meier. Isaac raised his head in instant recognition.

"Samuel ben Meier. Yes, I know him. A man of honor. How is he? Is he safe?"

"No. He was killed. With everyone else."

"And Rachel?" Isaac asked anxiously.

"Killed as well."

Throughout this conversation Rebecca had not said a word, her eyes fixed on the ground. At the mention of her parents she began softly to whimper, then to sob, and then to weep. Inconsolably. Miriam placed her arm around Rebecca's shoulders. Isaac and I looked straight ahead, saying not a word. We waited until her emotions were spent. I was grateful for this release, therapeutic I hoped. After a prolonged silence, "Father Oderic", Isaac said, "we must attend to business. A Christian pilgrim traveling with a Jewish merchant will bring scrutiny and questions from the soldiers should they return, and I am certain they will. And this might provoke unhelpful questions from my companion merchants. They haven't noticed you yet. I trust them to a point. But I am a Jew and they are gentiles. Their loyalty is not limitless. You must discard your pilgrim's garb for that of a Jewish trader. I have extra clothes which should roughly fit you. I shall pass you off as my nephew who has just joined me tardily from Rheims. You must take a Jewish name. I propose 'David'."

I shook my head. "'David' was the name of Rebecca's husband."

"'Moshe' then." I nodded.

"Finally, while you are traveling with us, we shall speak only in Hebrew. Oderic . . . I mean 'Moshe' . . . I'm going to have to get accustomed to your new name, you can speak Frankish if necessary. That will arouse no suspicion since you are from Rheims. It would be seen curious if, as a merchant of Francia, you knew only Hebrew. My companions in the caravan are all from Germania and likely do not know that language. But the less they know of you, the safer you will be."

Looking at Rebecca, "It's different with you. Speak only Hebrew, nothing else. I shall translate for you both. Your new name is Esther."

News from the Rhineland

It was near sunset, only three days from Semlin in the Kingdom of Hungary. The caravan had camped for the night, the wagons circled and a small communal fire built in the middle. As all of us were sitting around in conversation, there came the sound of an approaching horse. My instinctive reaction was Emicho's men coming to arrest us. Moments later, a rider on foot appeared dimly visible in the glow of the fire walking toward us. He asked if he could warm himself and camp with us overnight. We invited him to join us, one of the merchants fetching a stool for him. We were naturally curious what brought a solitary rider on the road. Other than saying he had ridden from Mainz and that his name was "Hermann", he was decidedly guarded in his answers to our questions, revealing little. Nothing about him at the beginning betrayed the fact that he was a Jew. Isaac somehow knew immediately. It became apparent to me as well a bit later, and probably to the merchants though they said nothing.

As random conversation proceeded with "Hermann"—he never revealed his true name—he became more voluble with each cup of wine Isaac served him. Isaac wanted information and understood how to pry it out of him, just as he had with me. Finally, Isaac could wait no longer. "What news from the Rhineland? We've heard nothing since entering Hungary several days ago."

Herman was still hesitant but the soothing effects of wine and the fact that Isaac and I, by our garb, were Jews, loosened his tongue. He had decided to drop his pretense. "The news is terrible. Eleven Jews killed in Speyer. The entire Jewish community in Worms, Cologne and Mainz too, wiped out by Count Emicho."

Isaac interrupted. "That can't be! I heard that the bishop of Cologne saved the Jews by sending them off to neighboring villages where they hid in safety."

"That's true. For a time. But Emicho learned of this ploy, returned to Cologne, and scoured the countryside hunting them down. Every one found was killed."

Until Hermann's appearance the mood of our small company in front of the fire had been quite amiable with a certain amount of good-natured teasing—after all, we had been traveling together for several days. But as Hermann spoke, it turned, dark and somber. All listened, acutely, to Hermann's every word, no one speaking except for Isaac's tenacious interrogation.

"In Worms," Hermann continued, "Emicho disinterred Christian corpses buried thirty days before and paraded them through city claiming that Jews had done this. Even worse, he accused the Jews of boiling one in a vat of water and pouring it into city wells to poison inhabitants."

"Did not the bishop intervene?" Isaac asked.

"Yes, he tried. He gave refuge in his palace but it was attacked. All those inside were slaughtered. The rest, whole families, committed suicide. The community has been destroyed."

"How many survived? Do you know?"

"No," Hermann answered, slowly shaking his head as he looked at the ground, "but I was told eight hundred died. At Trier the bishop tried to protect the Jews but Emicho's force was too numerous. To save them, he begged them to convert. Some did. Others threw themselves into Moselle River. Twenty-two Jews were killed in Metz. There were massacres in Neuss, Wevelinghoven, and Eler. Other towns too but I don't know which ones or how many. The Jews in Regensburg survived but only because they were pushed into the river at swordpoint for baptism. At Xanten some were killed, others committed suicide."

"What about Mehr?" Isaac asked. "I have a cousin there."

"I'm not sure. All I know is that the bürgermeister feared attack and tried to persuade the Jews to convert. They refused so he handed them over to Emicho. I know not their fate, but I can suspect."

I needed to know about Kalonymos. Remaining true to my new persona, I asked the question in Hebrew, Isaac obligingly translating into Teutonic. I knew that Hermann could understand Hebrew well enough but it appeared he wanted to continue to mask his identity, however thinly disguised, replying also in Teutonic.

"Ah, Kalonymos. Yes, the rabbi. With some members of his council he followed the archbishop to Rüdesheim where he, the burgrave, and garrison soldiers had fled. Kalonymos implored Ruthard to keep his promise, return to Mainz and prevent further destruction of the Jewish community. Ruthard agreed, but only if he and all the Jews of Mainz converted. I'm told that Kalonymos in fury pulled out his dagger and flung himself at the archbishop. Kalonymos and all his councilmen were put to the sword."

These communal firesides had been infrequent enough. When they did occur, Rebecca and Miriam never joined us. But overhearing from their wagon that a visitor had arrived with news from the Rhineland, they quietly slipped in, sitting off to the side. After Hermann's first report, they began softly crying. But as his narration continued their emotions could not be stayed despite their efforts to muffle themselves with hands over their mouths. Isaac, increasingly distraught, began bobbing his head murmuring a Jewish prayer. By the time Hermann finished Isaac had placed his arms across his knees, laid his forehead down shaking his head as though in disbelief. I too was overcome with emotion. And the faces of the merchants, Christians all, were tight and drawn. Perfectly silent.

After a long pause, Isaac looked up. "Was all of this done by Emicho?"

"No, not all. Some by two priests, Volkmar and Gottschalk. Each has his own followers. They are in Hungary now, doubtless hunting for Jews."

"What about Emicho? Where is he?" Isaac asked.

"In Hungary too, somewhere. I'm sure doing the same."

There was nothing more to say. The fire was dying down. We all stood to retire. The merchants, one by one, walked up to Isaac, saying not a word, gently touching him on the arm, hand, or shoulder in gestures of sympathy. The night was over.

Emicho hunts for Us

Two days later at midday two horsemen appeared from the south, the same ones who had visited the caravan earlier. Emicho's men. They motioned for the caravan to stop, dismounted, and began inspecting each wagon. The inspections went quickly enough until they came to Isaac's wagon, the fifth in line. Scrutiny seemed to intensify. What aroused their curiosity was the fact that several days before when they passed only Isaac and Miriam were traveling. Now there were four. And we appeared to fit the profiles of the fugitives they sought. I was sitting on the perch with Isaac and Miriam; Rebecca was driving our cart just behind.

One of the soldiers approached. "Who are you?" he demanded, glaring at me.

I shook my head as though not understanding the question. Isaac intervened. "Sir, this is my nephew, Moshe ben Judah, a spice merchant from Rheims. He speaks only Hebrew, unless you speak Frankish. With your permission I'll translate."

"Let him answer for himself. Where are you really from Jew?" glowering at me.

Again, I feigned not understanding. Realizing that he would get nothing out of me, the soldier directed the rest of his questions to Isaac.

"Who's the whore with him?" pointing to Rebecca, still sitting in the cart.

"His wife, Esther, Sir."

"They weren't with you before. Now they are." Isaac was about to explain but was immediately interrupted by the soldier. "Let *him* answer!" pointing at me.

Fortunately, Isaac and I had rehearsed our answers to possible questions should Emicho's men return. Again, Isaac translated. And again I explained in Hebrew. "Sir, he says that he had planned to rendezvous with us in Cologne but was delayed for two days in Rheims and only now caught up with us."

The soldier was exasperated. He was getting nowhere. He tried a different tactic. "I saw you in Mainz. What were you doing there Jew?" He was plainly fishing for an admission that I had been in the city. Isaac translated. I answered that I had heard there was trouble and had taken a side road around the city.

By now, the soldier's irritation was rising. He then turned his attention to Rebecca, no doubt thinking he might pry more revealing information from her. As he was walking toward her Isaac called out "Sir, Esther speaks only Hebrew. Would you like me to translate?" The soldier did not respond. I sensed that, however Rebecca answered, the soldiers were ready to take us both into custody. At least they would have something to show Emicho for their efforts. I unobtrusively reached for my dagger. I had already risked my life for Rebecca. I was prepared to do it again. Isaac gently placed his hand on mine in restraint. "Let's wait," he whispered.

Good fortune intervened. The rest of the merchants had descended from their wagons and began approaching. Each carried a dagger in his belt, their hands firmly wrapped around the hilts, and each bore a menacing look in his eyes. The soldiers did not mistake their intent. I have often wondered why these merchants, Christians all, were ready to risk their lives for Jews. I never asked them during the remainder of the journey. In the intervening days between the departure and return of the soldiers, word had passed through the caravan that they were Emicho's men. They had also listened to Hermann's tale of atrocities. I would like to believe—and I do believe—they were unwilling to suffer one more Jew killed. Outnumbered and on a lonely road, the soldiers quickly mounted their horses and as they galloped off one shifted around in his saddle and shouted "We'll be back!" They never did.

Massacre at Semlín

We followed the Danube River along much of the old "Bavarian Road", running in a relatively straight line paved with hewn stone or laid with sand deposits well stamped down. Every mile was marked with stones and there were even blocks for horsemen to mount their horses. Crossing streams was often a challenge. We always had three choices: find a ford, hopefully with a rope stretched from one bank to the other; or pass over a wooden bridge if one were present, though the craftsmanship of the bridges varied enormously—sometimes it was safer to dare the waters; or least frequently because they were so rare hire a ferryman to take us across. As we traveled, we would stop at the larger towns where the merchants in our caravan sold their wares, sometimes buying new goods for resale at the next. Our destination was Semlin, in the Kingdom of Hungary on the border with Bulgaria, a province of the Byzantine Empire. An annual fair, international in character, was scheduled. What goods they had left could be sold there and then they planned to load up their empty wagons with new purchases for resale at handsome profits on their return to Germania. Two merchants intended to travel a few miles further to Belgrade, the empire's frontier city, where there was a lively slave market, though these merchants swore they would buy only Turkish youth, no Christians they protested! When I asked, Isaac translating, to what use would these slaves be put, they merely shrugged their shoulders—they didn't know nor did they particularly care.

The days passed pleasantly enough. Rebecca and I took turns riding in Isaac's wagon and the cart. I enjoyed my conversations with Isaac, especially when we talked about spices: their origins; methods of cultivation and harvesting; culinary uses, especially in beef pottages. Above all, though, I was curious about their medicinal properties, a subject that had interested me since my reading of Galen and Geoffrey's, the Doctor of Physik, frequent references to him and my observations of his treatment of Father Benedict. At each of the cities we visited Rebecca and I would walk through the streets, exploring. As one day followed another, Rebecca slowly became more cheerful. The range of our conversations was almost limitless, from the divine to the profane: our concepts of God, the healing power of prayer, the differences between Jewish and Christian rituals, our youth together in Mainz, her education in a Jewish home and mine at the cathedral school in Rheims and then at La Charité, even our preferences in fish—she perch, I trout; she was quite obstinate on the question. And yet, there was a quiet understanding between us that the events in Mainz, especially the deaths of her two sons, would not be broached. And they never were.

We arrived in Semlin mid-June. There was minstrel music in the distance and our caravan moved toward it. The field, outside the city gates, was huge, perhaps ten bowshots in length and five in width. It was the first day. Wagons like ours were continuing to pour in: Byzantine merchants, international traders they, brought porcelains, carpets, precious jewels, silks, spices and perfumes, and glassware—all of the finest quality and unavailable in Francia or Germania; Flemish merchants came with their fine linen and cloths; Genoese and Venetian traders with their stores of Eastern goods; merchants from Hispania and Francia selling wines and oils; traders from Bavaria carrying furs and flax; English with rich fleeces of sheep and goats. The field was already filled with town inhabitants passing in and out of the city inspecting goods for sale. Also milling about were Peter's followers distinguished by the red crosses on their tunics, there I suspected more out of curiosity than to do business, or perhaps to pilfer. We parked our wagons along the perimeter and immediately set up trestle tables to display our wares, not even waiting to unharness the horses or set up tents. There were customers to be served and profits to be lost if we delayed.

I wanted to wander about the field and then into city. I asked Isaac if he minded; he waved me off with a smile. Rebecca decided to stay and help Isaac and Miriam. I wasn't needed. That morning, just before leaving our campsite, I had donned my pilgrim's garb. I no longer feared Emicho's pursuit. The field seemed to ferment with life. There was a flute player walking on stilts; a lutist prancing with light steps dressed in a clown's costume of blue and orange; a woman standing on the shoulders of a man, her arms waving as though in a dance; jugglers throwing balls and pewter cups in the air; acrobats doing somersaults and leaping through hoops. Children were everywhere, boys wrestling or fighting mock battles with wooden sticks, others playing hide and seek or stickball. Itinerant peddlers, sacks slung over one shoulder and display cases over the other, loudly hawking their wares: belts, colored ribbons, kerchiefs, scarves, and other sundries. Shopkeepers from the city were pushing three-wheeled barrows filled variously with bread, cakes, dried fish, competing with the peddlers for attention while trying to steer around children running helter-skelter throughout the field. I was uncertain whether this was a market fair or a festival. Both I supposed. The effect on me was dazzling. The last time I saw such an event was as a boy in Rheims, but even that couldn't compare.

I wandered toward the gates. There was a commotion near the city wall. Curious, I quickened my pace. A crowd had gathered below the wall —all followers of Peter the Hermit who had arrived the previous evening, some soldiers, most pilgrims—pointing upwards. Hanging from the parapet were helmets, shields, swords, hauberks, gambesons, breeches, even undergarments. I counted the property of sixteen men-at-arms. I asked a pilgrim standing by me what this was about. He told me that soldiers of Walter the Penniless, who had split off earlier from Peter's group wishing to make speedier time to Constantinople, had been assaulted by garrison guards in the city's marketplace, beaten, stripped of their clothes, and expelled naked.

"Whose fault was it?" I asked naively.

"Well, the city's naturally" came the scoffing reply.

The crowd was becoming increasingly agitated, inflamed by one man clad in armor, a captain by his appearance with a hundred infantry men immediately behind him. He was shouting up at two guards on the parapet as they responded with whistles and catcalls. "Remove the armor you godless vermin. Remove them all now!"

"No!" came the curt answer.

"What was their offense?" not a question but an accusation.

"They were thieves," came the quick answer, "like the rest of you scum. They refused to return stolen goods and we dealt with them accordingly. As we shall do with you!"

"You lie! A stinking, rotten lie! Take them down *now* or I'll climb up and take them down myself!" the captain shouted back, pulling out his sword halfway then slamming back into his metal scabbard. The wall defender just grinned at the captain, responding with a rude gesture of contempt by placing his finger and thumb on his forehead.

Each exchange provoked more anger from the crowd. When I thought it could not be more frenzied, silence suddenly descended. I looked to my right. The crowd, including the men-at-arms, were parting to make a path. Through it strode a short unkempt man, Peter the Hermit. He walked up to the captain.

"Brother Geoffrey. Peace. Restrain yourself," placing his hand on Geoffrey's shoulder. "King Colomon allowed us safe passage through his country and free access to markets on my promise of our good behavior."

"Father. This is insolence. It must not go unanswered!"

"Geoffrey," he responded serenely, "we are messengers of God. I too am displeased. Let me speak with the governor for an explanation and negotiate a solution."

Geoffrey would not be pacified. "What was their offense? Just purchasing supplies in this hellhole of a city? This insult cannot be endured! A lesson must be taught!"

Fate now intervened, with tragic results. A man came running out of the city gates up to Peter.

"Father, there's trouble in the city. You must hurry." Peter raced into the city, followed by Geoffrey, his foot soldiers, and other pilgrims. In the market square a crowd had gathered before a shoe shop. Two groups were shouting at one another, one townspeople and the other pilgrims. Peter, Geoffrey, and his soldiers pushed forward. Two garrison soldiers stood on either side of a pilgrim, his hands bound with rope.

"What's going on?" Peter demanded.

"This miscreant refused to pay for a pair of shoes so we arrested him," one of the soldiers answered. "He will answer to the city magistrate."

"I didn't steal anything!" the pilgrim protested. "I was cheated by this man," raising his bound hands pointing toward the shopkeeper.

"You're a bad liar and a clumsy thief," the shopkeeper retorted.

"That's enough," said one of the garrison soldiers. "We'll take him to the magistrate. He can sort this out," and at that they began pulling him away.

"Stop!" Geoffrey ordered. Looking to his own men-at-arms, "Release the pilgrim! And he can keep his shoes."

The garrison soldiers objected. Geoffrey drew his sword, pointing it at one of their throats. "Get out! While you can."

As the two were hurrying away, one of them, when safely out of reach, turned, "The governor will hear of this!"

"Sooner than later!" Geoffrey shouted back.

At that, Geoffrey signaled his men, some of whom were arbalists carrying crossbows, to follow him. "Geoffrey, stop!" Peter pleaded. "What do you plan to do? We are soldiers of Christ. We *cannot* make war on other Christians. This is not the pilgrimage I had hoped for."

"Maybe not. But it's the pilgrimage you have," Geoffrey crisply replied.

As Geoffrey began running toward the city's garrison, both soldiers and pilgrims following, Peter shouted after him, "Geoffrey Burel. You are a hothead. You will bring destruction down on us. Now or later." Geoffrey, without turning around, merely waved his hand dismissively. Peter's words proved prophetic. Only later, in Anatolia.

By the time Geoffrey reached the garrison, its gates were shut and the defenders already manning the parapets though their numbers seemed thin. "Find ladders!" Geoffrey ordered. While his soldiers were scouring the city, both attackers from below the parapets and defenders from above were relentlessly mocking one another. Soon, Geoffrey's men returned with five ladders seized from a church undergoing construction, suffi-ciently tall and sturdy for the task. They began laying the ladders against the wall. Geoffrey was in luck for the garrison's defenses were surprisingly minimal: no moat and only a single wall, rather unimpressive it seemed to me, built less to withstand a siege than opportunistic thieves.

Peter had now caught up. "Stop this! I forbid it!" he shouted. No one paid attention.

"Cover me," Geoffrey ordered his arbalists, ignoring Peter. They began unleashing a volley of bolts at the defenders as the latter ducked behind the merlons, upright stone blocks on the parapet, peering out through the crenel open spaces returning fire when they could. Geoffrey, fol-lowed by other men-at-arms, clambered up one of the ladders and, on reaching the top, leapt onto the wall-walk along the parapet, his sword flashing. Soldiers were climbing up the other ladders, they too reach-ing the parapet. I could hear shouts from inside, gradually abating until there was quiet. And then the garrison's gates flew open. Geoffrey's men rushed in. Gleeful pilgrims were milling about in front of the gates ready to follow but were stopped by Drogo, standing among them, who began yelling and pointing to one house after another lining the city street. I couldn't hear what he said but his message was clear: pillage! Which they executed cheerfully. Clubs and daggers in hand, they broke down doors, pushed through, beating or stabbing anyone who resisted. From within came shrieks of victims and wild and frenzied shouts of looters who only moments later raced back out, their arms full of spoils. Soon, Geoffrey Burel's soldiers, having ransacked the garrison, realized they were missing opportunities outside the garrison's walls. City inhabitants were fleeing through the city gate, some to the Danube where most drowned; others to the forest. Those unable to escape were pursued and killed either by pilgrims or Geoffrey's soldiers. I was left unmolested, the red cross on my tunic proving I too was a pilgrim, like them. But I wasn't like them.

Peter began racing up and down the streets begging his followers to stop. His rhetorical skills were no match for raging lust. He finally surrendered, walking slowly down the middle of the street, alone, head bowed, his cowl pulled tightly over it. As I followed Peter from a respectful distance I could hear wild and raging howls of looters and the screams of their victims. Hundreds, perhaps thousands, of Hungarians died that day.

Retribution at Nish

After passing through the city gates Peter rejoined his followers, at least those whose appetite for pillage and murder was now sated and had returned to their camp. I walked to the market field. Only a short time before it had been so alive. It was now almost empty, most of the merchant wagons having hurriedly departed. Our caravan was still there but the merchants including Isaac were hastily packing up. Rebecca was standing in front of the wagon anxiously waiting for me. She obviously wanted to hug me but restrained herself, perhaps for fear of improprieties.

Isaac approached. "Well young pilgrim. I'm glad you're safe. We're leaving, as you can see. You and Rebecca are welcome to return with us if you wish."

I made an inquiring look of Rebecca. She answered simply, "I'm staying with you. I have nothing left in the north."

I turned to Isaac. "It seems our fate lies in the south."

The four of us embraced with a kiss of peace. "I shall never forget either of you," I said. They nodded. I then approached each of the merchants as they were loading up to bid farewell and thanked them for their companionship. They seemed shocked at seeing me dressed as a Christian pilgrim, even more that I spoke Teutonic. I saw no point in continuing the ruse. They all had the same unspoken question on their minds, and to each I answered "It's complicated." They seemed to accept this vague explanation.

Rebecca and I climbed into our cart. In the distance I saw thousands of Peter's followers gathering up their belongings as quickly as they could—most walking, the rest in wagons and carts—heading for the Sava River bridge to Belgrade, the frontier of the Byzantine Empire, only two or so miles from Semlin. Peter had ordered an immediate evacuation fearful of certain retaliation by Colomon, King of Hungary. The stone bridge was a narrow one and already full of pilgrims, thousands of them, crossing as quickly as they were able. We had to wait our turn. My fear was that we would not be able to cross in time before Colomon's troops arrived. We did. All of Belgrade's inhabitants had already fled, taking their herds and flocks with them having heard of the massacre at Semlin. Even the garrison was abandoned, vastly outnumbered as it was by Peter's men. On entering the town I saw pilgrims looting homes and shops, setting some on fire. I urged our mule forward. Our destination was Nish, provincial capital of Bulgaria, seven days distant. I had hoped our troubles would end once we entered the territory of the empire. They only followed us.

Remembering the uncertainties of pilgrim companions—the goose and the goat came to mind—I decided it would be more prudent to remain with the baggage train in the rear which included a wagon carrying Peter's treasure chest full of coins and other valuables collected from donations through the Rhineland. We finally reached Nish, the city and its markets opened for us though the military governor Nikitios had required Peter to surrender Geoffrey Burel as a hostage for good conduct. We all camped outside the city walls near the Morava River. I picked a spot for Rebecca and me, remote as I could find, by chance close to the treasure wagon. I worried for Rebecca. She had enjoyed the relative comfort of Isaac's covered wagon sleeping with Miriam. Now she would have to sleep without cover under the open sky with only a tarp for a bed. There was no choice. I saw Peter riding his "holy" donkey come to the treasure wagon, dismount, and open the chest for distribution of coin to his people enabling them to purchase supplies in the city. A line immediately formed, hands cupped or empty purses opened as Peter filled them, each met with an expression of gratitude. I joined it. When it was my turn Peter looked at me closely with recognition but uncertain.

"I know you. From somewhere . . . "

"Yes," I answered, "I saw you preach at a small village not far from the Loire River in east Francia."

He pondered. "Ah, yes, you were a monk and sitting in a cart next to a more elderly one."

"That's correct, Father. He was the prior of La Charité sur Loire where I served. I was deeply inspired by your preaching and left the priory to join you to Jerusalem."

Looking at the badges on my hat, "I see you are well traveled."

Deciding not to disabuse him, I merely answered "Yes I am."

"Your name brother monk?"

"Oderic."

Those behind me in line were becoming restive at the delay. "Maybe we can talk later," Peter said. We would, but much later. I thanked him and left.

Rebecca and I walked into the city and as was our practice explored the streets and shops. I purchased some bread from a bakery and fresh mutton for dinner. We returned to our cart, I gathering some kindling, making a fire, and cooking our meat over it. As always we engaged in diverse conversation. I tried, yet again, to persuade her of the virtues of trout but again without success. I could see other camp fires not far from us, numerous, lighting up the night sky, and hear people singing.

It was a sultry evening and neither Rebecca nor I could sleep. There were several mills along the side of the river, their wheels turning slowly in the current grinding grain for flour. Rebecca suggested we walk over to them. She wanted a closer look. The sky was clear and the moon half-full, enough light to make our way. As we strolled, Rebecca gently placed her arm inside mine, and then held it tightly. With every passing day my affection for her had deepened. But I was a monk, sworn to my vows. Yet being so close to her, touching her, I couldn't withdraw my arm. If Rebecca sensed my conflict, she gave no indication. We approached the mills. I could hear quarreling. The words were indistinct—some of the voices were in Teutonic, the others I didn't recognize but assumed they were Bulgars. I suggested we turn around. Rebecca agreed. That night we slept in the open air on tarps and under blankets generously given to us by Isaac.

Before we retired messengers on horseback from Peter rode through the camps to inform us that Geoffrey Burel had been released on the promise that we would leave the next morning. We must be ready to depart. Not long after sunrise I was awakened by shouting. "Geoffrey Burel has attacked the garrison. We need to help!" As I arose, I saw the mills ablaze and thousands of pilgrims from their camps racing toward the city. Rebecca was soundly asleep. I shook her vigorously. "Rebecca, wake up. We need to go!"

As I quickly packed and harnessed our horse I looked back over my shoulder to see pilgrims within fifty paces of the gates. But then they suddenly whirled around fleeing back. Just emerging from the gates in flight were Geoffrey Burel's soldiers yelling "*Run! Run!*" and behind another group of Peter's followers trying to outrun the city's garrison soldiers just behind them, swords in their hands slashing the backs of every pilgrim in reach, leaping over fallen bodies to attack the next. And yet again, behind the garrison soldiers, were townspeople wielding clubs, hammers, and daggers beating or stabbing to death those missed by the soldiers. They knew of the slayings at Semlin and the burning of Belgrade. Yes, Hungarians, not Bulgars, had died but the Hungarians were neighbors. And Christians too. And they understood what fate awaited them at the hands of these pilgrims if action were delayed. Geoffrey Burel's men, the first to flee out of the gates, turned left to the river and to safety I supposed. The terrified pilgrims after them were less fortunate, running to the river, to the forest nearby, to the hills, wherever they could find refuge, pursued by Nish's troops and its townspeople. Those with wagons or carts were frantically harnessing their animals; those whose animals were already harnessed were furiously shaking the reins racing away in all directions. Everywhere were shrieks of panic and screams of pain. From the Bulgars, distinctive in clothing for the iron chains around their waists used as belts, came shouts of homicidal fury. There was complete chaos. It felt to me like God's judgment from the Old Testament. Pitiless. I later thought of the Book of Numbers, when the Israelites beseeched God to give them victory over the Canaanites, and the Lord said: "*Destroy them all and their towns.*" This was retribution.

Rebecca quickly jumped into the cart. I held firmly onto the reins uncertain in which direction to flee. And then I heard the sound of galloping hooves like thunder and trumpets blaring from behind a slight rise in the distance. I looked. Over it came a company of horsemen, a hundred I think, all carrying maces, shafts of wood with spiked iron balls on top, deadly "morning stars". Their pronged helmets were trimmed in fur attached to which were plate guards over their cheeks down to the chins, wearing no other armor, only shirts, breeches, and knee-length leather boots. They didn't need armor for their purpose was to kill simple peasants. These were Pechenegs, wild Turks from the north of Constantinople, mercenaries of the empire. They formed themselves in a single line, side-by-side, to ensure that no one escaped their onslaught and then spurred their horses to full speed into the fleeing pilgrims—men, women, children—the Pechenegs were indifferent—swinging right and left; the few able to dodge the mace were trampled by the their destriers, heavy warhorses. Those in wagons and carts fared no better than those on foot. The Pechenegs chased them down, one by one, smashing the drivers' heads, toppling them from their perches, then chasing the next just as ruthlessly.

I continued to hold the reins. Frozen. There was no escape. In the entire field it seemed Rebecca and I were alone. Bodies were strewn everywhere. Thousands. And then I saw a squadron of five Pecheneg horsemen heading directly for us no more than a hundred paces away, each twirling his mace, a frolic for them, their mouths open in wide grins. We were the sport, perhaps our cleaved heads intended for some form of Turkish stickball on a horse. But in that instant I thought of what my father had taught me one day in my youth on a hike in the forests outside of Rheims inhabited by mountain lions and bears. "My son," he said, "understand the nature of a predator. When the prey flees, the predator gives chase and kills it. Never run. Stand and face it. Don't move. Don't flinch. Back up slowly. It will be confused. And in that moment you may be able to escape."

I couldn't back up. Instead, handing the reins to Rebecca, I stood, straightened my tunic and hat, spread my legs akimbo, my left elbow extending straight out with a clenched fist on my hip; my staff, upright, in my right hand, arm outstretched, the spike resting diagonally beside my foot. I stood there erect and motionless, trying to strike the pose of a Greek god. I looked directly into the eyes of their leader, their sergeant I assumed, as he raced toward me. My father was right. Confusion filled his eyes. He pulled up his horse, raising his hand for his men to do likewise. We stared at one another, his eyes glaring and mine steely and unblinking. He lightly booted the flanks of his horse, ambling forward to within a few feet of the cart. We did not lose eye contact. I decided to take control without weak gestures or timid speech.

"I am Oderic of Rheims, Ambassador and Papal Legate of His Holiness Urban II, Pope of Rome. I am on a mission to Alexios Komnenos, Emperor of Constantinople. I have a letter from His Holiness for your Emperor. You will escort me immediately to his city where no doubt you will be rewarded handsomely." I spoke in Greek, surprised at how fluently the words came to me not having studied the language since my days at the cathedral school in Rheims. The sergeant was clearly flummoxed. He had not expected to be confronted by a speaker of Greek let alone such a dignitary. He just sat on his saddle, staring blankly at me as I stared back.

Finally, he regained his composure. "What credentials have you? How do I know you are an emissary of . . . what did you say his name is, 'pope'?" The sergeant's ignorance was obvious. This, I thought, could be to my advantage. The next few moments would tell.

"These are my credentials," I said, pointing first to the scalloped pilgrim's badge, that of Santiago de Compostela, on my hat. "It bears the insignia of the Pope of Rome. And this," pointing to my other badge, that of the Three Kings, "was given to me by Henry IV, King of Germania and Emperor of the Holy Roman Empire."

He was clearly mystified. "Then let me see this letter."

I reached into my satchel to produce Samuel's letter of introduction. Pressing his knees against the horse and with a slight shake of the reins he nudged his horse closer to within an arm's reach of me, resting his mace over his saddle. I handed him the letter. He unrolled the parchment, pretending to read. It was written in Hebrew, a script and language I was certain he could neither recognize nor decipher. His attention seemed focused on the bottom of the letter where Samuel had impressed his ring seal in red wax. He rolled it back up and placed it in his saddlebag.

"Who's this whore with you?"

"Beware, sergeant. I won't tolerate your insolence. This is Ingrid, Princess of Bavaria and daughter of Emperor Henry."

I was uncertain what this charade would yield but decided that more theater was required. I looked down at Rebecca who was trying to conceal her fright. She of course could understand nothing of the exchange between the sergeant and me as we spoke in Greek. "Rebecca," I said quietly, "you are a princess. You must act like one. Say anything you like but use the words 'Ingrid', 'Bavaria', and 'Henry'. Our lives depend on it."

Rebecca nodded. She slowly stood up and assumed the most regal and imperious bearing she could muster. Speaking Hebrew, she began reciting a Jewish psalm, the only thing that came to her mind, throwing in the words 'Ingrid', 'Bavaria', and 'Henry' at the beginning. The sergeant understood not a word except those three. He had lost control and his anger was rising.

"What in the fucking hell did she say?"

"She said, as I told you, that she is Princess Ingrid of Bavaria. That she has a message of friendship and comity from her father, Henry IV, to your Emperor. But her message is for his ears alone and can only be delivered in person. Now, escort us to your superior or you shall be dearly held to account!"

"So tell me this," the sergeant answered with a sneer. "If you're such a high and mighty ambassador and she a princess, why are you riding in a cart?"

"We had horses, the finest, and a company of soldiers. But this rabble," my hand sweeping across the field of dead and dying bodies, "stole them from us and killed our bodyguards. We were left only with this."

The sergeant's frustration was palpable. He could neither kill us, as he wanted, nor release us. "Follow me," he ordered curtly. "The *Strategos*, governor of this province, will have to decide."

Our Deception Exposed

We were led to the governor's palace in Nish. The sergeant accompanied by three of his men took us into an office. It was quite spacious but rather dark, only two windows, illuminated primarily by lighted torches holstered in wrought iron brackets fastened to the walls. A man, evidently the governor, was seated at a desk. We stood silently as the sergeant reported the successful attack on Peter's followers and his capture of Rebecca and me. The governor stared at us with obvious interest but without acknowledging our presence.

"What were the credentials this ambassador provided you?" he asked of the sergeant.

"The badges on his hat", he answered. "They looked official."

"And the letter? Do you have it?" The sergeant handed him Samuel's letter. The governor unrolled it, gave it a quick glance, rerolled it, and holding it in one hand began gently slapping it in the open palm of the other. He was thinking.

"Sergeant. You can leave us now."

"But Your Excellency . . ." clearly fearful of leaving us alone with him.

"Oh, I think I'll be safe with an ambassador and a princess. Leave us."

The governor waited until the sergeant and his men had left and the door closed , and then broke out in unrestrained laughter, not mocking but genuine mirth.

"My Pechenegs," shaking his head, "fierce warriors but ignorant as the ass Peter the Hermit rides. Ambassador," looking at me with a wry smile, "since when did the pope begin writing letters in Hebrew to a Greek emperor? Some new practice of the papal chancellery, is it?"

This was not going well, I thought to myself. "Your . . . Excellency," I stammered, "I don't know. This is the letter I was given."

"So," the governor continuing his interrogation, "your credentials. From the pope and the king, are they?"

I said nothing. I had nothing to say. Yet I sensed not the slightest ill will from the governor. "Some years ago I lived in Rome, part of a commercial mission. Your badges are nothing more than proof of pilgrimages, one to

Santiago I'm sure and the other to Cologne if I'm not mistaken. Why don't we cease this pretense. I am Nikitios, military governor of Bulgaria."

"I am . . ." beginning to respond.

Nikitios interrupted. "I know who you are Father. Do you think for a moment we have agents only in the Empire?"

"You mean spies?" I inquired naively.

"No, we prefer to call them 'agents' but you may assume what you will. We have them everywhere, in Hispania, Germania, Francia, wherever the Empire has interests. Yes, I know who you both are: you're Oderic, a monk, and she's Rebecca, a daughter of Mainz. You are being sought by Emicho, Count of Leiningen," Nikitios continued, "for an assault on Thomas of Marle, Count of Coucy, and the murder of his captain." Setting down Samuel's letter, he began thumbing through a stack of papers on his desk. "Let's see . . . oh, yes, here it is," pulling out a document, "a warrant from the count for your arrest. Although the count has no authority here, it is the practice of the Basileus to honor such requests, especially against criminals. I think you qualify."

My heart sank. Rebecca had endured such horrors and suffering. I had risked my life for her. All for naught. Everything was now undone. I knew our fate with Emicho once we were delivered to him. Perhaps I should not have tried to escape from the Pechenegs. Death in the field of Nish by a crushed skull would be more merciful. Nikitios continued talking, his back to me as he walked to the hearth standing over it.

"This warrant says you stabbed Thomas of Marle in the eye. Pity you didn't push more deeply. He still lives. You see, I know everything." And to my astonishment he placed the corner of the warrant in the fire holding it until it was almost completely burnt throwing it in. Turning back to Rebecca and me "There is also a practice of the Basileus, unwritten, that sometimes military governors, when justice demands, may ignore such warrants." To my further surprise he began speaking in Hebrew, albeit broken but intelligible enough. "I am half-Jewish myself." Looking at Rebecca, "I knew your father and your mother Rachel, but only by reputation, even here. I am deeply sorrowed by their passing." Rebecca began gently shaking, tears in her eyes. Turning to me, "And Father Oderic, I know of your brave service to the Jews of Mainz."

I nodded in gratitude. "Your Excellency, may I ask you, what has happened to all of Peter the Hermit's followers here at Nish. Do you know?"

"Many thousands of them were killed. Others were taken captive; they will serve usefully as slaves for the Empire. We also seized Peter's treasure chest.

This will compensate us for our troubles. I believe about seven thousand fled into the forests and have now regrouped. They are on their way to Sofia. I could hunt them down but there's little damage they can do between here and there. I will wait instructions from the Basileus how to deal with them."

"I've heard there are other pilgrim groups in Hungary, the priests Gottschalk and Volkmar, Emicho too. What happened to them?"

"Well," Nikitios answered, now speaking again in Greek, a language with which he obviously felt more comfortable, "Volkmar attacked Jews east in Bohemia. From there he went into Hungary. At Nitra he attacked more Jews but the townspeople rose against him, slaying or capturing most or all of his followers. Volkmar's fate is unknown. We've heard nothing more but I'm confident he received the death he deserved."

"Regarding Gottschalk," Nikitios continued, "he initially received the favor of King Colomon with open markets. But his men abused the privilege, pillaging the countryside, drinking, stealing wine and grain. When they impaled a Hungarian lad in the marketplace with a stake, the king had enough. He arrived with his army promising immunity and safe passage if Gottschalk's men surrendered their weapons. They did. Colomon's army fell upon them, slaughtering every one. Gottschalk tried to flee but was captured, I assume later executed." Nikitios wasn't done. "Now, Emicho is more interesting. His army besieged the walls of Wieselberg in Hungary for weeks. They even had siege engines. They had just broken through the castle's wall when, for some inexplicable reason, they panicked and began fleeing. His army was pursued and destroyed. Emicho with some of his retainers, Thomas of Marle and a man called William 'the Carpenter' among them, survived but only because they had swift horses. I'm told Emicho returned home. Thomas and William joined another expedition to Constantinople. That's all I know."

"But," Nikitios continuing now in Hebrew because he was addressing Rebecca as well, "I must deal with the two of you. Drop this pretense of being an ambassador and a princess. In the imperial court the truth will become immediately apparent and it will go hard for you. Perhaps, however, you both could be of service to the Empire. Father Oderic, I know you were a copyist at some monastery in Francia." I continued to marvel at the extent of Nikitios's intelligence. "Literate in Latin, I assume. What languages do you speak in addition to Greek?"

"Frankish, Teutonic and Hebrew," I answered.

"Excellent," Nikitios answered. "A translator perhaps. A scribe maybe. I shall give you a letter of introduction to Chancellor Demetrios Doukas, my cousin. The chancery employs scribes and translators fluent in all languages of the East: Arabic, Persian, Turkish; even languages of the Pechenegs and Cumans though they cannot read. Also every language of the West. I think you could be useful. And, Rebecca," turning to her, "you would be welcome in Constantinople. There is a lively community of Jews there, over two thousand living in Galata. And our laws forbid discrimination against Jews. I shall also recommend that Demetrios find a position for you in the court. You can pick up my letter when you leave. Oh, lest I forget it, here's Samuel's letter of introduction," handing it back to me. "Yes, I knew what it was. Two days hence a company of my men, Pechenegs under the command of the sergeant who nearly killed you, will be escorting the Bishop of Nish to Constantinople. You shall join them." I blanched at the mention of the sergeant. "Don't worry," Nikitios smiled reassuringly, "you will be traveling under my protection. He's not quite as evil as you may think." At that he rang a bell on his desk. A servant immediately opened the door. "Have the chamberlain attend to all the needs of my guests, accommodations, food, and clothing."

We were about to follow him out of the office when Nikitios made the sign of the cross in the Greek fashion. "May God bless and protect you. You leave in two days."

* * *

In the time that followed during our journey to Constantinople I had many opportunities to reflect on events of the last two months: The massacre of thousands of Jews in the Rhineland and along the Danube. Many hundreds, perhaps more, Christians slain at Semlin. The pillaging and burning of Belgrade. The foolish assault on Nish, thousands of pilgrims perishing needlessly. The atrocities of Emicho, Volkmar, and Gottschalk. All this at the hands of "Soldiers of Christ". I believed so deeply in their goodness. But Prior Damian's counsel had been right: "*Beware of them for they will fail you.*" It was too late to turn back. At best I would suffer severe censure and ignominy at home; at worst excommunication. I must chart a different course. But I knew not what. I trusted in God to guide me.

This ends Book V of *Jerusalem Falls!* Book VI begins.

BOOK VI

The PEASANTS CRUSADE

Journey to Constantinople

Our journey to Constantinople with the Bishop of Nish escorted by Pecheneg troops took two weeks. In the first two days after leaving Nish south along the Danube we passed some of Peter's followers straggling on the road but I saw even more returning north to their homes, thin, haggard, discouragement and dismay on their faces. They knew they would never reach Jerusalem. I felt nothing for their plight. I had seen just too much.

We passed through Sophia, Philippopolis, and Adrianople, enjoying the hospitality of the empire's palaces and castles; otherwise we camped. The Pechenegs, including their sergeant, treated Rebecca and me correctly but indifferently, their attention showered upon the bishop. For those two weeks he and I rode beside one another in animated conversation. I think he preferred my company to that of the Pechenegs whom he described as "brute animals devoid of culture". And for me this was an opportunity to improve my Greek. After serving in the bishopric of Nish for five years, the patriarch had summoned him for a new appointment which he hoped would be in Constantinople, the "Queen of Cities" as he called it, a city he obviously loved. We rarely spoke of theology. Rather, he expounded tirelessly on his "City" as though there were no other in the known world: its cosmopolitan character with Slavs, Armenians, Syrians, Jews, Venetians, Bulgars, Muslims, all living together harmoniously; international merchants in the commercial quarter of the Golden Horn—Muslims with spices, porcelains, and jewels; from Italia tin and wool; from the north honey, wax, amber, and wool; magnificent silks woven in Constantinople, prize of the empire, from silkworm eggs smuggled in during the time of

Emperor Justinian; Byzantine silver objects of craftsmanship unrivaled in the West; its bathhouses, pride of the city though the bishop warned me that some were dangerous where iniquitous and vile "favors", as he called them, were freely bought and sold. But above all the bishop expatiated with the greatest fervor on Constantinople as the center of the Christian world: its hundreds of churches and monasteries but most especially the thousands of sacred relics, including Christ's Crown of Thorns, the stone pillar on which Christ was scourged, the red marble slab on which His body lay after the crucifixion still bearing the tears of His mother, the Virgin Mary's robe and a lock of her hair, two heads of John the Baptist—I tempered my curiosity on this issue.

In time I became weary of hearing about the glories of the "Queen of Cities", although soon I would come to understand that indeed it is. Another subject interested me. "Your Eminence. Tell me about the barbarian Turks. Who are they? As wicked as I've heard?"

"Wicked? Well, yes, perhaps," pausing in thought. "Worse than my own Byzantines? Worse than your Latin princes? They all slaughter without remorse. Ransom captives when they can. Sell others on slave markets. They appear to me all the same." His sober judgment reminded me of Prior Damian.

"But tell me about them," I insisted.

"Yes, the Seljuq Turks. I am only crudely informed of their politics. However I do know this much: The East is a snake pit of hissing vipers full of dissension and intrigue. It would be easier to explain the interlocking of colored glass in a mosaic than Turkish politics, or Byzantine for that matter. They were a nomadic people, sheep herders, from lands far to the east of Persia, migrating there two hundred years ago. They call themselves 'Seljuq' after their founder. His empire grew beyond Persia, to Baghdad which he captured some forty years ago, and then all of Anatolia after defeating our Byzantine army in 1071, even seizing our Basileus whom they ransomed back to us. Anatolia was then lost to the Empire. After that the Seljuqs expanded, reaching into Palestine and beyond to the frontiers of Egypt. But as is the nature of great empires, it eventually began to crumble, splintering into competing principalities. In Anatolia and Syria the land was divided, Qilij Arslan establishing his own kingdom, the Sultanate of Rum with its capital at Nicea, and the brothers Ridwan who inherited Aleppo and Duqaq who inherited Damascus. All are relatives of the Seljuqs' greatest leader Malik Shah, who died a few years ago. They have always contended with one another, sometimes warring.

So long as they remain fragmented, your armies from the West may be successful. But," releasing one of his hands from the reins and wagging his finger at me, "if they unite, you are doomed." At the time, those names meant nothing to me. That would change later.

"And how does the emperor deal with all this?" I asked.

"With difficulty and caution. The Empire is always under assault, from every direction. Pechenegs from above the Danube invaded, reaching the walls of Constantinople. Alexios bribed another barbarian tribe, the Cumans, into becoming an ally. They virtually destroyed the Pechenegs six years ago. Those who survived transferred their loyalty to the Basileus. But now the Cumans are a threat. And the loss of Nicea in the north of Anatolia means all communication south, with those parts formerly part of the Empire and still loyal, is lost."

"So what can the emperor do? What is he doing?"

"It's really quite simple. Alexios has enlisted the aid of your pope, Urban. I was a member of the Basileus's embassy to his council at Piacenza last year. Our message was that we needed help to save Christendom from the heathens."

"True?" I asked. "Did you?"

"Well, the state of affairs was not quite as dire as we portrayed them, although there was some truth to it. But I suspect, quite strongly, that the Basileus's true purpose was to obtain Western troops to retake Anatolia, restore the Empire to its former borders. Alexios is indeed a pious man but never mistake. He will sacrifice piety in a moment if it means saving the state."

"Well," I answered, "Peter the Hermit and his army are on their way."

"Not the aid he had in mind."

Constantinople

We arrived in Constantinople in mid-July, year of Our Blessed Lord 1096. I digress for a brief description of the city's lay. It is shaped as an inverted triangle, bordered on the west by the Sea of Marmara and on the east by the Golden Horn, coming to a sharp point in the south at the shore of the Arm of St. George, a narrow strait separating the city from Anatolia to the south. The north is protected by two "Land Walls", as they are called, the outer is the Wall of Theodosius, over four miles in length stretching from the Marmara Sea to the Golden Horn. As we approached, even from afar, I was stunned by the wall's massive size, fourteen feet thick and thirty feet high with ninety-six similarly massive square towers every two hundred feet. In my journey from Rheims until Constantinople I had never seen such a fortification. There are ten gates, one reserved for the emperor, guardhouses at each strictly regulating the number of visitors entering the city at any single time and ensuring they bring no weapons. We passed through the Gate of Adrianople into fields of grain, vegetable plots, orchards, and vineyards. Another two miles further we came to the inner wall, Constantine, equally massive, both walls constructed of mortared rubble faced with blocks of fitted limestone and reinforced with courses of layered bricks. The deep moats, sixty feet wide, are lined with bricks. I could not imagine a more impregnable city.

Past the Wall of Constantine we entered the city proper on its main street, the Mese, which leads through the city's center ultimately to the Great Palace, *Boukoleon* to the Greeks, on the Sea of Marmara. As we rode, my astonishment only quickened. Rebecca's mouth was agape at all she saw. I was told later that Constantinople holds perhaps 300,000 inhabitants and occupies eleven square miles. No city in the West can compare. We passed the imposing Aqueduct of Valens to our east carrying fresh water from Thrace, then through a triumphal arch leading into the huge Forum of Theodosius surrounded on all sides by a colonnaded peristyle. Further on is the Forum of Constantine enclosed by a portico in front of which are marble statues of Greek gods and goddesses, including one of Pallas Athena, bronze, thirty feet tall. And finally, into the Augousteion Square abutted by the Basilica of Saint Sophia, the grandest cathedral I had ever seen, its dome, almost two hundred feet high dominating the skyline of the city, its interior columns each able to cure a different disease simply by rubbing it. Close, to the west, is the famed Hippodrome with its obelisk from Egypt and Chariot of the Sun, seating for 100,000, the scene of chariot races wheeling around the central *spina*, public executions, and battles between wild animals. All entertaining nourishment for the masses, a dubious legacy of Rome I thought. Before leaving my description, I must report on one other remarkable curiosity of the square, the *Horologion*, a mechanical clock with twenty-four doors, each flying open at the appropriate hour.

At the Forum of Constantine the bishop took his leave for the monastery of Saint John Stoudios where he was to stay. We went further down the Mese through the Brazen Gate, massive bronze doors with reliefs depicting the victory of the Emperor Justinian in Italia and Africa, into the walled Great Palace. My most immediate sensation as we neared it was the cool breeze and smell of salt water from the Sea of Marmara, refreshing, bringing some respite from the hot sun. In the distance, on the sea, were hundreds of fishing vessels plying their trade, nets full of fish, tuna, and mackerel especially, for sale at the markets along the Golden Horn. Below me was a harbor for the emperor's personal use, marble steps, the Stairs of Chalcedon, from the palace to the water's edge defended by two lions, sculptures of bronze burnished to a fine sheen, their mouths open as though roaring.

The bishop had only briefly mentioned the Great Palace. I was expecting a single structure, albeit a magnificent one. Quite the contrary. It was a complex of buildings, gardens, and pavilions, two square miles in size, all connected with perfectly hewn and polished marble slab walkways. The palace was used by the emperor for ceremonial occasions and imperial administrative affairs staffed by hundreds of bureaucrats, his residence, *Blachernae*, located on the Golden Horn to the north. Rebecca and I were led into the anteroom of the chancellor's office. Greeting us was an assistant who asked our business. I explained that we had come at the instructions of the military governor of Nish. He did not answer except with a nod, turned to a door directly behind him, opened it to say something inaudible to a person inside, and then waved us in. The sergeant and his troops who had escorted us from Nish departed.

The bishop had advised me that the emperor's staff, particularly his most senior officers, are eunuchs, trusted because by virtue of their physical mutilation are prohibited from occupying the imperial throne through a coup. Some came as captives of war, others as gifts from foreign ambassadors, or yet others castrated as babies by ambitious parents to assure lucrative positions in the court. I did not know the history of Demetrios Doukas, nor did I ask, but his "nature", if I may use that term, was easily identifiable: in physique rather tall, flabby, and somewhat corpulent; a smooth colorless face, sleek and soft; scrupulously dressed in a silken robe and his person redolent with the scent of perfume. But he was pleasant enough, soon overcoming my initial aversion. By now I had completely abandoned our earlier pretenses, introducing myself simply and without embellishment as Oderic, a monk of La Charité sur Loire, and Rebecca as a survivor of the massacre of Jews in Mainz and under my protection. He made no inquiries about our relationship although doubtless questions swirled through his head. Perhaps he already knew. The Byzantines knew everything. I handed him the letter of introduction from Nikitios. He read it.

Looking up, "Yes, I received a message from my cousin that you would be coming. A bit later than I expected but you're here. Nikitios believes you could be of service to the chancellery. Tell me about yourself." I told him of my education at the cathedral school of Rheims and my work as a scribe translating Galen; copying the life of Saint George; and chronicling the history of Saint John the Martyr, omitting the fact that my narrative was more invention than verity, an insignificant detail I decided. He seemed intrigued by my work on Galen, perhaps because bureaucrats serving the empire are expected to be thoroughly trained in the Greek classics. But what clearly interested him was my linguistic skills.

"You appear to have a gift for languages."

My instinct was to express modesty, but the stakes were high. "Yes, I'm quite adept," I answered simply but accurately.

"Good. We have a hundred translators and scribes fluent in all languages of the known world. One even from Cathay whose written language is as impenetrable to me as hieroglyphics. He's a merchant who brought porcelain from that distant land but chose to remain with us. The Basileus and Cathay's emperor exchange correspondence and the merchant translates. The Basileus seems most curious about their science, especially some device with a rotating arrow for navigating the seas day or night by pointing to cardinal directions. Very odd but I'm sure useful. The bulk of our correspondence is in Latin with the West, especially prelates of your church. A priest such as yourself with a formal education, familiar with the protocols of proper address, salutation, and linguistic subtleties critical for persuasive correspondence can always be of service to me. So, yes, I can use you. Be here tomorrow, midday. The master of the *scriptorium* will be informed of your arrival."

He then turned to Rebecca, I translating. "And Rebecca, tell me of yourself." The passage of two months had not soothed her grief, raw as ever. It was impossible for her to speak of herself without reference to her family, and the very instant she became even remotely close to the subject her voice would choke. In my many conversations with Rebecca I knew how to avoid the subject. Strangers didn't.

"I was married and have no skills," she answered quietly.

Demetrios merely nodded, suggesting to me he knew much more than he allowed. "Then I think you might make a fine lady's attendant. We have wonderful women here who would welcome your service."

"But I'm Jewish."

"Rebecca, my dear," he smiled, answering gently, "you are in Constantinople now. We have people of many faiths. All are respected and protected equally under our laws. Let me think about your situation. No decision is necessary now."

Turning back to me, "I have arranged for you to stay in two apartments, adjoining, here in the palace guesthouse. I hope they're not too modest." They were not. "There is also a common dining room. Our cuisine is different from what you're accustomed to but you will soon adjust. Later we can find more permanent accommodations." With that, he motioned to his assistant standing in the corner who wordlessly led us out of the office. As I reached the door Demetrios called out, "Father Oderic, I'll see you tomorrow midday." I turned, bowed, and thanked him for his kindness.

The next day I found my way back to the chancellery through the maze of walkways and arcades. Fortunately, the day before I had memorized the route which we had been taken to the guesthouse. I arrived at the appointed time. Demetrios's assistant, waiting, led me to the *scriptorium*. Like everything else in Constantinople I was stunned by its cavernous size, grandeur, and lavish architecture: marble floors; a dome in the ceiling with several glazed windows allowing sunlight to stream through; sixteen columns of green Thessalian marble, their capitals carved in vine tendrils entwining various animals; and mosaics of Old Testament scenes covering the walls. An infectious joy and industry seemed to permeate, scribes conversing and laughing as they worked at their writing desks, others consulting their colleagues on the correct translation of particular words, yet others fetching blank sheets of paper from cabinets, not parchments made of sheep hides but of silk manufactured in Baghdad which they called *bombazine*. This was so different from the silence and solitude of La Charité. The prefect of the *scriptorium*—I can neither pronounce nor spell his title—after a warm greeting guided me to my desk. My first task was to translate from Greek into Latin a letter from the Patriarch of Constantinople to the Bishop of Nimes. I undertook the project with enthusiasm, remembering only now the pleasures of exquisite calligraphy and perfect translation. Other assignments followed. All were welcome.

During the day I was occupied with my labors at the chancellery. I had stored away my pilgrim's garb in favor of Greek dress, less conspicuous I thought, allowing my hair to fill out and trimming my beard in the Byzantine fashion. Rebecca, through the intercession of Demetrios, had learned of a cousin living in Galata across the Golden Horn, crossing it daily in a ferry to visit with her. We reunited in the evenings and, as was our custom, explored this magnificent city, walking along the Mese and its side streets, each one segregated for particular trades: perfumery, shoes, hats, jewelry. I recall one vividly, a narrow street flanked with wretched small shops, the last place one would expect to find precious wares. We strolled into one to see jewels stored in oaken coffers bound with iron hoops in front of the shop containing stones of every kind: lapis lazuli, sapphires, opal necklaces, emerald pendants, rubies. But as we walked I was reminded of the prefect's admonition to be watchful, for Constantinople, while it excelled in riches, equally excelled in vice and squalid tenements standing cheek by jowl with brothels and gambling halls, haunts for brigands and thieves. We could always find a quiet tavern, play chess—the better ones always had a set—and enjoy a glass of wine together, Rebecca excitedly telling me of her new friends and I of my scribe's work that day. She always showed great interest though feigned I'm sure. These are cherished memories.

An Unexpected Meeting

It was perhaps a week after starting work that the prefect happened to be standing near my writing desk where I was speaking with one of the scribes. He was translating into Teutonic a letter from the emperor to King Henry of Germania and was uncertain about a proper verb—letters from Alexios had to be impeccably correct. I explained the difference between present and future conditional tenses. Satisfied, he thanked me, returning to his writing. The prefect ambled over to me. "I didn't know you were fluent in Teutonic. I thought only Hebrew, Greek, and Frankish." I told him of my apprenticeship under Samuel ben Meier in Mainz where I had learned the language. I expanded on that saying that I had visited it recently. At the mention of the city's name the prefect's interest was immediately piqued.

"Were you present at the carnage there?" he asked.

"Yes," doubtful how much more I wanted to disclose, his intent in the question unclear.

"And then later at Semlin and Nish?" His knowledge of events surprised me, creating more anxiety for me which I tried to suppress with affected indifference.

"Yes."

"And did you meet this man called 'the Hermit'?"

"Yes." I feared I had already revealed too much.

He smiled and to my relief asked no more questions. Later in the day the prefect visited me again to say that "someone" wanted to meet with me. Anxiously, I asked if I were in trouble. The prefect placed his hand on my forearm in a comforting fashion, "I'm sure not. You will be met here tomorrow at this time." Without further explanation, he wandered off to inspect the work of another scribe.

Rebecca's and my excursion that evening did not hold the same pleasure as they had in the past. I was worried. Why had the prefect asked such questions? Whom was I to meet? Rebecca did her best to reassure me but I could not be cheered. The next day I was too distracted to focus on my work. And then three Pechenegs, one of them the sergeant from Nish, strode into the *scriptorium* up to my desk. Wordlessly, the sergeant merely motioned for me to follow. They had a horse ready. Flanked by two horsemen and led by the sergeant we entered the Forum of Constantine then turned east to the sea wall following it north until we reached the northeast corner of the city where the Wall of Theodosius met the Golden Horn. The streets were teeming with people, on foot and horse; stalls crammed with exotic wares competing for business with street vendors selling more mundane goods; elegant ladies borne in curtained litters or seated on sedan chairs, eunuchs, whips in hand, running alongside them clearing the path; noblemen on white horses sitting on saddles embroidered with gold thread accompanied by servants on foot using sticks instead of whips. Twice I asked the sergeant our destination. He was mute throughout. I had a deep foreboding.

Finally, we arrived at a magnificent palace, *Blachernae*, the emperor's personal residence, surrounded by stout walls. There were four guards, huge men, axes slung over their backs, helmeted with aventails down to their shoulders and mail hauberks to their thighs. These were Varangians, mercenaries from the land of Rus in the far north, the personal guards of the emperor, fiercely loyal. As we approached twin iron gates the guards merely nodded at the sergeant, opening them; we passed into the courtyard and then dismounted. Attendants, waiting for us in the yard, took our horses. The palace door opened and a eunuch emerged signaling for us to follow. He led us through a labyrinth of corridors—I had now accustomed myself to the complexity of Byzantine architecture—paved with differently colored marble slabs, canted and perfectly flush with one another, yielding a stunning herringbone effect; the walls were cloaked in mosaics. As we walked my attempts at conversation with him were as futile as with the sergeant.

We came to a door, the eunuch knocked and from inside I heard "come". In front of me was another eunuch, evident from the smooth features of his face but much more masculine—stout of build, swarthy in complexion betraying some Turkish ancestry, but most astonishing wearing over his nose a gold plate shaped in the form of a nostril, the result he told me later of a military campaign. He introduced himself as Tatikios, *kuroplates* and military adviser to the Basileus Alexios. Was Tatikios the man I was supposed to meet? I was puzzled. "You'll see," he said. Followed by the Pechenegs, he led me down a passageway lit by scented beeswax candles standing in candleholders some five feet tall into a resplendent audience hall, mosaics on every wall except one. There, painted in fresco, was an immense mural of a man, stunningly lifelike, dressed in regal costume wearing a diadem with a bright golden nimbus behind his head sitting on a throne depicting him as the vicar of Christ at the Last Judgment deciding the eternal fates of weeping supplicants prostrate before him.

"Who is he?" I asked Tatikios in wonderment.

"The Basileus Alexios Komnenos."

We walked through the hall into a splendid garden. Tatikios ordered the Pechenegs to remain at the entrance. Varangian guards stood at attention in all four corners. In front of me sat a man on a curved, ornately carved marble bench flanked on either side by huge white and blue glazed porcelain vases painted with serpentine dragons and rising phoenixes—from Cathay, I wondered? Each vase contained a golden dwarf tree, their leaves glittering in the refracted sunlight of the garden. He was dressed simply in a leather jerkin, sleeveless, reaching down to his waist, wool breeches, and flared riding boots the length of his calves up to his knees—the costume of a soldier at leisure. I recognized him immediately from the mural, an unmistakable likeness. The emperor.

I digress again to speak of this great man from information provided by the Bishop of Nish and my own acquaintance. Alexios was born into a patrician family of Constantinople, his father even having been offered the throne, an offer he declined. Alexios seized it for himself years later in a coup, becoming emperor in 1081. Yet he was a warrior first, both before and after ascending the throne, leading imperial forces in battles throughout the empire including against the Seljuqs in Anatolia. His most formidable challenge was the Normans of southern Italia led by Robert Guiscard and his son Bohemond who seized territory along the eastern shore of the Adriatic. After several initial defeats, Alexios eventually triumphed. Yet his successes did not depend on military skills alone but also on his ability at enlisting allies against imperial threats. Hence, the bishop said, his appeal to Pope Urban. His personal habits were those of a military man—severe and serious in temperament, disinclined to small talk. His living quarters had no mirrors for he believed the only adornments a warrior required were a sword and purity of life. He was devout, his principal relaxation reading the Bible, often staying up late at night studying the Scriptures.

On recognizing the man in front of me, I was flustered. How was I to conduct myself before an emperor? "The niceties of protocol are relaxed here," Tatikios whispered, apprehending my disquiet. "A simple bow will suffice." The emperor's gaze was focused on two lovebirds—both red, yellow, and green—sitting beside one another on a tree limb preening each other. Hearing us enter he looked up and motioned for us to approach. He was about fifty years old, of medium build, muscular, with a distinct military bearing, mitigated only by a slight lisp, and a gaze both sharp and penetrating but not without a certain kindness.

"Your Majesty," Tatikios began, "this is Oderic, the priest and monk of whom I spoke. He is here to answer your questions." Alexios sat studying me, assessing. I stood there waiting.

"I have heard stories of a certain 'Peter the Hermit'. I'm intrigued. You know him?"

"Your Majesty," bowing deeply, "my acquaintance with Peter may have been exaggerated. Yes, I have met him. And, yes, I traveled with him and his company down the Danube. But I'm hesitant to say 'I *know* him'."

"Then tell me what you *do* know."

"Your Majesty, please forgive my impertinence, I mean no offense, but may I inquire why you're interested?" Tatikios, standing beside me, tugged sharply but discreetly on my sleeve, offended by my impudence. Alexios dismissed Tatikios's concern with a wave.

"Not at all. Perhaps more information would be helpful. My military governors have kept me quite informed of Peter's movements—in the Rhineland, Hungary, Bulgaria, and south. He and several thousands of his followers will arrive here in Constantinople within a week. Behind him will come other waves of your Latins, though rather later. I need to know what to expect and how to prepare for them. I'm informed that Peter is regarded as divine, even the donkey he rides. Is this true?"

"Yes, it is true. He is a pious man and claims to possess a letter from Christ Himself instructing him to liberate Jerusalem from the Muslims. I saw it. He is middle-aged, short, walks barefoot, rather begrimed in personal hygiene, and consumes only fish and wine but neither bread nor meat. Yet for all that, he possesses an unequaled eloquence and attracts followers wherever he speaks. They revere him."

"Yes," Alexios musing, "a leader of men?"

"Venerated, yes," I answered slowly, "a leader, no. Peter counsels restraint in the conduct of his men but he's ignored."

"Then tell me about his men."

"Rabble," I answered without equivocation. "Undisciplined, gluttonous, rapacious brigands and thieves. He cannot control them."

"Then can I expect trouble when he arrives?"

"Yes."

"And what do you know of Walter, so-called 'the Penniless'? He's already here with two thousand of his people and even now another two thousand Lombards have crossed the Adriatic to join him"

"I know little of him other than he was part of Peter's company but, frustrated with the pace, split off. He commands only a few men-at-arms, the rest peasants."

"Are they any different?" Alexios asked with a smile.

"Well," I answered, "different faces and different names. Same rabble."

"When I sent emissaries to Piacenza last year to solicit Pope Urban's support against the Turks I had hoped for soldiers, not peasants versatile more in swinging a scythe than a sword." Turning to Tatikios, "General increase our vigilance, more patrols. Father Oderic, I could use your services as a translator when I meet with Peter. More important, you've met and traveled with him. The meeting may yield insights for you which escape me. Thank you for coming."

Alexios Meets with Peter the hermit

Peter arrived in Constantinople August 1, a month after the events at Nish. He and his followers, under guard, camped outside the city walls and were supplied daily with open markets. Three days later the same Pechenegs who had escorted me earlier to Alexios again came to the *scriptorium*. "You're summoned. We leave now," the sergeant commanded in his usually terse manner. During our ride to *Blachernae*, I made no effort to engage him in conversation for I understood its futility. I was guided to the same garden as before. Alexios was again seated on his marble bench, Tatikios standing beside the armrest to his left. Tatikios motioned me to stand beside him. I had no sooner taken my position when Peter—his appearance precisely as I had earlier described—entered with a knight, I assumed Walter the Penniless, his scabbard empty, escorted by two Varangian guards who posted themselves on either side of the entrance. The Pechenegs stood beside them. Tatikios began with an introduction, Peter bowing clumsily, Walter following suit but in a more practiced manner. Peter glanced at me. He recognized me instantly, perhaps thinking he had found an ally in these intimidating and unfamiliar surroundings. I smiled, trying to reassure him.

"My dear Father Peter," Alexios greeting him with a cordiality I had not expected, "I trust you had a pleasant journey through our Empire and that you have been well treated?"

"Yes . . . yes, Your Majesty," Peter stammered. "You have been very generous and I thank you. But . . . except for . . . Nish . . maybe."

"What about Nish?" Alexios asked, his tone of voice amiable but with an unmistakable edge.

"Well . . . your soldiers . . ." Peter continuing to stammer, turning around to look back at the Pechenegs.

"Yes, my soldiers?" Alexios interrupted. "What of them?"

"So many good Christians killed . . ."

"Oh, I see," Alexios replied sardonically, "like the *good* Christians killed at Semlin? Or the *good* Christians your followers tried to kill at Nish?" It was difficult for me to translate Alexios's questions, drenched as they were in sarcasm, but I think Alexios succeeded in doing that quite well by himself.

"Your Majesty, I was not responsible," Peter pleaded. "I couldn't control them. And besides, our treasure was stolen."

"Ah, yes, treasure, what you pilgrims seem to prize above all else." Motioning to one of the Varangians at the entrance, "Captain . . ." The captain stepped into the shadows of the door and barked an order. Two eunuchs appeared instantly carrying a small wooden chest bound with iron ribs setting it down in front of Peter, opening the lid.

"Maybe this will help," Alexios said, his tone softening. Peter and Walter stared incredulously at the chest's contents. A hundred gold bezants.

"I believe this should cover your loss. Now, what further do you need from me?"

"I'm . . . I'm . . . at a loss. But to answer your question," Peter, now regaining his composure, "I hope you will transport my people to Anatolia where we can continue our journey to Jerusalem and cause you no further vexation or offense."

"You *really* want to invade Anatolia? *Peasants*? Untrained in arms. Against Turkish archers and swordsmen? This is supreme foolishness! Listen to my counsel. In only a few months princes, dukes, and lords from your lands will be arriving in Constantinople with their armies. Wait for them. Have patience. Then cross."

Walter had said not a word, until now. "Your Majesty. We march under God's flag. We are doing His will. Defeat is not possible. We must get on with the Lord's work."

At that moment, a eunuch walked quickly into the garden, urgency in his step. He anxiously motioned to Tatikios, who came over, the eunuch whispering in his ear. Tatikios turned to the emperor. "Your Majesty, I have just received word that Peter's men have evaded our surveillance and are now ravaging the countryside, burning barns, stealing livestock, setting fire to homes, ripping the lead off the roofs of churches to sell in city markets. Thus far, no one has been killed but that may change."

Alexios's demeanor until this moment had been genial and controlled. His face reddened with anger. "Peter, this is how you repay my kindness? My generosity? Pillaging my people as you have pillaged everyone else whose lands you passed through? I have heard enough. I shall grant your wish. In two days, no more, my ships will start transporting you across the Arm of St. George to the Gulf of Nikomedia and then to Civitot where you will be regularly supplied with open markets. Our prices will be fair. But under no circumstances are you to molest the local Christian communities there. You will need their support. Nor are you to engage the Turks. The fight will be unequal. You must stay there until your Latin armies arrive. And in Anatolia, you shall enjoy whatever fate God intends. Tatikios, see to it!" The meeting ended.

Peter the hermit to Anatolia

As I was about to leave, Tatikios stopped me and beckoned the Pecheneg sergeant to approach.

"Father Oderic. I want you to accompany Peter's men to Anatolia and to inform me regularly by letter of events as they occur. A boat will be available at the port in Civitot to transmit your messages. I shall inform the Basileus of your intelligence when appropriate." Turning to the sergeant, "Georgios Vardanes, you and three of your best soldiers will serve as Father's personal guard. He will have no command over you," glancing briefly at me to ensure no confusion about his instructions, "but you will protect his life with your own." Georgios, saying nothing, nodded. I sensed he would have preferred a more congenial assignment.

I returned to the Great Palace and informed Rebecca that in a few days I must depart. She was distraught, sobbing. "Oderic. No. You mustn't go! We have endured so much together. And now to be separated. I fear for your life. You will not return. You will *never* return. Please, please don't go!"

Rebecca's tears lowered my defenses, defenses to which I had clung tightly for so long. I took her in my arms, caressed her hair lightly kissing both of her cheeks. "Of course, I shall return," trying to comfort her. I released my embrace, stepped back, my hands on her shoulders, looking her in the eyes. "I could never leave you. While I'm gone, stay with your cousin in Galata. Wait for me there."

In the following evenings we continued our excursions through the city and then to our customary tavern for chess and wine. She did her best to disguise her alarm, as always sharing her day's adventures in Galata. But something was different. As we walked through the streets, she wrapped her arm around mine. All quite regular. Except that she hung onto me much more tightly than usual, releasing only when necessary, otherwise clinging.

On the day appointed a fleet had gathered in the Golden Horn at a harbor outside the Phanaria Gate just below the *Blachernae* Palace. A chain, thousand feet long, stretched across the Horn at its lowest point before entering the Arm of St. George used as a barrier against raiding ships, was withdrawn to permit ships to cross into the Sea of Marmara and then the Gulf of Nikomedia, Pelekanum the point of disembarkation. I had been excused from my work at the *scriptorium* and rode out daily to observe the departure of pilgrims, horses, wagons and carts on transport galleys, each with two decks of rowers, and then returning empty to transport more. It required four days. Georgios, mute as ever, always accompanied me, less for pleasure than to obey Tatikios's instructions. Georgios, his three Pecheneg soldiers, and I followed in a vessel, a lanteen with a triangular sail, sufficiently large for our horses and equipment and navigated by three sailors. Georgios had suggested we sail directly to Civitot but I demurred preferring to follow Peter's company in order to have a complete report for Tatikios. It proved to be the correct decision.

After disembarking on the northern shore of the Gulf of Nikomedia at Pelekanum we marched down a road running east towards the city of Nikomedia and then west along the gulf's southern shore to Civitot. We were in the rear. Georgios, with his typical barbarian impetuosity, wanted to move quickly to the front. I was satisfied riding in the shadow of the train, better to observe. As we passed, I saw endless destruction along the road: burned churches and villages, some still on fire, others smoldering. There were no animals grazing in the fields; looking ahead I understood the reason, pilgrims driving them off. Village inhabitants were either dazed or hiding behind any concealment they could find, children wide-eyed with fear crouching behind their parents. Georgios, no stranger to mayhem, was shaking his head in disgust at its wantonness. Even for

Pechenegs there had to be some larger purpose for rampage. None was evident here. Why had Peter not prevented this? I asked myself. My most charitable explanation was that he may have been at the front and ignorant of the depredations behind. Less charitably, he knew but felt powerless to prevent it, not even trying.

We reached Civitot, a modest port on the gulf with a small fortified outpost manned by only six soldiers, there more to demonstrate an imperial presence than to defend it. The pilgrims pitched their tents, thousands of them, the Pechenegs and I finding quarters in the outpost to which pilgrims were denied access. Every day I ventured out with my guards visiting the pilgrim camps to gather intelligence for Tatikios, sent daily to him by the ship which had taken us to the gulf, now docked in Civitot's harbor. I was struck by how the pilgrims had segregated themselves into three divisions of camps: Lombards, Franks, and Teutons. There was little concourse between them, as separate from one another as they had been in their own lands. There was one exception. A Lombard noble, Rainald by name, fluent in Teutonic, moving easily and frequently between the Lombards and Teutons, chatting and joking expansively with them. The Teutons seemed responsive to him. He had a certain charismatic charm, evident to me even from a distance. On several occasions I drew closer to listen but I heard nothing disturbing, certainly nothing to require action or a report to Tatikios. What was his purpose? Later it became clear.

* * *

We had been in Civitot for only a few days. Peter's troops and pilgrims were becoming restive, their nature to roam and pillage with little effort to deny that nature. Every day, with increasing frequency, I saw them leaving Civitot and then returning, wagon drivers munching on apples, dates, plums, and pears stolen from orchards; livestock in tow; wagons often full of household furniture, farm implements, tin pans and utensils—of little value to them in Anatolia, just plunder for plunder's sake. I saw no effort to control this and decided to confront Peter. I approached his tent. He was outside, sitting on a stool before a brazier holding in his hand a skewer, the opposite end resting on a forked branch planted in the ground, turning the meat over a fire as he periodically seasoned it with salt. I dispensed with pleasantries.

"Father Peter. Yet again, you've lost control over your rabble. They're raiding villages, *Christian* villages, no less. You heard the emperor. This is forbidden. I will have to report it. Every day ships arrive with supplies, sold to you at fair prices. There is no need for plunder. He will likely end his succor. You must end this. *Immediately!*"

Peter did not respond, just turning his meat over the flames without looking up. "Father, did you *hear* me?"

Finally, after more moments of silence, "Oderic. What can I do? They're *not* rabble. Perhaps somewhat undisciplined, yes. But *rabble*, no. All they need is God's guidance. A sign, perhaps. They'll soon behave."

"*Somewhat* undisciplined?" My voice rising in anger. "They are no different than the barbarians we're here to fight. No different!"

"What would you have me do?" Peter implored.

"Summon the nobles for a council. All of them. Lombards, Franks, and Teutons. They must lead and put an end to this foolishness."

"But will they listen to me?"

"Father Peter, I have heard you preach. Your eloquence is unrivaled. They will listen."

They didn't.

* * *

The next day all the nobles gathered outside Peter's tent, not enough room inside. I was present, Georgios beside me. "My Lords," Peter began, "we have lost our way. God did not intend for us to ravage Christians. We behave no better than barbarian Turks. We will have to answer to Our Lord, and there is much to answer for, not just here but at Semlin and Nish as well. His judgment may not be merciful." The nobles began shifting uneasily. "I confess that I have lost control. You have as well. You are weak. I too. The question before us is simple: Do we *lead* or are we being *led*? Discipline must be restored."

Peter had listened to me after all. Regrettably, his rhetoric was not equal to the task. The nobles felt Peter's stinging rebuke like a sharp needle in their thighs. And it showed on their faces. They did not take it well. The mood did not improve when Peter reminded them of Alexios's generosity in providing open markets both in Constantinople and in Civitot, of Alexios replenishing their coffers, and of his command not to molest our fellow Christians in Anatolia. There was at first silence.

Then Rainald, the Lombard noble, stepped forward. "I thank our estimable Father Peter for his guidance. But I must disagree. We cannot trust the Greeks. Effete. Dainty. Light of step. Governed by malformed eunuchs, an offense to God. Their licentious monks frequent the taverns and brothels of Constantinople. We've all seen them. They worship so-called 'saints', unknown to us, names we can't pronounce. Their pope, who lives in luxury worthy of a Baghdad sultan, does not recognize the supremacy of our own, or even of Rome. They do not comprehend the Eucharist, eating leaven not unleavened wafers. They cross themselves in a manner acceptable only to Satan, not to God. Why should we answer to their emperor?"

There were murmurings of assent from the nobles, growing stronger as he spoke. Rainald had not quite finished before Geoffrey Burel stepped forward. "My Lords. I concur with Lord Rainald. But I have more reasons why we must set our own course. We have all suffered to be here, some have died. There are riches to be had in this land. We came to this wretched country to cleanse it of the godless Turks and to save it for Jesus Christ. Why should we not also profit? Muslim caliphs, viziers, and sultans live with their many wives and harem whores in magnificent palaces, dining on plates of gold encrusted with precious jewels. Their captains, captured in battle, will bring rich ransoms. They possess fine horses for our knights, fat sheep and goats for roasting. Heathen mosques are filled with censers and candelabras of silver. Their youth, the comely ones of course," Geoffrey breaking out in an insidious smile, "can be sold to wealthy Christian families and saved from damnation by adopting a righteous faith."

The murmurs of agreement that initially greeted Rainald's speech now grew into shouts. "God wills it! God wills it!" Geoffrey's appeal to cupidity had trumped Rainald's to theology.

"This is not God's will," Peter appealed, "I know God's will. He delivered to me a letter in my own hands, not yours, commanding me, not you, to lead our people to Jerusalem. I . . ."

Geoffrey, fury in his eyes, "You are no messenger of God. You have lost His favor. We were victorious at Semlin, despite your objections. We suffered defeat at Nish only because God abandoned you. You fawn on the emperor as a supplicant, like one of his perverse eunuchs. You can no longer lead us! Tomorrow, at dawn, we Franks will march south under the flag and cross of Jesus Christ Himself. We shall claim what is rightfully ours and God's, not yours Peter, not the emperor's!" There were loud shouts from Geoffrey's captains and with that they turned in unison, storming out.

Peter was speechless, rather novel for him. His head bowed, standing motionless. I looked at Rainald. He seemed stunned by the turn of events.

He had been in control—until he wasn't. I had wished to intervene but no opportunity, at least one that could have altered the mood, presented itself. None of this augured well for the crusade. The next morning I was awakened by trumpets and shouts from the Franks' camp. Looking over the walls of the outpost I saw a modest company of horsemen, pennanted spears in hand, leading a large contingent of rejoicing pilgrims on foot, some in carts and wagons, singing hymns praising God and invoking His bounty and blessing.

* * *

A week passed. In those days I continued my practice of wandering amongst the pilgrims, the Franks having departed leaving only the Lombards and Teutons. They were becoming restless. It was too quiet for them. For sport they collected red and white ants from their respective colonies and set them against one another, placing a light daub of honey between them, laying wagers on the surviving "force" by tossing copper coins on one side or the other. Idleness is a dangerous pastime. There was little else to plunder in the area. They wanted adventure. And then Geoffrey's company returned. Shouts of glee from even three miles away reverberated from the hills. Through the dust kicked up by hooves I saw horses, goats, sheep, cows, and as they drew closer wagons laden with tin and pewter household utensils, and one wagon full of treasure—silver and gold crosses, chalices, candleholders, censers—pillaged from Christian churches. There were other wagons filled with grains, breads, vats of wine especially, and shiny trinkets of little value themselves except for their gleam in the sun's reflection. Geoffrey dismounted, climbed up onto the treasure wagon throwing gold and silver coins out by the handfuls, the soldiers gathered below scrambling to pick them up. The rest of the pilgrims started pushing and shoving to the other wagons in a frenzy grabbing what they could. That night Geoffrey's men were drinking and singing in front of their camp fires and braziers boasting of the villages and churches they had sacked almost to the gates of Nicea and of the "false" Christians they had killed. I wandered among the Lombards and Teutons. There was palpable resentment and envy over the plunder they had been denied. I knew that Rainald would have no choice but to satisfy their lust.

And he did. To their destruction.

Betrayal and Death at Xerigordos

It was only a few days later that a person who identified himself as a Greek Christian farmer had come to Civitot, seized by Lombards and brought before Rainald. He explained that he sought sanctuary from a band of Turkish brigands marauding throughout the countryside. Too small, he assured Rainald, to present a threat to us making it unnecessary to send out a scouting party. He reported the presence of a castle, Xerigordos, not far from Nicea, the capital of Rum, its sultan the Turk Qilij Arslan. According to the farmer, the sultan, on hearing of the presence of the crusaders, had secreted there all the treasures of Nicea including thousands of gold bezants. That night Rainald summoned his Lombard captains for a secret council in his tent, inviting the Teutonic nobles with whom he had sedulously curried favor. He shared the "farmer's" report and proposed a ruse, that they tell the Franks they were embarking on a mere foraging mission, their true objective the riches in Xerigordos. The plan was met gleefully. They would leave the next day.

I learned of Rainald's plan from Georgios who had a spy within Rainald's inner circle of captains—the Byzantines, as I had already come to know, were quite expert in the black arts of espionage but Georgios refused to give me the spy's name. The fewer people who knew of his existence, Georgios explained, the safer the spy would be. Georgios was skeptical of the farmer's report. He was familiar with the Turkish practice of sending spies into enemy camps both to gather intelligence and to plant false information. He warned me against going. It would be very dangerous. He expressed surprise that Qilij had so far seemed to tolerate crusader incursions into his territory, perhaps because their raids were limited to Christian targets. But now it was going to Nicea and beyond. He would surely respond. I had not joined Geoffrey Burel's expedition so my report to Tatikios was necessarily secondhand. This time I felt the need to witness events for myself.

On the following day Rainald's men were brimming with excitement at the prospect of adventure, singing bawdy songs as they marched out of Civitot. The Pechenegs and I followed in the rear, this time at Georgios's suggestion. We saw burned out villages and churches, Geoffrey's work several days earlier, the surviving villagers hastily burying their dead, hundreds of graves marked with no more than freshly turned dirt. As we passed, they had looks of panic fearing more massacres. They were left unmolested—they possessed nothing more to steal. We passed Nicea from a distance, an imposing fortress but no evidence of Qilij or his troops. The quiet seemed to me ominous. Rainald had now allowed word to spread of the Greek farmer's report and the promise of great wealth soon to be had at Xerigordos. Shouts went up when we sighted the castle, not especially imposing with only a single curtain wall and a ditch in front. We could see no defenders on the battlements. The gates were open. Perhaps Georgios was right—this was a trick. As we entered we saw to our astonishment that the castle was deserted, but only very recently for the cellars were well stocked with provisions.

The pilgrims, frenzied, began either racing throughout the castle, from room to room with hammers attempting to break through what they thought to be false walls, or digging holes in the castle grounds, all expecting to find chests of gold, those bezants they were promised. The Pechenegs and I dismounted and leading our horses by the reins wandered about the bailey. I walked to a small stream under one of the walls feeding into a cistern, half full, in a corner of the castle. No water flowed and yet the bed was still muddy with some standing water indicating the flow had ceased within the day. Had it been diverted? My apprehension increased.

It was at this moment I heard military horns blaring from a distance outside the walls. I raced through an arched passageway, up a tower to the parapet. There, coming toward the castle, were a thousand Turkish horsemen, perhaps more, in a slow cadence to the steady beat of drums. This had indeed been a trap. Qilij Arslan knew us well. Gold was the bait. We were the prey, caged. Georgios had been correct. That was no Greek farmer at all but a Turkish spy. This would be the first, but not the last, time I experienced the cunning deceptions of the Turks. Panic gripped the pilgrims. Greed was no longer a priority. It was survival. Geoffrey's men raced up to the parapets, crossbows in hand, spanned, ready to release their bolts at any Turk within range. But the Turks showed no interest in assault. Instead, they merely posted squadrons before two posterns to prevent escape, the bulk of the force in front of the main gate. They pitched their tents and settled in. Every night I scaled steps up to a turret watching them as they sat in front of their campfires, laughing with one another, female voices, musical instruments playing, Turks and their women dancing. Merriment. They were just waiting. There was no hurry.

Although it was late September the heat was insufferable. There was little respite from the sun except refuge in the cool of the castle rooms. Within two days the cistern had run dry. As days passed the pilgrims became more frenzied for water, dipping their clothes into the moist bed of the stream, squeezing out the muck, sucking what water they could; laying in the bed covering themselves with mud; urinating into the cupped hands of their comrades, drinking it to satiate thirst; bleeding their horses and donkeys, sucking out the blood; frantically digging into the ground, this time not for bezants but for water. One evening we received a light rain, more a sprinkle. The pilgrims raced out, stripping off their shirts to feel the wet on their skins, opening their mouths to taste the water, greedily licking their lips. The situation had become desperate. I too suffered like the rest, listless, my muscles aching, nauseous. I could see that Georgios and his Pechenegs suffered as I but their warrior ethos forbade them from showing it. It was only a matter of time. This was not a stalemate. It was checkmate.

It was the seventh day. I was resting, my eyes closed, in a corner of the castle where there was intermittent shade depending on the shifting clouds. The interior rooms were already full of fugitives from the scorching heat. I saw Rainald mount his horse, with difficulty raising his foot to slip into the stirrup and then on the third attempt finally lifting himself into the saddle. He was handed a spear with a white kerchief tied to its point. Accompanied by two horsemen he passed through the gate toward the Turkish camp, their horses as unsteady as Rainald. I was intensely curious and slowly, step by step, resting on every third, climbed up to the parapet and looked out. By then Rainald had already entered the enemy's camp riding to a tent, pennants hung at each corner drooping without a breeze, the quarters of their commander. With help he dismounted and entered. Some time passed and Rainald reemerged, mounted his horse, and returned to the castle. News of the visit had spread quickly; the pilgrims, some crawling, left their cool refuge to gather in the courtyard. He entered the castle and from atop his horse addressed us, though his voice so weak that I strained to hear him.

"My friends. I met this day with the sultan's captain, Elchanes, under a flag of peace. He has agreed to our safe passage in exchange for surrender of the castle."

Cries of joy poured out. "We're saved!" "God has not deserted us!" "We shall live!"

Rainald raised his hand for silence. "Yes, God is still with us. Tomorrow, at dawn, we shall march out under Turkish escort. But the captain exacted a condition. You are to bring nothing with you, especially weapons. We are to leave our swords and spears, any implements that could be used for attack, in a pile here in the castle. I agreed to that."

His voice now rising, trying to summon up what strength remained in him, "God has again shown His mercy. Tomorrow. Daybreak." We all fell to our knees in a prayer of thanksgiving, all except the suspicious Georgios and his Pechenegs.

I returned to my corner, exhausted, and fell asleep to be wakened shortly after by Georgios shaking my shoulder. "Oderic. I will come for you after dark. There's news." He said nothing more. Darkness fell and as promised Georgios came to fetch me. By this time the pilgrims had left the cool of the castle rooms for the greater warmth outside to sleep. Georgios, followed by his Pechenegs, led me into a room. Waiting for us was one of Rainald's captains whom I recognized from the council meeting with Peter days earlier. This was Georgios's spy, a Lombard minor noble.

"Rothari, tell us what you know," Georgios ordered. "We haven't much time." After returning to Civitot later I asked Georgios how he was able to recruit him. He simply pulled out a pouch of coins and jingled it. Fortunately Rothari, to my surprise, was rather fluent in Greek having been raised in Sicily, once a Byzantine colony.

"Rainald has betrayed us," he said, "all of us. It's true he asked for safe passage and the request was granted, but only for Lombard and Teutonic nobles and their men-at-arms. We will be permitted to march out without harm but once beyond the gates we must surrender to the Turks. Then, we either renounce our faith or be executed. Those who convert will be taken to Aleppo, or Damascus, or Baghdad—I don't know where—and sold into slavery. Only the nobles and their captains are informed of the plan; the soldiers know nothing. Elchanes insisted that it must be all or none of us, the better price the sultan can obtain at the slave markets."

I was astonished by the base treachery. I had come to suspect Rainald's duplicitous, cunning, and self-interested character. But I never dreamed of his capacity for betrayal of this magnitude.

"And did his lieutenants agree?" one of the Pechenegs asked.

Rothari merely shrugged his shoulders and lifted his arms, palms upraised. "What alternative did they have? Slavery or our lives. How would you have chosen?"

"Why are *you* here?" I asked.

"I have no desire to spend my life as a slave to heathen Turks. Better to die a Christian warrior than live as an apostate. At least with you there's a chance. A small one, I suppose, but a chance."

"What about the rest of the pilgrims? What does Elchanes intend?" I asked.

Again, Rothari shrugged his shoulders. "Rainald asked. Elchanes merely answered that he would deal with them as he sees fit, that they must answer for the destruction they inflicted earlier on the sultan's land. They will remain in the castle after we leave. Rainald is under no illusion what 'sees fit' means."

We all became silent, stunned by this information. "Does anyone have an idea what we are to do?" Georgios asked. "Our choices are few."

From one of the Pechenegs "It's dark. Perhaps we can escape."

"We're surrounded, by over a thousand Turks," Georgios answered. "And our horses are weak, no strength to race through their camp and outrun them if they pursue us, as they surely will. That won't work."

"Then," said another, "let's fight. Hopeless, I know, but better to die as a glorious warrior."

In in those moments, my mind raced. I knew that, after our troops left the castle, its gates would be closed and there would be a merciless slaughter of all within. No one would escape. Only a bold plan, a very bold one, might work. I thought of Nish. We would each have a role to play. Before we parted for the night Georgios asked if I still had the letter of introduction from Samuel ben Meier. I handed it to him.

* * *

Sleep eluded me. I both dreaded and looked forward to the morning, the uncertainty of our fate too much to bear. It came soon enough. At dawn the gates were opened to admit a company of Turkish cavalry. They all dismounted except for their captain Elchanes and his sergeant. Elchanes motioned with the sweep of his hand for his troops to post themselves around the perimeter of the castle, the Turks looking at the throng of pilgrims quite indifferently, betraying not the slightest sense of what was to follow. Rainald's men, disarmed, were already either mounted or on foot in formation. The pilgrims, anxious yet joyful, had gathered behind them expecting to follow Rainald and his men out of the castle. Elchanes, his horse standing steady beside the gate, motioned for them to pass through. They did. The pilgrims started to follow but in that moment the gates closed and Turkish soldiers repositioned themselves in front facing the pilgrims, hands on their swords. Their demeanor had in an instant changed to a grim and steady glare. Confusion now gripped the pilgrims. They were frozen, bewildered, uncertain what would happen or what they were to do.

I heard from outside the walls the clatter of horse hooves. The gates were opened and through it came hundreds of Turkish cavalry, whooping, laughing, their swords drawn. The slaughter began. On seeing the Turks gallop in some pilgrims fell to their knees, their hands clasped in prayer, either looking down to the ground in prayer or toward heaven imploring God's mercy. Others began fleeing in every direction, but where to hide? Those not immediately cut down sought refuge in the castle's interior, cowering in the rooms, the Turks following, bloodlust in their shouts and terrified shrieks from pilgrims. Others ran up the steps to the parapets chased by Turks, crawling over one another, pulling those ahead out of the way and pushing them over the stairway to the ground below. Those who reached the top raced along the wall-walk or leapt over the battlements, dying either way. The only survivors were the loveliest boys and girls who were rounded up for the soldiers' own wicked pleasures or to be sold in slave markets. It seemed over in the wink of an eye. Silence descended except for moans of pain from some of the fallen. They were dispatched immediately. The slaughter, but for the youth, was complete. Though not quite.

As Rainald's men were forming, the Pechenegs, Rothari, and I mounted our horses unnoticed, backing them up into a darkened corner facing the courtyard. Georgios was in front, one of his Pecheneg soldiers to his side slightly behind; Rothari and I, our hands bound in rope behind our backs, brought up the rear with the other two Pechenegs flanking us. We watched the slaughter quietly without moving. And we waited. One of the Turkish horsemen, the sergeant I think, trotting along the perimeter and over the fallen bodies looking for any yet alive, noticed us. He called out to his captain, who turned his head in our direction, obviously surprised to find any survivors. Elchanes approached. Georgios was impassive, his eyes expressing no more than curiosity, not fear. Elchanes addressed him. The Pecheneg next to Georgios was fluent in Turkish, his mother a Turk, translated for us.

"This is Georgios Vardanes," the Pecheneg introducing Georgios, "Captain of the Imperial Guard, Protector of the Supreme Basileus Alexios Komnenos of the Roman Empire." Georgios had promoted himself.

Without waiting for a response from the Turkish captain, Georgios intervened. "I have a warrant signed by the Basileus himself with his seal for the arrest of these two miscreants," turning in his saddle to glare at Rothari and me. "They fled from imperial justice, trying to conceal themselves among these marauders. But we tracked them down and they are now our prisoners."

I could easily tell that Elchanes was perplexed by this turn of events. He just stared at Georgios. "What offense have them committed?"

"Treason. They conspired to assassinate the Basileus. I intend to take them to Constantinople where they will be fairly tried and then executed. Slowly, I expect. The 'four splits.'" With that, Georgios turned his horse and nudged it beside my own, drew his sword and with its pointed end poked me in the chest and then, for full measure, delivered a solid blow with the flat side of his blade to my back, more vigorously than I would have hoped—perhaps repayment for the humiliation I had inflicted on him at Nish but enough that its force knocked me forward onto my horse's neck and head. "This one's the ringleader; the other his accomplice. Here's the warrant," pulling Samuel ben Meier's letter from inside his jerkin and handing it to the captain. Elchanes studied it. This was the decisive moment I feared. At Nish, I had been confident an unlettered Pecheneg soldier would not recognize Hebrew. I was uncertain now. Even without understanding the exchange between Elchanes and our Pecheneg I sensed he was an educated man, less likely to be deceived by such a simple artifice as had Georgios.

The captain rolled the letter back up and returned it to Georgios. "Well, I don't know. I can't make a decision without the sultan's permission. He's in Nicea. I shall take you there."

During our time at Civitot, over a campfire, Georgios had once told me that only my absolute confidence and imperiousness had saved me at Nish. He had learned. "These men have committed treason. The Basileus demands speedy justice! Turks and Byzantines have lived in peace. Not two years ago my Basileus warned your sultan of a plot against him, saving his life. Harboring traitors to the Empire would be regarded as an act of war. Whether I live or not, he will learn that his officers were arrested by the sultan in the lawful pursuit of their duties. Kill us or release us. You have a choice, Captain. Make it! Now!" Elchanes said not a word, sitting quietly, thinking. He motioned for his men to let us pass.

The Battle of Civitot

The ride back to Civitot was slow, our horses weakened as much as we from thirst. We found water in the streams and some food in burned out village homes. My back ached from Georgios's blow but I held no grudge. I owed my life to him. Perhaps its severity was necessary for theatrical effect. That, however, did not relieve my pain. We had just arrived at Civitot, its outskirts, and there on a broad field crusaders were massing, apparently for another expedition. I saw Peter speaking with Geoffrey Burel and other nobles. I spurred my horse toward them, dismounted, and walked up to Peter, pulling him by a sleeve to move out of earshot of the others.

"What's happening here?" I demanded to know. By this time my deference to Peter had sorely diminished.

"Geoffrey Burel . . ." Peter began to answer.

Geoffrey heard his name mentioned and stomped over. He was in an angry mood, for what reason I couldn't tell. "What is it you need Oderic? Father Peter and I were talking. I'm certain you have better things to do, like writing letters to that imposter of an emperor. Oh, yes, I know. You serve better as a scrivener of falsehoods than as a warrior in service to God. And right now, it's warriors we need. Go on about your monkish business. Write a letter. Leave us!"

My belly now reeked of Geoffrey Burel. I had lost patience with him, though I confess I'm uncertain whether I ever had any. "What in the name of holy Jesus are you doing?" I retorted. "Another hotheaded adventure? Have you not caused enough trouble. And yet you never seem satisfied. When will this end?"

"If you must know, my puerile monk, we have just received word from Greek farmers that Rainald has captured both the castle of Xerigordos and more importantly Nicea. And now, as I spend idle time talking with a foolish knave of a youth, he is claiming for himself their riches, treasures that belong to God and that should be shared with us. We are leaving to take what is ours. Tell that to your godless emperor!"

"Geoffrey Burel," I replied angrily, "you are indeed a fool. At Semlin. At Nish. And now at Civitot. Those 'Christian farmers', as you call them, are Turkish spies. Probably the same ones who promised Rainald that the sultan had secreted gold at Xerigordos. There *was* no gold. It was a trap. We just returned. Rainald betrayed us and opened the castle to the Turks. He is now a captive. The pilgrims are all dead. Slaughtered. This is the same deception."

On hearing this Peter's knees buckled, sinking down. "No! No! This can't be true. All dead?"

"Yes. Every one. And now this buffoon," turning to Geoffrey, "wants to lead your people into another trap. And a trap it will be. Father Peter," this time my voice softening, "it is time for you to assert your leadership. Call a council. Let it decide."

"Yes. Yes. You're right. A council," Peter answered meekly without the solid conviction I had hoped to hear.

Geoffrey could bear this no longer. His fury was uncontrolled, anger fever pitch. With his clenched fist he hit me in the side of my head, knocking me to the ground. Georgios, only five steps away, moved quickly forward but without drawing his sword. Georgios was going to beat him to death with his hands. I knew that. I raised my head, looked at him, understanding his intent. "No Georgios!" He stopped, helped me regain my footing, all the time glaring at Geoffrey, looking for an excuse, any excuse, to attack.

The council convened later that day. All the Frankish nobles attended. Geoffrey too, though he stayed in the back. This was *my* meeting. I would command it. "My Lords," I began "you have been deceived by Turkish spies. My Pecheneg sergeant," turning my head to acknowledge Georgios beside me, "and I have just returned from Xerigordos. Rainald betrayed us. All were killed. We passed by Nicea. It is fully intact. If you engage in this foolish expedition you can expect the same fate as befell our brothers and sisters. We must wait for aid from the emperor. I shall write him a letter." Turning now to Peter, "You will leave for Constantinople with my letter. A ship awaits you in the harbor. You must go immediately! I do not doubt that, as we speak, Qilij Arslan is plotting his assault on Civitot. We *must* prepare defenses."

"Yes." Peter responded, less with resolution than with a whimper. "I agree. My Lords, give me but eight days. I shall return with a Byzantine host. Do nothing until then. What say you? Eight days?" There was a murmur, but only a murmur, of agreement from the nobles. Perhaps a grumble? I couldn't tell. They had clearly not understood the gravity of their situation. The promise of plunder by the Turkish spies, despite my unmasking, was burning in their bellies. I feared we would be fortunate to restrain them even for eight days. I quickly returned to the outpost and wrote a letter to Tatikios, then racing delivered it to Peter waiting for me at the dock.

"Peter. Make haste! No delay!"

The days passed with no sign of Qilij Arslan. And with each day the sense of urgency to prepare for his attack waned. Slowly, news of the massacre at Xerigordos filtered further and further through the crusader ranks, the stories becoming more preposterous with each retelling: that captive Christians, one by one, were released into a field outside the castle for Turks to improve their bow skills on moving targets; that they impaled the women, naked, burning them alive over spits and eating their flesh; that live babies were thrown into the air, the Turks competing with one another who could slice it more cleanly before it fell to the ground, the prize a Christian woman for the night. The truth was horrible enough. Anger was slowly but incrementally swelling. I feared it could not be quenched. And it wasn't. Eight days passed. Then nine. And now ten.

Geoffrey Burel saw his opportunity. He called a council. I was not invited but I came nonetheless. Georgios urged me against it. My mind was set. He conceded but, understanding there may be hostility against me, insisted that he and his Pechenegs be present. The deliberations were brief.

"My Lords," Geoffrey began, "Peter vowed he needed no more than eight days to return with an imperial army. Ten have passed. The emperor has no intention of coming to our aid. Wrongs against our people must be righted. And righteous anger can only be assuaged with the sword. *This is the time for action!*" His bombast was answered with cheers from the nobles.

Walter the Penniless urged caution and patience. "My Lords. Yes, it has been ten days, but the emperor *will* come. Has he not been faithful to his promise of providing an open market for provisions, ships arriving daily? Did he not replenish our coffers?"

He was shouted down. "Open markets?" jeered one. "Yes, but why should we pay for *anything*? He wants only to recover his own lands. He brought us here as fodder for the heathens who feed on us like foragers." Another: "Those coffers he *'replenished'* were *our* coins, stolen by his troops. We owe the emperor not a whit." And another: "We need *nothing* from the emperor. We have God on our side!"

Walter tried to continue but was interrupted by Geoffrey, sneering, his lips curling, rising to one corner in disgust, "My Lord Walter, you have but two or three thousand *peasants* under your command. Few men-at-arms. Why do we even listen to you?"

Walter's strong voice at the beginning was reduced to a sniffle. "Let us at least send out scouts before venturing forth. What if Qilij Arslan *is* waiting for us?"

"If this Turk had wanted to attack, he would have done so," Geoffrey retorted, casually dismissing Walter's sensible suggestion. "He fears us. He fears our God. Enough talk! Tomorrow we leave at dawn for Nicea. We will first rescue our comrades seized at Xerigordos and the Turks will pay dearly for their slaughter of Christian martyrs. After that, Nicea! Is there agreement?" The nobles erupted into shouts: "*God wills it!*" The meeting concluded. They would be satisfied only with blood vengeance and plunder.

* * *

The day broke, October 21. At the front was Geoffrey Burel leading all his men-at-arms on horses, armored in mail, six abreast, their spears raised with pennants flying, horns blaring. They were followed by pilgrims on foot, their carts and wagons empty expecting to fill them later with booty; and then priests chanting hymns, holding clerical staffs. They numbered in the thousands. There was glad rejoicing among the army, eager for revenge and especially the promise of treasure in Nicea. They had no idea how impregnable the city was. Even had they known, they likely would not have cared. The only persons left behind were the old, the sick and wounded, women, and youth too young to fight. I had wanted to join them but Georgios strongly urged against it. This was folly, he said. Only evil will come of it. He had advised against me accompanying the crusaders to Xerigordos. I hadn't listened. He had been right. This time I accepted his counsel.

Georgios and I followed the army on our horses. Civitot itself sat on a plain. Three miles out the terrain gradually changed into more mountainous country, all the way to Nicea. At that point we stopped to watch. They entered a long, narrow defile, forcing the soldiers to reform, now three abreast. There were escarpments on both sides with barren strips at their rise, twenty feet wide, behind them thick forest. Geoffrey and his retainers had fallen back to bring up the rear, Walter the Penniless, the reluctant warrior, apparently with a change of heart, led the vanguard. It had nearly reached the top of the pass where I saw two fallen trees blocking further advance. The horsemen slowed and then stopped just before the trees considering the best way around them I supposed. And while they were motionless, Turkish archers on their horses, bows in hand and quivers full of arrows hanging from their saddles, quietly emerged from behind the trees to the edge of the escarpment. Without any order being given, at least that I could hear, they began unleashing a hail of arrows directing them at the horsemen in front. They did so methodically, without apparent hurry. Walter was the first to fall.

Panic and chaos followed. The cavalry at the front turned their horses and began galloping back into the horsemen just behind, who wheeled their horses around doing the same. They were cut down by arrows as they fled, their riderless horses continuing to run. And then more Turkish horsemen appeared on the rise further down and began releasing volleys. The sky was black with arrows. Soldier after soldier, pilgrim after pilgrim fell. The wagons and carts couldn't be turned, blocking those behind.

Arrows now depleted, the Turks slung their bows over their shoulders, guided their horses down the escarpments, swords drawn, attacking any crusader still standing. Those pilgrims at the rear, those who had not yet entered the pass, fared no better. The Turks were waiting for them unseen behind a small hill. As Geoffrey and the pilgrims began fleeing back to Civitot, Turkish horsemen emerged from around the hill, in two extended lines abreast, archers in front and lancers behind. The archers with the same methodical precision as I had seen moments before, without dismounting, began discharging all their arrows. Finished, they pulled their horses right and left making a wide opening for the lancers, their spears couched under their arms, galloping at full force into the throng of crusaders. They were then followed by the archers, now reformed, their swords swinging.

Rescue by Emperor Alexios

Georgios and I galloped back to the camp shouting that our army had perished and that the Turks would be in Civitot at any moment. We needed to escape. Hundreds of pilgrims had remained in camp. None was a warrior. They were peasants. We were defenseless. At that moment Geoffrey Burel and five of his horsemen, the sole survivors, came galloping into the camp. Before he had even dismounted I ran up to him. "What do we do?" He just stared down at me, his body quivering, shaking his head in despair, mumbling incoherently. Pilgrims had gathered around Geoffrey's horse as well, looking up to him expectantly for leadership, waiting for an order, any order. None came. I looked into their eyes, blank, terrified, and in shock. In that instant I recalled a moment from my youth in Rheims when I was searching for a flock of sheep attacked by wolves outside the city. I found them not far in the forest, huddled together, just staring at me, the same blank, terrified, and shocked expression. Our plight had now worsened—no soldiers, no commander. We were doomed for I knew Qilij Arslan would not ignore us. I never saw Geoffrey Burel again. He had much to answer for. There was no Christian charity left in me, at least for him. I hoped God's judgment would be speedy and merciless.

Georgios quickly strode up to me. "I will take command. You translate." He stepped forward, turned to the pilgrims, I translating as quickly as I could alternating between the languages of the Franks and Teutons. "Look!" Georgios exclaimed, pointing to dust clouds in the distance. "Those are Turks! They will soon be here. We must escape!" But to where,

I wondered? Not to the outpost. It was too small to hold us all, its narrow gate closed and no time for Georgios to negotiate sanctuary with its commander. Georgios had a different idea. "Over there," pointing to an abandoned fortress a quarter mile away. "Leave your belongings! Run!"

No persuasion was needed. The pilgrims in mass began racing for it leaving the others behind. Mothers and fathers picked up their crying babies running as fast as they could to catch up; parents frantically scoured the camp, shouting the names of their children; young boys and girls either huddled together for mutual protection or concealed themselves in the undergrowth. Their wails still ring in my ears even now, many years later. It will never pass.

It was a small fortress—I never knew its name—no more than a half-bowshot in width and length, dilapidated from lack of service, its walls only partially intact, the ashlar blocks having been cannibalized by local villagers and carted away to build their own homes. We raced through the gate, stout oak yes but each door hanging obliquely and tenuously by a single rusty hinge. Georgios saw a metal bar leaning against a wall. With help from his Pechenegs he shifted the doors so that they were flush and then slipped the bar into the gate's metal brackets securing it. Before the gate closed, I looked at Civitot. The Turks were already there, galloping through the camp, cutting down or trampling everyone before them not sparing even the few priests who were left ministering to the pilgrims, praying over them as they were kneeling and sobbing. The only ones to survive were the youth. I dare not think or speak of their fates. Work in the camp completed, the Turks now headed for us. They paused in front of the fortress, careful to be out of bowshot range not knowing what weapons we possessed. Had they known we had none, they would have pressed the assault without hesitation. Instead, and from the safety of distance, they began unleashing their arrows, one after another, high into the air, their arc ending in the middle of the fortress. "Arrows!" Georgios shouted. "Take cover!" We did, but the command came too late for some.

By good fortune, the sun was setting and the rain of arrows ceased. Daylight on the morrow would bring them back. It wouldn't take long. We would be finished. There was a half-moon that night partially illuminating the castle's interior, sufficient to find our way about. Georgios continued to take charge. The castle lacked any battlements, the walls no more than ten or so feet tall, simple enough to scale with ladders and hooked ropes had the Turks possessed any. Worse, there were gaps in the walls, easily penetrated. Fortunately, a number of ashlar blocks were scattered about the courtyard, thrown down by villagers to be scavenged later. Georgios motioned for the pilgrims to follow him. He walked the interior perimeter of the walls, at every gap assigning a small team to clean out the cavity and plug it with blocks or timber. In the meantime, one of the Pechenegs had discovered an armory, a few rusted swords and some spears, their hafts half-broken with rusted heads but at least their points were sharp. They were distributed to the pilgrims strong enough to use them, the others told to find wood and metal for clubs and even rocks for throwing, whatever they could use to defend themselves. Georgios gathered them in the courtyard, those not at work reconstructing the walls, organizing them in a loose formation ten lines front to back and instructing them in the rudimentary uses of their weapons—the thrust, the swing, the parry— his Pechenegs serving for demonstration. But these were peasant farmers, butchers, tradesmen. Not warriors. They handled their new weapons awkwardly though with a sense of purpose. Georgios continually encouraged them, praising their "skill" to boost confidence, but he had no illusions. Yet he was determined we would not go down easily.

That night the Pechenegs and I gathered faggots for a small fire. The days had been excruciatingly hot. The nights equally cold. The five of us sat cross-legged around it. I listened as they exchanged stories of battles with the Cumans, their lives in the north before joining the imperial army, their wives, their children. One of Pechenegs inquired about my past. I tried to deflect but he would have none of it. He continued to press. I spoke of my life at La Charité, events in Mainz, and the stabbing of Thomas of Marle with my pectoral cross, an act for which I felt no repentance. This brought hearty laughter. "Hmm," one Pecheneg mused, "Oderic, the warrior-priest." I never forgot those words. Georgios wanted to know about Rebecca. On that subject, I was more reticent, unwilling to reveal my heart merely answering that she was under my protection, no more. My reluctance betrayed my feelings. "Your 'protection'," Georgios smirked though without the slightest hint of mockery. The Pechenegs chuckled. Georgios let the subject drop. He and I then reminisced about Nish and how thoroughly I had deceived him. We both laughed, whatever grudge he bore had eroded as time passed. He even apologized, in his Pecheneg fashion, for striking me so severely at Xerigordos, then quickly adding with a grin "You deserved it".

Before retiring for the night, Georgios withdrew a dagger from his leather scabbard and handed it to me. It was a Pecheneg dagger, double-edged, ten inches long, almost a small sword, its quills curved downward, the grip made of some exotic wood I could not identify—Georgios himself didn't know—the detail of its carving quite breathtaking. "This belonged to my father and to his father before him. You'll have to return it to me after we kill the Turks. If not, you will find my father in Constantinople. Tomorrow, you stay behind me. The Basileus has entrusted your safety to me. I shall not fail him," then pausing, adding simply, "nor I shall fail you."

* * *

We retired for the night, without blankets, drawing as close as possible to the warmth of the fire. Daybreak came. Georgios was the first to rise and immediately shouted for the pilgrims to man their posts at the walls, the remainder to assemble in the same battle-line formation practiced the previous evening. That was where he expected the primary assault to come. Georgios stood in front, sword in hand, alone, facing the gate only feet away. The Pechenegs and I were directly behind him, they beside me on the left and right. They drew their swords, I the dagger Georgios had given me. Knowing the attack would come at any moment, he turned to the throng of pilgrims behind him. "My friends. We shall fight to the death. These Turks will soon understand our Christian mettle!" And, with that, he turned around to face the gate again, thrusting the point of his sword into the ground, holding it at arm's length. Just waiting. Watching. Georgios was a natural hero, his indomitable spirit coming as easily to him as his taciturn manner. I had never met anyone like him. He seemed afraid of nothing.

The attack did come, and quickly. We heard Turkish shouts and the sound of timber beams pounding against the gate. Thud, after thud, after thud, reverberating throughout the castle. The gate shook with each blow. But it held. Silence followed. It seemed the Turks had become impatient with their makeshift battering ram. Then we heard a scratchy noise, dry brush being set against the doors. Smoke began drifting through the gaps in the doors above and below. Then flickers of yellow between the crevices of the doors' vertical planks. The gate, dry as tinder, was on fire! In the meantime, Turks were trying to squeeze through the stones piled in the walls' gaps, pushing them through. As each face appeared, a pilgrim pierced it with a sword or spear. The Turks changed tactics, now releasing arrows at the defenders through narrow chinks as other Turks continued to clear openings. It would not be long. In what I believed to be my last moments I thought of Rebecca. Who would take care of her? Why were we punished by fate, she a Jew and I a Christian. And how I would die without ever feeling her embrace again, her love. Thoughts that rushed through my mind so quickly it takes more time to write than to think of them.

The fortress gate was now in flames. Turks had successfully squeezed through the wall gaps, only a few within but more following, pilgrim defenders lying on the ground pierced by arrows. It was over. But in that instant I heard the sound of a trumpet, two long blasts and one short, Turkish I thought by its timbre, unfamiliar to me. In that moment the Turks within the walls began rushing back into the wall gaps trying frantically to squeeze through. The Pechenegs cut every one down. A ladder lay on the ground not far from me. Setting it against the wall, I climbed up. The Turks were mounting their horses and galloping away to the east, to Nicea. My gaze turned to Civitot. There, I saw a fleet of imperial warships, *direma*, ten I counted, three decks of rowers propelling them gently into the harbor, each capable of holding two to three hundred men. They were docking two-by-two at the wharf for it could accommodate no more at any one time. Turcopole mercenaries were disembarking, leading their horses down the gangplanks.

Alexios had arrived! We were saved.

* * *

Thus, on October 21, 1096, Peter the Hermit's noble dream of a crusade of *pauperes Christi*, "the Poor of Christ", to liberate Jerusalem from the Muslims ended. I believed in that dream, though in time I became convinced that the Holy Land should be shared by all "People of the Book," as the Muslims called Christians and Jews, living together peacefully. Peter I'm sure, although we never discussed it, would have agreed. In the end his vision was corrupted by men, vain and covetous, leading the poor who followed blindly yielding to their own baser instincts. He objected to my description of them as "rabble" claiming they were merely "undisciplined" and needed God's guidance. Both are true. But they paid mightily for these failings. Of the many thousands who followed Peter, only a few hundred survived, their privations to continue later during the march through Anatolia. After the "Battle of Civitot" as it has been wrongly named—less a "battle" than a massacre, expertly and mercilessly executed—Peter's role in the crusade changed. Still venerated, yes. But without influence. I think of Proverbs:

> *The integrity of the upright will guide them,*
> *But the crookedness of the treacherous will destroy them.*

This ends Book VI of *Jerusalem Falls!* Book VII begins.

hOMAGE TO The EMPEROR

Reunion with Rebecca. house of Apollo and Aphrodite. Alexios
Komnenos Meets with Lord Bohemond and Count Raymond.
Emissary to Duke Godfrey. Duke Godfrey Attacks Blachernae.
Crusader Princes Pledge Their homage. My Next Adventure.

Reunion with Rebecca

In the two months since leaving for Civitot Rebecca stayed with her cousin in Galata, meeting more cousins and their friends. Though Jews, none knew Hebrew or only enough to recite prayers. This forced Rebecca to learn Greek, they patiently schooling her. She would also stroll into shops to practice with strangers. By the time I returned she had achieved passable skills. I had periodically sent her letters, invariably minimizing the dangers I encountered, reassuring her that I was under the protection of Georgios and his Pechenegs. But rumors were rife, of Xerigordos and the battle at Civitot. Rebecca lived constantly in fear for my safety. Tatikios then sent her word of my return on the following day at the harbor of the Great Palace, generally reserved for the emperor, a single galley for the surviving pilgrims landing in the Golden Horn. As our ship slowly eased into the wharf Rebecca was waiting for me, a white handkerchief in her hand waving when she saw me. I leapt over the gunnel onto the floating dock, steadying myself as I raced to her. She jumped into my arms, I lifted her, she placing her face into my neck and I kissing her cheek. "Oh Oderic. I've been so scared. Afraid you would die. That you would never return. The Lord has blessed me."

"I promised I would come back," I replied tenderly. "And I have."

From the side of my eye I noticed Georgios standing rather awkwardly a few paces away as the other Pechenegs walked down the dock, nodding goodbye to me as they passed.

"Rebecca, this is Georgios Vardanes, Captain of His Majesty's Pecheneg Guards." I had decided to accept Georgios's self-promotion declared at

Xerigordos. I was not wrong. Tatikios promoted him the following day. Rebecca offered her hand and in Greek, to my surprise, greeted him. "Captain Georgios. My undying gratitude for protecting the life of Father Oderic. I am endlessly in your debt." He blushed slightly, bowed his head indicating thanks were unnecessary, and in his inimitable fashion turned to follow his companions without saying a word.

Hand in hand Rebecca and I walked to a tavern which had become our favorite. We shared our adventures of the past two months and, dispensing with wine that evening, drank *Tsipouro* brandy, its anise flavor so seductive that one glass inevitably led to another. Involved as we were with one another's company we had not noticed our condition but did so on rising unsteadily from the table. Arm around each other's waist for support, we stumbled back to our apartments.

house of Apollo and Aphrodite

Months passed. It was now April 1097. I continued working at the *scriptorium*. Under the tutorship of a chancery grammarian of Turkish I began studying the language, thinking it might enhance my value. The prefect agreed and generously modified my working hours in the afternoons. During that time Demetrios Doukas had found Rebecca employment in the household of a lady, wife of a member of Alexios's court. We continued our evening excursions. Tatikios arranged for us to use a modest coach from the palace stable reserved for administrative staff but generally available when we needed it. Thus we were able to explore more of the city, even visiting Rebecca's cousins and her new friends in Galata, crossing the Golden Horn by ferry.

Rebecca received an invitation to a wedding reception for one of her relatives at an inn not too distant from the Great Palace serving wealthy merchants visiting from other lands, a dining hall on its second floor prepared that night for the party. I was conflicted over apparel—what to wear? Shortly after returning from Civitot Tatikios had given me some finery in appreciation for my service: a double tunic, one worn over the other, of silk, the outer garment decorated with an intricate pattern of stars and moons in all their different phases; loose, billowing breeches in the Persian fashion made of woven *balzarine*, light cotton and wool; a flowing *chlamys* for a cloak, pinned with a golden brooch at the shoulder; and blue slippers trimmed in miniver fur and gold thread. I was accustomed to wool and linen, nothing this splendid. Now would be my first opportunity to wear them. I couldn't resist. I looked magnificent, at least in Rebecca's eyes. Too magnificent as events played out that evening.

The inn was north up the Mese and then down a side street, the Via Egnatia, named after the renowned Roman highway from the Adriatic to Constantinople. It was a warm night perfect for walking. We became lost in conversation passing one street after the other without noticing, continuing forward until we reached the Aqueduct of Valens. The *scriptorium's* prefect had warned me that this neighborhood was known for "villains" and "homes for wayward women," his sensibilities too delicate to call them "brothels". We walked down a side street believing this to be the Via Egnatia, then down another, and one more. I was completely disoriented. We came to a lane, dark, tenements five stories high served by broken stairways with brambles reaching to their eves, lights in their windows but otherwise no evidence of life on the street except for dogs running freely, feeding on street rubbish, growling at one another. I sensed evil lurking in every corner, at any moment a robber springing out from behind a closed door. We turned around and began hurriedly walking back. There were peals of laughter close by. I followed the sound. We needed directions. Perhaps they could help.

We came to a public bath, "The House of Apollo and Aphrodite" its sign read above the door. Rebecca wanted to remain outside and wait for me but I hesitated to leave her alone. Taking her arm I led her inside, reassuring her that we were there only to seek directions. Through the vestibule we came into a large colonnaded room lit by torches bracketed to the walls, the steam so thick I was at first unable to see. My eyes quickly adjusted. There were two pools, one larger than the other. In the former, seated by each other, were men and women and men and men caressing one another; in the second men and boys. Terracotta statues, the lips of each painted in magenta and their cheeks in an orange rouge, lined the walls: one of Apollo, a laurel garland on his head, his member upright and stiff, far out of proportion to his physique; Medusa, two adders wrapped around her neck sucking on her breasts and a third around her waist probing her cavity; and a third, man and boy, in an embrace too repulsive for me to describe. Along the walls between the statues were cubicles, only partially concealed by curtains, with writhing bodies and sounds of grunts and moans.

All of this I absorbed in a moment. But what particularly caught my attention was a man, tall, thin, stooped, a long black beard woven in five braids, on his head a tall linen hat, his eyes narrow and dark. I thought immediately of Beelzebub, prince of evil. With his left hand he was grasping firmly the wrist of a young boy, shapely, hair down to his shoulders, naked, fear clearly in his eyes. To his right a rather portly female, not unattractive in face, unclothed from the waist up trying to appear as seductive as she was able, her thighs undulating back and forth and with each movement her oversized breasts shaking up and down. He seemed to be negotiating with a well-dressed Greek who handed him a small pouch of coins and then roughly grabbed the boy, leading him toward a flight of stairs up to the second floor. This was indeed a brothel about which the prefect had warned me, and a dangerous one at that. We had to leave. But it was too late. The man noticed us and walked over followed by two others whose appearance was as ominous as his. He stopped in front of me, closely examining my clothes. Rebecca slipped behind me.

"Noble Sir," he began, his tone unctuous, bowing obsequiously, "I am Bardanes Laskaris, owner and your humble host. Welcome to the House of Apollo and Aphrodite. How can we serve you this evening? A bath perhaps? A private room?" glancing over at one of the cubicles.

"No, Master Bardanes," I answered politely, "My wife and I have lost our way. Perhaps you could direct me to the Via Egnatia. We're expected at a reception"

"A reception you say?" he replied slowly. "But you should be in no hurry. You just arrived. We have so many delights here to suit every taste," smirking maliciously. "A boy for you perhaps?" looking at me; "a man for her?" leering at Rebecca over my shoulder, "or one of our charming women quite proficient at satisfying every female desire?"

"No. Directions should be sufficient Sir."

At that he began stroking my silk tunic. "How fine. Magnificent even. My clothes are quite worn. How much? Or better yet, perhaps you'll permit me to borrow them. Naturally, they'll be returned."

I pushed his hand aside, and then straightening my posture as imperiously as I could, hoping that the same bravado which saved me at Nish would do so here. "This is a gift from the *Kuroplates* Tatikios, whom I serve, senior adviser to His Imperial Highness, the Basileus. We apologize for our intrusion and must be on our way."

"I know no *kuroplates* here. Is that what you call him?" My ploy had not worked. He looked back at his men. "Lads, how do you think I'd look in these clothes?" Without waiting for an answer his attention turned to Rebecca, still cowering. "Quite lovely. I think she would be a welcome addition to my stable. Our clients pay handsomely, especially for a beauty like her. What do you think Markos?" looking back at the man to his right.

"She would, Bardanes. And I know how to break her in."

"Yes," Bardanes answered, "I expect you do. She's yours."

"Rebecca! Run! *Run now!*" She needed no encouragement. "After them!" Bardanes shouted to his men. In the vestibule I grabbed a torch from its bracket, turned and began swinging it back and forth and then with a quick thrust hit the first in the face knocking him down, the second tumbling over him. That gave us a few moments. We reached the street. I had no idea where we were or which way to turn. I chose one. We ran as fast as we could, Bardanes's men, having regained their footing, in hot pursuit. By the merest good fortune around the corner we came to the Cistern of Arkadias, one of many in the city providing fresh water for household use. It had no door at the entrance for it was visited at all times of day and night by inhabitants. We scampered down the steps entering a cavernous underground vault, completely dark lit only by the torch in my hand. It was an imposing structure, four long rows of marble columns, each forty feet tall supporting three arches and a ceiling made of brick painted in gesso whitewash, the arches reaching to the back wall barely visible.

The floor was covered in water fed from the Aqueduct of Valens, tiny ripples shimmering in the reflected light from the white brick of the ceiling above. We stepped into it, water coming up to our waist, and waded forward as quickly as we could, water resisting every step. I could hear our pursuers racing down the steps. I looked back and in the dim light of my torch could see their daggers drawn. I waved my torch over the cistern to take a mental image of its configuration then doused it. Perfect darkness. "Don't worry," one shouted, "come back. We promise not to hurt you. We can be friends." We pushed ahead, I holding Rebecca's hand, groping from one column to another hoping to reach the cistern's end. In our haste, we could not avoid sloshing through the water. Bardanes's men would stop, listen, and then follow. I whispered to Rebecca to move as silently as she was able. They were getting closer. I slipped on the smooth marble floor, falling into the water up to my neck and in doing so released my grip on the torch which floated away. My only weapon. Rebecca helped me up. Recalling then the image I had taken of the cistern I led her to the side wall and from there groped my way forward. I bumped against something floating in the water. Feeling it, the object was a dinghy used by workmen to clean the cistern I assumed, its bow tied to a ring affixed in the wall. I continued probing the wall with my fingers and felt a small iron door next to the ring. It was bolted from the outside. Escape through that was not possible. I untied the knot. "Quick," I whispered to Rebecca, "get in."

I pushed the boat out and clambered aboard. There were oars lying on both sides but they would make noise so I crawled to the bow partially lying over it and with both hands paddled back to the entrance. When the splashing of Bardanes's men stopped, I stopped as well allowing the dinghy to glide; then after it began once more I paddled. Though the night was dark I could dimly see moonlight sneaking through the entrance onto the marble steps leading down. We were very close, ten paces away. Then Rebecca coughed, the dampness of the cistern affecting her. One of Bardanes's men, much closer than I expected and unseen by me, grabbed the dinghy's gunnel with his left hand and Rebecca's hair with the other trying to pull her out. She let out a scream. I looked back. There was enough light to see what had happened. I stood up, turned, seized an oar swinging it at his head. He released his grip on Rebecca. The boat began to rock side to side. I tried to maintain my balance, holding onto the gunnel with my right hand and awkwardly thrusting the oar at his face with my left. He warded off my blows. Then, straddling my legs on the sides of the curved hull to stabilize the boat, I held the oar in both hands, raised it and struck at the man's head once, then again, then again, and again, every strike delivered with equal fury but hitting water, not him. Until the last blow. I felt it bouncing off a hard object, his head. He slipped under the water. Unconscious or dead, I didn't care.

I helped Rebecca out of the dinghy and with my arm tightly around her waist assisted her up the steps into the street, coming to the Mese and then the Great Palace. We were just outside the Brazen Gate when Rebecca began limping. She had lost a shoe in the cistern and her foot was bleeding from walking on the rough pavement. I picked her up and carried her through the gate to her apartment, the guards allowing us to pass without challenge. I gently laid her down on the bed. With a cloth moistened from a ewer I washed her foot and covered her with a blanket. Her eyes were closed all the time. I sat on the side of her bed. She appeared so seraphic, so pure, the countenance of an angel. I tenderly kissed her forehead and was about to stand up when her eyes opened. She raised her hand to caress my cheek, gazing at me. "Yet again, my beloved Oderic, you've saved my life." I murmured something in response which I can't recall. "Please don't go."

I stayed.

Alexios Komnenos Meets with Lord Bohemond and Count Raymond

Two days later the prefect informed me that Tatikios wished to see me. I entered his office in the Great Palace. Tatikios was there and to my surprise Georgios as well, standing off to the side without acknowledging me. Georgios will always be Georgios. This was the first time I had seen him since Civitot.

"I heard of your adventure in the cistern," Tatikios began. "You wandered into dangerous territory, even by my city's standards. Seems like I *just* can't trust you to protect yourself," he said smiling. "You're too important to the Basileus; future service will be required of you. I've decided that Georgios will serve as your bodyguard." I looked surprised thinking this another uncongenial assignment for my new hero. "Oh, he volunteered," Tatikios said, sensing my uncertainty.

I looked at Georgios in surprise. He nodded but as always saying nothing. I looked back at Tatikios. "Well, he will be fine company for me," I said, an exaggeration but perhaps I did need protection after all.

Tatikios came to the point. "Great lords from the West are arriving in Constantinople with their armies every day now. They've taken three routes: some sailing from Italia across the Adriatic to the port of Dyrrachium, then on the Via Egnatia to Constantinople; others on the Bavarian Road along the Danube through Hungary and Bulgaria, the same route followed by you, your friend Peter the Hermit, and Duke Godfrey of Bouillon; and a third group, a Frankish army from southern Francia, through Italia then north around the Adriatic and south into Slovakia, land of the Slavs. They wish imperial ships to transport them across the Arm of Saint George into Anatolia."

"The emperor must be pleased," I said. "This is exactly the assistance he sought from the pope."

"Perhaps not." Tatikios replied. "You may know that we have suffered recently from a plague of locusts which have devoured our vines but not our wheat. Curious. The Basileus's oracle, a monk and his spiritual adviser, has divined that the Franks are like the locusts but instead of ravaging vines they will slay the sons of Ishmael in Anatolia, refraining from harming Christians. He believes this to be true. I, however, am sure they are indeed locusts but here to feed on *our* vines. I do know this much: the Basileus was hoping for experienced mercenaries, *soldiers*. These armies are filled with too many peasants; not our problem I suppose. The Basileus is ready to assist these crusaders in crossing the strait. In return he will demand a declaration of homage and loyalty from each prince that all lands they conquer in Anatolia, formerly part of our Empire, be reclaimed and held in his name."

"How does the emperor intend to accomplish that?" I asked.

"Well, they cannot cross into Anatolia without our ships. And besides," Tatikios said with a sly smile, "the Basileus can be very persuasive when he chooses. He understands what motivates these Latins. Negotiations will be held with each prince separately. He requires a translator. He asked for you."

I was baffled. "These negotiations will be complex," I protested. "The chancery already has so many translators, all more experienced than I. Why me?"

"True, but the Basileus trusts you. He was impressed with your candor when the two of you met. And besides, you *are* fluent in Frankish and Teutonic. More important, there is already suspicion between both the princes and the Basileus. Your role is unique. You understand the customs of the West and, because you are a monk, can earn their confidence. You will begin tomorrow when the Basileus meets with Bohemond, Lord of Taranto, at *Blachernae*."

"You wish me to act as a spy?" I by now understanding the Byzantines' insatiable appetite for intelligence.

Tatikios lingered silently over the question, answering carefully. "A spy? No. But if you can gain their trust and in doing so glean information which could usefully contribute to mutual understanding between our peoples, the Basileus naturally would be grateful." Yes. A spy. Before taking my leave, Tatikios advised me to resume wearing my pilgrim's garb. He thought I looked too Greek for these meetings. I did so and had my tonsure cut and my face shaved. I was a monk again.

The next day Georgios, my new guardian, and I rode to *Blachernae*. We entered the audience hall, I standing below the dais on which Alexios's throne was set. Bohemond entered accompanied by his nephew Tancred of Hauteville. They both bowed. Bohemond looked at me briefly, his glance displaying surprise at seeing a Latin monk and pilgrim present, let alone translating. He made no comment. Bohemond was a striking figure. Some forty years of age, he was much taller than most men and unlike others wore his black hair down to his shoulders giving him the appearance of a Northman: muscular, broad of shoulders and chest, yet a slender waist; his eyes blue, clear as sapphires; beardless; and walking without swagger, his posture straight as a spear. A warrior, as indeed he proved throughout our crusade.

"Welcome to New Rome, Lord Bohemond," Alexios greeted him. "We have looked forward to your arrival. It is a pleasure to see you once again and in more pleasing circumstances than in the past," he said smiling. Alexios was referring to Bohemond's invasion of his empire along the Adriatic coast years before. Bohemond had won every battle except the last, the decisive one, at Larissa. His invasion failed. Bohemond understood Alexios's implication.

"Your Majesty, I too am pleased to see you again. I come as your friend and ally."

Pleasantries followed, too inconsequential for me to relate. Alexios steered the conversation to the matter at hand. "Lord Bohemond. Your purpose here?"

"Your Majesty," Bohemond answered, "I ask your aid in transporting my army to Anatolia. And then we march to Jerusalem to liberate it from the pagans."

"Yes," Alexios responded, "I understand that. But we are intrigued about your intentions in Anatolia."

"I have no intentions except to defeat the Turks who surely will oppose us."

"Yes, of course they will. Lord Bohemond, we are both soldiers, men of action. Subtlety and indirection do not suit us. What do you plan with territories you conquer?"

Bohemond had plainly not expected this question nor the blunt manner in which it was asked. Alexios had a reason. He understood the nature of the Normans: skilled in war but wily, unscrupulous, and avaricious in character. Bohemond had invaded his empire before. But perhaps most important in Alexios's mind was the fact that Bohemond's patrimony had fallen to his undeserving younger brother, Bohemond holding only the territory of Taranto won by himself in war. He had no other estates. The emperor could not ignore Bohemond's ambitions. Alexios's suspicions later proved correct. Stammering, fumbling for an answer, "Your Majesty . . . I have not . . . given consideration to that."

"Come now," Alexios responded sharply, "We're quite sure you have. These lands were part of our Empire seized by the Turks. We do not object if you Latins establish your own principalities and rule them yourselves. But you will do so as satraps of the Empire, answering to us. No less."

"What do you wish from me?" Bohemond asked.

"The matter is simple. You and your fellow princes will pledge homage to us. This pledge will include a vow, sworn on a sacred relic, that all lands in Anatolia which belonged to the Empire will be reclaimed and ruled in its name. In return, we shall provide you with ships and open markets."

As Bohemond stood there silently, thinking and weighing, Alexios signaled to his Varangian captain who in turn motioned to a steward. The steward clapped his hands and immediately two chests were brought into the hall and set before Bohemond. Their lids were opened and even from several paces away I saw the glittering reflection of gold and silver coins, pendants with precious stones, bracelets, and other treasures. Bohemond simply stood there, dazzled, bewildered by such wealth. Alexios waited, watching him.

Turning to the emperor, "Your Majesty, I would be pleased to offer my homage and restore to you all territories wrongly seized by the pagans. But I would like to make a trivial request. Numerous armies are arriving from the West. They follow different lords. A single leader is essential if we are to be victorious. With great humility I would suggest you appoint me 'Grand Domestic of the East'. With that you can be assured of our fealty," he paused, "and of mine in particular."

Alexios was surprised at such a bold request but said nothing for moments. "We understand the wisdom of your request. But it requires more thoughtful consideration than we can give it now. We thank you for coming." The appointment never came.

* * *

In the days following Alexios invited crusader lords to *Blachernae*, meeting with each privately and separately: Robert, Count of Flanders; Hugh, Count of Vermandois, called "The Great"; Stephen, Count of Blois; Robert, Duke of Normandy; and others. I was present for each. They all agreed to pledge their homage to the emperor and in doing so were rewarded handsomely. But thereafter comity between Alexios and the Latins, some at least, frayed.

It was ten days after Alexios's audience with Bohemond that Raymond, Count of Toulouse and St. Gilles, leader of the army from Provence in southern Francia, met with Alexios. Adhémar, Bishop of Le Puy, the papal legate, accompanied him limping as he walked into the hall leaning on a cane. Like Bohemond, Adhémar's face expressed both surprise and curiosity at seeing me, a Latin monk, present and serving as translator.

Raymond was indifferent. Raymond was the oldest of all the princes, in his fifties, stout, gray of beard, and a scar across his face. But what most distinguished his features was a single eye with no patch, the socket merely empty. It was said that it had been cut out in Jerusalem for his refusal to pay Turks a tax and that he carried the eyeball in his pocket to remind himself of their cruelty. I never saw it.

Alexios greeted them genially. "Welcome to *Blachernae*, both of you."

Raymond stood there stiffly, without bowing, a glare in his eyes. "I demand an explanation!"

"For what?" Alexios asked serenely.

"Your Pechenegs without cause attacked my troops at Rodosto in Thrace, not four days from here, as we were making our way peacefully to your city. Worse, they assaulted the papal legate," nodding to Adhémar. "He was wounded. This is an outrage, insufferable. I demand an explanation!"

Alexios could barely conceal his astonishment at Raymond's insolence. I too was shocked, so much that my translation initially faltered. "My apologies, Your Eminence," Alexios looking sympathetically at Adhémar. "Our troops mistook you. We regret your injury. Have you seen our physicians?

"Yes I have. They've helped me."

"Good. We are pleased to hear it. General Tatikios, house the legate in our Great Palace. He will be more comfortable there than suffering the miseries of life in a tent outside the city. We wish our personal physician to attend to him daily. See to it." Tatikios bowed. The emperor turned his attention to me. "You too will attend to the legate's needs. He must be denied nothing. I wish you to accompany the legate as a guide to our glorious city. He may especially enjoy visiting the Chapel of the Holy Virgin of Pharos. It holds many relics."

Raymond's countenance had not changed, still grimacing. "This alters nothing. You have given me neither an explanation nor an apology."

Alexios's composure remained steady but fire was in his eyes. "Let me remind you, good count, that it was *your* men, not mine, who seized the town of Rosso and looted it. You conveniently forgot to mention this. They then marched to Rodosto, attempting the same. Our punishment was severe but just. Expect no apology." Alexios's tone now became gentler. "What do you wish of me?"

Raymond was visibly stunned by the rebuke but his truculence was unabated. "I demand your assistance in transporting my troops to Anatolia."

"You demand?" Alexios half-rising from his chair, glaring at Raymond.

"You *demand* of the Basileus? Bohemond greeted us only days ago. He made no demands. His conduct was modest and honorable. Yours, that of a rustic." Alexios was mincing no words. In mentioning Bohemond he had in mind a more subtle calculation. Alexios understood men. He sensed a rivalry between Bohemond and Raymond and he chose now to exploit it. And exploit it he would.

"Yes, I know of your meeting," Raymond replied. "You appointed him leader of our armies. There was no consultation with the rest of us. This arrogance is insufferable!"

Alexios ignored the insult. "It is true Lord Bohemond asked for such an appointment. We are considering his request." He wasn't.

Raymond responded with indignation. "If such an appointment is made, it must be to *me*. I am here under the aegis of Pope Urban himself with his personal legate. And of all the armies gathered in Constantinople mine is the largest. I shall *not* serve under that Norman."

"You ask too much. You '*demand*' transport across the Arm of St. George. Of course, we can provide that. But in return an oath of homage to us is required. Otherwise, you can rot on our shores. We care not."

"I won't give it. My fealty is to my God, my pope, and my king." Raymond was seething with anger.

Alexios had lost patience. "You are annoying us Count Raymond, like a gnat flying around our head. This audience is complete. General Tatikios, please escort our guests out. Your Excellency," looking at Adhémar, "we trust your new accommodations will be satisfactory."

Shortly after the emperor's audience with Raymond, I was told to cease compositions entirely and spend my mornings serving as a companion and guide for Adhémar. I welcomed the respite from the labors of the *scriptorium* especially bending over a writing desk all day until my back ached. My time with Adhémar was spent enjoyably, a man of prodigious learning and kindness in equal measure. We visited the many monuments of the city, Georgios always in attendance following three paces behind: the Hippodrome, Saint Sophia, the forums. Adhémar seemed to delight especially in tasting the food of street vendors—spiced chunks of beef skewered with sticks and whole fish grilled over braziers. Yet, of all these charms, it was the Chapel of the Holy Virgin of Pharos in the Great Palace that excited his greatest enthusiasm for it held, under close guard, the most treasured relics of the empire: the Crown of Thorns, two sections of the True Cross, the sandals of Jesus Christ, His tunic worn at the time of His passion, and a small silver phial containing His blood. I particularly recall Adhémar lingering over the Holy Lance with which the Roman soldier Longinus pierced the body of Christ, carefully inspecting its point for evidence of blood. He found it, fell to his knees, his head bowed in silent prayer. Months later I came to understand the significance of that moment.

Emissary to Duke Godfrey

The "snake pit of hissing vipers", as the Bishop of Nish described the politics of Constantinople, became deeper. Suspicions of Emperor Alexios were rife amongst the crusaders. After Bohemond's audience, the emperor sent his personal chef to Bohemond's tent to prepare for him a sumptuous meal. Bohemond refused to taste it, suspecting poison, and ordered instead his attendants to eat it and on the following morning inquired as to their health. Then there was Godfrey of Bouillon, Duke of Lorraine. He had arrived but refused several invitations from Alexios to meet with him. Tatikios learned that Count Raymond had warned Godfrey against meeting with the emperor because of some unexplained "malevolent" design the emperor had on Godfrey. The emperor hoped that I, a Frankish monk, might allay doubts and persuade Godfrey to meet. Naturally, I accepted the mission though doubtful how successful I would be.

I rode out with Georgios across the Fortified Bridge north of *Blachernae* to Perra, across the Golden Horn, and readily found Godfrey's camp. I saw one tent, larger and more splendid than the others, pennants flying above its four corners, a fringed canopy set on poles over its entrance. I assumed this was Godfrey's. "Greeting" me, perhaps a charitable word, was a husky man, tall, a scar from his cheekbone to his jaw, fierce eyes, his head shaped less like a man's than one of those gargoyles that adorned the Cathedral of Rheims, not so much misshapen as evoking pure evil. He wore a cloak of thick, coarse black fur, bear I thought, tied at the neck with a metal clasp.

"Who are you, monk?" challenging me. "What do you want?"

"I am Oderic of the Priory La Charité sur Loire and presently emissary of His Majesty Alexios Komnenos to Godfrey, Duke of Lorraine."

"What is your business?"

"My business is with the duke," I replied sharply.

"No. Your business right now is with me!"

I was about to turn my horse around and return to the city when a man emerged from the tent "Richard, what is it?"

"This monk wants to see your brother. Says he's from the emperor."

"Whose emperor? What emperor? We know no emperor here," he scoffed. I knew immediately who he was, Baldwin of Boulogne, younger brother of the duke. Yet, despite the mockery, he opened the flap of his tent and motioned for us to dismount. We did so. As we approached the tent's entrance Richard roughly pushed me forward. "Only you monk. Get in!" Georgios immediately slapped his arm down. Both grabbed for their swords until Baldwin shouted "Enough!" Their grips relaxed.

Baldwin's tent was sumptuously furnished: velvet cushions; paintings of obscene art hanging by hooks on the tent walls; and three ornately carved chairs all facing a single one, even grander, with a high back and a painted coat of arms carved in relief, resembling almost a throne. He walked directly to his chair and assumed his seat. I was about to sit when Baldwin glared at me for my presumption. I remained standing.

"That was Richard Iron-hand" he began. "The story goes, and one he loves to tell, is that when he was in a forest hunting alone he came across a bear. He loosed an arrow but not fatally. The bear charged. Richard stabbed it twice with his sword but the bear was still alive and clawed him in the face. Richard struck the bear with his fist, knocking it unconscious. He is not to be trifled with," Baldwin warned, his tone ominous.

"I can see that, my Lord, but nor is my Pecheneg companion," I answered, not to be intimidated. This interview was proceeding awkwardly. I tried to lighten the mood, if only slightly. "The cloak that Richard wears, is that the bear?"

"Yes," he answered curtly. "Now tell me your business monk. No prevarication here. You are the emperor's boy." I was about to object when suddenly Baldwin changed the subject. "La Charité sur Loire, you said? Yes, I remember the name. A Cluniac priory. I heard it mentioned during my studies at the cathedral school of Rheims."

This was my chance to relieve the tension. "You attended the cathedral school?" I asked with affected incredulity. "I too was a scholar there. Did you have Father Anthony? He tried to teach me mathematics, beating me with a stick for every error of calculation. I still bear the welts," I said smiling.

Baldwin's demeanor changed immediately, now more animated. "Yes. Yes. Anthony. Vile man. Annoying. He was one of the reasons I left the school. But in any event there was no profit for me in education." We then reminisced over our experiences at the school for which there is no purpose to relate here. "It seems we have things in common," Baldwin said. "So, young monk," his tone now mellowed. "What is your mission?"

"My Lord," I answered in the most obsequious tone I could muster suspecting, rightly, that he preferred servility to fortitude, "with the deepest apologies but I have been instructed under threat of punishment to deliver my message directly to your brother."

"Wait here," he answered. He returned shortly. "The duke will see you." We walked to a separate tent twenty paces away and entered. It was far more simply furnished than Baldwin's. In front of me stood a man in his late thirties, roughly the same age as Baldwin but slightly older. That's where the similarities ended. Godfrey had inherited the family estates; Baldwin, as the youngest of three sons, was directed by his father to enter the priesthood, a vocation for which he possessed not the slightest temperament. Godfrey was shorter than Baldwin, finer in physique, fairer in complexion, and as chaste in his personal habits as Baldwin was venerous. Godfrey was a devoted follower of Christ, dogmatic even; Baldwin a slave to Baal and morally flexible. Godfrey's nature was genial; Baldwin's haughty and cold. But what truly distinguished them, as later events proved, was this: Godfrey's true quest was the liberation of the Holy Land; Baldwin's, without estates, to claim a principality for himself, whatever the cost.

I was about to introduce myself when Godfrey interrupted. "Yes, I know who you are Father Oderic of La Charité. Baldwin told me. Please sit. Refreshments first." Calling to his attendant standing at the tent's flap "Tea for us both, with honey please." We were served immediately. "There are few pleasures for me here in Constantinople, except this is one. From Cathay I think." Baldwin sat with us, he drinking wine. "So tell me, good father, what service do you provide your emperor?"

"I am a scribe in his chancery, copying books and translating letters."

"A scribe, you say? 'Of making many books there is no end. And much study . . . '" he faltered trying to recall the rest of the passage.

"is a weariness of the flesh'", I finishing. "Ecclesiastes."

"Yes. Indeed. You know your verses, Father."

"Well, I studied in Rheims," winking at Baldwin who grinned back. "I am here at the emperor's request. As we are of a common faith, yours and mine, he hoped that a message given through me might be generously received."

"And what is this message from your emperor?"

"My Lord, he wishes to meet with you. Thrice he has sent you an invitation and thrice you've refused. He's perplexed and wonders if he's offended you in some manner."

"No, not yet," Godfrey answered quite calmly. "I have been warned that he has designs on my person. Perhaps in his palace when he serves me tea, not from Cathay but from mandrake berries. Or I wear a cloak soaked in poison. Or I mysteriously disappear in one of his palace caverns. No, I'm safer here. If he prefers, you may serve as his messenger. You're a man of God and I trust you more than one of his eunuchs."

Discussions were leading nowhere. A different course was required, blunter. "My Lord, the emperor is as resolute in his faith as you. He is a godly man." That was true. "But he does insist that you cease pillaging his land. Yes, I know, he has denied you open markets but this was only because you refused his invitations. Those markets can be immediately restored if you agree to an audience and pledge your homage. In return, you will be provided ships to Anatolia and richly rewarded as Lord Bohemond and others were."

"'Insist' does he?" Baldwin jeered, now interjecting. "There is no treachery of which this Byzantine is not capable. He may be lucky to keep his throne." At that Godfrey fired a sharp look at Baldwin as though to say "you've said too much".

"Good monk," Godfrey said, "you will always be welcome here but I see no profit to either of us in further discussion. Thank you for coming."

Duke Godfrey Attacks Blachernae

I reported the failure of negotiations to Tatikios and related Baldwin's dark warning but its intent was not entirely clear to me. The next morning was Friday, the day our Lord was crucified. Adhémar and I had planned to attend service at Saint Sophia. I was in the midst of ablutions at my apartment when Georgios burst through the door. "Oderic. You're needed at once. *Blachernae* is under assault. By Duke Godfrey!"

We rode quickly to the palace passing imperial troops rushing in the same direction. Abutting the palace is the Wall of Theodosius, its parapets already manned by soldiers. Standing there on the wall-walk with his soldiers was the emperor, Tatikios to his left, General Nikephoros Bryennios to his right, and beside Nikephoros two Varangian captains. Georgios and I ran up the steps to the battlements and looked through a crenel opening at Godfrey's force on the vast, barren field below: archers in front, behind them cavalry, and finally thousands of Lorrainer foot. When we arrived Godfrey's archers were unleashing their arrows directed at the top of the wall. Alexios stood there impassively, quite visible to the archers below, quietly studying them. I was uncertain of what service I was expected to provide and just waited several paces away for instructions. I overheard Alexios telling Nikephoros that this was the day of Christ's crucifixion and it would be a desecration of His memory for Christians to kill Christians. He ordered Nikephoros's archers on the wall to shoot over the crusaders' heads to frighten them.

"Your Majesty," Nikephoros asked, "what about our war elephants? They can be saddled quickly. That might frighten them."

"No," Alexios answered. "Archers."

Nikephoros turned to one of his captains relaying the emperor's orders. The imperial archers, their bows already spanned and arrows notched, unleashed their own volleys. At that moment, while Alexios was standing resolutely at the parapet, an arrow flew within a span of him striking one of the Varangian captains behind, throwing him over the wall-walk to the ground below. Alexios did not flinch, fearless. I took cover behind a stone merlon between two crenels as I could hear metal bodkins either whistling over me or clinking against the stone. Georgios, on the other hand, followed his emperor's example standing just as defiantly, unprotected.

I could not fathom Godfrey's strategy. He had no siege engines or ladders. I could see no purpose except one: He was challenging Alexios to engage him in battle on the open field. Alexios obliged. He gave another order, which I could not hear, to Nikephoros who left immediately, hurriedly running down the steps. Shortly after there was the sound below me of clanging chains and metal bars, the rasping of pulleys and hinges, the creaking of enormous wooden doors. I peeked, carefully, around the merlon and over the crenel looking down. The raised drawbridge in front of the moat at the Gate of Saint Romanos was slowly lowering as the gate opened, then the clattering of heavily armored mounted lancers, their spears upright, over the bridge's wooden planks followed by light infantry, the *peltasts*, clad in stiffened leather jerkins holding shields and javelins filing out.

Leading them was Nikephoros himself wearing a plumed helmet and over his mail hauberk a cuirass of lamelar plates covering his front and back tied by straps over his shoulders, all of bronze and polished to a lustrous sheen, glittering in the sun. He rode a pure black horse, also burnished lamelar plate armor over its head and neck, leather straps and a saddle both dyed red, its forelegs rising in a stately prance. There were no trumpets, no drums, no howling from the troops to excite courage in each other or fear in the enemy. Except for the steady beat of hooves and boots, an eerie silence prevailed, almost ghost-like. Godfrey's archers at the same time ran left and right to open their ranks for the cavalry to charge through.

When the imperial force was fully deployed in the field, Nikephoros stopped, motionless. Suddenly archers poured out of the gate, arranging themselves on both sides shoulder-to-shoulder against the wall. Nikephoros seemed to know when they were in place without even looking back. He pulled his sword from its scabbard and thrust it upward. The archers immediately raised their spanned bows, all notched with arrows. He lowered his sword and in that instant a rain of missiles fell on Godfrey's cavalry but in a targeted fashion, all directed at the horses which began falling one by one, their death screams deafening. He then raised his sword a second time. His cavalry immediately couched their lances as Nikephoros spurred his horse charging forward at a full gallop, his sword at arm's length pointing directly ahead, the cavalry at break-neck speed following in a wedge formation.

Godfrey's army was thrown into confusion. Horsemen tried to free themselves from their fallen animals, those still on their mounts charging chaotically to meet the imperials but then, thinking better of it, wheeling around to race off. Godfrey's infantry, seeing the flight of the horsemen and facing this widening wedge of Byzantine horse, turned and ran in every direction throughout the field.

Nikephoros raised his sword and pulled back on the reins. Alexios's object was not to kill. It was to subdue. The battle was over. It had truly not even begun.

Crusader Princes Pledge Their homage

Two days after the failed assault on *Blachernae*, Godfrey, penitent, agreed to declare his homage to Alexios. In return Alexios rewarded him as he had the other crusader princes, all except Count Raymond, recalcitrant and proud, ever obdurate. A council of crusader princes was held to persuade Raymond to yield. He refused, insisting that the crusaders wage battle against Alexios to avenge the "wrongs" done him at Rodosto. That is, until the other nobles, including our greatest warrior Bohemond, warned him that they would support Alexios. Under this threat, and with no other choice, Raymond conceded, though truculently.

Three days later Alexios summoned the crusader nobles to his throne room, *Magnavra*, at the Great Palace. Tatikios requested I serve as translator. The hall excited wonder in the crusaders the instant they entered: its marble columns and floors, the mosaics and tapestries covering the walls. All the crusader nobles, perhaps two hundred, were assembled, even those from obscure and minor estates, their only claim to nobility a title, occasionally bestowed on themselves. The great princes stood in front, before them two immense brocaded curtains stretching across the entire hall and decorated with tigers, elephants, and unicorns concealing all behind. At both ends of the curtains, near the walls, were golden lions, ten feet tall, their mouths closed. Next to each was a golden tree, glittering leaves, silver birds perched on its boughs.

The nobles were milling about, conversing in whispers for the hall commanded awe, even reverence. Unnoticed by them was an enormous brass gong suspended by silver chains from the ceiling. Beside it a Nubian slave wearing only a loin cloth and slippers holding a mallet, its wooden shaft some three feet long, the brass head resting on the floor. The Nubian raised the mallet and struck the gong, producing a resounding echo throughout the hall. A door opened. Through it entered a tall, rather elderly man, his white beard flowing down to his navel wearing a red silken gown with a golden staff in his hand. The hall became quiet as the nobles stared at him with a mix of curiosity and wonder. This was the *Protospatharios*. He walked to the curtain, turned, paused to ensure silence, and then raising it above his head pounded it three times on the marble floor. "Behold noble sirs, Alexios Komnenos, Basileus and Autocrat of All Romans! He welcomes you to Byzantium. The Prophet Ezekiel foretold your arrival:

> *You will come from your place out of the far north,*
> *You and many peoples with you,*
> *All riding on horses,*
> *A great company and a mighty army.*

A hush then fell over the hall. What followed was the most specular scene I had ever witnessed or would surely again for the rest of my life. The curtains slowly withdrew, one to the left and the other to the right. Organ music began to play. All the Greeks in the hall fell to their knees, heads bowed. The Latins remained standing, their eyes focused on the separating curtains. To the astonishment of us all the mechanical lions burst out in terrifying roars, their mouths opening and closing synchronized perfectly with the roars, tails flying up and down. And as the lions roared the birds began singing, each in a distinctive tone and with a different song. I, we, *every one of us*, was dumbstruck. The curtains were now completely withdrawn to reveal a large platform, six steps, on which rested a magnificent throne of gold encrusted with sparkling jewels. On it sat the emperor dressed in a purple robe trimmed with fox fur, a loose *chlamys* covering his right shoulder clasped with a silver *fibula*, and over that a long scarf embroidered with gold thread and precious stones. He wore a diadem on his head decorated with gems flared with pendants and golden chains hanging over his temples down to his cheeks. On his feet slippers of purple velvet resting on a golden stool. Behind him, in a semicircle, stood Varangian guards in golden helmets and lamelar armor over their leather jerkins, silver axes slung on their backs, standing motionless, not the slightest quiver.

The spectacle was not over. To audible gasps and as the lions continued to roar and the birds sing the throne began to rise, slowly, six feet, the emperor gazing down impassively at the assembled nobles. The roaring and singing then ended. The *Protospatharios* pounded his staff. Two monks entered the hall carrying on poles a silver reliquary, cherubs on its lid at either end kneeling to one another reminding me of a miniature I had seen of the Arc of the Covenant in the Book of Exodus. They set it down below the throne.

"Behold!" the *Protospatharios* declared, his left hand pointing at the reliquary, "the sainted head of John the Baptist. On this," looking at the great princes, "you, the *principes* of many Latin nations, shall make your vows of homage to the Basileus. Approach!" It was the custom of the imperial court for ambassadors to walk forward, prostrate themselves, arise, walk forward again, prostrate themselves once more, and then a third time. Alexios had relaxed this protocol for the princes. Stepping forward were Bohemond, Lord of Taranto; Robert, Count of Flanders; Robert, Count of Normandy; Stephen, Count of Blois; Baldwin of Boulogne; Eustace, Count of Boulogne; Godfrey, Duke of Lorraine; Richard of the Principate; Hugh, Count of Vermandois. Count Raymond followed them.

"Place your right hand on this holy object," the *Protospatharios* instructed. They all bent on one knee before the reliquary their hands resting on it. Raymond alone remained standing. The *Protospatharios* was shocked, confused, uncertain how to proceed. He looked up at Alexios for some direction. The emperor was expressionless. The *Protospatharios* decided to continue. "Do you swear your homage and allegiance to Alexios Komnenos, Basileus and Autocrat of All Romans, that you will faithfully and fearlessly fight for Our Lord Jesus Christ, that you will free Jerusalem from the godless Muslims, that all lands between here and there you conquer will be reclaimed in the name of the Basileus and restored to his Empire. In return, the Basileus, in his munificence, pledges to support you with troops and provisions. This you vow. Say 'I so pledge.'" They all did in unison, stood up and stepped back.

Raymond, still standing behind the others, came forward, bent his knee placing his hand on the relic. "I swear my homage and allegiance to my God, my Pope, and my King. That I shall faithfully and fearlessly fight for Our Lord Jesus Christ to free Jerusalem from the godless. I pledge to respect the life and honor of the Emperor and swear that neither I nor my men will do anything injurious to him or to his Empire. I shall give neither aid nor comfort to his enemies and shall restore to him all lands rightfully his that I may conquer." This was not quite the oath of homage that Alexios sought but he seemed satisfied. The throne now slowly descended as the curtains were gradually drawn.

"The Basileus invites you to a banquet in the Hall of Nineteen Couches," the *Protospatharios* announced. "This audience is now concluded."

My Next Adventure

Shortly following the ceremony I returned to my former routine. Adhémar, after thanking me for my service as his guide, excused himself from further tours. His attention had now turned to preparations for the march to Nicea. While I had enjoyed his companionship, and I think he mine, I was pleased to return to the chancery. I spent the mornings translating occasional letters from the emperor to crusader princes and advising my fellow scribes on proper Latin syntax and idiomatic usages. My principal occupation, however, was to translate into Latin a Greek copy of *The Canon of Medicine* by the Persian physician and philosopher Avicenna which I happened upon in the chancery's library. Geoffrey, the Doctor of Physik, during his treatment of Father Benedict at La Charité, had referred to it several times, commenting that it was an essential part of the corpus of learning at his medical school in Salerno. However, neither he nor his fellow scholars could read Arabic or Greek. Thus their understanding of Avicenna's teachings was through Salerno's masters who themselves had never read the text. I was intrigued by this new undertaking. The prefect granted my request, he having a more liberal attitude toward medical science than had Benedict. In the afternoons, I continued my study of Turkish.

In the evenings, Rebecca and I resumed our evening walks, though not as frequently as in the past, her mistress often requiring her attendance even late into the night. Our excursions, however, became somewhat more adventurous. Tatikios had arranged for a skiff, moored in the emperor's harbor, for our use. It was now May and with the warmer weather the Sea of Marmara was calmer, though I was always careful not to venture too far from shore. This was a new experience for me. I first had to train myself: rigging the main sail and jib; trimming them in response to shifting winds; steering with a tiller; tacking at the precise moment, watchful of the swinging boom; and for me, the hardest, docking in our slip. Georgios, my faithful guardian, took no pleasure in these outings. He came from nomadic stock—the land, not water. But the sea thrilled Rebecca. She and I enjoyed the sun in our faces, the smell of salt water, the sea gulls circling above us, and the wind rushing through our hair. Following, Rebecca and I would find our favorite tavern for a glass of wine, Georgios always following at a discreet distance then standing outside the tavern door, watchful. But, after some coaxing from Rebecca—I saw that he had developed a loyalty to her almost as fierce as his to me—he would join us at our table and even converse so long as it was on a subject of interest to him. Otherwise, he was Georgios. Yet, we thoroughly enjoyed his company.

One morning, while absorbed in my translation of Avicenna, I was informed by the prefect that Tatikios had summoned me. I met with him immediately. That evening, Rebecca was free. We sailed and afterwards repaired to our tavern. The three of us sat at a table. I was looking for the right moment. At one point conversation ebbed.

"I saw General Tatikios today," I said.

"What about?" Rebecca asked.

"The crusaders are preparing to sail across the strait and then march to Nicea."

"Well, what has that to do with you?" Rebecca asked in almost a challenging tone.

"Well," I replied, "the emperor has ordered him to lead a regiment of two thousand Turcopoles to assist them."

"And ... and ... ?" Rebecca was becoming impatient, anxious to squeeze an answer from me.

"And he's asked me to join him. That's all."

Rebecca's irritation was beginning to erupt into anger. I'm sure I could have introduced the subject more artfully. "We're happy here, Oderic. You have your work. I have mine. Our life is contented. Complete. Are you really, *really*, thinking of going?"

"Yes," I answered simply. What I didn't reveal was my heart. I *was* happy in Constantinople with Rebecca. My work *was* important. And, yes, I had been more in love with the *idea* of the crusade than with its cruel reality. But since Civitot I had become restless, a longing for excitement, for adventure. I thought of an earlier time, the pleasures of working with

Samuel ben Meir but then, gradually, the need for a more spiritual life. And now the need for something more than a book in front of me and a quill in my hand. And I so wanted to explore beyond Constantinople. To see Jerusalem. *That* was the explanation I needed for Rebecca would certainly not be satisfied with any other.

"Rebecca, we are of somewhat different yet kindred faiths. Jerusalem is a holy place for us both, where Adam lived out his life, Solomon built his temple, the land of Abraham. It is sacred to Christians as well." I thought it politic not to mention the crucifixion. "I *must* see it."

"What will happen to *me*?" she asked softly, sniffing, her voice beginning to break.

"You have a family now in Constantinople. You can stay here, continue to serve your mistress until I return. And return I shall, just as I did after Civitot."

Georgios, sitting there quietly, listening, interjected. "Oderic, I too was summoned by the general after your visit this morning. He asked me to accompany you. I know the land of Anatolia. That was where I began my military career. And I know the Turks. There will be many perils and hardships for you between here and Jerusalem. We have become brothers, you and I. I took a vow this day at the altar of the Church of Divine Peace, where we Pechenegs worship, that I will protect you with my life."

I was touched. Deeply. To my soul. I had not expected such devotion. I sat across from him, I'm sure just staring, wordless.

"Then I shall go too," Rebecca announced firmly. I was about to protest but her tone and defiance told me she was unmovable. "We go", she said, "the three of us. We shall face all dangers together."

And we did.

This ends Book VII of *Jerusalem Falls!* Book VIII begins.

SIEGE OF NICEA

Meeting with Tatikios

Rebecca, Georgios, and I made preparations to depart for Anatolia. As promised, the emperor made ships available and between late April and early May 1097 the main body of crusaders and pilgrims with their animals and provisions were transported across the Arm of Saint George to the harbor of Pelekanum on the northern shore of the Gulf of Nikomedia, the same place where the followers of Peter the Hermit had disembarked. Before leaving, Georgios and I met with Tatikios at his invitation. We entered his office at the Great Palace. Tatikios was quite relaxed and greeted us without ceremony as old friends. Standing beside him was a Greek soldier dressed similarly to Alexios when we first met: a leather jerkin, woolen breeches, and high riding boots, by his military bearing and demeanor a man of significance.

"So, are you ready for yet another adventure?" Tatikios asked. "I hear your Rebecca," looking at me, "will be going too. Remember," he said smiling, "we have agents everywhere," Tatikios never willing to call them "spies" and I never forgetting he had them. "I'm not sure this is wise for a woman of her refinement. There will be hardships and dangers. Personally, I would not have permitted it."

"Yes, I understand," I replied. "But, to speak truthfully, her 'refinement' is molded in iron. She was quite obstinate on the matter."

"Then, if there's nothing to be done about it, let me tell you of my plans. But first I want to introduce General Manuel Boutoumites. He is leading a squadron of engineers and Turcopoles to Anatolia. You will sail with him to Civitot and serve as his translator." Both Georgios and I bowed, he responding with a perfunctory nod. "I shall accompany the Basileus somewhat later with two or three thousand Turcopoles to Pelekanum. You will be under Manuel's care."

"May I ask, General," I inquired, "and please excuse my ignorance, but why engineers? Are not our spears and swords sufficient?"

Tatikios laughed, perhaps more a giggle as though the question answered itself. "No, they are not enough. You Latins are experienced in assaults on small forts of wood built on equally small hills defended by ditches and modest palisades, also of wood. These are not what you will face in Anatolia or in Palestine. Fortresses there will not be so easily overcome. Their walls are constructed of thick stone, like ours here in Constantinople. Prayer and horns may have brought down Jericho; Nicea will not fall so easily. It is especially formidable. I know. Ten years ago I attacked it but without success. Even with ladders, siege engines, and sappers victory is uncertain. But without them failure *is* certain. Yes. You need our engineers."

Tatikios continued. "Let me give you more information. This may aid you in your service to General Boutoumites. Nicea is the capital of Qilij Arslan, Sultan of Rum, the northern part of Anatolia. As it happens, timing is fortuitous. He is currently away, occupied in a contest with the Danishmends much further south for sovereignty of that region. Nicea was lost to us in the battle of Manzikert in 1071. The Basileus wants it restored to the Empire. He is quite resolved on the matter. But the city is also vital to you Latins. The success of your march to Jerusalem depends on securing your rear. Nicea is essential to that." Tatikios bid farewell saying he was looking forward to seeing us again in Anatolia.

March to Nicea

Two days later we arrived at Civitot. Rebecca was anxious to see the abandoned castle where Georgios led the heroic defense against the Turks. Georgios was modest about his role. Tents which had housed the pilgrims months before were either frayed yet still standing or had collapsed. The dead were scattered about, their bones bleached by the sun, lying in contorted positions indicating the horrors of their final moments. Rebecca became distressed at the sight of such carnage. Tatikios had chosen Civitot as the supply depot for provisioning the crusaders and Manuel was tasked with ensuring it was clear of Turks before more imperial ships arrived. Confident it was secure, we left the next day to link up with the crusader army at Nikomedia bringing with us wagons filled with all the tools necessary for building engines and sapping walls. As we rode up the narrow defile where Geoffrey Burel had been ambushed we saw more bodies, some skulls still pierced with arrows; the fallen trees which earlier had blocked the pilgrims' forward advance still lying in place; and decaying wagons where they had been abandoned. It was a terrible sight. So many dead. And for naught. I grieved for them. There was no time to bury the bodies, Manuel being anxious to reach Nikomedia. Instead their bones and other obstacles were pushed to the side of the road as we proceeded.

We reached Nikomedia the next day. Duke Godfrey had been the first to arrive. There was an ancient Roman road to Nicea used later by the Byzantines. But over the last twenty years after the Byzantines were expelled from Anatolia it had become overgrown with vegetation. In preparation for the armies that would follow, Godfrey sent a large party ahead to clear it with axes and swords, marking the road with iron and wooden crosses. In the meantime Bohemond, his nephew Tancred, and Count Robert of Flanders disembarked at Pelekanum and then joined us at Nikomedia. Raymond, who commanded the largest force, and Duke Robert of Normandy were still in Constantinople waiting to be transported. Among those gathered at Nikomedia were thousands of noncombatants, either followers of Peter the Hermit who had survived the earlier foolish and deadly foray into northern Anatolia or of Latin nobles from Francia and Germania.

Duke Godfrey, leader of this expedition, decided not to wait for the others but to leave immediately. We began our trek. The road, laid with stone pavers once finely set but now over time separated, was rough. It was rather difficult, especially for those on foot, up one mountain and down another, I would surmise the highest five thousand feet. The oxen and mules pulling wagons loaded with provisions—dried beef and fish, fruits, and bread—and siege equipment labored particularly. Even those of us on horseback occasionally had to dismount and walk our animals to relieve them of the burden of carrying a rider.

Perhaps halfway to Nicea where the road began to level off somewhat, Rebecca and I, Georgios following, nudged our horses forward. I was curious about the size and composition of this expedition. We had not gone far when I saw Peter the Hermit ahead leading hundreds of peasants, primarily women. Walking beside him was a man vaguely familiar but obscured by other pilgrims around him. I was not anxious to renew my acquaintance with Peter, we slowing to a walk. One of the women close to us, barefoot, was stumbling on the rough stone, her young son struggling to support her. She fell, the boy unable to lift her. Rebecca quickly dismounted and helped her up. She was slender, a frayed wimple with a veil over her head indicating a married woman, striking red hair, thirty or so years old, and a beauty despite her face begrimed with dust. Her name was Miriam. Rebecca asked why there were so many women in Peter's column without men. She became tearful. "We are all survivors of Civitot. Our husbands died there, including my own. Peter promised to take care of us. There was no future for us in Constantinople and without the protection of men we cannot return to our homes in the West." Rebecca had no answer. She placed her arm around Miriam's shoulder, gave a hug, and remounted. She said little until nightfall. I did not intrude on her thoughts.

We arrived at Nicea on the sixth day of May. I was especially eager to see this holy city, the site of the famous council presided over by the saintly Emperor Constantine himself which revealed our Christian beliefs. The ancient city was truly as formidable as Tatikios had promised. Its immense curtain wall facing us, the city within, thirty feet high, was interspersed with hundreds of drum towers, no more than one bowshot from each other, their rounded contours extending beyond the wall itself with loopholes on three sides for archers. To the west the waters of Lake Ascanius lapped against the city's wall which rose directly out of the lake. The lake itself was so enormous I could barely see its shore on the opposite side—I thought it an ocean. Around the other three walls—north, south, and east—was a watery moat fed by the lake.

The siege began immediately. Bohemond and his Normans took a position along the north wall; Robert of Flanders with his Flemish troops and Godfrey with his Lorrainers and Teutons along the east; the south wall reserved for Raymond who had yet to arrive with his Provençals. The crusader princes had decided to take no further action until all crusader armies assembled. Until then, any attempt by the Turks to provision the city would be blockaded.

Turkish Spies

Rebecca, Georgios, and I camped near Manuel Boutoumites and his Turcopoles close to the south gate. Tatikios had generously supplied us with two tents, one for Rebecca and me and the other for Georgios, bedding, cooking equipment, and coins with which to purchase food at the market supplied regularly with ships from Civitot and then transported by wagon to Nicea. We had much idle time, often passing it during the following two days by strolling through the different camps, just exploring as Rebecca and I had done so many times, our favorite amusement.

On the second day after arriving, early in the evening, a very pleasant one, the three of us took another promenade, this time in a different direction. As we were walking Georgios noticed what appeared to be by their clothing two Greeks wandering about just outside the southern gate. What alerted Georgios was their sharp surveillance of the surroundings.

Georgios approached them. "Who are you?" he demanded.

They stiffened. "We're brothers," one replied. "Farmers. We grow dates not two miles from here. The best in northern Anatolia! Can you direct us to your market? We wish to see if there's interest in purchasing our delicious fruit. Here, have one, two even, please, taste them," the other opening a small bag and presenting it to Georgios.

"You're Greeks, aren't you?" Georgios asked.

"Oh yes," answered the one holding the bag, "Greeks. Yes indeed. Greeks." In that instant I wondered if they really knew who they were but the suspicion passed quickly.

Not for Georgios. He pressed. They were fluent in Greek, yes, but with an accent unfamiliar to him. "You speak strangely."

"Oh yes. You are quite observant, Esteemed Sir. Our father was a date farmer in northern Macedonia. He brought us here when we were children. We know only his dialect."

Their story was plausible. Despite Georgios's continuing suspicions, further examination would yield no better answers. There was, however, a different tactic. "You're Christians?" I asked.

"Oh yes. Christians. Both of us. We pray every day. Very good Christians."

"I'm pleased to hear that. Recite for me the Lord's Prayer."

They looked at one another in confusion. Not Christians at all. Turkish spies! One of them turned and ran, Georgios immediately in pursuit. The other pulled out a dagger concealed under his shirt pointing it at me. This was wholly unexpected and I stepped back out of reach without a weapon of my own. He then lunged forward, swinging wildly left and right, cutting my bare left arm, a shallow flesh wound but bleeding nonetheless, not even noticing in the heated moment. He lunged again, still slashing and then lost his balance, stumbling briefly, lowering his dagger. That was my chance. I struck him in the face with my fist as powerfully as I could. He fell back, still upright but dropping his knife. I wrapped my arms around his waist, lifted him until his feet were off the ground as he kicked furiously, and then threw him down landing on his back. I leapt on him, my knees straddling his body. The dagger was next to me, within reach. I grabbed it, pointing the tip of the blade at the Turk's throat. But I could not bring myself to plunge it, to take his life, a human life. This would violate not only my vow as a priest but as a man. Perhaps I was no "warrior-priest" after all I thought a bit later with some comfort. The Turk took full advantage of my hesitation, rolled me over, I then him, and he now over me. But the contest was in his favor. He was stouter than I, Georgios's size, my frame more slender. He ended on top, sitting astride me on my stomach, his knees spread and pressed tightly against my hips. He pried the dagger out of my hand and held it to my throat. He too hesitated but for a different reason. His eyes narrowed and face broke out into a smirk dripping with murderous intent. There was no escape. In an instant I would be dead.

Rebecca had been looking on in horror. As the struggle began she searched the ground for a weapon, any weapon, a rock, a tree limb, anything. There was nothing. The ground was perfectly bare except for a short, straight branch, less than a digit in width, both ends rounded and weather-worn. She picked it up, broke it in half with her raised knee, and sprang to the Turk thrusting the sharp end into his ear, screaming "*Mamzer! Mamzer!*" "Bastard!" "Bastard!". With each cry of "*Mamzer!*" she pushed harder and deeper. The Turk howled in pain, in a frenzy grabbing for the branch, releasing the dagger but still on top of me. In the meantime, Georgios had quickly caught up with the first Turk, knocking him down and pummeling him unconscious. The next thing I knew Georgios was standing over us both, his dagger in hand, the same he had given me at Civitot, seized the Turk's hair, pulled his head back, and with one slice cut his throat, blood spurting all over me. Rebecca knelt beside me, her voice trembling, her expression stricken, "Oh Oderic," as she wiped my face with her tunic between sobs.

We went back to the other Turk, both Georgios and I dragging him, still unconscious, to Manuel's tent only a short distance away. By now he had regained consciousness. Manuel was shocked as we entered, my tunic covered with blood, both Georgios and I breathless. We threw him to the ground, on his knees. After briefly explaining what had happened and our suspicions, Manuel immediately summoned three Turcopole soldiers who took positions over the Turk.

"What were you doing at the south gate?" Manuel demanded of the Turk.

"Nothing, most Honored Sir," the Turk protested. "I'm a date farmer. Greek. I came to sell my fruit. Only that. I swear it. These bandits attacked me."

Manuel was certain that, without more, prevarications would follow one after the other. More important, he sensed this spy had some immediate purpose. There was no time to employ the usual techniques of extracting information—beating, flogging, hanging him by his thumbs—until he revealed whatever sinister plot he was involved in. Something more dramatic and direct was required. Just outside his tent was a brazier, its flames heating a metal skewer resting over it, already red-hot, prepared to receive meat. Manuel ordered that it be brought into the tent. Manuel would manage this by himself. Wrapping the handle with thick leather he took the skewer and stepped over to the Turk, still kneeling, wailing, moaning, pleading his innocence.

"Stand him up!" he ordered the Turcopoles. He was roughly pulled to his feet, two Turcopoles on either side gripping his arms and the third his hair from behind. "Tell me Turk!" pointing the skewer directly at his right eye, only a span away. "First this eye, then the other," slowly moving it leftwards. "Next your ears. Then your nose. Tell me!"

"I beg you. I am but a farmer . . ." Manuel did not wait for him to finish. He pushed the skewer into the Turk's eye. The Turk emitted a shriek such as I had never heard, so loud and shrill that the tent walls seemed to shake. I was shocked by what I saw but didn't intercede, my usual sensibilities perhaps numbed by the savagery of his attempt on my own life. Manuel then pointed the skewer at the other eye. The Turk could bear no more. He revealed all: Qilij Arslan had recruited a large force from various cities of the sultanate. He was only a day and a half away. He knew that Raymond had not yet arrived and that the south gate, where Raymond's army was to be deployed, was unprotected. Qilij planned to attack the moment he reached the city before Raymond arrived, this spy and his companion ordered to scout out our defenses. But the Turk revealed something equally important. Qilij was overconfident. He assumed that, since Peter the Hermit's army had been so easily defeated, this new army would be little different.

Manuel called an urgent meeting of the Council of Princes. Apprehending the gravity of their situation it immediately dispatched a messenger with a string of two fresh horses to Raymond urging him to make haste. Raymond marched through the night, arriving in the morning of the following day. Georgios and I walked over to the Provençal camp to watch the troops set up their tents. Suddenly, without warning, a vanguard of Qilij's army, perhaps a hundred mounted archers, appeared. Leading it was their commander whom Georgios and I instantly recognized, Elchanes, the very captain we had confronted at Xerigordos. He probably expected easy access to the city through the gate but must have been surprised to see Raymond already there. Yet in this moment Raymond was vulnerable and unprepared. The vanguard charged, not attacking in a forward direction but in a continuous circle from right to left and then around again, the archers shifting sideways in their saddles loosening arrows. The instant the Turks had appeared, the crusaders, fortunately still wearing mailed hauberks and swords girded around their waists, mounted their horses and with javelins in raised hands poised to throw replied with a counterattack. Elchanes must have thought better of continuing this strike, badly outnumbered as he was. A trumpet sounded, two long blasts and a short one, the same signal of retreat I had heard at Civitot. The Turks turned and galloped off.

Qilij Arslan Attacks

The next morning I received a summons from Manuel. The Turkish commander of Nicea wished to see him. Manuel asked me to accompany him as translator.

"General," I protested, "I'm not fluent in Turkish. You will surely be disappointed."

Manuel dismissed this concern. "On the contrary, Father, I'm certain you will be sufficient to the task and meet my needs perfectly. As it happens, my command of their language may be better than yours. After all, I have spent years in Anatolia fighting Turks. But there's an advantage using you. As you struggle, perhaps, for an adequate translation, I shall have time to consider whatever this commander has in mind and my response. More important, however, Tatikios trusts you, the Basileus too; then of course I do as well. We leave now."

We rode into Nicea, guards at the gate expecting us, and were escorted into a palatial office. As we entered, a man sitting behind a desk stood up and came around, saluting in the Turkish manner, a hand slapped against the heart. Manuel returned this salute. "I am Hamza," introducing himself, "Commander of Sultan Qilij Arslan's Household Guards in Nicea."

"And I, Commander Hamza, am Manuel Boutoumites, General of Basileus Alexios Komnenos's Expeditionary Force." This was somewhat an exaggeration of Manuel's role for I'm sure the princes would have seriously challenged the extent of his authority over them.

"I congratulate you," Hamza said, "albeit with deep misgivings, for your victory over my sultan's army. I wish to discuss terms of the city's surrender." In fact, the sultan's army had not been defeated, only a small vanguard and at that merely forced to retreat. Moreover, a messenger had been intercepted with a command from Qilij to the commander that he must hold out at all costs, relief was on its way he promised. But Hamza knew none of this nor of course did Manuel correct him.

"What do you want in return?" Manuel asked.

"I wish safe conduct for the sultana and her children, my retinue, and garrison soldiers. Also the city's inhabitants must be placed under your personal protection. No others. Certainly not the Latins.'"

"I'm agreeable to these terms. But I have some of my own."

"No doubt," Hamza replied. "But not now. I'm not ready to discuss this further. Please return tomorrow at this time. We shall finalize negotiations."

The next day Manuel and I rode to the city's gate. It stayed closed, opening briefly to allow one of Hamza's attendants to come out. "The commander has no need for further discussion," he announced curtly. "Nicea will not surrender. Thank you for coming."

Riding back Manuel observed laconically "It seems the commander received a fresh report."

I shall summarize now the events that transpired. I was not an eyewitness, thus my account is based on what I was told by those who participated. We received word that Qilij Arslan was only a short distance away, across a hill in a narrow valley. Our crusader armies were prepared thanks to the intelligence extracted from his spy. Horses were quickly harnessed, knights and men-at-arms donning their armor. They marched out. At Georgios's urging, I did not join the troops and, like everyone else, waited anxiously in camp for word. Qilij's army, thousands of mounted archers, foot soldiers following, had entered the valley. The Provençal force was divided in two, one under the command of Raymond and the other under Bishop Adhémar. They attacked from the north; Godfrey and Bohemond from the east; on the west was Lake Ascanius. Thus, Qilij was hemmed in a confined space and unable to employ the usual mobile cavalry tactics at which the Turks were so skillful: hit, run, then hit and run again. Nevertheless, the battle raged the entire day. The crusaders would yield ground then retake it. So it went with the Turks. By nightfall, when fighting ceased, neither side had gained the upper hand, both having sustained heavy losses. The battle was expected to resume in the morning. The crusaders returned to the camp, marching out again at dawn the next day. But once on the field of battle there were no Turks. Qilij and his army had decamped in the night. The wounded and dead were left where they fell.

As we waited, just above a rise I heard joyous shouts. Our troops had returned, decapitated heads of Turks spiked on their spears or hanging by cords from saddle pommels. With them was a wagon with ropes taken from Qilij's camp with which the sultan intended to bind his Christian captives for the slave markets, so confident was he of victory; another full to the top of the wall boards with Turkish heads. The cavalry then paraded back and forth in front of Nicea's walls shouting taunts at the defenders as they raised their spears with the spiked heads, pumping them up and down. The pilgrims gathered to watch the spectacle, clapping their hands with enthusiasm.

I then saw one of the nobles, I didn't recognize him, amble over toward an especially loathsome looking lot—barefoot, soiled and ragged clothes, sores on their faces—who had gathered with the rest of us to welcome the crusaders' return. He leaned over to confer with one, the same man I had seen earlier with Peter on the road to Nicea but again from a distance unable to recognize him. The man turned, quickly giving instructions to the pilgrims who surrounded him. There were rumors that some of Peter's followers had organized into a separate band, calling themselves "Tafurs", a name unfamiliar to me, a more despicable race of Frankish and Flemish humanity never created—not by God but by the devil himself. They were led by their self-styled "king", his identity unknown to us. They suddenly ran to their tents returning with staff slings—slender poles three to four feet long, straps looped to their ends, leather pouches laced at the bottom of the loops. They raced to the wagons yanking out Turkish heads by their hair. The slings were powerful. They placed heads in the pouches, ran to the wall as they made bloodcurdling shrieks, whirled completely around two times for momentum flinging the heads over the walls, then racing back out of range of the defenders' arrows. They were paid one penny from the princes' common fund for each head successfully thrown over the walls. I was certain that this money would find its way into the "king's" coffers.

The Siege Begins

That afternoon Manuel sent an emissary to Hamza proposing surrender on the same terms previously agreed to. The emissary returned shortly after to report that Hamza rebuffed the offer without explanation—perhaps he was outraged at the desecration of Turkish bodies; perhaps his courage was fortified by Qilij's attack, albeit unsuccessful, hoping for his return. Manuel called for a council. Manuel framed the question thusly: the city was now fully invested. Nothing, most importantly provisions, could enter or leave,. Should we wait to starve it out or commence aggressive siege action? A spirited debate followed, some arguing for patience until the city was starved into submission; others to assault the walls but delay until siege engines were constructed.

Count Raymond had a different plan. "My Lords. We are the Holy Warriors of Christ. His Providence is all the protection we need from heathen arrows. With that we shall surely be victorious. I say we attack now! Let us take this godless city and then proceed to our destination, the Sacred City of Jerusalem. My Provençals are prepared to lead. We can scale these walls with ladders. The city will fall."

Opinion was moving in Raymond's direction. Manuel offered a diplomatic if cautionary response. "Yes, My Lords, you are indeed the Warriors of Christ. But you should know this. Ten years ago General Tatikios laid siege to this city. He was unsuccessful. I urge you to prepare properly by . . ."

Raymond, having none of this, interrupted. "No! Let us attack now! The Lord will guide us." The decision was made. I thought of Tatikios's admonition: We Latins may know how to assault a wooden palisade but not a wall of stone thirty feet tall. He proved to be correct.

Work began immediately. The hills were rich in forests. Pilgrims were sent out with axes, felling trees, hauling them back with oxen and mules. Ladders were quickly built. There were ten in all, sturdy enough. Two days later the assault began. At dawn Provençal men-at-arms, carrying the ladders each with hooks to be attached to parapets, raced to the southern wall. The defenders responded with arrows, some of the Provençals falling, but the attackers succeeded in reaching the moat, placing the ladders against the wall, then pushing them upward until their hooks caught on the parapets. Three knights led, there being great honor for the first to cross over an enemy's wall, men-at-arms close behind, all shouting "*God wills it!*" The crusaders had almost reached the crenels of the parapets when archers appeared, leaned over the embrasures and released their arrows beginning with the knights. They fell, tumbling down, one knocking over another, all falling like clay tiles set in a row dropping in rapid succession. The Turkish archers then trained their arrows on the crusaders waiting to climb the ladders. The arrows fell with such profusion that the crusaders turned and fled. But the Turks were not satisfied. To the disgust of the crusaders, they lowered ropes with iron hooks attached, grabbed onto the fallen crusaders, some swimming in the moat desperately trying to get a handhold on its bank before sinking under the weight of their armor. One by one they were pulled up. Each was decapitated, stripped naked, and then thrown back over the wall. The crusaders were outraged.

Nevertheless the princes were determined to try again. At dawn the next day the crusaders attempted the assault once more but using a somewhat different tactic proposed by Manuel. Pavise shields were brought in place just within bowshot range. They were made of tightly woven wicker reeds, twigs and slender branches, shoulder-length tall, in a convex shape three sides protected by the wicker, only the rear open. Each was manned by an archer—some with crossbows, others with long-bows—and by pavisiers who steadied the shield as the archer shot over its top. Under the cover of bolts and arrows, knights and men-at-arms shouting the same battle cry as the day before carried their ladders to the wall and commenced climbing, as always the knights leading. The Turkish defenders were prepared. This time, instead of arrows, they dropped large rocks through the crenels. Once again, crusader after crusader fell. And once again the Turks lowered their hooks, gleefully pulling the soldiers up but on this occasion only halfway, securing the ropes allowing them to dangle; those alive screaming in pain, their feet kicking wildly; those who were still mercifully dead. The attack had failed, not to be attempted again. A different strategy was required.

Rebecca Rescues Miriam

The days that followed were relatively quiet, broken only by defiant taunts from the Turkish posts on the battlements daring us to attack again and in the crusader camp by axes hewing timber for siege machines directed by Manuel's engineers. The crusaders expended their restless energy on the broad field behind the camp: mounted knights in mock charges carrying lances under their arms or throwing javelins from atop their horses; men-at-arms in swordplay, perfecting their shield walls, or tossing axes at rectangular wicker targets; and archers sharpening their skills aiming on popinjays, wooden birds set on poles. Georgios was a regular and avid spectator. Rebecca's and my interests were inclined differently. We walked along the shore of the lake or into the forest nearby, careful not to venture too far, or wandered over to the sites where siege engines were being constructed, I being particularly intrigued by the technique of their assembly.

We spent the evenings playing chess on a set borrowed from Manuel, Georgios drinking with the Turcopoles. After Rebecca retired for the night, I would retrieve my journal and by candlelight make my entries for the day.

One afternoon the three of us strolled through Peter the Hermit's camp, carefully surveying the surroundings to avoid what for me would be a disagreeable encounter with Peter. One group of tents, fifteen or so, attracted Rebecca's attention. They differed from the others by red ribbons fluttering from the flaps of their entrances. Soldiers were periodically entering and then emerging. Not just men-at-arms. I saw Duke Robert of Normandy, a man as well known for his indifference to Christian rectitude as he was for his skill in combat enter one of the tents. Rebecca, whose curiosity exceeded that of a cat, wanted to investigate. I urged her against it. I saw Tafurs, unmistakable for their manginess, all bearing daggers in their belts, strolling between the tents greeting every visitor, customers I assumed, with an obsequious bow, conferring briefly, collecting a coin, then opening the tent's flap allowing him to enter. I recognized one of them, Peter Bartholomew, the monk defrocked by Pope Urban two years earlier at the chapter meeting in the Abbey of Cluny for consorting with a local prostitute. I should not have been surprised, nor was I.

Rebecca was about to turn around when a scream emitted from one of the tents, a female voice in Teutonic, "*Please! Please! You can't! Don't do this!*"

Rebecca looked at me in horror. "I know that voice. From somewhere. She needs our help!" "Rebecca. No!" I commanded. "Those men are Tafurs. We don't know what's in there."

"Then I'm going to find out," she said firmly, hastening to the tent, Georgios and I without choice following. We entered. The tent was bare but for a blanket on the ground. On it lay a woman, arms bound behind her back, her tunic pulled up to her breasts. A young boy was huddled in the corner crying. Over her straddled a man, his breeches down to his knees, the same I had seen at Clermont, at the village near La Charité where Peter had preached, on the road to Speyer, and then only days before on the road to Nicea walking with Peter. He bore the brand of a "V" on his cheek. It was Drogo. He had not yet noticed us, too intent on his prey, bending over, roughly kissing her neck and pawing her breasts, she struggling to resist. "I like a woman with fight in her," he snickered. "Please. Please. You can't. Don't," he said in mocking mimicry. "Yes, I can and will. You are a prize. We have customers. They must be served. You will do nicely. But you need *real* experience."

Rebecca instantly recognized her from the road days before. "*Miriam!*

Miriam!" Rebecca screamed. Drogo, startled, looked up. Rebecca lunged at him with unbridled rage, knocking him off, and then throwing herself over Miriam shielding her body with her own. Georgios and I stood there, confounded, uncertain what to do next. Drogo rose from the ground, pulled up his breeches buckling them. He was defiant. "This is *my* woman! Get out!" he shouted at us. He drew a rondel from its leather scabbard hanging from his belt, pointing its narrow blade first at me, then at Georgios, and then at Rebecca. At the time I thought it was the threat to Rebecca which prompted Georgios to act, though later as I reflected I became unsure. Miriam perhaps? Georgios stepped forward and with his fist struck Drogo on the side of his head. As he staggered back, Georgios grabbed his wrist clutching the rondel, twisting it so violently that Drogo shrieked and dropped it. But this evil man was not done. He pulled Georgios down, the two of them rolling over one another, crashing against one of two flimsy poles supporting the tent bringing it down over all our heads. I quickly crawled out backwards, freeing myself. The canvas was shaking violently, Georgios and Drogo locked in combat. I yanked the canvas pulling it off the others and dragged it away. Drogo's face was bloodied, Georgios unscathed. I helped Rebecca up, then Miriam, and then the boy crying and shaking with fear.

The commotion had excited the attention of the Tafurs who immediately surrounded us, their daggers drawn and with terrible, menacing expressions stepped toward us. Georgios, now upright, his eyes red with fury and his face flushed with anger, held Drogo by the hair, the rondel against Drogo's throat ready to slit it as he had the Turkish spy. "One more move," Georgios shouted at them, "and he dies!" The Tafurs didn't understand Greek but his meaning was unmistakable. They stopped, just glaring. I stepped forward and speaking in Frankish, which I knew some would understand, "Release the woman and the boy at once. Otherwise this Pecheneg will sever this man's head. Do it now!" One of the Tafurs, growling and snarling, cut the ropes that bound Miriam. Miriam rushed into Rebecca's arms, each holding the other tightly.

Peter's tent was close. I had seen it earlier but kept at a distance. Peter was standing outside watching the spectacle. I turned to the Tafurs, "One move to hurt us, he dies." We walked as quickly as we could to Peter's tent, Georgios gripping Drogo's neck the rondel still at his throat, Drogo stumbling as Georgios pushed him forward. The Tafurs followed. We reached Peter's tent. I looked at him. "Inside!" I commanded. He knew of the brothel. He knew of Drogo's wicked exploitation of these poor women, bereft of their husbands, dependent on this "holy man". They had paid dearly for their trust. We all entered the tent, larger than the others around it, the Tafurs milling about outside. Georgios threw Drogo onto the ground in front of Peter.

"Peter," I demanded, "do you know what's going on here? This loathsome creature is running a brothel. Under *your* eyes! A sin against God. This will bring the Lord's wrath down on us. Do you really, *really* believe we can expect His mercy when we indulge in such evil?" Peter just stood there, returning my glower with a blank look. Weakness oozed from every pore of his body. He did not answer my rebuke except to shrug his shoulder as if to say "What can I do?"

Drogo stood up, straightened his clothes, defiant as before. "You sanctimonious monk. Do you know who I am? I am Drogo, sovereign here, 'King of the Tafurs'. And you will honor me as such."

"I know who you are. The devil. Yes, you'll be honored. In hell!"

"Do you think we service here only 'soldiers of Christ'? You're a pious fool. No. We provide amusements for all—princes, nobles, even monks like you, bishops too." I looked at him in astonishment. "He snickered. "Yes, bishops too."

"Enough!" I answered, barely able to control my anger. "I sin even using your name. In two days the Council of Princes meets. I'll be present. I shall report this whoring." This may have been bravado on my part. Could Drogo have been referring to Bishop Adhémar? Surely not. There were other bishops in our army. It must be one of them. I could not believe Adhémar was complicit. If he were, there would be no value in remonstrating before the council. I walked up to Drogo, facing him squarely, our faces no more than a foot apart, the stench from his mouth so foul surely rivaling that of the dragon faced by Saint Sylvester which could kill three hundred men with a single breath. "You will give us free passage out of here. If you do anything to us you will face the fury of General Boutoumites, whom I serve, and of his Turcopoles. They will not show you the same mercy my Pecheneg has." Drogo nodded and raised his hand waving us out of the tent, squirreling up his face with a smirk but a weak one. The Tafurs had been waiting outside for a signal from Drogo. Georgios had now drawn his own dagger, far more fearsome than the thin rondel. He intended to use it, on all of them. We were allowed to pass.

Miriam and her son Thoman accompanied us to our camp. That evening Georgios neglected his usual Turcopole company in favor of us. Miriam needed protection but, more than that, comfort. She was shaken, whimpering occasionally. Rebecca did her best. What struck us both was how attentive Georgios was to her. He would jump up from his chair as we sat outside sensing each of her wants, always without request and always grunting, though mildly, as though the task were disagreeable. We decided that he wanted to remind us he was a warrior first, a warrior forever. He was indeed our warrior but soon became Miriam's chief comforter. Though she was a Teuton and he a Greek, neither able to understand the other, his devoted attentions required no translation. It is curious how two roads, one Greek and the other Teutonic, could intersect and then seem to merge. Rebecca whispered to me "I think he loves her." I didn't know. But the next day he asked me to tutor him in Teutonic. I did so. Daily.

* * *

It was two days later. I woke up early. I wasn't sure why. Perhaps I was concerned about the meeting with the princes at midday. Or perhaps it was the stillness of the camp that disturbed me. I started a small fire underneath a tripod from which hung a kettle. Rebecca was still asleep in our tent. Georgios had surrendered his to Miriam and Thoman, he sleeping outside. I heard that a shipment of provisions had arrived the previous night from Civitot and I intended to buy some bread, butter, and fresh meat to make breakfast for us. On the night before I had hung my pilgrim's satchel on a pole outside our tent. I intended to empty its contents and make room for supplies. The air was still and yet the satchel seemed to vibrate, albeit slightly. I was about to reach in when Georgios, awakened by my activity, leapt up and shoved me out of the way, so roughly that I tripped and fell. I never learned what had alerted him. Perhaps Georgios knew that Drogo could not possibly allow me to live given my threat of a report to the council. Drogo would try something.

He grabbed the satchel's strap and threw it to the ground. No sooner had it landed than a Turkish black viper slithered out. I had heard of them, their fangs needle-sharp and venom deadly. It quickly coiled itself, its head at first hidden in its tail then rising, unblinking eyes focused on me, only two feet away. At any moment it would strike. I rolled over, then again, to make distance. Georgios raced back to his tent reappearing with a sword in hand and stood before the snake. Its attention was now diverted to him, rearing up, tongue flickering angrily. Georgios was uncertain how to attack. They faced each other, neither moving. But in the most peculiar way I sensed this viper knew the confrontation would end badly. It began slithering toward our tent, seeking sanctuary in its darkness. In that instant Georgios made two quick steps forward, raised his sword cleaving the snake in half. Drogo would try to stop me. At any cost.

The sun was now high. I was about to leave for the council. "Wait!" Georgios commanded. "That adder was a message. Not just for you but us all. If you persuade the council to close his brothel there will be certain retribution. And I cannot protect us."

"Yes," I answered, "but Georgios, I must do *something*. I'm a priest. This practice is abominable."

"I understand," Georgios replied sympathetically. "Truly. But consider this: The princes will *never* consent. Duke Robert himself uses it and I'm sure others under the cover of night. And you heard Drogo, bishops too. And, not least, your Latin princes are terrified of the Tafurs, Drogo most of all. This will all be for naught. But you will have sacrificed us. For what Father?"

I knew that Georgios was not fearful for himself. It was for his new family, all of us. He was right. I relented but it gave me no pleasure.

The Siege Continues

The princes had agreed on a new plan: a simultaneous attack against the barbican gatehouse and catapults against a tower nearby. The ram was a bosson, an enormous log, stout oak, brought from the forest and cut to a twenty-foot length. One end was tapered with iron plates hammered over it and secured with bolts. A penthouse, nicknamed the *vulpus*, "fox", ten feet wide and twenty feet long, an imposing structure, was constructed under the direction of two of Duke Godfrey's nobles, Manuel's engineers advising them on design. It reminded me of a tent, not of canvas but of wood, on wheels. The walls were made of vertical planks to protect those inside from defenders' arrows, the front and back open. It roof, the mantlet, was shaped like an inverted "V" of woven osier wicker covered with hardened ox hides, thoroughly wetted. Under the roof, just below its peak, was a squared horizontal beam stretching the length of the penthouse to which were attached six slings of looped rope. The bosson rested in the slings, four feet above ground, able to swing freely from back to front.

Twenty men-at-arms, Godfrey's soldiers, manned the penthouse gallery, the open space beneath the mantlet. They slowly rolled it over the rough terrain, inching their way to the barbican gatehouse, its twin towers flanking the gate. The drawbridge inexplicably had been lowered over the moat rather than drawn upright, a malfunction perhaps. This allowed the penthouse to be moved within only a few feet of the imposing wooden gate, thick and strong. The penthouse was greeted with a withering fire of arrows as it moved forward. Once in place, the soldiers began swinging the bosson back and forth, gradually gaining momentum until maximum velocity had been obtained and then with a tremendous push crashing it against the gate shuttering with each blow reverberating like thunder from the heavens. Crusader horse and foot had assembled just outside of bowshot range expecting the gate to disintegrate at any moment. The ram pounded again and again but it held fast.

The Turks' defense initially was ineffective. They hurled stones over the parapets onto the penthouse but they bounced harmlessly off the steeply pitched roof. They then began pouring a liquid, I think a mix of oil and grease, onto the roof followed by flaming arrows to ignite it. But this too was futile against the hides soaked in water. It was at that moment the worst happened. The Turks changed tactics. They lowered a rope with an iron hook attached, similar to those used to grab crusaders during the ladder attack, however its curved mouth much larger. I could see it from my vantage point but the cover of the roof prevented the crusaders in the gallery from detecting this new threat. The ram extended four feet beyond the cover of the penthouse. Its forward swing against the gate was always delivered with such force that it was too quick for the hook to snare, the ram bouncing back with even greater speed. But it was during the moments when the soldiers attempted to stabilize it for the next blow that the ram was vulnerable. Three times the Turks swung the hook back and forth to catch the ram, missing. On the fourth they were successful. The ram was caught. The Turks began immediately pulling the rope upwards. The ram rose higher and higher until it reached the pinnacle of the penthouse roof and then began breaking through. The beam holding the slings started to crack and then broke. With that, the entire penthouse collapsed, the roof and all the heavy beams supporting it crashing down on the men below. For good measure, the Turks recommenced pouring oil and grease on the penthouse, setting it on fire with their flaming arrows. Those unable to escape were either crushed to death or burned alive. This assault had failed and the crusaders did not attempt it again.

As the ram was pounding the barbican gate, two catapults, mangonels, on wheels were rolled into place two bowshots from the wall and fifty paces from each other. They were rectangular in form, the longer sides of two constructed of squared timbers bolted one over the other, single timbers at the front and back. The throwing arm, shaped—may I say this?—like an enormous spoon, its cup hollowed out at one end, centered between the side timbers. The butt end of the arm, placed in the middle between the side timbers, was wrapped in a skein of thick, twisted cord fixed to the side timbers. Another skein of twisted rope was attached to the cup, the rope wound around a horizontal roller, a windlass, at the back end. This rope was ratcheted down by two men holding iron pawl levers until the cup rested on the roller. A stone was placed in the cup and then released by a slip ring, hurtling forward with tremendous velocity. For two days the mangonels hurled their eight-pound stones, the largest the catapults were capable of handling, against the thick wall but without significant damage other than chipping away some mortar between the ashlar blocks. This assault too had failed.

* * *

The princes hurriedly met in council. Yet another plan was needed. The escalade with ladders had been disastrous. There was no faith in a battering ram—the princes were shocked how stubbornly the gate held. The catapults too were ineffective against the immense walls of a fortress which had been continually fortified for over six hundred years. The princes' faith in God's intervention was quickly waning. Manuel suggested that, rather than trying to break through the walls, they dig underneath, sap their foundations. The most ideal location would be below the point targeted by one of the catapults. It seemed to be more damaged than the other and perhaps sufficiently weakened that sapping there would be more successful. The princes agreed and Manuel began his work. A new penthouse, nicknamed the *testudo*, "turtle", was constructed. It was similar in design to the *vulpus*—a tent-shaped roof covered with woven wicker and wetted ox hides on a wheeled platform. But there were differences. One of the side walls, also of thick planks, was hinged at the bottom so that it could be freely opened and closed when it drew up to the foundation. It was long enough for five or more sappers to work side-by-side and transport picks, wedges, spikes, hammers, sledges, tools needed to dig underground and dislodge the stone blocks.

There was one other difference in this assault. The princes understood that the escalade and battering ram failed in large part because the Turks had been able with impunity to shoot their arrows and drop stones and hooks from the parapets on their attackers. They must be deterred. Fifteen pavises were constructed, more than had been used to protect the ladder-climbers, manned by archers. The catapults were raised at their fronts with wooden pedestals and then reoriented to the parapet directly above the location of the penthouse beneath. It was hoped that a continual barrage of arrows, bolts, and stones would distract the Turks from the sappers. Construction took three days. Under the cover of night on the day previous to the assault soldiers laid planks over the moat so that the penthouse could be rolled to the foundation. All was in readiness.

I had planned to watch, from a safe distance of course. That evening, like all evenings since Miriam's arrival, was spent sitting around the brazier cooking and talking. Our conversations were now in Teutonic. I had been tutoring Georgios in this language and he progressed with remarkable alacrity. I was uncertain who was the better linguist, Georgios or I. He could understand well enough though he occasionally faltered when speaking, Rebecca or I then translating when out of frustration he slipped into Greek. But he could always make himself intelligible.

At one juncture in the conversation he made an abrupt announcement. "I tell you. Tomorrow I join fight. Be archer." I had sensed that Georgios chaffed from lack of action, his encounters with Turkish spies, Drogo, and the black viper it seems had not satiated this need. But I had not expected this.

Rebecca and Miriam were even more disconcerted than I. "No, Georgios. Please. No." Miriam begged. "You may be killed. Then what will become of Thoman and me? We could not bear this. I couldn't bear this. How can you do this?" her voice a mix of censure and plea.

Rebecca joined, her eyes welling up, "Georgios. We can't lose you. It's not too late to withdraw."

A look of great compassion overcame him. I believe he had anticipated opposition and was prepared for that. But not this display of such devotion. "It my duty, my honor. I be safe behind pavise. I be safe. All be good."

I knew Georgios. The very instant he invoked "duty" and "honor", I realized he was resolute. Dissuasion was futile, even from me. I now switched to Greek, desiring total clarity in what I was about to say. "Who is your pavisier?"

"I don't have one yet. I'm sure I'll get one tomorrow."

"I doubt it," I answered. "I've heard that the pavises will be positioned dangerously close to the wall. You'll have trouble finding someone. What if you can't?"

"Then I'll handle it by myself."

"My Pecheneg friend, this is little short of lunacy. A pavise is heavy. It needs two men to carry it into the field. This is folly."

"Then what do you suggest, my good Father Oderic?" his tone less derisive than teasing, although the moment he asked I could tell he regretted the question. He fully knew how I would answer.

"I will brook no argument on this. My vows as a priest forbid me from serving as an archer. But I can act as your pavisier. A pavisier does more than carry a wicker shield into combat. He feeds you arrows. If you are wounded, he is expected to aid you. You've rescued me too many times, my loyal friend. I *shall* be your pavisier. What kind of bow will you be using?"

"I don't know yet, probably a longbow."

"What experience do you have with one?"

"Not much," he answered sheepishly. "I don't remember. But how much more difficult can it be than wielding a sword and an axe. I'm quite adept at both."

"Yes, I know. But a longbow is a different weapon. It takes years of experience to acquire even modest proficiency. You need a crossbow." Like all Byzantines, including the Turks, he knew little of this weapon, a fact I found very curious but its use had not migrated east it seems. "Here's why. The crossbow needs little experience. Merely point and shoot. It's just as dangerous as a longbow, maybe more. It does have one shortcoming: You can shoot five or more arrows from a longbow in the time it takes to span, notch, and release a bolt from a crossbow. But what value is there in firing more arrows if you only miss? Besides, as you shoot I can load a second." To my surprise, Georgios quickly accepted my suggestion.

At dawn, the archers with their pavisiers gathered on the field before the wall, Georgios and I with them. Georgios was quickly schooled in the use of the crossbow, I in how to load one. We were given two. At the signal given by a trumpet all of us grabbed the back straps of the pavises—there had been no time to build wheels for each—and carried them to our designated positions, half a bowshot from the wall. Some were manned by archers with longbows; others, like ours, with crossbows. As we raced forward, the Turks fired their arrows but the thick wicker shields protected us. The penthouse was slowly being rolled toward the wall, in the gallery Greek engineers experienced in sapping, pushing it forward.

As it advanced, archers, catapults, and even Tafurs with their staff slings immediately began unleashing a torrent of arrows, bolts, and stones at the parapets, the Turks taking refuge behind the merlons. Georgios loaded the crossbow by standing upright over it, his feet on the twin bows and pulling the string to its catch with his powerful arms, all the time stooping just below the top of the shield to avoid an unfriendly arrow. I, on the other hand, less muscular, had to sit on the ground, my feet on the curved bows and both hands firmly on the string pushing the bows forward with my legs as I pulled on the string until I was supine and the string was snagged in the catch. Georgios would rest his crossbow over top of the pavise searching with his keen eyes. He found his first mark. His shot was true. "Got him!" Georgios exclaimed with great delight, handing his bow to me for reloading as he reached for the second.

The penthouse reached the planks over the moat and was then swung lengthwise, the hinged sidewall now fully raised to a vertical position, the sappers only an arm's length from the foundation. They began their excavation, picks, hammers, and sledges striking the stone blocks as they dug under the ground with their shovels. By nightfall the penthouse and archers were pulled back, redeployed the next morning when the attack resumed. One block supporting the courses of other blocks above it stubbornly refused to budge. It had to be removed. One of the Greek sappers exited the penthouse, spike and hammer in hand, and quickly began chiseling the mortar around the block. Just as he completed his work, the block dislodged, the Turks noticed him and redirected their attention from the penthouse to him dropping a flurry of rocks over him. He hugged the wall with his back sidling to his left, looking up and dodging the rocks as they fell. He could not step out for fear of arrows. Then a rope, hook attached, was dropped on the Greek's unprotected head stunning him, he swaying back and forth. The hook seized his jerkin as he tried desperately to shake it loose, his hands yanking frantically on the rope. But he was caught and the Turks began pulling him up.

From my pavise I watched in horror. Without giving thought to danger, my instinct was to save another mortal. Reckless. I stepped out from behind the protection of the pavise and ran toward the wall. "Come back Oderic!" Georgios shouted. I didn't hear him, too intent on reaching the Greek. He was now dangling just above the ground, tugging on the rope to slow his ascent up the wall. The rope was just beyond my reach. I jumped and wrapped my arms around his waist and with my weight began bringing him back down. I had almost succeeded when a second Turk above took the rope. I was so occupied with saving the Greek I had not noticed another hook coming down behind me. I felt it catch my belt. I was being lifted up. I was doomed. I had failed to save the Greek and now would pay the full price for this rash act. For the moment the mangonel slingers, the archers, and even Tafurs had paused to stare in disbelief. I had to release the Greek but both of us were now hanging separately, our backs to the wall kicking helplessly, pushing our feet against the wall swinging forward then crashing back into the wall.

Georgios had picked up the second crossbow, now more skillful with this weapon novel to him, and aimed it at the Turk pulling me up. He missed but only narrowly, the whiz of the bolt so surprising the Turk that he momentarily loosened his hold on the rope, I dropping to the ground. But he instantly recovered his grip and began pulling me up again. There was only one course of action for Georgios. He left the pavise, sword drawn, and raced across the open field toward me. "Hold on Oderic!" Seeing Georgios's attempt, foolhardy as mine and surely as futile, the crusaders now resumed their attack against the parapets, redoubling their efforts. A veritable hailstorm of missiles pelted the Turks. But the Turks continued to pull us up, their speed gratefully slowed by the barrage. Georgios reached the wall. He could not save us both. He chose me. He jumped, releasing his sword, grabbing the hook with one hand and with the other reaching for his dagger to cut my belt but I was kicking too wildly for Georgios pull it from the sheath. Another Turk joined his comrade and I was being pulled up again, two feet above ground. Georgios dropped down, retrieved his sword, and with one tremendous leap, his sword swinging, slashed the rope with a mighty blow. I fell. I had never experienced before or later such a sweet sensation of feeling the earth under my feet. Georgios picked me up, threw me over his shoulder as though I were a sack of goose feathers, and still holding his sword ran back to the protection of the pavise, laying me down. Georgios said not a single word. He just took his crossbow, loaded it, and began firing. I lay there, for a time too weary to assist, but I recovered and recommenced reloading the crossbows. Sadly, the Greek was not so fortunate. He was hoisted up the wall, stripped naked, a noose placed around his neck, and then lowered again as he feverishly clutched the rope while descending trying to rip himself loose. But to no avail.

His life had not been given wholly in vain. By dislodging the ashlar, the course of blocks it supported was now fatally weakened. The sappers braced the blocks underneath with wooden beams and as they dug further placed more beams under the foundation. Their work now concluded, they filled the cavity with brush stored in the penthouse, lighting it on fire. By now the sun was setting quickly. The penthouse and all the pavises were again moved back. Hopefully for the last time. The next day would tell us if the tower had crumbled. Looking back I could see a fiery glow, growing brighter and brighter. We had succeeded!

Or so we thought. At dawn the crusader army, all its companies, had gathered, ready to charge over the broken mass of tower blocks. But to our chagrin, as we looked more closely, the tower had not fallen. It was still tall, firm, and manned by Turkish archers on the parapets jeering. Manuel suspected that while our sappers were mining underneath the wall, Turkish miners were counter-mining, digging their own tunnel, meeting ours, and during the night filling it with rubble, a defensive measure very familiar to him. All our efforts had failed. Utterly. Our strategies were exhausted. We would have to abandon the siege.

An Unexpected Discovery

That evening the five of us had dinner together. Earlier in the day Georgios took Thoman into the forest and laid rabbit snares which he fashioned. Later they returned to find two trapped rabbits, plump enough for us all. Rebecca dressed them with remarkable skill, gutting the animals and with her nimble fingers skinning and cooking them over a spit. Miriam made a lovely pottage of meat and some vegetables I had purchased at the open market, the bread rather stale but freshened when dipped in the broth. Conversations over dinner were always expansive: sharing our day's activities, gossiping about one crusader noble or another, our plans for the future and our past lives. Rebecca, however, would never talk about her sons, adroitly avoiding the topic. It soon became clear to Georgios and Miriam that this subject was not to be broached.

I was interested to see how relationships were developing between the five of us. Georgios and Thoman had become rather close, almost father and son. And Georgios continued to be attentive to Miriam's needs, though still trying to conceal it with mild grunts and grimaces but even then his tenderness was impossible for him to conceal. And she seemed to repay his attentions with her own, washing and sewing his clothes, cleaning his boots, never needing to be asked. And to my greatest surprise, Miriam and Rebecca had become close, one a Christian and the other a Jewess. In a curious way that difference seemed to draw them together. Before retiring for bed every evening they would kneel side-by-side in a nightly ritual, Miriam beginning with a passage from a Christian prayer in Teutonic, Rebecca repeating it. Rebecca, in her turn, would select a passage from a Jewish prayer and recite it in Hebrew, Miriam stumbling and stuttering as she tried to reproduce it. Rebecca would giggle softly, then Miriam too shaking her head in frustration. It was joyous for me to see them both so happy together. I chose not to invade these private sessions, praying alone. Georgios prayed not at all. I think he preferred to rely on his sword than on God's grace.

After dinner, before the sun set, we would stroll through the camps, into the fields, or into the forest, occasionally to the lake, Ascanius. This evening was somewhat different. It was much later than usual, we having been caught up in conversation.

"So, where shall we go tonight?" Rebecca asked. "I feel like a walk. I'm not at all tired."

"The open market?" Miriam proposed.

"I think it's closed by now," I answered.

In such deliberations Georgios never offered a suggestion. I'm sure he would have preferred we all practice throwing axes. "What about lake?" he offered this time. "We not there for time."

"Yes," Rebecca responded eagerly. "The lake. A perfect night for it. It would be fun to see it in the moonlight. It's not so far."

The decision was made and we set off. The moon was nearly full and the wide path clearly visible. Georgios, behaving more like a schoolboy, and Thoman engaged in short races in front of us. On the first Thoman announced "I'll count. One . . . two . . . three, go!", both sprinting forward. Thoman won, rather handily I must add.

"My turn, one . . . two . . ." and Georgios was off, Thoman trying to catch up.

"Not fair," he complained. It was amusing to watch.

We reached the lake. Georgios and Thoman began scouring the shore for smooth, flat stones, competing with one another for the number of skips over the water. The rest of us just watched with pleasure. As I was counting the skips I looked further out into the lake. In the moonlight I saw a small flotilla of skiffs, sails furled and tied to their masts—if unfurled the white canvas would reflect too conspicuously in the moonlight—all propelled by oars covered with cloth. There was no wind as though a cloak of silence had descended over the lake, only the slight splashing of muffled oars. We watched silently, Georgios and Thoman immediately ending their sport. The boats approached the west wall of the city and tied up at a dock in front of a postern gate which opened directly onto the lake. We heard the rasping of chains raising a portcullis with men appearing below it. The sailors began transferring sacks of what appeared to be grain and boxes, I suspected full of arrows of which the Turks seemed to have an endless supply. After one left, another tied up. I had discovered the answer to a festering question.

By the time we returned to our camp, it was already quite late. I was tempted to meet with Manuel immediately but he was probably sleeping. A Council of Princes was scheduled for the next morning so I decided to wait until then. I thought the entire council should hear what I had learned and decided to attend even without invitation. One came nonetheless earlier that day by a messenger from Manuel who wished me to translate. All the princes were gathered in Adhémar's spacious tent. I was the last to enter, Baldwin greeting me with a grin, Manuel with a nod motioning me to stand beside him.

Adhémar presided as always. "My Lords. We have a decision to make. I've asked General Boutoumites to frame the issues for our consideration. General . . . ?"

Manuel stepped forward. "My Lords. We must decide on our next course of action. We've tried scaling Nicea's walls. That failed. Our battering ram as well, and the catapults did little damage—they can do no more. Sapping will be no more successful. Our blockade has endured for several weeks and never once was the city resupplied. I can only assume they prepared for this siege and stored sufficient provisions to wait us out, certainly at least until Qilij Arslan returns, as he surely will, and this time with a more formidable army. Our spies inform me that, as we speak, he is recruiting another one."

Manuel paused, searching for his next words. "You have, I believe, two choices. First, continue this blockade indefinitely until the city is starved. But this will surely take us into the fall, winter perhaps, too late I believe for you to march south. We'll have to wait here for spring. Or we can abandon the siege and march south. But northern Anatolia will still be in Turkish hands and it will be impossible for the Empire to provision you from Civitot. I can think of no third alternative."

The princes responded with silence, reflecting, broken finally by Raymond. "I agree with General Boutoumites. He warned us the city would be formidable to take. It has been. Further effort here, it seems to me, is profitless. I propose we abandon the siege and move south. We have already delayed our march to Jerusalem by many weeks, longer than expected. I fear God does not want us to be victorious here. His mysterious ways cannot always be divined. But He will guide and succor us on our journey." Raymond's confidence in God's providence was unfailing.

There followed mumbling, perhaps more a grumble, but of reluctant consent. The meeting was about to conclude, the princes turning to leave, when I intervened. "My Lords. A moment please. We've all wondered how the Turks could be so well supplied. We assumed, as General Boutoumites explained, that they had prepared for a long siege before we even arrived. Yet, the sultan departed from the city with his army, leaving his family and treasure here. I'm certain—and forgive please my impertinence but I must speak my mind—he did not expect us at all. Or, if he did, he did not anticipate your valor and military prowess," a truthful statement but pandering somewhat. "Late last night my companions and I were on the shore of the lake. We saw Turkish boats unload cargo at a dock on the west wall. Grain and arrows, perhaps other provisions as well. That is how they've been supplied, probably nightly."

A roar of surprise and anger erupted: "Who was watching the lake?" "How could this happen?" "Who's responsible?" "What are we to do?" There was complete confusion.

Manuel said nothing but was obviously deep in thought as the rancorous back and forth continued. Finally he spoke, rather softly for attention, the princes straining to hear. "My Lords. I think with this new intelligence we can agree that Nicea will be able to hold out indefinitely. There is no choice but to interdict their supplies."

"Just how do we do that?" one of the nobles from the back of the tent shouted out.

"With our own ships on the lake," Manuel quietly answered. The princes immediately broke out in hearty laughter believing Manuel was jesting. Manuel was not smiling, his lips pursed. The laughter slowly died down as they stared incredulously.

"You can't be serious?" Baldwin exclaimed, sharing the disbelief of the others.

"Oh, I'm very serious."

"I've never heard anything more foolish," Baldwin retorted "The lake is landlocked. We can't get ships through to it. General, you're mocking us."

"Not at all," Manuel answered. "We *can* bring ships. It will not be easy, but it can be done. We transport ships overland on sleds from Civitot. We have horses and oxen. The road is difficult and it is long, yes, twenty or thirty miles. But it *can* be done."

The mood was beginning to shift. Raymond again broke the silence. "This may be God's providential answer after all. We must try."

"Just who will man these ships?" Godfrey asked, less a question than a challenge. "We're soldiers, not sailors."

"The Basileus is at Pelekanum not far from here," Manuel replied.

"General Tatikios is there as well with three thousand Turcopoles. They can, though we will not require nearly so many. But we must decide now. Your answer, my Lords?"

All shook their heads lacking confidence in the plan. There was no other option. "Agreed" each muttered, reluctantly.

"Then I shall immediately send a messenger to the Basileus. The ships can be at Civitot in perhaps ten days. In the meantime my engineers will construct sleds." The princes were about to file out when Manuel said "One more thing. We need to begin constructing siege towers. Two will be sufficient. And work must be done quickly and in sight of the city in front of its north wall for the Turks to see. This will be more of a ruse and will distract the Turks from our real plan, attack on the west wall adjoining the lake and interdiction of their supply line. Father Oderic, our thanks for this information."

* * *

A party of soldiers and pilgrims marched with horses and oxen to Civitot where under the direction of Greek engineers sleds were built. I was keen to join them, to see the ships moved onto the sleds and then pulled to Nicea. Georgios, however, was adamant about remaining. He feared for Miriam's safety, Rebecca's too. Drogo was still present and so long as he was he would always be a threat. I agreed and remained. The following days passed uneventfully. Word reached us that the ships had arrived at the western end of the lake and slipped into the water. That evening we walked to the lake. We could see what appeared to be hundreds of ships, their mast lights flickering in the distance, all at anchor, and hear the pounding of drums and blasts of trumpets. But this was another of Manuel's ruses. There were in fact no more than twenty, modest sloops powered by a single sail and oarsmen, the most that could be transported, outfitted with additional lanterns to give the impression of an armada, the drums and trumpets to reinforce the impression. The effect on Nicea's commander was dramatic.

The following morning I received a message that Manuel wished to see me. I hurried to his tent. "General, you sent for me?"

"Yes Father. I've received word that Commander Hamza wishes to confer with me alone, no crusader prince present. I suspect the reason. I need you to accompany me again, the same as before." We rode to the south gate passing through without challenge.

We entered Hamza's office. He began with a bluff. "General, I must compliment you on your extraordinary exploit, bringing so many ships overland. Quite a feat. But it will be to no avail. I too can summon ships."

"Yes, perhaps," Manuel replied coolly, "but presently you have none. And even if you did, we have 'fire'. Your ships will not survive." Manuel was referring to "Greek Fire", the empire's most closely guarded secret, able to be shot from a ship setting afire anything it touches, even water unable to quench it. "And besides," Manuel continued, "we're constructing towers, soon to be completed. Reinforcements are on their way from Pelekanum, three thousand Turcopoles, marching now, here this evening. You will be fighting on three fronts: the west, the south, and the north walls. Your city will be taken, Commander. You can be sure."

"My Sultan, the Magnificent Qilij Arslan," he answered, "will be here within two days . . ."

"No he won't!" Manuel now visibly irritated. "No he won't. My scouts tell me he's many days away and has yet to fully amass his army. Shortly we shall begin our assault. Your city will fall swiftly. I don't know why you called me here." Manuel stood to leave.

"Wait! Perhaps there's another way. While our treasury is limited, there's enough to reward you and your Latin princes if they will leave in peace without further disturbance."

"No!" Manuel answered curtly. "This city belongs to the Basilieus Alexios Komnenos. It will be returned to him. Nothing less is acceptable."

"Then what is it you want?" Hamza asked.

"Your complete surrender. In exchange, your sultan's family, you, and your troops will have my guarantee of safe conduct out of the city."

Hamza was doubtful. "Your Latins have a reputation, which I cannot ignore."

"I understand your meaning. You will surrender to me and to me alone. You will be protected by my Turcopoles."

"And our treasury? Surely it can be brought with us? Though of course we will leave enough for you and your Latins," Hamza asked without particular conviction.

"No."

Hamza was boxed in, his arguments exhausted and his pleas rebuffed. "Then it is agreed," Hamza answered, understanding further negotiations would be fruitless.

"Not entirely. For this to succeed," Manuel looking at me as though to assure himself of my discretion, "we need a plan. I shall report to the princes that you refused to surrender the city. My Turcopoles will assemble tonight before your south gate as though in preparation for an assault the next morning. That will quiet suspicions of their presence. At midnight you will admit them. They will assume control of the city and it will be safe."

As we left the office, Manuel turned to me. "No word, not a single one, must reach the Latins or else all will be undone. I'm trusting you."

"You have my pledge. Not a word." I gave it readily for I knew fully well the fate of the Niceans should crusaders gain entrance. I did not want to see a repeat of Semlin. Immediately on reaching the crusader camp Manuel called for an emergency meeting of the council. He proposed that an attack begin on the morrow. The crusaders should assemble in front of the south and north gates at daybreak. His Turcopole troops, those not manning the ships, newly arrived, would be camped that evening before the south gate. This will distract the Turks from the primary attack by ships on the west wall, he promised. All agreed. I rather admired Manuel's artful duplicity, rendered with apparent full conviction. For the princes, the prospect of an early assault and plunder all too sweet for them to detect the subterfuge.

The next morning the crusaders had gathered as planned. The Turcopoles were absent though no one seemed to notice. As they waited, hardly able to restrain their eagerness, a flag was slowly raised over the barbican, yellow with a black double-headed eagle, the flag of Byzantium, its twin heads symbolizing the empire's claim to the world, east and west. And as it was hoisted, Turkish soldiers on the ramparts suddenly withdrew replaced by Turcopoles. The initial reaction of the crusaders was muted, they only staring at the flag as it fluttered in the cool morning breeze. But the gates remained closed. The deception soon became apparent. There was unrestrained wrath. Soldiers raised their spears and then slammed them on the ground, their booted feet stamping on the earth, all the time shouting "Treachery!" "We've been betrayed!" "Greek bastards!" Some of the crusaders ran to the gate pounding it with their fists, maces, axes, spears, or swords, whatever was in hand, demanding entrance, the Turcopoles merely looking down with curiosity. The crusaders had spent six weeks in the siege. They had fought the Turks and paid dearly. They expected the city as their reward. It was not to be.

Manuel and his Turcopoles remained in the city reasonably fearful for their own safety. That afternoon I received word from Baldwin that the council required my presence immediately. It was known that I had accompanied Manuel in his meeting with the commander. I confess to being apprehensive. Georgios wanted to stand with me but I refused. If the princes wished to take revenge, my loyal companion could do little to help and would only sacrifice himself, as I too well understood he was ready to do. To my surprise, the council was less interested in my role in the meeting with Hamza than they were in summoning Manuel to personally appear before it and explain his "perfidy", the princes assuming I had some special influence with the general and could coax him out of the walls. I left immediately for the city. Manuel had no desire to meet with the princes. He did ask me to convey the following message: "The Basileus will meet you at Pelekanum, two days hence, where you will be generously rewarded for your service." I dutifully reported back. The council was clearly disgruntled by the response. It wanted an explanation for Manuel's conduct from Manuel himself. Now! Nevertheless, without choice and tempted by the rather vague promise of enrichment, they agreed.

Alexios Meets with the Crusader Princes

The evening prior to leaving for Pelekanum a rider came to our camp and announced that Godfrey and Baldwin wished me to join them at Pelekanum to serve as their translator. I was excited to go and agreed immediately. Georgios, ever watchful over our family, decided to remain. He did not object this time to my absence, confident that if Drogo sought revenge he would have tried before. He hadn't. The next morning the same rider came with an extra horse and we left, joining the Lorrainer nobles waiting for me. Baldwin and I rode side-by-side exchanging stories of our schooling at Rheims. Perhaps, I thought at the time, Baldwin was more genial than I had heard. I expected him to question me closely about Manuel's meeting with Hamza. He was either unconcerned or assumed I would betray nothing. Either reason was satisfactory.

We arrived at Pelekanum, its principal feature a large wharf, across the Gulf of Nikomedia from Civitot. Four warships were docked, camels and horses hobbled nearby. Crusader princes and other nobles had already gathered inside the emperor's tent. This was no ordinary tent. It was the size of a modest palace, the largest I had ever seen, magnificent, pennants flying above its five turrets. Inside, at the far end, was a makeshift dais, two steps, on which was placed a high-backed throne of gold gilt. For an instant I wondered whether it would be the same levitating throne I had seen in the *Magnavra*. It wasn't, to my disappointment.

The emperor had not yet arrived. When I entered the tent, I saw one of the nobles, a Norman, lounging on the throne, one leg laid over the armrest, boasting of his own courage and prowess in fighting Qilij Arslan outside Nicea and how feeble the Turks proved to be. At that moment, Alexios, surrounded by his Varangian guards, appeared. It was Bohemond, as I recall, who shouted "Ragenard, off the throne!" He jumped up and hurriedly joined the others who had gathered in front of the dais. Alexios sat without a word, fixing his gaze on the assembly. All the nobles bowed. Alexios saw me and with his finger motioned for me to come forward. I did so. He was accompanied by a translator from the chancery whom I recognized but for whatever reason Alexios sought my services.

"What did he say?" the emperor asked me.

"Your Majesty, he was boasting of the defeat of Qilij Arslan and how easy it will be to vanquish the Turks on the battlefield."

Alexios merely smiled but his expression scornful. "Father Oderic, we wish you to translate. Word for word. Miss nothing." I bowed, acknowledging his request. He then looked at Ragenard, pointing at him in an accusatory fashion. The Norman was obviously uneasy being singled out. "You *really* think you were 'victorious' at Nicea?" Alexios scoffed. "Your arrogance astonishes us. Yes, the Turks suffered heavy losses. So did you. And yes, the sultan left the field. But he did not flee. You will meet him again, we can assure you. He will be waiting, somewhere." Then turning his attention to all of the nobles, his eyes scanning the assembly, "Do not underestimate the Turks. They will prove to be worthy adversaries. We know. We've fought them for years. You Latins avoid open field combat, preferring to raid a countryside, what you call the 'chevauchée'. The Turks relish the field, ideal for their mobile tactics. Their skill with a bow on horseback is unsurpassed. They can reload their bows repeatedly without dismounting; in retreat they turn in their saddles and fire just as quickly at their pursuers. And in retreat they are the most dangerous. They will pretend to flee, provoking you to give chase. If you do, an ambush will be waiting. They will try to encircle you, or attack your flanks or your rear, anything to break your formation. If you break, the battle is over. You survived Nicea because, more by chance than by design, you met them in a narrow valley where they were restricted. The sultan underestimated you believing you as easy a prey as was Peter the Hermit's rabble. He won't make that mistake again. But let us change the subject," Alexios now in a more conciliatory tone of voice. "We greet you on behalf of the Empire. And we commend you for your victory over Nicea."

Alexios may have miscalculated the crusaders' mood. It was sullen, hostile even. Baldwin shouted out what doubtless all the other nobles were thinking: "*Your* victory. *Your* general, Manuel Boutoumites, betrayed us. He took Nicea in *your* name and deprived us of our rightful plunder. Shameful!"

Alexios fixed a steely look at Baldwin, his smile vanished. "You princes all assembled here swore an oath on a holy relic, the sacred remains of Saint John the Baptist, to restore to the Empire what is rightfully ours. Nicea has belonged to us for seven hundred years. But let us speak plainly as warriors. We knew well Nicea's fate if your troops were permitted to enter it. Pillaged. Razed. Its inhabitants slain. We will tolerate no further discussion on this subject."

The nobles were stunned by the severity of Alexios's rebuke. But they *had* to know he spoke truly. Baldwin, however, would not be appeased. "And what of *our* rights. We invested Nicea for six weeks. What have we to show for it? Nothing! No plunder. You gave the Turks safe passage out of Nicea. We now have no prisoners to ransom. You even provided an escort for Qilij's wife and his family and welcomed them in Constantinople. They would have been a rich prize for us, a prize no doubt *you* will collect. *You* got your city. *Our* pockets are empty!"

There were vigorous nods of agreement and grumbling among the nobles. Anger was rising, to a simmering boil. Alexios raised his hand for silence. "Yes, the sultana was welcomed in our city. But she will be returned by us with no claim for compensation. We do not hold women and children for ransom. But perhaps this will soothe you." He motioned, his eunuch retainers carrying in one chest after another, four in all, setting them down and opening their lids. They were filled with gold and silver coins, diadems, precious gems, richly brocaded robes trimmed in black and white fur. The nobles were dumbfounded. They had never before seen such treasure. "Here is your plunder, from the palace of the sultan himself. I have added gifts of my own. There is a chest here for each of your princes—Lord Bohemond of Taranto, Duke Godfrey of Lorraine, Count Robert of Flanders, and Duke Robert of Normandy—to be distributed as they choose. For your men I shall be generous with copper coins, *tarantarons*, and free provisions." Mutterings of discontent quieted immediately. The nobles continued to stare in disbelief.

But from the back came an angry shout in Frankish, a Languedoc accent indicating a Provençal from the county of Toulouse, "Where is Count Raymond's share?"

"Is the count not here?" Alexios asked in feigned surprise surveying the nobles assembled in front of him affecting a search for the missing prince. Alexios knew fully well that Raymond, still nursing all his grievances against the emperor, would be absent. "Well, perhaps not. Your princes no doubt will be eager to share their treasures with him." The princes were silent. No one offered. The Provençals realized they would not benefit from the emperor's largess.

"There is one more matter," Alexios added. "I expect all of you to renew your oaths taken at Constantinople. These gifts," pointing to the chests, "will then be yours." They did so without delay or complaint. The audience was now completed. The emperor stood up and surrounded by his Varangians left the tent, the Latin nobles bowing, all that is except the Provençals. The betrayal of Nicea's surrender to the emperor rather than to them was still a festering wound, though the emperor's generosity at Pelekanum was a partial salve. Nonetheless, bitterness still ruled the hearts of some, especially Count Raymond and his Provençals, the only ones to leave Nicea empty-handed.

* * *

In two days the crusader army would decamp to depart south, to Antioch. Jerusalem, the ultimate prize, was now closer.

This ends Book VIII of *Jerusalem Falls!* Book IX begins.

BOOK IX
BATTLE OF DORYLAEUM

Departure from Nicea

The princes were anxious to leave Nicea as quickly as possible. Crossing the deserts and mountains of Anatolia to Antioch would be challenging enough, worse when winter snows fell. There was no time to squander. But our fallen warriors needed to be honored in death. Burying them would require many days, all except the Turks who were allowed to rot where they lay. I confess to being deeply conflicted over this. Yes, they were pagans, errant in their faith to be sure, but they were after all children of God. I thought of Galatians: "*There is neither Jew nor Gentile, neither slave nor free, nor is there male and female, for you are all one in Christ Jesus.*" I said nothing, realizing that such reservations would be unwelcome. The Council of Princes decided a quicker solution was needed. Only the landed aristocracy would be buried, all the others cremated on wooden pyres, this decision motivated in part because the princes did not want the Turks to discover how many soldiers they had lost. Timber cannibalized from the two partially built towers, their slender boards suitable for coffins and crosses, were used for the nobles. So many had sacrificed their lives in service to Christ: Robert of Paris, Baldwin of Ghent, Tancred's brother William Marchisus, Lisiard of Flanders, Hilduin of Mazingarbe, Anselles of Caium, and others, all *milites Christi*. For the soldiers, pits were dug and filled with beams from the mangonels and towers to serve for pyres.

Pilgrims were dispatched to the valley where crusaders had battled Qilij Arslan to burn the bodies accompanied by priests to perform necessary rites. The labor was especially disagreeable for in the intervening weeks their bodies had partially decomposed under the hot sun. At Nicea, across the broad field in front of the barbican gatehouse where so much of the siege had occurred and soldiers had perished, separate pyres were erected: for the Provençals, Normans from the north of Francia, Normans from southern Italia, Lorrainers, and Flemings. Their respective princes, knights, and men-at-arms surrounded each. A mix of grease and rendered animal fat was poured over the wood and, as a drum beat rolled and a trumpeter blew a dirge, archers solemnly ignited the fires with flaming arrows. Swords were raised upright and then lowered, heads bowed as Bishop Adhémar recited a prayer from of the Office of the Dead:

May the angels lead you into paradise,
Martyrs receive you at your arrival
And bring you to the Holy City, Jerusalem.
May the choir of angels receive you
And with Lazarus, once a pauper.
May you have eternal rest.

The smell from the pyres was unforgettable: acrid and putrid, yet sweet at the same time. I was momentarily nauseated. As the flames rose ever higher, illuminating the entire night sky, soldiers raised their swords again shouting "God wills it! God wills it!" I wondered: Is this truly God's will? Or is it man's?

General Boutoumites was ordered by Tatikios to assume command of the city. He was given a modest contingent of Turcopoles supplemented with wounded crusader soldiers both to garrison the city and repair damage from the siege. Manuel had tried to persuade Georgios to remain with him as his adjutant but Georgios's fealty to his "family" was too strong to break. He fully understood the dangers ahead but believed his sword more valuable to us than serving as a bureaucrat. Tatikios had given us a wagon pulled by a single mule previously used to haul siege tools from Civitot. We loaded it with our tents, cooking utensils, and other belongings. Miriam, accompanied by Thoman, drove the wagon, the wife of a simple peasant much more confident handling a mule in harness than riding a horse, even a palfrey. Georgios, Rebecca and I rode. Tatikios had decided to join the vanguard of the army with the bulk of his Turcopoles and we joined them. Georgios delighted in being with his Turcopole friends again, often turning his horse back to ride side-by-side with them, joking and talking. But, as always, he kept a watchful eye on Miriam and Thoman.

We left on the 26th day of June, the remaining divisions of our army following over the next two days. Our destination was Dorylaeum, an abandoned Byzantine fortress. Two days later we came to a river crossing and there paused for the remainder of the army to join us. Once all the companies had reassembled, Tatikios called a Council of Princes. "My Lords,"

Tatikios began, "in the last couple of days I have received intelligence from my agents that Sultan Qilij Arslan has established an alliance with the Emir of the Danishmends, Malik Ghazi. This was unexpected. It is also ominous. The Sultanate of Rum occupies the northern half of Anatolia to the west and the Emirate of the Danishmends the northern half to the east. Their relationship has always been uneasy and most recently they have competed for suzerainty of land in the southern parts around the territory of the Armenians. But now they have concluded that you Latins present a greater threat to them than they do to each other."

"Do you know their plans?" Godfrey asked.

"Regretfully, no. Not at this moment. I do know this, however: As I speak they are moving west gathering a large army as they pass through cities either recruiting or conscripting troops. And they are heading straight for us."

"Then let them come!" Raymond declared with his customary bravado, always a blend of boldness, arrogance, and foolish piety, the balance depending on his disposition. "I will cheerfully meet them on the field of battle where they will face the sharp points of our lances and the keen edges of our swords. They won't be able to hide like cowards behind stone walls as they did at Nicea."

Tatikios's tone of voice and expression changed immediately, becoming rather severe. He would not suffer nonsense. "The Turks are at heart still nomads. They much prefer an open plain in which to live and fight. I can assure you, just as the Basileus did, that *Qilij Arslan*, not *you*, will choose the time and place of battle, both that serve his purpose."

"General, do you know the size of their force?" Bohemond asked.

"Again, no, Lord Bohemond, except that it will be considerable and not to be underestimated."

"Lord Princes," Bishop Adhémar said, now taking charge of the meeting, "we must decide on a course of action. How do we proceed?"

Quiet followed. Finally Godfrey broke the silence. "I propose we separate into two columns, perhaps a day apart, a vanguard and a rearguard, more convenient for foraging. If we meet Qilij Arslan, we meet him. Only God can determine our fate."

Tatikios objected immediately. "My Lords. I urge you against this. Your strength lies in a united formation. Divided, you are weaker and vulnerable to Turkish harassment. Don't divide!"

I shared Tatikios's misgivings. This was precisely the warning the emperor had given at Pelekanum. I wondered too how one day's delay would aid foraging. But the princes made their decision, assuring Tatikios that they would maintain constant contact. They didn't. We departed the next day. The vanguard, led by Bohemond, consisted of Normans from south Italia, Normans from northern Francia under Robert of Normandy, Tatikios with his Turcopoles, and the five of us following Tatikios. The rear guard was under the overall command of Raymond of Toulouse and included Provençals, Flemish, Teutons, and Lorrainers led by their different princes: Godfrey of Bouillon, Stephen of Blois, Robert of Flanders, Hugh of Vermandois, and Richard of the Principate.

Battle at Dorylaeum

Upon leaving the river we began a gradual ascent up to a plateau bounded by hills on both sides in the far distance. We met no opposition. The previous night Tatikios's scouts had reported seeing a small force of Turks some miles ahead. He feared this portended a larger army not far behind but his anxiety was dismissed by the princes believing this to be merely a raiding party. Nevertheless, the princes did decide, perhaps to placate Tatikios, to camp that night beside a marsh thus protected on one flank. Other than this single precaution, the princes were confident they could proceed unhindered the next day. They were wrong.

That evening Georgios and I pitched our tents. Tatikios had kindly provided Georgios with a tent larger than Rebecca's and mine that would more comfortably accommodate Miriam, Thoman, and him. Yet Georgios continued to sleep outside. The five of us gathered about the brazier to warm ourselves and cook supper. Georgios and Thoman had ventured into a nearby woods earlier in the day, Georgios with his crossbow. He had now become quite adept at the use of this weapon. They returned to camp, a large pheasant slung over Georgios's shoulder. "Mother! Mother!" Thoman exclaimed giddy with excitement, "look what Georgios has done. You should have seen it! We were creeping through the tall grass," Thoman hunching down and taking a couple of stealthy steps with both hands pretending to be clutching a bow, "and there was a flock of them. Right in front of us! They began flying off. But Georgios . . ." Thoman with both arms mimicking the press of the crossbow's butt against his shoulder, finger on the trigger, his left arm supporting the bow, raising it as though tracking the bird through the air, and then shouting "Zing! He got it! He got it!" A hearty laugh came from all of us.

Supper was over. "I think time go bed," Georgios announced. "We leave morning and need rest." He had laid his bedding outside Miriam's and Thoman's tent as before, ever their guardian. He rose from his seat and began walking toward it. "Georgios," Miriam called after him, "our tent is large enough for three. Perhaps you could stay with us. I know Thoman would like that and . . . " her voice lowering as she raised her head to look directly at Georgios, "I wouldn't mind. Besides the days are hot and the nights cold. Stay with us." Georgios was rather stunned. He began mumbling something I didn't understand but for one word "yes." He opened the tent's flap and the three of them, bending over, stepped in. Rebecca and I just smiled at one another.

The evening was pleasant. Georgios and Miriam had retired. Rebecca and I decided to walk, rather aimlessly. We wandered into Godfrey's camp, happening upon the same sumptuous tent used by his brother Baldwin in Constantinople. Baldwin was sitting outside with another prince, Robert of Normandy, the very noble I had seen using the services of Drogo's brothel at Nicea. There was a third man dressed in a rather fine cassock, a priest of some significance though I didn't recognize him. We were perhaps fifty paces away. I was about to turn Rebecca in a different direction when Baldwin noticed me.

"Father Oderic," waving me over, "please come join us. It's been a while." Without choice, we approached. "This is Duke Robert of Normandy, son of William the Conqueror," this last detail mere surplusage in the introduction, perhaps to give evidence, I thought, that he kept only the finest company. "No doubt you recognize him from the council at which you so ably translate," Baldwin said, smiling. I bowed to the duke.

"Yes, I know you Father Oderic," Robert said. "Let me introduce you to my chaplain, Arnulf from Choques, Bishop of Rohes, like you a man of God. He has a multitude of virtues, the most important for me is the efficiency with which he hears my confessions and presides over our private masses."

I bowed to the bishop with a brief "Your Eminence".

"My Lord," Arnulf responded, his tone servile, "your sins, such few as they are, are venial and permit more expeditious confessions. Besides, a mass needs no more than a bit of bread and wine and then a swift benediction to answer God's need."

"Indeed," Robert answered, "and you even light a candle for me every night. Very thoughtful, Your Eminence," he said with a wide, wry grin.

"Yes indeed, my Lord. In fact two, one for God and the other for Satan. One can never be too sure." Robert and Baldwin broke out in boisterous laughter. I smiled weakly, saying nothing. There was something about

Arnulf to which I took an instant dislike. He was short, obviously well fed from the bulge under his cassock. But it wasn't that. It was his deep-set eyes, thick black eyebrows, and especially his wide oleaginous smile reminding me of grease from a rendered mutton dripping from his lips down to his chin. It was only later I saw how ably he was by his unctuous manner to insinuate himself into the confidence of nobles, only men of consequence, despising those who were not.

I looked for an excuse to leave. Fortunately, Baldwin gave me one. "Father, it was nice to see you. Have a pleasant night."

The sun had just risen over the crest of the eastern hills. The sky was perfectly clear, a brisk breeze blowing through. I threw a cloak over my tunic for warmth. We had risen early and began to decamp, packing our belongings in the wagon, the mule already harnessed, when we heard shouts. In the distance I saw two riders, scouts that Tatikios had sent out the day before, galloping pellmell into the crusader camp. "The Turks are coming! The Turks are coming!" I could see behind them, over a rise to the east, what at first I took to be a dark swarm of locusts, infinite in number, countless. And as they cantered down the hill their number seemed to exceed the blades of grass over which they trod. Qilij Arslan was here! Tatikios had been correct. The sultan would be waiting for us and pick his own time and place. He had.

The Turkish army drew closer, a mass of mounted archers in front and behind them foot soldiers. Leading it was a rider whom I could see somewhat indistinctly, holding a pennanted spear in his hand, on either side of him a rider bearing flags emblazoned with silver crescents. That had to be the sultan, Qilij Arslan himself. He stopped and then with his spear pointed north and south, two companies of archers immediately splitting off in both directions. Their purpose: to encircle and annihilate. He paused and then raised his spear again, pointing directly at us. In that instant drums began beating furiously as one squadron after another of archers galloped forward. This seemed perfectly synchronized and the attack carefully planned. They wore *bashlyks*, felt conical hats, over their heads, a few trimmed in fur, sergeants I assumed; loose shirts over which were leather cuirasses and equally loose breeches tapering down their legs slipping into knee-high boots. I was struck by their horses, considerably taller than our own, sleeker, almost refined in their contours with long necks and backs, and most important faster than ours. But most terrifying was their bows, short, composite of wood, horn, and sinew, a fearsome weapon, exceeding our own in range and power.

They charged, screaming and howling in some daemonic language like devils from hell, "Allah akhbar" or some such. And then, from a considerable distance beyond the reach of our own bowmen, the archers rode from right to left shifting in their saddles unleashing a thick shower of arrows. Other riders, all holding javelins, raced directly for us, throwing them then racing off. Panic gripped our army. Total confusion. Never before had they seen anything like this. Bohemond tried to restore order but his commands could not be heard over the clamor of hysterical soldiers bolting in every direction. Thoman was almost trampled in the mêlée, saved only by Georgios who seized the boy around his waist and held him, his arms flailing forward and his legs kicking. Knights mounted their horses, grabbed lances handed to them by their squires, but in disarray.

Bohemond had to act. He saw a crusader flag, white with a red cross, planted in the ground. He leapt on his horse, jerked the reins and spurred it toward the flag yanking the pole up and holding it aloft for all to see, racing alone to face the Turks. Robert, seeing Bohemond, flung his helmet to the ground for his men to recognize him, and shouted "Normandy!" speeding forward to join Bohemond. The Norman knights, rallied, regaining their courage, and raced off to join their princes with whatever weapon they could seize in the moment: lance, spear, sword, or mace. Bohemond and Robert, their knights closely behind them, charged the Turks, not the premeditated attack Bohemond would have preferred but decisive, even reckless, action was imperative. The Turks refused to engage, wheeled around as though in flight turning in their saddles and firing from behind over their shoulders at the pursuing knights with the same rate of volleys as they attacked. Many of our men fell. Bohemond slowed to a walk, uncertain. The Turks immediately wheeled around again and resumed their attack, some galloping to Bohemond's right, others to his left, encircling our knights. We were outmatched, our weapons in hand unequal to their bows, they able to shoot at will from a distance. The pursuer was now the pursued. Bohemond, without choice, signaled by his flag for the Normans to retreat back to the crusader camp chased by Turks.

I learned later that it was at this instant Bohemond remembered Alexios's admonition: under no circumstances break formation. When Bohemond reached the camp, he flung the standard to one of his foot soldiers, turned about, and with his hand directed knights to form to his right and others to his left. He then shouted for his archers to move forward, in front of the knights. "Shoot at will. Kill the bastards!" The Turks' counterattack ceased and they moved back, out of range. Bohemond then raised his hand upright commanding his troops to hold. But one knight, Ragenard, the same arrogant Norman who had lounged on Alexios's throne at Pelekanum, broke ranks just too tempted by the "flight" of the Turks. He was followed by forty knights. Bohemond shouted "Ragenard! Back! Don't!" He either didn't hear or didn't care, galloping forward. The Turks yet again wheeled around but were now joined by two small squadrons of archers who began circling them unleashing their arrows. Ragenard was trapped, surrounded, no escape. His knights charged in every direction like wild boars attacked from different sides, lunging at one attacker then at another. Somehow only Ragenard was able to break out, two arrows in his back. A terrible, but perhaps salutary lesson for the others.

* * *

Georgios feared the situation hopeless for the crusaders. How many more Turkish attacks could they withstand? And we were too close to the front line for Georgios to be comfortable. We needed to find safety further back where Bohemond, on the arrival of Turks, had ordered pilgrims to seek protection behind supply wagons. We both knew that the rearguard was a day away. Would it come in time? "*We have to get them out of here!*" Georgios shouted at me over the din. "Back to the supply wagons!" I jumped into the perch of our wagon, Georgios leaping up beside me. I expected him to be girded with his sword only but this time he wore two baldrics, wide leather straps slung over each shoulder, one holstering a sword at his waist, the other a Pecheneg axe. He seldom carried the axe but seemed to anticipate a fearsome fight. He looked equal to the task. "Rebecca, Miriam, Thoman," I yelled, "*get in!*" I shook the reins and turned the wagon back through the camp, slowing only to avoid soldiers and pilgrims running helter-skelter. There were five enclosures, each surrounded by carts and wagons, their shafts and tongues lashed to one another, completing, if imperfectly, a barrier. I selected one, this having a gap in the circle just large enough for our wagon to squeeze in. Within the enclosure pilgrims—men, women, and children—were huddled in fear, children wailing as their parents tried to comfort them. Some priests, ten I think, had formed two lines facing each other singing the hymn *In Paradisium*, the requiem mass for the dead. Others, including the esteemed Bishop William of Orange, were ministering to the pilgrims, distributing communion and hearing confessions for none expected to survive.

My attention was drawn to one of the priests dressed in a white cassock with a richly embroidered pallium around his neck falling over his shoulders, clearly a priest of significance. It was Bishop Arnulf. He was bending over a peasant woman, rather attractive, it appeared receiving her confession. I left Rebecca, Miriam and Thoman in Georgios's care and hurried toward Arnulf, mightily curious about whatever he was saying for he was clearly bringing little comfort to the woman. In all the noise and confusion Arnulf had not noticed my approach.

"You have sinned, grievously, my child," I could hear Arnulf telling her. "Your vice and corruption in the brothel have brought you, all of us, in the eyes of God to this fate."

"But Father, I sinned *with* you. Surely God will forgive me. I was poor. My husband and child dead. No one to care for me. What else could I do?" I now understood who was the "bishop" using the services of Drogo's brothel. Arnulf himself. I was filled with disgust.

"Yes, I know we sinned together," Arnulf answered. "I repented. God forgave me. But Our Lord cannot pardon someone like you so easily for you tempted a priest into a mortal sin. I fear your soul is doomed."

At that the woman began to weep uncontrollably. "Oh Father. Please! Please! Find forgiveness in your heart. Then God may."

"There is no hope for the wicked. This will be God's Judgment, not mine, but I fear the worst for your salvation." With that, Arnulf raised himself upright and walked a few paces away to another woman, again bending over to speak with her. I could hear only indistinctly what he said but his message was similar: sin and damnation. "*The evil man out of evil treasure brings forth what is evil. His mouth speaks that which fills his heart.*" I could not bear this. I went over to the woman and knelt before her. "My child. I am Father Oderic. I overheard your confession and you needn't give it again. Our Lord is truly merciful. *Te absolvo.* Your place in Heaven is assured with your repentance. I promise you. Be brave, my child." With that I gave the sign of cross over her and placed both my hands around hers. I then went to others, one by one, hearing their confessions.

As the priests were singing, one of the soldiers whom Bohemond had left to guard us shouted "*the Turks are here!*" and in that instant he was struck by an arrow, falling to the ground. Wild shrieks and screams came from the pilgrims. I had just finished hearing a confession and looked up. There was a squadron of mounted Turkish archers galloping toward us. I recognized their commander, Captain Elchanes from Xerigordos. Georgios grabbed Miriam, in his haste throwing her under the wagon so hard that she struck her forehead against the wagon's sideboard. "Ow!" she cried out. But this was not the time for chivalry. I roared at Rebecca and Thoman, "*You too. Get under!*" As they crawled under the wagon Thoman began to whimper, trying his best to control himself, to show the same manly courage as Georgios. Georgios bent over to look at him in the eyes, "Brave, my son. I protect you." With that, he stood up, drew his sword with one hand, his axe with the other, his feet firmly planted in the soil, the same stance he had assumed at Civitot, ready to defend his family. At any cost.

Six Turkish mounted archers, perhaps more, Elchanes leading, jumped over the wagon tongues and rode into the enclosure, swords swinging, the Turks intent on killing as many Christians as they could. We were being overrun. Crusader soldiers left their posts outside the enclosure and sprinted in. One of the Turks dismounted. He had seen Arnulf, distinguished by his rich clerical dress, a delicious Christian victim for a Muslim warrior. Arnulf saw him draw closer, the Turk's design evident. Arnulf had just been "ministering", a term I use charitably, to yet another female pilgrim. As the Turk stepped forward, Arnulf fell to his knees, his hands clasped, looking up at the Turk. "I beseech you," he implored pitifully. "I am a man of God. I deserve to live! Spare me!" Of course, the Turk understood not a word; even had he it would have made little difference. A smirk came over his face, full of contempt. This Turk would show no more mercy to him than Arnulf had shown to the penitent women. Arnulf jumped up, clutched the hair of a woman next to him yanking her to her feet. Holding both her arms from behind, he pushed her forward, "*Take her! Take her!* She's a slut anyway! I beg you. *Take her!*" The Turk raised his sword but at that moment the Turk felt a Norman spear through his back. With God's mercy, the woman was saved. I was more conflicted about Arnulf's life. The bishop just slumped to the ground, whimpering, crawling to the wheel of a cart, wrapping his arms around its spokes as though it would protect him. Arnulf saw me and extended his hand for help to stand. I just looked at him scornfully and walked away. Had I not been a priest I might have dispatched him myself. He would not forget the slight. I had other problems.

Elchanes had been the first in. He recognized Georgios and immediately turned toward him, charging. As Elchanes closed Georgios stepped back and swung at the horse with his sword, slicing its neck. The horse instantly fell with a shriek, Elchanes under him. But the Turk was able to quickly pull himself free and stood opposite Georgios. Another Turk archer, seeing his commander, then turned his horse to join the fight against Georgios. My friend now faced two. On the ground within easy reach I saw a stout staff three feet long wielded by a pilgrim lying beside it. Within equal reach was a sword belonging to a fallen soldier. I hesitated for a moment and took the staff. Gripping it with both hands at one end I raised it to my shoulders, ran forward and drove it into the chest of the Turk, toppling him backwards over his horse. As he lay on the ground trying desperately to right himself I raised the staff and brought it down on his chest, then his head, again and again and again. I was going to send this Turk to hell. And I did. I stopped only when he was still, his eyes open and blank. Later, I prayed for forgiveness but without too much conviction. My consolation was that I had not used a sword, forbidden to priests, though I was uncertain that God would make that fine distinction.

But now a second Turk, having dismounted, ran toward me. Five paces away he stopped and began twirling his scimitar, then swinging it back and forth, playing with me just as Thomas of Marle had in Mainz. He wore the same vicious expression I had seen on the Turkish spy as he was about to pierce my throat. He lunged with a swing; I stepped back parrying his blade with my staff the best I could, unaccustomed to this weapon. And back and forth it went, he giving no quarter trying to close the gap between us as I thrust my staff, pulling it back, jabbing again to keep him at bay, all the time stepping back. Finally my staff was able to strike the haft of his sword which he dropped. At that moment I slipped and fell. The Turk leaned over to pick it up and as he rose, his face turning to me with a broad smirk, mocking, I heard a whirring sound as though something hurtling through the air. I looked up to see Georgios's axe protruding from the Turk's chest, its handle quivering as the Turk swayed back and forth and then fell. Georgios ran over extending his hand to help me up. We both looked around. The Norman soldiers had cleared the enclosure of the Turk invaders. In the meantime the Turkish archers had inexplicably ceased their attack, their horses outside the enclosure stationary, waiting for something. What was it? I didn't know. But for the moment we were safe.

I noticed a small squadron of Turcopole riders, five in number, gallop into the general area. They stopped at one enclosure, five hundred paces from ours, their sergeant cupping his hand over his eyes to shield himself from the hot glare of the sun scanning the people inside, searching for someone. He moved on to the second, and then to ours. He saw Georgios, dismounted, passed through the enclosure stepping over the tongue between our wagon and the next.

"Captain Vardanes," the sergeant saluting, "the Latin rearguard has arrived. General Tatikios has ordered the Turcopoles to assist it. He requests your presence immediately, I believe to lead a company. We have an extra horse."

The clamor of battle in the enclosure had subsided, Rebecca, Miriam, and Thoman crawling out from under the wagon. We were all standing around Georgios, none but me having heard the exchange between Georgios and the sergeant but they became alarmed by the expression on my face. "The threat is not over," I told Georgios. "Look," I said, pointing out to the field beyond the enclosure where the Turk archers, though motionless, were watching us. "They're still here. You can't go!"

"Father Oderic . . ." he began. That was always a bad sign. He only called me "Father" when he had something unpleasant to tell. "The Empire has summoned me. This is my duty. You fought well today. Like a Pecheneg. I can think of no man I would rather go into battle with than you. You have indeed become my warrior-priest as we Pechenegs foresaw." He thought this a compliment. I was less certain.

"Duty again," I exhaled, looking at the ground, shaking my head in disbelief. I said nothing more for I knew that when Georgios invoked "duty" further argument was mere empty rhetoric.

The sergeant stood, waiting for an answer. "In a moment," Georgios said, looking at the sergeant, who nodded and returned to his horse. Georgios stepped over to Miriam, kissing both her cheeks, hugged Rebecca, and then tousled Thoman's hair. "You care your mother," he instructed the lad looking down at him. "You man now. I be back." It sounded all so final. Without a further word he joined the squadron and galloped off, kicking up a cloud of dust obscuring him as he rode away. Would this be the last time I would see my friend and protector? I had come to despise Pecheneg honor.

It was just as Georgios rode off that the Turks did as well, in the direction whence Qilij Arslan had first appeared. I now understood the reason for their departure: to reinforce the main army with the arrival of the crusader rearguard. I remained with Rebecca and the others fearful that the Turks would return. Thus, the following account is of necessity based on interviews with several eyewitnesses. After all, I had promised Prior Damian to provide not just an accurate chronicle but a complete one.

Following Ragenard's debacle and before the rearguard had arrived, Qilij Arslan decided to throw his infantry at the crusader line. Bohemond ordered his foot soldiers to position themselves ten paces in front of the knights but no further. They would wait. Each carried a spear and a shield made of wood and covered with hardened leather, shaped like the kite I used to fly with my father in Rheims, broad at the top tapering down to a rounded point, many painted with differently configured heraldic designs, each the symbol of their lord. Swords and daggers hung from their belts. A few wore chain mail hauberks but most hardened leather jerkins; others metal helmets fashioned like simple bowls though most were bareheaded. They were formed in three ranks, in front the infantry, behind them archers, and then behind the archers mounted knights. Robert of Normandy, who had dismounted, stood with his foot soldiers, Bohemond on a horse with the knights.

As the Turks advanced, spears and scimitars in hand carrying round shields, smaller than our own, Norman archers fired arrows and bolts at the enemy over the heads of the infantry. "Hold fast!" Robert commanded. "Hold fast and wait!" The Turks were now closing, within fifteen or so paces. Robert raised his sword "shield wall up!" The Normans immediately closed ranks, sidling to their left until all shields overlapped, their spears raised shoulder-height resting over the shields. The Turks rushed forward. Robert shouted "*Normandy! Normandy!*" The Normans joined the cry and with perfect precision in an unbroken line, one step after the other, began moving forward, the shield wall impenetrable. There followed a thunderous clash of shields, spears, and swords. The Turks were being pushed back, slowly but inexorably, the Normans thrusting their spears into the Turks; when one broke the soldier would reach for his sword, cutting and slashing. But then a Turkish horn blew, and the Turks turned and raced back as though in flight. Bohemond could see in the distance detachments of mounted archers, bows ready, arrows notched, watching and waiting. The flight of the Turks seemed to him too well rehearsed, orderly. This was a trap.

Bohemond knew his Normans. Giving chase to fleeing Turks would be just too tempting. He spurred his horse through the ranks of the archers and infantry to the front, cantering up and down the line, "*Normans!*" he shouted, his sword at arm-length pointed downward as he waved it back and forth over the foreleg and flank of his horse, "*stand fast!*" The line held, remaining steady. The crusaders waited in its massed formation for the sultan to make his next move. He didn't. It was midday, the sun was scorching. Perhaps he was waiting for the crusaders to exhaust their strength from the heat. Relief for our soldiers came in the form of buckets of water brought from two springs carried continuously by pilgrim women who went up and down the lines, the soldiers greedily drinking from ladles. However, a sense of doom enveloped the crusaders. They had suffered serious losses, as had the Turks, yet they were still vastly outnumbered. No one, not even Bohemond, thought they could resist one more attack. Their only consolation, as one noble told me later, was that they would all suffer martyrdom together.

At that moment they heard the blare of trumpets. Godfrey and Hugh of Vermandois leading their knights rode out onto the field, Raymond and the other princes close behind, their knights holding either lances or javelins, all pennanted and upright, men-at-arms following. Bohemond had earlier in the morning, after realizing that the "raiding party" was in fact the advance guard of an army, sent a message to the rearguard several hours behind that their situation was perilous, the need urgent. The Norman foot and archers quickly fell back behind the cavalry line as the rearguard knights joined the Norman knights, forming a broad front, Robert of Normandy and Stephen of Blois to the left; Raymond of Toulouse, Robert of Flanders, and Richard of the Principate in the center; Bohemond, Godfrey of Bouillon, and Hugh of Vermandois to the right. We must have presented a terrifying sight to the Turks, like a ghost appearing just before death, a wraith, our knights wearing chain mail hauberks reaching down to their knees; some with chausses, mail leggings; to cover their heads mail coifs or conical iron helmets, nose guards to protect the face, secured by leather straps under this chins. Their shields, identical to those of the foot, were slung over their backs. The Turks had never before faced such a heavy cavalry, massed, tightly disciplined, their usual tactic of goading an enemy into pursuit to break its formation was unavailing. Our knights faced the Turks, disciplined, motionless, silent, staring ahead.

Bohemond nudged his horse forward in front of the line facing the Turks, sword in hand, ready to lead a charge. The Turks hesitated. They had apparently thought the vanguard was the entire crusader army. There was no movement on either side. And then, just above the rise of a hill, the crusaders could see flashes of light, the reflection of the sun on helmets and mail, like an apparition. It was Bishop Adhémar. Before taking the field, Raymond had split his force of Provençals, Adhémar commanding the smaller contingent. He had been guided by Turcopoles up a path over a small mountain and then to a hill flanking the Turks. He was clothed in armor, holding at arm's length a gleaming processional cross seated in a holster beside his stirrup, two priest attendants clad in vestments on either side of him bearing white banners emblazoned with red crosses.

The effect on the crusaders below was rousing and shouts erupted.

At Bohemond's command, the knights couched their lances or raised their javelins over their heads ready to fling them and began walking forward, then a trot, speeding to a canter, and finally breaking into a full gallop. Adhémar's troops too began racing down the hill. The Turks were thrown into confusion, attacked from the front and now the flank. They turned and fled, no blast of a trumpet signaling an orderly retreat, spontaneous and confused. This was no Turkish feint. It was flight. For two days our knights pursued them, killing every one they could outrun. I myself know the truth of this for, after leaving Dorylaeum, I saw the evidence, bodies for miles. In their pursuit the crusaders came upon Qilij Arslan's camp. There they found hobbled horses, mules, and camels; but more important chests of treasure—silver and gold coins and precious stones—with which the sultan intended to pay his troops, plunder indeed for our own. Victory was complete.

I Search for Georgios

News spread quickly. No longer in danger we headed back to our camp and waited for Georgios to return. Time passed. He didn't. I became apprehensive, anxiety increasing with every hour. I could bear this no longer and ran to the battlefield. I was shaken to see so many crusaders dead. Some Turcopoles were moving from one body to another, examining each, looking for their comrades in order to give them a proper burial.

"Do you know Captain Georgios Vardanes?" I asked one, dreading the answer. "Have you seen him? Is he here?"

"Yes, I know him. He's not here. I heard that on his way to the front lines his squadron was ambushed near the marsh." I began to panic. The Turcopole, seeing my reaction, added in a soothing tone, "But, of course, I don't know for sure. It's just what I heard."

"Where? Where?"

"Near the marsh. Somewhere."

I ran to the marsh, panting and near out breath. I scoured the road inch by inch but no evidence of Georgios or fallen Turcopoles. And then I looked out toward the marshy lake. To my horror I saw bodies floating on the water a hundred paces out. I waded in but with every forward movement the water rose until it reached my neck and yet I was still quite a distance from the bodies. The reeds became thicker and thicker, becoming increasingly difficult to push through them. I knew that if I went further I would suffer the same fate as Georgios. Heartsick, tears in my eyes, I had to abandon the search. What would I tell Miriam, Rebecca, and Thoman? Do I give them certainty of his death, knowing their reaction, or uncertainty for them to live in a vain hope? I didn't know. I was in no hurry to get back. I needed to think.

Finally, I returned to our camp. Standing between the two tents were Miriam and Rebecca wrapping their arms around Georgios, pulling him back and forth, he staggering under the press of their enthusiastic embraces and tugs, Thoman jumping up and down shouting joyously. Thoman saw me enter the camp. "Georgios's back! *He's back!*" I felt the blood rush from my head, dizzy, unable to maintain my balance. I fainted.

When my eyes opened I saw Georgios standing over me, smiling, "Get up priest!" as he grabbed my hand pulling me up and then placing his arm around my waist and my arm over his shoulder supported me to a seat. He was limping.

I had now recovered my senses. "Georgios. You're dead. I saw your body in the marsh. I *saw it!*"

"Not mine, Oderic. My comrades'" he answered quietly with evident sorrow.

"What happened?"

"We were ambushed."

"How did you survive?"

"Only the sergeant and I. But more Turks paid with their own lives." I could tell Georgios wished to talk about it no further. He had retreated under that Pecheneg dome of silence I had seen before. I asked no more questions and he offered no more information. It was already dusk. We were all exhausted. We went to bed without supper. None of us had an appetite.

We all slept late into the morning, to sext. We awoke when a rider came into the camp. "Captain Georgios," he called.

I could hear Georgios answer sleepily from inside his tent "Yes?"

"General Tatikios requests your presence when you are able. Today would please him, if possible."

"I'll be there."

Georgios dressed and rode off. He did not return for some considerable time. When he did, he was unusually quiet, even for Georgios. He was in deep thought, preferring solitude it seemed, just pacing around the tents. I didn't ask. He would tell me in his own time. And then, somewhat to my surprise, he walked over to Miriam. "We walk. We talk. Thoman too." And off they strolled, Georgios's hand in Miriam's, his other in Thoman's. I was filled with foreboding. An hour passed, more, an eternity it seemed, and with every moment my anxiety increased. They finally returned. Sober expressions. This did not relieve my deep unease.

"Rebecca, Oderic, please sit," pointing to the seats. Miriam and Thoman also sat, nothing said. Georgios now spoke in Greek, directly addressing me. By now his fluency in Teutonic had improved, speaking in Greek only when he had a complex message to deliver. I braced myself.

"As you know General Tatikios summoned me." I nodded. "General Boutoumites has renewed his request that I serve as his adjutant at Nicea. I accepted."

"You did *what*? I exclaimed. "Why? Why?"

"I asked Miriam to marry me. She has agreed," Georgios turning to look at Miriam, who nodded knowing, without understanding, what he had just said. "And Thoman wishes to be my son," as Georgios looked at him with a fatherly smile, he smiling back.

"But what will happen to Rebecca and . . ." I stopped myself. Too self-serving. Too weak.

"Yes, you and Rebecca . . . " he paused, comprehending what I was about to ask, "General Tatikios has not forgotten you. He proposed both of you return with us. General Boutoumites himself requested this. Your services would be valuable to him. Please join us, my dear friend."

This was wholly unexpected. I could only stammer, unable to form an answer.

"Listen to me," Georgios continued. "The army intends to leave for Antioch in two days. But before reaching Antioch you will have to march from Dorylaeum to Marash. This road through desert and over mountains will be difficult . . . " his voice trailing off, "no, unimaginably difficult. I know this land. You don't. I fear for the Latins. Tatikios does as well. However, the will of the princes is fixed. Many will die. That is certain. And I can't risk the lives of Miriam and Thoman nor can you jeopardize Rebecca's. The choice is yours."

"I must think," I answered, standing up, taking Rebecca's hand, the two of us silently walking off along the same path Georgios had taken.

A Deadly Journey

But I must now digress and take the reader, briefly, forward to September in the year of Our Blessed Lord 1099 when I returned to La Charité after the fall of Jerusalem. My beloved Prior Damian had passed not one month before I returned. To this day, decades later, I so profoundly regret not meeting him again before his death. If only I had hastened my departure from Jerusalem but I did not understand the urgency. There was so much to tell him. But I failed. Regret is a terrible burden. I shall bear it all my life. We shall meet in Heaven. Oh so many stories to tell. Perhaps not all of them.

Despite my sorrow, on reaching La Charité I was initially anxious to compose my chronicle as Prior Damian had enjoined me. As I began to write and reflect, my enthusiasm waned. There were too many conflicting emotions in my soul. Years passed. So did the number of priors, each eager to hear the story of this extraordinary pilgrimage from a true *Jerusalemite* who had witnessed all the great events: the splendor of Constantinople, surrender of Nicea, victory at Dorylaeum, capture of Antioch, and especially restoration of the Holy Sepulchre in Jerusalem to our faith, returning with a true palm branch in his hand cut from the River Jordan. However, I soon became weary and reticent. They wanted to hear of great deeds by righteous men. My story was more complex. I decided to retire to a small cell, outside La Charité, to live as an anchorite, alone. Five years later I emerged to labor in the *scriptorium* as a scribe, quietly and without complaint copying the lives of saints. I sought no familiar contact with other monks. I preferred solitude.

There was one young monk in the *scriptorium*, Brother Samuel, who displayed precocious gifts as a copyist and miniaturist, superior to my own, his talents rivaling those of the chancery clerks in Constantinople. His nature was excessively inquisitive. He wanted to know everything of the crusade, the "Blessed Pilgrimage" he called it, these persistent interrogations becoming rather tiresome. Yet, the lad possessed a certain irrepressible, youthful charm which I found soothing and increasingly unable to resist, though I tried. He did sense my occasional irritation which did not seem to deter him. He had read all the chronicles then in circulation. When I told him a story after his relentless imploring he might correct me citing some different account he had read, always a more heroic version. Yet his interest and knowledge spurred me to read these chronicles which previous priors had collected in our *armarium*. And then, one day, I erred. I told this young pest—even now, as I dictate, Brother Samuel is nodding in agreement—that I had kept a journal, four volumes lying dormant on a table beside my bed. That was enough for him.

Without consulting me, he approached the prior, Father Sebastian, requesting that I be relieved of my duties as a copyist and assigned to writing this chronicle, fulfilling a promise to Prior Damian. Such an act by a junior monk was not only bold, it was extraordinary, in violation of all Cluniac conventions. But lest I chastise him here too severely I am forced to admit that in my youth I too was capable of such foolishness. As it happened, Prior Sebastian had an insatiable interest in this pilgrimage and several times requested that I, the "famous Jerusalemite of La Charité sur Loire" as he delighted in calling me, a moniker I had neither sought nor relished, relate for his benefit the great tales. I declined each invitation. Despite my known reluctance and Samuel's egregious breach of monastic discipline, the prior approved. He had read my *Life of Saint John the Martyr*, enjoying the story without detecting its many inventions. He thought my literary talents, modest in my own eyes, sufficient to this new charge. The following day the claustral prior informed me of the prior's decision. I was without recourse and submitted. I asked only that, because of my age, Brother Samuel serve as scribe. The claustral prior readily assented. I ceased all work on lives of the saints, which even from my earliest days in the *scriptorium* I had never found congenial to my temperament. Samuel and I began our work immediately. To my surprise, I came to this assignment with some energy, even excitement. And I will say Samuel has thus far performed dutifully.

* * *

When I came to completing my dictation of the final part of this book, IX, the journey from Dorylaeum to Marash, I discovered my journal entries woefully inadequate. Not through indifference or indolence but hunger and thirst, too many days of hardships and deprivations just as Georgios had foretold. In the intervening years my memory had dimmed and I found it impossible to reconstruct events. Samuel had an idea. He had heard that pilgrims, crusader nobles and bishops alike, wrote letters back to their superiors or families. I forgot that I too had done so, missives to Damian. With my hesitant permission he asked Sebastian if he possessed letters from me. Sebastian searched his cabinet, finding four: two from Constantinople on arriving at the great city and then after returning from Civitot; the third relating the journey from Dorylaeum to Marash; and the fourth from Jerusalem. I knew there were others but these were all Sebastian could find. This is the third:

To the Most Reverend and Esteemed Father Damian, Prior of La Charité sur Loire, God's Blessings on you and all the monks of the Priory. I give greetings in the name of Jesus Christ, Our Lord and Savior. 16Th day of October, Year of Our Lord 1097.

I am composing this letter from Marash where we arrived yesterday after three and a half months following departure from Dorylaeum. I wrote you of our glorious victory over the Turks. The Lord, ever vigilant and merciful, ensured this triumph. Many valiant warriors, Soldiers of Christ, died. Bishop Adhémar performed a requiem mass speaking wonderful words assuring us that they are martyrs and will enjoy a special dwelling in Heaven. I pray that will be so.

Our army proceeded south from Dorylaeum. It was not many days later that we passed through a land such as I have never seen before: brown, barren, and lifeless, so vile that I believed it had never been touched by the divine hand of God. I had peered into hell itself. The heat was insufferable, suffocating. Nothing lived except for peculiar bushes dotting the landscape bearing a "fruit", if I may describe it as such, which we called "prickly pears". Our thirst became so great that we sucked on them, their tiny thorns blistering our lips. We chewed on their branches for any moisture they could yield. We marched, the pace gradually slowing from exhaustion. After three days horses and mules began to fail. Many knights were forced to ride even oxen. We loaded dogs and goats with our baggage. Our provisions gradually depleted. And as we trudged onward pilgrims, the older ones especially, began to fall. Soldiers too. There was nothing to do for them. I can write no more about this; it is too painful. We were woefully unprepared. Despite this, Father Damian, if you will believe me, our morale was still high. Having accomplished so much in His Name, we knew God would not desert us now.

We reached Iconium expecting Turkish resistance but they had withdrawn. Oh such fertile land: orchards, fields of grain, and streams of fresh, cool water; we drank deeply. We were now refreshed and purchased additional mounts for our knights. After several days of respite we continued south to Heraclea. There we encountered Danishmend Turks led by their emir, Malik Ghazi, the very force we had faced at Dorylaeum. Lord Bohemond immediately formed his knights, giving the Turks no time to plot their devilish strategies, and charged. They fled. Bohemond was intent on vengeance. We had lost so many men at Dorylaeum that he was fixed on bringing their emir to our Lord's justice. He pursued them for days but the enemy was too elusive. That horrid Turk will yet face judgment in another life. I must tell you of a wonderful event: a miraculous light in the sky, its bright tail falling across the sky, visible even in daylight. It followed us for a week, a sign that we were indeed favored by God.

The Council of Princes concluded that passage would be safer north around the mountains to Caesarea and then south through the land of the Armenians, Christians all, erstwhile vassals of Emperor Alexios, thence to Comana, Coxon, and after that Marash. This plan was encouraged by General Tatikios, his instructions from the emperor to restore all former territory to the empire. From Caesarea we passed through several Armenian towns which welcomed us as liberators. Such a joyful feeling. We reached Coxon, Marash now so close and after that Antioch, our destination.

Oh, Father, how can I describe our suffering on leaving Coxon? We had already endured so much in the desert of Anatolia but the journey from Coxon to Marash far exceeded it in privation and death, my powers of narration unequal to the present task. We climbed high mountains, deep gorges below us, only a slender ledge, part of it hewn from the rock years before by Byzantine engineers, on which to walk, so narrow that none dared to ride, never intended for an army. Our knights tried to sell their armor to the infantry—shields, breastplates, and helmets for three or five pennies, any price they could command; what they could not sell they discarded. Autumn rains began to fall, the dirt becoming thick and slippery mud so thick that it concealed the ledge of the lip. We lashed our baggage animals together but if one fell they all followed into the abyss far below. A single misstep, merely one, by man or beast and eternity beckoned. So many died. Neither soldier nor pilgrim was spared. Eventually we reached Marash, grateful our ordeal over.

I must add one disconcerting note. At Marash we heard rumors that the Turks had abandoned Antioch. This was joyful news. However, Count Raymond, without consulting the other princes, sent five hundred Provençal knights to the city. I do not know his purpose but I can only surmise—to claim Antioch in his own name. The rumor proved to be false; to the contrary, the Turks were bringing in reinforcements. Lord Bohemond had returned from his futile pursuit of the Danishmends. When he learned of this, he was furious, denouncing Raymond for his guile and treachery, these accusation receiving a sympathetic ear from the other princes. I am afraid this does not augur well for our unity of purpose.

I must conclude this letter with the greatest hope it reaches you. I have been called to attend to the Lady Godvere, wife of Lord Baldwin of Boulogne, who with her children is grievously ill. I fear my reputation as a *medicus* based solely on the translation of Galen and Avicenna has far exceeded my talents. I am not a learned Doctor of Physik like Geoffrey.

Do not fear for me. The Lord has protected me thus far. I am sure He will continue to do so. I shall write again when opportunity permits. The Lord's blessing on you.

This ends Book IX of *Jerusalem Falls!* Book X begins.

BOOK X
SIEGE OF ANTIOCH

I Become Medicus to Lady Godvere. Antioch. A Secret Mission.
Duqaq Attacks. Starvation, Desertion, and Repentance. Cleansing the
Sinful. A New Turkish Threat. Battle at Bridge Gate. Desecration
of Muslim Bodies and Retribution. Rebecca is Rescued.

I Become Medicus to Lady Godvere

It was at Dorylaeum, the day before the army decamped for its terrible march to Marash, that Georgios informed Rebecca and me he would return to Nicea with Miriam and Thoman. His entreaties for us to join them were heartfelt. I was deeply conflicted. I took Rebecca's hand and we walked. I was quiet, so many thoughts pouring like rain through my mind, Rebecca saying nothing, waiting for me to break the silence. I was deeply in love. In my youth at Mainz it was merely a boy's infatuation, but over time—from our shared dangers to the commonplace experiences of exploration and chess—genuine affection had taken root, deeply. But since leaving La Charité I had lost my way as a priest, a man of God, breaking my most sacred vows: killing and the vow of chastity. Those anxieties, however, were trivial against the prospect of losing Rebecca but even more exposing her to perils ahead.

"Rebecca, you know that the road to Jerusalem will be long and fraught with many dangers, possibly death. I cannot guarantee your safety. You should consider returning to Constantinople to be with your cousins. Perhaps, someday, I can join you."

"What do *you* want me to do, my love?"

"I don't want to lose you but . . . " staring at the ground, unwilling to look at her, uncertain whether I could maintain my composure.

"Then you won't," she answered quite firmly.

* * *

We survived the journey to Marash through the desert and mountains, exhausted. I had nearly finished my letter to Prior Damian when a well-dressed woman entered our tent.

"My name is Adelida, lady-in-waiting to Lady Godvere of Tosni, wife of Lord Baldwin of Boulogne. You are Father Oderic of La Charité sur Loire, are you not?"

"I am."

"My Lady has heard of you, a great *medicus*. She and her sons suffer terribly from a fever and require immediate attention."

"I think your lady greatly overestimates my skills. I am merely the translator of medical texts without experience myself."

Adelida dismissed my protest, likely thinking they false modesty. "We must leave now."

We hastened to Godvere's tent, more a pavilion, the same in which I met Baldwin in Constantinople. Outside were three female servants wringing their hands, wailing, pacing frantically back and forth. They looked in relief at seeing me and quickly ushered us inside. Godvere lay on one cot, two boys on cots next to her. Over her stood Godfrey's personal chaplain, Abbot Baldwin, unmistakable for the cross branded on his forehead. He had claimed this was the work of God Himself, a sign of His favor when he decided to go on the crusade. The more cynical, however, whispered that he had carved it himself to secure alms from the superstitious, a fraud for which he was richly rewarded. As we entered, the abbot was lecturing Godvere on God's punishment for her sins, now visited also on her children. She must repent and pray to the Lord for forgiveness, and to Patroclus, the patron saint of fever, to invoke his healing power provided, the abbot added ominously, he would listen. Happily, Godvere seemed to be paying little attention to him, her head raised weakly from the pillow gazing at her sons moaning piteously as she tried to comfort them.

I stopped, standing there, tentative, uncertain whether my services were desired now that she had a priest tending, albeit roughly, to her spiritual needs if not those of the body. Godvere saw me and even as Abbot Baldwin continued his harangue beckoned me forward. Just then I heard the clatter of horse hooves outside the tent and indistinct shouting. Baldwin rushed in, brushing me aside, stepping to each of his sons placing the palm of his hand on their brows, leaning over, whispering soothingly. He turned to Godvere, his tone reproachful. "Wife. How could you let this happen while I was gone?" She feebly mumbled something in response.

Turning to the abbot, "Priest, what are you doing for my family?"

"I am praying for Lady Godvere's repentance and God's Grace," he answered meekly.

"I don't think that will help. Father Oderic, what can you do?"

"I'm not sure. Only my best."

Godvere and her sons were feverish, their faces covered in sweat. I expected the worst. I remembered Geoffrey's methods in his care of Father Benedict at La Charité. He knew that Father's disease was fatal, beyond his healing powers. But he also understood the therapy of hope, of providing some diagnosis, any diagnosis, and prescribing a treatment even if ineffective. I would try to be a convincing, if not a genuine, Doctor of Physik. I pulled a stool next to Godvere, took her pulse, lifted her eyelids squinting at her glazed pupils, squeezed her limbs, doing the same with the boys. Baldwin and Godvere's ladies-in-waiting watched anxiously.

"As I thought," looking up at Baldwin trying to summon the most authoritative tone I could, "their humors are out of balance. The fire in their bodies is caused by an excess of yellow bile in the blood. It must be expelled. Adelida," looking now to her, "I saw a swampy pond not far from here. Surely you will find leeches there. Fetch as many as you can, at least eighteen. Rebecca, please cover my patients' faces with towels soaked in cool water. The fire's heat must be redressed with the cold." Suddenly recalling a herbal remedy Samuel ben Meier had taught me, a helpful antidote for fever, "I shall require mandrake, coriander, and sage for an elixir. Surely there's a herbalist in Marash. Lord Baldwin, please instruct one of your sergeants to acquire them; oh, and a mortar and pestle as well. Finally, we must adjust their diets with cold foods: a broth of egg yolks, perch and nuts, almonds if available, with cabbage and lettuce. I shall wait for the herbs. Finally, the great *medicus* Galen taught that disease is often caused by corruption in the air. The tent flaps must be kept closed."

I noticed for the first time Bishop Adhémar who had entered quietly, standing in the corner, observing. I bowed to him, he acknowledging me with a brief nod. As I waited for the herbs, Adelida returned with a wicker basket of leeches, a task which she clearly found distasteful. I placed them on my patients' foreheads, cheeks, and arms, careful to avoid the suckers. The herbs arrived soon after. I ground them, stirring the compound in cups of wine which Rebecca and I lifted to their lips.

"There is nothing more I can do. We must wait. I shall return tomorrow."

At midday Rebecca and I arrived at Baldwin's camp. Not far away I saw Lorrainers, including Baldwin and his brother Godfrey, standing beside three graves. Bishop Adhémar was presiding over a funeral mass and reciting the last verses of the penitential psalm De *Profundis*:

> With the Lord there is mercy,
> and with Him is plenteous redemption.
> And He will redeem Israel
> from all its iniquities.

The graves were filled by Baldwin's men-at-arms, Adhémar sprinkling holy water over each, and then the mourners silently dispersed. Adhémar was joining them when he saw me and walked over. I had expected to be scolded for relying on science rather than on God's grace in my treatment of Lady Godvere. Adhémar sensed my apprehension. "This was God's will. I knew it yesterday. There was nothing you could do. Indeed, after you left I administered the Last Rites." I mumbled something in response, a mix of gratitude for his understanding and apology for failing. "Father Oderic, I need your services. I already have a chaplain. What I require is a scribe, much like the work you performed at the imperial chancery in Constantinople. As papal legate, my duties as a correspondent are onerous, to Rome of course but also to various bishoprics throughout the Christian lands. Will you serve?"

"Yes," I answered without hesitation. "But there is my ward Rebecca to consider. She is under my protection."

"Yes, yes. I know all that. The Holy See no longer tolerates carnal intimacy between priests and women. I have no doubt, however, that your relationship with Rebecca is chaste and godly." I couldn't tell whether this was a declaration, a warning, or a question. I was about to answer but Adhémar moved quickly on, almost as though he didn't want an explanation. "The army departs for Antioch on the morrow. You will travel with me and the Provençals under Count Raymond. Be ready at daybreak."

Antioch

The journey of three days to Antioch was pleasant, a welcome contrast to that from Dorylaeum to Marash. Adhémar led the vanguard, a small contingent of Provençal troops, the rest of the army following. Rebecca and I rode with Adhémar. I shall attempt to describe the Bishop of Le Puy. Fifty years of age, only slightly younger than Count Raymond, the oldest of the crusader princes. Clean shaven, well-proportioned though shorter than most, his modest stature perfectly compensated by a certain regal bearing accentuated by his unalloyed white hair falling down to his shoulders, not cut since he left Le Puy. He was a complicated man, deeply pious, sometimes severely so, yet a piety tempered with a sense of justice and reason, though not always. He commanded the crusader princes not by virtue of his papal appointment but by the respect, even veneration, with which they accorded him. What I found most curious about Adhémar was his reputation as a "warrior-bishop", perhaps because he did not fear battle, carrying a shield and wearing chain mail though without a sword, only a scabbard. He once explained to me that he needed nothing more than his faith in Christ and his standard emblazoned with an image of the Virgin Mary. His scabbard was empty to signify that priests redeem souls and save lives, not take them. I did notice that a mace, its iron head round and smooth, was holstered on his saddle but I did not inquire.

We came to an arched stone bridge, called by us the "Iron Bridge", over the Orontes River, the walls of Antioch visible only a few miles in the distance. The bridge was fortified with two flanking towers at its far end and guarded by a small force of Turks. We were unexpected and the engagement was swift, they scattering back to the city. As they fled a caravan of Christian merchants, Armenian and Syrian, approached the bridge to cross bringing with them merchandise for sale in Antioch and driving large herds of camels, mules, horses, and cattle; flocks of sheep and goats; and carrying casks of wine. Over the irate reproaches of the merchants we confiscated them all. Our army feasted for many days.

We approached Antioch, the City of Saintly Apostles, in late October, Year of Our Lord 1097. Sitting on a plain, the city is shaped something like a cucumber: three miles long from north to south and a mile wide from east to west. Three mountains, each beside the other from north to south rising some thousand or more feet, border the city on the west. Perched on the middle one, Mount Silpius, is a citadel overlooking the city. An imposing curtain wall completely encircles the city. Along the eastern side of the city on the level plain behind the curtain wall is a second, interior wall, both then reforming into a single wall as it climbs up of the mountain slopes on the northern and southern sides of the city connecting at the crest of Mt. Silpius behind the citadel. It is regularly punctuated with towers, sixty feet tall, four hundred of them, all within a bowshot of one another. Within the enceinte of the walls are broad fields with crops, gardens and orchards, all flourishing, completely self-sustaining. On first beholding it, the city seemed to us impregnable by assault. We never tried.

Immediately on arrival, even before the army set up camp, Adhémar convened the Council of Princes to determine the next step. There were two competing opinions. Some princes, Tatikios too, argued that the siege should be delayed until spring—our troops were exhausted from the summer heat and the dolorous march through the Anatolian plain. They proposed expelling the Turks from nearby forts and there establishing winter quarters, in the meantime interdicting all merchant caravans with supplies for the city. Raymond argued for a different plan, insisting that the city should be invested immediately to starve it out. God would guarantee our success, he assured us, just as He had at Nicea, a poor example I thought. Raymond won the debate, Adhémar as always keeping his own counsel. I doubted the wisdom of this decision. We lacked sufficient troops to completely surround the city. Moreover, as events proved, the princes underestimated the ferocity of Syrian winters. They were seduced by the temperate weather in fall and this bountiful land: verdant fields; luxurious gardens; vines filled with plump, ripe grapes; granaries swollen with wheat and barley; limbs of orchard trees straining under the weight of their succulent fruits; boundless olive orchards; and not least vats full of wine stacked high, one on top of the other. Such a contrast to the desolate landscape we passed through from Dorylaeum. It was truly a *"land flowing with milk and honey"* which our Lord in *Exodus* had promised to Moses. There were five gates into the city. The strategy adopted was to blockade three of them, Bohemond establishing his camp at the northern end in front of what we called St. Paul's Gate; Raymond just south of him before the Dog's Gate, the source of that name uncertain to me; and Godfrey further south in front of the Duke's Gate. This secured the northern half of the eastern wall. But the Bridge Gate and St. George's Gate, south of the other three, were left unattended for reasons never satisfactorily explained to me.

A Secret Mission

The month of November passed relatively uneventfully except for periodic sorties of Turkish mounted archers sent out to harass us, each repulsed but with losses on both sides. For the most part, however, we just waited. Every morning I attended to Adhémar, sitting at my writing desk, sharpened quill in hand, my parchment scraped and prepared, ready for his dictations. One day was different. It began ordinarily enough with yet another letter. "To Manasses," Adhémar intoned, "by Grace of God venerable Archbishop of Rheims, greetings . . ." I had expected to particularly enjoy this task for writing to Rheims instantly brought back tender memories of home and my father. But then his voice trailed off.

"Oderic, we're not prepared. Not at all."

I laid my pen down, uncertain how to respond to such a cryptic remark. "Your Excellency, unprepared for what?"

"For winter," he answered. "Come. Let's walk." I followed Adhémar out of the tent and we strolled through the camps. Soldiers and pilgrims were gathered about open fires or braziers cooking pigs, sides of beef, goats and lamb over spits or in underground pits, the animals taken from merchants at the Iron Bridge or pillaged from local farmers. They feasted sumptuously. All were carousing, men and women alike, many stumbling drunk, flagons in their hands swilling wine with such thirsty gulps that it spilled over their mouths dripping down their chins, all the time singing bawdy songs. Adhémar walked, I beside him, he silently surveying the bacchanalia.

Finally, he spoke. "We sit idly before this great city. Oh yes, occasionally parrying skirmishes launched by the Muslims but otherwise merely devouring the fruits of this fine land with what can be seized." As we continued to stroll he looked at me. "I recall as a lad reading Aesop's Fables, in particular the story of the grasshopper and the ant. Do you know it?"

"Yes, Your Excellency. The ant stored food for winter. The grasshopper gorged itself instead and then had to beg for food from the ant."

"Exactly," Adhémar responded. "But recall that the ant refused to share. And we have no ant to whom we can turn. In council I have repeatedly warned the princes of the catastrophe that will come when winter arrives and our stores are empty. As surely as night follows day. But they are indifferent and express annoyance at my warnings. They merely offer excuses, especially that God is rewarding them for their privations of the past," then adding sarcastically, "as though they understand the will of God."

It was at that moment we came to a camp, somewhat remote from the others, fifteen tents each with red ribbons attached to their poles just as I had seen at Nicea patrolled by the same loathsome Tafurs. Drogo's brothel. Adhémar watched as men, swaying from drink, swigging earthenware jugs of wine, handed coins to the Tafurs who immediately opened tent flaps for them to enter. From within several tents we could hear raucous laughter, both male and female.

He looked at me incredulously. "What in heaven is going on here?" His question surprised me for I had always assumed he knew the vices that inevitably accompany military campaigns. Apparently not.

"It's a brothel." His face reddened with anger. He shook his head in disbelief. We walked on.

Adhémar proved to be as worthy a prophet as Isaiah. In the month following, into December, the granaries gradually depleted, the trees plucked of their fruits, the vats of wine emptying. Slowly, with every passing day, food for crusaders and fodder for our animals became more scarce. Foraging parties were having to search further and further afield for grain and livestock. We knew the Turks had informants in our midst, Armenians and Syrians who easily blended in with the traders routinely visiting our encampment. They were aware of our growing plight and we suspected, with reason, they were reporting such to the Turks for these foraging parties were regularly attacked, often lured into ambushes from which few survived. And thus our dilemma sharpened: to die from starvation or to die from foraging.

* * *

I had just completed a letter and was about to leave when Adhémar stopped me. "I have an urgent matter. General Tatikios has informed me that his spies"—I was about to correct him: they are 'agents', not 'spies'—"learned that Shams ad-Dulah, son of the Emir of Antioch Yaghi Siyan, together with the son of one of Yaghi's captains, has been dispatched on a mission south to the Emir of Damascus Duqaq requesting that he gather an army to relieve the city. It is absolutely imperative that we obtain intelligence on this embassy. You are fluent in Turkish, I understand?"

"Certainly not fluent but passable."

"And I recall," Adhémar continuing, "you once told me at Constantinople that your father was a spice trader and that you were apprenticed to one in Mainz. True?"

"True."

"To keep his mission secret, Shams has disguised himself as a merchant and is returning from Damascus with a caravan of traders. It is expected to pass through Meletine in Syria, several days east of here in two weeks' time. By fortunate coincidence I just received a letter from an old friend, himself a spice merchant, Menachem ben Yaakov. Three years ago Menachem had been a member of Emperor Alexios's delegation to Pope Urban at Piacenza where we spent much time together. He will be leaving from Meletine in a caravan bound for Antioch. He wishes to renew our friendship. I am reasonably confident this is the same as that which Shams joined. Posing as a Jewish merchant you may through charm or duplicity, a concoction of both perhaps, win Shams's confidence and learn more of Duqaq's plan. I am sure . . . well I hope . . . Menachem will allow you to accompany him. This would provide perfect cover. He has little affection for the Turks," then pausing, "and possibly even less for crusaders after the horrible events in the Rhineland. I shall give you a letter of introduction."

"It would help," I suggested, "if I could bring my ward Rebecca with me. She's Jewish, daughter of my former master at Mainz. It's likely Menachem knows her family. Jewish spice traders routinely transact business with one another. I also have a letter from her father urging all Jews to succor me."

"Good. Then it's settled. You must leave tomorrow. I shall have horses and provisions ready. Report to me immediately on your return. Good luck."

After returning to our camp, I told Rebecca of this covert mission and that it may involve dangers I was unable to anticipate. She could wait for me. But, as I expected, she would have none of it. She remembered vaguely that her father had mentioned a "Menachem from Meletine" who had sold him spices: saffron, cumin, and coriander she thought. She wanted to go, insisting she could help. Besides she was becoming restless and was ready for a small adventure, a welcome diversion she believed. I still had with me the clothes of a Jewish trader which Isaac ben Judah on our way to Semlin had given us to disguise ourselves from Emicho's hunters thinking that someday they might be useful. They were now. We arrived at Meletine just before dusk when the gates were about to close for the night. The city was modest in size yet sufficiently fortified to withstand attacks from the Danishmend Turks who long coveted it. We passed easily and unnoticed through the gates, a Jewish trader and his wife bringing little attention. The city was too small to support streets devoted to particular crafts but, inasmuch as it was located on the trade route from Syria to Constantinople, I knew it had to have a Jewish quarter which I readily found.

After an inquiry I was directed to the home of Menachem who greeted us genially albeit warily. His mood changed quickly after I produced letters of introduction from Adhémar and Samuel ben Meier. We spent that evening, the next, and then the following in conversation. Menachem remembered his dealings with Samuel, all by correspondence, and was particularly interested in his fate. Two years had passed since the deaths of her family and Rebecca could now, albeit still with a certain difficulty, talk about her parents and her husband. She could not speak of her children. I explained my mission and how important it was for the crusaders—I did not use that term, calling them "pilgrims" instead—to learn whether Shams had been successful in enlisting the aid of Duqaq. Menachem was fearful. If I were exposed it would go poorly for him once he was within the walls of Antioch and under Shams's fist. Thus, he queried me closely as to my knowledge of spices and all aspects of the mercantile trade to assure himself that my deception would be successful. He eventually became satisfied. We agreed on a simple story: my name was Moshe ben Judah, the same I had assumed on the road from Mainz to Nish; Rebecca was my wife; and I was Menachem's partner. Nothing more, we all agreed, was needed.

Menachem loaded his cart with spices and sacks of dried herbs. The caravan, destined for Antioch, arrived as scheduled and consisted of perhaps fifteen wagons and carts of trade goods with thirty or so merchants. Every evening we would gather over different campfires, segregated by language: Persian, Kurdish, Arabic, Aramaic, languages with which after two years in the East I was familiar enough to at least identify. Merchants, genial by nature and often conversant in several languages, would occasionally wander to other campfires, introducing themselves, sharing trade gossip and their latest adventures. On the first night after leaving Meletine my attention was drawn to a small company of Turkish speakers, conspicuous not simply for their language—Turks prize war and thus make unnatural merchants—but also because they made little effort to conceal their preference for privacy. Notwithstanding, this was my chance. I knew Shams was among them.

I ambled over, producing the widest smile of which I was capable. There were four of them sitting around a blazing fire: a man of thirty years, a lad of perhaps fifteen, and two others sitting somewhat apart distinguished by their surly looks and swords silhouetted from under their tunics. As I approached they both stood, placing their hands on the hilts of their swords less to draw than to threaten. The thirty year-old waved them off. This had to be Shams. He had a military bearing, short but stocky, with a scar that traced from his eyebrow down to the right side of his jaw, a relic of some past campaign surely. I introduced myself as Moshe ben Judah, a merchant from Meletine, on my way to Antioch to sell my spices. Shams gave his name as "Abbas", a dealer in tapestries also on his way to Antioch to replenish his stock. His young companion was "Hamid", his apprentice Shams explained, a youth of a pleasing appearance, tall and slender with long black hair, perhaps ten years younger than I. What struck me most was his shiny blue eyes, not Turkish at all, betraying a precocious intelligence although at the same time I detected a certain fearfulness the cause of which at the time eluded me. Shams ignored the other two. The conversation was rather perfunctory for my intention was merely to make an initial contact. I asked his permission to return the following night, this time with my "wife", a request he readily granted. Perhaps he found his companions tedious and sought more interesting conversation. Bringing Rebecca would prove to be a mistake. In my effort to perfect my persona as a simple merchant, I had placed her in grave danger.

After an enjoyable supper with Menachem, Rebecca and I walked to Shams's camp. On our approach he waved us over with what I thought to be an overenthusiastic welcome. I understood why as we drew closer to the fire, his speech slurred, swaying back and forth on his stool. He was holding a pewter cup of wine in both hands quaffing down one after the other as Hamid continued to fill them, punctuated each time by Shams ordering "fill it boy!" But I was immediately put on my guard when I saw how Shams leered at Rebecca. "By Allah," he exclaimed, "what a beauty! Like Safiyya, wife of Mohammad, may his name be revered for eternity."

I wanted to distract him from Rebecca. I thought his invocation of Islam would present a fillip for an affable conversation. "*Beyefendi* Abbas," adopting the formal usage, "tell me of your faith. I know so little of it. I would like to learn more."

Shams answered absentmindedly, merely disgorging from rote some homily no doubt he had heard from an imam. Hamid quickly detected my discomfort at Shams's attention to Rebecca and tried to divert. "Rabbi," Hamid thinking all Jews were to be addressed as "Rabbi"—he was never able to break this habit, once started—"tell me of your spices. Where do you get them? They can cure diseases, can they not? My father suffers from aches in his joints, especially the shoulders. It's quite painful. I've heard too they are even conducive to lovemaking," he immediately blushing, stammering "not . . . not that I know anything about that."

"I know little of their uses as an aphrodisiac," I answered, "but, yes, spices do have some curative powers, more often however they are used to relieve the symptoms of an ailment, pain especially. I know precisely what your father needs and it would be no hardship to mix a potion for him. Perhaps you could visit me at my cart."

Shams was visibly irritated. "No, boy, you will stay here. And shut your mouth. Fill my cup!" Now turning to me, "Moshe, you Jews are fortunate to have such beautiful women. I've never enjoyed the fruits of a Jewess. Tell me *Rabbi*," he fully understanding that I was not a cleric but employing the title with transparent scorn, "do their legs spread as widely as our Turkish women's? And can they wrap them around a man with the same enthusiasm as ours? I've heard they can and deliver even greater pleasure. Perhaps . . . " he almost falling off his stool, his lips curling in a lascivious grin, "perhaps you would allow me to enjoy her before we reach Antioch."

As Shams was speaking, his eyes still fixed on Rebecca, she started to slide closer and closer to me on the bench, our shoulders touching, her body quivering. She did not comprehend his words but fully understood his meaning. Duty or no, this was too much. "*Beyefendi*, my wife is feeling ill. We must take our leave. Thank you for your hospitality." I took Rebecca's hand to assist her up and as we turned to leave Shams called out "*Rabbi*," sniggering, "come back tomorrow. We can talk more." I said nothing.

* * *

For the next four nights I returned to Shams's camp, without pleasure and without Rebecca, hoping to learn something, anything, of his mission. I would inquire, as subtly as I could to avoid provoking suspicion, about his visit to Damascus, but Shams, always intoxicated, wanted only to expound on the glories of Islam and debate the relative sexual prowess of Turkish and Jewish women. We had camped for the final evening, Antioch only ten miles away, and would arrive there the next day. This visit, my last chance to gather information, was as fruitless as the previous. I had failed Adhémar. I returned to our camp, Rebecca and Menachem waiting anxiously for me. I said nothing, merely shaking my head in answer to their unspoken question.

And then Hamid stepped out from the darkness. "Hamid!" I exclaimed in surprise, "what brings you here? Does Abbas know? You may be in trouble. I sense he watches you closely."

"He does, Rabbi. I am *not* his apprentice. I am his prisoner. He thinks I've gone to the river to look for bright stones. He rarely lets me out of his sight but his guard is down. He's drunk and tomorrow we'll be in Antioch so he doesn't fear my escape. Since the Latins arrived, the emir, Shams's father, trusts no one. He knows that Antioch is too formidable to be taken by assault. But he knows also that the Turks took it some ten years ago from the Greeks by bribing guards, and the Greeks took it ten years before from the Turks in the same manner. He fears treachery every-where, especially from Christian Armenians. My father, Firuz, is captain of the Twin Sisters Towers. He is Armenian, not a Turk, and was once a Christian although he converted to Islam. Shams keeps me as a hostage wherever he goes, I guess to guarantee my father's loyalty."

"Then why does not Yaghi put your father in chains?"

"I don't know. He could, I suppose. Perhaps because he enjoys abusing my father. A plaything. My father has come to hate the Turks though he says nothing. But I can tell. The emir has spies everywhere who watch and listen, even my uncle Akhbar, also once a Christian, is now a fanatical Muslim. My father dares not be honest with anyone, even me. But I am *Armenian*, not a Turk!" he announced proudly. "And someday I will become a Christian."

I was now desperate. "Hamid, I must be plain with you. My life, and that of Rebecca's and my friend Menachem's, will now be in your hands with what I shall divulge. I'm not a 'rabbi', not even a Jew. My name is Oderic, a priest from Francia, here at the orders of the Latins to learn of Shams's—yes, I know who he really is—embassy to the Emir Duqaq. This information is vital to us. On my eternal soul I vow *never* to reveal that you are the source of whatever you may tell me."

"You are really a Christian? And a priest?"

"Yes."

Hamid hesitated. Before he answered I remembered from my days in Mainz, when I was in the back room grinding spices, that a customer had complained of aches in her bones and asked Master Samuel for a potion to relieve the pain, the same affliction as Hamid's father. "Brother Menachem," I called out, "please prepare a compound of two cups tumeric, a quarter cup of dried mandrake, some scrapings of ginger root. Oh, also, four slices of dry willow bark ground into powder." Menachem nodded. "Hamid, this will be for your father. It's not a bribe. A gift. Tell me all you can."

"I know very little, Rabbi, but maybe something. We had just left Damascus. Shams was full of drink that night and boasted of the success of his mission. He said that Duqaq agreed to immediately assemble an army to relieve Antioch. It will be a large force, *askars* without number. As we speak he is probably already on the march. Yaghi Siyan also sent emissaries on the same quest to Ridwan, Emir of Aleppo, and to Kerboqa, Emir of Mosul, the mightiest of them all. That's all I know."

Rebecca, seeing Hamid, walked over to greet him. Hamid in the moment was as awestruck by her beauty as he was the first time she had entered Shams's camp though he had tried to conceal it with furtive, yet telling, glances. She spoke to him in a soft, maternal tone. Translation was unnecessary. He was suffering from the same youthful calf love as I had when I first met Rebecca. I felt no envy, only the stirring of a sweet, distant memory. Menachem brought me a pouch of the dried spices I had requested. "Hamid. This is for your father. It should help. One spoonful every day mixed in hot green tea, not black." Hamid thanked me and left.

Duqaq Attacks

We arrived at Antioch the next day. Rebecca and I left the caravan, Menachem continuing into the city through the south wall's Dog Gate, still open to commercial traffic into and out of the city. I had been absent for a month. There was a disturbing silence amongst the camps, the cause of which I could not discern. I reported immediately to Adhémar. He was sitting at his desk reading some document.

"Your Excellency. The Emir Duqaq is marching now on Antioch. His army, I'm told, is formidable. I do not know when he will arrive but no more than a few days, perhaps less. Yaghi Siyan has also solicited aid from the emirs of Aleppo and Mosul. I cannot tell you anything more of that. I do know that Duqaq is on his way."

Adhémar seemed shocked. For moments he just stood facing me, his mouth agape, without a word. "Father Oderic, our situation is grave. Desperate. We are without food. Starvation has set in. The council ordered Lord Bohemond, Count Robert of Flanders with him, to lead a foraging expedition south toward al-Bara, a mere four hundred horse plus more foot soldiers, no match for Duqaq's force if it's as large as you've been told. The rest of the princes have remained here to continue the siege. Lord Bohemond must be warned. There is no time to write a message and find a courier to take it. You must go. Immediately! Toward al-Bara. There's a fresh horse outside my tent that was waiting for me. Take it! May you find Lord Bohemond in time. Hasten!"

I rode for two days pushing my horse to its limit though fearful it might expire under me. It was on the second that I encountered a small squadron of Provençals on their way to Antioch. Their leader was the very noble Rainald Porchet, I believe from Le Puy whence Adhémar hailed. I informed Rainald that I was on an urgent mission to Lord Bohemond to warn him of Duqaq's approach. Too late, he sadly told me, we have already met him. As we rode back Rainald related the encounter:

> "We were a few miles from al-Bara returning to Antioch after a successful expedition, our wagons full of foodstuffs and driving livestock ahead of us seized from pastures outside different fortresses, the Turks hiding behind their walls. We were joyful and confident. Too confident. We had not sent out scouts. Suddenly, Duqaq appeared over a rise with his army. We were greatly outnumbered. He immediately encircled our vanguard led by the Count of

Flanders, their horse archers firing arrows as their infantry rushed upon us. The Flemings were about to flee when Bohemond arrived. Courage now regained, the Flemings turned and with the Normans counter-attacked. It was a mêlée, close combat, our infantry cutting down their horses and slashing the Turkish foot while knights hurled javelins. The Turks appeared to be fleeing but Bohemond refused to press the attack, perhaps fearing an ambush awaited us. This is the favorite tactic of these vile infidels: pretend flight, hoping to be chased, drawing their pursuers into an ambush. I don't know. We thought God had given us a great victory. And then, inexplicable to me, Bohemond ordered a retreat. We left the wagons behind. But here is the shame of it: Knights on horses were able to outrun our infantry, leaving them behind. The Turks, seeing us depart the field, turned and massacred the foot. I heard their shouts and screams as I, along with the rest, rode away. Oh what an awful clamor. It still rings in my ears. I can speak no more of it."

As a foraging expedition, this was an utter failure. But Duqaq had enough, for now at least. He would trouble us again later.

Starvation, Desertion, and Repentance

Rainald and I then rode back in silence, he grieving for his comrades. On arriving at Antioch I immediately reported to Adhémar. Even as I entered his tent and before speaking a single word I realized he already knew of the expedition's fate. His face was ashen, his eyes swollen and red from tears. I waited for Adhémar to address me.

"Our circumstances are becoming more desperate by the day. Horses and mules are dying from lack of fodder. Provençals have only a hundred horses left, the other princes no more fortunate. The meadows, once rich in grass, have now been so grazed that they are barren. Horses fall, never to rise. Pilgrims stumble through the camps, enervated, lacking strength even to walk upright, too weak to forage in the countryside. Those who try often are killed by the horrid Turks. And those who do survive return only with thistles, dried straw, fig branches, dandelions and other weeds that even goats refuse to eat. They boil them in pots together with the soles of their leather shoes for a weak broth, that is if they can find firewood. The more fortunate, those still with strength in their bodies, fight among themselves over carcasses of dead animals, cooking their rotting flesh and chewing their hides. Even rats are not safe. We are dying."

"What about traders?" I asked. "Just today I saw two small caravans arriving in our encampment. Can they not help?"

"Oh, yes, they come. Yes, they come," he said contemptuously, "like locusts descending on a field of grain. Armenians and Syrians. Wicked men. Many are even Christians, Armenians especially, but devoid of the slightest Christian humanity. They sell their wares at usurious prices which only the wealthy among us can afford. A lamb, once sold for three or four pennies, now costs six shillings; bread, sufficient for no more than one day's meal, can be obtained, if at all, for two shillings. As though this were not enough, heavy rains, constant, rust our swords and spears and soak our tents, some already rotting. This is God's punishment," Adhémar sighed. "We have sinned grievously in His eyes. Gluttony. Fornication. Corruption. Games of chance, dice the most foul. And while you were away the Lord sent us unmistakable messages: An earthquake, a star in the sky, its long tail pointing east, reappearing every night and suspended like a lamp hanging from a ceiling. And, to the north, heaven on fire, flames—green, red, blue—all streaming from its core, so bright that we didn't require lanterns to walk in the dark. God is angry with us. We have forsaken Him and now He us. We must fall to our knees and repent."

"Lord Bishop, how do you hope to restore us to God's Grace?"

Adhémar's mouth tightened to a grimace. "It's really simple. I look for an answer to the Psalms: *Wash me thoroughly of my iniquity and cleanse me of my sin.* Tomorrow at dawn I, my bishops, and priests shall lead a procession of penance. It will then be followed by fasting for three days." For the barest moment I was puzzled. Were we not already fasting? Starving in fact? But I remained silent. "Then alms to the poor. After that, we shall fall on our knees and pray humbly, fervently, for God's forgiveness."

And so it happened. But prayer proved to be an elusive remedy. The famine and suffering continued. I walked among the pilgrims' camps offering solace and prayer where I could, especially to those within days of their demise, evident from their listless demeanor and bloated bellies. Those less fortunate, if I may use this dubious comparison, lay on the ground where they had taken their last breath, emaciated, ribs protruding through tattered clothes, skeletal faces with shriveled skin drawn tightly over bulging cheek bones. The scene was ghastly. I did not know whether to weep or flee. If there is indeed a hell, this was it, punishment not by fire but by frost and famine. Able-bodied pilgrims, such few as could be found, were conscripted to collect the bodies, two pennies for each, and throw them into wagons, heaped high, for disposition outside the encampment. The ground was too frozen for burial and too little wood for pyres. They were dumped instead into the Orontes River, their bodies carried down with the current. Such was our condition.

People had lost faith. All of them. I as well. Morale did not improve with numerous reports of desertion—to the hills, to the Port of St. Symeon twelve miles away. Mainly the poor but not only. There was the astounding news that Louis, Archdeacon of Toul, absconded with three hundred parishioners into the wilderness. We heard nothing more of them, though in the following spring, by chance, their bodies were discovered a few miles from Antioch, decapitated. Most astonishing was the rumor that Peter the Hermit and William, so-called "The Carpenter," Viscount of Melun, had fled; Tancred was sent by Bohemond in pursuit. It proved not to be a rumor. I was kneeling over a dying pilgrim administering the Last Rites when I heard a shout that Tancred was returning with fugitives. I raced to Bohemond's tent to see William and Peter, their hands bound in front of them pulled by a single rope tied to Tancred's pommel stumbling after him.

Bohemond stood waiting, scowling. "Scoundrels!" as they were shoved to their knees in front of him. "You especially," Bohemond pointing at William. "Coward! You deserted in Hispania before a battle against the Moors. And you flee again now." I was curious that he singled out William, ignoring Peter. Perhaps because he was a priest. Perhaps because his expectations of Peter's courage were so low, always met. If the latter, I shared that opinion. He turned to one of his sergeants. "Take a bucket. No three. Fetch me rubbish from the refuse pile and make a bed inside my tent." Turning back to William, "You will enjoy tonight the comforts of the slumber you deserve. The flaps will be left open for all to witness your dishonor as a Soldier of Christ sleeping on garbage worthier than you. Wretch!"

Turning now to Peter, "You have brought shame on yourself, Hermit. You may go. But I vow to Saint George, he of righteous retribution, that should you do this again, I will personally nail you to a post and let the crows eat you, morsel by morsel. Leave!"

Cleansing the Sinful

The following morning I entered Adhémar's tent. He barely noticed me as I quietly sat at my desk. Adhémar was pacing, his hands behind his back and head bowed in thought. He was mumbling indistinctly, I wasn't sure to whom: to himself? to God? He then stopped in front of me, his eyes narrowing, lips pursed, arms folded. "You've heard about Peter?" I nodded. "I think hereafter a different epithet, more fitting, is deserved. 'Peter the Godless', 'Peter the Apostate'. And William of Melun . . . " Adhémar just shook his head in disgust. He went silent, pacing again. "I think it not enough to pray and fast if the Lord is to be satisfied. Our eternal souls are still in peril, poisoned by iniquity. Sin, *all sin*, must be extirpated. Sterner, even ruthless measures are required. I have drawn up a list of offenses and their penalties." Adhémar then walked over to his desk and fumbled through some papers, selecting one. "Let's see," perusing the document, then reading from it. "There shall be no reveling, intoxication, games of chance, heedless oaths: for that two lashes. Chicanery, fraud in weights and measures, and theft, even for food—especially for food: five lashes. Blasphemy and false accusations against a bishop or priest: shaving of the head and branding on the cheek. Fornication and adultery: death. And finally, all prostitutes must be expelled from our encampment. They are a corruption on our body. It must be excised. This decree has already been sent to the princes and will be announced tomorrow by their heralds and the priests at mass." I was stunned. The reach was breathtaking. The backs of at least half of the crusaders—soldiers and pilgrims, nobles and princes, even priests and bishops—would be etched in blood.

Adhémar continued. "Courts shall be organized. Only priests will serve as judges. They will ferret out the iniquitous through fair but thorough inquiry and then render just, swift punishment."

My thoughts turned immediately to Rebecca. Would she be executed for my sin, not hers? Without thinking I blurted out "What about Rebecca? Does she die?"

"I have thought on this. The nature of your relationship has not escaped me but I shall not examine that here. I have a more important task for you. I was shocked to learn of a brothel in our midst. We both saw it. Do your remember?"

"I do, Your Excellency. Drogo's."

"You know him?"

"Yes. Unpleasantly."

"Then you are the perfect judge for his case. Of course," he now breaking out in a cryptic smile, speaking softly as though to communicate a private message, "as a judge you may bring charges against anyone you wish. Or exonerate. There should be proper limits to our investigations. This net is intended only for miscreants, the unregenerates, not the bewildered who may have strayed briefly from God's Law." A tide of relief came over me. I could protect Rebecca.

"But that limit does not include Drogo. He is like a boil on my thigh which needs to be lanced. You shall serve as the sharp point of my dagger."

"Lord Bishop. Please know Drogo is regarded by the Tafurs as their king. Soldiers will be needed to arrest him."

"Yes," Adhémar answered. "I shall assign a squadron."

News of Adhémar's decree spread throughout the camps like wildfire. Anxiety was palpable on the faces of all. Seven heavily armed Normans appeared at my tent. I directed them—they appeared to know anyway—to the location of Drogo's camp. In the meantime a makeshift courtroom in one of the mess tents, now seldom used, had been set up for the trials to be used by the priests. The design was rudimentary, less extravagantly furnished than the court I had once seen in a manor outside La Charité: a trestle table, a chair behind for me and a bench in front for the offender. Drogo's case would be the first. Drogo was arrested without incident. He entered the courtroom bound, Tafurs who followed him forced by the Normans to remain outside. He was defiant as always, the same sneer and arrogance I had seen at Nicea. He was escorted by two soldiers and pushed roughly onto the bench. I did not doubt that these Normans had been Drogo's customers but he was likely without allies because of wide-spread resentment over his exorbitant fees.

I began the trial following the procedure I had witnessed at a manorial proceeding. "Accused, your name?"

"Drogo, King and Lord of the Tafurs," he answered disdainfully. "And you priest, your name?" Drogo of course knew perfectly well who I was. "And by what right," he continued without a pause, "do *you*, a *mere priest*, sit in judgment of a *king*?"

I ignored his challenge. "Drogo, self-proclaimed 'King and Lord of the Tafurs', has been charged with conducting a house of prostitution, of enslaving women to satisfy the lusts of men, the penalty for which is death. You plead how?"

Drogo broke out in a wide, scornful grin. Before he could answer the tent flaps flew open. Entering was a corpulent man, his shape so large that he blocked light from the outside. Clearly, he had been foddered well while others starved. His voice was wheezing, out of breath, for he had been racing to the trial evidently alerted by the Tafurs. Bishop Arnulf.

"Priest!," Arnulf shouted at me as he stepped forward. "I am Arnulf of Choques, Bishop of Rohes, Chaplain to Robert, Count of Normandy." On

Robert's name the Normans, some of whom had been lounging beside the tent walls, leapt to attention. Arnulf was glaring at me, he surely remembering how I had witnessed his contemptible behavior during the battle of Dorylaeum where he had indicted himself for fraternizing with Drogo's women, "I shall preside over this so-called trial. Remove yourself!"

"Arnulf of Choques," I answered, my voice as firm and commanding as his, "I have been appointed by Bishop Adhémar, Papal Legate, to try this man. You may watch or you may leave. The choice is yours."

Arnulf, looking to the Norman sergeant, "Remove him!" The sergeant hesitated, confused, until Arnulf repeated the order, "In the name of Count Robert, your Lord, remove this priest. Immediately!" Between Adhémar and Robert, the sergeant submitted to the higher authority and beckoned two of his men forward.

"Arnulf," I shouted, "this is an outrage. I shall report it to the legate."

"You may do so," Arnulf answered scornfully. "Now *you* may watch or *you* may leave. The choice is yours." I decided to stay.

The "trial", if I may dignify this proceeding with the term, was brief and perfunctory. Arnulf took my chair. "Do you wish to call witnesses on your behalf?" he asked of Drogo.

"I do, Your Eminence," Drogo answered, his voice unctuous. "Any of the Tafurs outside this tent will suffice. They are Christian men, god-fearing, truthful."

Arnulf directed the sergeant to bring in two, picked at random. Each in turn was seated on the bench beside Drogo, their testimony the same: Drogo was righteous and godly; there was no brothel, a baseless rumor, a conspiracy to discredit their king. Arnulf made few inquiries, his questions designed to exculpate Drogo, merely nodding his head at their answers.

I watched this charade with increasing anger until I could bear it no more. "Arnulf of Choques, this is a travesty. I demand the right to testify. I was a witness to this man's deeds."

Arnulf was startled for he was about to dismiss the accusation. Then Drogo interrupted. "Your Eminence, may I ask a question?" Arnulf nodded. "Is it true that the penalty for fornication is death?" Arnulf nodded again. "Then may I bring my own charge?"

"You may," Arnulf answered, smiling.

"I charge this priest with fornicating with a Jewess. She is called 'Rebecca'. I demand to be released. This man must be tried in my place."

"Is this true, priest?" Arnulf asked, glowering at me.

I was stunned by the turn of events. I could only stammer "well . . . yes

. . . no I mean." A more vehement denial might have served me better but it was too late.

"Sergeant. Arrest this Jewess 'Rebecca'. Bring her before me. I shall interrogate."

I must save Rebecca for I well understood her fate, possibly mine too, with Arnulf as prosecutor and judge. But I thought only of her. I raced out of the tent, the Normans having no chance to seize me, running through the camps to our tent. I counted on the fact that the sergeant would have to search the encampment for our location. This would give me time. Rebecca was outside tending to a brazier in preparation for dinner. Grabbing her hand, tugging her after me. "Rebecca, you're in danger. We must leave, now! Forget your things." She made no protest. I thought first of seeking refuge with Adhémar but it was he after all who had launched this inquisition and decreed death for fornicators, although I did not think of Rebecca and me as such. I was uncertain of his power to protect us. But then I thought of the one man who could. Tatikios's camp was close by. The general was inside his tent as Rebecca and I rushed in. I explained the situation, Rebecca now trembling in fear at what she was learning for the first time. "General Tatikios, I beg sanctuary for Rebecca. Not for me. For her."

Tatikios needed no persuasion. "Of course. She may stay with us for as long as she likes. The Latins have no jurisdiction here. My Turcopoles will protect her. I shall arrange a tent for her."

For the next two days I stayed with Rebecca both to comfort her and to assist Tatikios in the event that either Normans or Tafurs arrived to arrest her, though I was uncertain what service I could provide. Very late that first night I returned to our tent, careful not to be followed, collected her belongings and for myself a dagger with which I used to sup but now to be employed for a different purpose if needed.

On the third day I returned at the usual time to Adhémar's tent to resume my duties. He seemed surprised to see me. He had heard about the trial and, without prompting, immediately on my entrance said "Arnulf is as corrupt as his lord Robert of Normandy. They deserve one another. But there is little I can do about him. He's under Robert's protection and the Normans love him. I'm uncertain why. Perhaps because he's as dissolute as his master. The Provençals sing songs about him, more appropriate to a tavern than a requiem mass." Then shrugging his shoulders, "There's nothing I can do. Is Rebecca safe? Where is she now?"

"She has been granted sanctuary by General Tatikios, thankfully."

"Good. Fortunately, it may not be needed long. I'm afraid my decree has succeeded only in spreading terror without relieving vice. Priests have been overzealous in their prosecutorial duties. Couples sometimes on the flimsiest evidence have been convicted of illicit conduct, paraded through the camps, children beating them with rods to the perverse delight of crowds without other amusements. Or people have been flogged for blasphemy, often of the mildest sort, merely for exclaiming 'by Jesus' or 'my Lord'. Yet, it is only the pilgrims who suffer, soldiers for the same offenses are protected by their sergeants and captains, the princes too. And my expulsion order of prostitutes has been ignored."

"Lord Bishop, you were certain that our suffering is due to our sinful ways and only by rooting them out would God's favor be restored. Do you think differently now?"

"I've prayed on this, Father Oderic. God has not answered me. And without divine guidance I must navigate my own course. Tomorrow I shall rescind the edict and issue a pardon for all those arrested. Leave Rebecca with the general, at least for a few days more. Drogo's and Arnulf's thirst for vengeance may not be quickly sated."

A New Turkish Threat

It was now February. We had heard nothing of Yaghi Siyan's embassy to the Emir Ridwan of Aleppo or for that matter to Kerboqa, Emir of Mosul. That is, until news came to us that Ridwan was approaching from the east with a large army. Adhémar summoned an emergency meeting of the Council of Princes. Adhémar introduced the scout, the first to sight them. His report was brief: Ridwan was twenty miles from the Iron Bridge leading twelve thousand horse and foot divided into a vanguard and a much larger rearguard no more than a half-mile behind. Panic gripped the princes.

"We have only seven hundred horses left alive," Godfrey exclaimed. "They're scrawny at best from hunger. With another two hundred donkeys for saddle, we can field no more than nine hundred knights. We have infantry but they, like our knights, are jaded from lack of food. These odds are overwhelming."

Raymond interjected quickly, not wishing Godfrey's words to fully sink in. "My Lords, we cannot despair. God's Providence has brought us this far. We must have faith in His protection. He will provide. We shall face these Turks directly under the Cross of Christ." By now, Raymond's pious assurances of 'God's Providence' had worn thin. At Nicea he promised that the initial ladder assault would succeed because God willed it. It was a disaster. He had insisted on an immediate siege of Antioch rather than taking refuge in winter quarters, relying on God's benevolent protection but again with even worse results. No one doubted his courage in battle. It was in his unquestioning reliance on faith to determine military strategy.

There followed an excited debate, each prince trying to talk over the other. Adhémar was silent, scanning the group until his eyes settled on Bohemond who stood quietly, in thought. Adhémar raised his hand for silence, the cacophony dying down. "Lord Bohemond, your opinion?"

Bohemond said nothing, merely looking back at Adhémar. Anticipation was building among the princes, all waiting for Bohemond to speak. "My Lords. Let us not rely blindly on providence but on ourselves." All present understood this as an indirect, if courteous, rebuke of Raymond—the enmity between the two senior princes was well known. "If God wishes to succor us, He will. But our situation now is indeed desperate. On hearing of Ridwan I rode out to reconnoiter the Iron Bridge and the road to it. I have a plan. I must tell you I cannot *guarantee* success." Bohemond went silent again, I think for effect.

"What is it?" Robert of Flanders asked excitedly. "Tell us!" the other princes responding almost as an antiphon, "Yes, tell us!"

"The Turks are victorious," Bohemond explained, "when they select the time and place of the field of battle, always an empty plain where they can outflank and encircle us and then at their leisure fire their arrows from a distance beyond our reach. This time, *we* pick the time, two days from now at daybreak, and the place, the Iron Bridge. We strike first and we strike boldly. Tomorrow night our army—only knights, all we can muster, men-at-arms to maintain the siege—will leave under the cover of darkness. Without a sound. The hooves of our animals must be muffled with cloth. The Turks have spies everywhere and Ridwan will get word." Bohemond then drew his sword and marked the Iron Bridge in the dirt. "Here's the road leading to it," drawing a straight line, "the Lake of Antioch here," drawing a circle beside the road, "and hills on the other side," marking them with three Xs one above the other. "The terrain narrows considerably the closer the road approaches the bridge. The Turks will be forced into a close formation unable to flank us at the lake to the north or the hills to the south. We divide our army into six squadrons, five of them leading and the sixth in reserve under my command. We conceal ourselves here," twisting the tip of his blade into the ground making a small hole behind one of the Xs. "Our first five squadrons will attack the

Turk vanguard here just before it reaches the bridge. Success depends on breaking the vanguard's formation, turning it back against the rear-guard. And then I shall bring my reserve into action and we attack with full force. To give the illusion of size, we must carry as many banners and pennanted spears as we can gather. That is my plan."

An apprehensive silence followed. Then gradually, one prince after the other, nodded in agreement. Not a word was said. No one had a better strategy. The fate of the crusade depended on this single battle. Anything short of victory, total, would seal our fate. The army left in the middle of the night as planned. For the next two days Adhémar was too distracted to dictate, just pacing back and forth in the tent, wringing his hands, then rubbing them together, then most oddly slapping them together. We waited. It was on the afternoon of the second day we heard loud, joyful shouts. Adhémar and I left his tent to see knights, their swords raised in triumph. Ridwan had been defeated. The course of battle went exactly as Bohemond had planned: Ridwan's vanguard, stunned by our ambush, turned and fled back, colliding with the rearguard which was in turn thrown into disarray as our knights continued their charge, pursuing them for miles, reaching their camp. There they found horses, camels, livestock, and wagons full of provisions intended for Ridwan's army but desperately needed by us. One wagon returned laden with Turkish heads, hundreds of them. Our men impaled them onto sharpened stakes in front of Antioch's walls shouting jeers and taunts met only with silence from the ramparts. We were saved.

Battle at Bridge Gate

Our circumstances began to improve. It was now March. Spring had arrived and with it the greening of pastures for our horses. The capture of Ridwan's supplies, sufficient for an army, relieved starvation among our ranks. And traders, their merchandise now less in demand, began reducing prices to more reasonable sums. I was in Adhémar's tent prepared to take dictation. "Not today," Adhémar said. We have learned that an English fleet has just arrived at St. Symeon under the command of an Edgar Aetheling, once a claimant to the English throne and a relative of its king, Edward, called 'The Confessor'. It brings needed supplies from Emperor Alexios, in particular tools, matériel, and mechanics for the construction of additional fortresses to complete our blockade of the city. The princes have just met in council and decided to send two companies, one under Count Raymond and the other under Lord Bohemond, as escorts from the port.

"Do you expect trouble?" I asked.

"I don't know. I've been surprised, even troubled, by the lack of retaliation from Yaghi Siyan after Ridwan's defeat. The quiet unnerves me. But the fleet is critical for us. We need to build these forts. Two gates are still open and through them pass caravans into the city. If we are to starve them out we must close and seal these holes. I shall be sending one of my own Provençal units, a small squadron, under the command of Rainald Porchet. I think you met him."

"I have Your Excellency. On the road to al-Bara. An honorable and genial knight, I thought."

"Yes," Adhémar answered, "virtuous and God-fearing as well."

"Your Excellency, I would like to join him. I remember walking with you at the harbor in Constantinople just below the Great Palace and watching ships on the Sea of Marmara, their sails full with decks of rowers. I have never quite lost my fascination with these vessels. I am also starved for news of that great city. And perhaps this Edgar Aetheling brings books, any books. I have read nothing in a year. Do you object?"

"No. They leave tomorrow. Stay close to Rainald. That is my condition."

It took two full days to transport supplies from the ships and load them on empty wagons we brought. Once the task completed, we headed back to Antioch. Raymond and his Provençals, a hundred knights and a similar number of infantry, escorted the convoy of wagons down the main road, Rainald Porchet and his squadron, twenty knights, with the Provençals. I rode with Rainald. Bohemond with fifty knights followed a different route, a narrow path over the hills to serve in reserve. The pace was slow, heavily laden wagons retarding progress, the mules laboring when ascending hills, infantry having to assist by pushing the wagons and knights lashing ropes from the wagons to the pommels of their saddles pulling them forward.

Rainald and I had an agreeable conversation as we rode, especially the prohibition against priests carrying bladed weapons. I don't remember who raised the subject. "Why is this?" Rainald asked. "I do know Bishop Adhémar carries only an empty scabbard when he enters a battle, just as he did at Dorylaeum where he brought up his knights over the hill outflanking and attacking the Turks. I was there. I think his sudden appearance was crucial to our victory."

"Yes," I replied. "I was at Dorylaeum too, but not in the field. Elsewhere.

I heard about it though. Adhémar once told me his scabbard is empty to show that belief in Christ is his sword and that, as a priest, he is forbidden to take lives. Something like that."

"I've often wondered how Adhémar would protect himself if he were personally attacked. What would he do? I wonder."

"I don't know. But church law," I explained, "prohibits priests from carrying bladed weapons, weapons that draw blood. That would be sinful."

"Perhaps," Rainald answered in thought, "there is another solution. The mace. It needn't be a 'morning star' with all its spikes which pierce the body. A club fitted with a smoothed iron ball could suffice. Such a weapon does not require the skill of a sword, only a well-directed blow. That would not violate church law, I believe. I could train you in its use."

I then remembered Adhémar's holstered mace. Perhaps Rainald was right. "I would like that," I answered.

We were approaching the main crusader camp, a mile away, concerns about an attack were now diminished when suddenly Turkish mounted archers rushed up at us from a ravine where they had concealed themselves, dividing to the left and right encircling our force, unleashing a torrent of arrows. Wagon drivers leapt from their perches and scampered into the woods. Our knights and foot soldiers panicked, the knights spurring their horses in the direction of the camp, the infantry racing behind them trying desperately to keep up, all pursued by Turk horsemen. Many of our men became martyrs in those moments. Rainald shouted at me to stay close—I needed no encouragement—as he waved for his men behind to follow. We galloped after the others toward the camp. But then the heavy, double-hinged doors of the city's Bridge Gate opened, a company of Turkish horsemen springing out toward the bridge over the Orontes River, so-called the "Fortified Bridge" because of the twin towers that defended it. Sentries opened the towers' gates to allow the company to pass through. If they crossed the bridge our escape would be cut off and we would face Turks both from behind and the front. Yaghi Siyan had plotted this strike skillfully.

Rainald immediately recognized the threat from the sortie. He raced ahead, his squadron following, and through foolhardiness or desperate courage, I don't know which, positioned himself just in front of the bridge facing the towers, Adhémar's standard bearer Bernard of Béziers beside him, I close behind. We were outnumbered but the narrow arched stone bridge, wide enough only for a single wagon, gave us some advantage against the mass of Turks. There was a hundred feet between us, too close to charge with lances and spears or the Turks for their bows. "Stay back!" Rainald ordered me and then signaled his knights to raise their shields, draw their swords, and they galloped forward meeting the Turks in the middle of the bridge, the clash of arms producing a noise that must have awakened all the saints in heaven. But the mass of Turks was too great and we were being pushed back when suddenly Bohemond appeared over a hill to our south. The Turks were now thrown into confusion and tried to wheel their horses around, back to the city, but they were too closely bunched together. Several of their horses reared, throwing riders over the bridge into the river or onto the pavement. In desperation, the fallen Turks began grabbing the manes or tails of our horses, attempting to pull the riders off.

I saw that Rainald himself had fallen, dropping his sword, lying on his back as he tried to parry with his shield the scimitar slashes of an unhorsed Turk. I was weaponless but I had to do something. Immediately. I saw an opening in this mêlée and spurred my horse forward straight into the Turk, knocking him over the bridge. I quickly dismounted helping Rainald to his feet. Bernard of Béziers too had fallen, his head bleeding profusely, unconscious, Adhémar's standard lying beside him. Pointing to it, Rainald shouted "Get the standard! We can't let the Turks have it!" As I was picking it up Rainald mounted my own horse, his having run off, stretching out his hand "Give to me!" Raising it up for his men to see he looked back shouting "We charge! *For God! And Paradise!*" I jumped out of the way, teetering on the edge of the bridge. It was at this moment that Godfrey, having heard the clamor of battle from his camp, was galloping to the bridge. The Turks were now in full flight back into the city, Rainald in close pursuit, Bohemond and Godfrey not far behind. Rainald was closing on them as the Turks raced through the Bridge Gate, still open. For an instant I thought victory was ours, that we had now penetrated the city's walls. But just as Rainald passed through, the gates quickly closed. Rainald, eight of his men and Adhémar's standard, were trapped within, prisoners of the Turks. As the bridge battle was waging, Raymond had reformed his lines and attacked the Turks who had seized our supply wagons and were leading them back to the city, massacring every one within reach of their blades.

Desecration of Muslim Bodies and Retribution

What I shall now relate is grim and I tell it with misgivings but I promised Prior Damian to be faithful in my chronicle. In the night we could see Turks carrying their dead to a Moslem cemetery just outside the Fortified

Bridge, on the crusader side of the river. Crusader princes ordered that they be left unmolested for these infidels, pagan as they were, deserved in death a decent burial. This view was not shared by their men-at-arms or the pilgrims, especially Tafurs, their lust for loot too great. The next day they went out to disinter the corpses. It was well known, or at least suspected, that Turks often concealed jewels and bezants in their mouths and other parts of their bodies, women too in concealed areas which good taste does not allow me to describe. The Turkish remains were placed on pyres and after the fires had died down these "crusaders", if I may use such a generous term here, raked through the ashes with sticks, hoes, spears or swords searching for treasure. I do not know what, if anything, they found for I was too filled with repugnance to witness these acts.

Retribution came swiftly. On the day following the cemetery's desecration we witnessed a terrible sight. Yaghi Siyan appeared at the ramparts above the Bridge Gate. Beside him was Rainald Porchet, his hands bound behind him with an iron collar around his neck, a chain attached which Yaghi held yanking it for effect as he spoke. I was standing next to Adhémar witnessing the atrocity that would follow. Yaghi, looking down at the crusader camp, began bellowing at us in a thunderous voice.

"What is he saying?" Adhémar asked.

"He wants to know how much ransom we will pay for Rainald."

Rainald, somehow understanding what Yaghi demanded, defiantly shouted out "No ransom! Not a shilling for me! My soul will be with God."

Yaghi yanked the collar chain, pulling Rainald to his knees just below the top of the parapet, no longer visible to us. I could hear Yaghi scream at him: "Convert or die. Face east. Toward Mecca. Renounce your pagan faith! Swear to Allah, infidel. Swear!" I couldn't hear Rainald's response but it was nonetheless clear—he would not renounce Christ. Yaghi then shouted at us, "You desecrate the bodies of my warriors. So I shall desecrate your own!" He unsheathed a dagger from his belt, held it over Rainald for all of us to see, then waving it slowly from right to left, toying with Rainald in his last moments, bent over. We could see nothing until Yaghi stood back up holding Rainald's head by his hair and then in a defiant gesture thrusting it forward at arm's length toward us dropping it over the wall. There was a gasp from the crusaders as they witnessed this gruesome scene. It was not over. Rainald's men, eight of them, were brought to the ramparts, each bound with a rope around his neck pulled by a Turk. The scene repeated itself. One by one the Turks bent over, then rising with a head throwing it over the parapet. Yet Yaghi even then was still not yet satisfied. The feet of the headless bodies were tied and lowered over the wall midway dangling upside down where they remained for two weeks. And as Yaghi's final act of defiance, Adhémar's standard, embroidered with an image of the Virgin Mary, was hung, also upside down like our crusader martyrs, over the wall to loud dismay. A standard, this one in particular, has near mystical significance for Christian warriors. Oh what a terrible price we paid for that cemetery.

Rebecca is Rescued

In all this time Rebecca had been the guest of Tatikios. I had visited her nightly, always careful to avoid being followed by Tafurs. But after Adhémar lifted his edict and with the passage of a few days my fear for Rebecca's safety had subsided. I brought her back to our tent. Yet I had a vague but uneasy sense of being watched, a feeling I tried to dismiss. One evening we took a walk to the outskirts of the crusader encampment, toward the river. Out of nowhere a detachment of five horsemen dressed as Normans rode to us, stopped, all dismounting wordlessly. I stepped forward to greet them when one pulled a club from his belt and before I could react hit me in the head. As I fell I could hear him bark an order to the others "Get her!" These were not Normans. They were Turks! I lay on the ground, unconscious, for hours perhaps. When I recovered, my head was throbbing from the blow, the feel of warm blood dripping down my face. I immediately raced to our tent to find Rebecca, my legs somewhat wambling and unsteady. It was empty. I ran to nearby camps frantically calling out "*Rebecca! Rebecca!*" The only response I received was "Not here." I needed help, Tatikios's. The general immediately ordered his Turcopoles to scour the camps. They searched for hours in vain. Rebecca was gone and I despaired, never to see her again.

For the next two days I did not attend to Adhémar. He sent a messenger to find me. I ignored him. Rather, I sat in my tent, alone, disconsolate, thinking of one plan after another to rescue her, each more fantastical than the last. She was surely in Antioch but where? Who took her?

Then I had a visitor, Hamid. "Rabbi, I've heard that your wife has been kidnapped. Shams did it. He was quite fixated and on our return to Antioch couldn't stop talking about her. He even said she would be a jewel in his harem. I would have warned you but I thought it mere loose talk. She's been locked in a cell in the citadel. I've seen her."

"Is she well?" I asked eagerly. "Has she been . . . has she been . . . ?"

Hamid understood my question though I could not bear to ask it plainly. "No. Her abductors would not touch her, under penalty of death. She belongs to Shams although he's been too distracted with you Latins to think about her. But joining his harem would be a more merciful fate than the one that awaits her.

"What do you mean?"

"The emir's thirst for Latin blood is now unquenchable. When your army was approaching the city he expelled all Christians. However, he recently learned that twenty women had concealed themselves. They've been rounded up and imprisoned in the citadel. He intends to burn them alive. Rebecca too."

I was shocked. "She's Jewish, not a Christian," I protested.

"For Yaghi, that is a fine distinction. Shams, I'm told, objected but what can he do? Even as we speak Yaghi is building a platform, just above the ramparts at the Bridge Gate, for the Latins to watch. They will all burn, the platform too but he doesn't care." I believed him for we had all heard the sound of axes and hammers at the gate without knowing its purpose.

"I need to get into the city," near weeping, my voice now lowering to a whimper, "I *must* get into the city."

"Rabbi. I know of no way. The gates are all guarded. The Turks closely question everyone passing in. *Everyone!*" he added for emphasis. "And getting into the citadel would be far more difficult than into the city through the gates. I can see no way."

I sat on my cot, head in my hands, in despair. Hamid watched me silently, with sympathy. "But . . . maybe . . . let me think . . . Yes, *perhaps* there's a chance. A small one but a chance. They have been taken to a jail underneath the citadel. It houses prisoners awaiting execution. It was constructed centuries ago by the Romans who used it to imprison Christians during the persecution. However, they secretly dug an underground tunnel from the jail out to an opening just beyond the western wall to escape. When I was young my father showed me the entrance. I could still find it."

"Will you take me there?"

"Yes."

We left immediately, climbing up along the south city wall to the top of Mount Silpius. Coming to a small grove we stopped, Hamid pointing to some bushes and vines at the base of the wall. I pushed them aside to reveal an opening, two feet wide and four feet high.

"I must warn you, Rabbi, though I have never walked the passage my father did once. I recall him telling me that it is very narrow in places, wide enough only for women and thin men."

As we walked back down, I asked him if my potion had done any good for Firuz. "Oh, yes, Rabbi. My father is feeling very well now. He would like to repay you."

"Unnecessary," I answered. "It was my gift." At the bottom of the mountain we parted.

I could not rescue Rebecca alone. I needed help and immediately thought, as always, of Tatikios. I told him of what I had learned from Hamid. Could any of his Turcopole warriors assist, I pleaded?

"I have only a small detachment of men left," he answered, "most having departed for Nicea. They are robust in frame and unlikely to squeeze through the passage if it's as you describe. However, I have two, slighter, much like you, but fearless warriors nonetheless. You must leave tonight. I've learned that the emir has completed his platform and intends to burn the Christians in the morning. There is great excitement among the Turks to see this." Tatikios then studied me intently as if to measure my courage. "Father Oderic, this will be dangerous. You're a priest, forbidden to carry a weapon. There will be only three of you and I have no idea what my men will face if they are able to reach the prison."

I nodded. I thought of Adhémar's mace and of Rainald Porchet's advice. I thought too of Heraclitus, *character is destiny*. Is this my character, my destiny, to become a 'warrior-priest' as the Pechenegs had foreseen? And then I thought of Christ's injunction *He that hath no sword, let him sell his cloak and buy one*. The lives of Rebecca and the Christian women were at stake. "General, I shall need a weapon, a mace I've been advised. Do you have one?"

Tatikios nodded. "I have some." He led me to a wooden frame against which several maces were neatly stacked. "Would any of these work?"

I examined each. Their heads were spiked or flanged with razor-sharp edges. "No. I'm a priest. I may not draw blood."

"Well," Tatikios replied, "these are what I have." He paused. "Wait. I may have something." He walked over to a chest, rummaged through clothes until he found what he was looking for. "This is a maul, not a mace. During our wars against the Pechenegs, before they became allies and mercenaries, I recovered it from one of their soldiers whom I killed in hand-to-hand combat. A brave and worthy fighter, Iskender after Alexander the Great. I kept it for myself and in his honor named it after him. I've never used it, too precious to lose in battle." He handed it to me, I turning it over in my hands. It was a double-headed hammer with a spike protruding up from the center, the metal burnished to a fine sheen, glistening. The haft, surprisingly heavy for its size, somewhat shorter than the maces, was made of hardwood, mahogany Tatikios told me. I was feeling the tip of the spike, Tatikios sensing my unease. "Just in case," he smiled. "This is indeed my most prized weapon but don't be confused by its beauty. Yes, it's designed to crush, not to cut, but it can be lethal nonetheless. Father Oderic, you have served me well. It is yours."

I was deeply touched, humbled. "Your kindness seems limitless. I accept it with the deepest gratitude."

"Two more things." Reaching back into his chest he pulled out a baldric throwing it to me. "Keep it," Tatikios said. It was a wide leather strap thrown over the shoulder, a small stitched loop at the waist in which to holster the maul. It was similar to the twin baldrics Georgios had worn at Dorylaeum, one for his sword and the other for his axe. I was proud to wear it and nodded in thanks. "Oderic, for a priest you are a man of great courage. Georgios once told me he would rather go into battle with no one but you. However, courage alone is not enough to wield *Iskender* skillfully. You will require training." Tatikios stepped outside the tent giving an order to his adjutant. Moments later two Turcopoles entered, both about my age and size. Tatikios made introductions, Adem and Ekbar. Tatikios then explained my mission making no effort to minimize the risks. Their faces were impassive, betraying nothing.

"And this is Father Oderic. He will accompany you."

"*Yassas*," I greeted them.

They were completely indifferent to me, studiously looking only at Tatikios. It was obvious my presence would be unwelcome. "He was companion to Captain Georgios Vardanes and is his 'warrior-priest'," Tatikios explained. Their countenances changed instantly, turning to look at me with considerable curiosity. They must have heard of me. "Ekbar, you will train Oderic in the use of the maul. Afterwards, Oderic, you and I shall dine together, share stories. You will leave at midnight."

Ekbar and I left the tent. Training began, I with my maul, he with a sword: the parry, the block, the thrust, the opening for close attack, assessing ones opponent's weakness, every maneuver repeated over and over again until Ekbar was satisfied—he rarely was—and then to the next. By the session's end I was exhausted but confident with the maul, now almost a part of my body as my arm. I saluted him in the Byzantine fashion, he just placing his hands on my shoulders with a wide grin. I had not disappointed him. That evening Tatikios and I supped on a congee of rice and mutton with bread, the portions modest but Tatikios believed no field general should eat better than his soldiers. Such fun we had, recalling our experiences from Constantinople to

Antioch, I momentarily forgetting the danger ahead. Time passed, too quickly. Ekbar and Adem appeared outside the tent. We had to leave. Tatikios provided me with a leather helmet, leather hauberk, woolen breeches, and boots fitting well enough. "Yes," Tatikios said slapping my arms, "you *do* look like a warrior-priest. Georgios would be proud. May Saint Mercurios protect you."

* * *

We trudged up the mountain taking the same path Hamid and I had earlier that day. The moon was full enabling us to make our way without difficulty. Each of us carried a torch soaked in pig fat. At the entrance, we lit them with flint and iron, Ekbar and Adem leading. The tunnel was dank and cold, in some places drips of water falling from crevices in the rock, in others rivulets. The passage was indeed narrow, at times we had to turn sideways to squeeze through. As we proceeded, the wails of women and the jeers of Turkish soldiers, first faint, became louder. We were now very close, no more than five feet away. But in the torchlight we saw a pile of rocks just in front of us, evidently placed there long ago to block the entrance from the jail. We could go no further. They had to be removed as quietly as possible. Ekbar in the lead lifted one rock, handed it back to Adem, and from him to me as I placed them in holes in the walls so that our escape back would be unobstructed. Despite Ekbar's care, twice some rocks tumbled down. We stopped, waited, listened. I was certain we had been discovered but the cries and jeers drowned out their noise. Finally, interminably it seemed to me, the tunnel was clear. We immediately doused our torches in the floor's standing water.

Through the opening I could see to our left cressets with standing poles burning charcoal, torches bracketed on the walls, and five gaolers sitting on benches against the wall facing barred cells on the right filled with women huddling in the corners. The Turks' taunts were cruel, telling the women with what relish they looked forward on the morrow to seeing them burned alive. With every taunt the women's wails became louder, subsiding until the next. We crept out of the opening still unseen, Ekbar's and Adem's swords drawn, I with *Iskender*. The air was almost insufferably putrid from the lack of sanitation. We were now in the full light. A Turk saw us, his eyes wide in shock, momentarily frozen but regaining his senses quickly, "*Infidels!*" he shouted to the others. The Turcopoles instantly leapt into attack, quickly dispatching two whose scimitars were only half-drawn. They then turned to the others.

I had followed them out of the tunnel but I must confess that I was momentarily paralyzed. Ekbar and Adem were warriors. I was not. Yet I was bursting with fury. I wanted to kill Turks, all of them. I attacked a third, swinging wildly from left to right. The Turk merely stepped back out of range, smirking. He knew the contest was unequal. Then I remembered my training. I stopped, waiting for his move. He thrust, I parried with the haft of my maul, pushing the blade aside. Another thrust, another parry. He then raised his scimitar over his head, both of his hands on the hilt, ready to bring it down with one crushing blow on my own. He was open. In that moment, that instant, I thought of plunging *Iskender* with its spike right through the Turk's skull. I couldn't bring myself to do it. Instead, I swung from my right the hammerhead of my maul striking the side of his exposed knee, mere breeches without mailed chausses. The Turk buckled over. Then I struck him on the side of his helmet. He fell back, and with each backward step I moved forward, one blow after another until he fell, unconscious. By now the remaining two Turks had drawn their scimitars and both my comrades were engaged in hand-to-hand combat, scimitar against sword. Adem had pinned his opponent against the wall and needed no help. But Ekbar had slipped and fallen, the Turk hunching over him, the point of his blade pressing against Ekbar's chest ready to impale him in an instant. I lunged at the Turk striking his head with my maul, knocking him away, and as he fell pummeling him again and again. I reached out my hand to Ekbar to pull him up. He looked at me, smiling "Georgios was right,"

The battle was over, the jail secure, but not for long. The women had to be evacuated quickly. I saw a ring of keys hanging on a hook secured to the wall and began opening the doors of the three cells, fumbling until I found the correct one. As I came to the third, Rebecca pushed her way through the other women pressing her face between the bars. "Oderic. You've come for me!" I said nothing. There was no time. I unlocked the cell, Rebecca the first through throwing her arms around me. "Oderic, Oderic."

"We must go," I answered, pushing her away. With that we began herding the women into the opening having first taken wall torches to guide us back through the tunnel. Some were too terrified to leave the cell, still huddled in the corner, weeping. I went to each, unceremoniously yanking her up, pulling her out of the cell, pushing her to the passage opening, then back for the next. Kindness would wait.

We led them down the mountain, the Turcopoles serving as a rear-guard, to Adhémar's tent. It was daybreak, he was up and emerged from his tent hearing a commotion. I whispered in his ear explaining who they were. His eyes glistened and as they stood in front of him, he making the sign of the cross over them, "*In nomine Patris et Filii et Spiritus Sancti*", then walking up to each tenderly giving them the kiss of peace. I took Rebecca holding tightly to my arm back to our tent.

* * *

It was two days later, midnight. I was already asleep when I heard outside my tent Hamid's whispered but excited voice. "Rabbi, come out. Yaghi Siyan is furious that the Christians escaped. He suspects treachery everywhere and is interrogating all his officers. My father will soon be one. He wishes to surrender the city to the Latins."

This ends Book X of *Jerusalem Falls!* Book XI begins.

BOOK XI

A NEW TURKISH THREAT

Intrigue and Extortion. Antioch Seized. Besiegers Become the Besieged. Desertion and Starvation. Arnulf's Ambition. The First Vision: Peter Bartholomew. Search for the holy Lance. The Second Vision: Stephen of Valence. City on Fire and a Plot. Kerboqa Defeated. Saving Bishop Adhémar's Life. The Citadel Surrenders.

Intrigue and Extortion

I was four days behind in my journal entries and I had not written to Prior Damian for several weeks. There had simply been too many distractions for me to devote myself to this daily task. I was up late writing for I understood the folly of delay on memory. Adhémar had kindly loaned me a stool and trestle desk in my tent which could be easily folded and set off to the side. I had retired to bed fatigued and fell asleep the instant I lay on the cot. I heard Hamid's agitated voice calling me outside the tent. I raised my head to listen, unsure between consciousness and slumber whether it was indeed he. I heard his call again and hurriedly dressed, careful not to wake Rebecca who needed rest even more than I, stepping outside, drowsy, stumbling slightly.

"Rabbi, Yaghi Siyan is furious at the escape of the Christian women. He suspects all his captains of treachery and has begun arrests and interrogations. My father is an Armenian and was once a Christian. He is now under suspicion and expects his turn will come shortly, especially because he commands the Two Sisters Towers. My father wishes to surrender them to Lord Bohemond. You have gained my trust, father's too. He was affected by your kindness with the medicine for his aches. He asks that you speak with Bohemond."

"What does your father want in return?"

Hamid answered quickly. "Safe conduct out of Antioch and fifty pounds of silver. A small price for delivery of the city."

"I shall do as Firuz asks. Bishop Adhémar plans on convening the

Council of Princes tomorrow, Bohemond of course will be there. I shall pass on this message."

"No!" Hamid answered quite adamantly. "Yaghi Siyan has spies throughout your Latin camps. This must be communicated to Bohemond, your greatest warrior, and to him alone. No one else. My father's life depends on absolute secrecy. There is little time. I will need an answer tonight."

With misgivings over the subterfuge, I agreed and instructed Hamid to wait. Careful to avoid being watched, I went to Bohemond's tent and informed the guard that I wished to speak with his lord. Recognizing me, he opened the flap, peered in announcing "Father Oderic is here to see you my Lord."

"Let him enter." Bohemond was awake and sitting behind his desk studying a map, two of his captains on either side.

"My Lord," saluting him, "I bring a message but it is for your ears alone." Bohemond, rather startled by the request, quickly dismissed the men. I explained how I had originally met Hamid and the message he had just brought from his father. I stressed also Firuz's demand for absolute secrecy and his terms for delivery of the towers.

Bohemond sat back in his chair, pensive, and then leaned forward, his folded arms resting on the desk. "Agreed. Tell this 'Hamid' to return tomorrow night with a plan from Captain Firuz. You must bring him to me. In the meantime, you will tell no one. Firuz is right to be mistrustful." I delivered Bohemond's message to Hamid who promised to return at midnight next.

It was midafternoon on the following day. I was on my way to Adhémar's tent for a meeting of the Council of Princes. I happened to pass by Tatikios's camp. There was unusual activity: wagons being filled with equipment, tents disassembled, folded, and thrown onto wagon beds. Tatikios was on the move, preparing to decamp. I found him close by directing the operation, barking one order after another.

"General," I asked anxiously, "what are you doing?"

He took my arm pulling me out of earshot of the others. "Bohemond came early this morning to warn of a plot against my life being formulated by the other princes. They blame me, the Basileus too, for all their sufferings especially the march from Dorylaeum and their starvation of recent months without the promised imperial relief of shiploads of food. They plan to kill me any day. I must leave."

I was shocked and told him I had heard nothing of this from Adhémar. He answered that perhaps Adhémar was not involved; if he were, then Adhémar would have thought better of informing me. Breaking my vow of secrecy to Hamid and Bohemond, I revealed all I had heard the night before.

Tatikios sat down on the edge of a wagon, deep in thought. "I believe I understand now. Bohemond knows that if he succeeds in taking Antioch, he will be bound by his oath to the Basileus to render the city to the Empire. He wishes Antioch for himself, perhaps with that as a base expanding his domain into a principality. With me out of the way, there will be no one to obstruct him, except perhaps Count Raymond." I protested that surely Bohemond had no such scheme. Tatikios merely smiled. "You are naïve, my young friend."

Tatikios's suspicion proved correct. Adhémar had just opened the meeting when Bohemond interrupted, apologizing but saying he had a matter of significance to raise. Adhémar permitted Bohemond to speak. "My Lords," Bohemond began, "I must be direct. We have besieged this city now for seven months and are no closer to taking it than we were in October when we arrived. I, like the rest of you, have lost men. Too many. My Normans are weary and worn. They want to return home. I have expended much money to feed and arm them and my coffers are near empty. And recently reports have reached us that a large Turkish force is on its way to relieve the city, much larger than the previous two if our intelligence is correct. I have decided to withdraw and bring my army home. There is little more I can say."

A stunned silence fell over the princes. They were all thinking the same thing—it was his military genius that enabled us to defeat the Turks. And now we would be facing the most formidable army yet without our greatest commander. All the princes, but one, understood this, Raymond.

"Lord Bohemond, you mistake yourself. Doubtless you think our successes, our triumphs, are due to you," his lips pursing into a sneer. "As always, you are wrong. It is God's Providence. Without Him, we would have been defeated long ago. So, I say, leave! Hide in Italia. We need you not."

It was unusual for Adhémar to speak at council. Yes, he was the papal legate and deputed by the pope himself to lead this crusade. Yet, he saw his role less as a leader than as a facilitator at council, ever endeavoring to build elusive consensus. On this occasion, recognizing the critical importance of Bohemond's announcement, he had decided to interject himself.

"Lord Bohemond. You understand the implication of your decision? All who have taken the cross made a solemn vow not to return home until Jerusalem has been taken. If you leave now you face ridicule from your countrymen, even possible anathema. Are you prepared for that?" Bohemond merely shrugged. I sensed he was engaged in a dramatic bluff.

The other princes were clearly not of Raymond's mind. They were shuffling on the floor, uncertain how to respond, looking at one another to be the next to speak. Raymond was after all the richest of all the princes and his Provençal force the largest. But his piety had become tiresome. And they needed Bohemond more than he needed them.

"My Lord Bohemond," Godfrey spoke, "what would it require to persuade you not to abandon us? I ask this plainly. Perhaps we could take up a collection," Godfrey, then turning with a sharp, almost rebuking glance at Raymond, "to replenish your treasury. Would this help?"

"Duke Godfrey, I thank you for your generous offer. I'm not a penitent seeking alms. No. But I would reconsider . . . well, perhaps . . . on a single condition: If I'm able to take Antioch through my own devices, the city belongs to me."

Raymond, his face flushed with anger, shouted "Do you not remember your vow to Emperor Alexios, taken on the sacred head of Saint John, that you, we, all of us, would restore to the Empire any lands we conquered. And yet you are willing to perjure yourself before God by breaking this oath? We must hand it over to General Tatikios."

"Ah, yes, General Tatikios," Bohemond replied disdainfully. "Have you not heard? The *redoubtable* general, he of the *golden nose*," his voice drenched in contempt, "has fled. To the port of Saint Symeon. I spoke with him this morning. He heard that a new Turkish army is on its way to Antioch, and the coward that he is, like all Greeks, was terrified. I tried to boost his courage, to face this new threat by standing with us. But he was quite insistent. We owe neither him nor the emperor anything!" I listened in shock. The deceit of it. Yet I said nothing. Even in time, with the opportunity to reflect, I don't know why I remained silent. Perhaps because it would be Bohemond's word against mine. I was certain who would be believed. Or perhaps because I was already too deeply implicated in the plot.

"Lord Bohemond, how do you plan to take the city?" Godfrey asked, more interested in Antioch's capture than in whose charge it would ultimately be placed.

"My plan is not yet fully formed. I cannot guarantee success. I can say nothing more except this: Without your agreement to my offer, I shall be forced to withdraw my southern Normans. Duke Robert will have to decide for himself whether or not he will follow with his northern Normans." Robert, though remaining silent, nodded in agreement. I must say I was impressed with the manner, exquisite in its subtlety and cunning, in which Bohemond practiced extortion on the princes. Robert's character was well known: courageous in combat, yes, when necessary, but more content caressing the bosoms of his courtesans of which he had several. He was always a reluctant crusader and there was a rumor, widely reported, that he wished to return to Normandy and all its sensual pleasures. Indeed, he had for many weeks been enjoying the fleshpots of the port of Latakia; it was only Adhémar's threat of excommunication that forced him to return. Both he and his chaplain Arnulf shared one thing in common, a lack of carnal disciple. Without the Normans, failure was assured.

At first, angry protests erupted from the princes, Hugh of Vermandois particularly challenging Bohemond. "We have *all* contributed to this siege. Each of us has spent treasure and sacrificed martyrs. We should enjoy the fruits of this city *equally*, not just *one* of us." There was resounding applause and "*hear! hear!*" from the others. But then the applause died down as each prince began contemplating his choices. There were none. Adhémar, sensing unspoken agreement, asked for a vote. All slowly raised their hands in favor of Bohemond's demand, only Raymond motionless. "It is done," Adhémar declared. "If Bohemond can secure the city, it is his."

The following night, late, Hamid arrived at my tent. I escorted him to Bohemond. We entered, Bohemond remaining seated at his desk, alone, not rising—this was just a boy and an Armenian at that warranting no deference. But he did listen, carefully, as Hamid spoke. Hamid's voice at first was quaking. He was, after all, in the presence Bohemond, Lord of Taranto, his fame having spread all over Anatolia. But his confidence soon returned.

"My Sultan," Hamid began, referring to Bohemond, bowing deeply, "my father Firuz, in service to Emir Yaghi Siyan and captain of the Twin Sisters Towers, proposes a plan. The towers control the entrance to Antioch at what you call St. George's Gate. The emir, because he suspects treachery everywhere, has ordered a doubling of all guards on the walls. They rotate every four hours. This will complicate things. However, my father can control their schedule. Before daybreak two days hence he will personally give a signal over the wall by waving a lantern slowly from left to right, twice. That will indicate the tower is unguarded. Your men must be ready below the wall with ladders. Complete secrecy and silence will be required lest other guards are alerted."

I had sensed from the beginning Bohemond's suspicion of Firuz. "Hamid, why does your father wish to betray his master and yield the city? I must know. Is this a trap?"

Hamid vigorously shook his head. "No, Sultan Bohemond, no trap. The emir, may his carcass be eaten by crows, has mistreated my father terribly. I myself two days ago discovered one of my father's wives—his second, not my mother," he emphasized quite firmly—"in bed with a Turk officer. My father remonstrated with the emir who merely laughed saying that he had profited because his wife was now more proficient in lovemaking, especially with a Turk. He should rejoice. This is only the latest of many insults he has received at the hands of Yaghi Siyan. No. He hates the Turks."

"Good. We will be ready," Bohemond replied, "but your father must do his part."

Hamid nodded. As he began to turn, "Oh, one more thing. You have agreed to fifty pounds of silver and your personal guarantee that my father and his family will be protected. My Sultan, is that still the understanding?"

"Yes. Your father will be paid and no harm will come to his family. I'll see to that." He didn't.

Antioch Seized

Hamid left to report back to his father. Bohemond asked me to stay behind. "Father Oderic, I have a ruse in mind. Tomorrow night we Normans shall march south on the pretext of a foraging expedition. If he knows that we've left Antioch, Yaghi Siyan may relax his vigilance. We shall secretly return ready to storm the walls. I wish you to join me. I'm unsure what we will meet once we climb to the ramparts of the towers. Will Firuz lose his courage? Will he betray us? I don't know. Hamid certainly trusts you and I assume his father also. Besides you speak the tongue of the Turks. I shall need you on that wall where Firuz will await us. Are you willing?"

This was an invitation I had not expected. Nor was it welcome. But it was too late for me to extricate myself. Moreover, the fate of our entire crusade might depend on the success of Bohemond's plan. I agreed. On the following day Bohemond, to ensure that Yaghi's spies would immediately report the departure of his army, dispatched heralds to all Norman camps, those of northern Francia and southern Italia, announcing with the aid of trumpets and drums that they were to prepare for a night's march south to al-Bara on a foraging campaign with the promise of plundering all the cities they encountered. Excitement at the prospect of booty passed quickly among the Normans. That night Bohemond and Robert of Normandy led their troops out of the encampment. I had donned the leather armor Tatikios gave me and of course *Iskender* secure in my baldric. After several miles, Bohemond redirected us back to Antioch. The troops were confused and clearly disappointed by this change in plans. Bohemond himself rode up and down the lines shouting the same message: "Normans! Soldiers of Christ! You will still have plunder this day! Not in the south but in Antioch! Be ready to fill your pockets." Rousing cheers followed.

Approaching the crusader encampment outside the city we slowed to a steady walk, the troops having been ordered to remain quiet. The silence was eerie and unnatural. A half-mile from St. George's Gate we all dismounted and tethered our horses. One of Bohemond's captains, Fulger of Chartres, led a small detachment, sixty men including me, on foot, carrying a single scaling ladder constructed the day before, to the base of the Twin Sisters. There we waited, hugging the wall to avoid discovery. We could hear the tramp of sentries above as they paced back and forth over the wall-walk, sometimes leaning over the battlements to peer below; they saw nothing. And then there was silence. No sentries. We looked up to see a lantern hanging from a long pole stretched out over the battlements, twice waving slowly from side to side. Firuz's signal. We immediately grabbed the ladder, leaned it against the wall, and began scrambling up. The honor of being the first to reach the ramparts belongs to Fulger. Other Normans followed. Fifteen had already succeeded in reaching the top, clambering through the crenel followed by more Normans, I among them. But the ladder's steps could not withstand the heavy boots of the soldiers. Three rungs, each above the other, halfway up, broke, the soldiers below tumbling down, one after the other, groaning from pain as they fell to the ground. I was only five feet up and was able to jump off in time.

I looked up and could see from the reflection of the lantern's light on Firuz's face as he leaned over a crenel that he was in distress, his plaintiff voice audible: "Where's Bohemond? He promised to be here. You don't have enough men!"

"Quiet!" I ordered Firuz. "It's me. Rabbi Oderic. I'll be up as soon as I can." I did not know how but I had to still him.

Our situation was indeed desperate. We had only the single ladder and it was now broken. The Normans already on the ramparts were isolated and the rest of us, forty or so, at the base of the wall were ready to flee back to Bohemond's camp. Fulger, now on top, left us leaderless. I would have to take command. "Wait!" I ordered. "I have an idea." The Turks had made periodic sorties from different directions, seldom leaving the city through its principal gates but from inconspicuous sally ports, many barely visible from a distance. I thought it was possible, *just possible*, that one was near. But it was pitch-black and we could see nothing. I walked up and down the line of Normans, they uncertain what to do next, whispering "Spread out along the wall, every ten feet, feel the wall for a gap in its stones and a wooden gate. No sound!" They did as I instructed. Suddenly I heard a hushed voice "I think I've found it." One of the soldiers waved to me. I rushed over. Yes, it was a hinged door wide and tall enough for horsemen in single file to pass in and out. The door was made of stout oak locked from the inside. We could not crush it for we had neither sledge nor club; even if we did the noise would raise an alarm.

The moment was critical. I feared that sentries would soon return to their duties on the battlements where Fulger's men waited. They would be executed as cruelly as had Rainald Porchet's. And then I had another idea, *Iskender*. Groping the door blindly I felt a hinge. To my enormous relief it was on the exterior. I removed my baldric, placed the strap under the pin to muffle the sound, and with my maul's hammerhead began gently pounding the pin upward, doing this with each of the three pins, all popping out more easily than I had expected. The door was flush with the wall, even slightly recessed. Two soldiers with their sword blades pried the door forward and off the hinges. We all began rushing through the postern into the street behind. In the meantime, unbeknownst to me, Fulger and his men had descended the stairs from the towers to St. George's Gate, surprising and quickly overwhelming the guards and then raising the heavy wooden bar from its brackets opening it. One of them blew a trumpet announcing to Bohemond that his men were in. The trumpet's blast and the sound of the thundering hooves of Norman knights racing to the gate awakened the other crusaders, who quickly dressed, grabbed their weapons, and either mounted their horses or raced on foot to the gates. The soldiers who had gained entrance through the postern had also opened the Bridge Gate not far from St. George's. The city would soon be ours.

Day broke. Bohemond had not appeared at the Twin Sisters Towers to provide protection for Firuz as he had promised. We would never have succeeded without his help and that of Hamid. It was my duty to defend them. I knew their fate should our soldiers reach them before I did. After passing through the postern I ran up the steps to the wall and down the wall-walk to the bastion at the corner of the eastern and southern curtain walls which quartered both Firuz's family and the towers' guards under his command. As I reached the bastion, I saw what I took to be Firuz, Hamid behind him, in front of a barracks door out of which guards were pouring. "Down there!" he shouted at them, pointing to the stairs leading to the streets. They took no notice of me. A look of desperation covered Firuz's face. "Where's Bohemond? He promised! Now there's only you." I started to reassure him when a bastion door opened, next to barracks door, I assumed leading into Firuz's quarters. A man emerged dressed as a Turkish soldier, his sword bloodied.

"Akhbar, my brother," Firuz exclaimed, welcoming him, "I have to get you to safety."

"Firuz," his face full of hatred, "you've betrayed us: Allah, the emir, and our family's honor. I know it all. There will be no mercy for you. I've already killed your whore wife. Now it's your turn" and with that, no warning given, he thrust his sword into Firuz's belly, Akhbar standing over his lifeless body. I was too shocked to react, one brother slaying another. I just looked at Firuz's body in disbelief. But Hamid was not as paralyzed as I and maintained his presence of mind. He pulled out a dagger from its sheath inside his boot and with two leaps plunged it into Akhbar's throat. Akhbar fell onto the wall-walk gasping for breath, Hamid on top of him pushing his dagger deeper and deeper screaming *"You killed my mother and father! Damn you!"*.

"Hamid!" I shouted, "We have to leave!"

The lad seemed dazed. I pulled him up and led him down the steps to the gate just below. As we reached it mounted knights, I thought Godfrey's, were galloping through. We couldn't delay. Hamid was in mortal danger of crusader wrath, even with me, too easily mistaken for a Turk. I needed another way out of the city. All of Antioch was awake now. Many inhabitants had emerged from their homes onto the streets to learn the cause of the disturbance. The crusaders, mounted and foot, were racing throughout slaying all they encountered without distinction—women, children, the infirm, the aged. It was a frenzied rampage. Every inhabitant unlucky enough to be in the streets was cut down. Other crusaders on foot smashed down doors killing everyone inside, screams following, and then running back out into the street with what silver or valuables they could snatch, raising their arms as though in triumph, then off to the next house for more killing and plunder. I thought of the massacre of Jews in Mainz and the Hungarians in Semlin. It was the same senseless horror, the same savagery, slaughter, and looting. Wails and screams resounded throughout all the streets.

As we ran down a street I had picked at random, Hamid in front more fleet than I, a Norman knight galloped down on us, his sword raised level to his waist ready to decapitate Hamid who stood there, disoriented, insensible to the danger he was in. But just as the Norman was only feet away I pulled Hamid back underneath the portico of a house, the Norman's sword missing Hamid by a hair's breadth. The knight then wheeled about for another charge shouting *"pagans!"* But now he was wielding his sword awkwardly in his right hand trying to swing from his left leaning well over in his saddle struggling to reach his targets, both of us. I leapt from the portico and before he could swing grabbed his leather hauberk and yanked him off his horse, he hitting the street's hard pavement on his head, unconscious. The horse stopped only a few feet away. I approached it quietly, took the reins, mounted, and quickly stretching my hand out to Hamid pulled him up behind me. I kicked the horse's flanks and we galloped off to Rebecca's and my tent outside the city. Hamid was safe.

Besiegers Become the Besieged

Just before passing through the Gate of St. George I looked back up at the citadel. Across from it, on the other side of a ravine, I saw Bohemond's standard, red with a black coiled serpent, planted. The city now belonged to him. But not the citadel. What few Turkish soldiers survived took refuge there under Shams ad-Dulah's command. Yaghi Siyan with some retainers was able to escape, the crusaders too intent on plunder to notice, into the hills outside Antioch. He may have eluded the crusaders but was unable to escape his fate, a fitting one for God's punishment. He was thrown from his horse, his retainers deserting him. He was soon discovered by some Armenian peasants who recognized him—Yaghi's features well known: a head of enormous size, ears wide and hairy, his hair white, and a beard that flowed from his chin to his navel. The Armenians decapitated him, whether dead or alive at the time I do not know, and brought his head to Bohemond for a reward. They received ten marks of silver. They then sold his sword, scabbard, and baldric to Bohemond for sixty more. A fitting reward for such a vile wretch and vindication for Rainald Porchet and his men, all martyrs for Christ.

The city was choked with bodies on the streets and in homes. The stench was becoming unbearable. They were thrown into wagons and dumped without ceremony into the Orontes River. Yaghi Siyan, may his soul be damned, as a gesture of contempt had forbidden Christian services in the Basilica of St. Peter and desecrated this holy place, founded by Saint Peter himself, converting it into a stable for his personal horses. Adhémar's first command was for clerics to cleanse it of animal filth and repair all damage. Services were soon resumed.

The city fell to us, more precisely to Bohemond though Raymond would not accept this, on June 3, Year of Our Lord 1098, after a siege of seven months. Yet, our troubles were only beginning. We received word two days later that Kerboqa, Emir of Mosul, with an alliance of various emirs and atabegs from Syria including the emirs of Damascus, Homs, and Manbij, had arrived from the east at the Iron Bridge, overrunning our garrison and slaughtering all our troops. Two days later he encamped outside the city walls at the confluence of the Orontes and Kara Su Rivers two miles north of Antioch. The citadel, still in Turkish hands, was accessible only from Mount Staurin to the north of Mount Silpius through the Iron Gate. Kerboqa immediately replaced Shams as commander with his own captain, Ahmad ibn-Marwān. I never learned Shams's fate but can only hope it was equal to the pain he inflicted on others.

I must interrupt this narrative with background information for it is critical to understanding subsequent events. In November of the preceding year a fleet of Genoese ships, thirteen in number, had arrived at St. Symeon and unloaded matériel for the construction of a fort. With the assistance of Genoese mechanics and craftsmen, a fort was constructed on the gentle slope of Mount Staurin opposite the Gate of St. Paul at the far north of the city. We named it *Malregard*, "Dirty Look". Four months later, in March of the following year, with matériel provided by Emperor Alexios and transported by the English fleet under Edgar Aetheling—saved from the Turks at the battle of the Bridge Gate—we built another, *La Mahomerie*, "The Mosque", using stone from the Muslim cemetery which our crusaders had desecrated. It was placed under the command of Count Raymond. And, in April, we built one more, the last, "Tancred's Tower," opposite St. George's Gate on an abandoned convent, under the command of Tancred for which he received four hundred silver marks collected from the princes. Now, the city was finally and completely sealed but for the Iron Gate on the slopes of Mount Staurin to the north and west, accessible only by horse or foot, not by wagon caravan. There was great rejoicing when the last tower was built for no food convoys could pass into the city and we would be able to starve it into submission. This proved not to be the blessing we had expected.

Kerboqa arrived leading an army far larger than our own. We, the besiegers, now became the besieged. Fighting began immediately. As soon as Ahmad took command of the citadel he launched a sortie which we repulsed. On the day following we responded with our own from a sally port, the same through which we had gained entrance to the city, but we suffered numerous casualties. The princes decided to abandon Tancred's Tower lacking adequate troops to man it. *La Mahomerie* was different. It stood astride the road to St. Symeon, the port vital to our survival should we be resupplied by Alexios. It's defense was entrusted to Robert of Flanders with five hundred Norman and Fleming troops. Kerboqa also understood the strategic significance of the fort and threw at least two thousand infantry at it in a relentless assault that raged for three days, our crusaders fighting valiantly. The story was told of Hugh, appropriately nicknamed "the Beserk", a Norman but whose Viking blood coursed through his veins, with but two comrades beside him fought off Turks trying to gain entrance to one of the towers. When one of his spears broke, he grabbed another; when that broke he picked up a third, then a fourth. Oh, with such ferocity he fought, eventually falling but he sent several Turks to hell before doing so. The odds against them were overwhelming. Robert knew he could not resist much longer and decided to abandon *La Mahomerie* under the cover of darkness, leading his men back into the city, setting the fort on fire as he evacuated.

Desertion and Starvation

Kerboqa's investment of Antioch was now complete. A sense of dismay, followed by doom, began to pervade the crusaders. I felt it too. I was on the ramparts and saw in the distance a large cloud of dust coming toward the city, Kerboqa's entire army I initially thought. But when they became visible there were only thirty mounted Turks. This was no army, I decided, but more likely a squadron sent to surveil our defenses. As it approached the city's walls, Roger of Barneville, a southern Norman renowned for his military prowess and reckless courage, led fifteen knights out of the Bridge Gate to engage them. News of this sortie quickly spread and crusaders raced up to the ramparts to watch. As the Normans cantered over the Fortified Bridge the Turks suddenly wheeled about galloping away as though in flight. Roger drew his sword and charged after them. There were shouts of "*hurrah! hurrah!*" from the ramparts. I alone was filled with a sense of foreboding, a trap. It was. Three hundred Turkish mounted, concealed and waiting in a draw below a small hill, emerged to attack the Normans who turned about to race back to the city. They all escaped safely but for Roger of Barneville. One of the Turks, holding a javelin, was able to outrun him and hurled it into his back, Roger falling to the ground but still alive. The Turk dismounted, drew his scimitar and with one strike cleaved his head from his body. He withdrew the spear, drove it into Roger's head raising it upward for us to see. We were silent, all of us sharing the same unspoken thought, an omen.

Morale only worsened as desertions followed. The first was Stephen of Blois who secretly took a contingent of men from Francia out of the city to Alexandretta. This news stunned us all for he was a member of the Council of Princes. But he was only the first, others following: William of Grant-Mesnil, brother-in-law of Bohemond, along with his brother Alberic of Grant-Mesnil; William of Bernella; Guido Trosellus; Lambert 'the Pauper'; and the traitorous William the Carpenter—may their names be recorded in the annals of infamy. They fled in the middle of the night lowering themselves over the wall by rope and thus came to be known, contemptuously, as the "rope dancers". We soon learned they had fled to the harbor of St. Symeon where Genoese ships were anchored ready to unload their supplies for the city. These contemptible fugitives told the Genoese captains that Antioch would fall to the Turks any day now and they must depart immediately, of course taking these traitors with them. Sails were immediately unfurled and just as they were departing Turkish troops appeared. Unable to attack the ships, they burned the harbor.

We were now cut off from the world. We could hope only that Alexios would bring an army by land to relieve us. We had heard nothing from him. It would require more than hope to save us. There were frantic rumors among the soldiers and pilgrims that all the princes would abandon Antioch in the night just as the "rope dancers" had, leaving them to face the Turks alone. Adhémar called an emergency Council of Princes and required each, his hand on Adhémar's bible, to swear an oath not to desert the city. Heralds were dispatched throughout the city announcing the pledge. For good measure, Adhémar and Bohemond posted triple sentries at all gates.

Following the execution of Rainald Porchet, Yaghi Siyan, his capacity for retribution seemingly limitless, had imprisoned John, called "the Oxite", the Greek Patriarch of Antioch, and then, I suppose depending on Yaghi's mood, would periodically have him lowered by a rope over the wall upside down, his solders beating John's feet with rods, or, when Yaghi was so disposed, placed in a cage for several days at a time suspended over the wall in view of us. One of Adhémar's first acts after our occupation was to release John and restore his patriarchy of the city. This was a gesture surely not welcomed by Bohemond who wanted little reminder of Greek sovereignty. In gratitude John offered Adhémar use of his episcopal palace. With the patriarch's permission, Adhémar invited Rebecca and me to move in, a welcome respite for us after two years living in a tent. We were assigned a small apartment, modest but far grander than our usual primitive accommodations. Rebecca was especially cheered by the change.

Hamid accompanied us. There was a small monastery adjoining the palace, perhaps twelve monks. The abbot agreed to employ him in the kitchen and as a gardener. In exchange for these services he was given a small cell just outside the monks' dormitory and allowed to dine with them in their refectory. Despite not knowing Greek, though he was quickly learning, it was his joyful disposition and readiness to undertake any task assigned to him that won the hearts of the monks. He after all wanted to become a Christian. What better preparation? And perhaps he would become as infatuated with the cenobitic life as I had at his age when father and I spent that night at La Charité. I resumed my duties as Adhémar's scribe.

With the appearance of Kerboqa, the death of Roger of Barneville, and desertion of crusader nobles, particularly Stephen of Blois, I thought our fortunes could not worsen. They did. Every morning at the regular hour I attended to Adhémar, taking dictation in his new office in the palace. I did not understand why he required my services any longer. Kerboqa's relentless skirmishes with our forces had abated. It appeared he had settled in for a prolonged siege, to starve us out. If in the past Adhémar was able to dispatch his letters with the assistance of Genoese vessels or trading caravans on their way north to Constantinople, Kerboqa's grip on the city was perfected. Nothing got in; nothing got out. We were sealed as tightly as the calfskin of a Marseilles drum. I supposed Adhémar found solace in routine, in sharing his thoughts with fellow clerics in the West surely understanding they might never receive them. Perhaps he was writing to himself. The tone of these letters became increasingly despondent.

It was one day in the latter part of June. "Oderic, I don't know how long we can hold out." "We are starving as badly as we were months ago. Discerning God's will is becoming increasingly difficult for me. He gave us victory over the Turks one day but three days later snatched it from us with even more Turks."

"Because of our sin?" I asked.

"I don't know. The provisions we brought with us into the city are now depleted. The princes had counted on regular supplies from St. Symeon but the road is controlled by Kerboqa and in any event the harbor has been burned. They were also certain that this wealthy city could provide for our needs."

"I'm not sure I follow, Your Excellency."

For an instant Adhémar displayed slight irritation at my question, one he thought too obvious to answer. Likely it was but I was ignorant of his meaning. "With the construction of Tancred's Tower two months ago our barricade of the city was finally complete. No caravans could bring in food-stuffs. The city's inhabitants thus had to rely on their personal stores of grain, salted fish and meat, probably expecting to replenish them with the summer harvests. What little they hoarded was ransacked by our soldiers, always slaves to loot and gluttony." He then shook his head in disgust. "With every home they broke into, not only did they kill, steal silver plate and uten-sils, whatever they could find, but every bit of food. There's nothing left."

I was shocked. Rebecca and I had so enjoyed the hospitality of Patriarch John in his beautiful palace that we rarely left its pleasures, cocooned like butterflies in a chrysalis. There was John's library, a feast of learning, books in Greek, Latin, Arabic too. It brought back cheerful memories of the hours I spent in the *armarium* at Cluny. I spent many hours in it, devoting myself to reading the *Physiologus* with its morality tales of beasts, each richly illu-minated. Rebecca, for her part, daily visited the palace's gallery with its splendid collection of paintings and sculptures, the latter delicately carved revealing in some detail the most intimate parts of the human figure, Greeks being rather more libertine in their artistic tastes than we Latins. Indeed, she became so fascinated that she asked permission from John for pen, ink, and paper manufactured by the monks from wild cane which flourished throughout the fields of Antioch, boiled and pressed at the monastery. She wanted to develop her own novice skills revealing a talent which surprised her; I too was impressed. The patriarch offered one of his monks, himself a skilled artist producing portraits of Greek saints, to tutor her, a bit more attentively than I would have preferred. When I expressed my concern, Rebecca teased me for my jealousy, I think daily over a week. I needn't have worried. In the evenings we joined Adhémar and John at the patriarch's table. The meals, though simple and served without pretension by palace servants, were ample in their portions.

Thus, I had no notion of the privations outside the palace walls. The following day I left the palace to see for myself. The situation was even worse than Adhémar described. I visited a small market not far away. Prices were exorbitant: a small loaf of bread cost a whole bezant; one egg, two bezants; a chicken, fifteen. I wandered through the public squares and saw homeless pilgrims—all houses now commandeered by soldiers who had vandalized them—listlessly sitting or lying in the shade of buildings to escape the summer heat, many chewing on old leather; others boiling vines, thistles, leaves in pots; yet others cooking the hides of horses, oxen, camels, and donkeys, slaughtered many days before, their flesh already consumed, for a meager meat broth. Knights tried to save their horses, cutting veins and sucking their blood rather than killing them, but without fodder the horses began slowing dying. Soldiers, though better housed, suffered as well. I saw sickness and death on every street, in every alley. The air was putrid from the dead. I walked down one particular alley and saw two emaciated men but for their swollen bellies, leaning against the wall. I asked them how they were doing, a question arising more from compassion than good sense. One asked me, deliriously, "Are you the bread god?" Another pleaded "Help me up! I must get back to the field or the steward will beat me." I could do nothing and left them alone. The sense of hopelessness was pervasive. Nothing but a miracle could save us. Without it, defeat was inevitable.

Arnulf's Ambition

It was two days later, morning, I was seated at my desk taking dictation for yet another futile letter from Adhémar, he pacing back and forth as he customarily did, contemplating his message and its tone. He was very alert to tone, usually gentle, sometimes rather more severe. There was a knock on the door.

"Enter," Adhémar ordered.

A palace servant carefully opened the door just enough to stick his head in. "Your Excellency, Arnulf, Bishop of Rohes, 'demands'—that is what I was instructed to tell you—an immediate audience. Do I allow him in?"

Adhémar hesitated for a moment. "Yes. He may enter."

The servant opened the door, Arnulf storming in. I rose from my chair, a gesture of protocol rather than respect. Glaring at me, "I see you still have your worthless priest. His Jewess whore must be somewhere close."

I had half sat down but then immediately raised myself upright, stiff, and took a step around my desk in Arnulf's direction. I was undisturbed by Arnulf's comment of me. His vile slander of Rebecca was quite a different matter. A solid slap across his face, better two, would be a salutary catechism in manners and I was ready to deliver it. Adhémar motioned for me to sit back down. Reluctantly I did so. I had seen Adhémar greet many visitors in the past, always graciously. But on this occasion he dispensed with the normal courtesies.

"Bishop Arnulf. What is your business here?"

"I'll tell you my business. The Lord's business. You have reinstalled that heretic John as patriarch of Antioch. This is a sin against God."

"You call John a 'heretic'? And what is his heresy?"

"Adhémar," punctuating each sentence with a kerchief cleaning his rheumy eyes and sweating brow, "I shall not demean myself with an idle theological dispute. But since, clearly, you are unlettered in Greek practices and beliefs," he continued disdainfully, "I shall say only this: They reject our Church's infallibility; the supremacy of our pontiff; that the Holy Spirit proceeds from the Father *and* the Son; their satanic rituals in mass, most particularly the use of leavened bread."

"That is mostly true," Adhémar answered, I thought his courtesy undeserving of a reprobate such as Arnulf. "but he was imprisoned for months by the emir. He was lowered over the city walls upside down, his feet beaten with rods until they bled, and then for further amusement stuffed in a cage suspended over those same walls. Do you not think he has suffered sufficiently for our faith?"

"Not as much as Christ suffered," Arnulf answered scornfully.

Adhémar had enough. "I can see from your magnificent frame how much *you* have suffered for Christ on our pilgrimage." Arnulf's face reddened, quite brightly. I was rather enjoying this spectacle. "What is it you want?"

"This false priest John is to be deposed. You will create the Bishopric of Antioch and appoint me bishop. You have that authority as papal legate. I have the support in this demand of Duke Robert, Lord Bohemond too, truly god-fearing men . . . unlike others." Arnulf's implication was quite clear, referring to Adhémar. "When can *we* expect your answer?"

"Now." Adhémar answered curtly. "Patriarch John remains. There will be no bishopric. And you *certainly* will not be its bishop. You may take your leave. My office needs to be aired."

Adhémar had made an enemy. I had as well.

The First Vision: Peter Bartholomew

It was another day of dictation, interrupted on this occasion by a palace servant announcing an unexpected guest. I thought it Arnulf, perhaps with Robert or Bohemond to force his will on Adhémar. I understood Robert's motive; after all Arnulf was his chaplain. Bohemond's less clear though I knew he wanted all evidence of Constantinople's suzerainty over Antioch to be erased thereby securing his own claim to the city. Instead, it was Raymond and one other, the latter especially catching my attention. Rather handsome, my age, dressed as a Benedictine monk wearing a black habit, his arms within its sleeves, his pate tonsured and head lowered. He had that same angelic countenance I had seen at the chapter meeting at the Abbey of Cluny during his trial before Pope Urban accused of "fraternization—shall we decorously call it that?—with a woman in a nearby village and whom I briefly saw at Drogo's brothel in Nicea. Peter Bartholomew.

"Your Excellency," Raymond began, bowing, "thank you for receiving us. I would like to introduce Father Peter Bartholomew, a man who hails from my own land of Provence, recently a monk of Cluny, a favorite I've been told of the eminent Abbot Hugh himself. Father Peter has received holy messages from Heaven. I would prefer that he explain them. They are beyond my understanding but I'm sure not yours. Father Peter . . ." turning to him for a response.

Peter bowed to Adhémar, even lower than had Raymond. "My Lord Bishop, I have received visions which I do not fully comprehend. But a holy priest of your wisdom and learning might be able to interpret their meaning." His introduction was fulsome, his tone unctuous, too much for me to stomach though I remained silent, just watching. I had seen that same behavior at his trial but I was unsure whether Adhémar would penetrate it as easily as had the pope and Abbot Hugh. "They began six months ago. I was alone in my tent. It was dark but suddenly the entire earth shook from a tremor so violent that I was thrown from my cot onto the ground. As I tried to feel my way back up in the darkness a bright light filled my tent, so brilliant that I was at first blinded. Two men appeared, an apparition I thought, both clothed in white raiments. I first took them for wraiths and was mightily afraid, prostrating myself, daring not to look up. One of them, the older, red hair with a bushy white beard, spoke: 'Be not fearful, Peter. We know who you are, a priest acclaimed even in Heaven for your virtue. I am Andrew, the Apostle, come to bring you wondrous news.' Saint Andrew did not introduce his companion, who stood silently. He was taller and younger than Saint Andrew but of a form beyond that of any mortal man, his countenance so luminous that I could not discern its features. 'You shall follow me,' Saint Andrew commanded.

"Before I could object, for I was clothed in a night shirt, I felt myself spirited through the air to a church. It was lit by only two cressets yet they produced an unnatural, incandescent glow illuminating the entire interior. He set me down inside a chapel before its altar and then with his bare hand, without the aid of tools, reached into the floor underneath the marble slabs to his elbow retrieving the head of a spear. 'This,' he informed me, 'is the Holy Lance that pierced the Body of Christ.' I immediately knelt down before it, my hands clasped and head bowed. 'You shall take twelve men, no more, to dig. Here you will find it. It must be tendered to the Count of Toulouse, intended for him for only he possesses the saintly character to lead the Soldiers of Christ against the pagans. No army which carries it into battle can be defeated.'

"I grasped the lancehead, tears of joy streaming down my cheeks. I could only protest that I was unworthy. Saint Andrew then took the lancehead and replaced it under the floor. 'Remember, this is for Count Raymond alone. Peter, God has chosen you because in merit and grace you stand above all men as the value of gold exceeds silver. Do as I command!'"

Adhémar could scarcely conceal his incredulity and I by Peter's brazen narcissism. "Where was this church?"

"The Basilica of Saint Peter," Peter answered.

"And the chapel?"

"The chapel dedicated to the Virgin Mary."

Adhémar stood silently, meditating, Raymond and Peter awaiting his answer. Finally, it came. "The story is astonishing. But if we are to search for the Holy Lance in the basilica, the princes should attend to witness this miracle."

Both Raymond and Peter could not conceal their anxiety at Adhémar's suggestion to invite the princes, in particular those allied with the Norman Bohemond I suspected. Peter interjected quite emphatically. "Oh no! Saint Andrew's instructions to me were quite specific. Only Provençal diggers and Provençal nobles. No others."

"Hmm. Why didn't you mention that earlier?" Adhémar asked, his skepticism growing.

Peter mustered up the most sheepish look he could. "I must have forgotten, Your Excellency."

"Alright," Adhémar answered. "But I insist that I and my scribe Father Oderic be present to witness this miraculous event and record it for the pontiff and his curia. I'm certain Saint Andrew would not object." Further remonstrations would have been futile and Peter well knew it. "When do you want to commence the search?"

"I think tomorrow, midday, at the Basilica of Saint Peter, of course only if you approve," Raymond answered obsequiously." Adhémar nodded.

After they left his office Adhémar began pacing. "Oderic, there is something very, very curious about this. You and I both saw the Holy Lance at the chapel in the Great Palace in Constantinople. Christ's blood was still on it. There cannot be two. And the priest's insistence that *only* Provençals can be present adds even greater peculiarity to this."

"Lord Bishop, may I speak?"

"Yes, of course."

"This Peter is no priest. A charlatan. He was defrocked at Cluny by His Holiness for fornication which he vehemently denied until the evidence against him was overwhelming making him a prevaricator as well. I was present. I also saw him using the services of Drogo's women at Nicea. There are widespread stories of his drinking and carousing. He is no instrument of God. He is the willing tool of Count Raymond whose purpose here is unclear to me."

"Yes," Adhémar answered, "I too have heard rumors of his moral incontinence, a man imbued with more *levitas* than *gravitas*. Which makes me wonder why Saint Andrew chose *him* to send God's message. Yet, he still may be of service. Tomorrow will tell."

Search for the holy Lance

On the following day Adhémar and I walked together to the basilica. Gathered in front of the northern door were diggers with pry bars, shovels, and picks and Provençal nobles, all members of Raymond's trusted privy council: Pontius of Balazun, Farald of Thouars, others, some I recognized, most I didn't. There were priests as well but they waited outside the basilica. Peter led us into the church. The air was thick with the smell of incense which thankfully smothered the foul odor of horse filth which lingered despite the cleansing efforts of priests. The interior was dimly lit, the narrow windows permitting only limited light so it was difficult for me to fully appreciate the basilica's grandeur except for the beautiful mosaics covering its walls, all featuring images of Greek saints, their eyes staring back at all who beheld them. We approached the Chapel of the Virgin Mary. It was similar in design to those I had seen in Constantinople but much larger and possibly more magnificent. A *templon* balustrade, constructed of wood so highly polished that I could see my own reflection and encrusted with mother-of-pearl, separated the chapel from the nave, a swinging gate permitting entrance. Two columns of red marble flanked the tavertine altar, over it draped a silk brocade, its filigree of gold and silver thread. On the altar stood a gilded chalice used for private masses and communion, behind it a gold cross embedded with precious stones. A silver *polycandelon* was suspended by bronze chains from the ceiling over the center of the chapel, its flat tray holding eight candles, all lit in preparation for our arrival.

Peter pointed to the floor about fifteen feet in front of the altar. "There", he announced. On Peter's instruction we stood outside the *templon* as the diggers set to work, lifting one marble slab after another with their bars. Then, with picks and shovels they began digging. Even with two teams of six working at a time progress was slow and laborious, the ground composed of heavy clay and rock. Every hour the teams rotated, the next jumping into the pit to resume digging. Hours passed and the candles began to flicker, burning down to the ends of their wicks producing now the barest of light. It was vespers. The Provençal nobles, so filled with anticipation earlier, were becoming restless, grumbling over the pace, Adhémar more forbearing. I was especially intrigued how this farce would end. The pit was now four feet deep but with no evidence yet of the lance. Some of the nobles began wandering out believing the search in vain. The diggers were becoming fatigued, their initial eagerness for the search waning. Just as the last team was helped out of the pit, unexpectedly Peter jumped in. It was impossible for us to see the pit's interior, the candles by now having burned out and we were several feet away behind the *templon*.

Suddenly Peter's head disappeared below the edge of the pit. All we could hear was the sound of Peter clawing and scratching loose dirt with his bare hands. Then it stopped. The suspense was too great. All of us rushed into the chapel, standing around the pit looking down. There we saw Peter on his knees holding what appeared to be the head of a lance, his hand triumphantly extended for all of us to see. He stood with his hands cupped and offered it up to Raymond, now on his knees, his hands also cupped to receive it. "My Lord," Peter exclaimed in a voice loud enough for all to hear "Saint Andrew instructed me to render this Holy Lance which pierced the Sacred Body of Jesus Christ to you," his voice now rising "and to you alone for you are the worthiest of all princes in God's eyes. With this you shall lead our *milites Christi* against the pagan Turks outside our gates. When you are victorious, Antioch will be yours to rule." Raymond began weeping as he clasped the lancehead to his breast. All the Provençals fell to their knees, making the sign of the cross as they mumbled prayers. Adhémar and I stepped back into the shadows of the walls to avoid attention.

Raymond handed the lancehead to his chaplain, Raymond d'Aguilers, who looking upward raised it as though presenting an offering to heaven. The Provençals broke out in ecstatic cheers, "*Toulouse! Toulouse!*" The chaplain, followed by Raymond and the nobles after them, Adhémar and I trailing behind, walked out through the basilica's doors. He presented the lancehead to the waiting priests who fell to their knees sobbing, crossing themselves, some even convulsing so great their emotion. They followed the chaplain in a procession through the streets of Antioch, arms swinging back and forth in unison and then upward to heaven, all singing *Te Deum laudamus*:

> *You are God: we praise you;*
> *You are the Lord: we acclaim you;*
> *You are the eternal Father;*
> *All creation worships you.*

Adhémar and I walked back to the episcopal palace, not joining the procession. We could hear in the near distance singing of the *Te Deum* and the loud rejoicing of Antiochenes who filled the streets. I was quiet. Finally, after passing through two streets, Adhémar spoke.

"Oderic, did you notice anything unusual about what we have just witnessed?"

Uncertain of Adhémar's purpose in the question, the answer being rather obvious, but I knew Adhémar must have something else in mind. I wanted to be careful in my reply. Adhémar was always a curious mix of the rational and the devout. I was uncertain where he leaned, prepared to be more forthright after I sensed his disposition. "Lord Bishop, surely a miracle. A message from God Himself perhaps?"

"Yes, yes. Of course. But anything else?"

I was prepared to go further. "Well the lancehead," I continued, "certainly different from those we use, not in a leaf-shape but rather flanged, similar to those I saw abandoned by the Turks on the battlefield at Dorylaeum. And rather fresh-looking, not rusted after a millennium in the ground as I would have expected but perhaps God intended to preserve it unblemished. After all, it did pierce the body of His Son."

"Anything else?" Adhémar asked.

"Well . . ." I answered slowly and carefully, "I thought Peter said Saint Andrew had replaced the lance down to his elbow, yet it required a pit four feet deep to find it. And . . ." I paused, hesitating.

"And . . .? And *what*. . .?" Adhémar impatiently waiting for me to complete my thought.

"And by the time we had dug to the bottom of the pit it was already very dark, difficult for us to see inside the pit, especially because Peter had directed the witnesses, Provençals all, to stand several feet away from the pit outside the *templon*. But I'm sure there is a satisfactory explanation."

"Hmm. Oderic, you disappoint me. You're answering my questions far too cautiously. Let me state plainly what you're thinking: This is a fraud. A clumsy, albeit perhaps effective, attempt to deceive the credulous. I was struck that Saint Andrew would appear to this dissolute rogue and by Peter's insistence that God intended this lance for the count *alone* because of his singular worthiness, only he deserving to lead our army against the Turks and thereafter lord of the city. The puzzle for me is Raymond's role: Is he complicit in a conspiracy or merely duped by a self-serving fraud of a priest."

"What do you plan to do?"

"I'm not sure. Nothing now."

The Second Vision: Stephen of Valence

News of the lance's discovery had spread quickly throughout Antioch, crusaders believing this a sure sign that God had restored His favor. They began agitating for the princes to march against the Turks, Count Raymond to lead it. Such feelings were heightened when, on the night of the discovery, a bright light was seen flying down from heaven into the camp of the Turks. Adhémar called for a meeting of the council the following day in the audience hall of the episcopal palace to determine their next action. Since becoming Adhémar's scribe he had required my attendance at all councils to memorialize discussions. He was quite exacting in his requirement that all his letters be accurate in their accounts. Adhémar had gained confidence in my abilities as a scribe, especially my ability to write sensible letters despite his rambling, discursive dictating style. The meeting began as they always did, Adhémar explaining its purpose. He had just finished when Arnulf, neither a member of the council nor invited, entered the hall accompanied by Stephen of Valence. This was unexpected and all eyes turned to Arnulf.

"Lord Bishop," Arnulf began without invitation, "discovery of the lance by Peter Bartholomew is of course wonderful news but also troubling. I must be frank. There are those—not I of course—who doubt its authenticity. Peter is a false priest. His 'visions' are perhaps the product more of imagination than revelation . . . or something more sinister. I bring with me a *true* priest who has received a communication *from Christ Himself*. I request the princes listen to him."

The nobles began murmuring among themselves, growing louder. Adhémar raised his hand for silence. "Father Stephen, you may speak."

"Your Eminence," bowing to Adhémar, "my Lords," bowing to the princes, "I am but a humble and unworthy messenger from Christ, but for reasons only He comprehends, He has selected me to deliver His instructions to you. Late last night my companions and I went to the Church of the Blessed Mary to pray. I kept vigils, sitting in front of the high altar as they fell asleep in the sanctuary. And then a great light illuminated the entire chancel, so brilliant that I was at first blinded. Before me stood a man, handsome beyond human form."

"My Lord?" I asked him.

"'Stephen of Valence, do you know me not?'"

"No, my Lord, I answered."

"'Who are these people who have entered my holy city?'"

"They are Christians, servants of Jesus Christ."

"'What do they believe?'"

"They believe that Christ was born of the Virgin Mary, that he endured agony on the Cross, was buried and arose again to ascend into Heaven."

"'And yet you still do not know me?' In that instant a cross appeared behind this man's head more dazzling than the sun. 'Do you still not know who I am?'"

"My Lord," I answered trembling, "you are the Risen Christ."

"'Your people have sinned grievously against me though I gave you the city of Nicea and many other victories. And yet you continue to sin, to lie with pagan women, the stench of this fouls my nostrils. You are undeserving of my Grace.'"

"In that moment, my Lords, a woman, her beauty defying my ability to describe, suddenly appeared. She knelt before Christ. 'My Son. These are Christians whose prayers to you fill Heaven. You cannot abandon them in this hour of their greatest need.'"

"The Christ then turned to look at me. 'Who is your commander?' he asked."

"We have none. Our Christian princes have their own armies."

"'Is one of these princes Lord Bohemond of Taranto, now King of Antioch, whose devotion to faith and prowess in battle against infidels is unequaled?'"

"It is, my Christ."

"'And yet you still fear the pagans? Stephen, you will listen carefully to my commands and report them to the esteemed Arnulf, Bishop of Rohes, beloved in Heaven, and all the princes. Bohemond must command your armies against the Turks. In five days he will lead you against them. On the day before you will sing *Congregati sunt*, priests to chant mass and distribute communion. You are greatly outnumbered by the infidels. Saint George shall muster a heavenly army to aid you.'"

"I shall do as you command, Lord."

"'There is one more thing. Antioch has suffered the stain of Turkish occupation for too many years. It can only be cleansed by establishing a bishopric with the worthiest bishop among you to assume the cathedral throne.'" Adhémar and I understood immediately whom Stephen had in mind. "'Do as I instruct. Otherwise I shall withdraw my Grace.'"

There seemed to be dueling visions and demands from God, each irreconcilable with the other: one for Raymond to lead the army against the Turks and govern Antioch; the other for Bohemond to lead that same army and govern Antioch. Anger immediately exploded among the Provençal nobles and Raymond's allies, all reviling Stephen, Raymond himself quietly nodding in agreement with each exclamation of outrage. The Normans then began shouting in return, impugning Peter Bartholomew. The clamor had become deafening.

Adhémar raised his hand for silence and then looked to Stephen for a response. "My Lords," Stephen protested so vehemently that despite my unspoken doubts I thought perhaps he was sincere. "I am ready to be tested. If you wish me to undergo an ordeal by fire, I shall do so. Or I'm ready to leap from a tower; if injured, you may behead me."

Adhémar clearly thought this excessive. "That will be unnecessary," he said. "It will be sufficient for you to swear on this crucifix," lifting one hanging on the wall. Stephen did so. Then Adhémar addressed the princes. He realized this was a critical moment for unity which only he could bring. "My Lords, enough! God has spoken to us through Saint Andrew and His Holy Son. We must listen. His messages are clear: We have the Lance that pierced our Lord and God's promise we shall be victorious with it in battle and that He will send an army to aid us. He has instructed us to march out against the infidels in five days. We shall do so, under Lord Bohemond's command. The question of Antioch can be decided later." It did not escape my attention that Adhémar did not address the issue of a bishopric for the city.

"There is yet one more thing, my Lords," Adhémar continued. "I have just received urgent word from General Tatikios who's with the emperor at Philomelium in the northern regions of Anatolia, the messenger able to slip through Kerboqa's cordon, that the traitor Stephen of Blois and the other so-called 'Christian' nobles who fled with him, renegades all, 'rope dancers', reached Philomelium and informed Alexios that Antioch would soon be overwhelmed, if it hadn't already been taken, by the Turks. Alexios intended to take his army south to relieve us but was persuaded the expedition would be futile. He decided to withdraw further north. We are now orphans dependent on God alone." A bewildered silence followed, whether because of the betrayal by Stephen of Blois or retreat of the Byzantine army. More likely both. "We have been offered hope with these visions. Yet I must speak plainly. God's Providence has been given one day to be withdrawn the next doubtless because of the faithless divisions among us. We *may* receive His Favor on the day of battle but there is no certainty. It all depends on His Will. What I *do* know is this: our situation could not be more desperate. I ask your agreement to send a delegation to Kerboqa to seek safe conduct for all of us out of Antioch. Do you disagree?" No one spoke. "Then it is done. I shall send Peter the Hermit. This is the decree of His Holiness Pope Urban through me, his legate. There is nothing more to discuss. Let us wait for Kerboqa's answer. In the meantime, prepare for battle."

The princes departed, Adhémar and I left alone. He was shaking his head. "Our internal discords are well known, probably to Kerboqa as well, but like a scab on a wound they have now been pulled off and the wound is beginning to bleed."

"Lord Bishop, with your permission I would like to ask you a question." He nodded. "Whom do you believe, Peter or Stephen?"

"Neither. Both are either scallywags or fools. What is more important is that the people believe them, that we possess the holy lance, and God's promise He will send an army from heaven to reinforce our numbers. They have served a necessary purpose. Hope and courage have been restored."

"Why did you send Peter to Kerboqa?" I asked.

"Simple. If I had sent any of our great lords, Kerboqa would surely have held him for ransom. Even under a flag of truce I cannot trust this infidel to honor it. This would be a great blow to our morale, something we can hardly afford at this moment. Moreover, it would be interpreted by Kerboqa, probably correctly, as a sign of our desperation. A minor noble would be quickly dismissed as an insult to the emir. Peter was the best choice out of several poor ones. His reputation as a holy man extends beyond our crusaders."

"Do you really think Peter will be successful?"

"No," he answered, "but perhaps . . . just perhaps . . . God will shine His Light on Kerboqa's pagan soul. We must try."

The following day, June 25, Peter rode out to the emir's camp, returning but one hour later reporting Kerboqa's curt answer: "Fight your way out." And so we did.

Adhémar summoned an emergency council in the palace. "My Lords, our mission to Kerboqa has failed. I myself thought there was little probability of success but an attempt had to be made. Now we shall face our most formidable foe yet. Lord Bohemond, your plan?"

Bohemond stood facing the princes. There was no weakness in the timbre of his voice as though his iron will were forged in a blazing fire. "My Lords. In three days we shall march out of the Bridge Gate, only that one. We all understand the odds we face. If we divide ourselves by attacking out of different gates we shall be dispersed. Victory depends on a unified, tight formation. We have lost most of our horses and our knights have now become foot soldiers. But most important," he continued with gritty resolution, "every man—able-bodied or not, knight, man-at-arms, pilgrim, Tafur even—must be rallied. We must gather the greatest host we can. Tomorrow morning we shall begin training in the fields within the city."

"Lord Bohemond," Robert of Flanders rising to speak, "our men have taken refuge in many houses. They appear to prefer the security of their new homes over combat with the Turks. I'm uncertain how we can dislodge them."

Bohemond's solution was simple. "I shall send out heralds throughout the city this afternoon to order they report immediately to their commanders. If they don't, I'll burn them out." The princes gasped at the thought of setting the city on fire. Bohemond ignored their consternation, returning immediately to his plan for the crusader attack on the Turks and the role each prince would play. He sought neither counsel nor approval. This was his war and he would lead it.

But then a curious thing happened. Raymond arrived late, carried into the audience hall on a litter claiming illness. Raymond had throughout our pilgrimage suffered from periodic ailments, the Normans often ridiculing him for cowardice suspecting they mere pretense. I did not share the skepticism. Yes, sometimes unwise in strategy dependent too often on faith but valiant in combat. Yet, looking back, on this occasion a pretext perhaps for a more ambitious plan he had in mind?

"Lord Bohemond, as you can see I am incapacitated, my legs weak and painful," at that trying to raise a leg, wincing in pain. "It will pass in a few days. Until then riding and walking are unbearable." Then quickly changing the subject, "Do you not think the citadel should be secure from an attack behind our lines?"

"I do Count Raymond, but . . ."

Raymond interrupted. "Good. Then it's settled. I shall personally command a hundred of my men to block any sortie from the citadel. They will be posted outside its gates. Bishop Adhémar will command the remainder of my troops in the field."

Bohemond had clearly been taken by surprise but Raymond's decisive intervention had given him little opportunity to object. Bohemond's suspicion of Raymond's intention was palpable. From the beginning Raymond had rejected Bohemond's claim to Antioch, wanting it for himself—occupation of the citadel was key to control of the city. Bohemond was right to be suspicious, just as Raymond was justified in his suspicion of Bohemond.

Adhémar closed the council. "My Lords, we shall meet again in three days on the field of battle in this our Holy War. Let not your faith in God falter. Listen to the prophet Ezekiel: *"They will know that I am the LORD when I disperse them among the nations and scatter them through the countries."* With faith and courage, we shall prevail," Adhémar's voice now rising, his arms outstretched, "God wills it!", all the princes raising their swords, shaking them back and forth, shouting *"God wills it! God wills it!"* We were again united: Normans, Provençals, Flemings, Lorrainers. We were now a single army of *all* Franks. At least for the present. It wouldn't last long.

City on Fire and a Plot

Rebecca and I were having dinner with Adhémar and Patriarch John when outside our window we heard shouts *"Fire! Fire!"* All four of us ran outside onto the street. Crusaders were fleeing their homes, most of wood, built cheek by jowl beside one another, many grabbing buckets of water trying desperately to douse the flames. The effort was futile. As flames erupted from one house, the wind which had picked up spread them to the next. In the distance I could see smoke billowing from different parts of the city. The city was ablaze. Bohemond had indeed succeeded in evicting idle crusader soldiers but well beyond his purpose. The fire burned for the rest of the night, destroying two thousand buildings, including churches. Fortunately for us the wind was blowing in a direction opposite from the palace and monastery. We were not in danger. Nevertheless, palace servants and monks from the monastery, Hamid among them, rushed out to deal with any threat to either. Hamid came running to me, ignoring Adhémar, John, even Rebecca.

"Rabbi," he exclaimed excitedly, tugging on my sleeve and pulling me away from the others.

"What is it Hamid?"

"Shams is no longer commander of the citadel. Emir Kerboqa replaced him with another, Ahmad ibn-Marwān. I don't know what happened to Shams. May he perish in hell."

"Yes, I know about the new commander."

"What you don't know, Rabbi, is that Shams had discovered how my father conspired with Lord Bohemond to deliver the city. He reported all this to Ahmad who ordered our entire family to be hunted down. Fortunately we left the citadel immediately after you Latins took the city and are now safe living with my mother's uncle only a few streets away. I think our house will be safe. Unfortunately my cousin Sahak—well, he's not exactly a close cousin, the son of my uncle's second cousin who. . ."

"Yes, yes," I answered impatiently, "what is it Hamid you wish to tell me?"

"Sahak was arrested and was certain he would be executed though he had nothing to do with Antioch's fall. But that's not what happened. Instead, Ahmad took Sahak into a private chamber and told him that he wished to speak with you, privately. Somehow Ahmad had learned of your role. He had also heard you are a godly man, a great warrior too, and can be trusted. Ahmad arranged for Sahak to secretly leave the citadel through the same passageway you took to save Rebecca from the jail. Ahmad will wait for you there tonight. He assured Sahak—this is what Sahak told me—that he wishes no harm to you, only to talk about 'something' which Ahmad did not disclose. But it must be this night."

I did not reveal this to anyone, even Rebecca. I made an excuse to leave the palace. Hamid had told me of a small sally port near St. George's Gate. I made my way through the chaos of the streets and found it, unguarded as I had hoped, the sentries probably engaged in suppressing the fire. Passing through, I made my way up the mountain slope to the passageway's opening, moonlight sufficient for me to see it. In my haste, I had forgotten to bring a torch but it was unnecessary for I was able to feel my way through. The opening at its end into the jail had not been closed. Standing inside was a Turk, a man near forty years, unarmed, the bearing of a soldier—tall, muscular, straight, his features not disagreeable but clearly one not to be trifled with. He looked at me without smiling or any formal acknowledgment.

"You are Father Oderic?"

I saluted him in the Turkish manner, he not responding with a return salute. "I am. You are Ahmad ibn-Marwān, Commander of the Citadel?" He nodded. "You summoned me Commander?"

He didn't acknowledge the question. "You don't look like a warrior, more like a callow youth. I expected something more."

"I am a warrior by force of circumstance, not by natural disposition."

"You were a companion of Georgios Vardanes of Constantinople, were you not?" I nodded. "A Pecheneg traitor who denied his Turkish blood and faith in Islam." I said nothing. "Yet a valiant fighter and a man of honor. We fought several battles against one another in Anatolia. Where did you get that puny weapon?" pointing to *Iskender.*

"It has served me well," I answered. "A gift from General Tatikios, taken in battle from a Pecheneg warrior whom he killed."

"Ah, Tatikios. My enemy but a great general."

"You summoned me, Commander?" I asked again.

"You know of course that your situation here is hopeless. You will die either of starvation or in battle. Emir Kerboqa is too powerful. Yet his alliances with the other emirs whom he recruited in this expedition are rather tenuous. And you Latins have been victorious in the past despite overwhelming odds. You may again, if Allah wills it. I know my own fate and the fate of my men if you do prevail. Your Latin reputation for Christian 'mercy' is well known to us," he said scoffing. "But I'm not sure we followers of Islam are any better."

"You summoned me, Commander?" I asked for the third time.

"Yes, to the point. I have spies in your camps. I know of Count Raymond's design on the citadel and then the city. It is not fortuitous that he has soldiers outside our citadel's doors. He wishes it for himself and will insist I surrender to him. I do not trust this Raymond. Men of his extreme piety are always the first to savage enemies in the name of their god. If you defeat the emir, I would be prepared to surrender the citadel to Lord Bohemond, and to him alone. He is reputed to be a practical man, one willing to sacrifice pious rectitude for expediency. In return he will grant safe conduct to me and my men. That is my message to Lord Bohemond. You will do this?"

"I will."

"Good. I shall send word through Sahak. I bid you good rest." He turned and left.

Once more I was caught in a web of intrigue between Turks and Bohemond, and now a crusader prince, Count Raymond. But I did as Ahmad had instructed reporting the entire conversation to Bohemond. We talked briefly. "Thank you Father Oderic. You will keep this between us." Smiling, "you will be compensated."

"I seek no compensation, my Lord. I do this for our pilgrimage and our faith. I desire nothing more."

Kerboqa Defeated

For the next three days and under Bohemond's watchful eyes knights, most now foot soldiers with few horses, and men-at-arms were drilled in tactics: the shield wall, unfamiliar to horsemen, and close combat swordplay; Hugh of Vermandois's bowmen practiced archery, always careful to retrieve their arrows, now more precious than ever. Bohemond had forgone cavalry maneuvers, the horses, what few remained, already jaded from lack of fodder. During those three days the priests fasted, Adhémar wisely exempting fighting men wanting to preserve their strength. Besides, Adhémar told me later, they had already 'fasted' for two weeks—God needed no further sacrifice from them. Daily, priests walked in procession from one church to another singing *Congregati sunt* and hymns of intercession. In the early morning of the battle, before the sun rose, priests said mass, distributed communion to all crusaders, and received confessions. We were ready to face the enemy.

It was the Vigil of the Apostles Peter and Paul, June 28, at dawn. We all stood in formation behind the doors of the Bridge Gate when it opened. The first to emerge was Raymond d'Aguilers riding alone bearing Raymond's trophy, the holy lance, brightly cleaned and polished, a shaft now attached to its head. Behind him came priests in white sacerdotal raiments, barefoot, chanting hymns, prayers, and benedictions to the saints. Bohemond had formed us into six divisions, columns of three, each carrying the standard of its lord: first the Flemish, primarily bowmen, led by Hugh of Vermandois and Robert of Flanders; the second composed of Lorrainers under the command of Godfrey; the third division, immediately behind, Normans of northern Francia under Robert of Normandy; then Raymond's army of Provençals under Adhémar; and finally the fifth and sixth of Normans from southern Italia led by Bohemond and Tancred in reserve. Adhémar was cloaked in burnished mail, dazzling in the sun—rather too dazzling, I feared, an inviting target for a Turkish arrow—his metal helmet shaped in the Norman fashion with a nasal guard; a white chasuble over his torso covering his mail; and an embroidered red pallium looped over his shoulders. He was riding the same white horse he had at Dorylaeum where he charged the Turks from over a hill. Adhémar had lacked a standard bearer since the death of Bernard of Béziers in the battle at Bridge Gate. Fortunately, his standard, captured and desecrated by the Turks in the same battle, had been recovered. Adhémar requested that I carry it and I was honored to do so. I was dressed in leather armor, *Iskender* hanging from my baldric. We rode side by side. As each division filed through the doors trumpets blared and drums beat furiously to crusader shouts "*God wills it! God wills it!*" Despite starvation, their spirits were fortified by the holy lance in front of them and by Stephen's promise of a divine army to reinforce their ranks.

As we were about to cross the Fortified Bridge in front of the Bridge Gate Kerboqa sent a company of mounted archers, two thousand, to confront us on the other side of the bridge unleashing their arrows. The priests immediately scattered, scurrying back to the city, climbing to the ramparts from which they shouted encouragement to us. Raymond d'Aguilers held firm, unflinching. Bohemond had anticipated this initial attack for which reason he had positioned Hugh's bowmen at the front of the army. They quickly reformed into two lines, the first kneeling and the second standing behind and over them, all discharging their own flurry of arrows. The Turks pulled back as we continued across the bridge. We turned right, to the north, the columns fanning out like fingers on a hand, two ranks, the foot in front, what few mounted knights we had immediately behind them. We marched steadily forward, carefully holding close to the river on our right to avoid being outflanked. Adhémar's Provençals held the far left of the line, more exposed. The Turkish army, mounted and foot, was massed in front of us, no more than a quarter mile away. Oh so many of them, countless, more than stars in the sky. Kerboqa dispatched detachment after detachment of mounted archers, passing in front us from left to right, loosening their arrows from a safe distance, riding off to be followed by the next. "Raise shields!" Bohemond shouted, our soldiers raising their wooden shields covered with thick and hardened leather over their heads creating a tight ceiling, continuing steadily to move forward. So many arrows rained on them that their shields resembled the quills on a porcupine. Our line did not break.

Kerboqa then sent his infantry against us. No more than twenty paces separated us, too close for Turks to use their bows. "Shield wall!" Bohemond shouted. Our soldiers sidled next to each other in perfect precision, shields overlapping, swords drawn and spears resting above the shields. We continued to march forward, step by step, in unison, close formation. Yet our situation seemed hopeless. The Turk infantry consisted of one rank after another, stretching back so far I could barely see, the landscape black with them. The sky was clear and blue, not a cloud above us, yet a gentle rain began falling, it seemed only on us, oh so refreshing, a welcome respite from the sun's heat. All felt the Lord was speaking to us. And as the rain fell shouts went up. "*Saint George! Saint George!*" I looked to my right and saw crusaders pointing to the sky in the distance behind the Turkish lines. I looked in that direction but saw nothing. Later crusaders who witnessed this miracle swore to me they beheld an army of horsemen descending from heaven, dressed in brilliant white led by three men riding black horses—Saints George, Demetrius, and Theodore, God's martial saints—just as Stephen had foretold, their swords drawn and behind them chariots with archers unleashing arrows at the Turkish rear lines. I never knew whether Bohemond actually saw them. But what he did see was that his men had taken heart. "*Charge!*" he shouted. And our soldiers did, throwing themselves heroically against the Turks with all of God's fury shouting "*Saint George! Saint George!*" The Turks pulled back. Suddenly, the grassy field separating our forces, dried from the hot summer, the wind blowing in our direction, was on fire. It was lit by Kerboqa. The flames were moving quickly toward us. As Kerboqa hoped, our soldiers began stepping back, our formation now breaking. In any moment they would turn and run. Bohemond saw the threat. Our mounted knights, some on horses, others on donkeys, mules, even camels, all scrawny, were in a line formation. "Cavalry!" he shouted, "Lances! Forward!" The knights couched their lances and galloped toward the enemy, trampling the flames with their hooves. The foot soldiers took heart once again and began racing behind them into the center of the massed Turkish infantry, behind them pilgrims, Tafurs too, with daggers, clubs, sticks, anything serviceable as weapons. The Turks were stunned, turned and fled, our crusaders slaying every one they could outrun. On the hill behind the Turkish lines the emirs who had joined Kerboqa began turning their horses and fled, Kerboqa the last to desert the field. Our army chased them for days.

* * *

Some of this account, including that of the heavenly army, is drawn from stories I heard shortly after the battle. My attention had been directed elsewhere. Kerboqa had directed one company of mounted archers and another of infantry to attack the Provençals commanded by Adhémar from our rear. Adhémar ordered his men, almost all infantry, to form a shield wall but just as he did was struck by an arrow in his thigh, just too irresistible a target. He was swaying back and forth in his saddle. I was beside him holding his lanced standard in my right hand and with my left reached out to steady him. I then saw a Turk spearman racing toward Adhémar, no doubt believing that killing an infidel general would bring him glory and passage into Muslim heaven. Adhémar weakly tried to pull his mace from its holster as the Turk closed, both his hands on the spear waist-high pointing upwards towards Adhémar's belly. I couched Adhémar's standard under my arm, leveled it at the Turk and spurred my horse forward. The Turk, an experienced soldier and more adept at handling a spear than I a lance, stepped aside and deflected my standard with such force that it dropped from my hand. I was no longer a threat but Adhémar, not I, was his prize.

He continued to move toward the bishop. I wheeled my horse around and pulled out my maul to attack his head from behind. The Turk heard me, turned, and with his spear point kept me at bay, jabbing it back and forth at my horse as he backed up toward Adhémar. I was without choice, my maul too short to overcome his long spear particularly from horseback. I leapt off my horse to face the Turk, spear against maul. Ekbar had trained me well. The match was still uneven but I had *Iskender*. He thrust, I flicked it away, he thrust again, another flick from me. And thus it went, thrust and parry until the Turk wearied of what he thought at first would be mere sport. He dropped his spear and pulled out his scimitar intending to draw me into closer combat. He still had the upper hand, the reach of his sword exceeding my maul's. He began slashing back and forth, I retreating step by step. He was dressed unusually for a Turkish foot soldier wearing mail from head to foot, even his leggings, the mail more tightly woven than our own, of Damascus steel, and an iron helmet. A captain perhaps? This would explain his armor and skill. I knew that a blow of my maul's hammerhead would at best bruise, not disable, the maul intended as it was for strikes against bone: an unprotected skull, an elbow, a knee. He raised his sword shouting "*Infidel! I'm sending you to hell!*" Death would come at any moment. Then I heard a voice. "Not today, pagan. Behind you!" The voice was mine. Startled, he turned his head to look over his shoulder. In that instant, as he turned back to confront me seeing no threat, I thrust *Iskender*'s spike into his face. He would face justice in the next life and I would seek God's forgiveness later for drawing blood. Or perhaps not.

Saving Bishop Adhémar's Life

As I was defending Adhémar, Provençals and Turks were engaged in hand-to-hand combat. Outnumbered, we were being forced back. I was certain our men would break and run but suddenly I heard a trumpet, two long blasts followed by a short one, the Turkish signal of retreat. They turned and fled, the Provençals pursuing them. My only thought was Adhémar. He was too dazed by the wound to be any further service in battle. I dismounted and checked his wound as he sat in his saddle. An arrow was deeply embedded in the left leg, the thigh, blood flowing from the wound. The arrow would be dealt with later. I pulled Adhémar's pallium from his shoulders and wrapped the band of cloth tightly around the wound to staunch the bleeding. After making sure Adhémar was secure in his saddle, placing both his hands on its pommel, I remounted, took the reins of Adhémar's horse leading it quickly to the palace's monastery where I was reasonably confident there would be an infirmary. I tethered our horses in front of the doors and shouted for help. Two monks opened the door, immediately recognizing the need they returned with a litter. We gently pulled Adhémar down and carried him to a cot in the infirmary.

An aged monk raced in. "I am in charge of this infirmary. "Who is this?"

"This is Adhémar, Bishop of Le Puy, the Papal Legate."

"What happened?" I explained and emphasized the urgency of Adhémar's condition requiring immediate attention.

"Yes, of course, I shall summon all the monks to pray for a speedy recovery. We will gather about the bishop's bed" Turning to an attendant sweeping the fireplace hearth, "Ring the chapter bell!"

Oh how memories of that fool of an *infirmarius* Guarin at La Charité flooded my thoughts, the same nostrum, hymns and prayer. I had just left battle and killed a man. I was in no mood for faith. "Have you no surgeon here?" I asked.

"No. We find convalescence and God's Grace sufficient."

"I am a Doctor of Physik and I alone shall tend to the bishop!" I replied quite firmly. The monk stepped back submissively. "You there!" pointing at the attendant, "you will stay here and assist me!" The monk quickly left, his absence welcome. "Bring me shears." He did so. I carefully cut the left leg of Adhémar's breeches and then untied the pallium. Adhémar lay on the cot quietly, but his head was shaking back and forth, moaning deliriously.

"Father Adhémar," I whispered in his ear placing my hand gently on his forehead, "it's me, Oderic. I'll take care of you." I had developed the same deep affection for my bishop as I had for Benedict. I could not let him die. I would have to summon all my knowledge of Galen, Avicenna, and Samuel ben Meier's herbal remedies. I began with Galen's injunction: first, close observation. My tourniquet fortunately had stopped the bleeding. The arrow was embedded in the leg without passing through to the other side. I didn't know whether or not this was a blessing. I had no choice but to extract it. Years later I found a quotation from the greatest of all physicians, Hippocrates: "*War is the only real school for the surgeon.*" On that day I thought he was proven correct.

The attendant approached me timidly, likely intimidated by the command I had now asserted over the infirmary and his superior. "Your name monk?" I demanded, in my present disposition feeling no need for normal courtesies.

"Brother Bardas, Your Excellency" a more elevated form of address than my station warranted. Now I was both an "excellency" and a "rabbi". I was satisfied with either.

"Bardas. We have little time. I shall need from your medical cabinet a forceps, the smallest you have; all your surgical probes, of different widths; and a lancet. They must be thoroughly cleansed in your best wine, fortified with brandy. I'll also need several pieces of linen, cleaned and washed. Honey and vinegar too."

"Do you also require holy water?"

"No. Useless. You may sprinkle it on him later if you wish. Do you have a medicinal garden?"

"We do, Your Excellency."

"Then you must have dried mandrake root, henbane and hemlock. I want them mixed in wine, soaked in a sponge. This must be done immediately. After I receive it, I shall begin surgery."

Bardas proved a capable assistant. The sponge came quickly, my instruments and the linen soon after. I placed the sponge to Adhémar's nostrils and held it there. His moaning subsided until it ended as he became drowsy then falling asleep. I wiped the blood from around the wound and with the lancet carefully cut about the arrow's shaft, continually wiping the wound with linen soaked in vinegar as blood emerged. I gently wriggled the shaft. It moved. A good sign, I thought. Perhaps I could withdraw the entire arrow. I then began gently pulling on the shaft just below the fletchings but it quickly separated leaving the head embedded in the leg. My only recourse was to use forceps. I would have to widen the hole to reach it. I selected the thinnest probe, wrapped it in linen smeared with honey, and nudged it into the wound to open it slightly. Then, doing the same with a larger one, continuing this procedure, each time with a wider probe, and as the hole gradually opened more blood flowed, every time sucking it out with my mouth, spitting it on the floor. Finally the arrow-head was visible and the wound now open wide enough for the forceps. Fortunately it was a bobkin, not barbed nor lodged in bone. I took the forceps, coaxing it further and further into the wound until it reached the arrow's point, gripped the handles tightly and began a slow and careful extraction. The arrowhead was now removed. I sucked out the blood until it was as clean as I could make it. Bardas brought me a poultice of butter, onion, and mandrake which I spread over the wound.

"Bardas. I must leave. You will feed the bishop mutton broth with leeks, onions, and cabbage, as much as he wants. Bread too. Not stale or moldy. Freshly baked. I shall return as soon as I am able. In the meantime, you will personally ensure that at every hour of the day and night either you or another attends to him. He is never to be left alone. I shall hold you, *you alone*, responsible. I've killed many men. I'm already doomed to God's Hell. One more will make no difference. Don't fail me" as I placed my hand on *Iskender* to reinforce the message. Walking out, I turned around. "Brother Bardas, you have served well. God's blessings on you. But remember . . ." I was certain he would.

Perhaps God would forgive me. I had taken one life. I may have saved another. I hoped the account was in balance.

The Citadel Surrenders

I had returned to the palace and just tethered my horse outside its doors when Hamid accompanied by a young man his age, Sahak I assumed, ran to me. "Rabbi, Commander Ahmad has ordered me to tell you that a Frankish count, 'Rimon', something like that, is now besieging the cit-adel and demanding it surrender to him. Sultan Bohemond must come. Otherwise Ahmad will have to surrender to this Rimon."

Oh how I wished I had never met Hamid. I was now an accomplice of Bohemond against Raymond but too deeply enmeshed in this conspiracy to extricate myself. I remounted my horse and rode off to alert Bohemond, finding him in a market square reveling with a small detachment of his men over the victory that day. "Lord Bohemond, Commander Ahmad requires you immediately at the citadel. Count Raymond is demanding its surrender to him." We were only a short distance from the citadel, up a single path leading from the city proper. Bohemond summoned his troops mounted and foot, including his standard bearer, to follow him. We quickly arrived at the citadel. I saw Raymond pounding on the door with the hilt of his sword demanding entrance and the citadel's immediate surrender. Behind him were a hundred Provençal soldiers ready to rush in the instant the doors opened. Raymond had certainly recovered from his infirmity, a "miracle" no doubt, one of many that day.

Bohemond dismounted. "Count Raymond. The city is mine. The citadel too. You will yield to me."

"And I should do that why?" Raymond retorted. "I was here first. I claim this fort. You may find others for yourself," waving his hand aimlessly toward the east, "somewhere, out there."

As this was occurring Provençals and Normans had formed themselves into two opposing lines, each it seemed ready to attack the other, the battle unequal with Raymond's hundred facing some thirty Normans. But for the moment they were merely hurling epithets against each other: "You Francones," a disparaging term for men from Francia, one Norman shouted, "dirty bastards with your false lance. It was Norman courage that won this day!" Provençals responded in kind, one shouting back "You Norman cocksuckers, victory was ours!" I will not recite more of the insults and jeers that passed back and forth, each becoming more vile than the last. Anger was growing on both sides. I quickly dismounted and walked between them to the citadel's twin doors where Bohemond with his standard bearer beside him and Raymond stood in confrontation. Ahmad now appeared over the ramparts just above calling down at us, neither Bohemond nor Raymond understanding.

"What did he say?" Bohemond asked me.

"That only you and I may enter."

A few moments later one of the doors opened, narrowly, Ahmad standing just inside, dozens of Turk soldiers behind him, their swords drawn. Raymond of course understood the significance of Ahmad allowing Bohemond with his standard into the citadel. As Bohemond started to pass through Raymond roughly grabbed him from behind to pull him back. "You've tricked me, you coward!"

Bohemond angrily whirled around pushing Raymond off. "Get away from me!" he shouted and then walked in taking his standard from its bearer, I behind him. The door closed. Bohemond and Ahmad saluted one another.

"Commander Ahmad," Bohemond began, "you wish to surrender the citadel to me?"

"I do, Lord Bohemond, but on a single term. You will grant safe passage for my men, those who wish it, out of Antioch. Those who remain are willing to convert to your faith and serve under you. I shall do the same."

"This is agreeable," Bohemond answered "You will please raise my standard above this fortress," handing it to him, Ahmad passing it on to one of his soldiers. "Replace that false banner with my own." Very quickly the emir's banner, black with a red crescent, was lowered and Bohemond's banner, red with a coiled serpent, raised fluttering over the highest point of the citadel. From outside I heard "hurrahs" from the Normans. And then the clash of arms. "Open the gate, quickly!" Bohemond demanded, and walked out with his sword drawn. "Stop this!" he shouted. "Now!" And to make the point he thumped a Provençal on his metal helmet with the broad side of his sword, doing the same to a Norman, other than stunning them inflicting no injury to either. Bohemond's quick action produced the desired effect. The fighting stopped. Raymond had in the meantime merely stood by watching, confident I think in his superior numbers, disinterested in intervening in the quarrel. Bohemond turned to Raymond. "You and your men may leave. *Now!*" Raymond was steaming with anger but he said nothing, leading his men away.

Antioch was now Bohemond's. But the enmity between Provençals and Normans would only become more bitter.

* * *

I returned to the palace, exhausted—from the battle, Adhémar's surgery, and the altercation at the citadel. All I wanted was sleep. Rebecca and I retired to our bed. Just as I was falling into a deep slumber I felt Rebecca's arm glide over my waist as she moved closer. "Oderic," she whispered tenderly, "I'm pregnant."

This ends Book XI of *Jerusalem Falls!* Book XII begins.

BOOK XII

PLAGUE, TRIAL, AND FLIGHT

Plague and Death of Adhémar. Election of William, Bishop of
Orange. Trial of Rebecca. Escape to Edessa. Baldwin's Triumph. A
Plot Unfolds. Rebecca and I Marry. Escape from Edessa.

Plague and Death of Adhémar

The days following Kerboqa's defeat were quiet. Much cleanup was
needed. The battlefield outside the city was littered with corpses.
Wagons, previously used to collect the bodies of those massacred in the seizure of Antioch a month before, were recalled into service.
Pilgrims were paid a *sous* for each collected. The remains of Turks were
dumped into the Orontes River, the bodies of crusaders burned on pyres
accompanied by suitable religious services. Reconstruction of the buildings
damaged by fire began. Priests were charged with cleansing all churches,
asperging their altars with holy water to rid them of any pagan stain.

Adhémar was recovering, thanks be to God, from his arrow wound,
albeit more slowly than I had hoped. For the first three days after bringing him to the infirmary I visited Adhémar twice daily replacing the poultice, cleaning any seepage, and changing his bandages. Rebecca took
upon herself responsibility for his diet, overseeing the preparation of all
his meals in the monastery kitchen, particularly ensuring ample portions
of beef and fish to fortify his body. When Adhémar couldn't feed himself
or denied an appetite, Rebecca would sit on his cot feeding him while
softly encouraging him to eat another bite. By the fourth day I decided
he could be returned to his apartment in the episcopal palace. Although
there were palace servants to attend to Adhémar's needs, Rebecca would
have none of it, personally supervising his care.

It was only five days after Kerboqa's defeat that Adhémar decided to
convene a council to determine the army's next move now that Antioch
was secure. I tried vehemently to dissuade him, his strength insufficient
to manage the sometime truculent princes, especially the increasingly

bitter dispute between Bohemond and Raymond over lordship of Antioch. Bohemond commanded almost the entire city, most importantly the citadel, but Raymond occupied the towers of the Fortified Bridge across the Orontes, Yaghi Siyan's palace, and the fort *La Mahomerie* even though largely demolished. The Fortified Bridge was particularly significant because it controlled the roads to St. Symeon and Alexandretta from Antioch. Neither was willing to relinquish his claims. Even Adhémar, the only member respected by the entire council, had been unable in the past to negotiate an accord between them. He hoped this time would be different and his mind was set. He answered my remonstrances quite simply, quoting the Psalms: "*Summon your power, God. Show me your strength as you have done before.*" Further efforts to dissuade him would be unavailing.

The meeting was held, as before, in the episcopal palace's audience hall. Raymond, predictably, argued for the army to immediately march south because God had shown His favor with their defeat of Kerboqa. With the power of the "holy lance" alone, he insisted—Raymond never reluctant to take credit for the victory with its "discovery" and never willing to credit Bohemond for his brilliant generalship—no Turkish emir would dare oppose them. The other princes were unpersuaded. It was July and they would face the summer's heat; moreover, water would be scarce. Better, they reasoned, to wait until early November and then reconvene to consider a strategy. At least they had learned a lesson from the disastrous death march from Dorylaeum to Marash.

And then disaster struck. Joyful news arrived that Venetian ships had just docked at the port of St. Symeon, now repaired, bringing fifteen hundred crusaders from Regensburg. They had made their way to Antioch but soon began complaining of fever and stomach ailments. Most died within days. Quickly, the disease spread throughout the city. More deaths followed, especially amongst the poor pilgrims. No one understood the cause. Panic gripped the city. Crusaders accepted death in combat but this enemy, unseen, was more terrifying. Daily, wagons drove throughout the city collecting bodies, drivers covering their faces and mouths to avoid contagion which they were certain was carried through the air. I continued to attend to Adhémar, monitoring his slow but steady recovery. One day was different. As usual I checked his wound. The seepage had ended. Removing the poultice I saw that he was healing nicely and needed no reapplication. I was very pleased until, in my examination, I felt his forehead, cheeks, and then his chest. He was burning with fever. I asked Rebecca to fetch towels soaked in cold water to wrap his head.

"We'll need to keep him cool," I told her. At every hour Rebecca brought in another set. His condition only worsened. Fever first, then stomach pain, weakness. In my mind I poured through the pages of Galen and Avicenna unable to recall anything describing these symptoms, let alone treatment. I had to do something.

"Lord Bishop, a plague has struck us. You may have contracted it. I don't know how. The princes are now assembling their armies and will soon depart, I think both to escape the plague and to assert their dominion over other parts of Syria and Armenia until the next council meets in November. I think you should join them as well, to leave the city while you are yet able."

Adhémar waved me off. "Oderic, I must remain with my people. If they suffer, I shall suffer with them. I am prepared for God's Judgment if He so wills. I stay." Yet again I confronted the implacable wall of his stubbornness. Patriarch John, having learned of Adhémar's illness, summoned monks from the monastery to maintain a continuous vigil over him, singing penitential hymns in Greek, Adhémar not understanding but taking some comfort in their voices. Rebecca continued to change his towels and to feed him meat broth, he too weak to feed himself. I was becoming distraught. I felt helpless. I eschewed fake diagnoses with urine examination, star gazing, astrology. I decided that faith was the most promising therapy, both Rebecca and I joining in prayer with the monks.

Days followed. Rebecca and I attended to him from morning to night until we retired to bed, then up again early to return to his chamber. Despite our attentions and prayers of the monks, his condition continued to deteriorate. Adhémar must have had a premonition of his death. One day as I was attending to him he pointed to a drawer in a cabinet and asked me to retrieve a "box". It was no "box" but a reliquary, magnificently fashioned of glistening silver and encrusted with precious jewels. From his bed he tenderly opened its lid and tipped it over for me to look within. It was lined with red velvet, a small piece of aged wood lying on the bottom. "This," Adhémar explained, "is a piece of the True Cross. I wish you to send it to the Pope." I promised to do so. The next day I showed it to Patriarch John. When he opened the lid and saw the Cross, he fell to his knees praying between sobs, so moved was he. "Oderic," he said, "this reliquary is almost as beautiful as the Cross it contains. It must be protected from damage. I know a craftsman powerfully skilled in carving fine wood. I shall ask him to build a box to hold it." I thought the suggestion sensible and agreed. Not three days later John presented the completed box to me, the reliquary nestled inside. It was lovely, made of exotic Turkish burled walnut he explained, finely carved in foliated designs, the incisions delicately painted in red, blue, and gold. I was overcome with its exquisite beauty. When I showed it to Rebecca, she was as affected as I and asked if another could be made for her. She begged. Once more I was powerless to refuse her. I went to John and passed on Rebecca's request, though explaining, apologetically, that presently I lacked the means to pay for it but would send him money when I was able. "Tut, tut, my son. I saw how tenderly Rebecca nursed Bishop Adhémar, my dear friend. Besides, the craftsman owes me another favor . . . now that I consider it, in fact several." The box was completed before we left Antioch for Maarat, identical in every detail to the original. Rebecca was thrilled.

It was the day of the Feast of St Peter's Chains, August 1. As usual we arrived early to Adhémar's apartment, Rebecca sitting beside him on his cot placing another cold towel on his forehead. She was about to rise when Adhémar, saying nothing, grasped her hand though weakly, just looking into her eyes, smiling. Rebecca remained at his side, returning his gaze as she murmured a Jewish prayer of lamentation. A new rotation of monks was filing in to begin hymns and orisons for God's grace. Rebecca and Adhémar continued to gaze at one another, not a single word exchanged. I was standing over Rebecca looking down at Adhémar. In that moment I sensed the worst. Adhémar mouthed one word to Rebecca, "Goodbye". His eyes closed. He had passed into the Lord's eternal care. Rebecca broke down weeping, her forehead resting on Adhémar's chest, her shoulders heaving. I was instantly brought back to Father Benedict's last moments. I too fell into indescribable sorrow.

Word spread instantly. Church bells began ringing. Pilgrims and soldiers came out into the streets, braving their fear of contagion, sobbing as they threw up their hands imploring God's mercy for Adhémar's soul. Deep mourning descended upon the city. Monastery monks ritually cleansed his body and dressed him in his sacerdotal vestments. On the following day his body was borne in the patriarch's ceremonial carriage, mounted knights in escort as it proceeded through the city to the Basilica of Saint Peter, the church overflowing with mourners. The service was conducted by Patriarch John in accordance with Eastern Greek ritual practices. No one seemed to object though I'm sure Bohemond was not happy for he wished to rid Antioch of every vestige of Greek presence and Alexios's claim to the city. He surely would have preferred that Arnulf, his obedient hound, presided. At the insistence of Raymond, never wishing anyone to forget the "miracle" of the lance, Adhémar was buried in the pit where Peter Bartholomew "discovered" it. Raymond claimed that Adhémar himself had requested this spot as his final resting place in a visit to him on the day of his death. This was a falsehood for neither Rebecca nor I had left Adhémar's side. I said nothing but sensed Raymond harbored a deeper plan. But what?

Election of William, Bishop of Orange

All was revealed the following day. The death of Adhémar had left us leaderless. Raymond called for the council to meet. I had not been invited but attended nonetheless out of curiosity, seeking the most unobtrusive spot I could just beside the door. After a brief prayer for Adhémar's salvation, he announced the purpose. "My Lords, we are gathered to elect a new spiritual leader for our pilgrimage. Surely His Holiness the pope will appoint a new legate as successor after word reaches him of Adhémar's passing. Until then, this void needs to be filled."

There was general agreement with the need for an election. The question was who? Silence followed as each prince mulled possible candidates in his mind. Raymond seized the moment. "My Lords," he continued, "may I propose the name of a holy man, not a bishop but one blessed by God Himself. It was Our Lord who sent Christ's disciple Saint Andrew to reveal to Peter Bartholomew, *and to him alone*, the location of the Holy Lance. God promised that with the Lance we would be victorious, *and we were*. I believe Peter has been anointed by God Himself to lead us. We *must* respect His Judgment." Raymond neglected to mention that Saint Andrew also told Peter God favored Raymond to govern Antioch, perhaps too transparent an admission of self-interest.

The princes were incredulous. It was well known that Adhémar doubted Peter's vision and the lance's authenticity, some of the princes, Bohemond and the Normans especially, sharing his suspicions. Moreover, they had all heard rumors of Peter's debauchery. I could not understand why Raymond would submit such a foolish candidature other than his vanity as the richest prince and his overweening ambition. The princes were speechless, each calculating a response, respectful but firm.

Bohemond broke the silence. "My Lords, our task is painful but I agree with Count Raymond that it must be done. Therefore, I nominate Arnulf, Bishop of Rohes. He serves as chaplain to the Duke of Normandy and is known both for his learning and piety. No one is better equipped to guide us through these perilous times, least of all a mere priest." Robert said nothing but nodded his head in agreement.

"My Lords," Arnulf volunteered, "what I now say I do so humbly. It would be an honor to accept this position, not to *replace* Bishop Adhémar, a man esteemed by God, but with humility to *follow* him. Indeed, before he died Adhémar told me he was considering a bishopric for Antioch and asked me to serve as its bishop." This of course was false, no deception beneath his serpentine nature. An uneasy silence followed. Arnulf's reputation for unbridled ambition and moral dissolution was well known.

An immediate objection came from Raymond. He understood Bohemond's ploy. With Arnulf as temporary legate, Norman leadership of the crusade would be complete and his own claim to Antioch, however tenuous and limited, would be threatened. He must have now realized that nomination of Peter would not meet approval. He had to find an alternative, quickly, and rather half-heartedly proposed Achard, Archbishop of Arles, a godly man, he asserted, "whose morality is unquestioned," a not too subtle rebuke of Arnulf. It was no coincidence that Achard was a Provençal. However, this bishop was unknown to the princes and no discussion followed.

The princes appeared to be at an impasse. That is, until Godfrey, of all the princes the least controversial and recognized for his genuine Christian piety, a virtue not shared by all of his peers, intervened. "My Lords, I agree with the Lord of Taranto that learning and piety should be the test for election to this office. For which reason I propose William, Bishop of Orange, esteemed by us all for the very qualities recommended by Lord Bohemond." There followed immediate murmurs of agreement, the princes grateful for a suitable candidate. William was known for his sense of justice in dealing with all the princes and his incorruptible character. His close relationship with Adhémar was itself a recommendation. Godfrey called for a voice vote, all expressing their approval with "ayes", Raymond, Bohemond, Robert of Normandy alone answering "nay". I glanced at Arnulf. His face showed how plainly annoyed he was by the decision, a public repudiation and humiliation. What his expression did not reveal was his determination to redeem himself by sacrificing another, Rebecca.

Trial of Rebecca

The princes began to disperse when Arnulf stopped them. "My Lords, there is yet one other matter which needs to be addressed. I understand your fears over this terrible plague. But we cannot depart before its source is eradicated, completely." The princes were puzzled. What "source" did

Arnulf have in mind? "I alone, Bishop of Rohes, understand the cause of our affliction which cruelly has taken from us so many lives, most especially our beloved and blessed Bishop of Le Puy. *Jews!* My Lords, you know well from our history that the godless Jews, a nation which denies the divinity of Jesus Christ, who caused Him to be brutally nailed to a cross, are a scourge of humanity. Our present suffering is God's punishment for failing to purge them all from our midst. There lives amongst us a Jewess, so-called 'Rebecca', whore to a false priest Oderic standing here now," pointing to me, "faithless scribe to Bishop Adhémar. Adhémar would never have suborned her presence but for her enchantments. She bewitched him with her diabolical skill in the arts so dark I may not describe. We *must* hold a trial of inquisition to examine this sorceress." It was well known to the princes, of course, that Rebecca was Jewish and that we enjoyed an intimate relationship. It was never questioned, perhaps because I was under the protection of General Tatikios and later Adhémar until his death. We no longer had a protector. That is, until Baldwin spoke.

"My Lords, I know nothing of this Rebecca's ancestry but I must report one fact. When my wife, the Lady Godvere, and our two sons were dying at Marash it was Father Oderic and Rebecca who attended to them. Rebecca most tenderly treated my family though ultimately her ministrations were unsuccessful. I cannot accept that Rebecca, Jewess or no, is responsible for this plague. She also risked contagion in nursing Bishop Adhémar. I have heard that the city of Regensburg before the arrival of its soldiers suffered a similar epidemic. Perhaps they carried it to our shore. I object to a trial."

There was a division among the princes: Raymond, having somehow learned of my role in the conspiracy between Bohemond and Ahmad ibn-Marwān for the surrender of the citadel, supported Arnulf. Bohemond, perhaps as compensation for my assistance with Firuz and Ahmad and despite his alliance with Arnulf, concurred with Baldwin's objection as did Duke Godfrey. William of Orange was silent. "My Lords," Arnulf continued, trying unsuccessful to repress his anger, "this is a *church* matter, not a temporal one for decision by the council. I brought this matter up only to bring you comfort that, after we burn this witch, God will be appeased and release us from this plague's grip. The trial will take place quickly, tomorrow, lest more die. I have instructed Thomas of Marle, Count of Coucy, to arrest this hateful Jew for trial."

I ran out of the audience hall down the corridor to our apartment. Rebecca was not there. Perhaps in the palace gallery, I thought. She was with her monk tutor, standing before a painting on an easel, a small container of yellow ocher paint in one hand and a thin brush in the other. Rebecca looked over at me as I entered. "Oderic, just in time. I'm nearly finished with . . ."

"*Rebecca!*" I blurted out, terror in my eyes. "Rebecca, they're coming for you. To burn you!"

"Oderic, slow down! What are you saying?"

I embraced Rebecca so tightly that she dropped both the paint and brush to the floor. "Rebecca, you're being blamed for the plague."

"Me?" she asked in disbelief.

"Because you're Jewish. That's enough. We must escape. *Now!*"

It was too late. In that instant soldiers bearing the escutcheon of three gyrfalcons descending on an angry boar, the arms of Thomas of Marle, poured into the gallery and grabbed Rebecca by her arms, pulling her out. As she was roughly pushed through the door she looked back at me, pleading with her eyes for help but there was nothing I could do. The memory of her face in that moment is seared into my brain, even now just as painful. I was determined I would do everything I could to save her.

I couldn't sleep that night, most of it spent in the patriarch's private chapel kneeling before its altar in fervid prayer. The trial was held in the former palace of Yaghi Siyan. As I walked through the market square fronting the palace I saw gallows used for public executions. More ominously, a partially burned wooden stake was just being withdrawn from a hole in the flagstones to be replaced with a fresh one I was certain intended for Rebecca. Soldiers were spreading faggots about the stake. I entered the palace into the audience hall. There, seated on Yaghi's raised throne was Arnulf, to his side a more modest throne used I assumed by Yaghi Siyan's wife sat the Bishop of Orange. Standing on Arnulf's right was Thomas of Marle in polished armor, a black patch over his left eye making him look more sinister than ever. He spotted me as I walked in, glaring with that single bulbous eye. Girding the hall was a line of armed soldiers. As I entered, princes, their captains and sergeants were drifting into the hall. Baldwin and Godfrey were standing side-by-side. Baldwin and I exchanged glances, his face full of compassion. Then I saw Drogo. What was he doing here?

The trial began immediately. "Bring in the accused!" Arnulf barked. The hall's doors opened. Rebecca, her hands bound, with two of Thomas of Marle's soldiers on either side tightly gripping her arms, the third pulling her by a rope around her neck as she stumbled forward. I was shocked by her appearance: clothes partially torn and bloodied; her beautiful long black hair unkempt and scraggly; cheeks red, swollen, and bruised; and she limping. Rebecca had been beaten! I coursed with anger. She was brought directly before Arnulf.

"Your name, accused!"

"I am Rebecca of Mainz, Your Eminence," her voice weak and quivering.

"You are accused of witchcraft, with your dark arts causing the death of Adhémar, Bishop of Le Puy, and of the plague that has resulted in so many deaths in this city. How do you answer?"

"I am innocent. I would *never* harm anyone, least of all the revered Bishop Adhémar, nor do I have the power to cause a plague. There must be some other explanation."

"Do you deny that you are a witch and a Jewess?"

"I *do* deny being a witch. I do *not* deny that I am Jewish," Rebecca answered defiantly.

"You admit to '*treating*,'" his tone derisory, "Bishop Adhémar. Do *not* lie to me, Jew! It will only go harder for you."

"I so freely admit. During the bishop's illness I supervised his diet and hand-fed him when he was too ill to feed himself. And I prayed over him daily."

"Now we are getting somewhere," Arnulf smirked. "You *fed* him and *prayed* over him, to your false god I suppose? And do you deny being a Jewish *whore*?"

"Your Eminence, I . . . I don't understand the question."

"Oh, you will," he answered cryptically. "I call the first witness. Drogo of the Tafurs."

Rebecca was yanked by the rope around her neck off to the side. Drogo came forward, facing Arnulf. "Witness, your name?" "I am Drogo, called by some 'King of the Tafurs.'" Suddenly I heard uneasy mutterings from the audience, "What's a *Tafur* doing here?"

"Do you believe in Jesus Christ, your Savior?"

"I do, Your Eminence, with all my heart. I believe in our Redeemer."

"Do you know the accused?"

"I do Your Eminence."

"How do you know her?"

"It was at Nicea. I was operating a hospital tent treating poor pilgrims. This whore," turning to Rebecca, looking at her scornfully, "came to me thinking my hospital was a brothel and begged, *begged* me to employ her promising that her particular skills with men, her ability to bewitch them, would yield handsome rewards for us both. Naturally, I refused. She pleaded further. I ordered her out of my tent. And then this false priest Oderic with a Pecheneg thug invaded my tent and wantonly assaulted me. I was taken before Peter, called 'the Hermit', who pronounced me innocent."

Arnulf's interest perked up. "The accused said she is able to 'bewitch' men?"

"That is what she said."

I was listening in shock, unable to believe what I was hearing. This was now too much. My fury boiled over. "YOU LIE! YOU LIE!" I shouted. "YOU BASTARD!" and with that I shoved aside those in front of me, grabbing Drogo. I wrapped one arm around his neck and with my other hand gripped his throat to choke the life out of this villain. He was gasping for breath as I squeezed tighter and tighter. I wanted to kill him. With my bare hands. Three soldiers pulled me off and flung me to the floor. I was in a rage, so much that one of them had to place his boot on my chest to restrain me. I then lifted myself up, the same soldier shoving me back into the crowd.

"I think the evidence is sufficient," Arnulf announced. "She admits to being a Jew. And the testimony is uncontroverted that she's a sorceress and whore as well. I've heard enough. Count Thomas, have your soldiers take her outside and bound to the stake. There she shall face God's Judgment," he said grinning.   The three soldiers were about to turn her around and lead her out.

"WAIT! I demand to be heard!" I shouted.

"No," Arnulf replied, his voice rising in anger, "you shall *not* be heard. Take her out, *now!*"   Until then Bishop William had been a silent albeit intent spectator. What had struck me was that under normal protocol it should have been William, not Arnulf, who presided. Perhaps he yielded out of political calculation, perhaps because he was hesitant to assert his new authority. I never learned. I did sense, however, he was discomforted by this proceeding. He then gently placed his hand on Arnulf's arm, looking at him with a smile. "Esteemed Bishop, I think he should be heard."

Arnulf was momentarily flummoxed by William's unexpected intervention but he was without a choice. "You may speak, false priest," he said grudgingly.

"Rebecca is pregnant," I said, "and under church law cannot be executed if she is with child."

This was unexpected for Arnulf. He pondered for a moment. "Are you the father?"

"I am."

"And were you married under our Church's laws?"

"No, but we would have been."

"The matter is then settled. This child is the conception of a false priest and a Jewish whore. Church law does not protect her. Take her away where punishment awaits."

"NO!" I shouted again. "I demand the right, under our customary laws, for a trial by combat to decide her innocence. I shall be her champion. Let God decide!"

"No!" Arnulf exclaimed, rising from his throne. "Verdict has been rendered. And by Church Law only clerics and Jews may demand a champion in such a trial. A cleric may not serve as one."

But then, to my continuing surprise, Bishop William again intervened. "Bishop Arnulf," he said very gently, "you yourself have declared this monk a 'false priest'. Under this circumstance do you not think he is exempt from the prohibition which you very correctly cited."

"But . . . but . . ." Arnulf stammered, "not by a *cleric*."

"I think I've answered your quite reasonable objection," William replied slowly. "You will now need to find your own champion to defend the Church's honor."

Arnulf was flustered. He had no answer or choice. "Then who will serve as God's champion against this pagan Jew?" looking up to Thomas of Marle.

"I shall do so," Thomas answered. "In humble service to our Lord."

"We should not delay. In one hour, outside in the market square, the two of you shall meet. God will render His Judgment there."

I raced back to the episcopal palace where I donned my leather armor and threw my baldric over the shoulder, kissing *Iskender* with a brief prayer, "Lord, bless it," before placing it back into the holster. As I was about to leave I thought of something else, the pectoral cross consecrated by the pope with which I had stabbed Thomas's eye. I am even today uncertain why I brought it, raw defiance likely. I quickly hung it around my neck and hastened to the market square. Rebecca was already tied to the stake, one soldier holding a lit torch ready to set it afire, beside him a bucket of pig fat, when the signal was given. The hall had already emptied into the square, Arnulf and William standing in front. William showed some surprise at my battle costume. An area had been cleared. There we would fight. Thomas was already in its center, waiting for me, a shield in one hand and a drawn sword in the other, the point of its blade resting on the pavement. I was without a shield; but, in any event, I had never used one. This combat, unequal to begin with for I had never fought a soldier with Thomas's reputation for skill in battle, was lost before it began. I walked into the center to face Thomas.

Then William intervened for the third time. "Bishop Arnulf, I'm certain our Lord would not approve of such a contest, a sword and shield against a single maul. The count must surrender one." Arnulf, clearly unhappy, said nothing.

Thomas, overhearing William, handed his shield to one of his soldiers. "It is of no matter. All of this will quickly be settled."

We faced one another, silently, both of us still. Thomas sneered and then pointed to his eye as if to say "I shall pay you back in full." I, in turn, pointed to my pectoral cross, grinning, more out of bravado than confidence, then slipping it inside my leather jerkin. I began circling Thomas to his left taking advantage of the blind eye. He too began circling me indifferent to my tactic though still wary, replying to each of my steps with one of his own, continuing to sneer in contempt, I trying to maintain impassivity but staring at him intently. "So, this is what a 'warrior-priest' looks like?" surveying my armor up and down. "Yes, I've heard of you. Stories. Fabrications as all here will soon learn." Thomas began playing with me just as he had at Mainz. He lunged then stepped back; lunged again, stepping back; and again, each time trying to startle me laughing with every feint. I didn't flinch but continued to circle him. He soon tired, trying a different strategy to intimidate me: twirling the sword in his hand, then waving it from right to left and back again. My concentration was focused, looking for an opening as Ekbar had taught me, tightly gripping *Iskender*.

Now the count was becoming more serious. He thrust his sword at my chest; I flicked it away. Another thrust and another flick of my maul. Thomas was visibly becoming angrier. This would not be the quick victory he had promised. I hoped, in his anger, he would make a mistake. He began slashing, I merely stepping back out of range not wishing to test my wooden haft against the direct strike of his iron sword. That morning there had been a light rain. The flagstones were moist and somewhat slick. In Thomas's anger, he slipped, momentarily stumbling. That was the opening I sought. With the hammerhead of my maul I struck the side of his left knee on his blind side, unprotected by mail. He bent over howling in pain. I then stuck his metal helmet, the sound reverberating throughout the square, stunning him. I struck him again against the same knee. He now fell on his back, dropping his sword. I set my boot on his chest to force him down and placed *Iskender's* pointed spike against his throat ready to plunge it, Thomas just staring back at me in disbelief. As much as I hated this fiend and wished him dead, I hesitated, uncertain whether I wanted to draw blood again. In my confusion I suddenly recalled a story my father once told me, how gladiators had sought approval from an emperor before delivering the killing blow. Instinctively, perhaps, I looked over at William. He looked back, saying nothing but slowly shook his head. I removed my boot, leaving him moaning on the pavement. The fight was finished. Rebecca had been saved.

Yet Arnulf, unable to accept God's judgment but without choice, could not repress his viciousness. "Release the *whore*." Rebecca staggered off the pile of wood, no one to assist her. I ran over and as she was about to fall catching her. She fell into my arms weeping. I led her back sobbing to the palace, her head nestled between my neck and shoulder holding her tightly around the waist. I had never loved her so as I did in that moment. I laid her gently onto the bed, covered her with a blanket, and laid damp towels over his wounds to reduce the swelling and then ran to the monastery infirmary for a salve of mustard, arnica, tumeric and ginger wetted in wine which I applied over her swollen face. I had just finished when the patriarch John entered our room.

Ever solicitous and gentle, he walked up to me not wishing to disturb Rebecca's rest and whispered "Yes, I heard about all of it. How is she?"

"She'll recover, I'm sure, a day or two."

"Oderic, you were the guests of Bishop Adhémar here at the palace. He has passed," with that John quickly made the sign of the cross. "But do not worry. You, both of you, are now *my* guests. You may remain here as long as you like enjoying my hospitality, however modest it is."

Escape to Edessa

The princes with their armies were already leaving Antioch. Their explanation was to escape the plague. Perhaps. But their designs were larger: to claim territory, even principalities, for themselves until the meeting on November 1: Robert of Normandy to Latakia doubtless to enjoy its female delights though his stay, only a few weeks, ended when he was forced out due to his onerous exactions on the population; Raymond to Cilicia where he seized the cities of Rugia and al-Bara either killing all their Muslim inhabitants or selling them on Antioch's slave market; Bohemond to Mamistra in Cilicia; and Baldwin to Edessa joined later by his brother Godfrey. I do not know where the others went. Rebecca and I remained in the episcopal palace believing we would be safer from the plague behind its walls than in the city, despite Adhémar's experience. But even had I wanted to leave, I would not know where to go.

It was two days later. I was in the *armarium* reading the *Physiologus*, almost completed and was thinking about my next book; Rebecca had resumed her painting in the gallery. Suddenly John rushed in, a panicked look on his face. "Oderic! One of my monks went on an errand in the city and passed by a group of pilgrims, a wretched looking lot."

"Tafurs, probably," I answered.

"Perhaps," John replied, "but he heard them plotting an attack on this palace to seize you and Rebecca. They may be on their way here, even now. I have no palace guards and cannot protect you. You need to escape, immediately! I've already ordered horses to be saddled in the stable. I'll meet you there."

I needed no more explanation. I was not surprised that Drogo was seeking retribution for my attack on him at the trial. I ran to the gallery. "Rebecca. Tafurs are coming! We need to get out. Now! There's no time to pack. Follow me." John had in the meantime gone to our apartment and stuffed whatever clothes of ours he could quickly gather into my satchel and a knapsack he provided. We ran down the stairs. I could hear the thunderous beating of clubs on the palace door and shouts "*Open up! Let us in!*" We had just passed John. "I'll try to delay them. Here," handing me the satchel and knapsack. "Go!" On entering the stable I saw one horse already saddled, the stable attendant buckling up the strap around the horse's girth of the second. Rebecca had not entirely regained her strength from the beating she had received. I lifted her up on the horse, mounted the other, and we rode out into a side street, dashing through the Bridge Gate and across the Fortified Bridge. There the road forked, south and west to St. Symeon, north to Alexandretta, and east to Edessa. I chose the last, to find Baldwin. Our sole chance of survival depended on his protection.

We rode for three days to Marash. There, as I hoped, we came upon Baldwin's camp just outside the city. I recognized his tent. We dismounted in front of it and walked in, the posted guard freely allowing us entrance. Baldwin was sitting at a desk speaking with one of his captains. I recognized him from Constantinople, Richard Iron-hand, the same with whom Georgios had a brief confrontation. Baldwin looked up, startled to see me.

"Lord Baldwin," placing my hand on my heart in salute and bowing, "Rebecca," nodding to her, "and I seek sanctuary with you." I had now dropped the pretense that she was my ward. All had been revealed at trial. "Drogo's Tafurs are hunting for us. It was only with God's providence that we escaped in time. May we have it?"

"Yes, of course," he answered without hesitation. "I saw you vanquish

Thomas of Marle. He is a mighty warrior. As clearly you are. I could use your services in my army. Do you not think so, Richard?"

"I'm not sure, my Lord, without his gutless Pecheneg," he replied petulantly.

I ignored the insult. "My Lord, my reputation, such as it is, exceeds my skills. But I am a man of God foremost. I fight only when forced to do so. I would serve you poorly as a warrior."

"Oderic, consider this: There are many possibilities in Mesopotamia, beyond the Euphrates River. Opportunities for great conquests in Armenia. I am without estates. My brother inherited Bouillon and other lands in the Lorraine. But I nothing. I shall tell you frankly. I became a pilgrim to serve myself, to become a great prince, greater than Raymond, Bohemond, and even my brother Godfrey. You too could profit, a bishopric perhaps? 'Bishop Oderic' . . . hmm, yes, the two words seem to have a 'harmonious euphony' as Father Anthony used to say during our school days in Rheims."

I was deaf to Baldwin's blatant appeal to the same greed and vanity he presumed I shared with him. "My Lord, I have no such need except, with your kindness, sanctuary under your protection and accommodations for us both. That's all. I would gladly serve you in any other occupation, a scribe perhaps, a translator, even a stable hand."

"We shall talk again," Baldwin responded. "In the meantime, Richard, see to it that they are furnished with a suitable tent, bedding, and cooking supplies."

Two days later Baldwin was on the march, south. He had a small force, no more than one hundred knights. We encountered cities and fortresses governed by Turkish lords but their garrisons either fled or surrendered on the news of our approach so fearsome the reputation of the Franks had become. Wherever we went, Armenian Christians, the majority of the population, lined the streets cheering our arrival as we passed through. Within two months Baldwin had firmly established his suzerainty right up to the Euphrates River.

* * *

It was late September. We arrived at the city of Ravendan. The Turkish garrison, including the regional governor, had fled. Baldwin commandeered the governor's palace in which we were assigned a comfortable apartment. That evening we were invited to a banquet in the great hall.

Our Armenian servants, particularly the males, were attentive to our needs, Rebecca's especially, I suspected smitten with her. Baths were prepared for us, the first we had in several weeks, and fresh clothes, all in the Armenian fashion, the *taraz*: a silk shirt, cotton embroidered waistcoat, wide trousers with a silken belt wrapped several times around my waist one end hanging down to my knee, and boots made of soft lambskin. Rebecca was more lavishly outfitted: a cylindrical hat trimmed with miniver fur from which hung silver coins over her forehead, a richly embroidered silk samite dress reaching down to her ankles, and a cotton apron decorated with different geometrical designs. I had never seen her more lovely.

We entered the hall. At the high table sat Baldwin, two beautiful and richly attired Armenian women lounging on either side of him, somewhat worse for wine and wrapping their arms around Baldwin nuzzling his neck and giggling. Below the dais sat Baldwin's captains and sergeants sitting at long tables, women laughing and fondling them. Present also was a handful Armenian guests, all dressed quite elegantly, prominent citizens of the city I assumed, sitting at a separate table. For an instant I thought I was back in the House of Apollo and Aphrodite. I took Rebecca's hand to guide her back out hoping not to draw attention to our quick departure until Baldwin stopped me. "Oderic, Rebecca. Where are you going? Sit, eat, drink," pointing to one of the tables. We had no choice. Servants colorfully garbed brought in trays upon trays of food: lamb meatballs braised in a tomato and yoghurt sauce, dried meats richly flavored, saffron rice, dumplings filled with spiced lamb meat, roasted eggplant stuffed with rice cooked in cardamom and coriander, flavors with which I was very familiar. For the moment, I was grateful that Baldwin had called us back.

Until Richard spoke. He stood up from his bench, swaying, a flagon of Armenian beer in his hand, belching, looking straight at me. "Whoosh that Turkish harlot wit you? Flesh from some Babylonia-something harem?" he slurred. "Make her tell us."

I never had patience with slurs on Rebecca. But by now I would no longer defend her honor with mere words. My instinct was to attack, however drunk the offender. I rose, stepped over the bench, and began walking toward Richard. "Richard Little-cock," I said mockingly, "this *lady* does not answer fools. Especially from the son of a stinking whore!"

Richard stepped over his own bench and began staggering toward me. "Captain," Baldwin ordered, "sit! You as well Oderic."

"My Lord," I answered with a slight bow, "our presence here seems unwelcome with some of your guests. With your permission we shall take our supper elsewhere."

Before Baldwin could respond, the massive oak doors of the hall opened, the rasping of their hinges grating on the ears. All heads turned to it. A guard approached the dais. "My Lord, a delegation from Edessa has arrived and appears to request an immediate audience."

"They may enter," Baldwin answered. The guard waved them in. Three Armenians, prosperous merchants evidenced by their elaborate flowing gowns, walked in approaching Baldwin. They bowed, their leader addressing Baldwin in a language with which I was unfamiliar, Armenian I supposed. Baldwin looked bewildered, the only word he recognized was "Baldwin". Baldwin looked to me for a translation, I merely shrugging my shoulders for I comprehended no more than he. But this was my opportunity to demonstrate the value of my service.

I stood. "Do you speak Greek?" I asked the leader.

"Yes, of course," he replied.

I stepped up onto the dais to be closer to Baldwin. "Please explain your purpose here."

"I am Aram, a merchant of Edessa." He then introduced his companions, names I've now forgotten, one a silk merchant and the other a tailor. "We are all members of our city's Council of Trade. Am I addressing Lord Baldwin of Boulogne?"

"You are," Baldwin answered, his curiosity piqued. "How can I serve you?"

"We are emissaries from Thoros, *Kuroplates* of Edessa, its sovereign. You Franks are known throughout our land. The *kuroplates* requests that you hasten to Edessa, the most splendid city in Mesopotamia, to relieve us of the vexations of the Turks who oppress us with tribute and take our children as hostages. Our Lord will reward you for your service."

Baldwin's abrupt, even imperious, answer rather surprised me. He possibly had something more ambitious in mind. "I know not this 'Thoros'. Does he think I'm some common mercenary ready to spill the blood of my men for a few coins? He mistakes me. We are Soldiers of Christ. And we go where God directs us. You insult me Sir."

"Oh no!" Aram protested anxiously. "The *kuroplates* is old and childless without an heir. If you will deign to attend him, he will adopt you as his son although," he added coyly, "the conditions must be favorable."

Baldwin was stunned. He expected great things from the expedition.

But this was beyond his dreams. Edessa was indeed a great city, one of the finest in Mesopotamia, fabulously wealthy. His mood changed immediately. "I am inclined to accept this invitation but I'd like to know what are these 'favorable conditions' of which you speak."

"My Lord," Aram answered, "I am uncertain. I know only what the *kuroplates* instructed me to tell you."

Baldwin hesitated, but only for a moment, the opportunity too tempting. "Then I accept Lord Thoros's invitation. We shall leave two days hence. Please have your Lord prepare for our arrival." The merchants bowed, turned, and left.

Baldwin's commanders appeared equally astonished by this dramatic turn of events. One of them stood to speak. "My Lord. Might this be a trap? Some kind of Muslim treachery? To imprison us and then offer a ransom to the highest Turkish bidder?"

Baldwin turned to the table of Armenians, directing his attention to one of them. "Your opinion Bagrat?" I had heard of this 'Bagrat' though I was unfamiliar with the particulars other than he had accompanied Baldwin from Antioch and was the one who persuaded him to come to Armenia, luring him with tales of wealth and opportunity.

He stood up, bowing. "We Armenians," he answered, "are *Christians*, not Muslims," he emphasized with some vehemence. "Yes, I know this Thoros. He is, as the merchant said, old and childless. Very unpopular with his own people, regarded as a heretic by most for he worships in the Byzantine manner unlike we Armenians who have separated from that faith and become Jacobite Christians. His taxations are onerous bringing him no love. Moreover he is surrounded by Turkish emirates on all sides, their emirs coveting each other's land but Edessa above all. I'm sure he wants to exploit the reputation of you Franks to preserve his throne and perhaps even to expand his kingdom."

"Do you know what 'conditions' the emissary was referring to?"

"No, I do not. But you must beware. Three years previous he served a Turkish emir, his lord. Thoros invited him to his palace and poisoned his food. Thoros then reclaimed control of the city. Thoros is indeed old but not to be underestimated. Care is warranted."

"Captains, we leave in two days," Baldwin announced. "Bagrat, you shall govern this city in my absence. I shall leave with you a detachment of my troops."

Baldwin's Triumph

We rode east with sixty of Baldwin's remaining knights, crossing the Euphrates on the next day. The closer we approached Edessa, the more villages we passed. News had spread quickly for the villagers came out lining the road to welcome us. Then we arrived at Edessa, a fortified city with imposing walls. It was as magnificent as we were told with a gatehouse guarded by two enormous lions, their mouths open baring long fangs and haunches down poised to pounce on any unwelcome visitor. We passed through the gate and heard a thunderous roar of people, some carrying large wooden crosses over their shoulders, singing, dancing, shouting in Armenian, I sensed "Welcome." Some even rushed up to the knights to kiss their feet or tug on the hems of their garments. We were all dumbstruck, even numbed, by this joyous, hysterical reception, almost religious in its fervor. They expected Baldwin to be their Christian savior. They did not realize that he had come not to liberate them but to enrich himself. They would come to understand this in the months that followed.

We came to Thoros's walled three-story palace, the gates to the courtyard open, a crowd of Armenians following us, all cheering. As we proceeded into the yard the palace doors slowly opened and coming out to greet us was an old man, Thoros, his gait unsteady and assisted by a guard; after him an equally aged woman, his wife. Baldwin dismounted, removed his helmet, walked up the steps and bowed to them both. Thoros embraced Baldwin with the kiss of peace, turned to the throng, clasped Baldwin's hand and raised both their arms as though to introduce Baldwin to his people. The crowd erupted into ecstatic cries, some even kneeling down, hands on their heads, weeping violently. Oh, such a sight! Thoros then put his arm around Baldwin's waist and led him inside, the doors closing after them. The rest of us dismounted, our horses led by attendants into a stable. Baldwin's soldiers were directed to their quarters in the citadel, just above the palace, Rebecca and I escorted into the palace itself to a rather commodious apartment facing the courtyard on the third floor.

We had barely settled in when one of Baldwin's men-at-arms rapped on the door and announced that Baldwin wished me to attend to him immediately. I was needed to translate. I followed the soldier into an audience hall. Thoros, Baldwin, and Richard Iron-hand were waiting for me. Thoros was indeed infirm, thin, leaning on a cane, toothless, his face purple and breath short, sometimes gasping for air.

"Lord Baldwin," Thoros began, speaking Greek, "I need your services quickly. There's a wicked Turkish emir, Balduq, only two days from here, at Samosata, who extracts excessive tribute from us, his raiding parties stealing our sheep and goats and seizing our children as hostages where he imprisons them in his castle. This is unendurable.

"And what of my reward?" Baldwin asked. "What do I get? Your embassy had promised that you would adopt me as your son and heir. My services do not come without cost."

"My embassy did indeed report that to you," Thoros replied, "but you will recall the message: 'only when conditions are favorable'. Those conditions may be *more* favorable if you can rid me of this presumptuous emir. I shall provide you with an Armenian force of one thousand men. We can discuss this matter after you return victorious."

"No. We decide now! I was told you would adopt me as your only son. We do not go until the adoption ceremony is completed and you agree to share one-half of all tribute and taxes you collect."

Thoros was quite surprised at Baldwin's blunt negotiating technique, in the East subtlety and indirection preferred. Nevertheless, he demurred again. "Not until you take Samosata."

"Listen old man. I am beloved by the people of Edessa. I can take you as my prisoner at any time and the people will love me. The adoption must be completed, in whatever manner you Armenians prescribe. Then I shall march to Samosata."

Thoros, plainly fearful, mumbled "I agree. Tomorrow at midday."

What followed was the oddest ceremony I have ever witnessed. It seemed the entire populace of the city had gathered in front of the palace, those unable to squeeze into the courtyard overflowing in front of its gates outside the wall. Emerging from the palace doors came Baldwin, Thoros, and his wife, all three wearing simple white shirts and wide trousers, behind them a Greek priest. The crowd erupted into thunderous shouts. The priest steered Thoros and Baldwin, side-by-side, to face the crowd. And this was what was most extraordinary: The two men removed their shirts, attendants taking them, and then turned to face one another, chest to chest against one another. The priest then placed an oversized chemise covering them both. He quietly gave instructions which I could not overhear and they began rubbing their chests against one another, Baldwin visibly embarrassed. The priest then removed the chemise revealing both men in their half-nakedness. More extraordinary yet, the ceremony was repeated with Thoros's wife, Baldwin's face now a very deep red. Baldwin and Thoros turned to face the crowd. Thoros raised his arms straight up expecting an enthusiastic response. Instead, he was greeted with silence, only scattered applause from a few. He was clearly nonplussed. Baldwin then raised his arms and the crowd erupted into shouts, only later did I learn they were crying "*Our King*". Thoros's demeanor changed quickly, irritation visible on his face. He whirled around and stalked back into the palace leaving Baldwin to bask in the warm light of Edessa's adulation. This was a moment of triumph for Baldwin, his arms continued to be upraised. He relished it all.

Baldwin besieged Samosata for a week but without success. The fortress was too formidable and well-defended, nor did he have siege engines or time to build any. He wanted to return to Edessa as quickly as possible. He feared duplicity from Thoros in his absence, recalling Bagrat's story of the emir's fate. Moreover he had left no one in Edessa to defend his interests. He did establish a small garrison several miles from Samosata on the east side of the Euphrates which immediately interdicted the Turkish raids from there to Edessa. But, most important, as a condition of lifting the siege Balduq agreed to release his child hostages, twenty-five of them. News quickly spread that Baldwin was returning with the children. Like everyone else in the city I joined the crowds lining the street as Baldwin entered through the city gates. He dismounted and led a child with each hand. Parents, hysterical with joy, broke from the crowd racing to their children, lifting them up in tight embraces, crying, shrieking. One could not witness such a spectacle without being deeply moved. Baldwin was now, indeed, King of Edessa. But what would Thoros do? I think that question was on Baldwin's mind as well.

A Plot Unfolds

It was late that evening. I had already retired to bed when I heard a knock on my door. It was one of Baldwin's soldiers summoning me to immediately meet with his lord. I dressed quickly and left the palace with him. As we walked he looked around furtively to ensure we were not followed. I asked the purpose of the summons, my inquiry greeted with silence except for "follow me". We came to the citadel through a dark corridor into a vault underneath. I was momentarily blinded by the light from five torches held by Baldwin's soldiers standing alongside either wall. The room was dank, a disused storage room with dilapidated chairs and tables littered about without care for their conditions. In front of me were five merchants, one of them Aram. Baldwin was present, Richard Iron-hand standing beside him.

"Thank you for coming, Oderic," Baldwin greeting me. "These men have something to tell me." He then nodded for Aram to begin.

"My Lord, we represent the people of Edessa. We have witnessed your honor and courage. The people rejoice in your arrival. They even welcome you as their redeemer. You delivered our children from bondage in Samosata. You . . ."

"Yes," Baldwin interrupted impatiently, "get on with it."

"Apologies, my Lord. We face many threats outside our walls. Balduq is only one. We require a strong leader, a new king to confront them, a *Christian* king such as yourself. Thoros is unloved. He's old and lacks strength. Yet he squeezes our lifeblood with more and more taxes. We wish to replace him. With you, as *kuroplates*."

There was no hesitation in Baldwin's response, no moral qualm despite the fact that Thoros and his wife had just adopted him as their own son and received him with honor and generosity. But that was not enough for Baldwin. His ambitions needed to be sated immediately.

"I accept this offer. Will his palace guards?"

"Oh, yes," Aram answered quickly. "They will. They've been bribed though I think even that was unnecessary for they will follow you regardless."

"Do you have a plan?" Baldwin asked.

"We do. Two days hence at noon is the feast of Sahak the Parthian, the patron saint of Edessa. There will be a celebration in the Basilica of Saints Cyprion and Candidus. Thereafter the patriarch, Amos, will lead a procession from the church through the city to the palace and gather in its courtyard. At that time you will arrest Thoros and surrender him to us. The patriarch will immediately anoint you as king on the steps of the palace. A formal investiture in the basilica can wait."

"What will you do with Thoros?" Baldwin asked, I think more out of curiosity than compassion.

"He will be dealt with appropriately," Aram answered grimly. "But you must ensure he is present in the palace."

"I shall do so," Baldwin answered firmly.

Aram and the others departed, Baldwin, Richard, and I left alone. "Surely my Lord," I protested, "you cannot be complicit in this murder. You are Thoros's son. In the eyes of God this is nothing less than patricide."

"My Lord Baldwin, ignore this fool of a monk," Richard retorted as he shoved me in the chest, I stumbling backward. "He can return to whatever monastery he came from. This is God's providence, a sign of His favor. You cannot ignore the opportunity."

"Father Oderic," Baldwin said. "I know this seems distasteful. Would this happen but for God's blessing on me? No, of course not. I know that. The Lord desires I protect these oppressed peoples. Besides . . .", Baldwin reflecting, "there are magnificent opportunities here in Edessa. For us all. Not least for you."

Rebecca and I Marry

In the days since arriving in Edessa Rebecca and I had explored this marvelous city. When I was absent, she continued to do so, discovering a thriving Jewish community occupying the northwest corner. She attended a service on a Friday night at the synagogue and afterwards mingled with the worshipers in the courtyard. Rebecca, normally rather shy, seemed to thrive being amongst her fellow Jews for the first time since Constantinople. She returned to our apartment quite excited. "Oderic, I have met such lovely people at service today. Especially the rabbi, Yaakov ben Josel, and his wife. They wish us both to attend evening service tomorrow and invited us to their home for a meal after that. Please, let's do. Please, let's do," she begged. "The rabbi, a very learned man, is especially interested in meeting you."

I had not attended a Jewish synagogue since Mainz and was at first hesitant but then quickly changed my mind. I had found such warm friendships with Jews, Samuel ben Meier especially but also Isaac ben Judah and Miriam on the road to Constantinople. I had missed their hospitality and genial company. "Yes. We'll go."

"Oh Oderic," Rebecca throwing her arms around me, "I just *knew* you would."

The next day we walked to the synagogue. It quite resembled that of Mainz, rather modest in its architecture. I wondered if it were for the same reason as in Mainz, the fear of arousing Christian envy though I doubted it. Rabbi Yaakov greeted us graciously outside on the steps, "*shabbat shalom*" he said, and then escorted us in. He offered me a kippah skull cap fitting snugly over the crown of my head which I willingly accepted. I had expected the service to be conducted partially in Armenian, the rest in Hebrew but it was entirely in Hebrew and thus I was able to follow it, at least for the most part for it had been so long since I spoke the language, Rebecca and I always conversing in Teutonic. But I welcomed the opportunity to polish my skills. The service was similar to that I had seen so often in Mainz: prayers, recitations from the Psalms, the cantor leading the congregation in hymns, and then the Torah brought from the Ark to the bimah which Yaakov unrolled on the lectern and began reading, each verse punctuated with multiple bowings from the congregationalists. Finally the rabbi gave a short homily exhorting the faithful to be true to God and live righteous lives.

After the service Yaakov and his wife Chana took us to their home. It was a very pleasant evening, the conversation expansive, from Armenian music to theology. As I suspected, Yaakov was particularly interested in two topics: my experience as a monk at La Charité and events in the Rhineland about which he seemed surprisingly well-informed. He was about to ask Rebecca a question about her family but then looked to me for permission, sensing the subject sensitive. I quietly shook my head. Yet, he could not repress himself from expressing grief over the destruction of so many Jews and then broke out in a passionate denunciation of the Gospel of John and its author blaming Jews for the crucifixion of Jesus, not the prefect Pontius Pilate, the source he exclaimed of all Jews' miseries. As I listened to him, I recalled a conversation with Prior Damian at one of our noon respites on the journey to Clermont when he had made a similar point. I said nothing though nodding in sympathy. We visited several more evenings for supper.

The last was especially memorable. Rebecca and Chana were involved in an animated conversation. Yaakov signaled for me to follow him into his study. We sat, sharing a glass of wine.

"Oderic, we have become friends. No doubt I am intruding on a delicate matter. I shall cease when you so instruct." I nodded for him to continue. "I see that Rebecca is pregnant. It of course shows plainly. Yours I assume?" Without waiting for an answer—he knew the answer—"May I inquire how you intend to raise this child, as a Christian or a Jew?" I was startled by the question and unprepared to answer. Rebecca and I had rarely discussed her pregnancy. Perhaps I was at fault, still conflicted over my monastic vows. "What I am about to propose will either astonish or vex you. You may want to consider it. I am uncertain of my motive but for this: Chana and I have become fond of Rebecca. Of you as well. I wonder if she wouldn't feel better if the two of you married, otherwise the child will be born a . . . a . . . "

"A bastard?"

"Well, yes. I was searching for a different word, but yes. I must be honest."

At that moment Rebecca walked in. After noting Yaakov's and my absence she had come looking for us and overheard our conversation. "Since this involves me," she said quite firmly, "I think I'm entitled to express my opinion."

"Of course," Yaakov answered uneasily but obligingly.

"Oderic," looking directly at me, "I so wish it. In what faith we raise our child is yet to be decided. But at least I would like the benefit of marriage."

Yaakov said nothing. I went deeply into thought. "You know that neither Christians nor Jews will accept this union as lawful. And I doubt that Rabbi would marry us unless I convert, which I cannot do."

"Oderic," Yaakov answered, "what you say is generally true. There could be no ceremony in the temple. But Moses married an idolatrous Medianite. That is sufficient precedent. I have only two necessary questions: Do you believe in our One True God? And do you vow to follow Our Lord's Commandments?" I answered in the affirmative. In time my adherence to the Sixth would become far more casual. "Then I see no impediment to this marriage. If you agree, I can perform the ceremony here and now."

"Yes!" Rebecca stated with certainty. "Oderic, you will do this for me. It would mean so much," her tone of voice more pleading than commanding. I could never deny Rebecca anything.

We returned to the solar where Chana was waiting. Yaakov walked to a cabinet, pulled out a prayer shawl which he placed over his head and a siddur prayer book. He motioned for us to stand in front of him, Chana holding a blue scarf at Rebecca's side. Yaakov intoned some passages from the siddur, took the scarf from Chana and wrapped it around both our wrists. "This is how we do it in Armenia," he said proudly. "You are now man and wife. Let us celebrate. With my finest Armenian liquor reserved for the *most* special occasions." And celebrate we did, after which Rebecca and I returned to the palace, admittedly a bit tipsy. But Rebecca was serenely happy. I wanted nothing more.

Escape from Edessa

It was now noon on the second day after the plot between Baldwin and the Armenians had been formed. Baldwin instructed me to be present in Thoros's Prospect Chamber overlooking the courtyard below the palace and the city beyond. It was bare of furnishings or tapestries, used only by Thoros to receive the adulation of his subjects, certainly all carefully orchestrated, from its balcony. Baldwin and Richard Iron-hand were already present, three soldiers each standing at attention against two walls. Thoros then entered followed by six of his household guards.

"*Kuroplates!*" Baldwin greeting him. "How delightful to see you! Thank you for accepting my invitation. But before we talk, listen!" Baldwin walked to the open balcony pointing to the crowd below. "The crowd is shouting your name, 'Thoros!' 'Thoros!' Lord Thoros what is this? They call to you like a god. They must adore you!" I too heard the voices. Not adoration. More savage. I was filled with disgust. Baldwin was amusing himself, barely able to conceal his mockery as though this frail man were a kitten, he dangling a role of yarn on a string in front of it.

Thoros's expression changed immediately, from affable to wary then to suspicious sensing Baldwin's mockery but his vanity was irrepressible. "Yes, they *do* love me, not so much as a god but as their father."

"Well, that may have been once but no more," Baldwin responded serenely. "They wish a new king. Soon they will be chanting 'Baldwin! Baldwin!' Arrest him!"

As Richard approached Thoros whirled around to face his household guards. "Seize these scoundrels, all of them. If they resist kill them." They stood motionless. "*Seize them! Kill them!*" Again, they merely stood, not a word, impassive. Now, Thoros fully comprehended the plot. He rushed to the door. Richard grabbed him. Thoros showed more spirit and strength than I had expected. He was squirming in Richard's arms, butting his head against Richard's, kicking him in the shins as Richard lifted him up Thoros struggling to break loose.

"Richard," Baldwin ordered, "take him to the balcony. Let's see if he *is* a god and can fly like one."

"No!" I shouted. "You can't do this. He is a creature of God," and with that I pulled Richard off, freeing Thoros. "My Lord Baldwin. This cannot be borne!" I shouted at Baldwin. Baldwin merely gazed at me, evidently unperturbed by what had just happened. Richard did not wait. "Seize *him!*" pointing to me. Two soldiers pulled me out of the chamber. As I looked back over my shoulder I saw Richard throw Thoros over the balcony to the frenzied crowd below, joyful screams following. My captors dragged me down the marble stairs, I assumed to a jail underneath the palace. We came to the main floor and then to a dark, narrow winding staircase barely wide enough for two men, the soldier in front pulling my left arm down the steps as I sidled against the wall and the one behind holding my right. I would soon be under lock and key. My moment must be now. I yanked back my left arm and lifting up my left leg thrust it straight out with my boot into his knee, sending him tumbling down the stairs. The guard behind me began pulling on my arm but he was unsteady on the step above my own, losing his balance. Stepping forward, I yanked him down between the wall and me, he stumbling down the stairs. One kick and he too tumbled down joining his companion at the bottom of the stairwell. I knew that once news reached Richard Iron-hand of my escape he would be sending out troops to search the palace. I raced up to the third floor. Fortunately, Rebecca was in the apartment. "No time," I shouted at her. "We have to go! Gather our things."

We ran out into the street in front of the palace. Where to flee? We had only one choice: the rabbi. We ran to his house. I pounded furiously on the door. Chana opened it and we roughly pushed ourselves in to avoid being seen. There was no time for etiquette. I urgently asked for Yaakov. He emerged from his study, startled to see us especially in our panicked state. I explained what had happened and that we needed to escape from Edessa for Richard would be sending out troops to scour the city once they determined we were no longer in the palace. "Follow me." We did, to the synagogue. There behind it was a small stable with but one mule and a dilapidated cart. He quickly harnessed the mule to the cart and told is to get in. He threw a tarp over us. "I can take you to Samosata but that's as far as I can go. After that you're on your own. That's the best I can do, my friends." We remained hidden, Rebecca shivering with fear, I trying to comfort her with whispers of affection and reassurance. We arrived in Samosata. Just as we were sliding off the cart to the ground Yaakov spotted a caravan ready to depart from the city. "Wait here." He ran over to one of the wagons and spoke quietly with a merchant standing beside it. Yaakov waved us over. "This is Abraham. He will take you to Antioch." We both embraced Yaakov with deep gratitude.

* * *

So many times I had felt the providential protection of God in perilous moments. This was another. Yet, our future was now more uncertain than ever.

This ends Book XII of *Jerusalem Falls!* Book XIII begins.

BOOK XIII

The ARMY MARCheS SOUTh

I Become Scribe to William, Bishop of Orange. Peter Bartholomew Threatens.
Siege of Maarat an-Numan. Treachery and Massacre. horror and a Final
Reckoning. Departure from Maarat an-Numan for Arqa. Ordeal by Fire. A
New holy Man and Search for the True Cross. I Steal the True Cross.

I Become Scribe to William, Bishop of Orange

On arriving at Antioch after our escape from Edessa, Rebecca and I went directly to Patriarch John's palace. He greeted us warmly and told us he had kept our apartment reserved hoping someday we would return. Walking up the stairs we happened upon Bishop William of Orange who had just opened the door to Adhémar's former apartment. He invited me to meet with him after Rebecca and I were settled. It didn't take long, being anxious to learn what William had in mind. The short of it is that William wished me to serve as his scribe just as I had for Adhémar. Though not a papal legate, he was deeply respected by the army and was treated as though he were Adhémar's true successor. William believed it his duty to continue Adhémar's practice of correspondence with the prelates of Francia, Germania, and Italia, especially Rome. Adhémar, he said, had valued my services in this regard, my ability to create coherence out of his rather rambling, discursive style of dictation but particularly my unswerving loyalty and candor, a "man of character" Adhémar had described me to William. Naturally, I was grateful for these kind words yet at the same time thought this description hyperbolic. I wanted William to be certain of his decision.

"Your Eminence, you know of my relationship with Rebecca. You must understand as well no inducement, *none*, would ever persuade me to surrender her." I chose not to reveal our Jewish wedding. "And how can you tolerate a priest in your employ who engaged in combat with a champion of the Church and was prepared to push a spike through his throat. Surely this gives you pause. I wish only that you are clear in your choice."

"Father Oderic," William answered with a wide, comforting smile, "rest easy my son. I confess I am uneasy over your relationship with Rebecca. That is for God to judge, not me. Yet it was your fierce devotion to her, your readiness to die protecting her honor and life, which so deeply impressed me. That told me all I needed to know about you." I was humbled, murmuring some nonsense which I don't recall. "Besides," placing his hand on my shoulder, "you're not half-bad with a maul."

"Then I accept your kind offer and shall serve you with the same devotion as I did Bishop Adhémar." I was faithful to that promise.

Peter Bartholomew Threatens

In early July 1098, after the defeat of Kerboqa, the Council of Princes had decided to reconvene in early November to plot a strategy for Jerusalem. They all returned to Antioch at the appointed time, all that is except Baldwin who now styled himself "Count of Edessa". He had no intention of joining the crusade. His abiding interest was expanding his lands and ferreting out intrigues against him, the Edessenes having realized that they had merely exchanged one tyrant for another, even a more ruthless one. The council met in the palace of Yaghi Siyan. As I walked into the market square and saw the stake where Rebecca had been bound, the painful memory of her near-death flooded my mind. But my attention was quickly diverted to a noisy crowd of soldiers and pilgrims in front of the square's gallows, apparently waiting for something. An execution? I lingered.

The crowd became silent and parted to allow a rather shabbily dressed priest holding a staff in his hand to pass through. It was Peter Bartholomew. He walked to the gallows and slowly, with self-conscious deliberation, climbed the steps to the platform and then stopped beneath one of the gibbets. He turned to face the crowd, which drew closer to hear. He displayed the same sense of drama as had Pope Urban at Clermont and Peter the Hermit in his many harangues.

"Fellow pilgrims," he began. "Friends all! I am Peter Bartholomew, a humble priest, unworthy of Our Lord's Favor, yet He bestowed it on me. God Himself appeared in a vision through his messenger, Saint Andrew the Apostle, who revealed to me, *and to me alone*, the very spot where the Holy Lance that pierced the body of Jesus Chris was buried in the Basilica of Saint Peter. With its power we defeated the pagan Kerboqa. This was a sign of His divine love and protection. And yet," he paused, gazing across the crowd, stamping the butt of his staff on the platform, "there are those who doubt my vision and that this Lance is truly sacred! Blasphemers all of them! Suspicions must be extinguished for they are born of Satan. Do you believe this was the true Lance? *Do you believe?*"

In unison the crowd shouted back "*We do! We do! We believe!*"

Peter paused, slowly surveying the crowd. "Fellow Christians. *I am one of you.* I've suffered as you have, grubbing for food in the fields, finding only dried stalks of grain; cupping my hands in putrid water to quench my thirst; marching over hot desert sands until my feet blistered and bled. Yet in spite of these sacrifices, our princes have pursued their vain and ungodly lusts, conquering lands to fill their coffers while Jerusalem languishes in the hands of heathens who despoil our holy sites." Stamping his staff once again on the platform, "How much longer can we endure this? *Answer me!*"

"No! No! came the unified response. Someone shouted *"Jerusalem! Jerusalem!"* The crowd erupted "JERUSALEM! JERUSALEM!"

Peter raised his staff for silence. After several moments, the crowd settled. "The princes are meeting now, over there" pointing to the palace with his staff. "If you agree, I shall speak on your behalf demanding we march south. If they refuse, let us tear this city down. Then, *and only then*, when forced, will they pursue the mission entrusted to us by God. *Do you agree?*"

Voices erupted in enthusiasm. "JERUSALEM! JERUSALEM!"

He continued to harangue the crowd, bringing them to frenzied excitement while I pushed my way through into the audience hall. Bishop William had just called for order and silence. After a brief prayer, he declared the purpose of the council.

"My Lords, we are here to set a date for departure to Jerusalem. We cannot have dissension on this matter. After all, we have taken up the Cross to discharge our duty to Christ. Is there agreement?"

There followed loud "ayes" and "God wills it." Except for silence from Raymond and Bohemond. This did not pass unnoticed by the other princes, nor especially by William who had been watching both closely.

"Lord Bohemond. You have not answered. Nor you Count Raymond. May I inquire the reason?"

"Yes, Lord Bishop," Bohemond responded immediately, "I must remind the council, and one of its members in particular," not mentioning Raymond by name, "that the council had agreed this city would be mine if I were able to take Antioch by whatever means. But what followed was base treachery. This very palace in which we are gathered, the Fortified Bridge, and *La Mahomerie* remain in the hands of Count Raymond who stubbornly refuses to honor the council's decision."

"*Stubborn?*" Raymond retorted angrily, "It is you, Lord Bohemond, not I, who has shown himself faithless to the oath you took in Constantinople, on the head of Saint John the Baptist, to restore all lands to Emperor Alexios. What few parts of Antioch I hold, I do so in his name. I at least am a man of integrity."

Bohemond's face reddened with anger, his own honor now impugned. They both reached for the hilts of their swords and stepped toward the other. "My Lords, *cease!*" William demanded. "You will take not one step closer."

It was at that moment Peter Bartholomew followed by the crowd from the square entered the hall. He stood there, silently, then stamping his staff on the marble floor for attention, its sharp clang echoing throughout the hall. His tone was arrogant and imperious.

"Bishop William, my Lords, I am here as the legate of the people," without turning pointing with his staff to the crowd behind. "We come not as supplicants but with righteous demands, not negotiable. I received a startling vision last night. Bishop Adhémar himself appeared to me. 'Father Peter, you so esteemed of Our Lord,' he said, 'do you not know who I am?'"

"My Lord Adhémar, Bishop of Le Puy, I answered. Yes I know you."

"'Do you know *where* I am? Do you not see the burns on my face and my clothes singed from fire?'"

"I think I do, Lord Bishop. You are in Hell."

"'I am and have been sorely whipped for doubting your vision of the Holy Lance. It was only through the prayers of Lord Bohemond and the payment of three *denari* as alms in honor of the Lance that God released me from Hell and gave me a place in Paradise. But this is not my only message from God. Let Lord Bohemond reign over all of Antioch as his own *provided* he agrees to march on Jerusalem.'"

Peter had not finished. "My Lords," addressing the princes, "we the people of Antioch demand that you leave for Jerusalem without delay. We are tired of this trifling dispute between Lord Bohemond and Count Raymond. God, through me, *His voice*, has decided in Bohemond's favor. If he disobeys God by perversely abandoning this sacred pilgrimage, we the people will tear this city down, stone by stone, brick by brick, until it is fit only to pasture goats," turning now to face Bohemond, "and you will have no city to rule. We shall begin today unless I see agreement. If there is none, Count Raymond is commanded to forfeit the Lance, surrender it to us, and we shall carry it to Jerusalem ourselves." Glaring now at the princes "For the rest of you, you must abandon your ungodly ways. If you do not repent, your journey to Jerusalem will take not ten days but ten years. This is God's warning through me, his faithful messenger."

Peter's arrogance, his sense of impunity, was shocking to the princes. I was beginning to think him deranged. Later I became certain. For reasons I could not fathom, he had now allied himself with Bohemond against Raymond, heretofore Peter's indefatigable protector. He was irrationally obsessed with doubts about the truth of his vision of the lance. And his latest vision, claiming that Adhémar, beloved by crusader rank and file, was suffering in the flames of hell because of his own mistrust would only increase popular suspicion of his credibility. Yet, Peter's bombast did produce its desired effect. Bohemond was now trapped, like a treed lion with howling dogs underneath. If he wanted his city intact, he would have no choice but to join the march south. Raymond too was cornered for he knew the pilgrims would not stop with the citadel; Yaghi Siyan's palace would be next, the Fortified Bridge and *La Mahomerie* after that.

Bishop William resumed control of the council, ignoring Peter but recognizing the opportunity presented by Peter's "vision". "Bishop Adhémar has spoken," William announced. "We can decide the issue of competing claims to Antioch later." Addressing Raymond, "Count, if Lord Bohemond agrees to march on Jerusalem, will you accept the council's decision on yours and Bohemond's dispute over Antioch?"

"I will, your Eminence, on my honor" Raymond answered, though it seemed to me without particular conviction.

"And you, Lord Bohemond will you do the same?"

"I shall as well, your Eminence, on my honor" replying just as unconvincingly.

"Then let us swear to it." William reached for a bible next to him, bringing them forward to lay their hands on it.

But before departure south for Maarat an-Numan both princes strengthened their holds on the city by fortifying their respective positions with additional troops, Bohemond even signing a charter with Genoese merchants for exclusive trading rights in Antioch. So much for honor, more a business transaction, easily broken.

Siege of Maarat an-Numan

The council decided to march on Maarat an-Numan, a rich prize. On the appointed day, November 23, 1098 the army departed Antioch. Bishop William requested that Rebecca and I join him on the journey. We bid farewell to Patriarch John with deep gratitude for his hospitality and protection. More difficult was our parting with Hamid.

"Oh Rabbi, Lady Rebecca, I shall so miss you," tears flowing from his eyes. "When shall I ever see you again?"

"Hamid, my friend," I answered, "this is in God's hands. You must serve the monastery well. Otherwise, I shall learn of it and return to beat you severely," I said smiling.

"Oh, yes, Rabbi. Hamid will be a good boy. I have become an oblate and the monks make me pray six times daily. Too much prayer. I much prefer working in the kitchen and tending their garden. But I do as instructed. I shall pray for you both."

Rebecca was now six months pregnant. I knew nothing of such a condition and I must confess I took peculiar comfort in my ignorance. Yet I was acutely aware of her need for comfort and care. Patriarch John, who had come to develop an affection for Rebecca, insisted that we use one of the palace's coaches, rustic but much more comfortable than the cart in which Prior Damian and I had traveled to Clermont. It contained two simple wooden benches on either side with cushions and unremarkable, colorless tapestries on the walls for shielding its occupants from the wind blowing through its poorly fitted plank boards. I protested that this was an excess of generosity. William assured me he had two others for infrequent visitations by the monks outside the monastery; this one merely an auxiliary and rarely used, he assured me. In the days that followed, as I drove the coach to Maarat with time to reflect, Rebecca sitting next to me on the perch snuggling for warmth in the cool air, I discovered that all past conflicts in my soul between love for Rebecca and my monastic vows had dissolved. I had beaten and killed men. I had conceived a child. And I was married, albeit in a Jewish ceremony but a true marriage nonetheless. Hereafter, my duty was still to God but it was above all to Rebecca.

We arrived in Maarat at the end of November. The city, two square miles in size inhabited by both Turks and Saracens, reminded me of Edessa: heavily fortified with thick walls and formidable towers. Investment began immediately, the princes taking up strategic positions entirely encircling the city. The Turkish governor, on learning of our approach, had collected all livestock and grain in the countryside. What they couldn't collect, they burned. For miles around the land was denuded and bare. It was as though a scorched-earth military campaign had passed through. The princes expected, after their seizure of Antioch and victory over Kerboqa, that the cities they encountered would quickly yield. Thus, no sooner had we encamped than Raymond dispatched a delegation of three knights to the city's main gate to receive its surrender, one holding the holy lance affixed on the head of a lance pennanted with a white flag emblazoned with a red cross, confident that the reputation of the Franks and the awesome power of the lance would compel the governor to capitulate. Instead the delegation was greeted with arrows, the knights wheeling around to escape out of range.

An ill-conceived and fruitless assault was immediately undertaken. Two scaling ladders were set against a wall, but the ladders, poorly constructed, one too short and the other too fragile to bear the weight of soldiers breaking just as only a handful reached the ramparts. They were either slain or leapt over the wall to the ground below. The princes then decided there was no choice but to lay siege and build engines, a tower and penthouse for sapping operations, both rather rudimentary for our crusaders lacked the engineering skills to build more sophisticated devices.

Treachery and Massacre

It was only a few days after the initial assault. Rebecca was lying on a bench inside the coach as I was cooking a stew of salted beef and vegetables scavenged from the garden of a local farmer's house now abandoned. A horseman rode up, a saddled horse in tow behind him. "Father Oderic, Lord Bohemond summons you. We leave immediately."

After assuring Rebecca that I would return shortly, I left with the messenger. We arrived at the Bohemond's camp and I entered his tent. He was standing in the middle, waiting for me, beside him a Saracen, not a Turk. In Constantinople I had learned to distinguish the two, Saracens from Arabia and Egypt bearing smoother facial features and slimmer physiques than the Turks.

"Thank you, Father, for coming so promptly. This is Abdullah bin Khouri from Maarat. He knows only a few words of Frankish. You must translate. I sense his mission significant."

I bowed to Abdullah, hoping he was fluent in Turkish, my command of the Saracen language no better than his command of Frankish. He explained his mission. "We Saracens once governed this beautiful city. Then the wretched Turks invaded and seized the city from us. They treated us poorly, as though we were loathsome . . ." He caught himself and began stammering.

"As though you were Christians?" I completing his statement.

He was visibly embarrassed and bowed, placing his hand on his heart, "My apologies Imam." I thought to myself how many clerical titles I had collected: "Father," "Rabbi," and now "Imam". "It is of no consequence," I answered. "What is it you wish of Lord Bohemond?"

"We know of Bohemond, the greatest vizier of your Latin army, a valiant warrior. We know also of his conquests: Nicea, Dorylaeum, and Antioch. Our family, the Khouri, have ruled Maarat for ten generations with firmness yes, but always with humanity. We wish to rule for another ten after the Turks are expelled. Thus we desire to place ourselves under the protection of Vizier Bohemond. We heard how he honored his agreement with Ahmad ibn-Marwān, commander of Antioch's citadel, granting him and his troops safe conduct out of the city. We hope for the same generosity of treatment."

Bohemond was attentive, intently so, this man of action coming immediately to the point. "Abdullah, what do you offer in return for my protection?"

"The Khouri family," Abdullah answered, "distinguished throughout Muslim lands, is not without means. You will be rewarded, of course."

"Then I accept this offer and you shall have my protection. How many are there of you?"

"Let's see," Abdullah eyes looking upwards in thought, his lips mouthing the names of his family as he counted on his fingers, "twenty-one, twenty-two, twenty-three . . . Yes, twenty-three, eight of them children."

"To ensure your safety you must all gather in a secure location. You will also bring all your valuables. *Everything.* Even though we crusaders are devout Christians, some in our army are neglectful of principle and not averse to ransacking homes. You can only safeguard your most precious possessions by bringing them with you. I don't know the city. Where would you suggest your family gather?"

"There is a mosque," Abdullah answered, "beside the governor's palace near the main gate. We will go there."

"I suggest you assemble there tomorrow. Secure the doors. Open to no one except Father Oderic. I shall send a detachment of Normans with him." I agreed to serve Bohemond yet again, believing that he would indeed show the same mercy to the Khouris as he had to the Turks in the citadel of Antioch when they surrendered to him. I was wrong. Abdullah bowed to us both and left.

As I was about to take my leave Bohemond stopped me. "The sapping operation under Maarat's city walls is proceeding more quickly than expected. I'm not sure when we shall break through but it will be very soon. Be ready."

* * *

It was December 11. The penthouse was rolled daily into place below one of the walls, sappers digging away at the foundation with picks and crowbars. It was attacked with arrows and burning tar, even beehives, dropped on it but without effect. During sapping operation the Provençals had filled in a dry moat before the south wall and rolled a siege tower, five feet taller than the wall, under the command of William of Montpelier. When close enough soldiers on the top story threw stones down on the defenders from the top story as Everard, called "the Huntsman", blew his horn to give our soldiers courage. The assault lasted the entire day into dusk. Neither side seemed to have gained a decisive advantage, although the sappers had succeeded in dislodging three stone blocks at the wall's foundation. As the sun set, both the tower and penthouse were rolled back to be repositioned the following morning. The penthouse was no more than fifty feet away when a section of the wall began gradually crumbling, then collapsing. The princes had decided to wait until morning light to assess the damage and, if possible, send troops over it. But the princes had no control over the pilgrims, especially the Tafurs, who rushed to the wall in the dark and clambered over the rubble. From the sound of their shouts they were now in the city. I could hear the shrieks of women and the cries of children as our crusaders ran through the streets, ransacking homes, massacring all they encountered. The voices were terrifying.

I heard the clamor throughout the night but in the dark could see nothing. At daybreak I was up to survey the city. The barbican's gate was open. There were still shrieks and cries, the Tafurs and others not yet have completed their rampage. The princes immediately dispatched their own troops through the barbican gate looting what meager spoils remained after the previous night's pillage and killing all inhabitants still alive. A Norman detachment of knights arrived at Rebecca's and my camp to escort me into the city. I noticed that several had linen bags draped over their shoulders, odd I thought but did not inquire. As we rode to the mosque Tafurs and others were running excitedly in the opposite direction back to their camps holding all their booty and shouting *"Glory to God!"*

What I shall now relate is a tale of duplicity of a crusade in which treachery was the common currency. We arrived at the mosque's heavy door and I pounded on it shouting "Abdullah. It's me. Imam Oderic. Open up. We're here." After some moments I heard a key open a lock, the door opening just wide enough for Abdullah's head to peer through. "It's you, Imam. Thanks be to Allah. Come in." In the corner the entire Khouri family was huddled, their faces showing terror at events outside the mosque. In another corner was a prodigious pile of glittering objects, most of silver, some of gold, tiaras set with precious stones, chalices, candelabras, bracelets and necklaces.

"Thank God," I said to Abdullah, "we're here in time. You're now safe under the protection of Lord Bohemond." The Norman sergeant, who evidently understood a few words of Turkish, whispered to me, his tone sinister, "Not safe." With that, he drew his sword, the rest of his soldiers behind him doing the same and began stepping toward the family.

"What are you doing?" I exclaimed. "Lord Bohemond gave his assurance of safe-conduct. I *heard* him."

"I know that," the sergeant answered with a menacing grin. "But my Lord has given me different orders." Turning his head back to the soldiers "Kill them."

I begged the sergeant, "You don't have to do this. Take their valuables, yes, but leave them alive."

His answer was curt, "I've been ordered to kill them all. Besides, they're only Muslims. Would rather spare a pack of dogs." With that, they began slaying every adult, the youth they herded together likely to be sold in Antioch's slave market. I watched helplessly as the soldiers thrust their swords through the bodies of their victims, laughing, a murderous frivolity for them. Their grisly work now completed, they began throwing the Khouri treasure into the linen bags they had brought with them carrying them off along with the children. I returned to my camp numbed by the treachery I had witnessed and in which I was unwittingly complicit.

The savage destruction of Maarat was thorough, so thorough in fact that even Turks and Saracens who took refuge in caverns under the city were not spared. The crusaders relentlessly pursued them, burning sulfur to smoke them out and as they tried to escape they were seized and tortured to reveal where they had hidden their valuables; the bellies of those who pleaded they had none were split open in the search for bezants.

horror and a Final Reckoning

In the days preceding the fall of Maarat provisions were already running low. Expecting an immediate surrender, the princes had given no thought to preparing for a sustained siege. Hunger already had begun. The sack of Maarat brought temporary relief but whatever provisions they found were quickly consumed. Knights, men-at-arms, pilgrims scoured the city and its environs for any food they could find. Just as at Antioch, our ranks began to be thinned from desertions. I wondered how many more starvations Rebecca and I would have to endure. But we were more fortunate than most, the princes having tithed some of their foodstuffs to Bishop William who generously shared them with us. The situation, however, gradually worsened for the rest of the crusaders. Desperation was on everyone's face.

I had come to develop an affection for Bishop William. Perhaps not as deep as I felt for Adhémar but sincere all the same. William was younger than Adhémar, in his mid-forties I thought. He and Adhémar were contrasting personalities: William deliberate in judgment and more taciturn, less willing to reveal his deeper thoughts; Adhémar lurching unpredictably from extremes, strident piety to judicious calculation. If Adhémar were inclined to attribute every misfortune to God's punishment for our moral failings, the only cures prayer, alms, and fasting, William preferred more earthly, practical explanations and solutions. I have always held William deep in my heart for his intercession with Arnulf in my duel with Thomas of Marle without which neither Rebecca nor I would have survived. But perhaps above all for not once challenging my relationship with her.

* * *

It was a few days following the capture of Maarat when I entered William's new office in the former governor's palace. William looked up at me with a shocked countenance. "Oderic, I have just heard the most horrifying report. There's no time to talk. Follow me." We walked out of the city, a short distance, to a campsite of Tafurs, immediately recognizable from the debris strewn about, the tattered tents, the naked, grimy children running about screaming, all free-range I thought. I tried to inquire our purpose. He said nothing, just shaking his head. We entered the campground. The Tafurs, obviously half-starved, looked at us suspiciously. They had gathered about a roaring fire with a spit set over it, some animal impaled on a skewer which two Tafurs were turning—deer, goat, mutton? I couldn't tell. What I did detect, immediately, was the same nauseating odor—acrid, putrid, yet sweet—I smelled at Dorylaeum when bodies were burned on funeral pyres. I dismissed my suspicions. Another Tafur was slicing blackened meat on a trestle table handing out pieces to Tafurs waiting impatiently in line, they then sitting on their haunches greedily devouring the flesh or gnawing on bone. What especially attracted my attention were three Saracen youth, two boys and a girl, all possibly twelve years old, completely naked, their hands bound, huddled together in the cold December weather to share warmth, faces terrified. As William and I silently surveyed the scene, both of us trying to make sense of it, Drogo emerged from his tent and approached us.

"Bishop William, how pleasant to see you," Drogo greeted him, ignoring me. I was content with the slight. "You're just in time to eat. Supper is already being prepared. There's more than enough for us. To what do we deserve the presence of such an eminent cleric?" he asked, his tone redolent with sarcasm, mocking him with an obsequious bow.

"Drogo!" William responded, trying to restrain his fury as he turned his eyes to the three children, "I have heard a report so vile, so repulsive, that I'm horrified even to repeat it. Who are these children?"

"Oh, them," he replied indifferently, "they're our guests. We met them in the city and they begged, *just begged*, us to bring them here. And because we Tafurs are so generous in Christian spirit, we obliged. That's all."

During this exchange, I wandered over to the children, bowing their heads on my approach afraid to make eye contact.

I gently asked if any spoke Turkish. One answered "some".

"Where do you come from? What are you doing here? Don't be afraid. I won't harm you."

"We were seized by these men a few days ago in the city. We tried to run but were caught."

Drogo overheard the conversation and burst out in anger. "What are you doing over there priest?" Before I could answer he stomped toward me placing his hand on the hilt of his dagger "Get away or you'll join them!"

I turned to squarely face him, "Join them in what, your majesty Drogo, King of the Tafurs?" I asked with a sneer. "Join them in just *what*?"

In that instant, both William and I fully apprehended the fate of these children. "*Drogo! What have you done?*" William screamed in disbelief.

"Oh, it's really quite simple," Drogo answered serenely. "We're tired of eating grass, twigs, and grain stalks. We're hungry. And these," nodding his head toward to the children, "aren't really people. They're Muslims. No better than goats. Tastier too" he said grinning. "Good eatin' at that."

William was in shock and began stumbling back in horror. Stricken. "*Enough!* Release them *immediately!* Or I shall report this atrocity to the council!"

By now the shouting had attracted the attention of the other Tafurs who began walking toward us, each bearing a menacing look. Drogo, with a sinister, twisting smile waved his men off and stepped up to William placing one arm over his shoulder as though with affection, pulling him closer, withdrew his dagger and without warning plunged it into William's belly yanking the blade upward into his chest. William's eyes bulged, his mouth agape, staring wordlessly into Drogo's face, then slumping to the ground. Drogo turned his bloodied dagger toward me laughing almost hysterically, "You both will make fine fodder for our dogs. They get hungry too." I was without a weapon, useless anyway. There were just too many Tafurs who were now starting to surround me. I turned and ran, Tafurs chasing me but I was too fast and they soon stopped.

I was determined, without anger, only an unwavering resolve there would be a final reckoning with Drogo, whatever the danger. I thought first of Rebecca—if I told her of my intention I was certain of her response and I would have no choice but to ignore her pleas. Fortunately Rebecca was absent. I quickly dressed in my leather armor and holstered *Iskender* in its baldric thrown over my shoulder. Now where? I couldn't face the Tafurs alone. My first thought, and only thought, was Bohemond. Yet I was deeply conflicted, my soul still haunted by his betrayal and slaughter of the Khouris. Still, I desperately needed his aid and he owed me too much. This would settle that account. I had heard he was leaving Maarat to return to Antioch. When I found him, his troops were just beginning to decamp. I was in time. A guard had been posted in front of his tent. There was no time for ceremony. I brusquely pushed him aside. Bohemond was startled to see me, especially dressed as I was. I blurted out what happened. In his response I saw he was much less interested in Tafur barbarity or the fate of the Saracen children than he was the murder of Bishop William, a challenge to princely authority. Moreover, like all the other crusading nobles he both hated and feared the Tafurs. He wanted to be rid of this pestilence. After reassuring Bohemond that the battle was between Drogo and me alone, his troops merely to hold the Tafurs at bay, he readily acceded to my request.

I was anxious to return to Drogo's camp as quickly as possible fearing for the three children I had left behind. When we reached it I saw only two. We dismounted, the Normans having drawn their swords standing behind me. The Tafurs, still eating, seemed confounded by our arrival. They stood up but made no threatening move. Drogo was not among them. I called out for him to face me. Moments followed. Still no sign of Drogo. Not a sound. All was quiet until from under the shade of a nearby tree I saw him, a sword buckled to his waist, mount a horse and spur it out of the camp. He would not escape so easily. I grabbed the sword of one of the Normans and leapt onto my horse holding the reins in my left, the sword in my right. I would hunt Drogo down.

He raced through one field after another, I chasing after him shouting for him to stand and fight. He continued to flee. Fortune favored me once more. Drogo had turned sharply into a copse of small trees possibly thinking he could conceal himself there but his horse stumbled over some thick vines throwing him headfirst over the horse's head. By the time I had caught up with Drogo he had disappeared, hiding certainly behind a tree or shrub. I dismounted and began taunting to lure him out into the open, "Oh Drogo, King of the Tafurs, *do* come out to play. Maybe you can chew on *me*. I'm damn good eatin' too." In my anger, I was fearless. I began slapping the trunks of the trees with the broadside of my sword as I continued my taunts, stepping carefully through the copse, listening. "Oh King Drogo, *do* come out."

I heard the rustling of bushes behind me. He stood facing me, sword in hand. There would be no quarter asked or given. Even today I remember, most peculiarly, that *Iskender* seemed actually alive and whispering to me, "Oderic, I'm ready." I have no explanation for that. I was untrained in swordplay and Drogo had been a Norman knight before he plumbed the depths of hell, certainly more skilled than I. I employed the same combat techniques with my sword as Ekbar had taught me with the maul, the only ones I knew. Drogo slashed; I stepped back carefully. He stepped forward again, slashing once more; I blocked his next swing with my blade, my turn to swing which he also blocked. And thus it went—swing, block; swing, block—the sound of clashing metal swords resounding throughout the woods. I was intent on finishing this. A different tactic was required. I stepped back three paces to make room between us, shifted my sword from the right hand to the left, pulled out *Iskender* with my right flinging it at Drogo's head as I hurled myself at him. In that moment, that instant, I could tell Drogo hesitated, weighing which was the greater threat: *Iskender* flying through the air straight at his face or my sword. It was too late.

Iskender struck. Drogo was stunned and stumbled back. I thrust my sword through him, pushing, pushing, pushing until it had passed through his body. I was not finished. He had not yet fallen. I withdrew my sword, held it horizontally with both hands, shoulder height, my arms outstretched, whirled around to gain momentum and severed Drogo's head cleanly from his body. It rolled for several feet. I walked over and spat on it.

On returning to the camp, I saw that the Normans still held the Tafurs in check. We took the Saracen children back into Maarat, one child riding behind me, the other behind a Norman, and released them in the city. I do not know their fate but surely it could have been no worse than what awaited them with the Tafurs.

With a blade I had drawn blood. My last monastic vow was now broken. Was I beyond redemption?

Departure from Maarat an-Numan for Arqa

I shall now recount briefly the events that immediately followed the capture of Maarat. Bohemond's troops seized the city's towers and ramparts and claimed the city for himself. Raymond angrily disputed this, declaring that the city belonged to him for without his tower and sappers the city would never have been taken. Raymond called for a council meeting at Rugia, the city he had taken three months earlier after the princes departed Antioch for new conquests elsewhere. Raymond shamelessly offered handsome bribes to the princes, all except Bohemond, in exchange for recognizing his claim, most rejecting them. The status of Maarat remained unresolved. When the council adjourned, Bohemond returned to Maarat, assembled his troops, and returned to Antioch, apparently deciding that Antioch was the greater prize and he needed to consolidate his rule. On arriving at Antioch he immediately seized control of Yaghi Siyan's palace, the Fortified Bridge, and *La Mahomerie*, expelling the Provençals. He now was the undisputed sovereign of Antioch and soon declared it the "Principality of Antioch," he its prince. And, like Baldwin, he easily forsook the march to Jerusalem, seeing no personal profit.

Raymond's hold on Maarat proved less successful. Before leaving for the Rugia council, Raymond ordered his Provençals to repair the damaged wall. For the army this confirmed Raymond had no interest in continuing the march to Jerusalem but rather to enrich himself with land and power. In Raymond's absence Peter Bartholomew inflamed public opinion further, loudly accusing Raymond of betraying the crusade. "Let us tear down

this wicked pagan city! Then the count will be compelled to march south."
And they did. Raymond, hearing of this, hurried back but it was too late.
Even as he approached, the Provençals were busy dismantling the walls.
Raymond shouted at them to cease. They ignored him and continued with
their work. Raymond had a choice: either march to Jerusalem or lose his
army. He chose the former course. In a display of penance, he walked out
of Maarat barefoot carrying his supposed "Holy Lance", priests following
him singing hymns of praise. The army followed. In a final act, to evidence
his pledge, he ordered the city burned. This was January 13, 1099.

* * *

With the death of Bishop William, Rebecca and I were once more without
a patron, a protector. We traveled south with the other pilgrims trailing
behind the army through Kafartab, Shaizar, Emesa, Rafaniyah, along the
way crusaders seizing thousands of head of livestock or purchasing them
at markets, including one thousand Arabian horses, quite magnificent,
much superior to our own. For the most part the army was unopposed.
Local emirs sent tribute of supplies and gold wishing to make accord with
Raymond having heard of the fall of Antioch and Maarat, particularly stories of crazed crusaders eating Muslim flesh. In mid-February we arrived
at Arqa some fifteen miles north and east of Tripoli, a formidable city
indeed with twin walls and a dry moat. Raymond decided to besiege the
city for reasons that completely eluded me inasmuch as it held little strategic value. It was a fateful decision.

Rebecca and I found a small campsite among the tents of pilgrims, fortunately without Tafurs. I heard they had dispersed after Drogo's death,
most remaining in Maarat to what purpose I did not know. I was becoming
increasingly concerned about our means. Our coins were almost depleted
and Rebecca's appetite was growing, sometimes even ravenous, and the
cost of food dear. One day I was in an open-air market served by local
Christian farmers. After selecting dried meat and vegetables, I reached into
my purse to pay but was without sufficient coin. I asked the farmer if I
could repay him later. He had been so very pleasant before, even servile,
when I first walked up to his stall but then turned instantly belligerent and
began loudly cursing me. It was at that moment Godfrey was strolling by,
two of his captains accompanying him. He overheard the vendor's outburst
and, curious, walked over. He recognized me and saw my predicament. He
asked the farmer what was owed and paid it himself. "Father Oderic. It's

been a while. Come visit me this evening. I may have use for your services."

I did so, anxious for employment. We talked at length, quite enjoyably, about many matters including my involvement with Baldwin at Edessa about which I concealed nothing. Naturally I was apprehensive, uncertain of his reaction—I had, after all, tried to save Thoros from his brother's treachery. He dismissed my concern. "I know all about it," he said. "I would have done as you did." He then told me he had lost his chaplain in Antioch to the plague and proposed that I replace him. I immediately agreed, thankful he had not asked me to serve as one of his warriors. Godfrey, unlike his younger brother, had an unimpeachable reputation for genuine piety and scrupulous impartiality. He had little need for my spiritual ministrations other than prayer and a private mass every morning. The question of Rebecca did come up, briefly, Godfrey kindly asking about her health. He had attended Rebecca's trial and of course knew she was both a Jewess and pregnant and would soon give birth. He was untroubled. Indeed, he volunteered two midwives, their husbands in his service, to attend to Rebecca.

Two months had passed since the siege of Arqa began. We assaulted the city with scaling ladders, sappers, siege towers; they replied with devastating effect employing mangonels and ballistae from their ramparts. The city would not yield. No progress had been made. It was now early April. One afternoon while I was feeding Rebecca by hand, she feeling too uncomfortable to do so by herself, that she cried out "Oderic, fetch the midwives. *Now!*" I did so and paced up and down outside the coach listening to her wails. I was so fearful, feeling helpless. Then I heard a baby's cry. One of the midwives opened the rear door calling to me, "Father Oderic. You have a son. Mother and child are well." She placed him in my arms. I kissed him on the forehead and then stepped into the coach, Rebecca holding out her arms to reclaim her child, holding him to her breast. He suckled greedily. I left the coach and wandered for hours, conflicted, not about my vows as a priest but confused about my responsibilities as a father. I returned, lay beside Rebecca, our son sleeping between us. The fog of confusion lifted.

Ordeal by Fire

With the lengthy and inconclusive siege of Arqa, doubts about Raymond's commitment to the crusade were growing again with the rank and file, no less with the princes. Duke Godfrey confided in me he suspected

Raymond's dogged insistence on this siege was to establish his lordship over Arqa and after that Tripoli, leaving Jerusalem to others, no doubt inspired by Baldwin's creation of the County of Edessa and Bohemond's Principality of Antioch. Godfrey's suspicions of Raymond's motives proved prophetic years later. Now, more than ever, Godfrey believed, the army needed the guidance of a spiritual leader who would be true to the mission of this pilgrimage: deliverance of Jerusalem.

There was no obvious candidate to replace Bishop William. Peter of Narbonne perhaps, recently installed by Raymond as bishop of al-Bara, but he was widely perceived to be Raymond's tool. Arnulf, "the Wicked", a moniker I hoped he would be known to posterity, saw an opportunity to assert himself. He was already favored by the Normans, after all Arnulf was himself a Norman and chaplain to Duke Robert of Normandy. Yet there was another candidate, to my mind even more unfit, Peter Bartholomew. Since the victory over Kerboqa at Antioch, Provençals to my astonishment were proclaiming him a saint. As the siege of Arqa dragged on, Raymond's influence diminished proportionately and Godfrey's rose, the army increasingly looking to him for leadership. For that reason, he convened a council to elect a successor to Bishop William. All attended including Raymond, Peter Bartholomew in tow, and Robert of Normandy with his chaplain Arnulf. I suspected, rightly, this to be a contest between Provençals and Normans, animosity between the two well known, and their proxies Peter Bartholomew and Arnulf.

"My Lords," Godfrey began, "we have languished here in Arqa for three months. The city thus far has repulsed all our assaults without a single indication of surrender. The Turks seemed well prepared for us and can likely hold out for months more. In the meantime, Jerusalem awaits. We no longer have the benefit of Bishops Adhémar's or William's wisdom. We need new spiritual guidance. I invite opinions."

Before anyone said a word Peter Bartholomew stepped forward.

"My Lords, I must speak. Last night Saints Peter and Andrew appeared to me. I recognized neither for they were dressed in tattered clothes. But in my astonishment I fell to the ground, shivering in fear. Saint Andrew extended his hand to lift me up. 'Peter, Beloved of God, we come to reveal to you the bounty that Our Lord grants to those who esteem purity over vanity.' And with that, my Lords, a bright, blinding light filled my tent and their apparel miraculously changed into raiments of gleaming white all trimmed in gold. 'Tell us,' Saint Andrew asked 'what is the condition of the army?'"

"We have assailed the walls of Arqa, I answered, for three months and yet are still unable to conquer the city. Andrew rebuked me. 'God revealed to you the Holy Lance. With it your army defeated the Turks. But you Christians have fallen from God's Grace. Thievery, adultery, fornication, gambling with dice, every kind of wickedness once again prevails among you. If you do not cleanse your ranks of sin, the Lord will no longer be merciful.'"

The princes were listening in silence until Peter said that God commanded the army to cleanse itself of sin. The princes began shifting uneasily, glancing at one another with alarm. Peter continued. "I asked Saint Andrew how we were to separate the wicked from the pure?"

"'In two days assemble the entire army on the field before Arqa,' he instructed. 'God will separate them into three ranks. The first will consist of the pure in heart. They are guaranteed eternal salvation. The second rank will be those whose deviation from the Path of Righteousness is due to weakness of faith but can be redeemed by prayer and fasting. The third will consist of the incorrigible, those whose souls are so wicked that their sins can never be absolved. You will be the hand of God. They must be executed immediately, without mercy. Only then will the Lord give you victory over Arqa.'"

The princes were shocked, even Raymond including his captains standing beside him. Peter Bartholomew had gone too far. I was now convinced he was thoroughly deranged. Arnulf saw his opportunity.

"My Lords, if I may. This man is a false priest, like some others I know," glancing at me with a grimace. "God is *not* talking to this miscreant, and neither is Saint Peter nor Saint Andrew. His 'visions' are decoctions of malice and fabrications, all designed to deceive the people, to enhance his reputation as a prophet, even a saint. The lance is a fraud. He leapt into a pit after diggers searched mightily and then under the cover of darkness withdrew a lancehead secreted in his tunic and proclaimed 'This is the lance that pierced the body of Christ!' I, Arnulf, Bishop of Rohes, have carefully examined it myself. It is *not* Roman. It is *Turkish!* Satan was once able to disguise himself as an angel of light. Peter Bartholomew's skills may exceed even his. A fraud, my Lords, duplicitous and cunning."

Murmurs of agreement emerged from the Normans, Lorrainers and Flemings too, only the Provençals were silent but they too were clearly agitated. "My Lords," Peter retorted, "this false bishop is a liar and a well-known fornicator. I have seen him frequent brothels in our camps. Gleefully." Peter conveniently forgot that he had done the same at Nicea. "Out of respect for Mother Church I did not mention that Saint Peter himself fingered Arnulf, *by name*, as one of the trespassers of God's Law.

He must meet God's Judgment just as all other depraved sinners."

Raymond's reputation was now in peril. He understood that Peter's demand for the execution of crusader soldiers was demented. His leadership depended upon faith in the lance. And now that leadership was imperiled.

"My Lords . . . Raymond began, stammering, immediately interrupted by Robert of Normandy. "My Lords, I share Bishop Arnulf's doubts. This so-called 'vision' is a fraud perpetrated by a false priest," pointing at Peter, "to inflate his own importance, that *he*, and no one else, is the true messenger of Our Lord. I support Duke Godfrey's suggestion that we select a spiritual leader, but a *holy* man, not a conjurer. I propose Bishop Arnulf."

Dissension arose immediately. All knew that Arnulf was no more chaste in body or soul than was Peter. It was now that the most extraordinary thing happened. "My Lords," Peter cried out, "I have been impugned by scoundrels! Be not deceived on that. I am indeed the true messenger to this army from God. Let Him judge me, not you. I shall willingly undergo an ordeal by fire. If I survive, *and I shall*, the truth will be revealed to all of you."

Though Arnulf's face was impassive I knew he relished the moment. "So be it," Arnulf answered instantly, not wishing to give Peter time to reconsider this preposterous test of faith. "This is a matter for the Church and the ordeal shall be conducted according to our Laws. Peter Bartholomew, you shall fast and pray for three days. I urge you to seek forgiveness for your grievous sins. On the fourth day you will present yourself before this council to undergo the ordeal. We shall soon learn whether you are truly favored by God."

Following the meeting, as Godfrey and I walked to his tent, both of us shared our astonishment at Peter's challenge, his readiness to face death to redeem himself. Even I was beginning to wonder—perhaps these "visions" were truly as he said and perhaps the lance was indeed the Holy Lance. But Godfrey as we walked proposed a different, more practical explanation, "Or perhaps, Father Oderic, Peter has become unhinged by the hot Syrian sun and believes his own delusional nonsense." I agreed this too was a possibility.

* * *

For three days Peter secluded himself inside his tent, fasting and praying. Word had spread within the army of Peter's call for the death of all sinners. The anger was swift. This was one vision too many. Even among the Provençals doubts about the lance were growing. On the day of the ordeal dried olive branches were piled four feet high along a path five feet wide and thirteen feet long through which Peter would walk. Priests made judicial benedictions as the fire was lit. All the soldiers had assembled, no one wishing to miss this spectacle. Soldiers formed two lines from Peter's tent, holding back the pilgrims behind them. One of the soldiers approached Peter's tent to announce that it was time. The flaps of Peter's tent opened as he walked out clad in a simple tunic, holding the lance in front of him with outstretched arms. There followed catcalls from most of the soldiers, jeering him; from the pilgrims a different response, many falling on their knees imploring God not to abandon this true apostle of Christ. The branches had been lit and flames were erupting skyward, almost an inferno, even from several feet away I could feel its heat and had to back away. Peter walked forward but then hesitated. I wondered whether he would truly go through with it, his better judgment prevailing. This only prompted more taunting from the soldiers. "Go on, priest. Wanna see how holy you *really* are." From another, "You want us killed? Enjoy the fires of hell." Ironically, Peter's courage may have been fortified by the ridicule. He began walking forward. The flames were too high for me to see him until he emerged at the end, stumbling, his tunic on fire, then collapsing. The pilgrims began screaming hysterically. "A *holy man!*" "*Behold Saint Peter!*" They rushed at Peter through the line of soldiers, some merely to touch him, others tearing his tunic into pieces, pulling out tufts of hair, grabbing his sandals, each now a sacred relic. If the fire hadn't already killed Peter, I'm sure the mob would have in its frenzy. It was only through the intervention of one of Raymond's sergeants and his soldiers that Peter was rescued. The soldiers lifted him up and throwing both of his arms over their shoulders, Peter shrieking in pain, supported him back to his tent as his feet dragged in the dirt.

Godfrey, knowing of my attempt to save his sister-in-law Lady Godvere and her sons, asked that I attend to Peter's injury. For twelve days I did so, applying ointments, salves, and poultices to his wounds. I had hoped that, in his debilitated condition, he might reveal to me the truth of his visions of the lance but he was delirious the entire time. I knew the burns were too severe for treatment, especially on his legs and chest. Peter had suffered other wounds in the pilgrims' zeal, broken ribs and arms. There was nothing more I could do for him. During those days, pilgrims, especially Provençals, milled about the tent praying for God's intersession and expecting him to emerge at any moment unscathed. He didn't. He died. Yet Peter's death did nothing to heal divisions within the army. For the skeptics his death only confirmed their doubts. For believers, the fact that he had succeeded in walking through the fire and survived for twelve days were irrefutable evidence of his sainthood, the truth of his visions and of the lance. The Provençals buried him where he had crossed through the fire.

There was, however, an unexpected outcome. Raymond's reputation, so closely connected to the authenticity of the lance, was now irredeemably tarnished. No longer would he be treated as leader of the army. The mantle passed to Duke Godfrey by common consent. Another casualty of the episode was Arnulf. He had preened and pranced to succeed Bishop William. But his challenge to Peter Bartholomew had excited the anger of Provençals. A detachment of soldiers went in search of him to bring him to Provençal justice. It was rumored that Raymond himself had given the order. Arnulf sought the protection of Duke Robert of Normandy and Count Robert of Flanders. I was certain that without it he would have been nailed to a cross.

A New holy Man and Search for the True Cross

It was early one evening shortly after Peter Bartholomew's death. I had gathered wood and lit a fire for the brazier; Rebecca was preparing a stew of fresh meat with rice kindly provided by Godfrey. I looked forward to her fried bread, especially when she was able to use butter. I was in the coach holding our son who was suffering from colic of some sort. To settle him, I softly sang melodies my mother had sung to me in my early childhood. I had never forgotten them. There was a rap on the door. It was Stephen of Valence.

A Provençal priest, Stephen was a singular fellow. In his mid-thirties, lean, almost gaunt, with an angular face, a sharp nose, and eyes so piercing they seemed capable of penetrating ones soul. He was rather tall, a full head above my own, reinforcing his ascetic appearance. He exuded piety like a water-soaked rag when squeezed, though of the most severe, unforgiving, and pharisaical sort. He wore a beard, black but for streaks of white, stretching down his neck to the upper part of his chest. He had been a hermit living in a hut next to a monastery in Valence. On learning of the crusade, he emerged vowing not to shave until Jerusalem was recovered from the infidels. Peter was among the five priest-judges, I one of them, recruited by Adhémar at Antioch during the great famine to try sinners. Stephen came to the assignment with unrestrained zeal. Despite Adhémar's injunction for us to cleanse the army of sinners, he also admonished us to hold fair hearings and, if the accused were found guilty, to determine a punishment proportionate to the offense. I recall so clearly Peter's objection: "Sinners against God are like poisonous tumors on our souls which need to be excised without pity! God can determine their eternal fate, on Judgment Day." Although reproved by Adhémar, Stephen nonetheless found every accused guilty, sentencing all to death even for the mildest offense. Adhémar intervened commuting their sentences, unfortunately too late for one. I recall too how he rejoiced over the slaughter of Muslims at Maarat. His only regret, he told me at the time, was that there were just too few of them to kill. But it was earlier at Antioch, during Kerboqa's siege, where Stephen, hitherto unknown, gained prominence when at a Council of Princes he related his "vision"— not from a mere apostle like Andrew who appeared to Peter Bartholomew but from Christ Himself and His Holy Mother —that the Lord promised victory over the Turks if Bohemond led our army and that He would send a heavenly army under Saint George to assist.

Stephen came immediately to the point. "Peter Bartholomew is dead. I feel no sadness. He was a sinner, otherwise God would have saved him from the fire. But that's not the reason I'm here. Bishop Adhémar has now chosen me, a worthier priest than the reprobate Peter, to receive messages from God." Had we merely exchanged one "visionary" for another? I suspected that Stephen had a different purpose in mind, to supplant Peter Bartholomew with himself. Were Stephen's ambitions the product of raw cunning or fanatical piety? Likely both.

"Brother Stephen, what do you require of me?"

"Bishop Adhémar appeared to me in a vision last night with a message for Count Raymond. You were the bishop's scribe and knew him well. Perhaps you can attest to the accuracy of his words."

"And what did he say?"

"You will learn soon enough if you come with me."

I was disinclined. I had not the slightest notion of how I could attest to this "vision" of Adhémar. I was certain too that Raymond harbored a grudge against me for accompanying Bohemond when he received the surrender of Antioch's citadel from Ahmad ibn-Marwān. And, finally, I mistrusted aiding yet another "visionary" whose motives were dubious. But, I was intensely curious. I agreed, seeing little harm.

We walked to Raymond's tent. Raymond was inside discussing some matter with his chaplain Raymond d'Aguilers and Adhémar's brother William Hugh of Monteil. As we entered, Raymond looked at Stephen suspiciously, clearly remembering the council meeting when Stephen announced Christ had ordered that Bohemond, not he, lead the army against the Turks. And he glared at me recalling my role in the citadel's surrender. Yes, Raymond forgets nothing.

"My Lord Raymond," Stephen began, bowing to the count, "I come with a message from Bishop Adhémar to you."

Raymond was startled. "What message?" he asked incredulously.

"Last night the bishop appeared to me in my sleep. He rebuked me, asking why I ignored his past commands regarding the True Cross of the Lord. 'It must be carried with the army,' Adhémar demanded. 'What relic is better than the Cross? Without it, the Holy Mother believes you have no wisdom.' In that moment, she appeared, standing beside her Saint Agatha and a virgin holding two candles. My Lord Bishop, I asked, may I have one of the candles to show the princes as proof this was no illusion. Adhémar then approached the Holy Mother who whispered something in his ear. He returned to deny the request. 'You have no need of a candle nor the ring on your finger. Rather, the ring should be presented to Count Raymond as evidence of your testimony. Mother Mary orders that, henceforth, the Sacred Cross must be borne by priests wearing sacerdotal clothes in front of the army.'"

"Where is the Cross, Your Grace? I asked."

"'Father Oderic of La Charité sur Loire knows. Inquire of him.' In that instant, a heavenly choir of hundreds of thousands voices sang out and Bishop Adhémar vanished. My vision ended."

All eyes turned to me. That Bishop Adhémar possessed a fragment of the True Cross was well known; it required no "vision". But by asking me to accompany him to Count Raymond, Stephen was hoping to force me into revealing its location, all in the service of Raymond who desperately needed a new relic to refurbish his reputation after Peter Bartholomew was discredited. Oh, what fluid allegiances these "messengers of God" attach themselves—Peter, once the supplicant of Raymond, then binding himself to Bohemond; Stephen, once in league with Bohemond, now seeking comfort with Raymond. As the wind shifted, so did fealty.

I explained how Bishop Adhémar, near death, had requested that I send the Cross and its reliquary to the pope and that Patriarch John commissioned a beautifully carved box in which to contain it. I held on to the reliquary until reaching Arqa, uncertain how to send it to Rome. It was there I learned by chance a certain priest, Justin of Rouen, a Norman, was on his way to Constantinople through the port of Latakia where a small Venetian merchant fleet was loading cargo for sale in the great city. I wrapped the carved box, reliquary inside, with crude linen secured by a leather strap to disguise its true worth, and gave Justin coin to deliver it to General Tatikios in Constantinople with a letter explaining that it was intended for the pope. All of this I related to Raymond, fortuitously, as it developed later, failing to mention that a second, identical box had been built for Rebecca.

"When did you give the True Cross to this priest?" Raymond asked.

"Two days ago."

"Do you think the Cross is still in Latakia?"

"Possibly, but of course I can't be certain."

Raymond turned to William Hugh. "William, you must hasten to Latakia and find it. The matter is urgent."

William agreed if he could bring a company of Provençal troops and if I would accompany him for only I could recognize Justin. To encourage me, Raymond offered me two silver marks. I was sorely conflicted. To accept money for a religious mission was anathema to me. I also fully understood Raymond's purpose here. His leadership had depended on his possession of the lance. With Peter Bartholomew's death and the lance now in disrepute among most of the army, even many Provençals, he needed a new relic. With that, he could reassert his dominance. This was not a spiritual quest and thus I accepted Raymond's offer. Before leaving, I arranged for one of Godfrey's midwives with whom Rebecca had developed a special affection to attend to her in my absence.

We left immediately, arriving at Latakia in the early evening and camped outside the city. The next morning we commenced our search, riding through the streets as I scrutinized every face. Justin could not be found. By late afternoon it seemed to both of us this hunt would be fruitless. I thought of the inns. On the third try we were successful. I dismounted and peered through the inn's door. Justin was sitting alone at a table, a plate of roasted game bird, rice, bread in front of him and a flagon of beer in his hand, a rather sumptuous meal for a mere priest. He was shouting as though disputing with an unseen companion, obviously drunk. I persuaded William to leave his soldiers outside and for him to stand unobserved in the corner, thinking Justin might be more pliant speaking with a fellow priest than intimidated by a show of force. I quietly sat beside him.

"Brother Justin," I began, trying to disarm him, "so nice to see you again."

Justin was startled and turned to look at me, suspiciously. "Whoosh you?"

"Don't you remember me, Father? I'm Oderic, formerly scribe to Bishop Adhémar. I entrusted a box. It was wrapped in linen. I asked you to deliver it to General Tatikios in Constantinople. Do you still have it?"

He looked at me quizzically, his eyes glazed. I wasn't sure if he were feigning or just too drunk to remember. "What crosssh? Not 'member. Never sheen no crosssh. Who you again?" I had not mentioned that the box contained the Cross. It became immediately clear that Justin had unwrapped it, saw the reliquary inside and then the piece of ancient wood within. He had divined the value of what he held.

I introduced myself once more and yet again he professed ignorance of the Cross as he began gulping down beer even more thirstily than when I first entered. He was clearly nervous. William had been watching with impatience. He walked over, pulled out a dagger, pressed the point of the blade into Justin's neck, "Maybe this will restore your memory." It did indeed and Justin immediately blurted out the truth, that he had sold the relic to three Norman soldiers, knights he thought, the day before. He had obviously been well compensated, evident from his lavish meal and the fat purse hanging from his belt which he repeatedly fingered.

"Are they still in Latakia?" William demanded.

"Think sho. Shaw 'em thish mornin'. Not far from here."

We left, but on rising from the bench I slapped him on the side of his face with my open hand as powerfully as I was able sending him flying over his bench onto the floor. He deserved much worse. "That's for betraying Bishop Adhémar!"

William and I recommenced our search up and down the streets. There was no sign of the knights until we came to an inn at the outskirts of the city, on the road north to Antioch. In front three destriers were tethered to a pole, these warhorses obviously belonging to knights. We dismounted and walked in. The inn was dark. I could dimly see three men sitting at a table, laughing boisterously, none wearing mail but rather quilted gambesons. In front of them, on the table, was the reliquary which they had taken out of the carved box, passing it from hand to hand, stroking it almost lasciviously as though expecting a handsome reward for its recovery. William summoned his troops. They filed in and surrounded the Normans.

"Sirs. I am William Hugh of Monteil, captain in the service of Count Raymond of Toulouse. I have been commissioned to recover the reliquary in front of you, formerly the property of Bishop Adhémar, Papal Legate. It was intended as a gift for His Holiness Pope Urban and entrusted to a priest who fraudulently sold it to you. I'm sure you purchased it unwittingly and so I shall spare you punishment. Nevertheless, it must be returned. Hand it here."

The Norman sergeant stood up, not defiantly, the odds severely against him, but more as a penitent. "Captain William, we paid good coin for this," looking down at the reliquary, "and we expect a worthy reward from our Lord Bohemond. Surely we should be compensated for without us you would not have recovered this relic."

William was unmoved. "I suggest you find that scourge of a priest who sold you this precious object and demand repayment from him. But do it quickly before he drinks and eats up all the coin you paid him."

I Steal the True Cross

We returned to Arqa. My anxiety over the role I played in recovery of the Cross only deepened. It would now go to Raymond, not to be used in the service of Christ but for his own personal advancement. Yet, had I not accompanied William Hugh, it would have fallen into the possession of Bohemond to be exploited just as covetously. Either result was repugnant to me. It belonged in Rome. I had betrayed Adhémar's faith in me and failed my bishop. I would make amends.

We reached Raymond's camp. He was pacing outside his tent evidently having learned of our imminent arrival. William dismounted, reached into his saddlebag withdrawing the carved box, reliquary inside, fell to one knee, head bowed, and offered it up to Raymond. Raymond accepted it, lifted the box's lid then the reliquary's gazing down at this sacred relic. He clasped the box to his chest, then holding it in both hands, his arms stretched upward to heaven, turned completely around presenting it to the excited crowd of Provençals who had gathered around him. "Behold! A miracle! The Cross of Jesus Christ! Tomorrow at midday when we depart for Jerusalem I shall reveal to you the Cross which will lead us to that holy city. But tonight I worship it in the Chapel of Saint Agatha." A scheme quickly formed in my mind. The chances were slender and depended on what Raymond did in the chapel. If he brought the relic back from the chapel to his camp, it would be closely guarded and I would have no opportunity to take it. But perhaps, just perhaps, things might transpire differently.

After Raymond received the reliquary I returned to the coach and dressed in my pilgrim's attire, a disguise of sorts: hat with the medallions of past "pilgrimages", woolen sclavein with its red cross of silk sewn below the shoulder, staff, and satchel. My plan, if the opportunity presented itself, was simply to snatch Patriarch John's carved box with its reliquary and flee. But I feared escape would be unlikely. I then hit upon another idea, to replace the box with Rebecca's. I scoured our campground for a stone about the weight of the reliquary and one that would fit snugly into the box. Eventually I found one. I stuffed both box and stone into my satchel. I hesitated to take it from Rebecca but there was a higher good.

The chapel was located outside the city walls, one of very few Christian houses of worship left unmolested by the Muslims. I then walked to Raymond's encampment watching his tent from a safe distance unobserved. I saw him appear, beckon two soldiers to accompany him. They mounted for the ride to the chapel, a short one. I followed them, running, a pilgrim on a horse certainly arousing suspicion. I soon came to the chapel and opened its door carefully fearful its creaking would alert the soldiers. The interior was dark, illuminated only by moonlight streaming through narrow windows. I hung back in the shadows. Raymond had withdrawn the reliquary from the box and set it on the altar, opening its lid. He kneeled in prayer, his soldiers standing leisurely behind him. He then stood up, placed the reliquary back into the box, closed the lid, and left it on the altar, the soldiers remaining to guard it. I could not understand why Raymond left the Cross in the chapel—perhaps he wanted God to know it was now safely in his own hands. This was, beyond reason, what I had hoped for. But I had to deal with the soldiers, something I had not anticipated.

There were only three of us in the chapel. The soldiers sat off in the corner cross-legged playing dice. One of them pulled out a goatskin of wine from under his cloak, concealed I suspected from Raymond. As the night wore on they became increasingly rowdy and drunk, throwing dice, shouting in delight when they won, tossing coins into a small pile between them, the loser accusing the other of cheating which immediately produced howls of laughter. I waited. After the longest time, the soldiers fell into a stupored sleep, snoring loudly. I walked stealthily up to the altar, keeping an eye on them, and slipped the box into my satchel and turned to step down from the altar. Disaster struck. I had leaned by staff against the altar. The hem of my tunic touched the staff sending it to the stony pavement awakening one of the guards, who drowsily lifted himself up. There was no time. I quickly pulled out Rebecca's box and placed it on the altar exactly where the other had rested and then stuffed the original in my satchel, standing over it, my head bowed as though in meditative prayer. Seeing me, the soldier leapt to his feet, staggering somewhat as he approached, drawing his sword pointed at me.

"Thief! Who are you? What are you doing? What have you stolen?"

I turned, bowed obsequiously, doffing my hat. "My Lord," I whimpered, "I am but a penitent sinner, a pilgrim to Jerusalem where I hope to see the sacred spot on which Our Lord Jesus Christ sacrificed his life for Mankind. See here my badges. This to Compostela and this to . . ."

"Enough! No care for your badges. What are you doing here?"

"I heard that the True Cross was here in this chapel. I merely wanted to be in its presence, to worship. If you wish, I shall leave."

The guard looked to the altar and saw the carved box. However, he seemed not to be satisfied. He stepped up to the altar, set his sword against it, and lifted the box, about to open the lid. I was certain to be exposed. The other guard had woken up and was walking toward us. I had to act.

"My Lord, if I am but permitted to remain here, to worship, I will pay." I then quickly untied my purse from my belt, held it up for him to see, shaking it up and down, coins jingling. His interest was piqued. He stepped toward me and snatched the purse from my hand.

"What's in your satchel?" seeing its bulge. "What did you steal scoundrel?"

"My Lord," continuing to whimper, "nothing. There's only a loaf of bread which is all I'll have to eat for two days. Please! Don't take it from me."

"Let me see inside. Then I'll let you go." He reached for the satchel but was stopped by his companion. "Lanval, he's already given us coin. Let's get back to the dice."

On the following morning, May 13, Raymond as promised assembled the crusading army to depart Arqa, the city still unconquered. Raymond believed his possession of the True Cross would be an affirmation of God's renewed favor. He stood alone in front of his troops formed in tight lines. Stephen of Valence, flanked by two priests, approached him, Stephen holding the box. Raymond took it in both hands, raised it upright for all to see, then opened it. It was empty but for a stone. He stared into the box, saying nothing for so long that the troops broke discipline and began whispering to one another. He silently closed the box, handed it back to Stephen, mounted his horse, and waved for his army to follow him.

* * *

Raymond had obstinately insisted on besieging Arqa for three months, the cost in lives considerable, all for nothing. The luster of the lance was now tarnished. And he was without the "true cross" with which to replace it. He would never again lead the army.

This ends Book XIII of *Jerusalem Falls!* Book XIV begins.

BOOK XIV

JERUSALEM FALLS!

From Arqa to Jerusalem. An Unexpected Question. A Peculiar hermit
and a Foolish Assault. Despondence and Deliverance. Another Visionary.
Rebecca Slain. Burial. Precipice of Defeat. Jerusalem Falls. Vengeance
and a Vision. Escape Through hezekiah's Tunnel. Plunder in the
Service of God. Greed, a Solomonic Solution, and Massacre.

From Arqa to Jerusalem

On May 13, Year of Our Blessed Lord 1099, the army departed Arqa. Among the crusaders feelings were conflicted: frustration that the city had not succumbed after a three-month siege; anger at Count Raymond for his insistence on prolonging the siege; sorrow over the loss of life in the failed effort; but joy the army was now marching to Jerusalem. Not long after leaving Arqa the princes met in council to decide on the route to be taken: through the hinterland or along the coast with mountains to the east and sea to the west. The latter would be quicker but more perilous for we would need to cross mountains through many narrow defiles easily defended by the Saracens. Moreover, we would pass a number of well-fortified port cities. Our army was much depleted over the past three years—from starvation, sickness, battle, and desertions. We lacked the strength to lay siege to each. More troubling was a rumor that the Fatimid Sultan of Babylon, al-Afdal, was leading a formidable Saracen relief army from Egypt to Jerusalem. There was no time to tarry. We took the coast route.

We marched first to Tripoli where the emir, under threat, released three hundred Christian prisoners and made a gift of fifteen thousand gold pieces, horses, mules, and fine garments. From there south, to al-Batrun, and then Jubail where the emir gave a tribute of five thousand gold pieces, more horses, mules, and an abundant supply of wine. We were well provisioned. Then to Beirut crossing the Dog river, the northern border of Fatimid territory, to Sidon, Tyre, Acre, Haifa, Caesarea, and finally Arsuf. The journey was, for the most part, uneventful. At Sidon we did encounter limited Saracen resistance though handled with relative ease. More deadly were vipers, doubtless the same "flying fiery snakes" that attacked the children of Israel when Moses led them into the land of Edom. Many died from their bites. For the other cities, however, we were unmolested, their garrisons poorly manned and the inhabitants happy to provide us with provisions so long as we left them in peace, which we did. At Arsuf we turned inland to the east, arriving at the city of Ramla, location of the Church of Saint George where that saintly warrior was buried. The garrison fled on our approach. We continued south into the Judean Hills. We were no more than nine miles from Jerusalem when a delegation of Christians from Bethlehem arrived beseeching us to liberate them from the Saracens. Tancred and Baldwin of Le Bourcq led one hundred knights to the town, joyously welcomed. Tancred placed his own banner above the Church of the Nativity claiming it for himself, a matter of dispute later.

* * *

The closer we came to Jerusalem the more I was struck by the land's desolation. Farms, yes, but all abandoned. The fields had been harvested and bare, gardens plucked of their produce, no livestock to be seen, orchards now mere stumps freshly cut by Saracens I assumed to prevent use for siege engines. The only human activity I saw was many scores of people, Christians by their dress, certainly not Muslims, wandering along the road and into fields, those not burned, gleaning what food they could. There were also makeshift camps, open-air without tents, scattered about. One Christian was walking toward us. I stopped, leaned over as he was just passing and speaking Frankish, which he understood, asked where were the inhabitants. His answer, I was certain, would be of interest to Duke Godfrey. Our coach was in the train of Godfrey's army. I invited the Christian to join me on the perch, and moved quickly to the front around the files of soldiers which Godfrey was leading. I hailed the duke who turned his horse on hearing my voice and dismounted. We both stepped down from the coach.

"My Lord, I think this man has information of value to you." Turning now to him, "This is Godfrey, Duke of Lorraine. Tell him what you just told me. First, your name."

He bowed awkwardly to Godfrey. "I am Bernard, formerly of Trier, a resident of Jerusalem for the last ten years."

"Bernard," Godfrey asked, "where is everyone? The land seems deserted except for wandering Christians such as you."

"My Lord," Bernard bowing again, "Jerusalem was formerly in the hands of the Turks. About a year ago, al-Afdal, Sultan of Babylon, laid siege to it and the garrison surrendered. The sultan left his governor, Iftikhar ad-Daulah, to rule the city. We were treated tolerably, that is until word arrived your army had crossed the Dog River and was heading south toward Jerusalem. Iftikhar ordered all the crops in the field be harvested; what couldn't be gathered was burned; all the livestock was herded into the city."

"And who are these people wandering about the fields?" Godfrey asked.

Bernard bowed for a third time. It was becoming annoying. I wanted to whisper to him to cease but restrained myself. "They are Christians, my Lord, Nestorians like me, Paulicians too, Jacobites from Armenia, others. Iftikhar ordered us all out of the city on a pretext to repair the moat next to the Jaffa Gate. We did as commanded but once outside the city the gate slammed shut. We were not allowed back in. He feared we would aid you Latins."

Godfrey was quite curious. "Would you?"

At this question Bernard seemed to cower a bit. "I'm . . . I'm not sure, my Lord. Until now we have prospered under Saracen rule. We are unsure of you Latins. There are stories, from the Kingdom of Hungary and Anatolia. None true, I'm sure but . . ." his voice trailing off.

"What stories?" Godfrey asked impatiently.

Bernard was clearly agitated by the question. He feared he had revealed too much and was anxious to change the subject. "Except the Jews." Bernard continued. "Iftikhar has allowed them to remain. He heard of their treatment in cities along the Rhine River and does not suspect their loyalty."

"Is he correct?" Godfrey asked. "Can we count on Jews to assist us?"

"I think not. I have a Jewish friend, a spice trader, Isaac ben Judah, a frequent visitor to Jerusalem with relatives in the city. I used to sell his goods in my humble shop before the expulsion." At the mention of Isaac ben Judah I perked up instantly, he and his wife Miriam, dear friends to Rebecca and me who had concealed us from Emicho's soldiers on the road from Mainz to Semlin. "He told me . . . " Bernard now hesitating, uncertain whether candor might be rewarded with a lashing.

"Go on," Godfrey urged, "you may speak freely."

"He told me that Jerusalem Jews fear the Latins far more than Saracens. No, you cannot rely on them."

I could not repress my excitement at hearing Isaac's name. "Is Isaac in Jerusalem now?"

"Yes. I saw him but two weeks ago. He's staying in the Jewish Quarter."

Now Godfrey's curiosity was piqued. "You know this Isaac ben Judah?"

"I do, my Lord. A very worthy man. He saved Rebecca's and my lives." I turned to Bernard, "Tell the duke what you told me about water."

"Yes, of course. The governor has poisoned all the wells for a distance six miles from the city, throwing dead carcasses into them. The springs, he buried under piles of rubble such that they no longer flow. And what few cisterns existed have all been drained. Only the Pool of Siloam outside the city, less than a bowshot from the walls within easy range of Saracen arrows, has been left untouched. Perhaps to pick off Latins."

"What of the city's water supply? And its provisions?" Godfrey asked.

"The city is abundantly provided with cisterns, all quite full, almost overflowing. And there is no dearth of food since Iftikhar ordered early harvests of the farms and their livestock herded inside the walls. I think another reason Iftikhar expelled the Christians was to reduce the number of mouths to feed."

The interview was over and I was about to escort Bernard away when he turned to Godfrey. "Oh, yes. One more thing. I almost forgot. There is a tiny community of hermits living on top of the Mount of Olives. One is reputed to be especially holy. I do not know his name nor have I met him. But for over a year rumors have circulated that he predicted your arrival and had even received a message from God with a strategy for the capture of Jerusalem. You may want to see him." I could tell Godfrey was intrigued but he said nothing.

As we walked back to my coach I was flush with excitement pummeling Bernard with questions: Where is Isaac now? Is Miriam with him? How are they doing? Where are they living? I wished to know everything.

"Isaac is well, as is Miriam. They are staying with a spice trader somewhere in the Jewish Quarter, on Spicery Row which is shared with the goldsmiths. Isaac had expected to leave Jerusalem but Iftikhar ordered the city gates closed not only to prevent Christians from returning but also anyone from leaving. Perhaps he was fearful they would reveal the city's defenses. They must still be there."

"Do you know of any way I can get in to see them?"

"Hmm. There are secret underground tunnels leading from within the city to outside the walls. The only one I know is Hezekiah's Tunnel, below the al-Aqsa Mosque. It carries water from the Gihon Springs to the Pool of Siloam near the Gate of Zion in the south. The tunnel was carved out of rock centuries ago I believe, very dark and narrow from what I've heard. But even if you get into the city you will surely be arrested. The governor suspects everyone lacking Saracen features of being a Christian spy. You'll be caught and executed immediately. I don't advise it."

An Unexpected Question

It was June 7. We had just passed through another defile, its trail the most difficult yet, steep and so gravely that our mule continually slipped, struggling to pull his load. We finally reached the summit and looked down. There in the distance was Jerusalem, our destination, the Muslim Dome of the Rock glimmering in the sun's light. After so much suffering for over four years—thirst, starvation, sickness, and death—gasps and cries erupted instantly. Oh what rejoicing there was on our first glimpse of this Holy City, the "Navel of the World". Women collapsed to the ground, lying prostrate, weeping, their arms outstretched to heaven crying to the Lord with gratitude. Even warriors, fearless in battle, fell to their knees, heads bowed in silent prayer, their hands clasped and eyes drenched in tears.

I shall briefly describe this magnificent city. Located in the Judean Hills, it sits on a high plateau with steep ravines on the east, west, and south. It is surrounded by some three miles of walls, fifty feet tall, ten feet thick, first constructed during the time of the Roman Emperor Hadrian and then strengthened over the next eight hundred years by a succession of conquerors. To my eye, the defenses were no less formidable than those of Constantinople, Nicea, or Antioch. It was only to the north and a narrow field to the south at the Gate of Zion that flatter ground allowed the approach of siege engines. But there, twin walls had been constructed with a moat in front of the outer one.

Immediately on arriving before the city, we laid siege. Robert of Flanders made camp before Herod's Gate; Robert of Normandy at the Damascus Gate; Tancred further to their south; and Duke Godfrey even more south in front of the Jaffa Gate next to the Tower of David. I positioned our coach close to Godfrey's camp. Rebecca and I, ever curious about new surroundings, decided to explore. In my youth I recalled my father having fashioned a sling made of a broad piece of linen which he tied behind his neck carrying my youngest brother. I made something similar for our son and as we walked through the different camps I would gently stroke his head and kiss his cheeks. In the evenings, we shared pleasant meals sitting around the brazier, Rebecca and I periodically passing him from one lap to another. But how we both missed the company of Georgios and Miriam.

I don't recall most of those excursions, except one, a poignant memory. It was a sultry evening and we walked to the Jaffa Gate admiring its imposing twin-towered barbican resolutely defending the drawbridge behind it. We gazed at it, the silence broken by an unexpected question.

"Oderic, do you feel married? I mean *really* feel married?"

The question took me aback. I deflected, not because I feared my answer but because I had just not given much thought to the matter. "Do *you*?" I asked.

"That's no answer, my husband. In your heart, the *depth* of your heart, do you regard me as your wife? I want you to answer truly."

"Rebecca, I'm surprised at the question. Have you ever doubted my love?"

"No, never," she answered emphatically. "You've risked your life too many times for me. No, I don't doubt that. Yet, after all, you're a priest—oh yes, some call you a 'warrior-priest' but a priest all the same. You are no longer celibate, you've married a Jewess in a Jewish ceremony, and now you're a father—priestly vows not merely broken but some may say even shattered. Do you regard me as your wife?"

I stood there quietly, plumbing not my mind but my heart. My mind was clear on the matter. But was my heart? Reconciling the two can be difficult. In the following moments of silence Rebecca becoming increasingly anxious. But she asked for the truest answer and I had to give it.

"Yes," I answered slowly. "Yes, you *are* my wife. I feel it to the depth of my soul. We are married for life. If anything should happen to you, and God willing nothing will, I would never take another. Besides," now trying to lighten the mood, "who makes fried bread as well as you? Though in the future, you might use more butter," I added with a smile.

Rebecca, normally quite buoyant, was unmoved and would not be distracted by clumsy humor. "But you're a Christian and married a Jewess in a Jewish wedding. Besides, I fear that at Edessa you were pressed into marriage. It was not your idea. It was mine."

I placed my arm around her and pulled her close. "Rebecca my love," I whispered in her ear," I regret nothing. You *are* my wife. Get this silly notion out of your head. But I still need more butter on my fried bread." She giggled, finally satisfied. I still remember that conversation as though it happened yesterday. It required no journal entry.

A Peculiar hermit and a Foolish Assault

It was two days after arriving at Jerusalem that Godfrey, following morning prayers and mass, asked me to accompany him to the Mount of Olives. He had summoned the other princes to join him, most agreeing. Godfrey and I joined them, riding down a gentle but narrow trail into the Kidron Valley just below the Temple of Solomon and then up to the Mount of Olives, much less a mountain than a large, sloping hill. We saw a grove of olive trees, hundreds of years old I estimated, standing in contrast to the denuded orchards through which we passed days before. They were all gnarled and bent from age, unmolested by Saracens probably because they had no military utility.

On the far side of the grove were several small caves used for burials I was told later. As we dismounted one hermit emerged followed deferentially by four others. He was taller than the rest, even more gaunt, dressed in a tunic so grimy and covered in dirt that I thought one could plant a modest garden on it. His hair, disheveled, was perfectly white stretching below his shoulders and a beard, just as white, reaching almost to his waist. There was a certain wildness in his eyes. He seemed more like a specter than a man.

"Noble pilgrims," he began speaking Frankish without bowing, making little effort at acknowledging the courtesies of addressing seigneurs, "I expected you. Welcome."

"Your name, Father Hermit?" Godfrey asked.

"My name is of no consequence," the hermit replied in a gravelly voice. "We dispense with such vanities here. They are the badges of pride and hubris. But I know who all of you are," turning now to Godfrey, "including you, Duke of Bouillon. I foretold your arrival in the Holy City long ago." At that, the other hermits vigorously nodded their heads. "And I know your purpose in today's visit. Last night, in a vision, the Archangel Michael informed me."

"Then you will know," Godfrey answered, "that we were told you have a message from God instructing us on a strategy for capturing Jerusalem. What is this message?"

"Ah yes, the capture of Jerusalem. Our Lord is very impatient with you. You spent idle months in the sieges of Nicea, Antioch, and Arqa, all the while ignoring the suffering of His people in Jerusalem under hated heathen rule. Yet God is just and merciful, *so long as you obey His commands*," he added quite sternly and without apology.

"What is God's command?"

"You shall attack the walls of Jerusalem tomorrow. After it has fallen, you will fast for three days, distribute alms to the poor, and then give thanks at the Church of the Holy Sepulchre. *That* is His command."

The princes made no effort to conceal their shock. Godfrey as well. Such a plan was preposterous, doomed to ignominious failure. We were unprepared. Crushing defeat was certain. "Father Hermit," Godfrey protested, "we can build but one scaling ladder by tomorrow with two walls to overcome. This is impossible!"

"Have you learned nothing in the last three years? Over and over you have despaired, fearful of defeat, yet always God intervened to give you victory but only when your heart was full of His Grace. At Antioch you moaned, wailed, and wept at the sight of a Turkish army. But God gave you the Sacred Lance that pierced His Son. Your faith in the Lord was restored and you defeated the pagans. I merely see before me today callow youth, trembling and faithless. Renew your faith! God will protect you! I have nothing more to say. But it must be tomorrow." He returned to his cave followed by his acolytes.

The princes were silent, most staring at the ground and then up at Godfrey. Godfrey too was silent, merely looking at them for comment. None came but for slow, unenthusiastic nods. "Tomorrow at dawn it is," Godfrey announced.

As Godfrey and I rode back to camp he was deep in uneasy contemplation saying nothing. We were about to part. "My Lord, may I speak freely, as your chaplain and spiritual adviser?"

"You may."

"I shall be direct. I fully understand that victory is ultimately possible only with God's Favor. But perhaps . . . just perhaps . . . God also expects us to depend less on Him than on our own resolve and intelligence, gifts which come directly from Him. I think of Antioch. We rejected the advice of General Tatikios and others to seek refuge from winter storms in nearby forts and instead decided to rely on the Lord's protection by camping outside the city. We endured unspeakable hardships and many deaths for that decision." I chose to ignore Godfrey's foolish assault on the walls of Constantinople three years earlier. "My Lord, I fear tomorrow's assault is reckless and is doomed."

Godfrey nodded. For an instant I thought I had reached him. That hope was quickly dashed. "The council has decided. We shall learn tomorrow what is God's Will."

At daybreak all the crusader armies were gathered before a wall close to Herod's Gate. We had but one ladder. No siege engines, not even wicker pavises behind which our archers could take cover. For hours our archers unleashed their arrows against the defenders on the ramparts while foot soldiers hurled spears but to little effect, all trying to dodge the flurry of arrows from the defenders. Then we placed a ladder against the outer wall and Tancred's knights began climbing up, the first Raimbaud of Chartres. On reaching the top, as he grasped the rampart's edge to pull himself up, a Saracen soldier drew his sword and severed Raimbaud's arm. He fell back to the ground below, dead. The initial enthusiasm for the attack, believing we were under God's protection, vanished. We withdrew to shouts and jeers from the Saracens. We suffered many casualties that day, martyrs not to God but to blind, credulous folly. May Our Lord grant them peace in heaven.

Despondence and Deliverance

Two days later the princes met in council. Godfrey asked me to attend, though I was uncertain of his reason which he didn't offer. For Bishop Adhémar I had served as a scribe taking notes on wax tablets as reference for his ceaseless letters to Rome and elsewhere. But by now all my tablets either were lost or so scratched and defaced that they were no longer serviceable. Godfrey required no such record. I sensed a change of mood among the princes, their earlier euphoria and confidence supplanted with melancholy. Not a single word about the previous assault was uttered as though by not mentioning it the painful memory would be erased. Predictably, early in deliberations Count Raymond invoked reliance on God's providence and faith. Godfrey quickly interrupted. "My dear Count," he said in an undisguised patronizing tone, "I believe our best course is to rely on our own resolve and intelligence. Whether God aids us is in His hands alone." Godfrey *had* listened to me. The princes had to confront the dismal reality that faith alone would not enable them to take this formidable city. Success depended on a practical solution: siege engines. Prayer, fasting, and alms were not mentioned. Yet, as discussions progressed the princes' despondency only deepened. We lacked matériel, especially wood but also tools and the skills with which to build sturdy towers and especially mangonels and a battering ram. Worse, food was growing scarce. Most threatening of all was lack of water, thirst exacerbated by incessant winds and insufferable heat. No plan emerged from the meeting because no plan was conceivable. The only "strategy" I could discern, if I may generously use that term, was to wait. But wait for what?

Two days passed and the army's mood only darkened. We scoured the fields and orchards around Jerusalem for what wood we could find to build scaling ladders. But ladders alone could not succeed in crossing a moat and two immense walls, each taller than the other. It seemed hopeless. The day was June 17, ten days since arriving at Jerusalem. I had just completed mass with Godfrey when a rider galloped up to his tent without dismounting and shouted "Duke Godfrey, help has come. Ships are now docking in Jaffa's harbor. They're Christian!" We both rushed outside. The rider was almost breathless, his horse wheezing and covered with sweat. "My Lord, there are six ships, two from Genoa, the rest from Anglia. They carry provisions and materials from Constantinople. I have just left the harbor where they're unloading cargo. But you must send help. Saracens are everywhere. I had to evade two patrols." The rider then wheeled his horse around to give the same message to the other princes. Godfrey did not wait. He ordered his adjutant to instruct one of his captains, Raymond of Pilet, to assemble his company and ride posthaste to Jaffa, some twenty miles away, with wagons.

Two days later sailors and wagons laden with heavy beams, rope, adzes, hatches, hammers, nails, rivets, and much else arrived at the crusader camp together with blacksmiths and carpenters, in addition stout and tall masts cannibalized from the ships, useful for constructing the towers. They also brought bread for our hungry soldiers. The return journey had not been without danger. The convoy was attacked by a company of Saracens but fortunately defeated by Raymond Pilet, every Saracen killed, except one. Persuaded by torture, he revealed that al-Afdal was leading a Fatimid relief army to Jerusalem expected in less than two months. The spy was held captive and later rewarded for his intelligence by being hurled from a mangonel against the city's walls on the first day of the assault. We learned too that our ships had barely unloaded their cargo when a Fatimid fleet, there to support al-Afdal's army, arrived at Jaffa and seized the harbor. Our preparations for the siege now assumed urgency. But there was a serious problem—other than the wood transported from the ships no other was available. We were informed by local Christians that small copses of trees could be found about six miles away. However, they proved insufficient for heavy construction. Samaria, we were told, a considerable distance away, contained substantial woodlands. Muslim captives, initially captured for ransom, were dispatched under heavy guard with mules and camels to cut the heavy timber and haul them to Jerusalem. Work began at a swift pace. Logs were hewed and sawed to their proper shape and length; blazing iron forges produced armor, arrowheads, hinges and other metalwork. Priority was given to constructing engines: mangonels, two siege towers, and Godfrey's battering ram. William Embriaco, the Genoese captain, was commissioned by Raymond to build his tower; Gaston of Béarn, a valiant Provencal noble who had defected to Godfrey, to build Godfrey's. Livestock, especially oxen, which had died of thirst were skinned, their hides dried and sewn together for use as protective shields. Women and children gathered twigs and branches in the fields to be woven into wattle shields for pavises, the towers, and Godfrey's penthouse housing his battering ram.

Another Visionary

In early July, during preparations for the siege, Bishop Arnulf called for a meeting of princes and senior clergy. Godfrey knew nothing of the reason but he was wary. I did nothing to allay his suspicions. We all gathered in an open field in front of Arnulf's tent. While waiting, milling about expectantly but uncertain of just what, Arnulf emerged from his tent followed by a priest unknown to me. I was intensely curious why he was present.

"My Lords, your Graces," Arnulf began, "I thank you for answering my summons. We have received an urgent message from Heaven. It was conveyed to Father Peter Desiderius, chaplain to the Count of Die. I shall let him explain. Father Peter . . ."

Peter stepped forward with a slight bow to Arnulf and the assembled nobles and prelates. "Last night I was awakened by a tap on my shoulder. I opened my eyes. Standing over me was our beloved Bishop Adhémar dressed in the purest white cotton raiment, a golden mitre on his head wearing white lambskin gloves. He motioned for me to stand. I was astonished, fearful and trembling. Your Eminence, I exclaimed, is it truly you?"

"'Yes, it is. I bring a message from Our Lord to your army. Victory is at hand. But the Lord is angry at the selfishness and corruption within the army, especially among the princes. At Antioch I warned you that your privations were the result of sin. You heeded the warning and the Turks were defeated. Yet since then you have reverted back to your indolent manners and failure to strictly observe God's Laws.'"

"What would you have us do? I asked the bishop."

"'You must demonstrate your fealty to the Lord. Only then will He be certain of your faithfulness. Fast for three days. Then every prince, knight, soldier, and pilgrim must walk barefoot to the Mount of Olives where Jesus preached and wept over the fate of Jerusalem. Blow your trumpets, beat your drums as did Joshua at Jericho. Shed your tears as you march in joy to this sacred mountain, kneel in prayer, repent your sins. And if you do these things, nine days hence the walls of Jerusalem will fall as did those of Jericho.'"

"'But this is not all,' Bishop Adhémar admonished. 'You seize Muslims and hold them for ransom or sell them on the slave markets. This displeases Our Lord. They are the sons of the wicked Ishmael. They stain the earth with their filth and foul the air of Heaven with their stench. They must be exterminated. Only then will God be satisfied. This is the Word of Our Lord.'"

Peter was finished and stepped back behind Arnulf. It was now Arnulf's turn. "My Lords, you have heard the Word of God. We shall be victorious—after fasting, repentance, and the death of all Muslims. But what after that? There is great anxiety among the prelates assembled here. Jerusalem is a city, yes. The 'Navel of the World' certainly. But it is the *House of God.* Heaven and Jerusalem shall soon be united. It is here that God and His Son shall soon sit on their thrones and judge the pure and the sinful. As Our Lord promised the prophet Zechariah:

> *I will return to Zion and dwell in Jerusalem.*
> *Then Jerusalem will be called the Faithful City,*
> *And the mountain of the Lord Almighty will be called the Holy Mountain.*

"The hour of Judgment is nigh," Arnulf continued. "Jerusalem must be ready for Their Coming. It cannot be governed by a king. It can be ruled only by a devout minister of the Lord, a patriarch." I fully understood who Arnulf had in mind as the "devout minister of the Lord".

From the prelates there followed vigorous nodding and murmurs of strong agreement. Reaction from the princes was very different, Tancred in particular whose motive in his response was quickly exposed. "Your Grace," the word "grace" rendered rather disdainfully, "it is *we,* the Soldiers of Christ, who have suffered broken and severed limbs, even death, to reach Jerusalem. And it will be taken, God willing, with more sacrifices—*our* sacrifices. It is *ours* to govern! You priests are adept at receiving confession, distributing communion, and kneeling in prayer. You have no experience in governance. Once Jerusalem falls there will be other Saracen armies to face. How do you priests intend to battle them," his mouth curling in a mocking sneer, "by donning your sacerdotal robes, marching out against charging spearmen throwing hymnals at them as you sing?" With that the princes broke out in laughter, none disguising his mirth.

"We need only the protection of Our Lord," Arnulf retorted. "He is our sword and our armor. The dissolution of God's Kingdom has already begun, By *you*, Lord Tancred. *By you!* In rude defiance of God's Will you seized Bethlehem and with unholy arrogance raised your banner over the Church of the Nativity. This is unendurable. A devious scheme, perfectly transparent to us all, to claim not merely Bethlehem for yourself but Jerusalem as well. You shall renounce this claim immediately, *now!*, and any designs you have on the Holy City. Otherwise you will face God's Judgment and I shall offer no prayer to mitigate your sin."

Tancred's face flushed with anger. "The Bethlehemites came to *me* imploring protection from the Saracens. At great risk to me and my men we chased the heathens out of the town and for that they offered it to me. I shall *not* renounce my claim." Tancred said nothing about his designs on Jerusalem, inadvertent perhaps; or perhaps not. He, like Bohemond and Baldwin, had no inheritance in Italia or Lorraine and, like them, surely had ambitions beyond Bethlehem. The princes were solidly in support of Tancred's objection to clerical rule of Jerusalem. They were less supportive of his refusal to renounce his claim to Bethlehem. He recognized it but was obstinate on the matter nonetheless.

The mood of the council had now turned rancorous, nobles and prelates trying to shout over each other. Godfrey intervened. "My Lords and Your Graces, I propose we defer a decision on this matter of a patriarch. It's premature. Jerusalem has not yet fallen. Let us wait. Tancred," turning to him, "I believe we all agree you must reconsider your action at Bethlehem. That too can wait. Let us concentrate our attention and energies on this siege. In the meantime, however, we have received instructions from Bishop Adhémar for three days of fasting and on the fourth a procession of penance and thanksgiving. The entire army will assemble here in four days and proceed barefooted to the sacred Mount of Olives. There we shall seek God's blessing."

On this, there was finally unanimous agreement. The army gathered except for a few detachments in front of the gates to guard against surprise sorties. The clergy, dressed in their sacerdotal raiments holding crosses aloft, led the procession singing hymns of praise and tearfully calling out the names of saints. As we passed by the walls of Jerusalem, Saracens fired arrows through the battlements, harmlessly for we were out of range, taunted us, running along the wall-walk to continue their invectives, whistling, blowing trumpets, shouting and jeering. Most obscene were soldiers who pulled down their trousers and urinated on crosses hung upside down on the wall. If they believed this would cripple our spirit, they were mistaken. Our will was only fortified. At the summit of the mount we gathered in a half-circle, those in in front sitting as the rest stood, to listen to hortatory orations from Peter the Hermit and Arnulf. This was the first time I had seen Peter since Civitot where he had led his peasants to near total destruction by the Turks. His reputation was so blemished that I assume he had taken refuge among the few followers who remained with him. But now he was reemerging, for better or for ill, from purposeful obscurity, perhaps to rehabilitate his reputation. But it was clear that he had lost none of his masterful eloquence inspiring the spectators with a rousing speech, they responding intermittently with shouts of "*God wills it!*" After him Arnulf spoke. I must confess—though I am conflicted over this admission—that Arnulf was no less eloquent than Peter, he too animating the army with his rhetoric. We returned to our camps, Saracens still abusing us as we walked past, to continue constructing siege engines and preparing for battle.

It was midday, July 10, Duke Godfrey summoned a council. "My Lords," he began. "we have already settled on attacking Jerusalem from two directions: the south at the Gate of Zion under Count Raymond, the north under my command. We need to agree on a date for the assault. My Lord Raymond, perhaps you can begin by reporting on your attack plan."

"William Embriaco has nearly completed construction of a siege tower and mangonels," he answered. "We also have five scaling ladders prepared. But we must fill in the moat otherwise my tower will be unable to close in on the wall."

"How long do you think that will take?" Godfrey asked.

"Three days, I believe. I have begun already paying pilgrims a penny for every three stones they throw in. It will be dangerous for they will be exposed to Saracen bowmen. However, our pavises are now prepared and we have an abundant supply of arrows. Under the archers' covering fire I believe they can manage the work. Yes, three days."

Godfrey nodded approvingly. "I have been constructing my own tower in front of the Tower of David. That is where they expect me to attack and that's where they have placed their mangonels. However, I have a different plan. I shall attack elsewhere, near Herod's Gate. The wall seems weaker there, more susceptible to my battering ram. My engineer, Gaston de Béarn, has built the tower in an ingenious fashion permitting it to be disassembled, transported, and then reassembled with relative ease. On the eve of the assault I shall move the tower, battering ram, and mangonels there. I too must fill in the moat in front of that wall, three days I think. This robs me of complete surprise but my hope is that Iftikhar will be confused as to the real direction of my attack and be forced to split his defenses, especially his mangonels."

"Then when do we launch our attack?" Tancred asked.

"Lord Raymond?" Godfrey turning to him.

"July 13, at daybreak," Raymond answered confidently.

"I agree," Godfrey responded. "Daybreak, three days hence. May God be with us."

Rebecca Slain

For the next three days all crusaders, without distinction of rank, worked night and day both at Herod's Gate and the Gate of Zion carrying stones to fill in the moats, readying our attack. Two days earlier Rebecca passed away. By daybreak of the 13th we were prepared with . . . .

It is now that I, Brother Samuel, must take up Father Oderic's narrative for the subject of Rebecca's fate was too painful for him to relate, extracted by me only with perseverance. I laid my quill down and looked at him in quiet astonishment. "Father Oderic," I exclaimed quite excitedly interrupting him, "I've read your journals. You mentioned nothing of Rebecca's death. And now you pass over it as though it were a mere inflection point, one of many, in your account. She was your *wife*! What happened? You *must* tell me."

Father said nothing, staring at the wall, still and motionless. I waited. He was unable to respond. "Father, what happened to Rebecca?" I insisted. He broke down into sobs, tears flowing uncontrollably, placing his head in his hands, mumbling "my Rebecca, my Rebecca" over and over again. I concluded nothing would be gained further from him that afternoon. "Father, let's resume tomorrow morning," I gently suggested.

Tomorrow came. In the meantime, I had approached Father Sebastian, Prior of La Charité and the one who had so encouraged me to record Father Oderic's pilgrimage to Jerusalem. I cryptically explained to the prior there was a "significant gap" in Father's chronicle though refusing to explain other than it was "sensitive". I revealed no more. Sebastian offered a practical solution, not one I expected, that the priory's cellar contained a special vintage of wine produced three years earlier, flavored with spices and cherries grown in one of the priory's deaneries, reserved only for visiting prelates. He thought on this occasion it would be well served to "loosen Father Oderic's tongue" as he put it. "The cellarer will help you."

Usually, Father was punctual in meeting with me but not this day. He clearly was dreading it. He finally walked into the room, bleary-eyed, stumbling for his chair, settling in.

"Father," I said, "you appear ill. Are you alright?" He merely nodded in response focusing his eyes on the blank wall in front of him. I was determined to pursue this inquiry. I filled two beakers of wine, one for me, the other for him.

"Father, you know how relentless I am. I approach this subject with some disquiet. However, the story is not complete without knowing Rebecca's fate." He sighed, taking another sip of wine, very slowly telling his story which I now report faithfully as given in his own words:

In the days preceding the assault, he began, Rebecca and I joined women, children, and elderly men in collecting stout twigs and branches, dried cane stalks as well, to be used as wattle. Rebecca had been a seamstress in Mainz and was particularly adept at weaving them into sheets later to be tied together. I lacked such talent, more proficient at skinning the hide of dead animals, a rather disagreeable task, some having putrefied under the hot Palestinian sun but I became accustomed to the odor. It was July 11, two days before the assault. Duke Godfrey, following our simple mass in the morning, asked me to join him on the top floor of his tower. He had witnessed my combat with Thomas of Marle and heard of other exploits, some rather exaggerated with the retelling. He needed a man of my "martial skills", he explained, beside him. Of course, I was gratified by his confidence but politely refused. These masses which I performed, albeit somewhat perfunctory, revived nostalgic memories of my life at La Charité as a priest serving the Lord. I wanted to be free of my reputation as a "warrior-priest" and become simply a priest once again, albeit a married one. How I could accomplish that yet eluded me but I would never leave Rebecca.

We suffered from lack of water, as did others. Even though there were daily convoys to springs miles from the city, the water had to be distributed amongst all of Godfrey's soldiers and camp followers. There was never enough. You cannot imagine our thirst. It drove men mad. The only source within walking distance of the city was the Pool of Siloam. Soldiers and pilgrims thronged there, animals too, at night to avoid Saracen arrows. The weak crawled to the pool's edge begging for help, a simple ladle of water. They were ignored. Some died right there, their hands dangling in the pool. The soldiers fared better though but little.

I was without choice and decided to join a small detachment of

Lorrainer knights, five in number, escorting several camels with their drivers, empty wineskins tied over the camels' flanks. Saracen patrols had attacked previous missions. Protection was required. I debated within myself whether to ride my mule, leaving Rebecca and child in the coach. Rebecca insisted that they accompany me despite my warning of danger. She was ever fearless and did not want to be left alone. To my profound regret, which I shall take with me to my grave and beyond, I acquiesced. I knew better and that compounds my guilt. We reached a spring, probably eight miles from Jerusalem, feeding into a small pool, no more than ten feet in circumference but deep with sufficient water to meet our needs. I positioned our coach thirty or so paces away, on level ground. While feeling secure in the protection of our guards, I nonetheless slung *Iskender* over my shoulder despite Rebecca's gentle mocking of my fearfulness. I took our two wineskins to the pool filling them, careful to avoid leeches which inhabited these pools; if swallowed they clung to throats chocking the drinkers. Many perished. I had just filled them and was returning, a skin in each hand. It was then that I saw seven Saracen horsemen gallop into our area. Two dismounted; the others drawing their swords and from horseback attacked our knights. My attention was drawn to them. I held onto the wineskins uncertain how to react. Then I heard a woman scream from within the coach. It was Rebecca! I dropped the skins, unholstered my maul, and raced to the coach, up the two steps, the door already open, rushing inside. I roared at what I saw, my fury indescribable.

Father Oderic then went silent, wiping tears away with the cuff of his habit. He appeared to seek solitude, reaching back to pull the cowl over his head, retreating into a very dark place, only his pained face, glistening eyes, and tightly drawn mouth visible. He had by now emptied his beaker of wine which I refilled, taking another draught, a deep one, just staring at me, more through me as though I were invisible. "Father," I asked anxiously, "*what* happened?" He now returned to the moment, his head still covered, and continued his narrative:

Inside the coach were two Saracens. One of them was just . . . just . . . withdrawing his sword from . . . Rebecca's belly. She had placed both hands over the wound, looking down at it, and then up at me, her face wracked in pain and horror, and fell back onto the bed. The Saracen had heard me enter and turned to face me, his bloodied sword pointed directly at my chest, holding it steadily. I was oblivious to the danger. I had but one thought: to kill this monster. With my arm I pushed the blade aside and thrust *Iskender*'s spike into his throat, driving it ever deeper. He fell back over Rebecca, blood spurting over me. I had no time to pull him off for I had to deal with the other Saracen. Our child was lying in a crib made for us by one of the Genoese carpenters, crying woefully. Both of the Saracen's hands were wrapped around his sword's hilt, raised straight up to his head, ready to plunge it into our child, not yet baptized and thus denied the prospect of Eternal Salvation. In that instant the Saracen saw me before he could strike. He had no room to swing and instead began jabbing his sword back and forth, I flicking each aside. My sole thought was to kill this beast as quickly as I could and attend to Rebecca. Just as I had parried the third or fourth I thrust *Iskender's* spike into the Saracen's chest hoping that its thin point might pierce his chain mail's links. It didn't, only surprising him. That gave me the advantage, for only an instant. I made a hammer blow to his knee. He buckled bending slightly forward. Before he could right himself I struck him in the side of his head. Dazed he stumbled backwards. I pummeled his head from right to left and then again from left to right until he fell unconscious to the floor.

Father took another long draught of wine, emptying the beaker, I refilling it, and then continued his story:

I pulled the first Saracen off Rebecca. She was still conscious, lying on her back, looking up at the ceiling. Her countenance was serene, almost sublime, as though reconciled to her death. I knelt beside her and placed my hand under her head, gently lifting and turning it to me. My eyes were so filled with tears that she was only a blur though I could feel her own fixed on me. At first she said nothing, her breast heaving, but then began whispering. I bent my ear to her mouth to hear. "Oderic, protect our son. Never leave him. Promise me." Choking with emotion, barely able to speak, I whispered back, "I . . . I . . . I promise." She gave a weak smile, still concentrating her eyes on me, filled with love. And then those deep brown eyes, once sparkling, became blank. With the same tenderness I had lifted her head I lowered it and placed my fingers over her eyelids closing them for an eternal sleep. I was sobbing without restraint, burying my face in her breast. I heard the second Saracen groaning, regaining consciousness. I arose, stepped over to him consumed with a furious rage and began hitting his face and head over and over with my maul, each blow tearing away his flesh, nose, cheeks, then his forehead until I heard his skull splinter. He looked as though he had been attacked by a pack of savage, ravenous dogs. I then turned to the other Saracen, knelt over him, my knees astride his waist, both my hands on *Iskender's* hilt, raising it above my head and then plunging its spike into his body over and over and over until my fury was spent.

I then heard shouting from outside. I quickly stepped down from the coach to see a battle raging between our knights and the Saracens. One of the Saracen horsed lancers saw me, some twenty paces away, lowered his spear and charged. I had left *Iskender* in the carriage and there was no time to retrieve it. It was of little consequence for my maul likely would have had little effect against his spear. I quickly stepped around the corner of the coach, hugging the wall, my arms fully extended. I heard the lancer pull up his horse in front of the coach's door. He turned his horse and cautiously nudged it forward to follow me. Just as he turned the corner, his spear leveled and extending beyond the side of the coach, the lancer himself not yet visible, I grabbed the spear with both hands yanking it from his hands and with its blunt end rammed it into the lancer's chest with enough force that he fell backward over his horse. As he lay on the ground and before he could rise I flipped the spear and with its sharpened metal point drove it into his chest, once, twice, thrice, more. I don't recall. Like the other two, this Saracen was now a worthy one. Destined for hell.

I was listening intently to Father Oderic's description, furiously scribbling, I'm sure my eyes wide open in bewilderment. "Father, have you no regret, then or now, for these killings. You were a *priest*! A man of God!"

No regrets, he answered. None, he answered coldly, his eyes narrowing as he gave me a piercing look. I would do it again, he said. In that moment I was *not* a priest. I *was* a husband and a father. Perhaps this was not God's punishment. But it was mine. And they paid dearly. Not dearly enough. I am prepared to answer to God.

By now, the Lorrainers had either killed or routed the rest of the Saracens. I pulled the two out of the coach, down the steps onto the ground, leaving them where they lay. Dazed and numb, I retrieved the wineskins, removed my baldric replacing it with a sling, picked up my son placing him in the pouch. He was still wailing despite my efforts to soothe him. I climbed up the coach's perch, shook the reins, and returned to Jerusalem. On the way back there was time to reflect. Why had God deserted me? For my sins? Why should Rebecca have paid for them, not me? I had no answer. My soul was barren.

Burial

On arriving back to our camp I wiped down the interior of the coach, splattered with blood as it was, Rebecca lying peacefully on the couch. I was familiar, though only casually, with Jewish burial ritual from my years in Mainz and tried my best to follow them, though without benefit of a rabbi to advise or from whom to receive comfort. Rebecca's body had to be buried as quickly as possible and in a simple coffin, an *aron*, without metal—*For you are dust, and unto dust you shall return.* I went immediately to the worksite of the Genoese craftsmen all putting finishing touches to Godfrey's tower.

One of them was leaning against the tower, resting. I introduced myself.

"Yes, I know who you are, Father," he answered smiling though I detected a hint of sorrow.

"Master Carpenter, I apologize for interrupting your work. However I require a coffin, preferably of pine. Could you build one?"

He answered quickly, "Yes. We are well supplied with pine planks. When do you need it?"

"By tomorrow," I answered, "but there is a special requirement: It must be built without nails, no metal at all. Is this possible?"

He hesitated, thinking. "Hmm. Father, we have all heard of your wife's death. Terrible. News spreads quickly. Stories about you too, your exploits are well known, even to us Genoese. Yes, that will take more time. But as it happens I have extra pegs and a fine auger. Sharpened it just yesterday, I did. I'll have to start immediately. It should be ready by tomorrow, midday."

I expressed my deep appreciation which he dismissed with a nod, smile, and wave of his hand. I returned to the coach to perform the *taharah*, the washing and purification of Rebecca's body. I cleansed her wound, the blood now dried, then her head, arms and legs, finally gently ladling water over her body for purification, purified too with my tears I hoped. After ablutions I dried her body with a linen cloth and wrapped her in a shroud, not white as Jewish custom prescribed but a gray woolen blanket, all I had.

At midday I returned to fetch the coffin. It was ready. "I would like to help you carry it, Father," the carpenter said apologetically, "but completing the tower is my urgent task. It must be ready for tomorrow." I nodded, expressing gratitude for his work and offered him coin which he declined. I began dragging the coffin over the ground with much difficulty. I had gone only a few paces when two of Godfrey's captains, Gilbert of Tournai and Roland, the junior officer, passed by. They too had heard of the previous day's combat and of Rebecca's death. Without a word, they picked up the coffin and carried it to the coach, I following silently. They laid the coffin just below the coach's steps. I was about to enter to carry Rebecca out. Gilbert shook his head. "We'll do it." They lifted Rebecca up respectfully and carefully carried her down lowering her into the coffin. "Roland, we'll need two spades, a hammer, nails for the lid, and two ropes," Gilbert ordered. I countermanded that instruction. "No nails." He soon returned.

It would have been Rebecca's wish to be interred in a Jewish cemetery but the Jewish Quarter was behind Jerusalem's walls. I had no choice but to bury her here. Not far away I saw a solitary scrub bush, the only living plant in this barren field, with a magnificent, unobstructed view of Jerusalem. It was there Gilbert and Roland dug the grave, Gilbert forbidding me from helping. The ground was hard, dry as bone, almost the texture of mortar. Yet both men dug without complaint, their faces dripping in sweat. Once the grave was dug, I picked up the lid to place it over the coffin, lingering for a moment to gaze at Rebecca, my farewell. I placed pegs in the lid's holes and began hammering, too often missing, my eyes so bleary with tears. Gilbert offered to relieve me. I just shook my head. It was my job to finish. Gilbert and Roland lowered her into the grave with ropes. We had no headstone, instead gathering rocks and piling them one over the other. We each took turns filling the grave, I tamping it down with a shovel's broad blade. The three of us, my son in my arms, stood silently over the grave. I tried to perform the funeral service, the *Levayah*, as well as I could relying on distant memories. I recited in Hebrew the single passage from the *Kaddish*, the only one I remembered: "*May the Lord be blessed and praised, glorified and exalted*." Then the 23rd Psalm, the "Lord's Prayer," the soldiers responding with "Amen". Finally, the *Hesped*, eulogy, simple and brief, my voice breaking and capable of no more than a statement of my undying love delivered without the rhetorical flourishes as a rabbi would have. I concluded with Proverbs: "*A wife of noble character is worth more than rubies*" and with the Jewish funeral benediction, also given in Hebrew: "*May Hashem comfort you among the mourners of Zion and Jerusalem.*" I knew in time her gravesite would disappear from wind and under sand but I took comfort that Rebecca was now in the bosom of God's Love. I hoped only that she would forgive my derelictions from Jewish custom. Gilbert and Roland shook my hand expressing words of condolences and left.

I interrupted his narrative. "Father, have you thought of her since? After all, it's been thirty years."

He sighed. "Memories are a curse. Not a day passes without grieving.

Every year at night, on the anniversary of her death, I light a candle allowing it to burn until it's extinguished in its own melted tallow."

* * *

Immediately following I went to Godfrey's tent. "My Lord, I can no longer serve as your chaplain and priest. I shall become your warrior and join you in the tower." I gave no explanation nor did he ask for one. He seemed to know. I wished for only one thing: to slay Muslims, without mercy."

Precipice of Defeat

All through the night of July 12 we pulled Godfrey's tower, battering ram, and three mangonels with horses and mules to Herod's Gate. I left my son in the care of the same midwife who had developed a close relationship with Rebecca. She had heard of her death and was pleased to assist. I fully understood our son was now half an orphan and the consequences for him if I did not survive. But there was a debt to settle and I was committed to settling it. All was in readiness for the next day's assault. Both Godfrey's and Raymond's towers were impressive: some sixty feet tall exceeding the height of the walls by perhaps ten, three stories, all sides except the rear protected with wattle shields and hardened leather soaked in vinegar. We had been warned by Christian refugees that the Saracens had developed some flammable liquid, not Greek Fire but similar, which could be doused only with vinegar. Godfrey's battering ram was no less impressive. The bosson was an enormous log, massive, the largest I've ever seen, hewed with axes to a rounded point and faced with iron newly forged by blacksmiths from Anglia. It was housed in a penthouse and suspended by ropes from a transverse beam just under its roof. The penthouse was set on a wheeled platform with an angular roof and walls shielded, like the towers, with wattle and vinegar-soaked hardened animal skin. Scaling ladders were in readiness, on this occasional sturdily constructed, the crusaders now having learned lessons from previous assaults with faulty ladders unable to bear the weight of soldiers.

At dawn the siege of Jerusalem began. I stood with Godfrey, Robert of Flanders, Robert of Normandy, and Tancred next to the tower watching as the assault unfolded, waiting for the battering ram to breach the outer wall, the tower then to be pushed through to the inner wall. The sky was clear and cloudless, the air cool. Sweltering heat would follow soon. Just as the sun rose the attack was announced with the blare of trumpets, beating of drums, and priests loudly singing hymns of praise. Archers carrying bows or crossbows shouting "God *wills it!*" sprinted forward, their pavise shields covered with wattle carried by pavisiers moving into position in two lines behind each other. Three mangonels on wheeled platforms had been pushed forward and then secured by ropes and spikes hammered into the ground to steady their aim, ox-drawn wagons filled with stones collected during the days before following closely. The archers and mangonels opened fire on defenders standing on the ramparts. Under this cover, the penthouse was pushed slowly over the moat, now filled in, to the outer wall, Saracen mangonels hurling stones against it, fortunately bouncing harmlessly off the roof and walls protected as they were by wattle and hardened leather. Soon, the ram was in place against the outer wall, too close for the enemy's mangonels to be effective. Inside the penthouse soldiers grabbed a rope swinging the ram in unison, back and forth, shouting "*heave! heave!*" until the correct momentum had been achieved then flinging it against the wall, the ground shuddering with each blow. The Saracens began dropping heavy stones on the penthouse and throwing buckets of a gelatinous substance over the roof, I assumed the mysterious liquid which the Christians had warned us about, followed by flurries of flaming arrows in an attempt to set the roof on fire. But the leather skins, freshly soaked in vinegar, were impervious.

Godfrey's ruse had succeeded, at least in part. Of the five Saracen mangonels initially placed on the ramparts at the Tower of David, Iftikhar was able to move only two, lowered down the wall, through Jerusalem's narrow streets, and then hoisted up again to the ramparts at Herod's Gate before the assault began. The battle raged all day, the northern wall slowly cracking. Raymond had made less progress. Iftikhar was prepared for his attack, stringing bags stuffed with straw and other chaff over the wall cushioning it from Raymond's mangonel stones. With the advantage of height the Saracen mangonels silenced two. Frustrated by his inability to inflict damage on the wall, he ordered an attack with scaling ladders but this too was easily repulsed. By twilight it was clear that we had gained little advantage. Our success appeared to depend on Godfrey's battering ram. We would have to wait for morning.

The battle began again at daybreak to trumpets, drums, and the cheering of priests as the day before. The wall had weakened from the previous day's attack. The soldiers manning the ram redoubled their efforts, one blow after another. Slowly, the cracks began to widen until blocks were tumbling down. We had now breached the wall to loud "*hurrahs!*" from the soldiers inside the penthouse. Godfrey ordered the soldiers assigned to the tower to ready themselves for the push through to the inner wall. But the breach was not large enough for the tower. It would have to be widened. The penthouse was pulled back and then turned slightly to the left and pushed forward, continuing its strikes until finally widening the breach. In the meantime Saracen defenders furiously poured flammable liquid over the penthouse, shooting lit arrows. Under the hot Palestinian sun the vinegar-soaked leather had dried out. The penthouse was now on fire. Wineskins of vinegar had been stored at the back of the penthouse. Soldiers lugging the skins climbed up onto the roof dousing the fire, some falling from Saracen arrows. Soldiers inside the penthouse began pulling it back to allow the tower through the breach. The path to the inner wall was almost cleared when one of its wheels rolled over a particularly large rock breaking it. The penthouse was now immobile. There was not enough room for the tower to squeeze through. Godfrey's tower was blocked. The penthouse would have to be burned. Our soldiers frantically ripped off wattle from its walls, gathered it into piles and lit it on fire. Now, the Saracens, so eager earlier to burn the penthouse, wanted to save it and from their ramparts poured water over the roof successfully extinguishing most of the fire, the rest still burning. Night fell. Our second day's assault had failed. This was a disaster.

That evening Godfrey called for a council of nobles allied with him and all their captains. Godfrey came directly to the point.

"I fear we are on the brink of defeat. Count Raymond through a messenger informed me that his tower has suffered such damage from Saracen mangonels it had to be withdrawn from the field. It will take several days, likely more, to repair. Several of his mangonels are either destroyed or barely functional. There is small hope he can smash through the walls on the south. Our circumstances are little better. The penthouse has partially burned and in any event is immobilized. Our own tower sits idly. The situation has become worse," Godfrey continued. "The army is demoralized. This evening, before council, I strolled through my camp and of others. I heard wails and cries of despair. I thought at first these merely the bawling of pilgrims. Yes, that too. But most came from our own soldiers! Many believe the cause is lost, that God has deserted us. They are also suffering cruelly from thirst. There is talk of desertion. Indeed, a company of Provençals has already left for the Jordan River, to be rebaptized I'm told, and will then go to Jaffa to take a ship back home. This is just the beginning, I fear."

"But what about Adhémar's promise that our victory was certain?" Gilbert of Tournai asked. "I heard Peter Desiderius say so. Have we indeed been deserted by God?"

"We already have too many visionaries in our army," Godfrey replied dismissively. "I would prefer more warriors. God will aid us if we first rely on our own resources." Turning to Gaston de Béarn, "Captain, you built the tower. Your assessment?"

Gaston paused to gather his thoughts. We waited anxiously. "My Lord, unless the penthouse is either removed or completely burned it will be impossible to pass through the breach. That is the simple answer. I have no other."

"It's burning now, is it not?" Godfrey asked.

"Yes," Gaston answered. "But the bosson is huge and of green wood. It will take days before it's burned away. In the meantime the Saracens will surely repair the outer wall."

"We don't have time," Godfrey responded impatiently. "The Fatimid army will be here in less than a month, maybe sooner. Is there *nothing* we can do?"

Gaston pondered. "Then we must pull the penthouse out. I see no alternative. Understand, my Lord, the risks are substantial. Our men and mules will be within range of Saracen mangonels and bows. You may be sure they won't ignore us."

"Does anyone have a better solution?" Godfrey asked. None did. "We have journeyed for four years, suffered unimaginably, overcome enormous challenges, defeated our enemies against terrible odds. Yet, here we are, victory within our grasp but on the precipice of defeat. We can no longer rely on Count Raymond's army. Success depends on us alone. We can't afford to wait. There will be more desertions. We move the penthouse tonight."

Work began under a crescent moon, slender, just enough light to see, no more. Ten mules were harnessed with ropes attached to their breast collars in a file two abreast following each other. Genoese craftsmen, who understood the precise points on the axles and platform of the penthouse to tie the ropes, grabbed their ends and raced to the penthouse protected by pavises carried over their heads. Saracen mangonels and archers flew into action, the pavises offering little protection against the stones hurled against them. Two Genoese fell before they could reach the penthouse. The ropes were tied and they raced back to safety. The Saracens then concentrated their arrows on the mules, the mangonels unable to redirect their aim. Three mules fell. They were unharnessed, their ropes retied to the others, and then pulled out of the way. Saracen arrows rained down; darkness was our principal protection. I watched with growing anxiety as the mules struggled to pull the penthouse despite curses and lashes from the muleteers. The situation was desperate. Gaston shouted at the soldiers waiting beside the tower waving them over, *"Take the ropes and pull!"* They rushed forward, I as well, all braving the arrows, grabbing ropes and pulling. Slowly the penthouse moved, inches, then three feet. Just enough.

Jerusalem Falls

Just as the sun rose above the crests of the Judean hills, the path was cleared to the inner wall. I joined the soldiers inside the tower pushing it with every ounce of energy we could muster past the smoldering penthouse and through the wall's breach. We no longer feared the enemy's mangonels as they were all placed on the outer wall and posed no threat. Saracen archers on the ramparts of the inner wall unleashed barrage after barrage of arrows but doing little damage against the tower's shield of wattle and hides. We had closed in on the wall, only three feet distant, close enough to lower the drawbridge. I had joined Godfrey, his brother Eustace, Robert of Flanders, Robert of Normandy, and Tancred on the tower's top story, a small detachment of Godfrey's archers with us. From narrow slits they fired on the Saracens, Godfrey showing unusual skill for a nobleman with his crossbow. The archers removed the wattle and leather covering the tower's drawbridge ready to lower it over the ramparts.

Their attention was focused on the Saracen archers without noticing a log attached by two chains descending down the wall to the foot of our tower. I saw it but was unable to discern its purpose until I saw a Saracen archer shoot a flaming arrow at the log setting it instantly on fire. In only moments the tower's base was burning. The log had been soaked in that mysterious flammable liquid. I could hear soldiers' shrieks from below. I sprinted down the tower steps to the first story. They were fleeing the tower, the quilted gambeson jacket of one ablaze. Each story had been supplied with skins of vinegar and water. I quickly threw water over him but didn't wait to see the effect, turning my attention to the log. The tower's wattle shield immediately in front of the log was now on fire. I kicked it out of the way, grabbed skins of vinegar pouring one after the other over the log quickly extinguishing it. The danger was not over for the upright posts supporting the tower's structure were now burning. In moments the entire tower would be in flames. I scrambled back up the steps to the top floor. "*Lower the drawbridge! Now! The tower's on fire!*" I shouted. Godfrey looked at me in astonishment but in that moment smoke was drifting up through the floor. I didn't wait, rushing to the drawbridge, unfastened the heavy hooks holding it in place and pushed it over onto one of the rampart's merlons. With a loud shout of "*Jerusalem! Jerusalem!*" Gilbert of Tournai was first across the bridge. He was felled immediately by a Saracen arrow but the tower's archers followed him across, their swords drawn, slashing wildly at the Saracens. Soldiers from the second floor raced up the steps and crossed the bridge. In the meantime a company of Godfrey's soldiers had set scaling ladders against the wall and were climbing up, some already on the ramparts. We now controlled the wall. The Saracen defenders took flight, fleeing down the steps to the street below and to the safety, they thought, of the Dome of the Rock and the al-Aqsa Mosque. One of Godfrey's soldiers opened Herod's Gate and another Zion's Gate. Crusader soldiers poured in beginning their rampage.

Vengeance and a Vision

What followed was a savage massacre, on a scale worse even than Antioch or Maarat as if that were possible. As the crusaders passed through one street to another they slaughtered all in their path without distinction, often pausing to slit open the bellies of their victims, dead or alive, in search of bezants, no life spared, no opportunity for pillage ignored. And I was a participant, an eager one. May the Lord forgive me. I was among the first across the drawbridge. I chased a Saracen soldier down the wall-walk and struck him with my maul's hammer; he tumbled over to the pavement below. Without stopping I attacked the soldier running just in front also hammering him over the wall-walk. I was not satisfied. There were more Muslims to kill. I scampered down the steps to the street and saw three Saracen soldiers fleeing, one behind the other, down a particularly narrow street. I gave chase, undeterred by the odds, my hatred white-hot. I caught up with the first, he having no sense of being pursued, and thrust *Iskender's* spike through his back. He fell screaming like a gelded boar. I leapt over him and without pausing chased the second. He had heard the shrieks of his companion, stopped to face me but before he could raise his spear I was on top of him, my hammer striking his forehead followed by another to his cheekbone, crushing it. He too fell. The third had turned and was ready for me, scimitar drawn. While I was confident in *Iskender's* ability to handle this weapon, I did not want to engage in lengthy swordplay—thrust, parry, thrust, parry. I was impatient. There were more Muslims to kill and I wanted my share. I holstered *Iskender*, picked up the second Saracen's spear, gripped its haft with both hands, raised it waist-high, and rushed screaming "*murderers!*". He was so startled by the ferocity of my attack that he failed to sidestep. The point of my spear penetrated his chest. A third heathen dead. I welcomed their journey to hell.

I was filled with bloodlust, maniacal and unforgiving. I ran down the street to find more Muslims, indifferent to whether they were men, women, or children. They were the same to me. At the end of the street I saw two young women huddled together sitting against a wall, each wrapping her arms tightly around a child, weeping piteously begging for their lives. I did not understand their language. I understood their pleas. I didn't care. I unholstered *Iskender* and with it motioned for them to stand. I stepped forward to attack but then hesitated. They were identical twins with a striking resemblance to Rebecca in age, beauty, complexion and their children the same age as ours. What I shall relate now will sound extraordinary. I have always dismissed visions as the concoctions of either fevered or too often self-serving imaginations. Yet in that instant of hesitation I experienced my own. It was Rebecca, her face less than an arm's length from me, somewhat indistinct, gauzy, as though shrouded in gossamer-thin silk. She said nothing, merely smiling. I reached out to stroke her cheek but my hand slid through her face as though it were vapor yet without distorting her visage. She continued to smile. "Oderic, my dearest. Enough. Return to be the man I love. I'm waiting for you. Someday. But not now." She faded and then disappeared before I could respond. And in that moment all my hate and anger drained from my soul as quickly as she did. I have no rational explanation. I holstered *Iskender* and surveyed the street. There was an open door of what appeared to be a private home no more than a few paces away, the inhabitants having probably fled. I spoke to the women in a tender, reassuring voice, beckoning them to follow me and pointing to the door. They did though still trembling. The first needed encouragement to enter. I placed my hand on her lower back gently nudging her through.

The second was about to follow when I heard a loud, angry voice behind me. I turned. It was a Provençal soldier. "What are you doing?" he demanded. "I have already claimed this house. You can see my mark," pointing to an "X" chalked on the door. "Get them out!" He then paused, reflecting. "Now that I think on it, they can stay. They're handsome wenches, even for heathens. They will please me mightily." By now my bloodlust was spent. I had a surfeit of death. But this time I was without choice. I could threaten this soldier, even beat him; I knew he would return. These women would never be safe. I pulled out *Iskender* for what I hoped would be his final service and stepped forward briskly. The Norman drew his sword but clearly had not expected this contest. Nor was he prepared. He made a swing at me but before he could bring the sword back around for another I stepped inside and thrust my spike straight though an eye driving it to his brain. I did so without anger but equally without remorse. I was insensate to feeling except for these women. They had been watching the combat fearfully from the door. I returned to them. They were still trembling but I sensed gratitude. I took each, tenderly holding their cheeks with both hands and kissed their foreheads. With a gesture of my hand I instructed them to bolt the door. They nodded. I left the "X" on the door hopeful that marauding crusaders would respect it as was their custom.

Escape Through Hezekiah's Tunnel

Physically exhausted, I leaned back against the door, *Iskender* still in my hand, my arm hanging down, to rest. I could think of nothing else than Rebecca. Was she an apparition, an illusion, the result of torrid heat or feverish delirium? Despite these doubts, I knew in my heart that Rebecca had returned to me, if only for a thrice. In the midst of this reverie my thoughts flowed to Isaac ben Judah and Miriam, still in the city. The memory of the wanton killing of Jews in Mainz had remained fresh. I knew their fate at crusader hands. I had to save them. I raced to the Jewish Quarter, in Spicery Row from what Bernard had told me. The Jewish Quarter was west of the Temple of Solomon, visible to me over city roofs. I ran there. As I entered the quarter frantic Jews were streaming in the same direction.

I grabbed one by the shoulder "Where is Spicery Row. I seek Isaac ben Judah."

"Leave me!" he shouted back. "We're taking refuge from you Latin butchers in our synagogue. He'll be there." He hurried off to join the others.

I followed them to the synagogue, a single-storied rectangular building faced with brick, just as unimposing as the synagogue in Mainz but much larger. There was a throng of Jews in front of its twin doors all desperately shoving through the entrance. I pushed my way in, the Jews seeing my armor and maul making way for me fearful I was yet another crusader marauder. I shouted Isaac's and Miriam's names but my voice was lost in the clamor within.

I continued to push through until I spotted Isaac. "Isaac," I shouted over the din, "it's me, Oderic. 'Moshe'" using the name Isaac had given me on the road from Mainz, hoping to jog his memory. "You and Miriam are in danger. You must get out. *Follow me!*"

Isaac looked back at me in confusion. He hesitated. Then his faced opened into a broad smile. "Moshe, *it's you!* You've come for us."

"Yes. No time to explain. You must leave. Trust me!"

Isaac did as I ordered, grabbing Miriam by the hand as I elbowed my way back out. We had just passed through the doors when I heard it slam shut and bolted behind me. I looked out into the square facing the synagogue. I immediately understood the reason. Crusader soldiers were running to the synagogue carrying loose faggots in their arms and then spreading them in front of the door, another with a lit torch in his hand. The synagogue was to be burned with all the Jews in it! I could hear terrified screams behind me but there was nothing I could do. All perished.

Our only hope of escape was through Hezekiah's Tunnel. We hurried toward the Temple of Solomon through narrow, winding streets, up and down a myriad number of steps, arriving finally just below the al-Aqsa Mosque as Bernard had directed. I could see above me, on the plaza of the Temple of Solomon, crusader soldiers swarming like flies over a dead carcass. But where was the tunnel's entrance? Isaac was rather infirm, walking too slowly. There was no time to lose. I had to find the tunnel quickly. "Isaac," grabbing his shoulders quite firmly, "stay here. Don't move! I'll be back. *Wait!*" With that I dashed through the streets, a confusing labyrinth unlike the orderly streets of Constantinople arranged as a grid, up one and down another hunting desperately for anything resembling a tunnel entrance. I saw none and was about to abandon the search when I saw close-by a Saracen family, father, mother, and two daughters, in front of a small archway of stone, no more than three feet high, partially obscured by brush, ivy, and rubble. The father, doubtless trying to escape rampaging crusaders, was roughly shoving his family through attempting to hush the cries of his daughters. I watched until they disappeared into the opening. This had to be Hezekiah's Tunnel. I returned with Isaac and Miriam and led them through the tunnel's entrance. "It will be dark and narrow," I warned them, "and we'll have to feel our way through but there's no choice." Miriam was shaking with fear, Isaac whispering encouragement in her ear.

We bent over and stepped through the archway. Once inside, the tunnel's ceiling opened and we were able to walk upright. But only a few feet from the entrance it turned sharply to the left. We entered a dense, impenetrable darkness, dank, cold and perfectly silent except for muted echoes of children's cries in the distance. "Isaac, take my hand," reaching behind me with my left as he fumbled to find mine. "Miriam, take Isaac's." I stepped forward carefully probing the wall, my fingers feeling the scars incised into the rock from pickaxes cut centuries before. Before each step I gingerly tapped the floor for steps descending down into the tunnel, certain we would encounter some. At times the tunnel walls became so constricted we were forced to sidle through, lightly scraping our backs. I finally felt an edge in the stone floor, the toe of my shoe extending downward. "Be careful. Steps." Progress was slow, interminable I thought. Soon we began wading through a stream of water fed from the Gihon Springs, at first up to our knees then gradually subsiding to our ankles. I began to wonder whether I had missed in the darkness a side tunnel leading to the egress. Deciding this was a dead-end and that we needed to retrace our steps, I saw to my joy a glimmer of light ahead and then an opening. We emerged into a courtyard paved in hewn stone surrounding a cistern, three steps leading down to it. The Pool of Siloam.

The Saracen family was nowhere to be seen, surely having hurried off to find safety elsewhere. The yard was full of people desperately drinking from the pool, some on their knees with faces in the water, others greedily drinking from cups or ladles dipped into the water or filling wineskins. They paid no attention to us. Miriam had calmed down, soothed by the warm sun and the pool's courtyard. Both she and Isaac were exhausted. I knew they lacked the strength to walk further. They would not be safe until we reached Godfrey's camp where they would be secure under my protection. I ran to the camp, harnessed the coach's mule grazing on what little grass was available, fetched them and returned to my camp. When I opened the coach's door, they were both slumbering. I let them rest.

Plunder in the Service of God

I returned to the city. I wasn't quite sure of the reason. My thirst for killing had been sated. Curiosity perhaps? Or possibility my promise to Prior Damian that I would write a complete account of the crusade, not yet completed. The Saracens had taken refuge at the Temple of Solomon. I headed there, stepping around or over bodies lying on the streets, some dead, others dying. I ascended the steps, coming to the Dome of the

Rock. I gazed at this marvelous structure, its exquisite architecture rivaling anything I saw in Constantinople, octangular walls faced with blue and red ceramic tiles and the dome covered with gleaming copper. To my surprise, I saw perhaps three hundred Saracens—men, women, and children—standing precariously on a ledge that encircled the dome at its base. Flying above the dome was Tancred's banner. The doors of the shrine were wide open, Tancred's soldiers recognizable by their crest hurrying out clasping treasure in their arms—candelabra, vases, ewers all of silver and whatever else of value that could be easily pilfered.

I walked inside, the interior as breathtaking as the exterior, reminding me of the Basilica of Saint Sophia. The shrine encased a broad, flat rock in the center where Abraham was said to have laid his son Isaac to be sacrificed and where the Muslim prophet Mohammed was supposed to have ascended to heaven. The rock was surrounded by two colonnades, an ambulatory between them, supporting the dome, each column veneered with marble its veins sinuous in colors of green and red on the bottom half and mosaic tiles of purple, yellow, and red on top. Splendid mosaics and rich tapestries of silk covered the walls, none depicting a human or animal form, instead geometric designs interspersed with inscriptions in Arabic script, passages from the Muslim Koran I presumed, each framed with precious gems. Light streamed into the interior from windows at the base of the dome. I was stunned by its opulence.

Suspended from the ceiling by silver chains were chandeliers of gold and eight huge lamps of silver. Tancred's men stood on scaling ladders unhooking the vessels and removing the tapestries to eager hands below. Other soldiers were prying out precious gems with their daggers. Tancred was supervising the dismantling of the shrine. I walked over to him.

"Oh Oderic, what a marvelous day for the Lord. His will has been done and Jerusalem now belongs to Him."

I gave a perfunctory response. "Yes, God's will indeed."

"This heathen church shall be returned to the service of God. I claim it . . . I mean dedicate it of course in His name," quickly correcting himself.

"Then I assume, Lord Tancred, you design to convert this magnificent building into a church for the service of God."

"Oh, yes," he answered quite emphatically.

I confess I was now trying to bait him. I was weary of "pious" princes masking raw cupidity with protests of service to the Lord. "I'm certain that is so," I answered. "But, I'm curious. Why strip"—I was pleased with myself for using the term—"this shrine of its lustrous adornments? Would not Our Lord be pleased with such a glorious church as it is?"

Tancred was nonplussed by the question. "Oh, that," looking up at one of his men on a ladder handing down a particularly fine lamp, struggling for an answer, "they are stained with pagan filth. For them to remain in a consecrated church would be an offense to God."

"Could they not be cleansed and made holy with blessings and prayers of purification?" I asked in the most guileless tone of which I was capable of rendering. I quite expected the answer I received.

"No, Father, the stain is indelible and will taint all Christians who see it. It can be purified only in the forge of hot fire and melted down."

"Into coin, I suppose?"

"Well, yes, maybe," pausing, "probably." His coin, I knew. I didn't bother to ask him about the tapestries.

"My Lord, I saw Muslims above, on the dome's ledge. What will happen to them?"

"Oh, them. They are under my protection. They sought sanctuary there. I ordered them to remain until the ardor of our crusading soldiers wane. Not all of our princes are as full of God's grace as I. Their lives will be spared in exchange for rich ransoms. God is merciful."

I could endure the hypocrisy longer. "I must leave. May the Lord be with you." I knew He would not.

"And with you," Tancred responded obligingly. I feared Tancred probably was wrong.

Tancred's expectation of ransom proved misplaced. On the following day crusader soldiers, angered at having been deprived of booty, assembled below the shrine and with arrows shot every Saracen on the dome's ledge, a sport for them despite Tancred's furious protests. They then clambered up the dome peeling off sheets of the polished copper, in their ignorance thinking them gold. Raymond fared better. Iftikhar had taken refuge with his retainers in the Tower of David. In return for safe conduct out of the city he surrendered his entire treasure to Raymond and was later escorted under Provençal guard to Ascalon on the coast. They were the only Muslims ultimately to survive. I hoped the two Saracen mothers survived as well, but I never knew.

Greed, a Solomonic Solution, and Massacre

Two days passed. The city was suffocating under the stench of putrefying Saracen bodies in the streets. Duke Godfrey summoned the council.

"My Lords, there is an urgent matter requiring consideration. The city is strewn throughout with rotting corpses. Pestilence will soon follow. They must be removed immediately. Some of you hold Muslim prisoners, I assume for ransom. They can be used to haul the bodies out of the city to be burned. What say you?"

There was broad agreement, all the princes nodding, until Bishop Arnulf, Peter Desiderius standing beside him, spoke. "My Lord Godfrey, I concur with your proposal. But that solves only part of the problem. I have invited Father Peter to join us. He has another message from God." Godfrey beckoned for him to speak.

"My Lords," Peter began, "Bishop Adhémar appeared again last night in a vision." I wondered who else found Peter's "visions" as annoying as I.

"'Beloved Father Peter,' he said, 'the princes will meet in council tomorrow.'"

"I know nothing of this Your Eminence, I responded meekly.

"'No, you don't but I do. They will discuss the disposal of Muslim bodies and will decide to use Muslim captives to take them out of the city. I approve of that—Muslims lack the tender feelings we Christians do in care of the dead. But after that they must all be slain. By obstinately refusing to accept Jesus Christ as their Savior, they have forfeited the right to live. They are no better than dumb beasts. This is God's Will. Announce this to the council.'"

Audible gasps followed, then angry remonstrances, especially from Robert of Flanders and Robert of Normandy. "This is intolerable!" Robert of Flanders exclaimed. "Some of us have profited from Jerusalem's capture and have enriched themselves with plunder, from a certain Saracen shrine for example. What booty did the rest of us gain? Pittances! Plates of pewter, cups of bronze. Our prisoners will bring fine ransoms, just rewards for our service to the Lord. I for one shall not surrender them. I believe the Count of Normandy is in agreement." The count nodded.

Tancred visibly chaffed from this thinly disguised rebuke. Even though his name was not mentioned, all understood to whom Robert of Flanders referred. "My Lord Count," Tancred rejoined, "you mistake yourself. Yes, I claimed the Dome of the Rock and even placed my banner on it. But this was for the Glory of God. Three hundred prisoners were taken under my protection. Yet your men, others too, killed them all! They were intended for ransom. I shall suffer mightily from this loss of revenue. I too have given much for this pilgrimage. Compensation is only just. But that has been *stolen* from me!"

"Oh, how *mightily* you have suffered, beyond calculation I'm certain,"

Robert scoffed. "My heart weeps for your loss. Yet," Robert pausing, "only this morning I saw several camels being led out of the Dome laden with gold and silver objects of all kinds. Yes, I do *grieve* for you. And let us not forget your 'claim' to Bethlehem made without consent of this council." Tancred, despite quickening with anger, said nothing.

Raymond broke his silence. "I too promised sanctuary to Governor Iftikhar and his men with the guarantee of safe conduct out of the city. That was my Christian duty. I too refuse to surrender them."

The Duke of Normandy was particularly vexed. The animosity between Normans and Provençals ran deep. "Oh, dear Count, how *very, very* Christian of you," he said mockingly. "And may we presume you profited not at all from granting safe-conduct, your *Christian* duty as you put it?" The duke knew very well the answer.

"Well, yes . . . no, not exactly," Raymond stammered.

"Yes? No?" Robert continuing his mockery. "Surely, despite your age, even *you* can recall." The dispute had now turned personal, more rancorous than any council I had witnessed in the past.

Raymond became quite agitated, his face reddening. "If you *must* know, my dearest duke," Raymond repaying Robert with his own biting sarcasm, "the governor did relinquish his treasury to me. But that had nothing to do with my Christian duty."

The entire council broke out in laughter at Raymond's shameless hypocrisy, excessive even for the princes, fortunately relieving the tension. Peter Desiderius was listening intently, visibly annoyed. His "vision" had been ignored. Worse, *he* had been ignored. "My Lords, I remind you that I am the messenger from God. No one else. I have announced to you His Will. Pray renounce your selfish desires for ransom. Submit yourselves to Our Lord. These heathens, *all of them*, must die. Let their carrion nourish the bellies of crows and wild beasts. A worthy end for them all."

The council was deadlocked. Godfrey decided to break it. Turning to Tancred. "Lord Tancred, you have indeed been deprived of ransom for your prisoners. Yet you have been well rewarded with rich plunder, more than any other member of this council. I ask you to tithe a portion of that treasure to the church and a similar amount to the other princes, all except Count Raymond, to be equitably distributed. And renounce your claim to Bethlehem. This cannot be countenanced. Count Raymond," looking now at him, "you made a Christian promise of safe-conduct to Iftikhar. That must be honored. But you too should tithe your treasure to the church and another to the other princes." I thought Godfrey's solution worthy of Solomon. Until his final decision. "Regarding the prisoners, I agree they must remove bodies from the city. After that, may God save His own."

That afternoon the Saracen prisoners under guard collected all the Muslim bodies in Jerusalem piling them in wagons, through the Jaffa Gate, placed on pyres and burned. When the last pyre was set alight the crusader guards pulled their swords and slew them all. After the fires died down soldiers and pilgrims raked through the ashes searching for bezants and jewels they suspected the Muslims had swallowed. A "glorious" capstone of the conquest of Jerusalem. Or perhaps not.

* * *

Jerusalem fell. The army marched to the Holy Sepulchre where it gave prayers of thanksgiving. I did not join them. I wished only to return to the peace of La Charité sur Loire, there to seek solitude and redemption. But what to do with my son?

This ends Book XIV of *Jerusalem Falls!* Book XV begins.

BOOK XV

MY JOURNEY ENDS

Election of Duke Godfrey. A Secret Mission. Torture and Arnulf Deceived.
Baptism and Purification. Arnulf's Deception Exposed and a Fraudulent
Election. A Compact with Duke Godfrey. The Final Battle. Audience
with Pope Paschal. Return to La Charité and A Revelation.

Election of Duke Godfrey

I returned to the coach after my visit with Tancred at the Dome of the Rock, on the way retrieving my son from the midwife. She handed me a horn of a small cow, its tip punctured with parchment wrapped about it to form a nipple for feeding. "It's full of milk," she said. "Tomorrow I'll send over a wet nurse. After he's weaned, feed him soft oat porridge, very soft," she admonished. "He'll grow strong." I expressed deep gratitude for her care paying with coin which she happily accepted. Isaac and Miriam were awake, sitting outside on trestle chairs waiting for me. I had purchased some dried fish, oatcakes, and bread which we shared. As we sat eating I related the pillage of the Dome but they were more interested in the fate of their fellow Jews in the city. Despite my efforts to deflect, they insisted—did any survive the synagogue's burning; are Jews left alive in the city? I was unable to comfort them. They sat in numbed silence, broken when Miriam looked upward "Thank you Lord for Father Moshe. He saved us. Truly a man of God." They also inquired about Rebecca, not seeing her. I was able only to mumble something, that she had been killed. They asked no more.

It was two days following our victory that a Council of Princes and senior clergy was convened at the al-Aqsa mosque, I'm uncertain at whose request. Now that Jerusalem had been taken the question burning in all minds was who would govern it, deferred at an earlier meeting because of clerical animosity to a "king". There were pressing issues to be resolved: taxation, rebuilding of walls, control of the Tower of David now occupied by Count Raymond, restoration of the expelled Christians to their former homes, but most important leadership of our army to face Sultan al-Afdal, his arrival expected soon though date uncertain. Initially the princes milled about uneasily, none ready to broach the subject for fear of creating an impression he sought the election for himself.

Finally Count Robert of Flanders spoke. "My Lords. We are all aware that a king of Jerusalem must be elected without delay. I wish only to return to my home as soon as reasonably possible. Duke Robert of Normandy similarly intends to return to his duchy. Thus I am free to speak without self-interest or deception. There are only two of the senior princes possibly in contention: Count Raymond and Duke Godfrey. The matter is delicate because we all know the inestimable qualities of both. But a choice must be made. I suggest . . ."

Bishop Arnulf interrupted, rudely and without apology, "My Lord Count. You forget yourself. I am shocked you would believe the election of a king should precede a much more important appointment, patriarch of Jerusalem. This is the House of Our Lord, not some estate in Flanders from which to suck taxes and peasant services. There can be no election without a patriarch to consecrate it. Let us begin with that. And, because selection of a patriarch is a church matter, it is not subject to consent from the princes. Only the clergy may decide. And we are prepared to do it today. I believe we all have someone meritorious in mind." Of course, the "someone" was Arnulf. His narcissism and ambition were limitless.

The clerics all nodded their heads in vigorous agreement. The princes shook theirs just as vigorously.

Tancred, an implacable foe of clerical rule, spoke first. "My Lords, Your Graces, like Count Robert I too harbor no design on Jerusalem and I have already freely renounced my claim to Bethlehem." That was true though not done quite as "freely" as he declared. Moreover, he certainly understood there was little chance he, a junior prince, would be elected king. "Selection of a patriarch can be deferred," he continued, "his Eminence Bishop Arnulf having made clear that election of a patriarch is a matter for the church. So be it. But so is the election of a king a matter for us, the nobles of our army. It does *not* require clerical blessing. Let us proceed immediately."

The same rancor between princes and bishops as occurred previously on this issue erupted again, each shouting at the other. Before anyone else could intervene, Peter of Narbonne, a Provençal, appointed bishop of al-Bara by Count Raymond and thus no champion of the Norman Arnulf, spoke. "My Lords and Your Graces, I must dissent from Bishop Arnulf. This question of selecting a patriarch, important indeed, requires discernment, reflection, and prayer. There are so many worthy bishops among us and a hurried decision would displease Our Lord. I agree with

Lord Tancred that we defer this matter until later." Arnulf, so confident he would be elected, was visibly discomposed, his crude manipulation failing. Otto, Bishop of Strasbourg completed it. "I concur with Bishop Peter. Let us agree on a king today. A patriarch later." Dispute ended.

Count Robert after this interlude continued. "As I was saying, we must elect a king. I propose Count Raymond of Toulouse, a pious man and valiant warrior, known to us all. Council, what say you?"

Perfect silence greeted this nomination. There seemed little enthusiasm, even among Raymond's own Provençal nobles. Raymond's prestige had suffered over many months: his support of Emperor Alexios, the prolonged and unsuccessful siege of Arqa, the discredited lance, Raymond's obdurate support of Peter Bartholomew, and not least his annoying and undisguised pretensions to leadership of the crusade. All of these had tarnished his reputation. Whether Raymond understood these reservations I never knew.

Raymond hesitated. "Count Robert, I thank you for your confidence. But I am a humble man of God, far, far too unworthy to even *pretend* to rule this holiest of all cities. No. It can be governed only by the most saintly of all men. If you find one, I certainly will not oppose his election." He had raised the bar so high thinking, I'm certain, that by his pious but unconvincing expression of humility and prescribing the standard as the "most saintly of all men," none would be audacious enough to assert claim to the title. Count Robert smiled and nodded. He turned to Godfrey.

"My Lord Duke. It was after all you who broke through the Saracen defenses allowing us to take this city. Would you consider becoming king?"

Godfrey, unlike Raymond, did not hesitate. "Count Robert, I agree with Count Raymond that no mortal man such as I is worthy of being anointed 'King of Jerusalem'. However," pausing in thought, plainly for effect, "we *do* need a leader to ensure the safety of this holy city. I would accept a different title, *Advocatus Sancti Sepulchri*, 'Advocate of the Holy Sepulchre'."

Raymond had outwitted himself. He was playing with one set of gaming cards. Godfrey, cleverly and simply, chose a different one. Raymond would soon regret his decision. He had always coveted leadership of the crusade, never masking it. His anger at Bohemond for contesting his primacy was still raw. Yet, that obsessive ambition which had so bedeviled him for four years, now within such easy reach, slipped from his hands. By acclamation Godfrey was elected 'Advocate of the Holy Sepulchre'. All kneeled, everyone except Raymond who had not taken this well. Godfrey ignored the slight. Raymond, however, was not finished.

"My Lord Duke, or should I now call you 'My Liege'?" Raymond began scornfully. "There is yet one matter unresolved: the Tower of David. Jerusalem is yours to rule. But you should know the tower is mine and I will not relinquish it."

This was a direct challenge to Godfrey's authority. There could not be two masters of Jerusalem yet this was exactly what Raymond was demanding. The tower was more than Jerusalem's principal citadel. It was itself a fortress surrounded on all four sides by strong walls and a dry moat. It also commanded the Jaffa Gate, the principal route to the sea.

"Count," Godfrey replied coolly, "you understand of course that I could take the tower by force if necessary." This of course was mere bluster—the crusaders had little appetite for another siege, particularly against a fellow-Christian prince. And Raymond knew this.

"Then try it," a defiant challenge delivered quite serenely.

This was an impasse and a dangerous one. Godfrey became pensive. "For the last four years all of our decisions have been made by consensus of the council. That has served us well. Let me propose this: We submit the question to it, not now but for later adjudication. In the meantime, as a gesture of good faith, you will evacuate the tower and surrender it to a person of your own choosing. A member of our senior clergy perhaps? What say you?"

"I agree," Raymond responded, far too carelessly as events proved. "You say a cleric of my own choosing?" Godfrey nodded. "Then I choose Bishop Peter of Narbonne. I shall deliver the tower's keys to him but to him alone."

A Secret Mission

The morning following his election Godfrey moved into Iftikhar's palace. He invited me to meet with him there. He had heard, I'm uncertain how, of my combats with the three Muslims after I had crossed the drawbridge onto the ramparts of Jerusalem's walls and congratulated me—likely he had not heard that I had also slain a crusader soldier, a Provençal, though just as likely he would not have cared. I told Godfrey that I repented of my role in such killings and wanted to return to my former life at La Charité.

"So, you no longer wish to be a 'warrior-priest' but a simple priest again?"

"I do my Lord."

"Would you be willing to return as my chaplain until you leave for home?"

"With joy," I answered.

"Father, you have a reputation for discretion. I now rely on that. There are two matters that trouble me deeply. I have spies in the Provençal camp. There is a great deal of unrest among them after learning that Raymond is determined not to surrender his claim to the Tower of David. They wish to return home to the Provence. I have arranged for a small group of them to 'encourage', let me say, Bishop Peter to surrender the tower to me. If he resists, they are to employ other means. This did require a bribe, of course, but only a modest sum for they were only too happy to cooperate. That will solve one problem. But I have another, Bishop Arnulf. You know him well, do you not?"

"I do my Lord, without pleasure. A loathsome creature. Corrupt. Lacking a single Christian virtue."

"I share that opinion. There is a rumor that a piece of the True Cross, once belonging to Bishop Adhémar, was recovered in Latakia, that you were a member of the search party, and that it was given to Count Raymond disappearing soon after. Do you know anything of this?"

"Yes. It is in my possession. Hidden."

Godfrey was rather startled by my answer. "You must tell me someday how that came to be. It is imperative in the meantime it remain hidden. Arnulf believes this sacred relic is in the city, concealed from the Saracens by Greek monks, at the Monastery of the Holy Cross I believe, its very name suggestive of the Cross's location. He is now searching for it. His reputation suffered, at least among many clerics, from public doubts, even denunciations, about the authenticity of the holy lance, doubts in truth I shared. Worse, he is the bastard son of a priest in Flanders. And, as if that were not enough, there are salacious stories, even songs, about his philandering."

"My Lord," I asked, "what is your concern?"

"Simply this. All of his transgressions will be overlooked if he is able to recover the Cross. He will proclaim that his possession is evidence he is favored by God to become patriarch of Jerusalem. It will be a powerful argument. I cannot allow this. He is already talking about restricting access to the Holy Sepulchre to only those observing Latin rites. This would mean excluding all other Christians: Greeks, Nestorians, Jacobites, Copts. Count Robert of Flanders and Duke Robert of Normandy intend to depart soon for their homeland. Our crusading force will thus be sorely diminished. It will be challenging enough to protect Jerusalem from future Saracen attacks, and they surely will come. The task will be even more difficult if the Christian community is riven by dissension. I must govern a *united*

Jerusalem. It is imperative he not be elected patriarch. I need your help."

"I shall try, my Lord. While in Antioch the patriarch John gave me the name of the *archimandrite*, abbot of the Monastery of the Holy Cross, Demetrios, here in Jerusalem, a friend of his. The abbot may be inclined to help. Regretfully, the Greeks have as little affection for our Latin Church as our Church for theirs. However, this can be turned to advantage, especially if the *archimandrite* understands Arnulf's purpose. I'm sure he will have as much incentive as you in the election of a truly worthy patriarch. Let me try."

"Thank you, Father Oderic. "But understand. The will occur soon. Haste is imperative. Tell no one."

Torture and Arnulf Deceived

I walked immediately to the monastery. Recognizing me as a crusader even without my armor, the monk at the gate was reluctant to admit me. His suspicious were allayed after I told him I carried a message from the Patriarch of Antioch, escorting me to Demetrios's office. Demetrios was an elderly man, in his sixties he appeared, rather thin even frail, with a full black beard contrasting with his white hair but withal a kindly face. He stood up to greet me.

"Reverend Father," bowing to him, "I am a monk from the Priory of La Charité sur Loire in Francia, for four years now a member of the crusader army on its pilgrimage to Jerusalem. I bear greetings from His Eminence John of Antioch. He asked me to convey his solicitudes."

"Ah, John. Yes. It's been years. We were novices together in Constantinople. He was somewhat headstrong . . . well, as I. We were often in trouble with the master. Many nights in penitential prayer on our knees, the stone so rough that, like Saint James's, both of ours came to resemble those of a camel. But we survived," he said with a smile. "How is my old friend?"

"He is very well though he suffered mightily at the hands of the Turks in Antioch. However, he has recovered and been restored to his patriarchy. Reverend Father, I have a matter of some urgency requiring your guidance. Recently . . ."

Demetrios stopped me. "Father Oderic, we receive such little news here, bits and pieces, only from caravans and even then always conflicting. I'm anxious to know *everything*. We can discuss later your mission. Please favor me with information. How did you find Constantinople, surely the

'Queen of all Cities'?" I agreed with him. I was anxious to turn the conversation to Arnulf but Demetrios was insistent. For the next three, perhaps four, hours I related my journey, from Mainz to Constantinople, through Anatolia to Antioch, and then through Palestine to Jerusalem, giving particular emphasis to the iniquities of Arnulf. He listened without interruption enabling me more quickly to turn to the matter at hand.

"Reverend Father, I am chaplain to Duke Godfrey of Bouillon, just elected Advocate of the Holy Sepulchre, a pious man and great warrior. Bishop Arnulf has learned that your monks secreted the True Cross in this very monastery. He is certain it once belonged to Bishop Adhémar and wishes to find it thinking this will ensure his election as patriarch. If that occurs, Duke Godfrey fears the worst for all Christians in this city, including Greeks, excluding only those who do not practice Latin rites from worshipping at the Holy Sepulchre. I believe Arnulf will stop at nothing to extract information. Do you have it? I must know."

Demetrios rose from his chair and began pacing back and forth, without a word, silent but for the flapping of his sandals on the stone floor, gently stroking his chin, his forehead furrowed in thought. He then stopped to look at me. "Oderic, I have no choice but to trust you. Yes, we do have a piece of the True Cross but not that belonging to Bishop Adhémar. Antonios!", he called out. Almost immediately the door opened and a monk peered in. "Antonios. I'm going to the crypt. I'll need a torch." He soon returned with one. "Follow me." We walked through the cloister, then the refectory into the kitchen, a thick oaken door at its far end. He opened it and pointed the torch inside revealing circular stairs winding down around a single column. "Watch your step," Demetrios warned. We descended entering a vaulted room bare of furnishings except for a pile of broken tables, desks, and chairs in the corner, probably to be repaired in the future. There was, however, one curious feature, a mural, some six feet tall and five feet long, against the far wall made of rough vertical planks flush with each other. It was whitewashed, covered with the signatures of past monks scribbled over it in black ink, a memorial of some sort to their lives here. Demetrios walked to the side of the mural, felt behind and with a tug the mural swung open on hinges to reveal a secret room behind. Demetrios motioned for me to enter. "Only the senior monks know of this." The room was surprisingly spacious and in the torch light I saw the reflected glitter of chalices, candelabra, plates, vases, all of silver and used for the sacraments and religious observances.

"Beautiful, aren't they? From antiquity this holy city has been occupied by one invader after another. Since the foundation of this monastery centuries ago we hid these valuables here on the arrival of every new conqueror, waiting until safe to bring them out. We did the same when last year the Saracens took the city. Here they are."

"But Reverend Father," I objected, "we Latins have taken the city. Surely now you can be confident." Demetrios looked at me with a bemused smile as though no explanation were necessary. "They remain here," he answered firmly. "I need to show you something else." Demetrios walked over to a cabinet, reached in with both hands lifting out a box encrusted with jewels, ornately carved, trimmed in silver, in most respects similar to Adhémar's reliquary. He reverently opened the lid. There, on red velvet, lay an ancient piece of wood. "This is a piece of the True Cross. We have held it since the beginning of our monastery."

I noticed another box inside the cabinet, rather similar in size, pushed to the back. I reached in. "May I?" Demetrios nodded. The box was crudely constructed without ornamentation. Inside was a piece of ancient wood not dissimilar to the cross preserved in Adhemar's reliquary. "What's this?" I asked.

"Oh that. One of my predecessors, fifty or so years ago, paid dearly for it without investigation on the assurance, given under oath on the Bible, that it contained a piece of the True Cross. We later learned that the scoundrel was selling various relics throughout Jerusalem. A fake. We keep it just to remind ourselves of the ease of fraud."

I suddenly had an idea. "Reverend Father, you *must* trust me. Arnulf will stop at *nothing*, even torture, to steal your reliquary. It will make little difference to him whether it belonged to Adhémar or to this monastery. If you don't succumb, he will then turn to your other monks. In the end, he will surely find it." I pulled out my small knife used for eating and behind the false cross carved "OR", replacing the object in its box. Demetrios asked no questions. I took the box and we walked back out. I stopped him in the cloister.

"Here, take it. But this is important: Success of my plan depends on deception. Arnulf will not be fooled by a rude box such as this holding a piece of the True Cross. Do you have anything finer, more ornate?"

"Hmm. Yes, I think so. The Greek Church, like your own, forbids cremation. But our monastery has been in existence for hundreds of years. Some time ago we ran out of space for burials in our graveyard. We were then forced to cremate the bodies of our deceased monks. But," he added somewhat defensively I thought, "we honor them with the *same* burial rites and place their remains in wooden boxes which are preserved in a magnificent mausoleum at the corner of the cemetery. The urns are rather impressive, intricately carved by one of our monks, quite a talented woodsmith. He always has one in readiness. But I warn you they're fashioned without precious metals or gems. Not like our reliquary, or likely Bishop Adhémar's. So, I don't know if . . . ."

"That will have to do. Have it lined with red velvet. I shall return tomorrow morning and then reveal all. In the meantime, you must think of a cavity in your monastery, behind a wall or under a floor, plausible for concealing a precious relic. Arnulf must not become suspicious."

The next morning I returned to the monastery. Demetrios was in his office, the urn with the counterfeit cross inside sitting on his desk. "Where shall we hide it?" I asked. Demetrios led me into the refectory, lifted a stone slab, the ground underneath recently excavated. As I bent over to place the 'reliquary' in the hole, I was filled with unease. However elegantly carved with rosettes and embellished with swirls of colorful enamel, it was, after all, a box unequal to the breathtaking beauty of Adhémar's reliquary. But this was all I had. I fervently hoped that Arnulf, in his eagerness, would not question its authenticity. We returned to Demetrios's office. He took his seat behind his desk; I sat opposite him, my back to the door.

I was in the midst of explaining my scheme when suddenly Antonios barged through the door. "Reverend Father, there's some cleric at the door. He calls himself 'Arnulf'. He's brought troops. He demands to see you."

"Let him in."

"No! Not yet!" I burst out. "Reverend Father, you *must* resist Arnulf's interrogation, though only to a point. It may be rough. If you surrender too easily, Arnulf will surely suspect. He *must* believe this box contains Adhémar's cross."

"I understand," Demetrios replied. "Let this Arnulf enter."

Arnulf stormed in, a detachment of Norman soldiers behind him. He wasted no time. Looking at Demetrios, "You are Demetrios, so-called abbot of this monastery?"

Without rising Demetrios answered "I am. Who are you?"

"Not that it's your business but I am Arnulf, Bishop of Rohes. You shall address me as 'Your Eminence'. You, like all Greeks, are clearly ignorant of proper courtesies. Your monastery holds the True Cross, once the property of Bishop Adhémar of Le Puy. Do not deny it, apostate! Reveal it now or it will go badly for you!"

"I know nothing of this cross. Surely you're mistaken."

"I have no interest in idle debate or your lying protests. Sergeant bring him to me." Two soldiers strode behind Demetrios's chair, roughly yanked him out of it, and brought him to face Arnulf. Arnulf slapped his face, twice. "*Speak!*"

"I . . . I know nothing."

"Sergeant, persuade him." The sergeant than hit Demetrios in his stomach. Demetrios doubled over in pain. "Again," Arnulf ordered. The sergeant hit him once more in the stomach and then lifted Demetrios's head from under his chin and struck a fierce blow to his face. Demetrios's lips began to bleed and his nose gushed with blood. "*Speak!*" Arnulf demanded. Demetrios said nothing. "Again. More vigor this time!" The sergeant delivered another blow to his stomach, even more violent than the first two and then lifted up his chin and hit him once more in the face. Demetrios, though covered with blood, stared defiantly at Arnulf. "Let's be rid of this apostate. We'll find another more pliant." With that the sergeant pulled out his dagger, its tip at Demetrios's throat ready to thrust it.

I had instructed Demetrios to resist for effect only. Not to surrender his life. I rose from my chair and turned about. "Your Eminence," I whimpered, feigning to shake with fear. "Spare this godly man. If you do, I will reveal the cross's location. I know where it is. I put it there myself."

Arnulf had not noticed me, my back to him. "It's *you*, the *false* monk. Always where you're unwelcome." Arnulf looked at the sergeant and shook his head, "not now". The sergeant put his dagger back into its sheath. Glaring at me, "Find it!" As I led Arnulf and his soldiers out of the office, Demetrios was stumbling back to his chair. I took them to the refectory, Arnulf roughly pushing me forward. I wiped away the dirt over the slab, pulled it out setting it aside and retrieved the box. Arnulf grabbed it from my hands, opened its lid, looked inside, then closed it again. "This is it. We're finished here." My hoax had succeeded.

Baptism and Purification

In my solitary walk from the monastery to the coach, my thoughts turned to a question which had long disturbed me: Was Rebecca's and my son a Jew or a Christian? He was a Jew yet never circumcised. He was a Christian yet never baptized. I was indifferent to his ultimate choice. I think Rebecca as well. We cared only that he professed faith in God. To coax him to sleep Rebecca would softly tell him stories of great prophets from the Old Testament, none of which he understood; I sang Christian hymns. Those were his catechisms. We never discussed the question, perhaps believing it might cause discord between us. The only thing that mattered was our love for each other and our son. By the time I reached the coach I had resolved on a course of action, a peculiar one certainly. That evening I discussed my decision with Isaac.

"Master Isaac," I began, "my son is neither Christian nor Jew yet the blood of both faiths courses through his body. Someday he will have to choose. Until that day I wish him to have the benefit of both—to be baptized as a Christian and purified as a Jew."

As I was speaking Isaac had just put a spoonful of stew prepared by Miriam into his mouth. He was so astounded that he dropped the spoon into his bowl, almost chocking on his food, his eyes widening in astonishment. He just sat there staring at me, confounded how to answer.

"Moshe, this is impossible. Your son has not been circumcised and I suspect he will not follow Jewish dietary practices as he matures. He can never be a true Jew nor can he be purified as though he were one. Our Law is very strict on this."

"I know that Master. Your answer is not unexpected. To perform such a ritual may be regarded by your rabbis as a sacrilege. But to receive a blessing according to your custom is important to me and would be to Rebecca if she were alive." Invoking Rebecca's name was a sincere if devious effort to invoke an authority higher than my own.

"Yes, I suspect she would. I miss her so, Miriam especially. A treasured woman." Isaac was softening as I had hoped.

"Master Isaac," not wishing to allow this opportunity to be squandered, I pressed my argument forward. "Rebecca and I were married in Edessa, by a rabbi, in his home and not a temple, and I a Christian. Not a true union in the eyes of either of our faiths but a true one in our own. The rabbi was satisfied with my profession of belief in God and obedience to His Commandments. Despite these encumbrances he performed the ceremony nevertheless."

Isaac continued to shake his head. Miriam now intervened. "Dear husband, I must speak. Moshe's request is of course contrary to our Laws as you say. But surely there is a higher good recognized by the rabbi in Edessa. Rebecca was a godly woman and Moshe a godly man. On the road to Constantinople we risked our lives for them. In Jerusalem he risked his for ours. And you love their son as though you were his *sandik*. I'm sure God, the final judge, will forgive you. I pray you do this."

Isaac sat in thought. I decided to pursue my request no further. He would have to decide. "Then it will be done," he announced firmly. And with a smile, "Afterwards I too shall need to purify myself of sin."

The next morning we departed for the Jordan River. We camped close to the bank. Isaac and Miriam slept in the coach, my son and I in a tent as we had done since Isaac and Miriam stayed with us. I was pleased with the arrangement for I would hold my child in my arms as we both fell to sleep. We walked to the river so storied in biblical history. I expected it to be magnificent, at least the size of the mighty Rhine. To my surprise it was but a stream, a large one yes, but unimpressive I must say. It was enough, however, that it was the Jordan River, sacred to both Christians and Jews—where Christ was baptized and where God had drained its flood waters allowing the Israelites to pass into Canaan.

Both ceremonies were performed quickly but reverently. Isaac began immediately searching the river for a *mikveh*, normally a stone-faced cistern into which people stepped for ablution and purification, its principal requirement that it be fed by fresh but not flowing water. Isaac had an unconventional solution. He decided that a quiet slough would suffice and found one close by, no more than two feet deep and placid. I handed my son to Isaac as Miriam and I stood watching. Isaac turned himself to face Jerusalem and then chanted the *Shemoneh Esreh*:

> *"We acknowledge You, Oh Lord, that You are our God,*
> *as You were the God of our ancestors, forever and ever.*
> *Rock of our life, Shield of our help, You are immutable from age to age.*
> *We thank You and utter Your praise,*
> *for our lives that are delivered into Your hands,*
> *and for our souls that are entrusted to You.*

He then dipped my son into the water up to his armpits probably knowing that full immersion would follow with me and one was sufficient. Yet it was too much for my child as he began wailing, probably from the shock of the cold water. I took him, Isaac and Miriam watching from the bank, carried him into the river, treading carefully unsure of the river's depth. I held his head with one hand and his legs with the other upright above the water presenting him to God.

> *"I baptize you, my son,*
> *in the name of the Father, the Son, and the Holy Spirit.*
> *May you live faithful to Our Lord and obedient to His Laws."*

And then I quickly submerged him into the river immediately lifting him up. If he had been wailing before, he exploded into a full-bodied scream, loud enough I'm certain Rebecca heard him in heaven. He soon settled down and the four of us returned cheerfully to Jerusalem. Before leaving I cut four palm branches: one for the pope, the second for Prior Damian not then knowing he had already passed, one for my son, the other for me. I still have it.

Isaac and Miriam longed to return home. I had searched all the stables in the Jewish Quarter but was unable to find their wagon. In the meantime, Godfrey invited me to stay in his palace. I no longer had need for the coach and gave it to them. We spent a joyless evening before their departure knowing it would be our last. The next morning I removed all my possessions, not forgetting Adhémar's reliquary, *Iskender*, or my journals, the fourth and final almost full with only three blank pages remaining. We made our tearful farewells. Before they climbed up to the coach's perch I handed Isaac my purse of coin, uncertain whether it would be sufficient for their journey but it was all I had. Isaac of course refused to accept it, surrendering only after my relentless insistence. The three of us embraced. Isaac placed his arms on my shoulders, looked squarely in my face and blessed me, tears in his eyes:

"May God, our God and the God of our fathers
lead you in peace and direct your steps in peace,
guide you in peace, support you in peace,
and cause you to reach your destination in life with joy."

I watched the coach until it was out of sight never to see them again. I was now as destitute as they had been. But I had my son.

Arnulf's Deception Exposed and a Fraudulent Election

A few days later a council of senior clergy was convened in the al-Aqsa Mosque at the summons of Peter of Narbonne. All the bishops and chaplains to princes and lesser nobles were present. I was surprised to see Peter Desiderius. My attention was especially drawn to a monk, unknown to me, Norman I thought, who hung back in the shadows. There was something suspicious about him, nothing I could identify but present.

"Your Graces," Peter began, "we are convened for the solemn task of electing a patriarch for Jerusalem. I trust you have used this time fruitfully in discernment and prayer. I have no interest in assuming this sacred role and thus disavow myself as a candidate. There are so many other bishops more experienced and worthy of consideration. I invite discussion."

In the silence that followed, Arnulf, Bishop of Marturana, a thoroughly unctuous, disreputable man, seized the moment before any but his own nominee could be named.

"Your Graces, I am but a humble servant of the Lord, unlearned in the texts of antiquity and lacking the rhetorical skills of many of you gathered here." He was perfectly correct in admitting his lack of learning and rhetorical skills. Unmentioned was that he and Arnulf of Rohes were intimate companions sharing many an evening delighting in the fleshpots of the crusader camp. "There is but one man here sufficiently virtuous and irreproachable in character to sit on the throne of the See of Jerusalem, Arnulf, Bishop of Rohes. I propose," turning to Bishop Peter with a bow, "that we dispense with futile debate and move directly to the election of Bishop Arnulf."

Bishop Peter demurred. "Thank you, Your Grace, but I am loathe to move precipitously. We should hear from others."

"Your Grace," the Bishop of Marturana responded, unwilling to yield easily, "your wisdom certainly exceeds my own. And yet before there is further discussion our colleagues must know of a miraculous event, a gift from God himself. Bishop Arnulf has recovered the True Cross, once in possession of the Blessed Bishop Adhémar, discovered in a Greek monastery in this very city. This is truly a sign of the Divine Grace with which Our Lord favors Bishop Arnulf."

Before Peter could respond Arnulf stepped forward. "This is true," Arnulf began. "The Holy Spirit enveloped my soul and directed me to a Greek monastery and the very place where Adhémar's True Cross was secreted even from us Latins, their devious purpose unknown to me. I have it here," one of Arnulf's attendants handing him the monastery's urn. Arnulf opened the lid and gazed inside with feigned reverence, his eyes glistening in tears. It was dramatic theater; worse, believable and well-rehearsed. There were gasps from the clerics all straining their necks as Arnulf tipped it, turning from right to left for all to see. Some of the bishops even fell to their knees, heads bowed, crossing themselves.

"This is indeed glorious news," Peter cried out. "Thanks be to God. Perhaps we *should* proceed directly to election."

I watched this farce with growing disgust, anger rising. This was the moment to act. "Your Graces, this cross was not '*discovered*'. It was seized *by force*! The Holy Spirit played no part. Arnulf deceives you!" I no longer wished to honor him with the title of "Bishop".

Arnulf's anger equaled my own. "You, Oderic of Rheims, are a false priest, a prevaricator. There is a special place in Hell for the sinful likes of you!"

"Wicked am I?" I retorted. "And you a notorious fornicator!" This was now a race to the bottom for invective. "Do you deny torturing, nearly to death, the abbot of the Holy Cross Monastery and then placing a dagger at his throat? I witnessed it. *Do you deny this?*"

"I do deny it. I remind you again that Hell welcomes liars and sinners. And I look forward to learning you are burning there, your flesh on fire as you feast on worms and vermin. The company should suit you."

Excited murmurs erupted from the clerics. Bishop Peter raised his hand for order. "While the circumstances of this discovery appear to be in dispute, what I think important is whether this is indeed the True Cross once held by Bishop Adhémar. Bishop Arnulf, what say you?"

"I can tell you with absolute certainty it is. Count Raymond of Toulouse sought it and sent his liege man to Latakia where it was found. Father Peter Desiderius, here today, personally presented the reliquary to Count Raymond of Toulouse at Arqa. It then disappeared under circumstances, it appears by a mysterious pilgrim at the Chapel of Saint Agatha. I'm sure Father Peter can authenticate it."

Peter stepped forward, examined the box and looked inside. "Yes, this is the very reliquary that belonged to Bishop Adhémar and the same piece of the True Cross that I saw before. Yes, this is it," he declared quite unequivocally.

"Then I think this settles the question," Bishop Peter said. "We can now proceed to . . . "

"No!" I shouted out, "This matter is *far* from settled! Peter Desiderius lies. What Peter holds in his hands is no *true* 'reliquary'. It is a box built by a monk at the Monastery of the Holy Cross intended to be used as an urn. This, your Graces, is the *real* one." I then pulled from my satchel Adhémar's reliquary and lifted it up for all to see. "Can anyone deny that this has all the exquisite craftsmanship, encrusted jewels and silver trim of a precious reliquary? *This* is the one that belonged to Bishop Adhémar who entrusted it to me to be delivered to the pope in Rome. I was that 'mysterious pilgrim' who rescued it at Saint Agatha's chapel and have held it since. It, *not* that urn, contains a piece of the True Cross."

"Oderic," Arnulf shouted, "you're a fool but a cunning one. Anyone can purchase such a box, or in your case more likely steal one, common thief that you are. This proves nothing."

The mood of the clerics seemed to shift like the tide, one moment flowing in my direction, the next ebbing. It was now flowing toward Arnulf. I needed to change that.

"The Monastery of the Holy Cross indeed possesses a piece of the True Cross," I answered calmly. "I knew Arnulf would attempt to take it. It was I who hid the urn, the very one you see in Peter's hands, underneath the monastery's refectory floor and placed a false cross inside. Bishop Peter, I ask you to inspect the cross and turn it over." Peter did as requested. "Your Grace, what do you see?"

"Initials, 'OR.'"

"Yes, 'OR' for 'Oderic of Rheims' which I carved myself. This is no genuine relic. It is a villainous scheme for which Abbot Demetrios nearly paid with his life. All in the service of Arnulf's overweening ambition."

The mood ebbed once more, now against Arnulf and would not flow again in his direction. Peter had enough. "Your Graces, I propose we consider other worthy candidates." I had noticed moments earlier out of the corner of my eye the monk who had first attracted my attention sprinting out the doors. Almost immediately a company of Norman soldiers burst in and rushed to take positions around the perimeter of the interior, all facing impassively the clerics in the center.

"Your Grace," the company's sergeant addressing Peter, "you will pardon this intrusion. I am confident there has been sufficient time for deliberation. We Normans propose Arnulf, Bishop of Rohes, for election as patriarch. Perhaps you would ask for a show of hands. I think now would be convenient." Peter was shaking with fear, too terrified to speak, merely nodding his head. All hands slowly raised, nary an objection.

I was just standing there, in shock at the audacity of this move by Robert of Normandy. Arnulf slid past me, snarling in my ear, "I'll find you. Wherever you are." Godfrey's fears for the election of Arnulf came to pass—his first act as patriarch was to deny all Christians, except those following Latin rites, access to Holy Sepulchre.

A Compact with Duke Godfrey

Immediately following the "election" I hurried to Godfrey's office and was ushered in by an attendant.

"It's you Father. Come in. Come in."

"My Lord, perhaps you heard of Arnulf's election today. I failed you. For that I apologize deeply. There's nothing I can say."

"Oderic, my loyal friend, yes, I just heard about it from one of my Lorrainer chaplains. No apology is necessary. No. You are *not* to be blamed. And truthfully, I am quite in awe of your ingenuity, a ruse which nearly succeeded. In truth it *did* succeed. Adhémar's Cross is still safe?"

"Yes my Lord."

"What do you intend with it?"

"Bishop Adhémar requested before he passed that I deliver it to His Holiness in Rome. I promised to do that and I shall. However, I must petition you, a petition I submit with deep reluctance and even deeper embarrassment."

"What is that?"

"I rescued a Jewish spice trader and his wife from the synagogue before it was burned. Through what is called 'Hezekiah's Tunnel'. I was in their debt."

"Yes I heard a little about this. You were seen emerging with an elderly man and woman into the Pool of Siloam. Tell me about it." I did so, relating all the circumstances with a detailed description of the tunnel."

"Quite daring, I must say. I admire your courage and devotion to your friends. I shall find the tunnel's entrance and rock it over. If you were able to escape from the city to the outside, someone with motives less pure than yours might use it to infiltrate within the walls. Now, what is your petition?"

"My Jewish friends lost everything in Jerusalem. I gave them my coach and a full purse, all I had. I am now . . . now a . . . "

"A pauper?" Godfrey completing my sentence.

"Yes, my Lord, in a word, a pauper."

"You need say nothing more. Father, I think in years to come your fame in this great pilgrimage will eclipse even my own. I actually welcome that. It's well deserved. Your purse will be replenished and then some."

"My Lord, I am deeply grateful. I shall repay you when I am able, though I cannot foresee when. I ask only for your patience."

"Father, this is the very least I can do. I dare say that without you my tower would have burned and we would never have taken Jerusalem. I also grieve for the loss of your Rebecca. You intend to meet the pope?"

"I do. I wish to leave as soon as possible. After his 'election', if I may use this term far more generously than deserved, Arnulf threatened to find me. I do not fear for myself, only my son."

"I shall assist. There are ships in Jaffa, two of them Venice-bound. I shall today send one of my captains to arrange for your transport, at my expense. But there is something you can do for me."

"My Lord?"

"Pope Urban has passed. The new pope is His Holiness Paschal. You require no letter of introduction from me. I'm quite certain your very name will be admission enough. When you meet with him I ask only that you report the truth of Arnulf, a pestilence, a blight on Jerusalem. I think no one knows his iniquities better than you. Will you do that for me?"

"My Lord, I shall undertake this with enthusiasm. His base character *must* be exposed."

"Good. We have received word that the army of Sultan al-Afdal is encamped outside the city of Ascalon, forty miles from here. I suspect he assumes we shall hide behind the walls of Jerusalem. His army is considerably larger than our own. Our victory depends on surprise and taking the battle to him. The army leaves Jerusalem in two days but without Count Raymond and the Duke of Normandy. Raymond was humiliated by my election as Advocate of the Holy Sepulchre and then became consumed with anger when Peter of Narbonne surrendered the Tower of David to me. Both of them, their armies too, are in Jericho where Raymond is sulking. I am perplexed why the duke joined him. I sent them a message two days ago that al-Afdal is at Ascalon and their aid was urgent. Their answer was rather curt: 'Reports of al-Afdal at Ascalon are unconfirmed. We shall remain where we are.' Whether they will join us is uncertain. Without them I fear the worst."

Godfrey now changed the subject. "I remember in Constantinople you told me you were keeping a daily journal. Are you still doing that?"

"I am my Lord."

"To write a chronicle telling of our great deeds?"

"Some," I answered cautiously.

"When you judge the past, remember this: Great deeds, like the actions of great men, are never unblemished. They are two sides of the same coin. Without one the other cannot exist." Godfrey paused in thought. "And how will I fare in this chronicle of yours?"

"You will figure well, except . . ." I had said too much.

"Except? Except?" Godfrey asked, more out of curiosity than intimidation. "Oh yes. My attack on Constantinople. Yes. Pure folly on my part. Or perhaps something else?"

"Something else," I answered simply. It was too late to evade the next question, certain to come.

"Then I think I know. It was my order to slay the Saracen prisoners after the siege, was it not? I saw it on your face at council."

"It was, my Lord."

"I understand Father. But you must understand this: I did not order their execution because they were heathens. That of course made the decision easier. No, not that. We shall face a formidable force in al-Afdal. My scouts tell me they outnumber us, by two to one, perhaps more. I could not afford leaving troops to guard them. Worse, if they escaped they would join al-Afdal or possibly form a second line of attack behind us. That would mean fighting on two fronts, not just one. I hope that is included in your chronicle."

"I promise it shall be."

The Final Battle

On August 9 Godfrey marched out of Jerusalem with the Count of Flanders to meet our foe on the field of Ascalon. On the day before the army marched barefoot to the Church of the Holy Sepulchre and then to the Temple of Solomon. Arnulf, shamelessly holding aloft the counterfeit cross, led the procession—first the priests singing hymns of praise and prayers for God's intercession against the pagans, then the princes, and after them their soldiers followed by pilgrims. We headed east to Ibilin, inland, south of Jaffa and north of Ascalon. To our surprise we encountered a herd of cows, sheep, and goats, two hundred in number, al-Afdal's animals to feed his army. The herdsmen were killed, saving one because of the intelligence he offered though only after seeing his fellow herdsmen slain and he threatened with torture. Al-Afdal indeed expected the crusaders to remain in Jerusalem. Siege engines had been transported by Fatimid ships to the port of Ascalon and were now being unloaded. He planned to decamp on the 13th for Jerusalem having no idea we were so near. All was working in Godfrey's favor. Most concerning, however, was confirmation of earlier reports Godfrey had received of the size of al-Afdal's army—even if reinforced by Raymond and Robert we would still be greatly outnumbered. Godfrey sent another urgent plea to both princes. There was no reply.

The following day, the 10th of August, we continued our march south closer to Ascalon. Al-Afdal had become complacent, confident that we would remain in Jerusalem and had dispatched no scouts, thus ignorant of our approach. We had the element of surprise. Such a wretched night we spent without tents, bread, or wine. We did have plenty of fresh meat so our bellies were full. I found a cow with a calf not yet weaned. I milked her to feed my son. Our march recommenced the next morning. What was most curious was the herd—it followed us instinctively, requiring no one to direct them, stopping when we stopped, continuing forward as we did. If Raymond and Robert would not join our ranks, perhaps these animals would, reinforcements sent by God some believed.

At midday on the 11th Godfrey and Robert of Flanders held a council of their captains. There was agreement that our attack would have to be the next day as al-Afdal planned to decamp the following. Morale of the captains was low; Raymond and Robert of Normandy had still not come. Godfrey and Robert did their best to raise it, unsuccessfully. But then we heard the sound of trumpets. The Provençals and Normans had finally arrived to the hurrahs of the Lorrainers and Flemings, Raymond and Robert now convinced from their own reconnaissance that Godfrey had not exaggerated the threat. Even though our army was at full strength, we were still greatly outnumbered. But at least we were united.

Just before daybreak on the following morning, August 12, we formed into three squadrons of three lines apiece, in a curved shape, the knights in the first line and behind them the foot. In front of the army was the herd, new "recruits" to our army. Having forsworn my role as a "warrior-priest" I remained behind. The attack was launched with the blare of trumpets. The animals, frightened by the sound, stampeded forward goaded by the lances of knights behind poking their tails. The hooves of the animals stirred up such dust that the Saracens must have thought this was an army far in excess of its true size. On the plain in front of Ascalon's city walls I could see Saracen tents without number, soldiers tumbling out on hearing the trumpets and thunder of hooves. Hell had arrived. The animals crashed through the Saracen camp tearing down tents and trampling all in their path. Behind them came our knights, their lances couched or hurling javelins, and finally the foot with spears or drawn swords. The Saracens panicked without time to organize a defense. They fled instead. Those not killed in the initial attack sought safety in a grove of trees which they climbed to conceal themselves. They were discovered, crusader arrows settling their fate. Others fled to Ascalon's gates rushing through, many suffocating under the crush, those behind clambering over their bodies. The battle was soon over. Then plunder. And what rich plunder it was: large chests of gold and silver coin, jewels, weapons, and horses. Our soldiers raced from one tent to another seizing everything of value. No soldier returned to Jerusalem empty-handed. There was great rejoicing that night. Al-Afdal had taken refuge in the city. A few days later he returned to Babylon with his fleet.

On the following day, victory complete, the army marched back to Jerusalem. I was about to turn my horse to Jaffa when a small detachment of Godfrey's knights found me. "The Lord Advocate wishes to speak with you."

Godfrey was in the midst of supervising the transport of bullion plundered from the Saracens. He saw me and with a wide grin shouted "Oderic! Victory! Over here!"

I dismounted and handed my son to one of the knights who accepted him easily, surely a father himself. "Lord Advocate," congratulating him, "a great victory."

Godfrey embraced me. "Indeed," Godfrey answered. "I have little time now. Too much to do. My soldiers will escort you to Jaffa where a ship awaits. Arrangements have already been made for you with special accommodations. If you are not treated well, I'll hear of it. But I've made certain you will be. It will depart in two days for Venice. A wet nurse, the same who nursed your boy in Jerusalem, will accompany you. She is healthy enough to feed two on the voyage. Sadly, her husband was killed in the siege and she wishes to return to her home in Italia, just north of Rome where you'll be going. And finally, a gift. Rainald" calling out to his adjutant who reached into his saddlebag extracting a silver goblet, the most exquisite I've ever see, filigreed in gold. "Father Oderic, this is for you with my eternal gratitude." And then with a giggle, "It actually is a gift from Sultan al-Afdal I found in his tent. I'm certain he'd be delighted to know it now belongs to a Christian priest." He then lingered in thought looking at me quite intently, "If you ever tire of being a priest, there is always a place for you here in Jerusalem beside me."

"This is too much," I protested quite sincerely. "I cannot accept."

"You *must* and you *will*. I am, after all, the lord of Jerusalem whose will cannot be refused," he answered smiling. "You have given too much, Father, in the service of our pilgrimage, I know often with misgivings and yet always fearlessly. Remember my request: When you meet His Holiness spare no detail about Arnulf. This is not about retaliation but about the future of Jerusalem." Godfrey embraced me, his lips close to my ear "And in your chronicle be generous to this poor servant of God who made the best decisions he could."

Audience with Pope Paschal

I reached the port of Jaffa. As promised a ship was waiting. Its captain greeted me genially and provided his own cabin for my use. The voyage took only three days, a calm sea and a brisk wind behind us. We arrived in Venice. The last time I was there was when I accompanied Samuel ben Meier many years before on a trading mission. I so wished to explore this wondrous city but Rome called and then La Charité after that. I was anxious to return home. I hired a modest carriage to take us to Rome. On reaching it, the Lateran Palace was my first stop. The gates were closed and guarded.

"I am Oderic," I announced, "a monk of La Charité sur Loire bearing a gift of the True Cross for His Holiness from Bishop Adhémar of Le Puy, formerly Papal Legate."

The guard from behind the bars of the gate peered at me quite suspiciously, responding with a gruff "Wait here," strolling casually into the palace.

I waited but not long. The palace doors swung open and two priests, their black cassocks flowing behind them, came springing down the steps bounding across the piazza, the guard doing his best to keep pace. "Father Oderic," one shouted at me, waving his hand, "don't leave! His Holiness awaits you. Follow us." They led me into the palace down a passageway to a modest audience hall in the pope's private quarters. Two attendants stood by the door. Without choice I handed my son to one of them who took him rather clumsily with a bewildered look. I decided he would be safer in my arms.

Paschal was sitting on an upholstered chair covered in red velvet, a priest standing beside him. He beckoned me forward. I knelt before him and kissed his ring which he extended to me.

"Oderic of La Charité sur Loire. We have heard so many stories about you, even here in Rome. A 'warrior-priest', we've been told, surely a singular epithet, the most famous of all Jerusalemites. We are delighted to meet you. Who is this young one with you?"

"My son, Your Holiness. I apologize for bringing him into your hall but I was hoping for your blessing."

"Your son?" he queried, more out of curiosity than the censure which I rather expected. "Present him to me." I lifted him out of the sling and with my hands under his armpits stretched him out before the pope. "*In nomine Patris et Filii et Spiritus Sancti*", making the sign of the cross with two fingers over his head. Gratefully my son was quite peaceful, looking up at Paschal as though studying his features. "A fine looking boy." I stepped back in respectful silence. "Father Oderic, we have so much to discuss. I want to know everything."

"Your Holiness. I would be pleased to tell you my story. But with your permission I have two gifts." The pope nodded. Reaching into my satchel I withdrew the reliquary. "This precious object contains a piece of the True Cross. It was entrusted to me by Bishop Adhémar shortly before he died to be given to you."

"You mean Pope Urban," correcting me. "But we are humbled to receive it. We grieve for Bishop Adhémar's passing." I handed the reliquary to the priest beside him who in turn passed it to the pope. "Magnificent," lifting the lid gazing briefly inside then closing it. Perhaps he had already seen too many "True Crosses". "Father Anthony, please take it to my chapel. I wish to pray before it this evening."

"And this", I said, retrieving the palm branch from my satchel, "from the sacred River Jordan." I handed the branch to Anthony who again passed it on to the pope, Paschal fingering it with curiosity.   "Shall I put it in the chapel, Your Holiness?" Anthony asked. Paschal nodded.

"Please bring a chair for Father Oderic. Father, I wish to hear everything. From the beginning."

And from the beginning I began, starting with my decision to join the Great Pilgrimage. Paschal seemed particularly intrigued with Peter the Hermit and his followers. I decided not to describe them as "rabble". Then through the Rhineland. Occasionally Paschal would interject either comments or questions. "Yes, we mourn for the Jewish community in Mainz. Murderous. Unforgivable. Pope Urban received a dispatch from Bishop Ruthard of Mainz which I have read reporting your attempt to protect it." I did not mention Ruthard's betrayal of the community. That would be fully exposed in my chronicle later. "I heard too that you succeeded in rescuing a Jewess from Thomas of Marle, a thoroughly wicked man, no less a scourge in Francia today than he was in Mainz."

"Rebecca was her name," I replied.

"Whatever happened to her? I have heard she accompanied you to Jerusalem."

"That is true. We married but she was slain."

"No doubt in a Christian ceremony. Curious. It is very rare for a Jew to convert to our faith."

I was prepared to blur or elide over certain events. Not about Rebecca. "No Your Holiness. She did not convert. In a Jewish ceremony, at Edessa."

Paschal looked at me in astonishment, grimacing. "I have never heard of such a thing. A *priest* married to a *Jewess* by a *rabbi*. Unthinkable!" I fully expected to be immediately dismissed from his presence. He leaned back in contemplation, staring at me. "You loved her, I assume?"

"Deeply, Your Holiness. I grieve for her even now and will for the rest of my life." Looking down lovingly at my son, "This is our child."

"Father Oderic, you have suffered much and given much. While I cannot condone such a marriage neither shall I condemn it. That is for God though . . ." looking at me kindly, "I suspect He will be merciful. Until then and while it is within my power I give you absolution, "*Te absolvo*," waving the sign of the cross over me. "No penance is required. Please continue."

I proceeded through to Antioch and the defeat of Kerboqa. My son was beginning to fidget and then cry. He was hungry. "Your Holiness, my son has not eaten. I have a wet nurse waiting in a carriage outside your gates. May I . . ."

"Yes. Certainly. Anthony, please arrange chambers for Father and the nurse, a repast as well. May we continue tomorrow morning?"

"It would be my honor, Your Holiness."

The next morning I was summoned to Paschal's hall. I completed the story, through to the battle of Ascalon. Though I had often phrased my story carefully, I spared no detail about Arnulf: his debauchery, the obscene songs sung about him, the sham trial of Rebecca for witchcraft, his torture of Abbot Demetrios, his "election" by force of arms. All was revealed. I had delivered on my promise to Godfrey and I took much joy in it.

"We have heard many rumors of Bishop Arnulf's infidelities to the Mother Church. I had hoped they were unfounded gossip but you have confirmed them all. This Arnulf is unworthy to be a priest, let alone a bishop, and even more the patriarch of Jerusalem, a most uncanonical election purchased by intimidation. I shall immediately send a letter to Daimbert, Archbishop of Pisa, now Papal Legate to the Holy Land. He shall be instructed to remove Arnulf from his office." I had hoped he would be defrocked but was satisfied with this result.

"Father Oderic. We are grateful for your service to Our Lord and not least for your service to us these two days. Tomorrow you shall depart for your priory. I shall provide an escort of our papal guards—there are brigands on the road—and a carriage. On the way I ask that you stop at the Abbey of Cluny. I'm certain Abbot Hugh will be keen to hear your tales. I shall send a courier to advise him of your visit. And then to La Charité where we hope you will find peace and rest. May God be with you, always."

Return to La Charité and a Revelation

The journey from Rome through Italia and then to Francia was quite pleasant. I stopped at Cluny for two days meeting with Abbot Hugh. And then to La Charité. Passing through the priory's gate the same porter was there, evidently having survived the chamberlain Roderick's ill temper, doffing his hat and waving. All the monks had gathered in the priory's courtyard, alerted to my arrival, forming a double line singing hymns of welcome and bowing as I passed through, a ceremony reserved for popes, abbots, and priors—not for a common monk. Prior Bernard was standing on the steps of the portico waiting for me. As I stepped down from the carriage he and the monks began clapping and breaking out in cheers *"The Jerusalemite has returned!"* And I had.

* * *

Father Oderic thought his chronicle now complete. "Brother Samuel," he said to me, "I think this concludes my story. I have so enjoyed my time with you and am now thankful for your insistence, even if obstinate, that I tell it," he said with a twinkle in my eye.

"Father, your story is *not* concluded, not yet," I protested. "What happened to your son? You haven't mentioned his name. Not even *once*. Nothing is done until it's done. And we are *not* done."

"Ah . . . my son . . . Yes. I placed him in a nunnery near Cluny. Abbot Hugh made the arrangement with the abbess, his sister, to care for him until he would enter the abbey as an oblate. She was reluctant to receive him but Abbot Hugh can be quite persuasive when he chooses. As it happened one of the sisters had been a midwife, herself a mother, taking the vows after her husband passed. I left him there confident he was in good care. Later, at the age of seven, he was admitted to the abbey. He is now a monk. Quite a learned one I'm told. He has done well."

"Why did you never name him?"

"Oh we did. Rebecca picked it."

"What did you name him?"

Father shifted uneasily. "Remember the peculiar hermit at the Mount of Olives, that names are without consequence?" It was an evasive answer, clumsy at best. I'm sure he hoped it would suffice. It didn't.

"Hmm, Father you're concealing something. I'm uncertain what is your reason. Like your son I too was raised in a nunnery close to Cluny, 'Queen of Angels'. I recall a palm branch in my room. No one seem to know, or refused to tell me, how it came to be there other than a 'monk' had left it with me when I was brought to the nunnery. I remember also that when I entered the abbey as an oblate Abbot Hugh himself interviewed me, quite kindly as I remember, the only occasion I was told he had done this. Thereafter, the abbot took an unusual interest in my training and education."

"Well, I'm certain a man of your intellectual talents and spiritual qualities merited such attention, even in your tender years," Father answered. "Samuel, I've become rather weary and should probably retire."

For two months I had faithfully recorded Father's dictation, only rarely interrupting. For the second time, the first when I insisted on knowing the fate of Rebecca, I adopted a rather belligerent tone. "*Not yet*, Father! We're not finished. There's more here. You're hiding something. I think I know what it is. I remember now that at Cluny the Master of Novices was about to punish me for an infraction, something, I don't recall what. He spared me because I was the 'son of a famous Jerusalemite'. And then, for reasons never explained, the day after I professed my vows as a priest Abbot Hugh called me to his office, extremely unusual by itself, and requested that I *agree* to being transferred to *this* priory. He explained only that it would 'please him mightily'. Such a request from an *abbot*, especially to a newly professed monk, was remarkable. And finally, you said that Rebecca had selected your son's name. Rebecca was the daughter of *Samuel* ben Meier. She was my mother. You are my father."

He sat there silently. Not a word. There was little point in denial. "Your mother would be proud of you," he answered softly. "As I am."

"But why have you tried so hard to conceal this from me? I don't understand."

"I feared that if you knew, you would become too personally invested in this account, losing the detachment necessary to write an authentic chronicle. I regret you have discovered my secret."

"But that does not explain why, in the many years we spent together at the priory, that I never had the sense I was special to you."

"The answer is simple. If I paid unusual attention to you questions would be raised. There are so many tales about me, I'm certain my relationship with Rebecca and the birth of a child conceived in an unholy wedlock, a Christian priest and a Jewess, among them. This would be rich fodder for the wags in our priory and you would be subject to malicious gossip. This would serve you ill. So, I maintained a prudent distance. Yet, in these years I watched you closely, albeit from a distance. Do you remember twice when you committed serious breaches of discipline and were about to be reported to chapter? I intervened, discreetly. There are privileges to being a 'famous Jerusalemite.'" I did recall that and how the charges just seemed to disappear.

"Samuel," Father Oderic continued, "my end is near, God's will, *Deus vult*. The manuscript is now in your hands to complete. Always remember as you write, the truth is incontrovertible. Ignorance may attack it, malice distort it, but truth is never to be compromised."

Tears began streaming down my face. "My father . . . my father," my voice breaking, "I deeply hope you are wrong. But I vow to complete the chronicle without gloss and with integrity, just as you dictated it. Someday it will be published to the world. On this I am committed, with devotion."

He knew I would.

* * *

Father Oderic of Rheims, the "Jerusalemite of La Charité sur Loire" as he came to be known, died two months later in the Year of Our Lord 1130 and was buried in the priory's cemetery next to his beloved Father Benedict. Two weeks later a memorial service was held, unique in the history of La Charité. Peter "the Venerable", then abbot of Cluny, personally attended as did the son of Count Robert of Flanders, the count having passed. Pope Honorius sent two cardinals as his representatives. And of course all the monks of our priory were present, they especially in deep mourning. I regretted his passing so soon after our dictation ended and not having the opportunity in earlier years to spend more time with him. Yet, I am so grateful for those many weeks together, day after day. Joyful memories.

This chronicle, *Jerusalem Falls!*, is the work of a true Jerusalemite, an heroic warrior, God-fearing priest, a faithful husband, and my father.

This ends Book XV of *Jerusalem Falls!*

APPENDIX

EPILOGUE

Most of the surviving crusaders after the battle at Ascalon, their pilgrimage completed, straggled back to Europe, generally impoverished but for the distinction of now being honored as "Jerusalemites". Many carried back relics of the Holy Land: pieces of the True Cross and the Holy Lance, stones from the Holy Sepulchre, a ball of the Virgin Mary's hair as she witnessed the crucifixion of her son, clippings of Jesus's beard, body parts of several saints including John the Baptist. Churches and monasteries were flooded with them. Godfrey of Bouillon, "Advocate of the Holy Sepulchre", was left with a slender force of a few hundred knights and perhaps two thousand men-at-arms. He made urgent appeals to Pope Paschal II for reinforcements. Paschal answered by announcing a new expedition, known in history as the "Crusade of 1101", also referred to as the "Crusade of the Faint-Hearted" because of the number of participants who had abandoned the First Crusade before reaching Jerusalem and were reviled at home. The response was as enthusiastic as it was to Urban II's at Clermont. The armies—French, northern Italian (Lombards), and German estimated to be as large as the previous—began departing from Europe in September 1099 and assembled at Constantinople. From there, they crossed the Bosporus with Count Raymond of Toulouse as adviser and guide. Raymond brought with him the Holy Lance. By now, the sultans and emirs, led principally by Qilij Arslan, had learned their lesson from the previous crusade, that only by setting aside their personal ambitions and uniting could they defeat the Christians. In the summer of 1101 the crusader armies were decimated in battles at Mersivan and Heraclea in Turkey. No more than a few hundred crusaders reached Jerusalem.

The subsequent sequence of events in Palestine, Syria, and southern Turkey is too complicated to trace here. The following is a summary: In 1100 Duke Godfrey fell ill following a banquet hosted by a local emir. It was suspected that he had been poisoned; more likely he died of typhoid. By now, the remaining crusaders wished to restore customary usages, to be ruled by a "king". Before his death, Godfrey named his younger brother, Baldwin of Boulogne, then Count of Edessa, as his successor. Baldwin was crowned "King of Jerusalem" on Christmas Day 1100. He ruled until his death in 1118. The kingdom itself survived until 1187 when the famous Saladin recaptured the city. The County of Edessa fell earlier to the Turks in 1144 prompting the unsuccessful Second Crusade (1147-49), the Principality of Antioch to the Mamelukes (Egyptians) in 1268, and the County of Tripoli to the Mamelukes in 1289. In 1291, when Acre, the last refuge of crusaders, fell to the Mamelukes, the crusader presence in the Holy Land after almost two hundred years disappeared.

The following is a brief description of the fates of the significant characters appearing in this novel:

- **Alexios Komnenos**: The success of the First Crusade enabled the Byzantine Empire to reclaim lost territory in western Turkey. However, this required Alexios to continually defend this land from Seljuk Turks in addition to dealing with palace intrigues at home. He died in 1118 from disease.

- **Arnulf of Choques**: At the end of 1099 he was deposed as Patriarch of Jerusalem because of the "uncanonical" nature of his election, not least because he was the illegitimate son of a Flemish priest. Daimbert, Archbishop of Pisa and papal legate, was elected in his place though shortly after he too was removed by a new papal legate over questions about the regularity of his election. In 1112 Arnulf was restored to the patriarchy, losing it again in 1115, regaining it the following year, dying in 1118.

- **Bohemond of Taranto**: After the fall of Jerusalem Bohemond attempted to expand his principality but was captured by Turkish Danishmends at the Battle of Meletine, Turkey, in 1100. He was released three years later after an enormous ransom was raised. In 1104 he returned to Europe where he encouraged a crusade against Emperor Alexios Komnenos whom he believed to be a serious threat to his rule over Antioch. The "crusade" ended in surrender to Alexios in modern day Albania. He then retired a broken man to his estates in southern Italy dying in 1111.

- **Hugh "the Great" Count of Vermandois;** Hugh, brother of Philip I, King of France, had been dispatched by crusader princes from Antioch to plead, unsuccessfully, for Alexios to send reinforcements. Rather than return to Antioch he left for home but suffered such ignominy that he joined the Crusade of 1101. He died from wounds at the battle of Heraclea in that year.

- **Peter the Hermit**: Peter returned to his homeland soon after Ascalon. It is generally believed he founded an Augustinian monastery named for the Church of the Holy Sepulchre at Neufmoustier in Flanders where he died in 1115 and was buried.

- **Raymond, Count of Toulouse and St-Gilles**: Raymond participated in the disastrous Crusade of 1101, barely escaping. He went to Constantinople and thence to Antioch where Tancred, the regent, imprisoned him. After release, Raymond embarked on a siege of Tripoli (Lebanon) dying in 1105 before its capture in 1109. He is credited with founding the fourth crusader state, the County of Tripoli.

- **Robert, Count of Flanders**: Robert left Palestine soon after Ascalon bringing back a relic, the arm of Saint George, a gift from Emperor Alexios. He became involved in local wars and was killed in battle in 1111.

- **Robert "Curthose", Duke of Normandy**: Robert left the Holy Land shortly after victory at Ascalon and returned to his duchy in Normandy which he had inherited from his father, William the Conqueror. He became embroiled in a dispute with his brother, Henry II, King of England, claiming the throne for himself. Robert was defeated by Henry at a battle in Normandy, 1106, imprisoned and died in captivity at Cardiff Castle in 1134.

- **Stephen, Count of Blois**: Stephen was one of the "rope dancers" who deserted Antioch during Kerboqa's siege, returning in disgrace to France. His wife Adela, daughter of William the Conqueror, was so shamed by his conduct that she forced him to return to the Holy Land to atone for his sin. He joined the Crusade of 1101. In 1102 he accompanied Baldwin, now King of Jerusalem, in an ill-fated attack on an Egyptian force at Ramla and was killed.

- **Tancred of Hauteville, known also as the "Prince of Galilee"**: Tancred served as regent of the Principality of Antioch during Bohemond's captivity from 1100 to 1103. On Bohemond's release, he was relieved of the regency but then restored when Bohemond left for Europe, a position he held until his death in 1112 at the age of 36 from a typhoid epidemic.

- **Thomas of Marle, Count of Coucy**: Thomas returned to Coucy following the crusade. His penchant for brutality continued unabated, engaging in ruthless wars to expand his domain. So rapacious was his conduct both on the battlefield and his treatment of prisoners that he was excommunicated and Louis VI, King of France, launched a series of attacks against him. Thomas was mortally wounded in one. It was said on his deathbed in 1130 while receiving the Eucharist he broke his neck.

HISTORICAL NOTES

Book II: My Life at La Charité sur Loire

The Priory of La Charité sur Loire, located in the medieval town by the same name in Burgundy, France, was founded in 1059 by Cluniac monks and was the eldest daughter-house of the powerful Abbey of Cluny. Historical information is quite sparse. Monasteries were often funded by lords out of their manorial lands generally in return for absolution of sins and regular prayers by monks for their eternal salvation. La Charité was likely no exception.

Medieval medicine has long fascinated me. The Church's view was that sickness was the consequence of sin cured only by repentance and prayer. Galen, the Greek physician and philosopher (129-200 AD), found a more "scientific" explanation, that illness was the result of an imbalance of the four "humors". Layer on that astrology as a diagnostic tool and we have nearly a complete medical manual for the Middle Ages that prevailed for centuries.

Finally, the belief in relics, generally the body parts of saints, is one of the more fascinating features of medieval culture and of the credulity of the age. In the tenth and eleventh centuries especially there was a thriving industry in their collection by the Church. They attracted pilgrims, particularly for their healing powers, and with them came rich donations to churches and monasteries, eager purchasers seldom if ever questioning their authenticity despite widespread fraud. The story of the hand of Saint John the Martyr, fictional, is emblematic. The power of these relics is a continuing theme of this novel.

Book III: Journey to Clermont and Cluny

There were three principal reasons for the enthusiastic popular response to Pope Urban II's call for a great crusade (for the nobility, as one emeritus historian of the First Crusade wrote, it was "plunder, conquest, and adventure"): famine, lawlessness, and penance through religious pilgrimage (the third to be explained more fully in the Historical Notes to Book IV). France, in the north especially, had been devastated in the years prior to 1095 by drought and consequently famine and plague. Ergotism, a fungus that affects barley, rye, wheat and other grains, was particularly devastating, one of its most prominent symptoms blackened limbs, hence the name "Holy Fire" (later known as "St. Anthony's Fire"), in extreme cases dementia. Conditions were so severe that the chronicler Guibert of Nogent, a contemporary, wrote: "Masses of poor people learned to feed often on the roots of wild plants since they were compelled by the scarcity of bread to search everywhere for some possible substitute."

Another feature of the age was lawlessness and banditry throughout the country. Again, Guibert of Nogent: "At that time, before people set out on the journey [to the Holy Land], there was a great disturbance, with fierce fighting throughout the kingdom of the Franks. Everywhere people spoke of rampant thievery, highway robbery. Endless fires burned everywhere. Battles for no discernible reason except uncontrollable greed." No one was safe.

The name of Peter the Hermit is indelibly imprinted on the First Crusade. A powerful, eloquent preacher, he aroused near hysterical enthusiasm wherever he went. One modern historian estimated he had 40,000 followers by the time he reached Germany, more after that. He was venerated as a holy man, his donkey as well. Guibert of Nogent marveled: "Even the hairs of his mule were torn out as though they were relics, which we report not as truth but as a novelty loved by the common people."

Book IV: Massacre of Jews

Pope Urban II was overwhelmed by the response to his call for a crusade. What he had not expected, nor welcomed, was that most of the crusaders were not soldiers but poor peasants without military training. Arguably the single most important factor motivating their near hysterical enthusiasm was the religious fervor of the age. From about 1000 AD a profound religious sentiment penetrated all levels of European society, in particular an overwhelming sense of sin as the cause of all misfortune, especially illness, which could be purged only by prayer and pilgrimage. Related to this was the growth of the cult of saints and belief in the curative power of relics. It was truly an age dominated by credulity and superstition. There is no better example of this than stories of the goose and the goat. One contemporary wrote: "[Pilgrims] asserted that a certain goose was inspired by the Holy Spirit and that a she-goat was not less filled by the same spirit. These they made their guides on this holy journey to Jerusalem. Those they worshiped excessively and most of the people followed them like beasts believing with their whole minds that this was the true course."

The pogrom of Jews in the Rhineland is the single most doleful, tragic feature of the march through the Rhineland. One modern historian opined that, in general, the goal of crusaders was conversion rather than annihilation. I am less certain. The Church in Rome was opposed to forcible conversion; in any event it was seldom successful for Jews swiftly returned to their faith. Some bishops did try to protect Jews, arguably less for reasons of conscience than bribes and the revenues these communities provided from taxation; others betrayed promises of protection. The Bishop of Speyer John and the Archbishop of Mainz Ruthard are examples of both. The principal collaborators were local parish priests, monks, and leading municipal merchants, the burghers, though there were exceptions to the last.

One notable feature of the pogroms was the readiness of Jews to commit ritual suicide rather than fall into crusader hands, shocking even to medieval minds. One Hebrew chronicler tells the story of Rachel in Mainz, the mother of four. A female friend came to Rachel's home where she sharpened a knife to ensure it had no nicks. Rachel enjoined her "Have no mercy on them [her children] lest the uncircumcised ones come and seize them alive and raise them in their ways of error." The friend killed three, Rachel the fourth. "Then [Rachel] placed them all on her arms two children on one side and two on the other and they quivered beside her till the enemy captured the chamber and found her sitting there lamenting over them." Rachel was killed. Her story inspired mine of Rebecca. The Jewish communities in the Rhineland were decimated, those of Mainz and Worms, possibly others, eradicated. One modern historian estimated three thousand Jews died, another five thousand. I incline toward the latter figure.

Book V: Butchery on the Danube

Crusader armies began leaving Europe in the spring of 1096, some later. They followed three principal routes to the point of rendezvous, Constantinople. One was down the Danube River (taken by Oderic); the second was from Italy embarking at Brindisi or Bari, across the Adriatic Sea by ship to Dyrrachium or Durazzo on the western coast of modern-day Albania and then along the Via Egnatia, an ancient Roman military road; the third was from southern France, over the Alps, through northern Italy, circling the head of the Adriatic and then south through the land of the Slavs who gave crusaders no little trouble.

Peter the Hermit's "army" entered the Kingdom of Hungary peacefully until it reached Semlin. The sources generally agree that a small number of Walter the Penniless's men-at-arms who had passed through Semlin earlier had gotten into an altercation with Semlin merchants, the men-at-arms expelled, their clothing and armor hung from the city walls. When the bulk of Peter's force arrived and saw this, it flew into a rage, Geoffrey Burel especially. This was followed quickly by a dispute over the purchase of shoes resulting in crusader attack on the city's citadel and inhabitants, according to one source four thousand Hungarians killed. What is disputed is whether Peter encouraged the attack or tried to restrain his followers. Fearing retribution from the King of Hungary, he ordered his people to leave immediately. On the way they pillaged Belgrade, just across the river. Upon reaching Nish Peter's followers burned some mills and attacked the city. Byzantine Pechenegs and Bulgarians responded with a counter-attack and Peter's followers were routed, many killed or captured.

Roughly at the same time Count Emicho and the priests Gottschalk and Volkmar led different armies through Hungary pillaging along the Danube River as they hunted for Jews. Their fates were as described in this novel. One emeritus historian of the Crusades wrote of the European response to the collapse of these three campaigns: "To most good Christians it appeared as a punishment meted out from on high to the murderers of the Jews. Others, who had thought the whole Crusading movement to be foolish and wrong, saw in these disasters God's open disavowal of it all."

Book VI: The Peasants Crusade

Book VI tells the story of the "Peasants Crusade", also variously known as the "People's Crusade" or the "Paupers Crusade", terms that only came into use centuries later. Modern historians rely on contemporary or near-contemporary chronicles. Yet none of the chroniclers was an eyewitness, their accounts based on second-hand, perhaps third-hand, reports probably provided by the remnants of Peter's army who returned to Constantinople. Thus they differ considerably. There is, however, general agreement about certain key events: pilgrims pillaging Greek Christian villages as they marched to Civitot; and then on reaching Civitot more pillaging raids south and in the region of Nicea held by the Turks two days from Civitot. The sources also agree that Geoffrey Burel, leader of the French, led a successful raid almost to the gates of Nicea, again targeting Greek Christians. His success excited the jealously of the northern Italians (Lombards), led by Rainald, a minor noble about whom little is known, and the Germans. Rainald launched his own expedition, reaching "Xerigordos" in the general vicinity of Nicea, its specific location never identified. Thereafter the details become rather murky: whether Xerigordos had been deserted or the crusaders besieged and captured it; whether the Turks stormed Xerigordos or whether the crusaders, through lack of water, were forced to surrender; also Rainald's ambiguous role in the crusaders' surrender, though there is some suggestion in one of the chronicles that he betrayed the crusaders to save himself. Nevertheless, it is clear that Rainald's force—other than those who surrendered and renounced their faith to be sold into slavery—was destroyed. It is clear too that there was rising anger amongst the crusaders over events at Xerigordos. Geoffrey Burel left Civitot to exact revenge and to pillage but was met by an army of Qilij Arslan near Civitot and decimated. Similar to descriptions of Xerigordos, broad outline is clear but details provided by the chronicles are impossible to reconcile.

We do know, however, that the Peasants Crusade ended in catastrophe. Against the sober advice given by Emperor Alexios Komnenos, Peter decided to cross the Bosporus into Turkey where they faced trained, hardened Turkish warriors. The result was predictable. One military historian of the period estimated that of the many thousands who embarked on the crusade, perhaps three thousand survived. I suspect even that figure is rather overstated. Thereafter, Peter becomes a peripheral figure in the history of the First Crusade.

Book VII: Homage to the Emperor

The attempted abduction of Rebecca at the Temple of Apollo and Aphrodite and flight to the cistern is of course fictional, except for this: Bathhouses were celebrated in Byzantine poetry, second only to the Hippodrome. But in some cases there was a blurred distinction between a bathhouse and a brothel. Those in the vicinity of the Aqueduct of Valens were especially notorious. The cisterns of Constantinople are some of the few magnificent architectural monuments of the Byzantine Empire still remaining in Istanbul. The Basilica Cistern, near the Hagia Sophia, was featured in the James Bond movie *From Russia with Love*.

Alexios did greet the crusader princes cordially but required a pledge of homage from each that they would restore to the empire lands which the Turks had conquered in Turkey. In return, they would be transported across the Bosporus and richly rewarded. I limited my description of Alexios's audiences to two, with Bohemond and Raymond. Both were the greatest leaders of the First Crusade but the rivalry between them was intense, each wishing to be the supreme commander of the various crusader armies, their mutual animosity intensifying over time. Bohemond gave his oath easily, though later he broke it just as easily. Raymond resisted, agreeing essentially to pledging his allegiance to Alexios but not his homage, and this only under threat from the other crusader princes. Yet, curiously, of them all he proved to be Alexios's most faithful ally, to Raymond's cost.

Another feature of the two-months sojourn of the crusaders in Constantinople was their deep mistrust of Alexios. Bohemond, according to Alexios's biographer Anna Comnena, rejected food prepared for him by Alexios's personal cooks suspecting it to be poisoned. Godfrey too refused the emperor's several invitations for an audience having been warned about the emperor's capacity for treachery (including a poisoned cloak). The reason for Godfrey's assault on *Blachernae* is unclear, especially because the walls of Constantinople were almost impregnable and Godfrey lacked any siege engines. The Greeks suspected that Godfrey intended to usurp the throne. Latin sources blame Alexios for attacking the crusaders and initiating the fighting, glossing over the fact that Godfrey's men were pillaging the countryside.

And finally, the audience with Alexios in his throne room, the *Magnavra*. No doubt a reader will suspect that my description of the ceremony—roaring mechanical lions, singing birds, an ascending throne—novelistic invention. It is not. Long before Alexios Komnenos, ambassadors to the Byzantine court reported them, marveling at the spectacle. Emperors intended that it impress, strike awe, and it invariably succeeded. Except for the fact that an oath was taken in the throne room, there is no reliable description of the ceremony itself. Mine is an effort to reconcile the sparse and somewhat contradictory accounts.

Book VIII: Siege of Nicea

The crusader armies crossed the Bosporus Strait ("Arm of St. George") to the Gulf of Izmit ("Gulf of Nikomedia") in waves, beginning in mid-April, the last in early June 1097. It is impossible to estimate the size of the force with any accuracy. Contemporary sources, as always, are notoriously unreliable and of marginal value. Necessarily, therefore, the estimates given by modern historians, specialists all in the period, are based more on intuition than evidence. Unsurprisingly, they differ considerably, but at least they provide a rough sense of dimensions, ranging from a total force of 40,000 to 100,000 of combatants (horse and foot) and noncombatants. The plurality of opinion settles on around 70,000. Two historians estimate that eleven to seventeen percent (8,000 to 12,000) were fighting men. To give a sense of scale, it's been estimated the army of William the Conquer who invaded England in 1066 numbered 7,000; the English army at the Battle of Agincourt in 1415 about 12,000. Whatever the precise count, all historians agree this was by medieval standards a prodigious force the size of which stunned Europeans of the time.

The first wave, led by Godfrey, Duke of Lower Lorraine, gathered at Izmit ("Nikomedia") and from there marched to Iznik (Nicea), arriving on May 6. The chronology and description of events once the crusaders arrived provided by the primary and secondary Latin sources are, in large measure, irreconcilable. Even historians differ considerably in their accounts depending upon which source they rely. I have done my best to bring some coherence to these contradictions and to relate what I believe to be the most probable story. Nevertheless, there is general agreement among the contemporary or near-contemporary sources on the following: Duke Godfrey cleared the road to Nicea; Qilij Arslan, who had been absent, returned to Nicea and unsuccessfully attacked the crusaders; the crusaders returned from the battlefield with the heads of Turks on their spears or hanging from their saddles; the discovery of ropes brought by Qilij to bind his prisoners expecting a comfortable victory, a matter which all chroniclers gleefully reported; the twin strategy of blockade and siege warfare: escalade, battering ram, sapping (almost successful), use of catapults (the "mangonel"—the earliest recorded use of the "trebuchet" catapult, popularized in movies powered by counterweights instead of torsion as the mangonel, was in 1199); and finally the transport of Greek ships overland to Lake Iznik ("Ascanius Lake"). It is most probable, if not certain, that this was what finally persuaded the city to surrender and then solely to the emperor, not the crusaders, a wound salved but not totally healed by the emperor's largess at Pelekanum, June 22.

The reader is introduced for the first time to the "Tafurs", their nature and disposition described in this novel. Little is known of them or of their self-styled "king," whom I named "Drogo." Contemporary sources do agree that they were feared by crusaders and Turks alike for their barbarism and reputation for cannibalism.

Book IX: Battle of Dorylaeum

As always, the sources are inconsistent in their descriptions of the battle with Qilij Arslan. They do broadly agree, however, on the following: After leaving Nicea the crusading army divided, the vanguard consisting primarily of Normans, the rearguard of Provençals, Lorrainers, and Flemish. On the morning of July 1, 1097 Qilij Arslan's army appeared and immediately attacked the vanguard with his mounted archers. Crusaders were terrified and panic spread quickly through the ranks. They were vastly outnumbered. But even more important, the cavalry tactics of the Turks, the same used so successfully by the Mongols a century later, were completely foreign to them and they were unprepared. One eyewitness wrote: "Meanwhile the Turks were howling like wolves and furiously shooting a cloud of arrows. We were stunned by this. Since we faced death and since many of us were wounded, we soon took to flight. Nor is this remarkable because to all of us such warfare was unknown." Another: "When the Turks initiated a battle, our men were almost reduced to despair by the novelty of their tactics in battle; they were not accustomed to their speed on horseback, nor to their ability to avoid our frontal assaults. We had particular difficulty with the fact that they fired their arrows when fleeing from the battle." It was only through the heroic and steady leadership of Bohemond, described by one distinguished scholar of medieval warfare as "one of the finest commanders of the age", and Robert of Normandy that the Normans held. Had Bohemond not maintained the tight discipline of a massed formation, refusing to being lured into Turkish feigned retreats, the outcome would have been different. But similarly the Turks had never faced a European massed charge of heavy cavalry. Neither was prepared for the other. For the first time in history East met West on the battlefield.

The Normans waited for the rearguard to rescue them. Bohemond had placed the noncombatants behind the lines for their own protection. They "trembled" in fear as bishops and priests heard their confessions and administered the sacraments. The Turks attacked them nonetheless, killing all they could before leaving. Several hours after Qilij Arslan's initial attack, the rearguard arrived. It seems the appearance of Bishop Adhémar over a hill leading a force of Provençals outflanking the Turks was decisive. The Turks fled, leaving their treasures for crusader plunder. For two days the crusaders pursued the Turks. The reputation of crusader prowess at Dorylaeum and especially later at Antioch excited both hope and fear throughout Anatolia and Palestine, Christian Armenian cities in southern Turkey welcoming the crusaders, Turkish cities with a couple of exceptions readily capitulating. But victory at Dorylaeum came at a heavy cost to the crusaders. One historian estimated 4,000 Christian dead 3,000 for the Muslims, though yet again these numbers are based more on intuition than solid evidence.

The crusader army departed Dorylaeum on July 3, 1097 reaching Marash on October 15, Antioch five days later. All sources agree the journey, two and a half months, across the Anatolian desert and then over the Taurus Mountains from Coxon to Marash especially, was horrifying. As always, details are lacking but the sense of the journey is clear. "[We traveled] through a land which was deserted, waterless and uninhabitable and from which we barely emerged alive. We suffered greatly from hunger and thirst and found nothing to eat except prickly plants. We survived wretchedly enough on such plants, but we lost most of our horses so that many of the knights had to go on as foot soldiers." And another participant on the trek from Coxon to Marash: "[We had] to cross a damnable mountain which was so high and steep that none of our men dared to overtake another on the mountain path. Horses fell over the precipice and one beast of burden dragged down another. As for the knights, they stood about in a great state of gloom, wringing their hands because they were so frightened and miserable." An emeritus historian of the period estimated, I think reasonably, that more crusaders died during the journey from Dorylaeum to Marash than were killed by Turks at Nicea and Dorylaeum.

Book X: Siege of Antioch

After arriving in Antioch on October 21, 1097 the crusaders had given little thought to preparing for winter. Some princes argued for establishing winter quarters in the general vicinity and begin the siege in the spring. However, Count Raymond's argument for an immediate investment prevailed. In the month or two prior to winter setting in, the crusaders "enjoyed the high life so that they ate only the best cuts, rump and shoulders, scorned brisket, and thought nothing of grain and wine," wrote Raymond d'Aguilers, chaplain to Count Raymond. But when the winter cold and rains came, the effects were devastating. Fulcher of Chartres, another eyewitness, wrote: "Then the starving people devoured the stalks of beans still growing in the fields, many kinds of herbs unseasoned with salt, and even thistles which because of the lack of firewood were not well cooked and therefore irritated the tongues of those eating them.

They also ate horses, asses, camels, dogs, and even rats. The poorer people ate even the hides of animals and the seeds of grain found in manure. The people for the love of God endured cold, heat, and torrents of rain. Their tents became old and torn and rotten from the continuous rains. For this reason many people had no cover but the sky." Ralph of Caen, author of The Gesta Tancredi, not a participant in the crusade himself but who drew much information later from interviews with Bohemond and Tancred wrote: "Everywhere there was want, calamity, and desolation."

There was a general belief that the famine was God's punishment for the sinful habits of the crusaders. This belief was fortified by an earthquake on December 30, lights in the northern sky at about the same time, explained by modern historians as an aurora borealis, and a comet reported by a Syrian chronicler. Adhémar's response was typical for his age: prayer, penitential processions, alms for the poor, and fasting. Despite these measures, the famine not only persisted but worsened. Adhémar decided on a more severe solution: he would purge the crusaders of their sin through inquisition and harsh penalty. "In the course of this siege the strength of Christian law flourished greatly, and if anyone was convicted of a crime, he submitted to the severe judgment of the leaders of the army. Moreover, sexual crimes were punished with particular severity, and this was just." William of Tyre, many years later, wrote: "During the siege of Antioch there was a famine and pestilence. The elders saw these troubles arose from sins of the people and the Lord was angry. Bishop of Le Puy ordered a fast of three days, also to put away from the camp all the light women of ill repute. Adultery and fornication of every description was forbidden under penalty of death and an interdict placed on all reveling and intoxication."

Latin chroniclers all agree that, following the battle at Bridge Gate, the crusaders disinterred the bodies of slain Muslims to search for gold, silver and other valuables. Fulcher of Chartres wrote: "I saw great many of the Saracens who were killed there put in a pile and burned. The fetid odor of their bodies bothered us greatly. These wretches were burned for the sake of finding the bezants which some had swallowed and others had hidden in their mouths next to the gums, not wishing the Franks to get anything."

The monk Tudebode, not a participant but writing shortly after the crusade and generally a reliable chronicler, is the only source for the detention of Christian women. He claimed that Yaghi Siyan, in retaliation for Rainald Porchet's refusal to convert, ordered one hundred Christian women stripped naked, bound, formed in a circle, firewood and hay piled around them, and then burned. Whether their fate was as Tudebode described is uncertain—he wasn't present—but very possibly Christian women in the city were indeed rounded up and at a minimum imprisoned.

My description of the battle at Bridge Gate is a conflation of Latin accounts of Yaghi Siyan's attack on the crusaders on December 29, 1097, he taking advantage of the absence of Bohemond and Robert of Flanders on their foraging expedition to al-Bara, and the battle at Bridge Gate on March 4 the next year when Bohemond and Raymond were returning with supplies from the fleet commanded by Edgar Aetheling.

Book XI: A New Turkish Threat

The plot of Firuz, captain of the Twin Sisters Towers, and Bohemond in the fall of Antioch is undisputed. What is unclear is Firuz's reason for betraying the city to the crusaders—Latin sources claim that he had discovered his wife *in flagrante delicto* with a Turkish officer. Bohemond's ruse of leading his army away from the city, then returning late at night, is well attested as is the near failure of the assault with the collapse of the scaling ladder. One eyewitness reported that it was only the fortuitous discovery of a postern gate that allowed the crusaders entrance into the city. Also well attested is the massacre that followed when the crusaders entered the city. The anonymous author of the *Gesta Francorum*, an eyewitness, wrote: "All the streets of the city on every side were full of corpses so that no one could endure to be there because of the stench, nor could anyone walk along the narrow paths of the city except over the corpses of the dead." Another wrote in a letter home: "[We] did not take captive any of those whom [we] found."

The precipitous departure of Tatikios from Antioch is interesting. Latin chroniclers, all virulently and inflexibly hostile to the Greeks, explain it was due to Tatikios's cowardice on news of Kerboqa's imminent arrival. However, Anna Comnena, daughter of Emperor Alexios, admittedly also a partisan, states in the biography of her father, *The Alexiad*, that Bohemond falsely warned Tatikios of a plot against his life. He knew Tatikios would resist his claim to the city as a breach of the princes' vow to restore all lands formerly held by the empire to Alexios. With Tatikios out of the way, Bohemond could accuse Tatikios of cowardice and the emperor of violating his pledge to aid the crusaders, thus releasing the princes from the oath they took at Constantinople. I believe Anna's accusation more credible.

By mid-June crusaders were desperate. There had been desertions of nobles, Stephen of Blois being the most notorious and affective. Worse was the starvation that followed. When the crusaders seized Antioch, they had given no thought to husbanding their resources—"[We] gormandized sumptuously and splendidly as [we] gave heed to dancing girls." But soon stores of food, the city having been tightly barricaded since April, were depleted. One chronicler wrote: "People ate poisonous food: celtic nard, hemlock, hellebore, sorrel, darnel and cockle. They died while eating in order to live. Old soles of shoes and whatever leather were thrown into pots of water. There was dysentery and death everywhere." And another: "The crusaders cooked leaves of figs, vines, and trees in water and ate them. Some put the hides of horses, asses, camels, oxen and wild buffalo, dried for five or six years into water for two nights and a day, and after mingling them with water boiled ate them. We suffered starvation and fear for 26 days."

Morale was now at its lowest ebb. There was a pervasive belief that they were doomed. That is, until the "visions" of Peter Bartholomew and Stephen of Valence. They are described in some detail by the chroniclers, which I generally followed. They differed in content: Saint Andrew appearing to Peter Bartholomew and revealing the location of the holy lance; Jesus himself—a form of visionary "one-up-manship" I suspect—to Stephen of Valence promising aid from a heavenly army. The more interesting feature of these "dueling" visions was their political partisanship, never explicitly conceded by any of the chroniclers but intimated by at least one: Peter asserting Raymond's claim to Antioch and Stephen to Bohemond's competing claim.

Adhémar's doubts about the authenticity of the spear were well known for he had seen one in Constantinople recovered centuries before by Helena, mother of the Emperor Constantine, his skepticism also fueled by the questionable circumstances under which it was "discovered" in the dark pit at the Basilica of Saint Peter. But his reservations were somewhat muted because he saw its effect on crusader morale. It was these two visions, reinforced by the sight of a meteor falling into the Turks' camp, that galvanized the dispirited crusaders and was likely the critical element leading to their victory over Kerboqa. The anonymous author of the *Gesta Francorum*, wrote: "Peter found the lance as he had foretold and they all took it up with great joy and dread and throughout the city there was boundless rejoicing." The crusader princes, in a letter to Urban II, wrote: "We were so comforted and strengthened by finding [the lance], and by many other divine revelations, that we, who before had been afflicted and timid, were then most boldly and eagerly urging one another to battle." Yet the issue was a sore one for many crusaders. The Provençals believed it was a sign of God's favor on them alone; the Normans, by contrast, mocked it. Regarding Stephen of Valence's "vision", it too was doubted, particularly by William, Bishop of Orange, second only to Adhémar in reputation and respect. Adhémar likely shared his suspicion but the sources do not say.

Bohemond's collusion with the citadel's commander Ahmad ibn-Mar- wān for its surrender is nowhere mentioned or even suggested in the sources. Yet, Kenneth Setton, emeritus scholar of the crusades, argues it is likely. Control of the citadel was key to control of the city. And Raymond, immediately after victory over Kerboqa, attempted to force it to surren- der to him. The Turk commander refused, insisting he would deliver it only to Bohemond. I agree with Professor Setton.

Bohemond plotted a brilliant strategy for fighting Kerboqa. He knew the crusaders could not survive much longer and that the moment must be seized. But he feared that crusader soldiers were too comfortably lodged in their homes and would not turn out. To evict them, he set the city afire. The tactic worked but at a terrible cost to the city itself, beyond what Bohemond had anticipated. The course of the battle against Kerboqa on June 28 is quite confusing. The sources, and consequently modern historians, describe it differently. I have tried to bring some coherence to it. What is certain is this: The crusaders were vastly outnumbered by the Turks. One historian estimated the size of Kerboqa's force at 35,000 soldiers and the crusaders at 20,000 which included noncombatants. Another estimated a disparity of two to one. More ominous for the cru- saders was the fact that that most of their horses had perished from star- vation. What had formerly begun as an army of cavalry and infantry was now an army of infantry, knights serving more in an auxiliary role. There was a grass fire although its significance to the outcome of the battle is unclear—one chronicler explained that the Turks lit it, another that it was the crusaders. Finally, reports of crusaders sighting Saint George leading an army from heaven is well attested. Again, the *Gesta Francorum*: "At that moment appeared from the mountains a countless host of men on white horses with white banners. When our men saw this, they did not know who it could be until they realized this was the help sent by Christ, whose leaders were Saint George, Saint Mercurius, and Saint Demetrius [martial saints]. This is quite true for many of our men saw it."

And finally, Oderic's surgery on Adhémar. There are several books on medieval medicine but few describe the treatment of battle wounds, perhaps because most or all of these "physicians" were barber-surgeons, many barely literate leaving few records. My description is based largely, although not wholly, on the account by John Bradmore, a London physician, unusually detailed by standards of the time, who extracted an arrow lodged in the head of the future Henry V in 1403. It was believed at the time that vinegar, honey, and wine were helpful antiseptics, although their understanding of infection was limited.

Book XII: Plague, Trial, and Flight

The plague that followed the defeat of Kerboqa is well attested. Historians generally attribute it to typhoid, common enough in the ancient world, even today in developing countries. It was a devastating disease, claiming the lives of one-third of Athens in 430 B.C. including that of the great Greek statesman Pericles. On August 1, 1098 it took the life of Adhémar.

The trial of Rebecca is my invention. What however is not invented is the belief in the Middle Ages that Jews were responsible for all plagues.

Sources agree that Thoros invited Baldwin to Edessa and that Turks fled as he traveled to the city, the crusaders having now acquired a fearsome reputation after the defeat of Kerboqa. They agree too that Thoros adopted Baldwin in a public ceremony, rubbing of naked chests which fascinated Latin chroniclers. What is also undisputed is Thoros's unpopularity with the people of Edessa and that Thoros was violently killed shortly after Baldwin's triumphant arrival welcomed as the city's liberator. What is disputed is Baldwin's complicity in Thoros's death. All sources agree that a plot to overthrow him began with overtures from prominent citizens to Baldwin. Fulcher of Chartres, Baldwin's chaplain and the sole Latin eyewitness to all events, reported that Baldwin refused to participate in the plot. This is partisan nonsense. As a cadet son, he had no claim to family title or lands. His situation was similar to that of Bohemond. Like other young nobles, he came to the Holy Land perhaps for reasons of piety and adventure but certainly to enrich himself. This was too great an opportunity for Baldwin to ignore. Shortly after Thoros's death he created the County of Edessa, the first crusader principality created in *Outremere*, a term used to describe crusader states established in Turkey and Palestine.

Book XIII: The Army Marches South

Maarat an-Numan is often cited in the histories of medieval sieges. It was notable for several reasons: Most medieval sieges required months to starve out a city; if capitulation occurred sooner it was generally due to surrender, not by assault. Maarat required only two weeks to fall, albeit by storm. Another feature is the savagery that followed. The anonymous author of the *Gesta Francorum* wrote: "Our men entered the city, and each seized his own share of whatever goods he found in houses or cellars, and when it was dawn they killed everyone, man or woman, whom they met in any place whatsoever. No corner of the city was clear of Saracen corpses, and we could scarcely go about the city streets except by treading on the dead bodies of the Saracens." Another is the severe starvation of the besiegers. Raymond d'Aguilers, chaplain to Raymond of Toulouse, also an eyewitness, wrote: "It grieves me to report that in the ensuing famine one could see more than ten thousand men scattered like cattle in the field scratching and looking, trying to find grains of wheat, barley beans or any legume. Despite the continuing work on assault machines, some of our people, impressed by the misery around them and the audacity of the Saracens, lost hope of God's mercy and turned tail."

However, above all, Maarat's particular notoriety is the reports of cannibalism which circulated widely at the time. Tafurs especially had a reputation for this practice. The *Chanson d'Antioche* ("Song of Antioch"), written in the late 12th century, describes Tafurs sitting about eating Saracen flesh. Fulcher of Chartres, not an eyewitness for he was then in Edessa, wrote: "I shudder to tell that many of our people harassed by the madness of excessive hunger cut pieces from the bodies of the Saracens already dead, but when it was not yet roasted enough by the fire they devoured it in their savage mouths." The anonymous author of the *Gesta Francorum*, a participant in the siege, wrote: "While we were there some of our men could not satisfy their needs, either because of the long stay or because they were so hungry, for there was no plunder to be had outside the walls. So they ripped up the bodies of the dead, because they used to find *bezants* hidden in their entrails, and others cut the dead flesh into slices and cooked it to eat."

Turning to Arqa, curiously the chroniclers wrote little about the siege other than it occurred over three months until it was finally abandoned. However, the most singular event was the ordeal by fire of Peter Bartholomew, confirmed by all sources. Over time, Peter had become the voice of the people, frustrated with the princes' lack of zeal to reach

Jerusalem. Yet, at the same his visions—reported in detail by chroniclers Raymond d'Aguilers and Fulcher of Chartres—had become increasingly erratic, for example, that Bishop Adhémar, revered by all crusaders, was burning in hell for doubting the lance. Especially unhelpful to Peter's reputation was Saint Andrew's command that all sinful crusaders were to be lined up and executed. Chroniclers agree that Peter was able to complete his walk through the fire. Agreement ends there. Did he die the next day or twelve days later? Was his death due to burns or wounds from fanatical pilgrims who rushed at him, tearing his clothing and body believing him holy? For some, the very fact he succeeded in walking through the fire was evidence of his sainthood. For others, the majority, his very death merely confirmed their doubts about his visions and the authenticity of the lance.

Raymond d'Aguilers, Count Raymond's chaplain, likely present, left a rather detailed description of Stephen of Valence's vision of Bishop Adhémar regarding the true cross as Stephen reported it to Raymond. I have been generally faithful to his relation though so much of it makes little sense to the modern mind. Nonetheless, Raymond was convinced and dispatched Adhémar's brother, William Hugh of Monteil, to the port city of Latakia north of Arqa to retrieve it.

Book XIV: Jerusalem Falls!

Estimates of the size of the crusader army when it reached Jerusalem vary, complicating the count is whether it includes noncombatants. Most modern historians accept the count of Raymond d'Aguilers, a participant, that there were 1,200 to 1,500 knights and 12,000 foot soldiers. Whatever the number, the attrition rate from disease, starvation, combat, and desertion over four years was enormous. Two scholars have calculated a loss of three out of four. A near-contemporary source gave ninety percent.

One of the oddest episodes of the siege of Jerusalem was the initial assault on June 10 undertaken on the promise of victory given by an obscure hermit on the Mount of Olives, yet one more in a plethora of visionaries. Crusader princes were skeptical for which the hermit rebuked them severely for lack of faith. They acquiesced, to their cost. It did teach them, however, that victory depended less on faith than military strategy, a lesson lost on subsequent crusaders.

The assault on Jerusalem, from July 13 to 15, occurred much as described here although, as always, I'm forced to reconcile disputing accounts. However, all agree on the essential events. Without the unexpected arrival of Italian and English ships at Jaffa and its craftsmen, the crusaders lacked the necessary skills to build siege engines, especially towers, a battering ram, and mangonels. It is highly improbable they could have taken the city, particularly in time before the arrival of the Fatimid army from Egypt. This begs the question: why had not the crusaders anticipated this need in advance? The likely answer: blind faith in God's providence. By the second day Count Raymond's assault at the Gate of Zion collapsed, his tower and mangonels no match for Iftikhar's defenses. Success depended on Duke Godfrey's battering ram and tower. The ram must have been enormous, able to pierce the thick walls of Jerusalem. But the initial breach was not large enough for the tower to pass through and had to be widened. It then broke down, the cause disputed, but it blocked the tower's advance. The crusader set it on fire, defenders trying to save it. Modern historians accept the chroniclers' explanation that it was burned. I think that less likely than the account given in this novel: the penthouse dragged away. It would have taken several days for the ram to burn and in the meantime Saracens would have repaired the wall. Moreover, with the imminent arrival of the Fatimids, urgent action was necessary.

Finally, the massacre of Muslims and Jews in the city. The carnage was horrendous, indiscriminate and rapacious. The Muslim world never forgot. Raymond d'Aguilers, an eyewitness and a particularly virulent critic of Islam, wrote with satisfaction: "With the fall of Jerusalem one could see marvelous works. Some of the pagans were mercifully beheaded, others pierced by arrows from towers and yet others tortured for a long time and burned to death in searing flames. Piles of heads, hands and feet lay in houses and streets and men and knights were running to and fro over corpses." Fulcher of Chartres, writing of the refugees on the Dome of the Rock, seems more conflicted: "Many of the Saracens who had climbed to the top of the Temple of Solomon [modern "Temple Mount" to Jews and Christians; "Haram al-Sharif" ("Noble Sanctuary") to Muslims] in their flight were shot to death with arrows and fell headlong from the roof. Nearly ten thousand were beheaded in this Temple. If you had been there your feet would have been stained to the ankles in the blood of the slain. What shall I say? None of them were left alive. Neither women nor children were spared." Similarly Guibert of Nogent: "[A] general slaughter of the pagans took place. No one was spared because of tender years, beauty, dignity, or strength: only inescapable death awaited them.

* * *

The Franks chased the fleeing pagans fiercely, killing everyone they came upon, more in slaughter than in battle, through the streets, squares, and crossroads until they reached what was called the Temple of Solomon. So much human blood flowed that a wave of damp gore almost covered the ankles of the advancing men. That was the nature of their success that day."

It is impossible to know with certainty how many Muslims were killed. The Arab historian Ibn al-Athir (1160-1233) estimated 70,000 including imams and Muslim scholars. A modern Western historian reckons 40,000. What we do know is that few, if any, Jews or Muslims survived other than Governor Iftikhar and his retinue. Fulcher of Chartres wrote that on December 11, even five months following the siege when he arrived in Jerusalem "Oh what a stench there was around the walls of the city, both within and without, from the rotting bodes of the Saracens slain by our comrades at the time of the capture of the city, lying wherever they had been hunted down!"

Book XV: My Journey Ends

After the fall of Jerusalem it was rumored that a piece of the holy cross had been hidden by Christians somewhere in the city. Bishop Arnulf did begin a search probably to enhance his chances for election as patriarch of Jerusalem—he did, after all, enjoy an unsavory reputation. A new relic might accomplish that. The sources differ on the circumstances of its discovery. Was its location revealed only after torturing some unidentified local inhabitants or from information provided by a Syrian? Where was it found—in the Holy Sepulchre or elsewhere? It's uncertain. Regarding the election itself, we know only that it occurred. My story of interference by Robert of Normandy is speculative.

Modern historians generally agree on the respective sizes of the Fatimid (Egyptian) and Crusader armies at Ascalon: the army of al-Afdal, "Sultan of Babylon [Cairo]" numbered 20,000; Duke Godfrey's 1,200 knights and 10,000 men-at-arms, the crusaders outnumbered two-to-one. It was because of al-Afdal's numerical advantage in the field that Godfrey decided to take the initiative and bring the battle to him. All agree that the Fatimids were unprepared and routed. The disagreement lies in whether Saracen soldiers were able to mount some form of resistance or whether the surprise attack was so complete that they folded immediately. The loss of crusader life was certainly minimal. Regarding Fatimid losses, Ibn Al-Qalanisi (1071- 1160) in his *Damascus Chronicle* estimated that 10,000 Muslims died.

The most peculiar feature of the battle was discovery of al-Afdal's herd, which obediently followed the crusaders south. Raymond d'Aguilers wrote: "God multiplied our numbers. Miracle came when animals formed herds and followed us, stood when we stood, ran when we ran." It does appear that the herd played some role, albeit unclear, in the attack on the morning of August 12.

FRANCE

EASTERN EUROPE

CONSTANTINOPLE

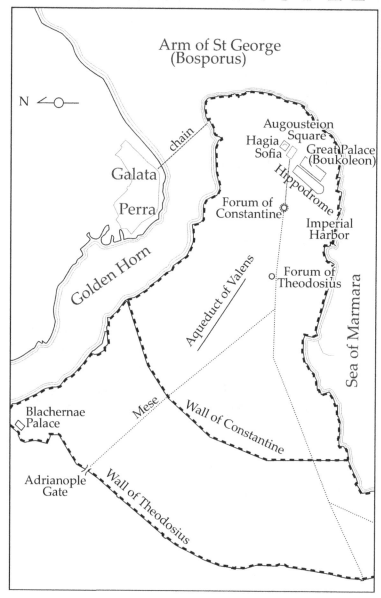

ANTIOCH

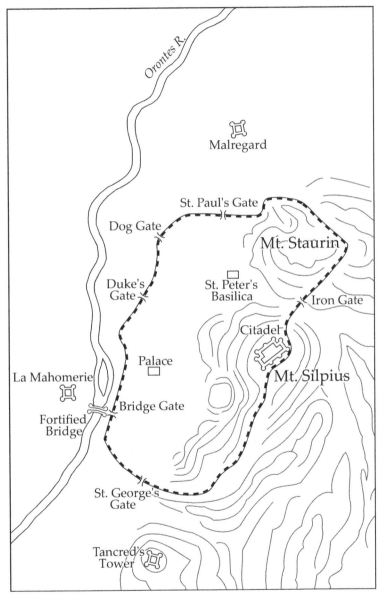

WESTERN TURKEY

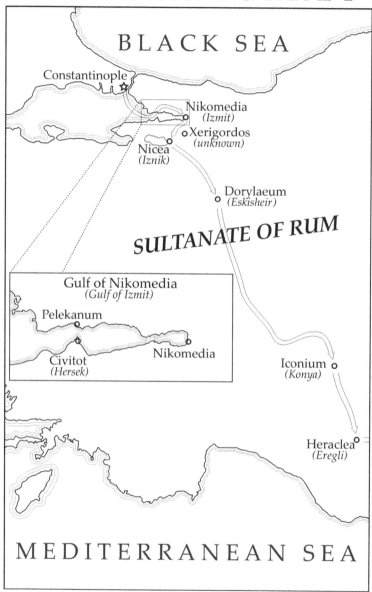

BLACK SEA

Constantinople

Nikomedia
(Izmit)

Xerigordos
(unknown)

Nicea
(Iznik)

Dorylaeum
(Eskisheir)

SULTANATE OF RUM

Gulf of Nikomedia
(Gulf of Izmit)

Pelekanum

Nikomedia

Civitot
(Hersek)

Iconium
(Konya)

Heraclea
(Eregli)

MEDITERRANEAN SEA

EASTERN TURKEY

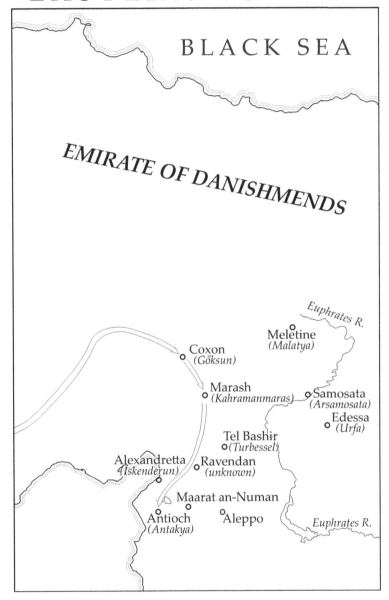

BLACK SEA

EMIRATE OF DANISHMENDS

Euphrates R.

Meletine
(Malatya)

Coxon
(Gőksun)

Marash
(Kahramanmaras)

Samosata
(Arsamosata)

Edessa
(Urfa)

Tel Bashir
(Turbessel)

Alexandretta
(Iskenderun)

Ravendan
(unknown)

Maarat an-Numan

Antioch
(Antakya)

Aleppo

Euphrates R.

PALESTINE

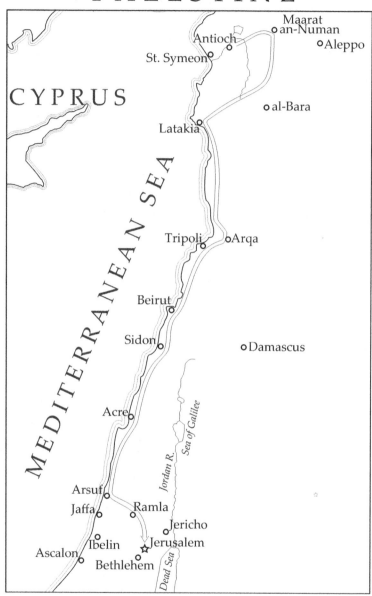

JERUSALEM

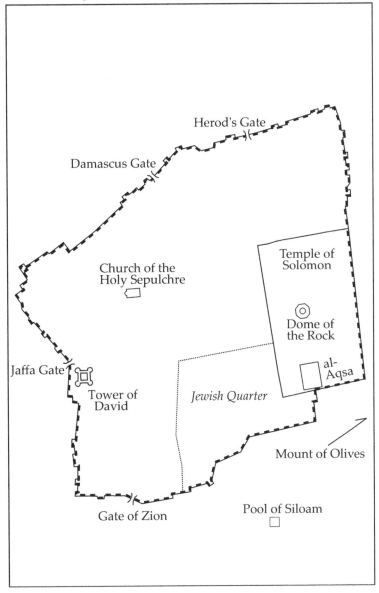

Herod's Gate

Damascus Gate

Temple of
Solomon

Church of the
Holy Sepulchre

Dome of
the Rock

Jaffa Gate

al-
Aqsa

Tower of
David

Jewish Quarter

Mount of Olives

Gate of Zion

Pool of Siloam

Made in the USA
Monee, IL
01 December 2022

19228262R00262